BLUE GIANT

TENOR SAXOPHONE | MIYAMOTO DAI

SHINICHI ISHIZUKA

5-6

CONTENTS

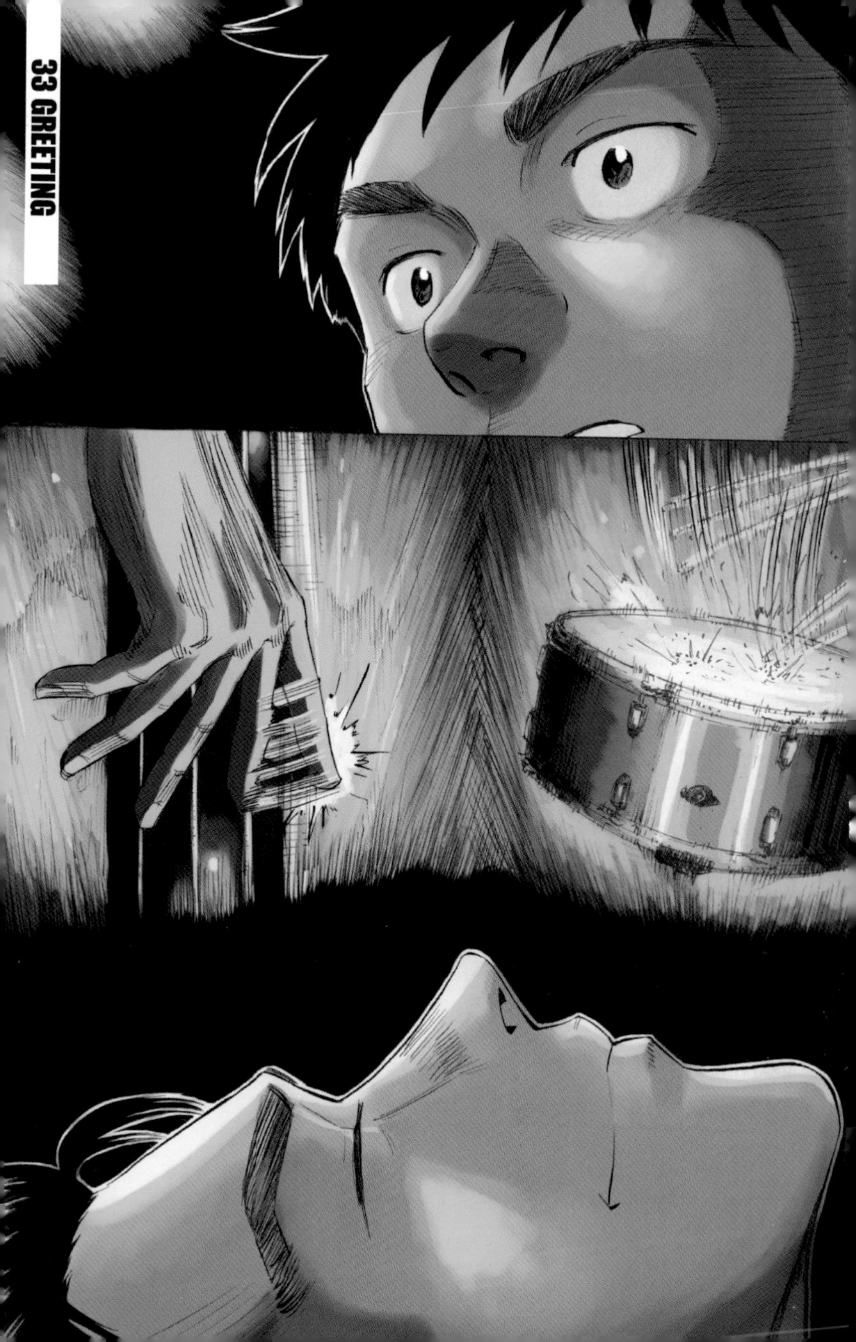
33 GREETING

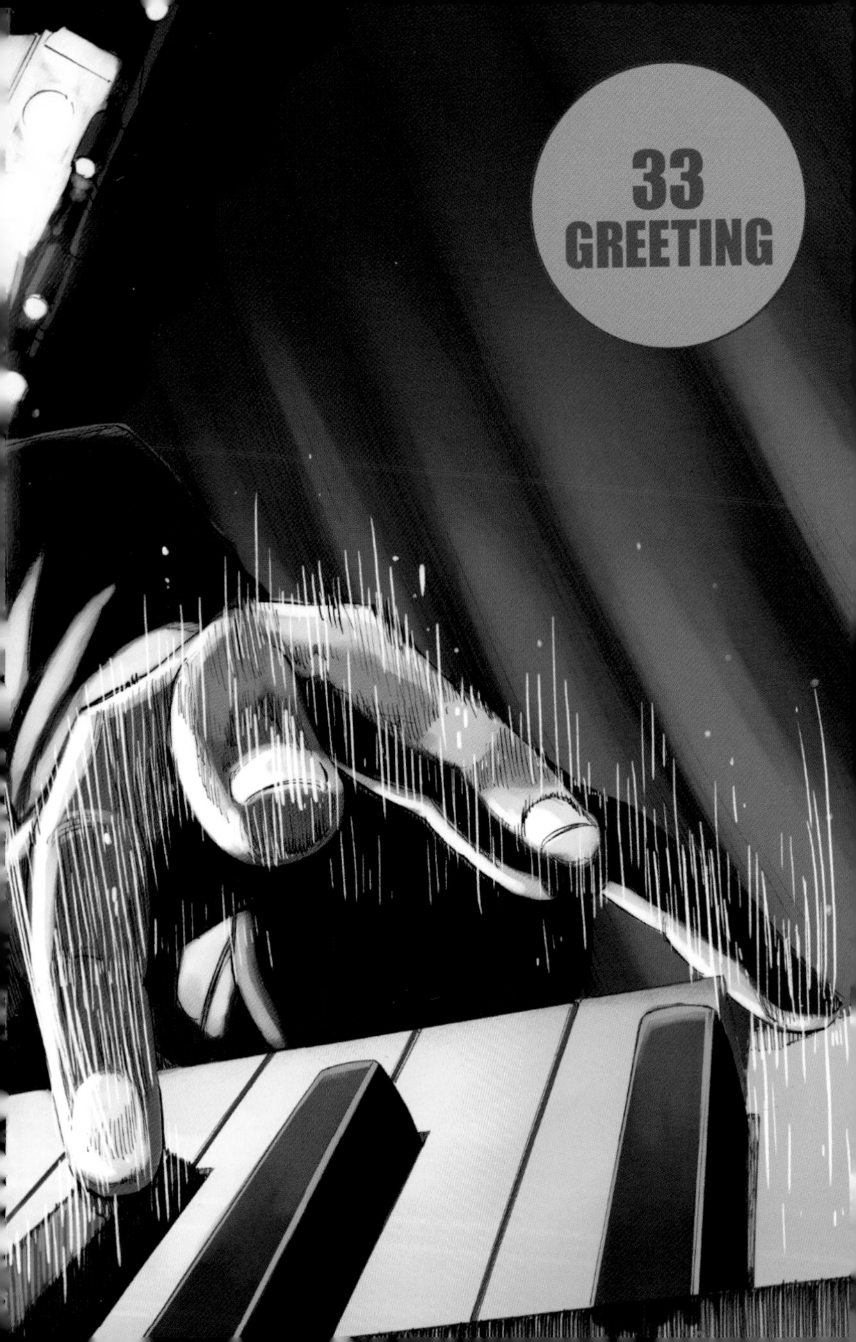
33
GREETING

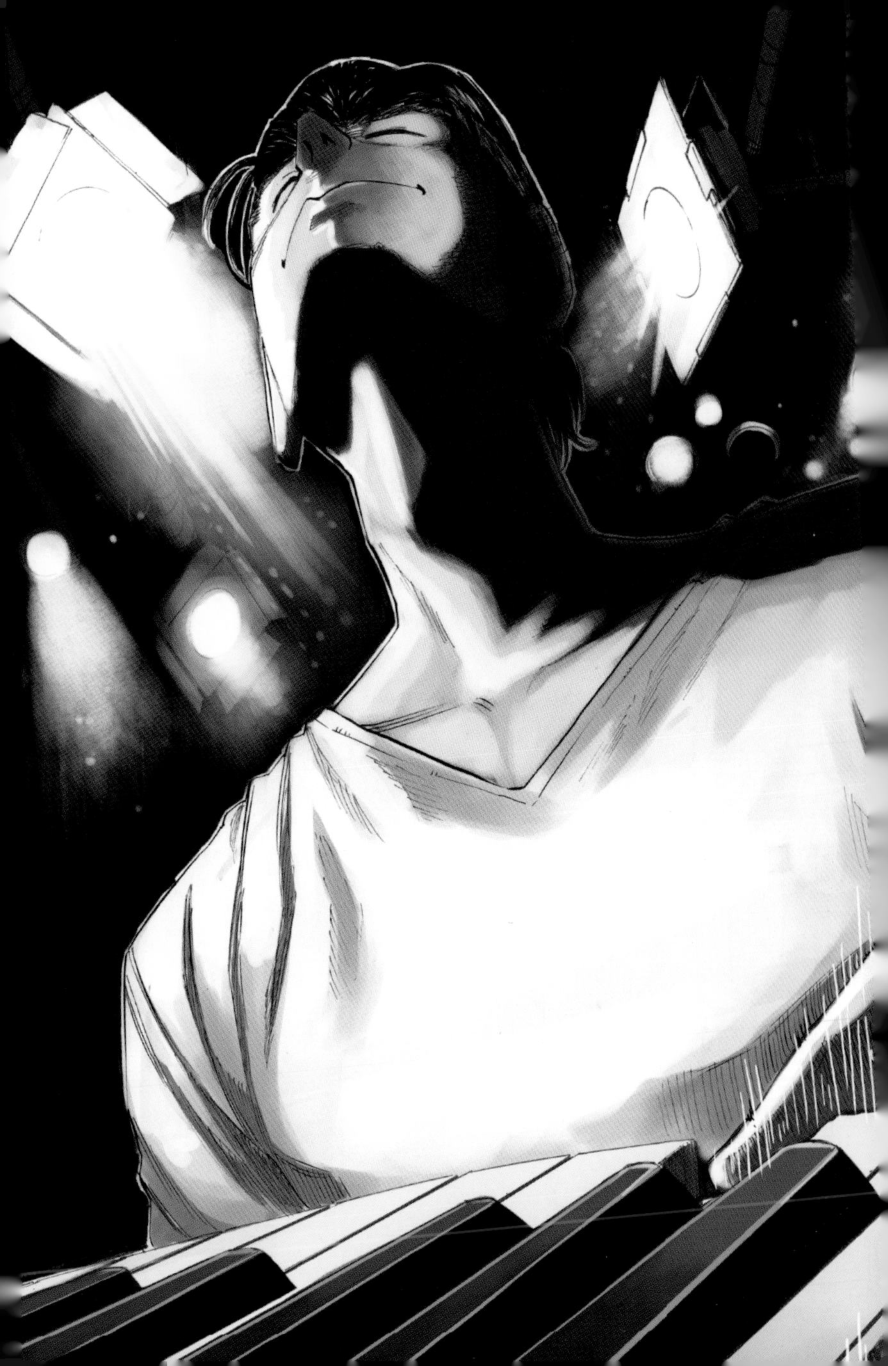

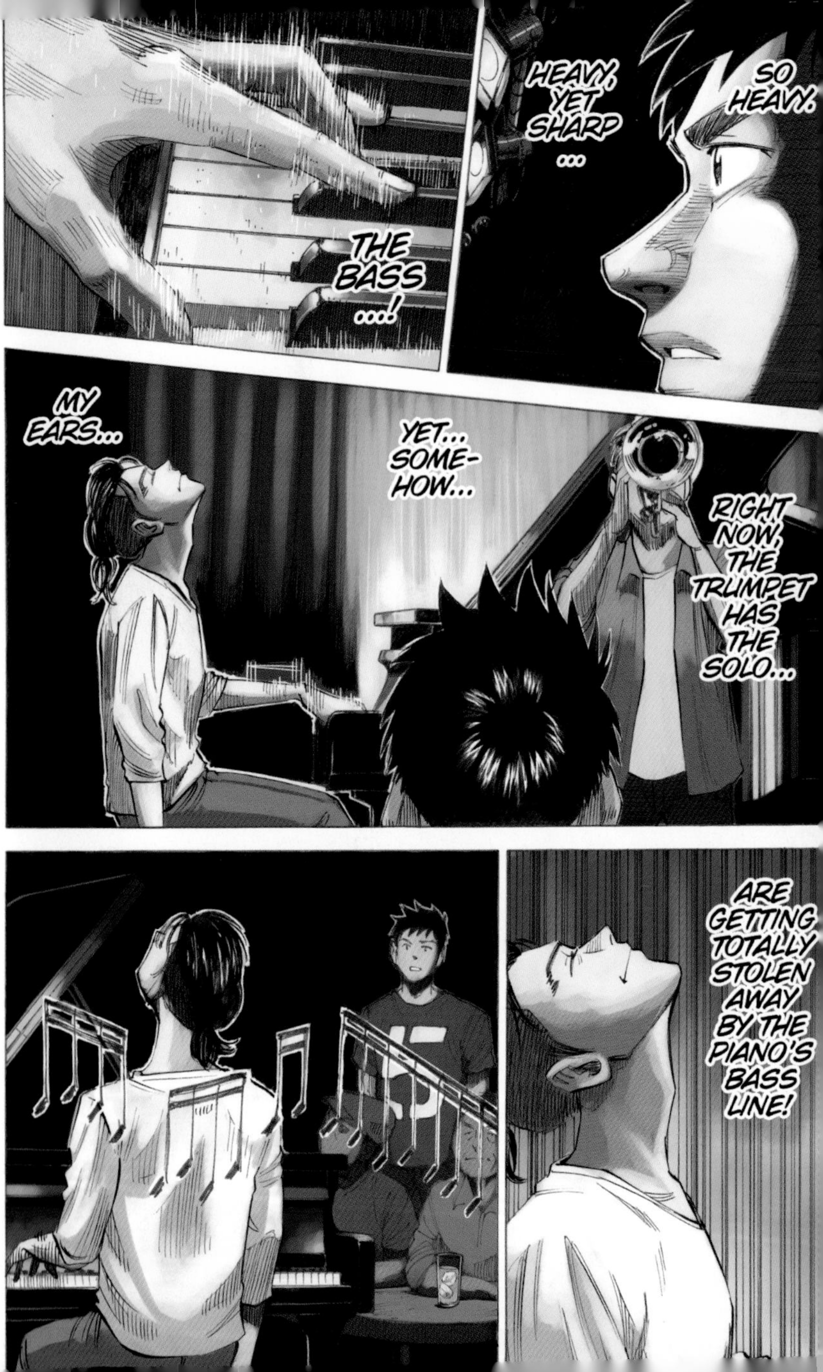
SO HEAVY.
HEAVY, YET SHARP...
THE BASS...!
RIGHT NOW, THE TRUMPET HAS THE SOLO...
YET... SOME-HOW...
MY EARS...
ARE GETTING TOTALLY STOLEN AWAY BY THE PIANO'S BASS LINE!

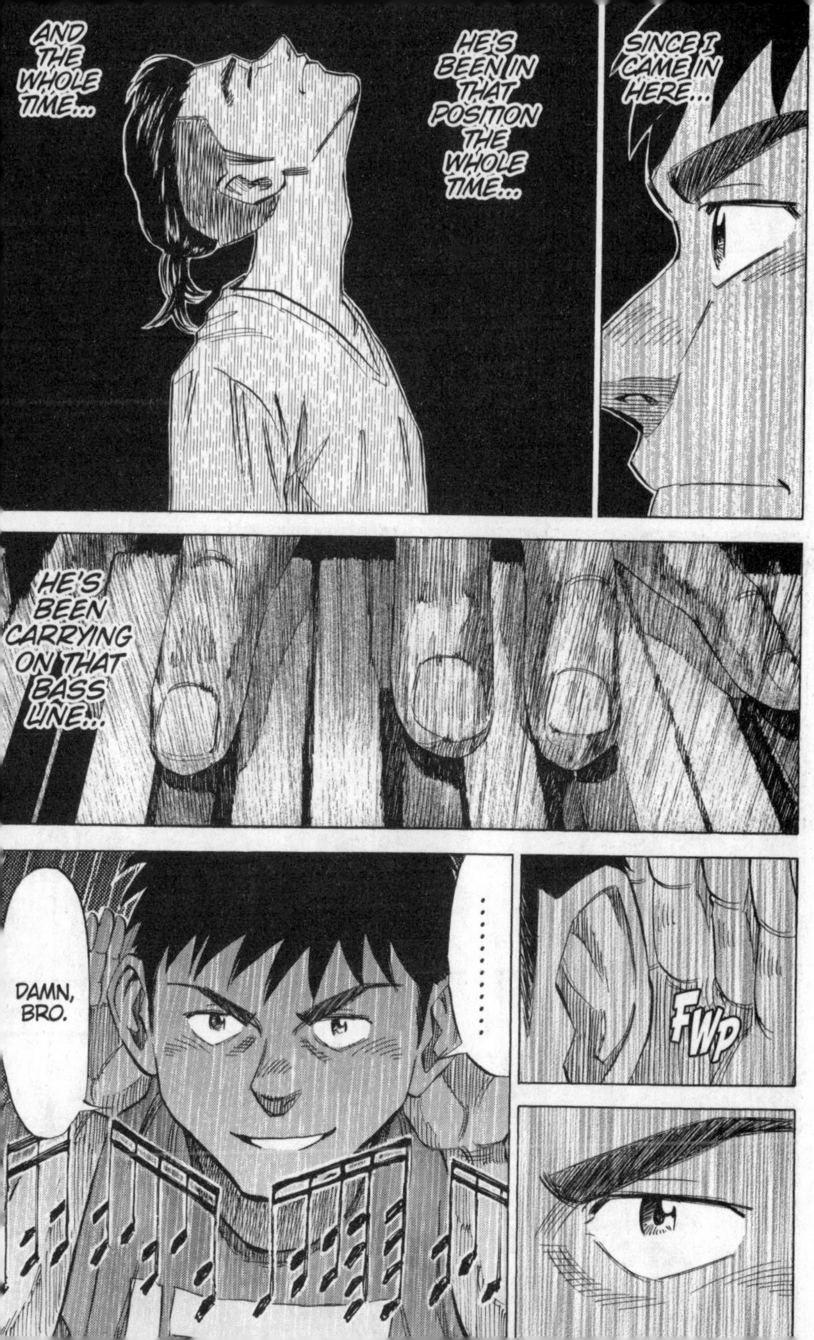
SINCE I CAME IN HERE...
HE'S BEEN IN THAT POSITION THE WHOLE TIME...
AND THE WHOLE TIME...
HE'S BEEN CARRYING ON THAT BASS LINE...
FWP
......
DAMN, BRO.

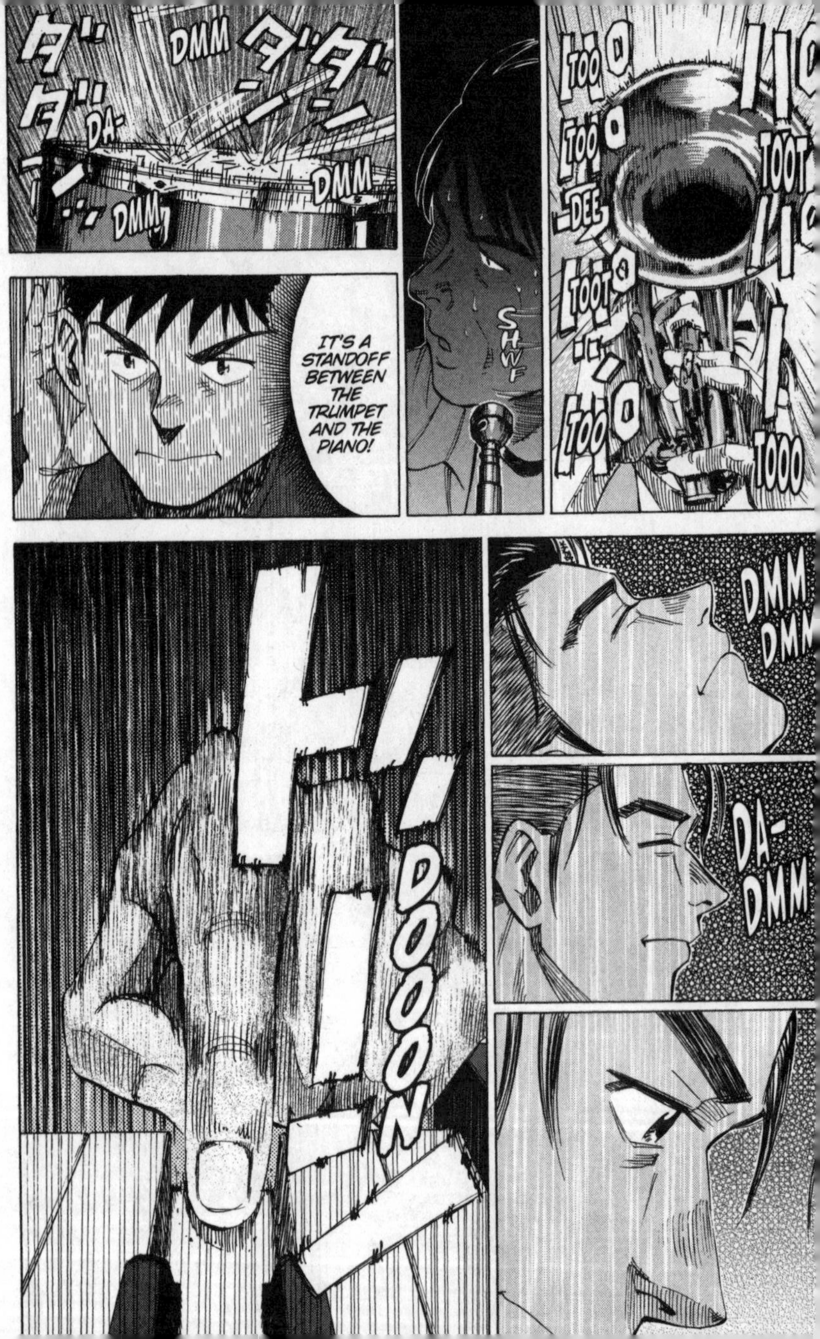
TOOT
TOOO
TOO
TOO
-DEE
TOOT
TOO
SHWF
DMM
DA-
DMM
DMM
IT'S A STANDOFF BETWEEN THE TRUMPET AND THE PIANO!
DMM DMM
DA-DMM
DOOOON

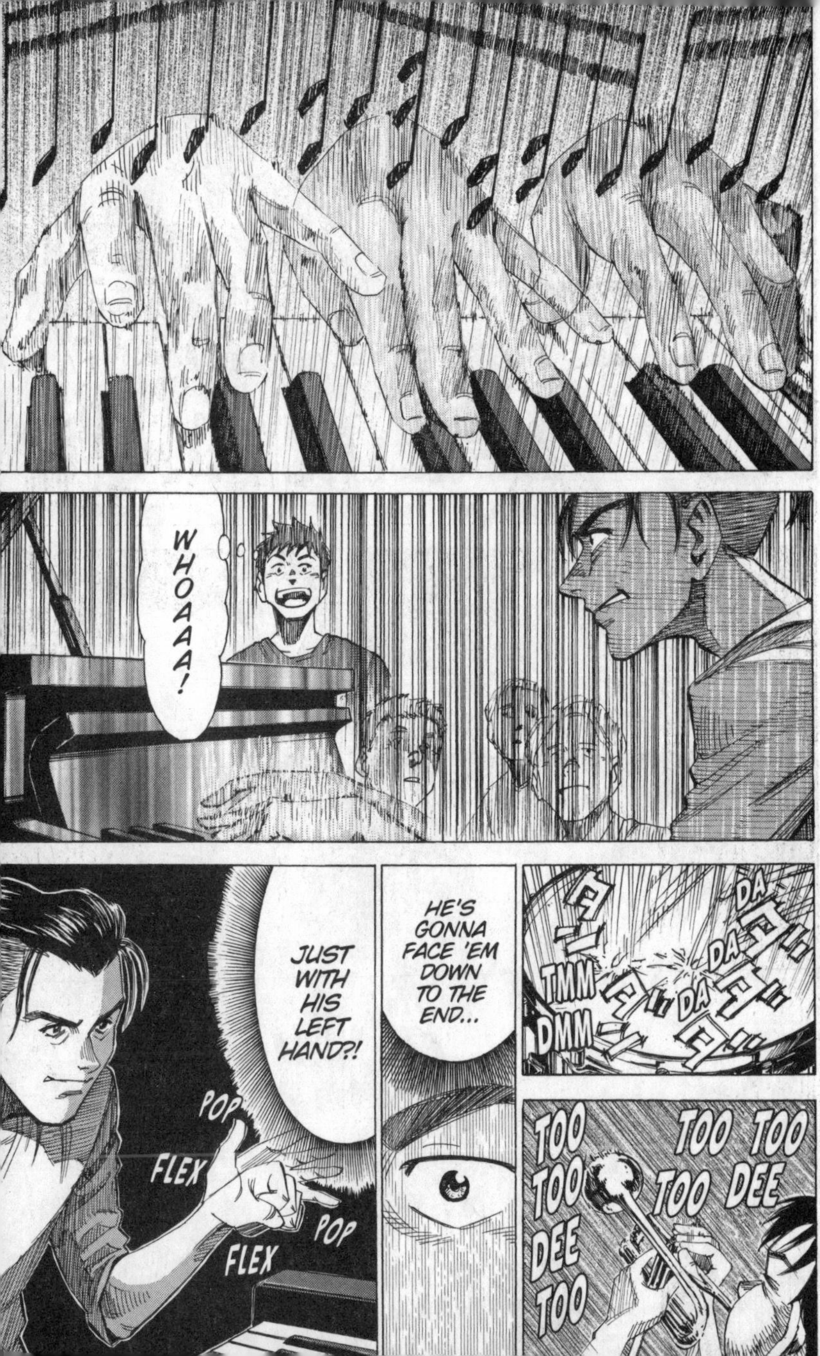
WHOAAAA!
DA DA DA
TMM DMM
TOO TOO TOO DEE
TOO TOO DEE TOO TOO
HE'S GONNA FACE 'EM DOWN TO THE END...
JUST WITH HIS LEFT HAND?!
POP
FLEX
POP
FLEX

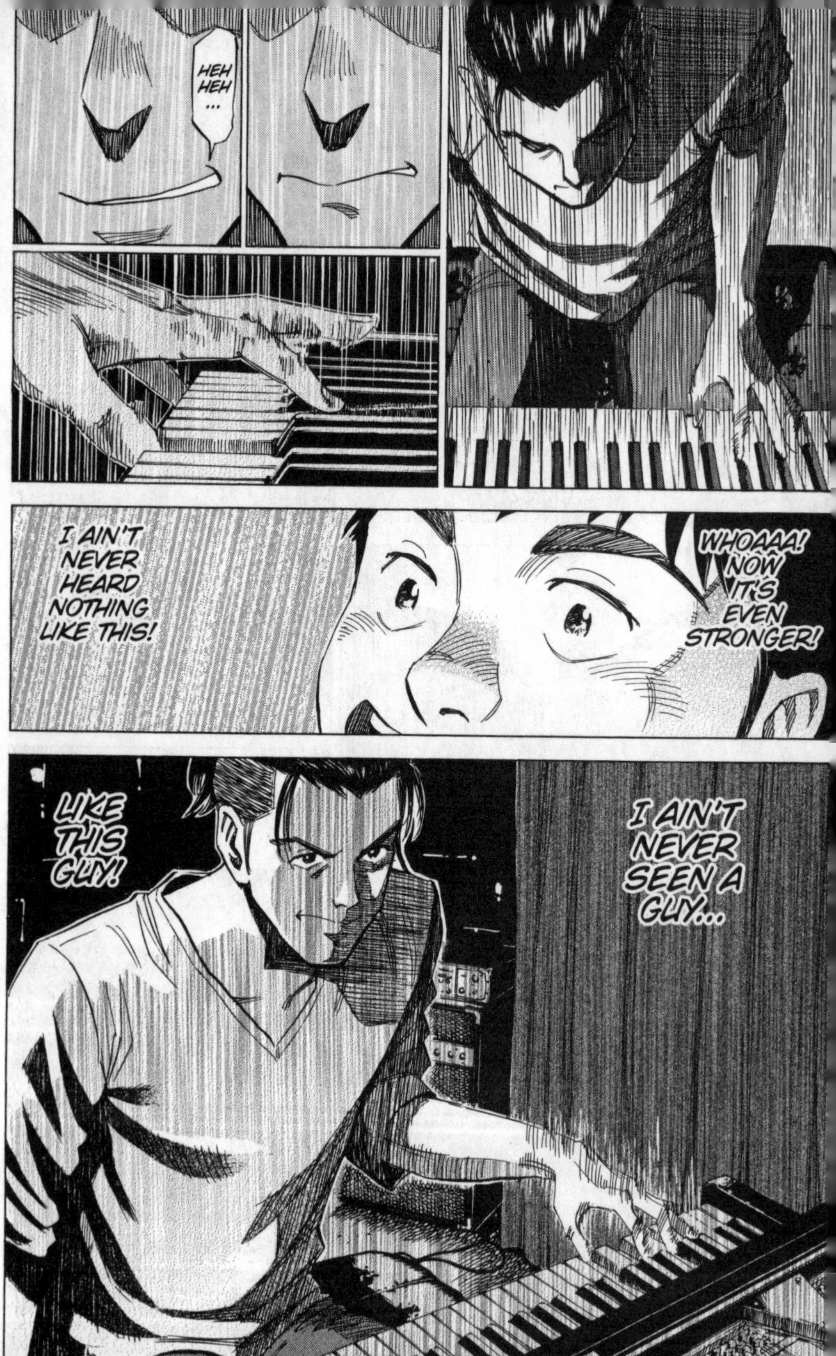
HEH HEH ...
WHOAAA! NOW IT'S EVEN STRONGER!
I AIN'T NEVER HEARD NOTHING LIKE THIS!
I AIN'T NEVER SEEN A GUY...
LIKE THIS GUY!

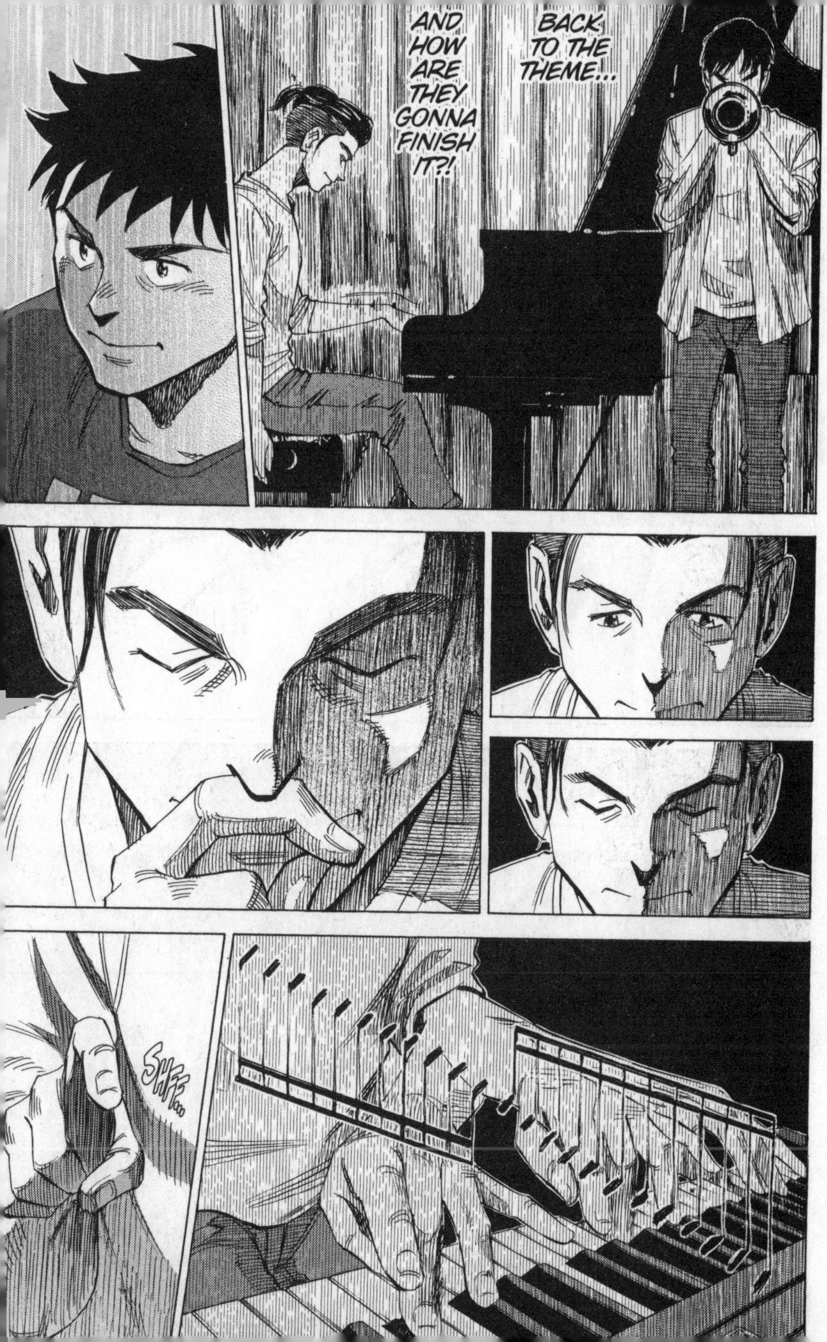
BACK TO THE THEME...
AND HOW ARE THEY GONNA FINISH IT?!
SHFF...

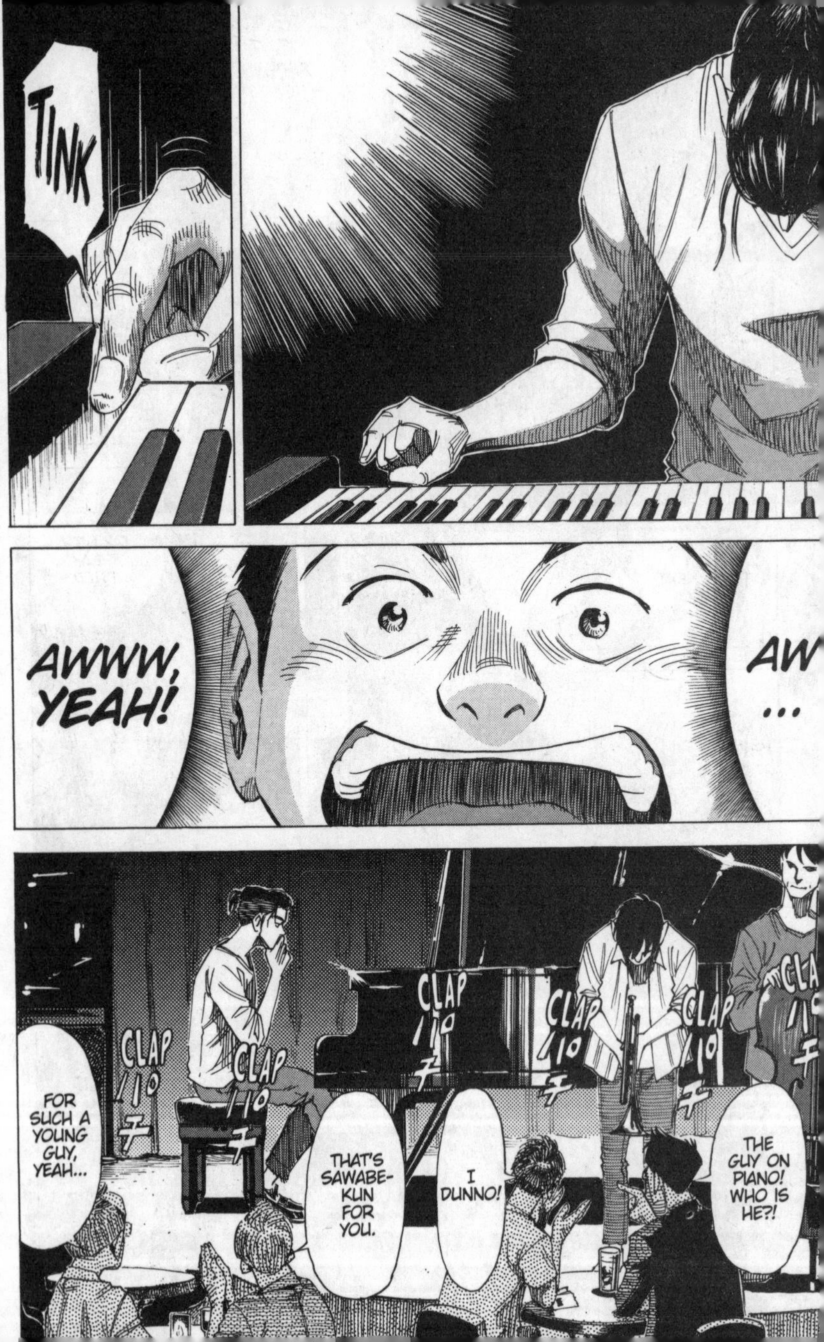
TINK
AW ...
AWWW, YEAH!
CLAP
THE GUY ON PIANO! WHO IS HE?!
CLAP
CLAP
CLAP
I DUNNO!
THAT'S SAWABE-KUN FOR YOU.
CLAP
CLAP
FOR SUCH A YOUNG GUY, YEAH...

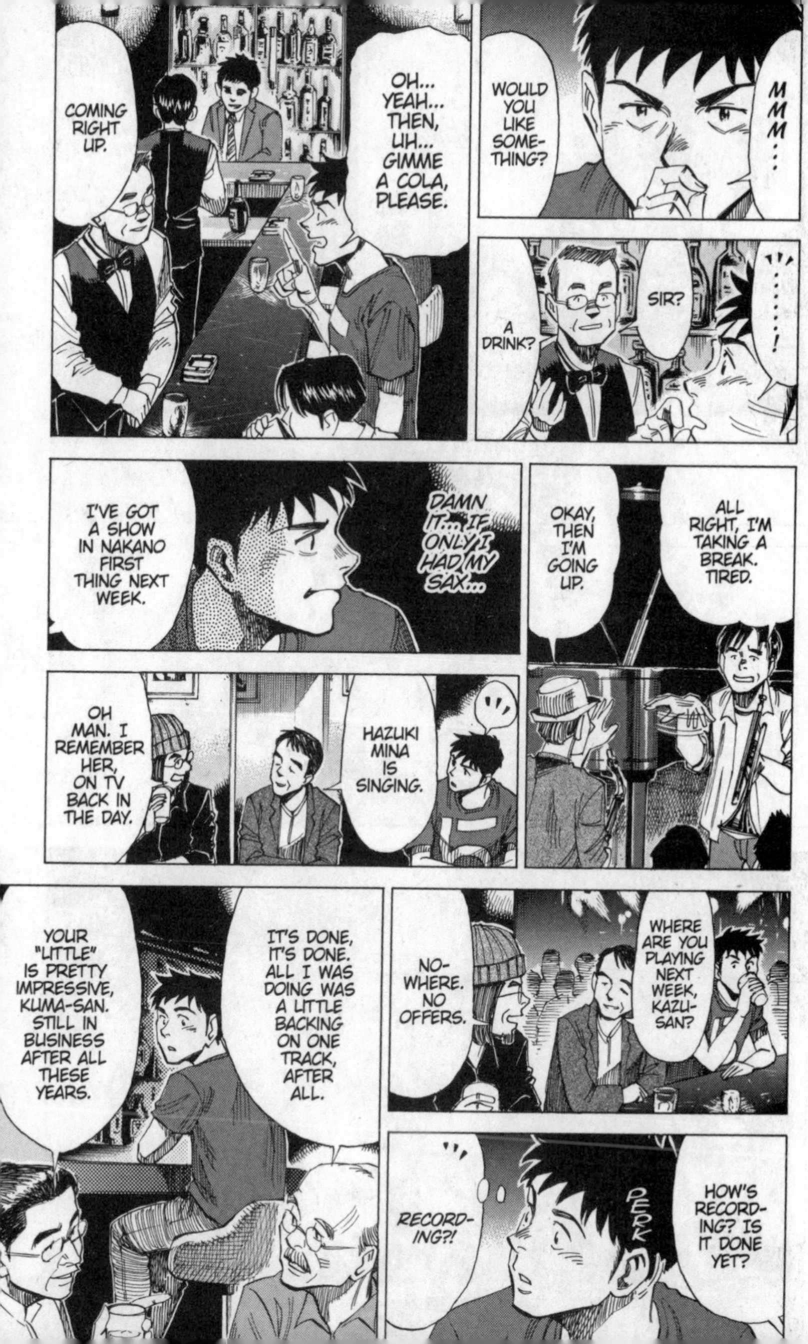
MMM...
WOULD YOU LIKE SOMETHING?
...!
SIR?
A DRINK?
OH... YEAH... THEN, UH... GIMME A COLA, PLEASE.
COMING RIGHT UP.
ALL RIGHT, I'M TAKING A BREAK. TIRED.
OKAY, THEN I'M GOING UP.
DAMN IT... IF ONLY I HAD MY SAX...
I'VE GOT A SHOW IN NAKANO FIRST THING NEXT WEEK.
HAZUKI MINA IS SINGING.
OH MAN. I REMEMBER HER, ON TV BACK IN THE DAY.
WHERE ARE YOU PLAYING NEXT WEEK, KAZU-SAN?
NO-WHERE. NO OFFERS.
HOW'S RECORDING? IS IT DONE YET?
PERK
RECORDING?!
IT'S DONE, IT'S DONE. ALL I WAS DOING WAS A LITTLE BACKING ON ONE TRACK, AFTER ALL.
YOUR "LITTLE" IS PRETTY IMPRESSIVE, KUMA-SAN. STILL IN BUSINESS AFTER ALL THESE YEARS.

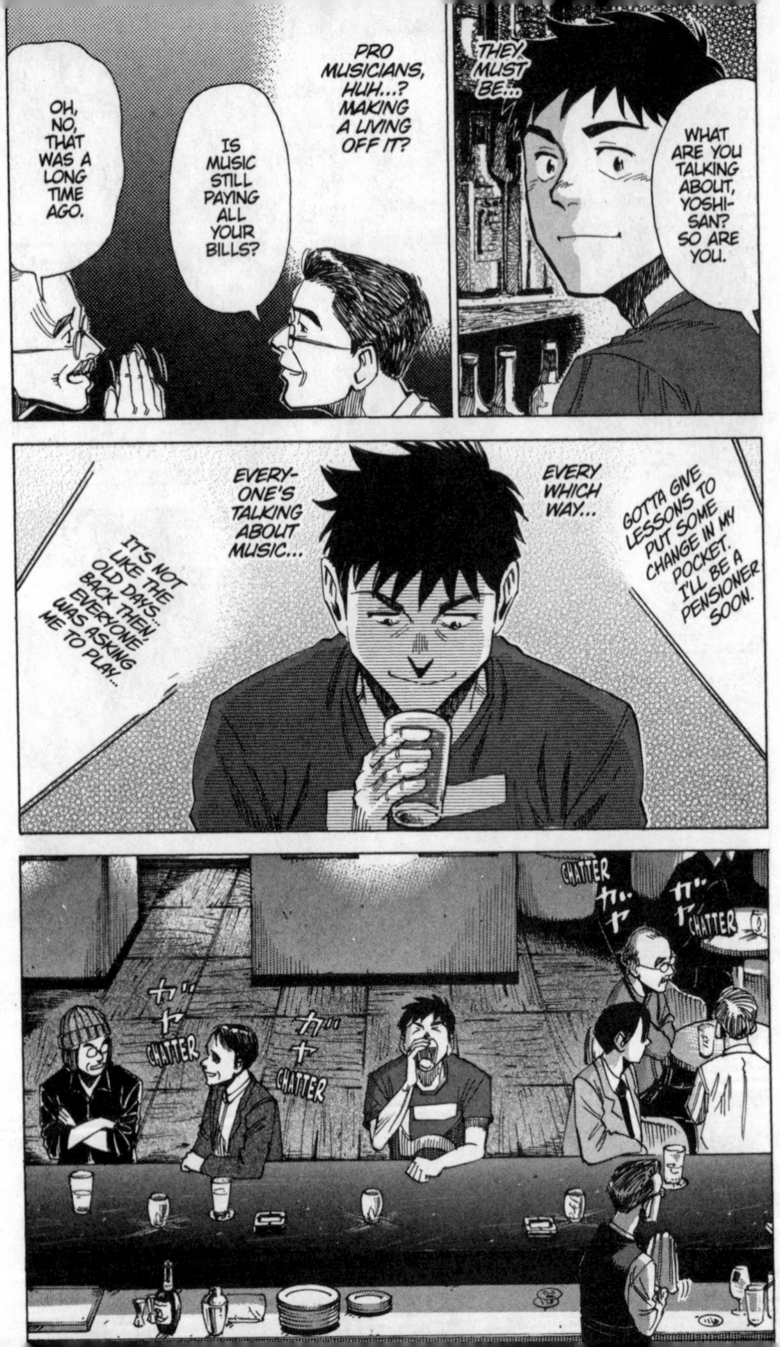
WHAT ARE YOU TALKING ABOUT, YOSHI-SAN? SO ARE YOU.
THEY MUST BE...
PRO MUSICIANS, HUH...? MAKING A LIVING OFF IT?
IS MUSIC STILL PAYING ALL YOUR BILLS?
OH, NO, THAT WAS A LONG TIME AGO.
GOTTA GIVE LESSONS TO PUT SOME CHANGE IN MY POCKET. I'LL BE A PENSIONER SOON.
EVERY WHICH WAY...
EVERY-ONE'S TALKING ABOUT MUSIC...
IT'S NOT LIKE THE OLD DAYS... BACK THEN, EVERYONE WAS ASKING ME TO PLAY...
CHATTER
ガヤ
ガヤ
CHATTER
ガヤ
CHATTER
ガヤ
CHATTER

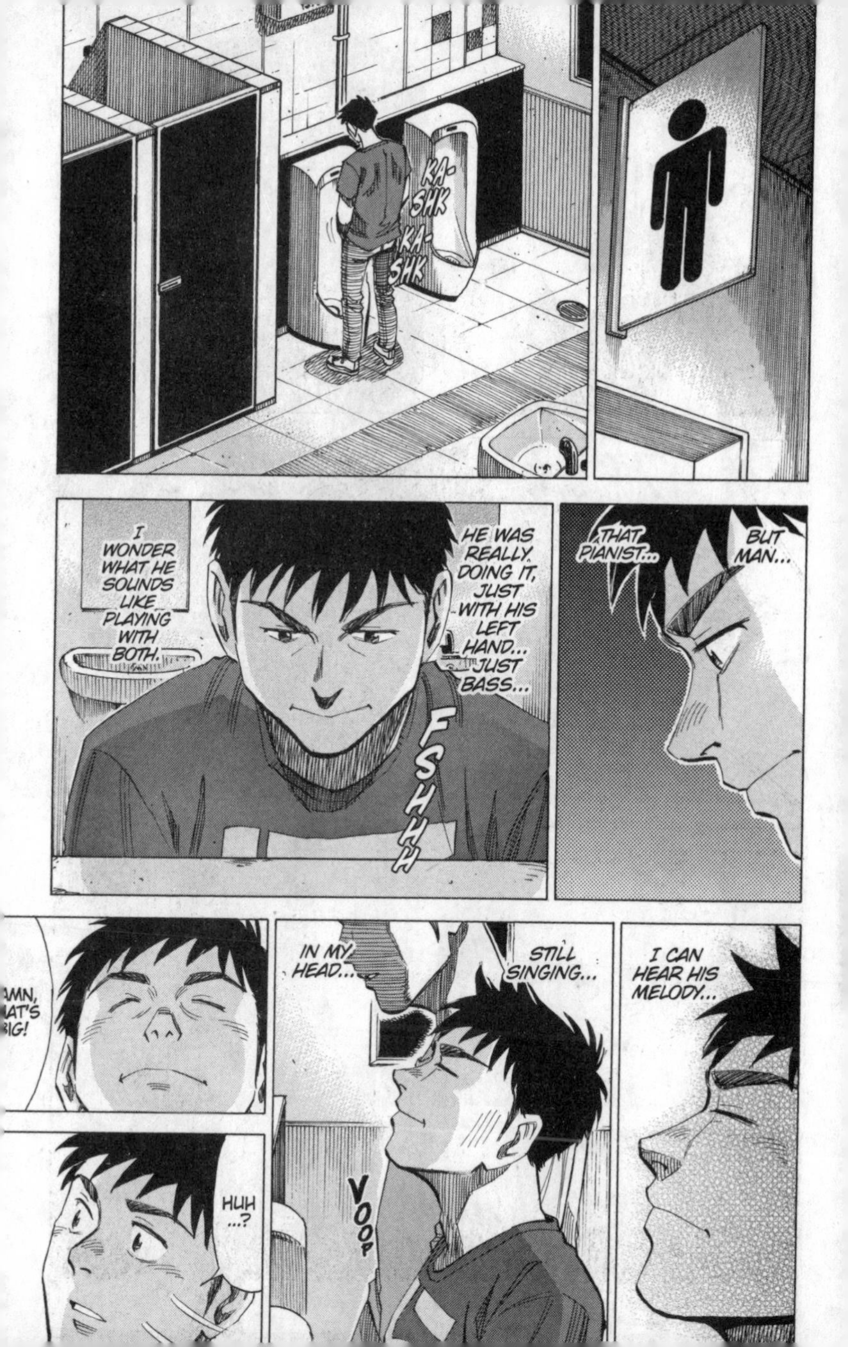
KA-SHK
KA-SHK
BUT MAN...
THAT PIANIST...
HE WAS REALLY DOING IT, JUST WITH HIS LEFT HAND... JUST BASS...
I WONDER WHAT HE SOUNDS LIKE PLAYING WITH BOTH.
FSHHHH
I CAN HEAR HIS MELODY...
STILL SINGING...
IN MY HEAD...
VOOP
AMN, AT'S BIG!
HUH ...?

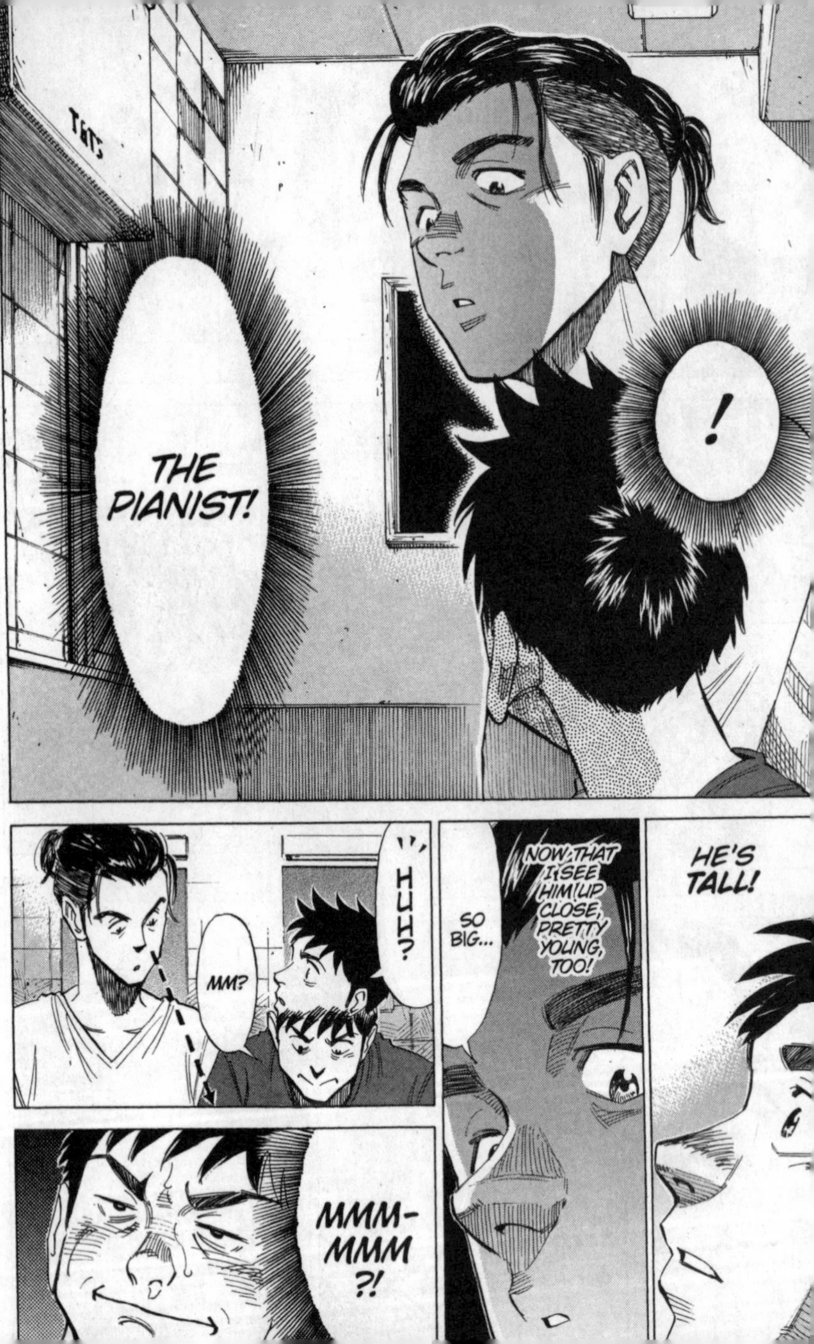
!
THE PIANIST!
HE'S TALL!
NOW THAT I SEE HIM UP CLOSE, PRETTY YOUNG, TOO!
SO BIG...
HUH?
MM?
MMM-MMM?!

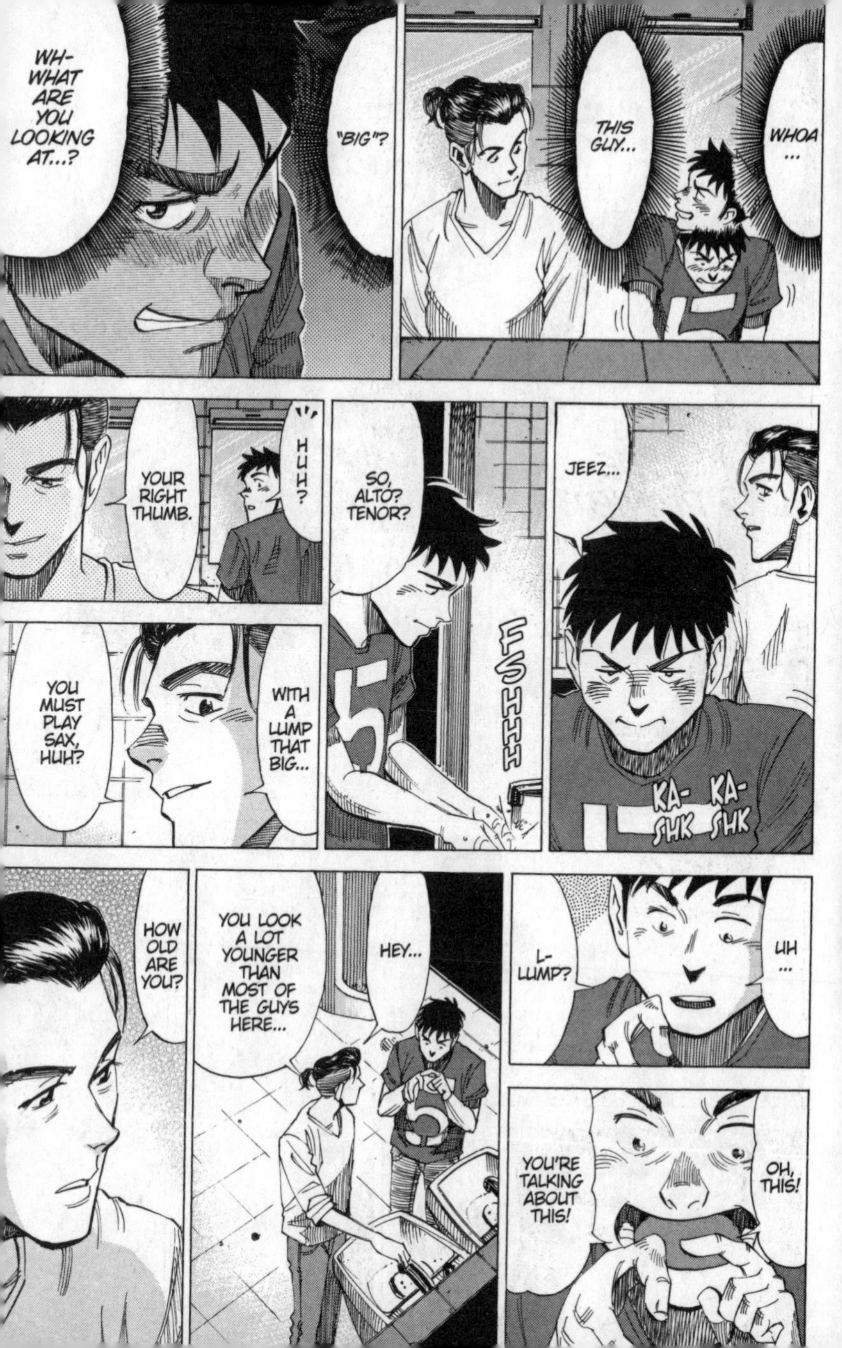
WHOA...
THIS GUY...
"BIG"?
WH- WHAT ARE YOU LOOKING AT...?
JEEZ...
KA- SHK KA- SHK
SO, ALTO? TENOR?
FSHHHH
HUH?
YOUR RIGHT THUMB.
WITH A LUMP THAT BIG...
YOU MUST PLAY SAX, HUH?
UH...
L- LUMP?
OH, THIS!
YOU'RE TALKING ABOUT THIS!
HEY...
YOU LOOK A LOT YOUNGER THAN MOST OF THE GUYS HERE...
HOW OLD ARE YOU?

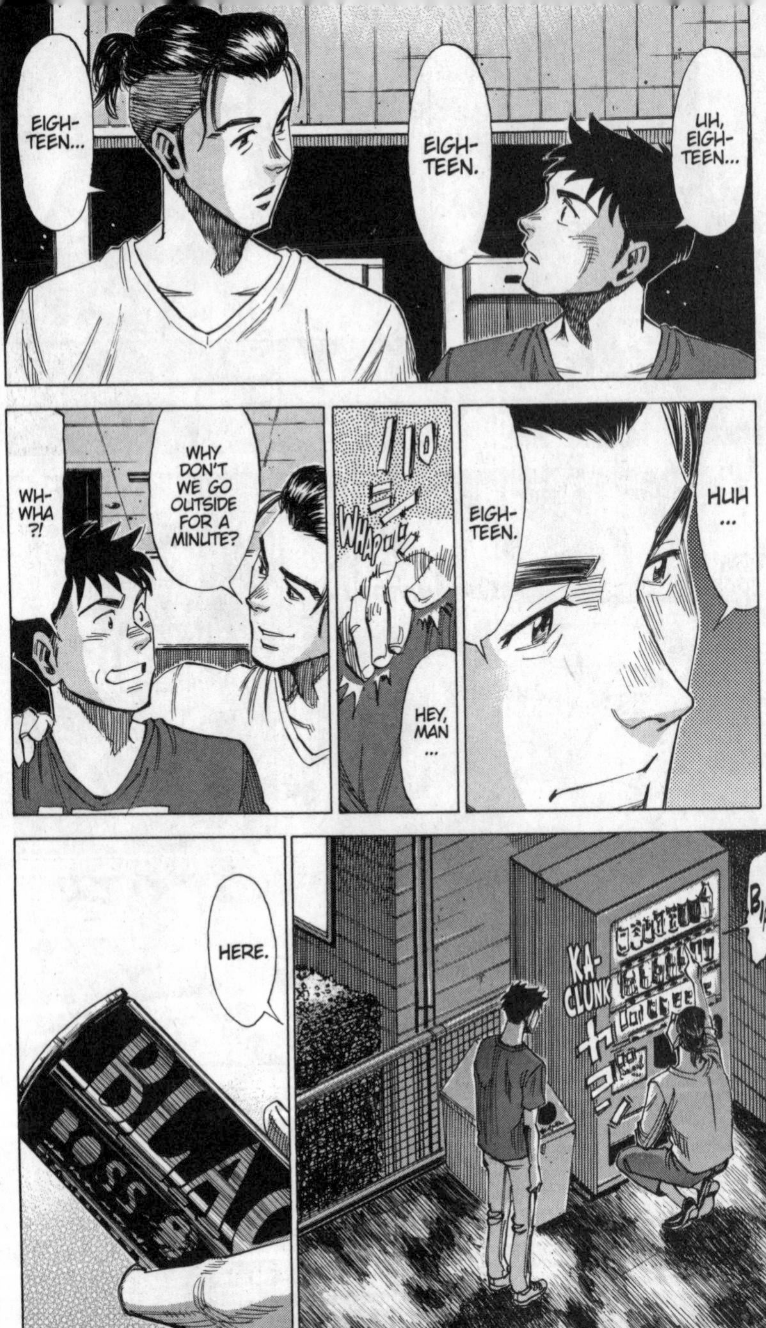
UH, EIGH-TEEN...
EIGH-TEEN.
EIGH-TEEN...
HUH ...
EIGH-TEEN.
WHAP
HEY, MAN ...
WHY DON'T WE GO OUTSIDE FOR A MINUTE?
WH-WHA ?!
BIP
KA-CLUNK
HERE.
BOSS

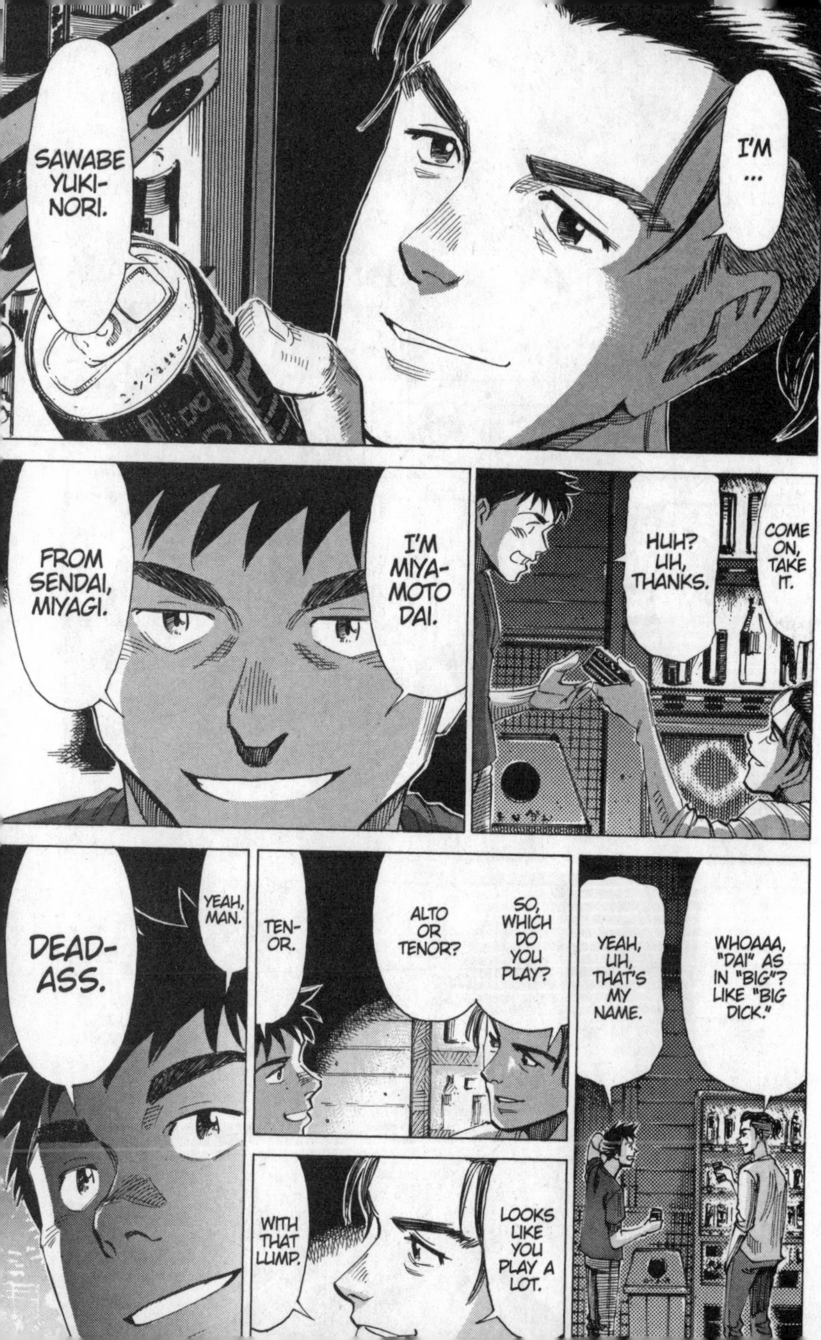
I'M ...
SAWABE YUKI-NORI.
COME ON, TAKE IT.
HUH? UH, THANKS.
I'M MIYA-MOTO DAI.
FROM SENDAI, MIYAGI.
WHOAAA, "DAI" AS IN "BIG"? LIKE "BIG DICK."
YEAH, UH, THAT'S MY NAME.
SO, WHICH DO YOU PLAY?
ALTO OR TENOR?
TEN-OR.
LOOKS LIKE YOU PLAY A LOT.
WITH THAT LUMP.
YEAH, MAN.
DEAD-ASS.

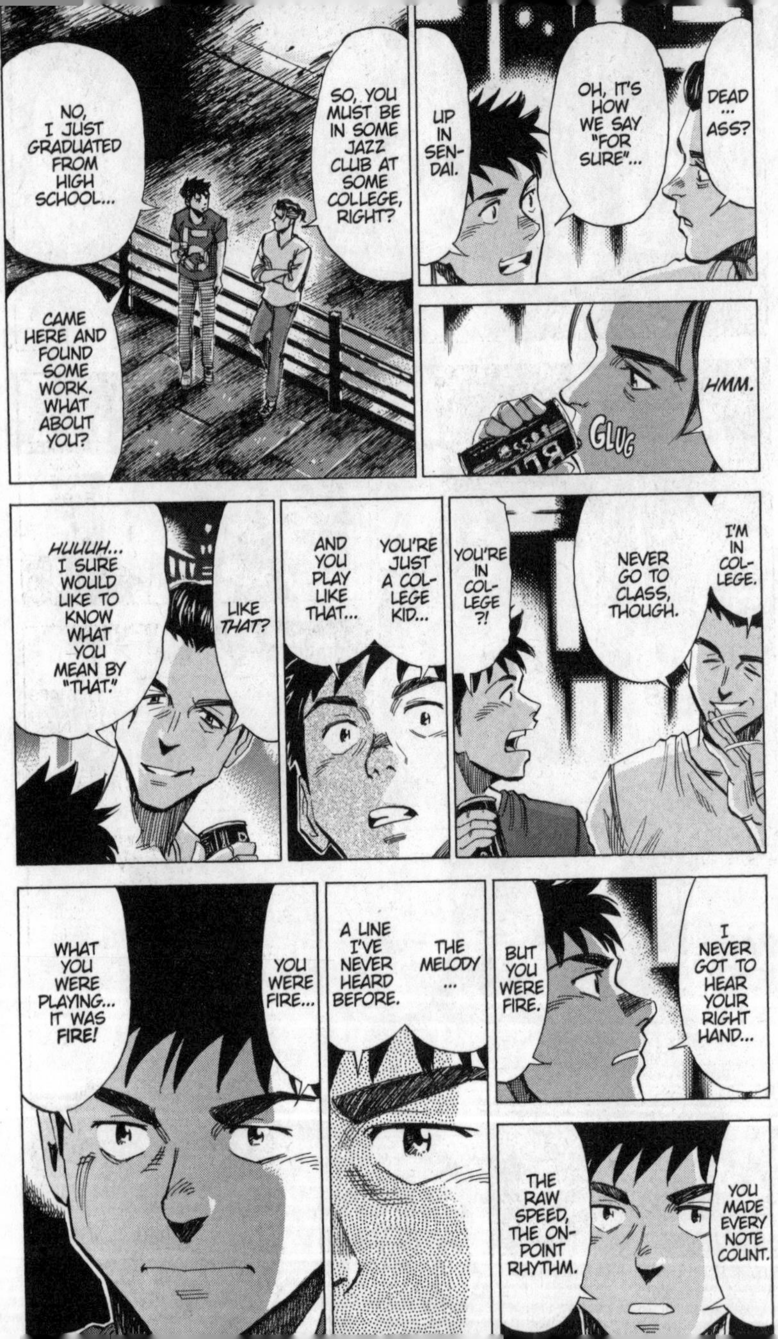
DEAD ... ASS?
OH, IT'S HOW WE SAY "FOR SURE"...
UP IN SEN-DAI.
HMM.
GLUG
SO, YOU MUST BE IN SOME JAZZ CLUB AT SOME COLLEGE, RIGHT?
NO, I JUST GRADUATED FROM HIGH SCHOOL...
CAME HERE AND FOUND SOME WORK. WHAT ABOUT YOU?
I'M IN COL-LEGE.
NEVER GO TO CLASS, THOUGH.
YOU'RE IN COL-LEGE?!
YOU'RE JUST A COL-LEGE KID...
AND YOU PLAY LIKE THAT...
LIKE *THAT*?
HUUUH... I SURE WOULD LIKE TO KNOW WHAT YOU MEAN BY "THAT."
I NEVER GOT TO HEAR YOUR RIGHT HAND...
BUT YOU WERE FIRE.
YOU MADE EVERY NOTE COUNT.
THE RAW SPEED, THE ON-POINT RHYTHM.
THE MELODY ...
A LINE I'VE NEVER HEARD BEFORE.
YOU WERE FIRE...
WHAT YOU WERE PLAYING... IT WAS FIRE!

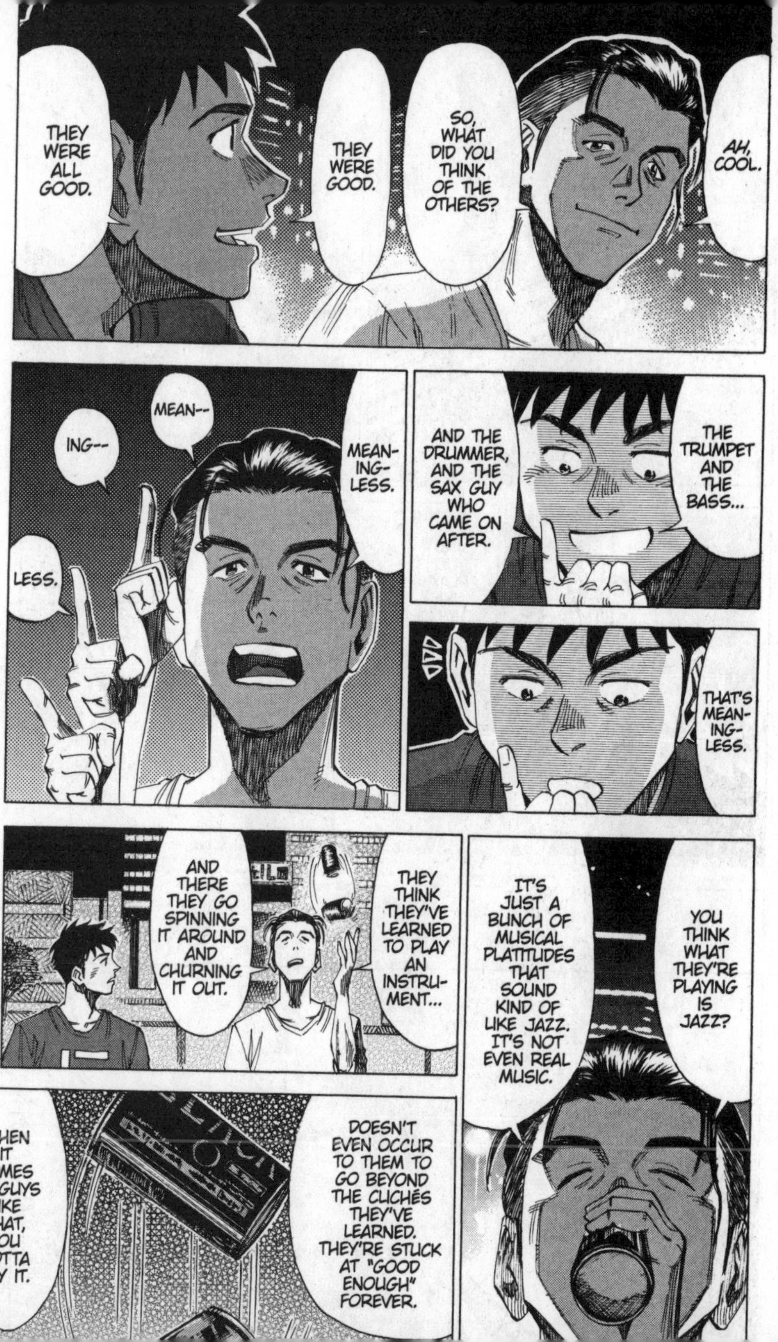
AH, COOL.
SO, WHAT DID YOU THINK OF THE OTHERS?
THEY WERE GOOD.
THEY WERE ALL GOOD.
THE TRUMPET AND THE BASS...
AND THE DRUMMER, AND THE SAX GUY WHO CAME ON AFTER.
THAT'S MEANINGLESS.
MEANINGLESS.
MEAN--
ING--
LESS.
YOU THINK WHAT THEY'RE PLAYING IS JAZZ?
IT'S JUST A BUNCH OF MUSICAL PLATITUDES THAT SOUND KIND OF LIKE JAZZ. IT'S NOT EVEN REAL MUSIC.
THEY THINK THEY'VE LEARNED TO PLAY AN INSTRUMENT...
AND THERE THEY GO SPINNING IT AROUND AND CHURNING IT OUT.
DOESN'T EVEN OCCUR TO THEM TO GO BEYOND THE CLICHÉS THEY'VE LEARNED. THEY'RE STUCK AT "GOOD ENOUGH" FOREVER.
WHEN IT COMES TO GUYS LIKE THAT, YOU GOTTA SAY IT.

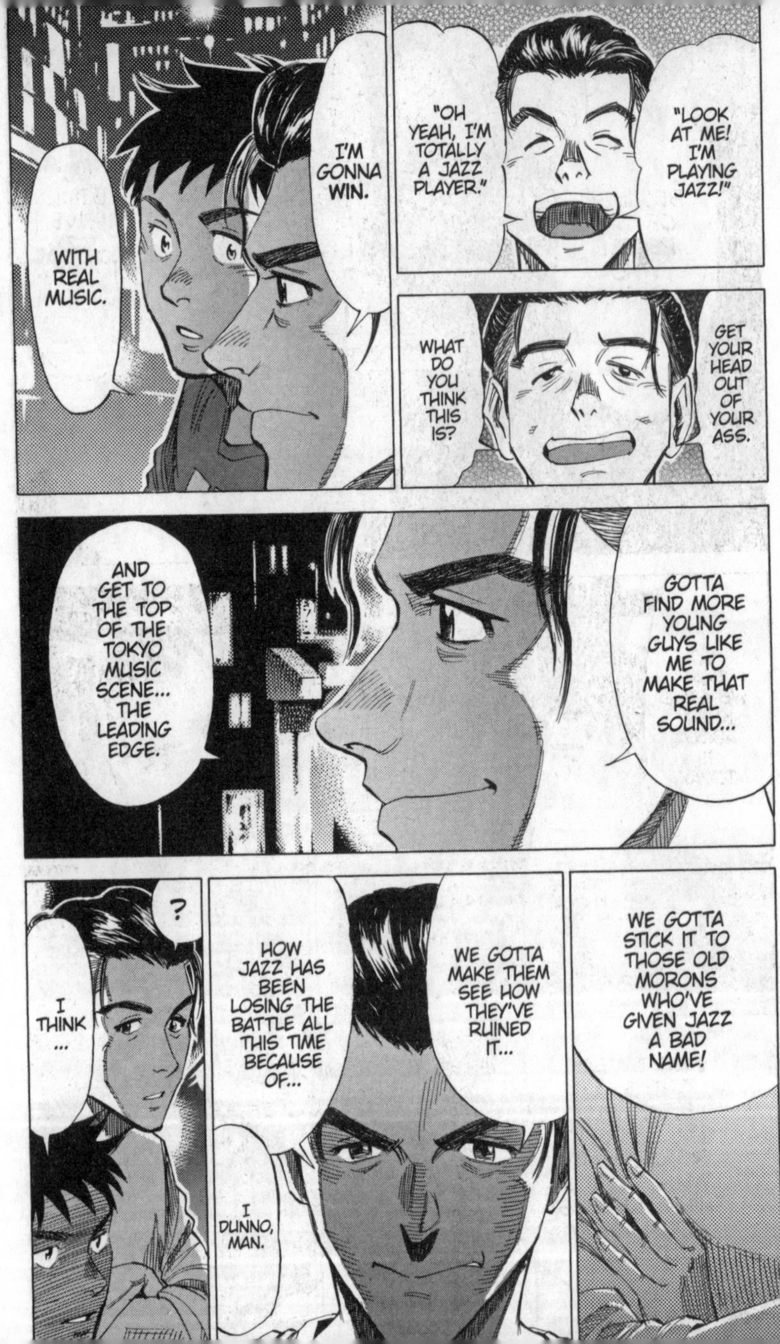
"LOOK AT ME! I'M PLAYING JAZZ!"
"OH YEAH, I'M TOTALLY A JAZZ PLAYER."
GET YOUR HEAD OUT OF YOUR ASS.
WHAT DO YOU THINK THIS IS?
I'M GONNA WIN.
WITH REAL MUSIC.
GOTTA FIND MORE YOUNG GUYS LIKE ME TO MAKE THAT REAL SOUND...
AND GET TO THE TOP OF THE TOKYO MUSIC SCENE... THE LEADING EDGE.
WE GOTTA STICK IT TO THOSE OLD MORONS WHO'VE GIVEN JAZZ A BAD NAME!
WE GOTTA MAKE THEM SEE HOW THEY'VE RUINED IT...
HOW JAZZ HAS BEEN LOSING THE BATTLE ALL THIS TIME BECAUSE OF...
I DUNNO, MAN.
?
I THINK ...

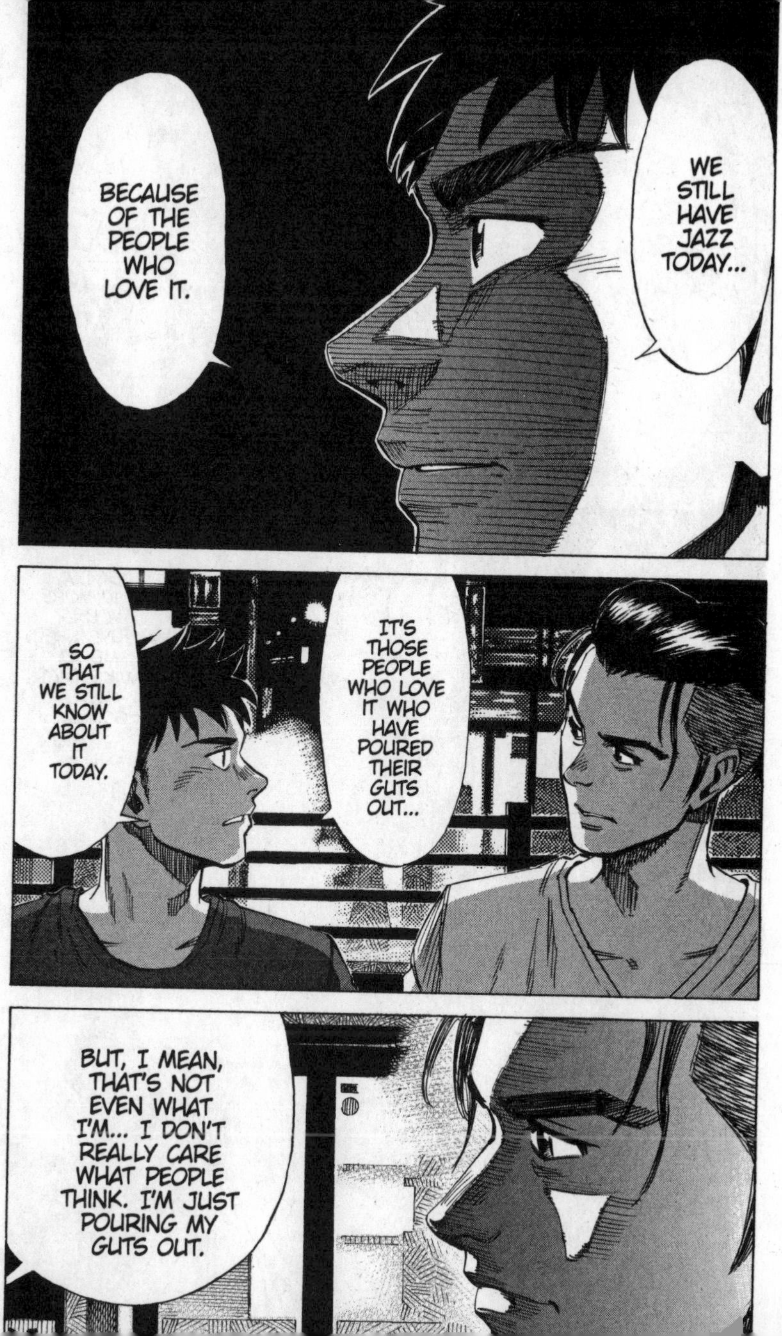
WE STILL HAVE JAZZ TODAY...
BECAUSE OF THE PEOPLE WHO LOVE IT.
IT'S THOSE PEOPLE WHO LOVE IT WHO HAVE POURED THEIR GUTS OUT...
SO THAT WE STILL KNOW ABOUT IT TODAY.
BUT, I MEAN, THAT'S NOT EVEN WHAT I'M... I DON'T REALLY CARE WHAT PEOPLE THINK. I'M JUST POURING MY GUTS OUT.

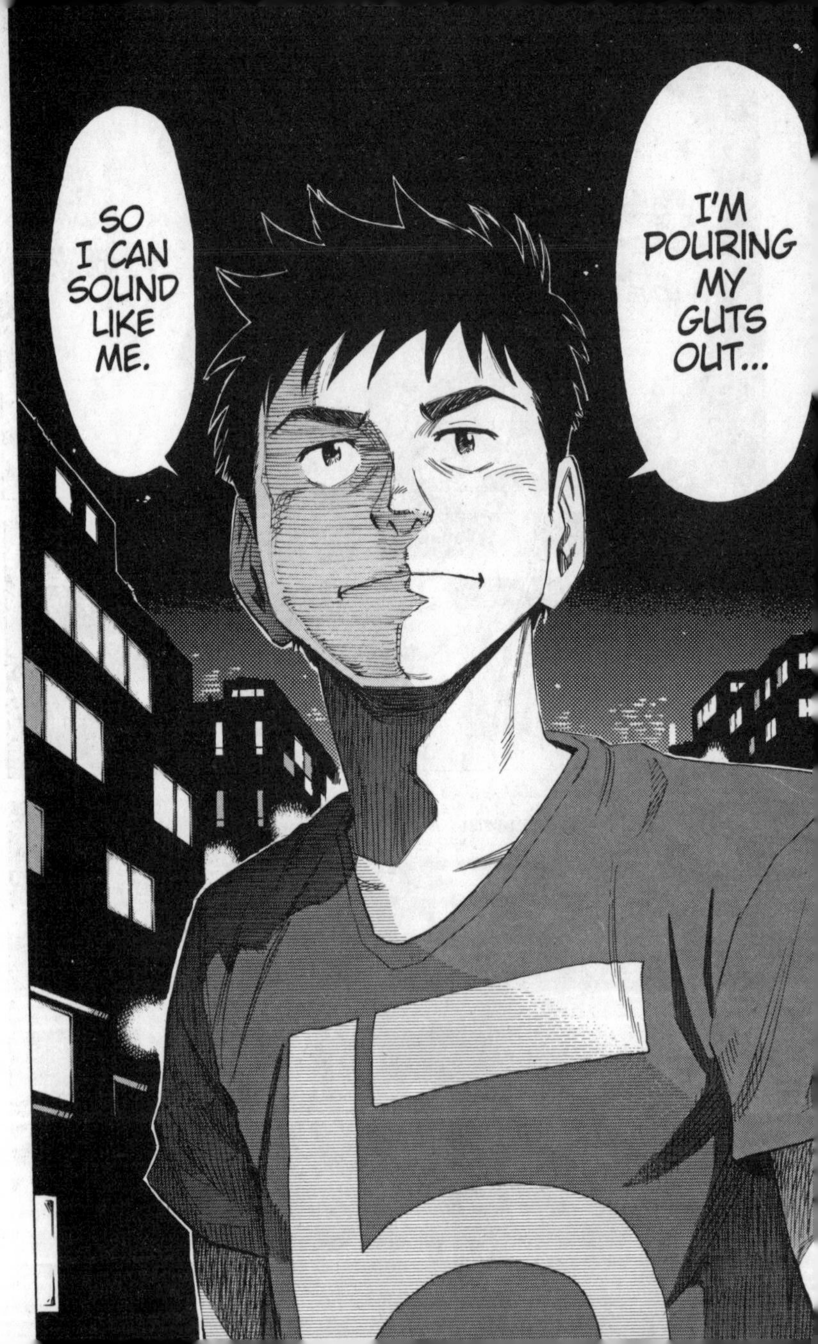
I'M POURING MY GUTS OUT...
SO I CAN SOUND LIKE ME.

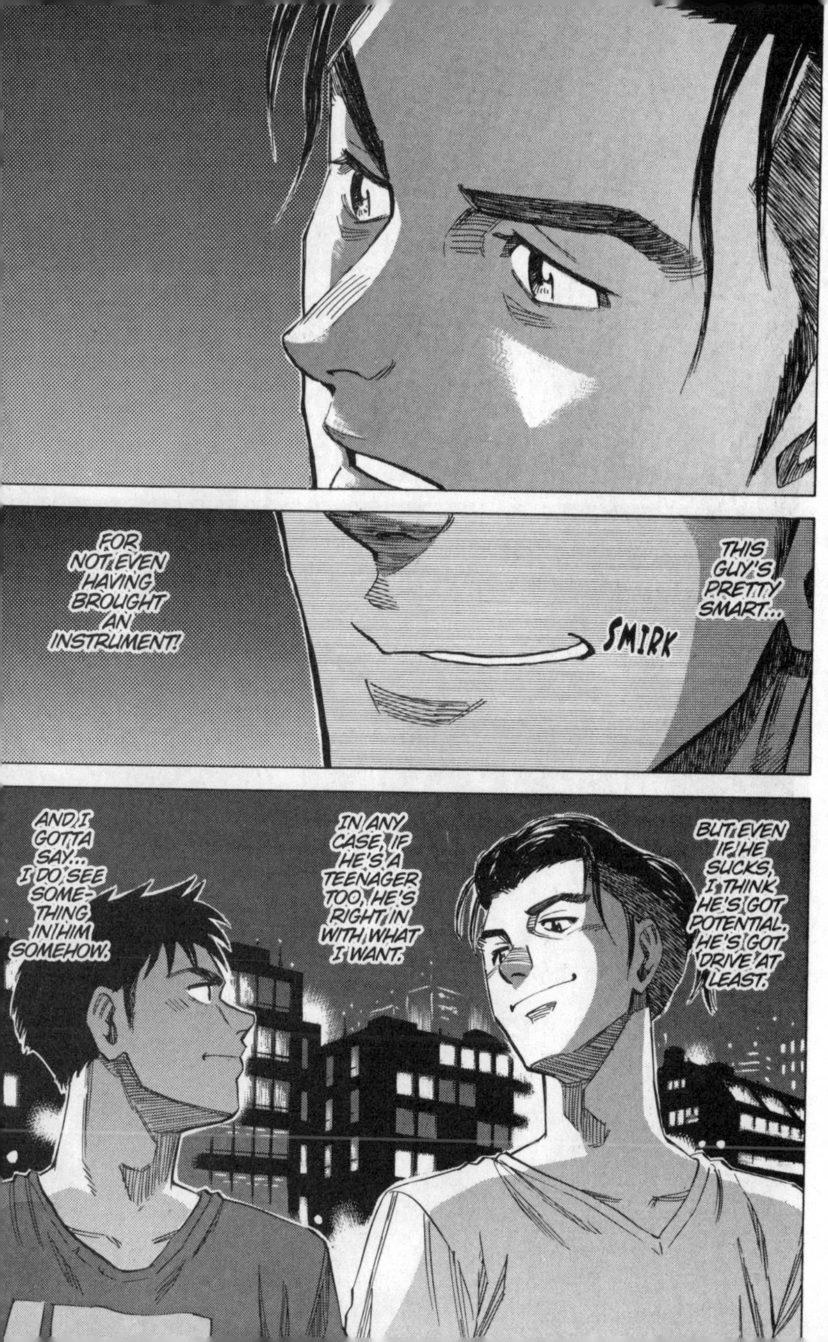
THIS GUY'S PRETTY SMART...
SMIRK
FOR NOT EVEN HAVING BROUGHT AN INSTRUMENT!
BUT EVEN IF HE SUCKS, I THINK HE'S GOT POTENTIAL. HE'S GOT DRIVE AT LEAST.
IN ANY CASE, IF HE'S A TEENAGER TOO, HE'S RIGHT IN WITH WHAT I WANT.
AND I GOTTA SAY... I DO SEE SOMETHING IN HIM SOMEHOW.

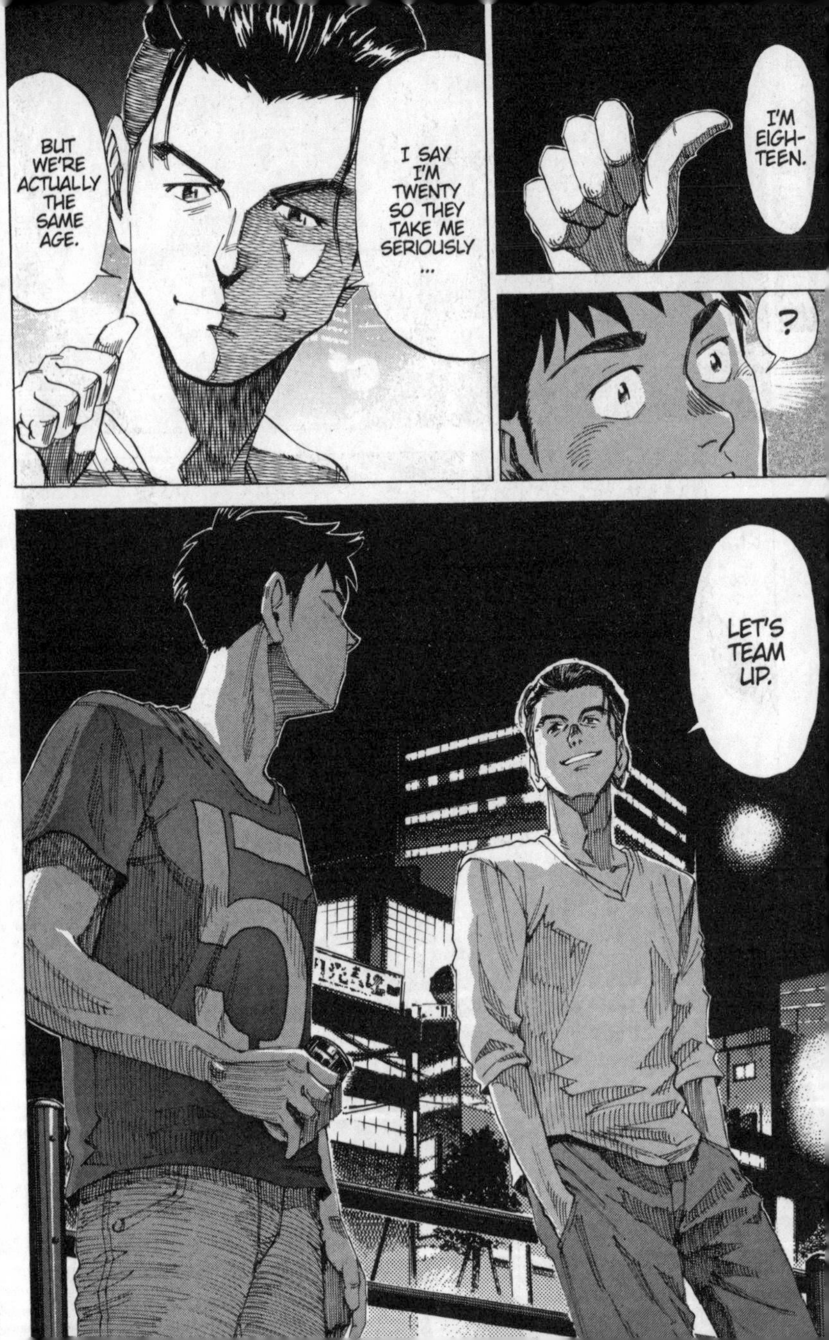
I'M EIGHTEEN.
?
I SAY I'M TWENTY SO THEY TAKE ME SERIOUSLY ...
BUT WE'RE ACTUALLY THE SAME AGE.
LET'S TEAM UP.

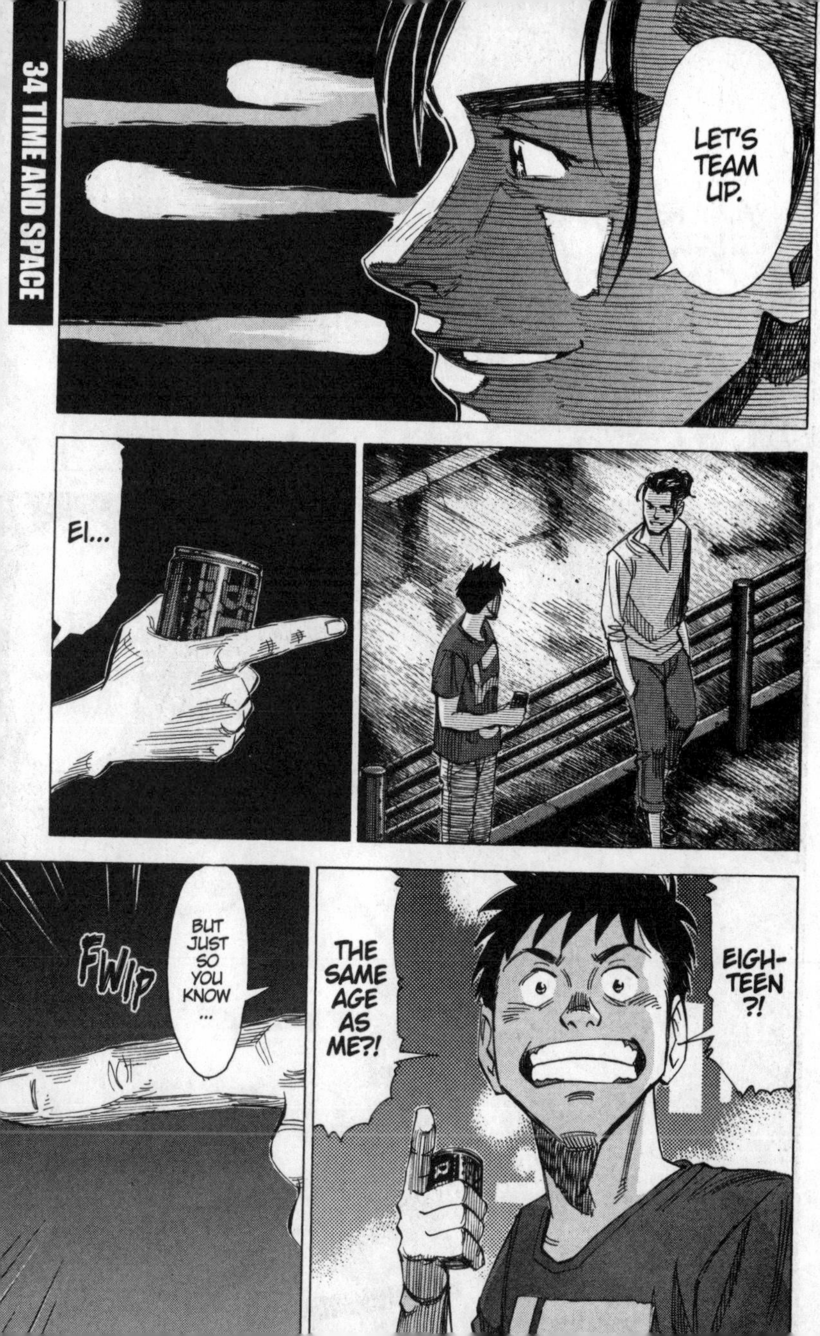
LET'S TEAM UP.
EI...
EIGH-TEEN?!
THE SAME AGE AS ME?!
BUT JUST SO YOU KNOW...
FWIP

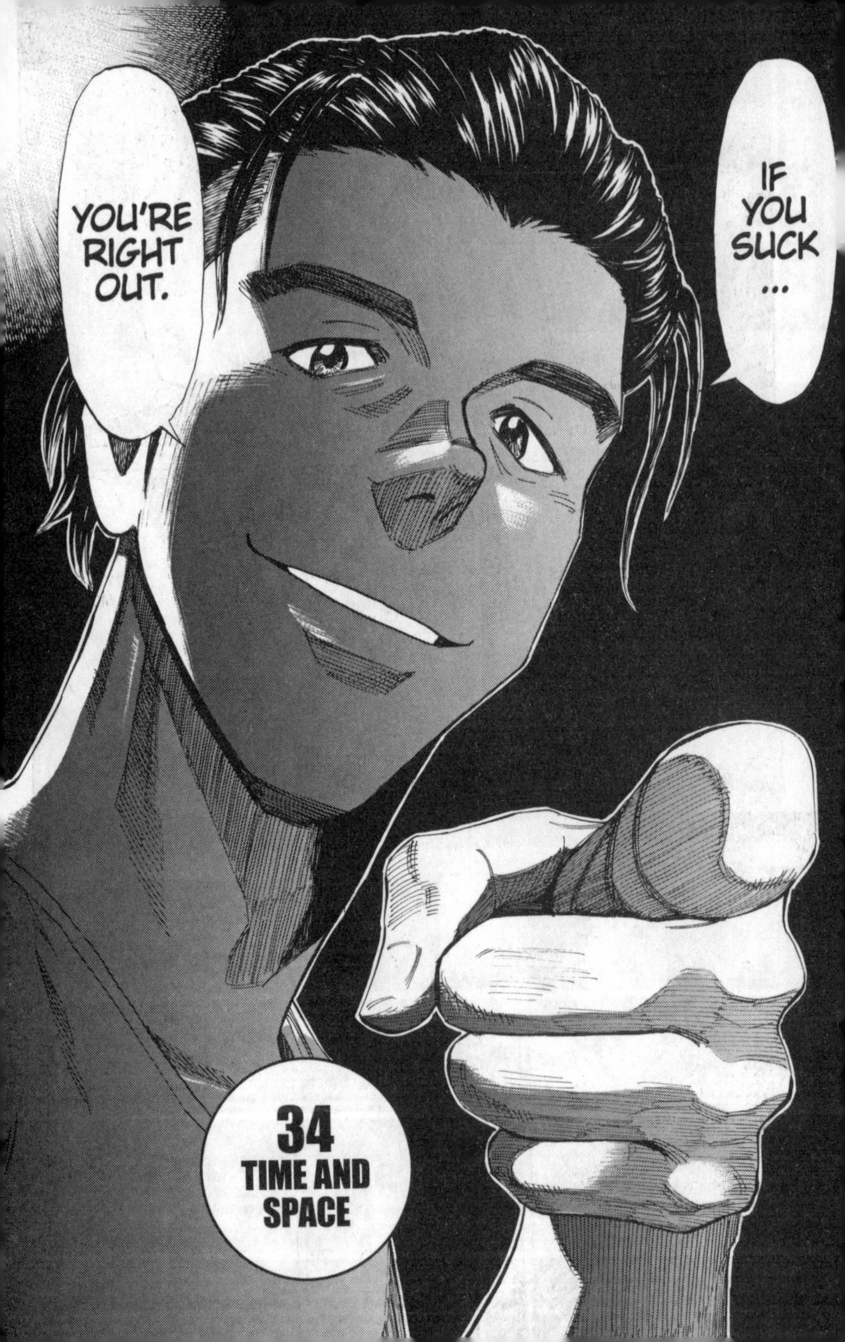
IF YOU SUCK ...
YOU'RE RIGHT OUT.
34 TIME AND SPACE

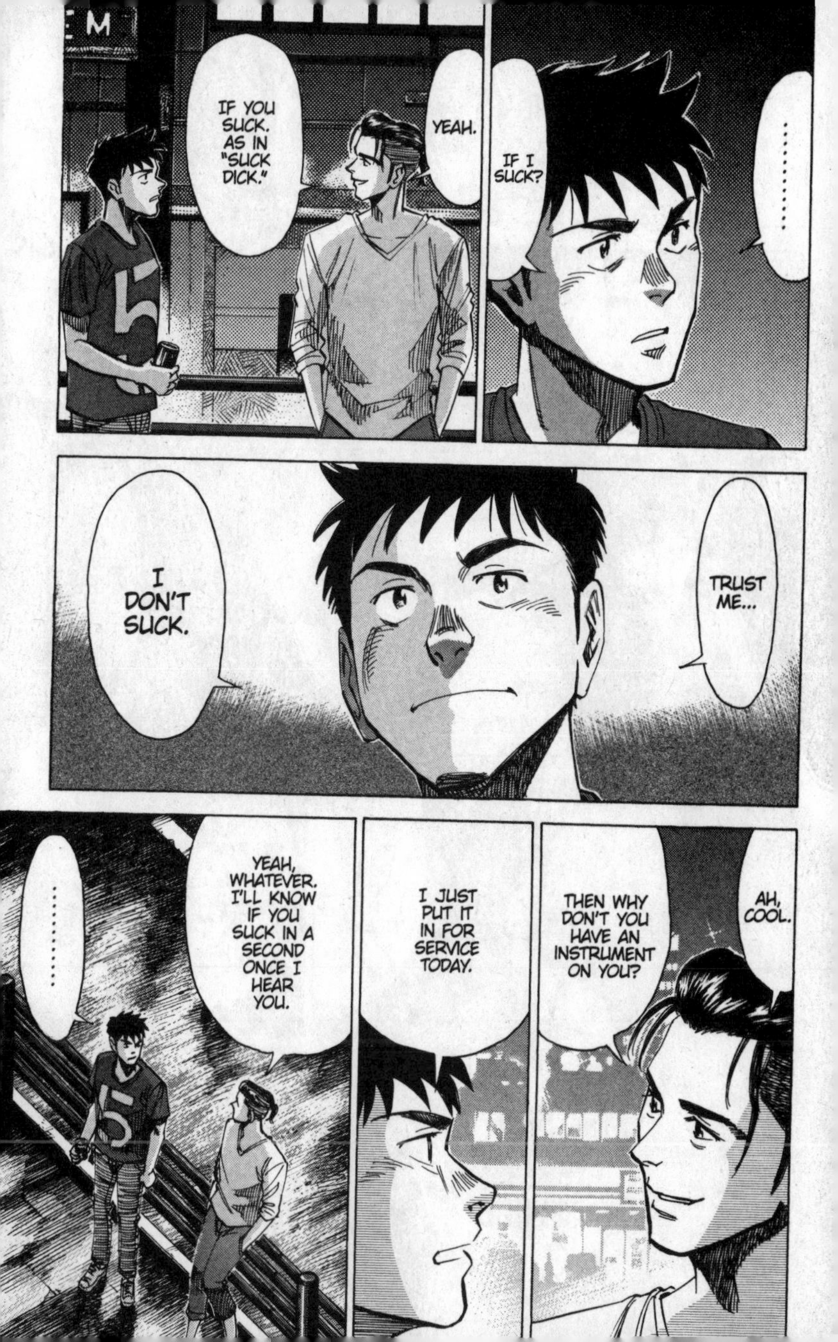
......
IF I SUCK?
YEAH.
IF YOU SUCK. AS IN "SUCK DICK."
TRUST ME...
I DON'T SUCK.
AH, COOL.
THEN WHY DON'T YOU HAVE AN INSTRUMENT ON YOU?
I JUST PUT IT IN FOR SERVICE TODAY.
YEAH, WHATEVER. I'LL KNOW IF YOU SUCK IN A SECOND ONCE I HEAR YOU.
......

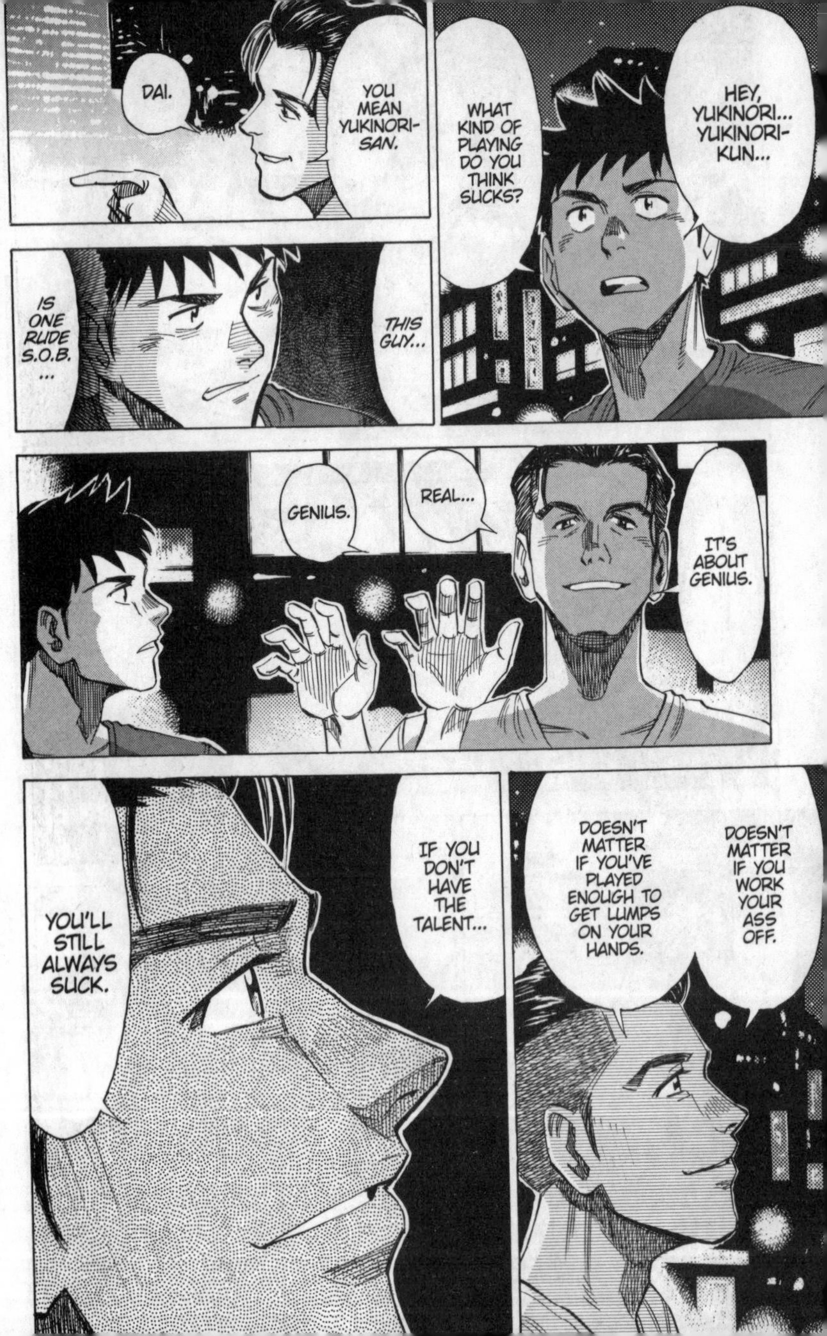
HEY, YUKINORI... YUKINORI-KUN...
WHAT KIND OF PLAYING DO YOU THINK SUCKS?
YOU MEAN YUKINORI-SAN.
DAI.
THIS GUY...
IS ONE RUDE S.O.B. ...
IT'S ABOUT GENIUS.
REAL...
GENIUS.
DOESN'T MATTER IF YOU WORK YOUR ASS OFF.
DOESN'T MATTER IF YOU'VE PLAYED ENOUGH TO GET LUMPS ON YOUR HANDS.
IF YOU DON'T HAVE THE TALENT...
YOU'LL STILL ALWAYS SUCK.

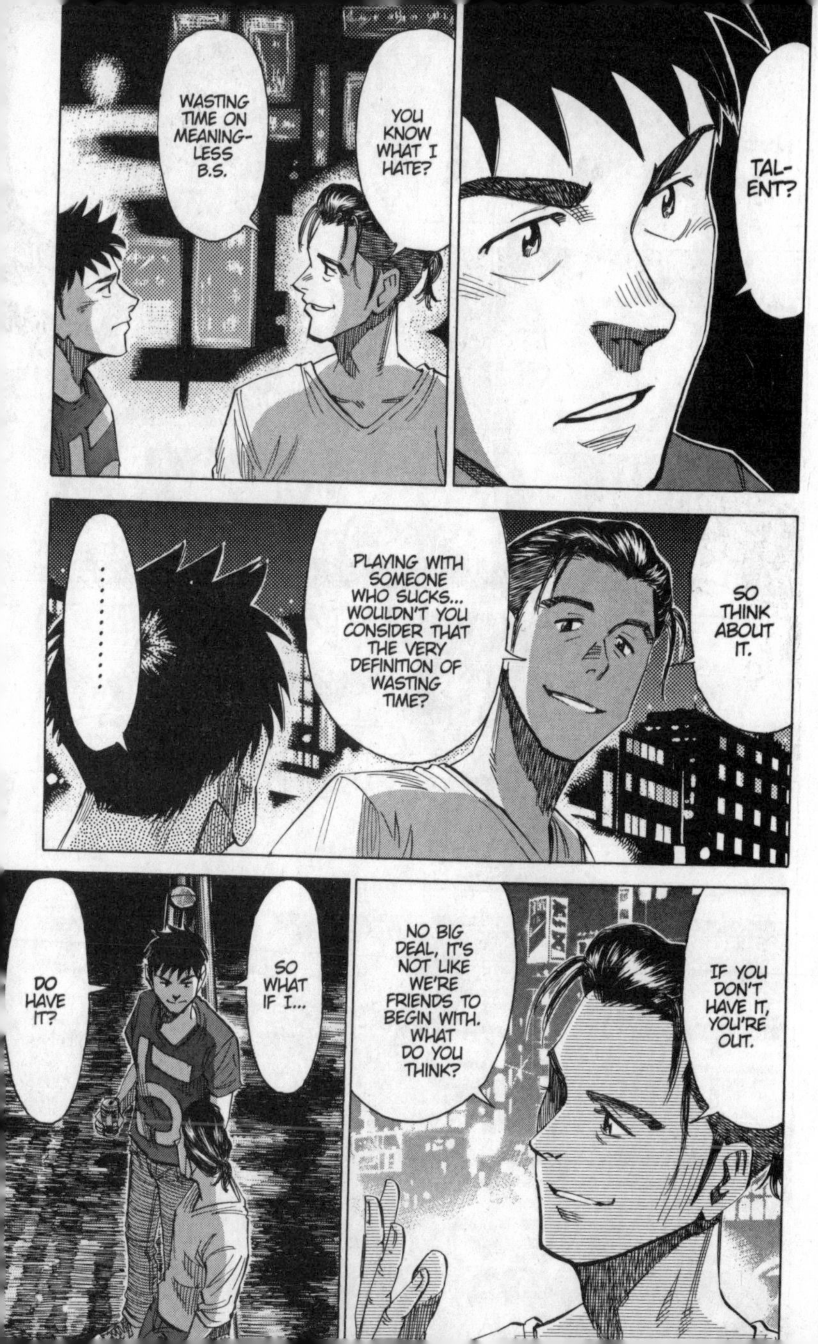

TAL-
ENT?
YOU KNOW WHAT I HATE?
WASTING TIME ON MEANING-LESS B.S.
SO THINK ABOUT IT.
PLAYING WITH SOMEONE WHO SUCKS... WOULDN'T YOU CONSIDER THAT THE VERY DEFINITION OF WASTING TIME?
......
IF YOU DON'T HAVE IT, YOU'RE OUT.
NO BIG DEAL, IT'S NOT LIKE WE'RE FRIENDS TO BEGIN WITH. WHAT DO YOU THINK?
SO WHAT IF I...
DO HAVE IT?

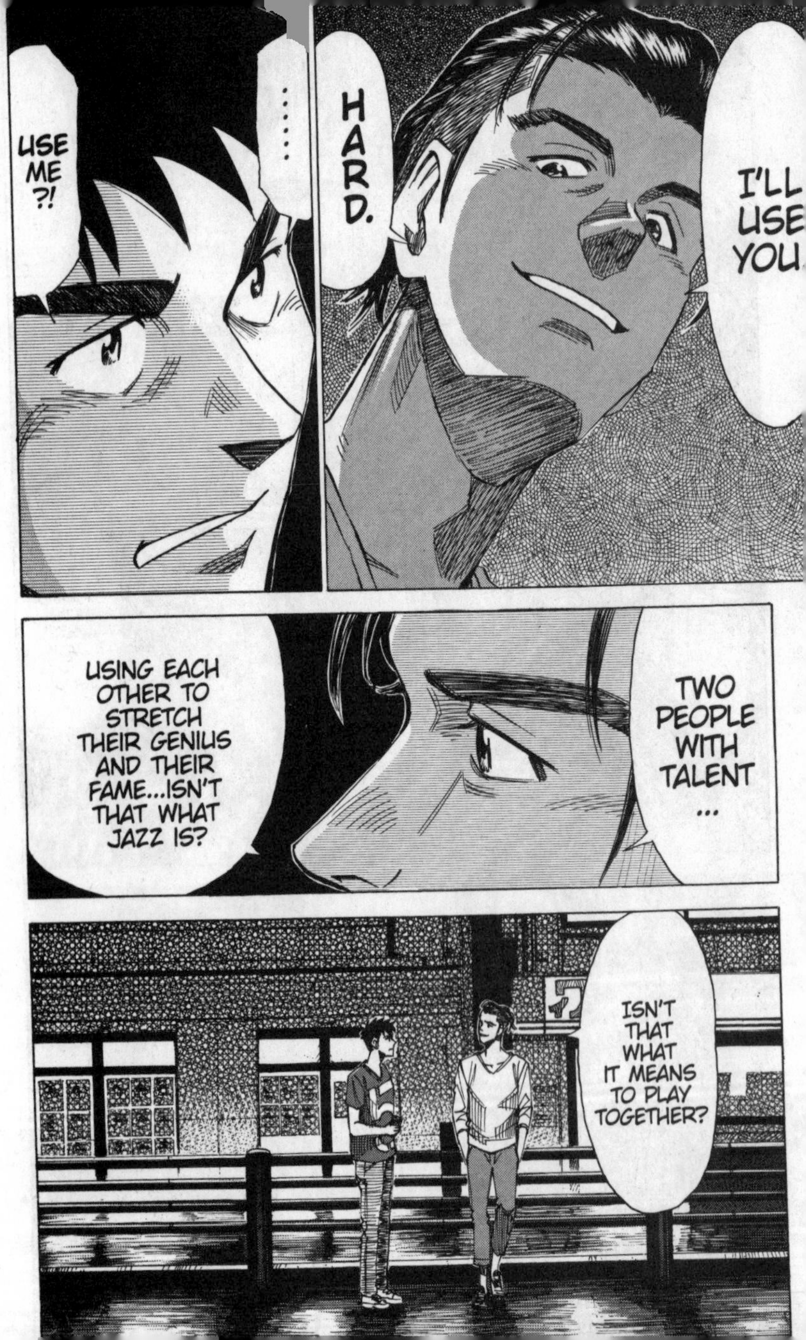
I'LL USE YOU.
HARD.
......
USE ME ?!
TWO PEOPLE WITH TALENT ...
USING EACH OTHER TO STRETCH THEIR GENIUS AND THEIR FAME...ISN'T THAT WHAT JAZZ IS?
ISN'T THAT WHAT IT MEANS TO PLAY TOGETHER?

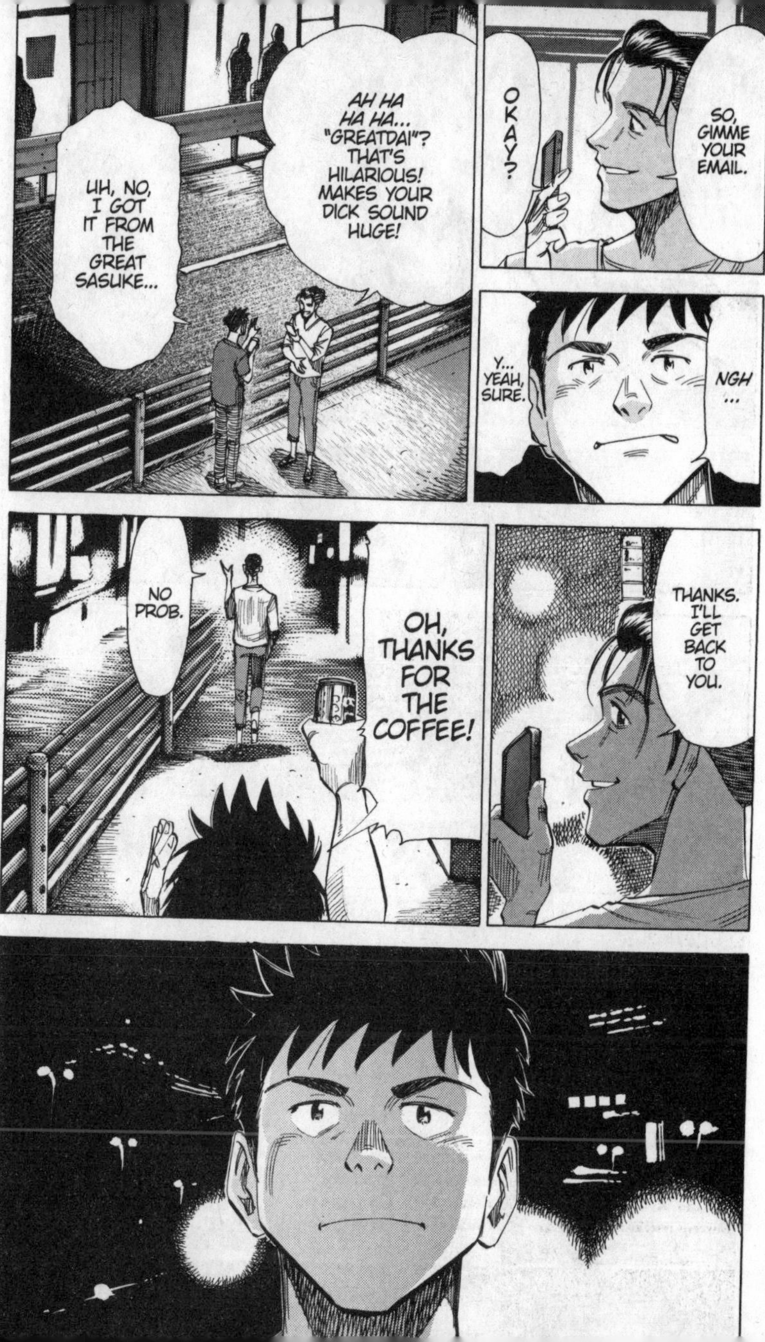
SO, GIMME YOUR EMAIL.
OKAY?
NGH...
Y... YEAH, SURE.
AH HA HA HA... "GREATDAI"? THAT'S HILARIOUS! MAKES YOUR DICK SOUND HUGE!
UH, NO, I GOT IT FROM THE GREAT SASUKE...
THANKS. I'LL GET BACK TO YOU.
OH, THANKS FOR THE COFFEE!
NO PROB.

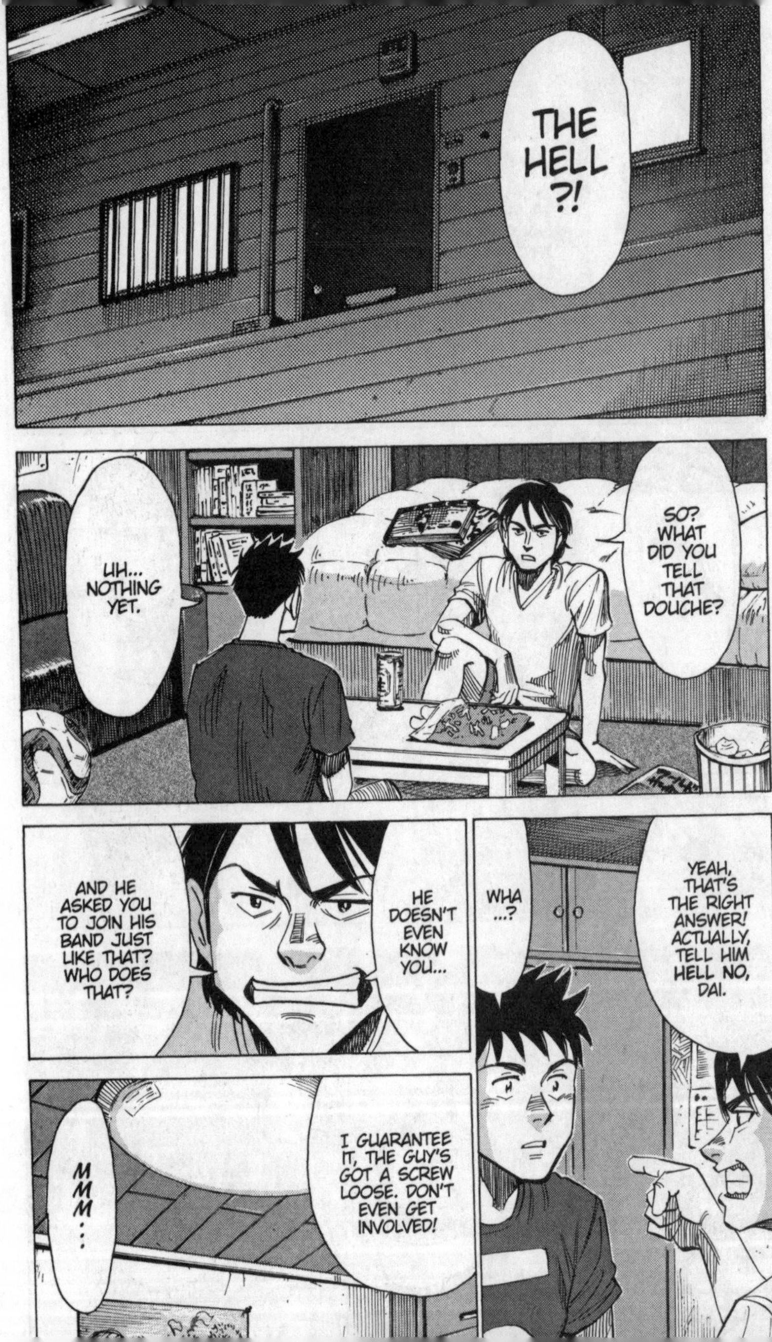
THE HELL ?!
SO? WHAT DID YOU TELL THAT DOUCHE?
UH... NOTHING YET.
YEAH, THAT'S THE RIGHT ANSWER! ACTUALLY, TELL HIM HELL NO, DAI.
WHA ...?
HE DOESN'T EVEN KNOW YOU...
AND HE ASKED YOU TO JOIN HIS BAND JUST LIKE THAT? WHO DOES THAT?
I GUARANTEE IT, THE GUY'S GOT A SCREW LOOSE. DON'T EVEN GET INVOLVED!
MMM...

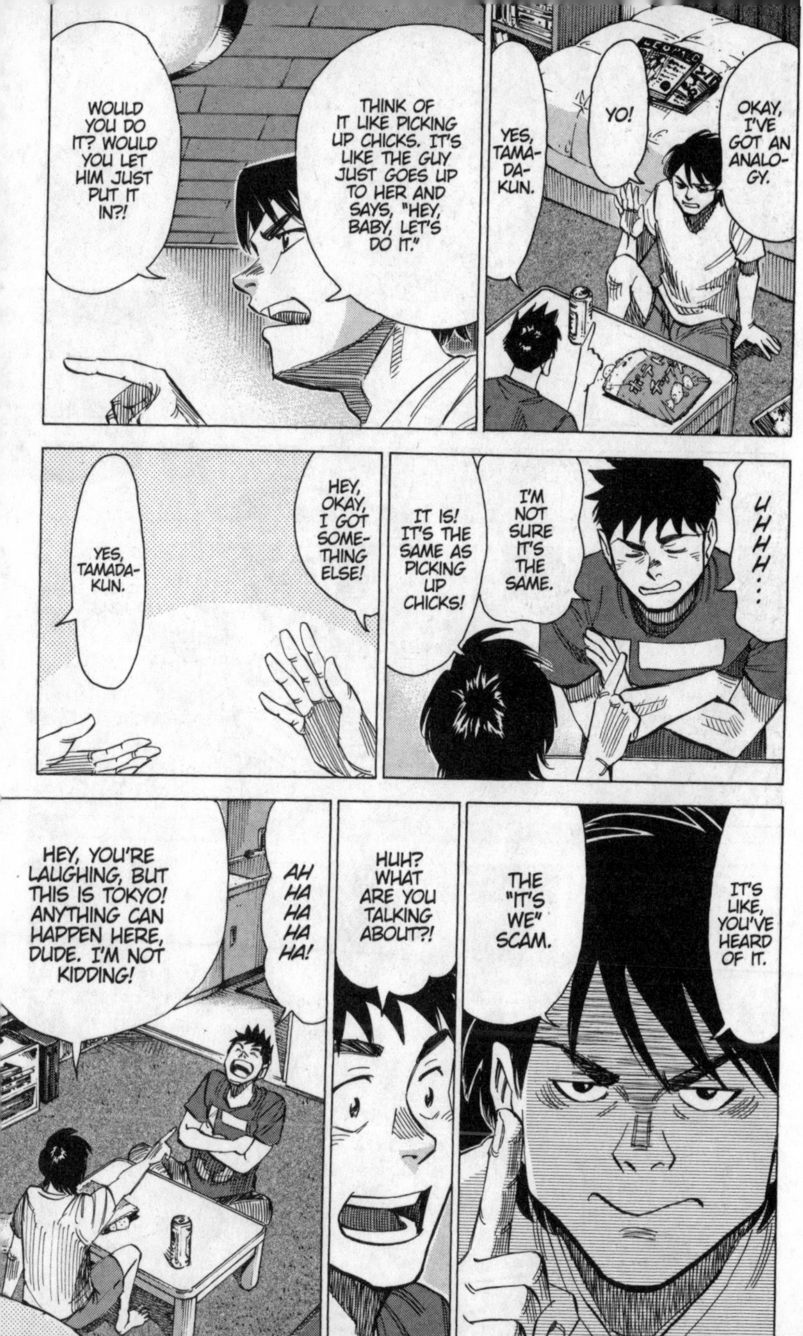
OKAY, I'VE GOT AN ANALOGY.
YO!
YES, TAMADA-KUN.
THINK OF IT LIKE PICKING UP CHICKS. IT'S LIKE THE GUY JUST GOES UP TO HER AND SAYS, "HEY, BABY, LET'S DO IT."
WOULD YOU DO IT? WOULD YOU LET HIM JUST PUT IT IN?!
UHHH...
I'M NOT SURE IT'S THE SAME.
IT IS! IT'S THE SAME AS PICKING UP CHICKS!
HEY, OKAY, I GOT SOMETHING ELSE!
YES, TAMADA-KUN.
IT'S LIKE, YOU'VE HEARD OF IT.
THE "IT'S WE" SCAM.
HUH? WHAT ARE YOU TALKING ABOUT?!
AH HA HA HA HA!
HEY, YOU'RE LAUGHING, BUT THIS IS TOKYO! ANYTHING CAN HAPPEN HERE, DUDE. I'M NOT KIDDING!

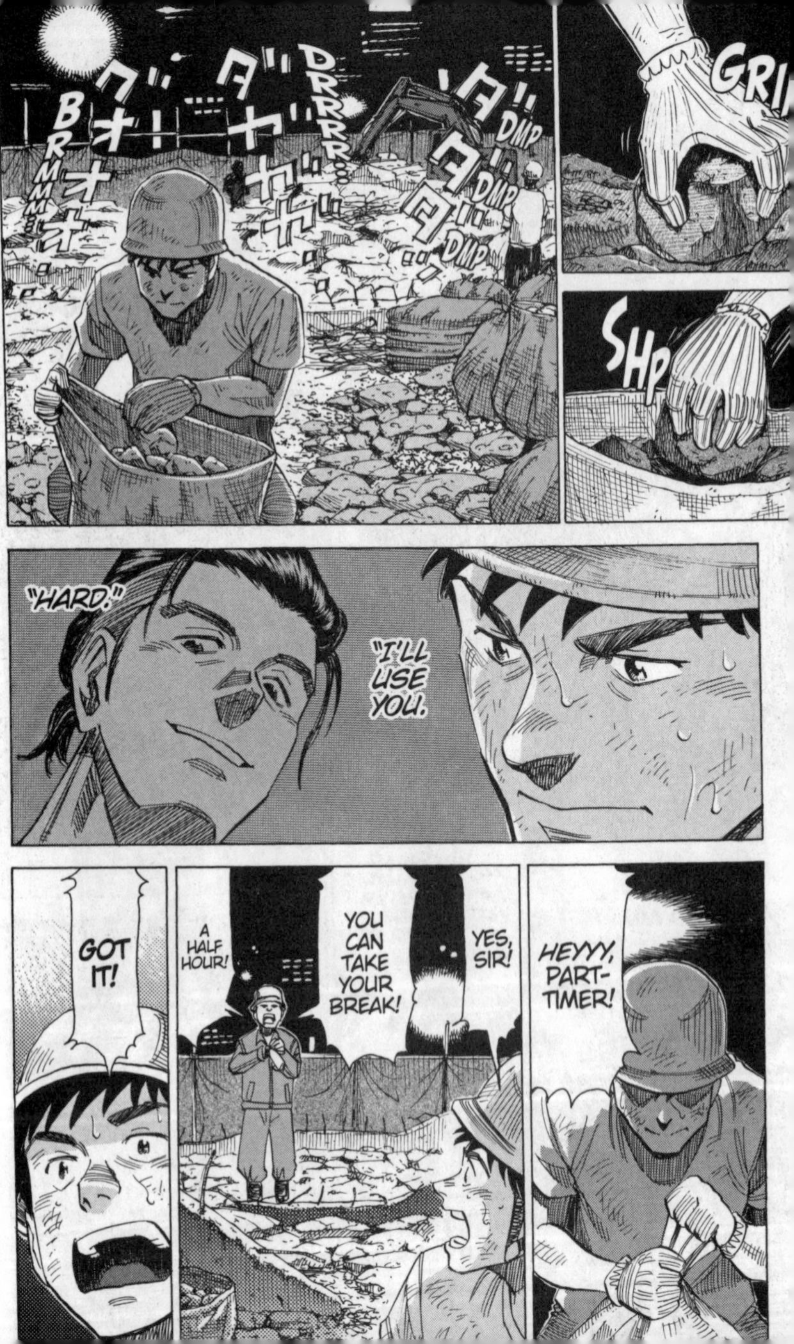
GRI
SHP
DMP
DMP
DMP
DRRRR...
BRMMM...
"I'LL USE YOU.
"HARD."
HEYYY, PART-TIMER!
YES, SIR!
YOU CAN TAKE YOUR BREAK!
A HALF HOUR!
GOT IT!

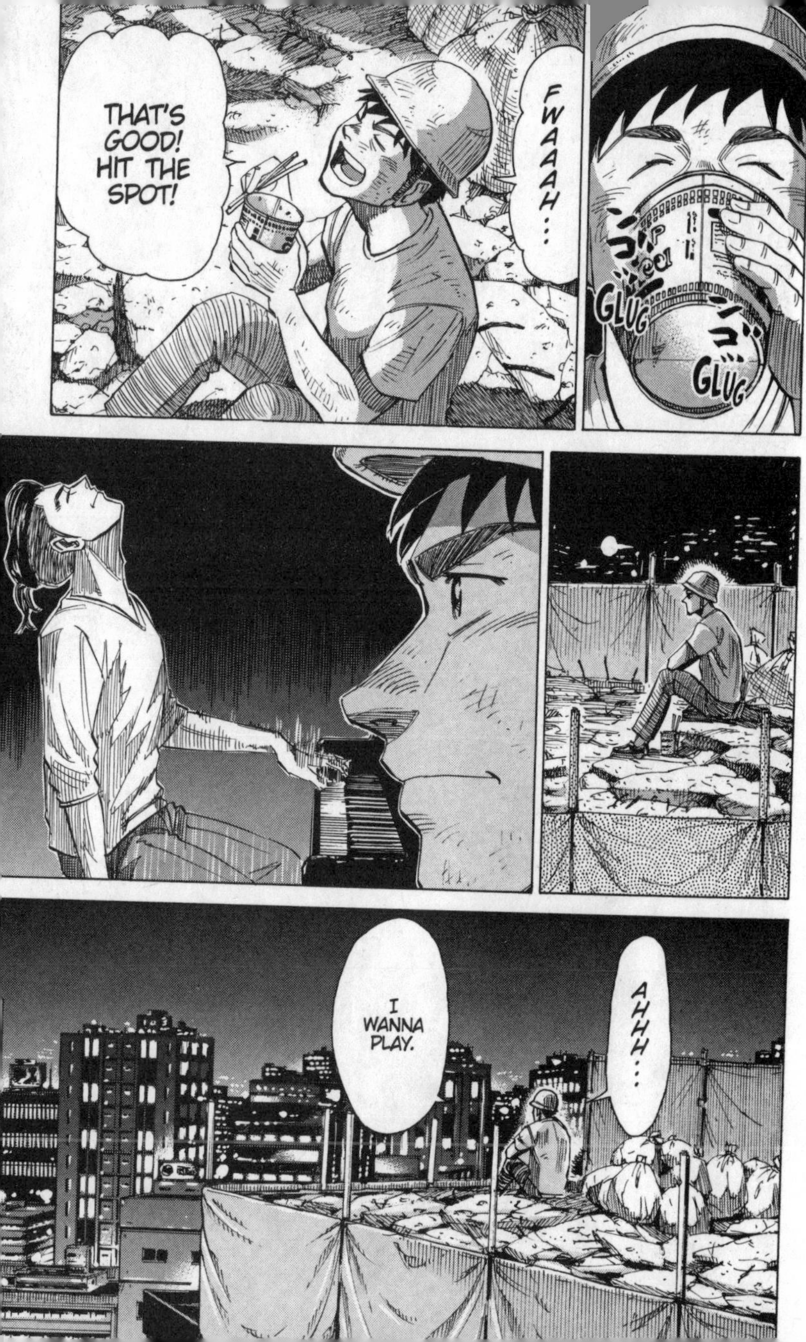
GLUG
GLUG
FWAAAH...
THAT'S GOOD! HIT THE SPOT!
AHHH...
I WANNA PLAY.

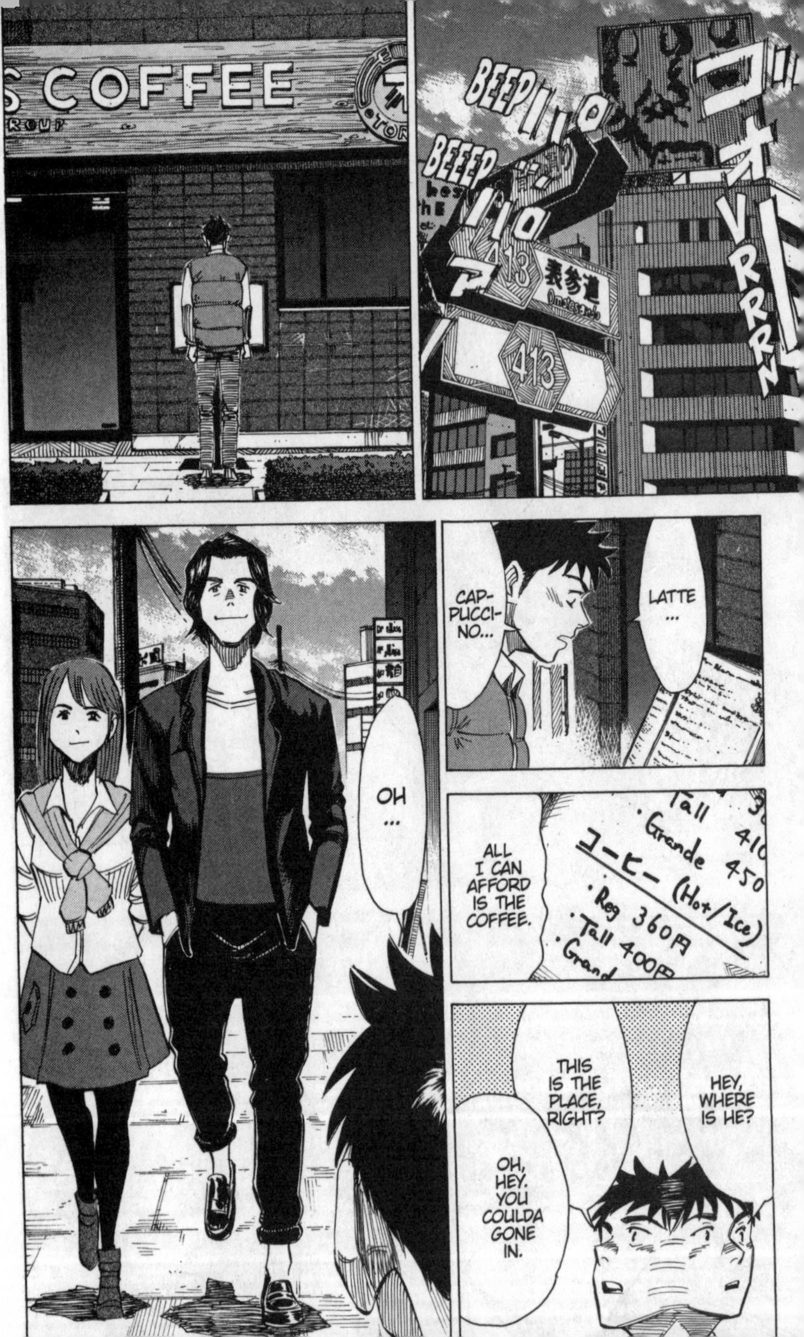

BEEP
BEEEP
VRRRN
413
表参道
Omotesando
413
S COFFEE
ROUP
LATTE ...
CAP-PUCCI-NO...
ALL I CAN AFFORD IS THE COFFEE.
Tall 410
Grande 450
コーヒー (Hot/Ice)
Reg 360円
Tall 400円
HEY, WHERE IS HE?
THIS IS THE PLACE, RIGHT?
OH, HEY. YOU COULDA GONE IN.
OH ...

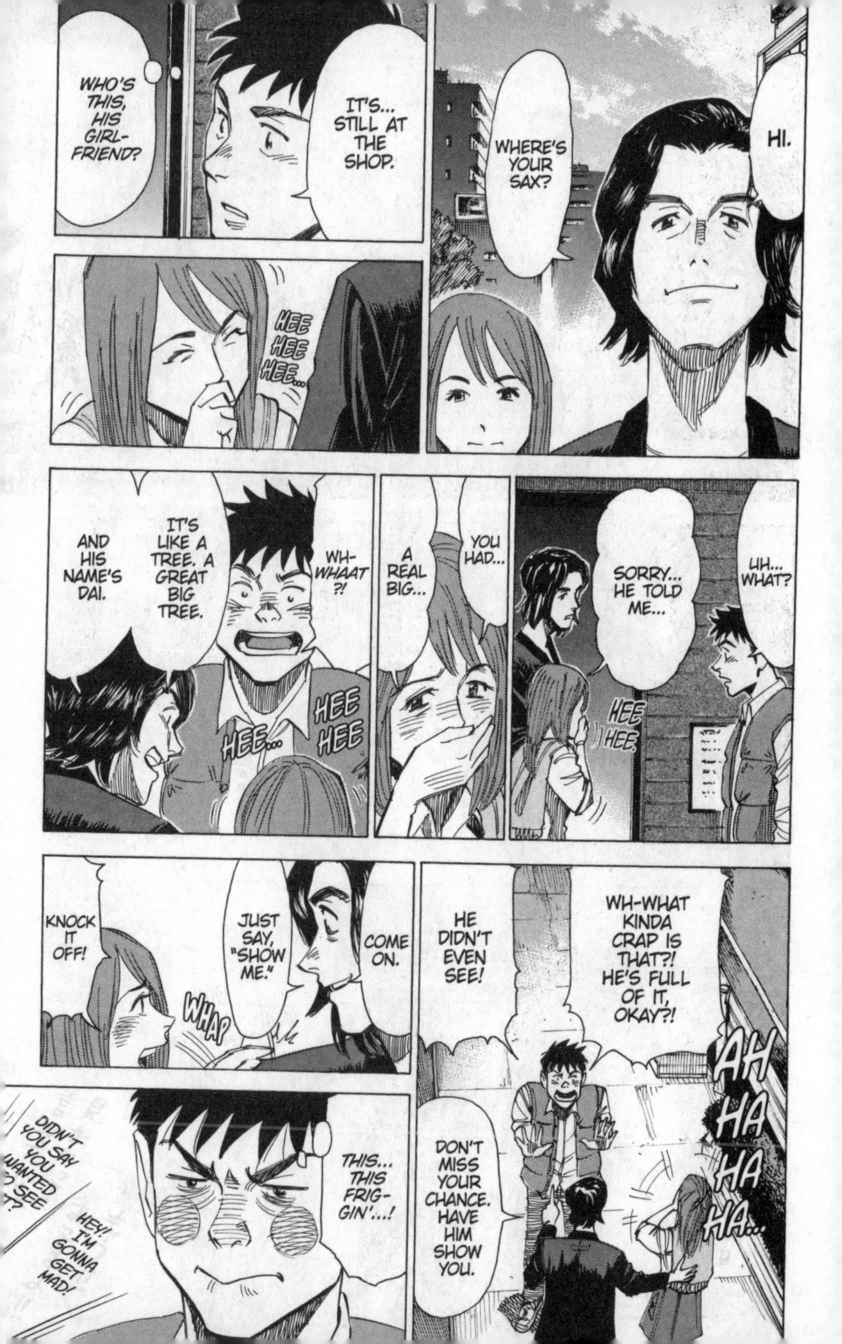
HI.
WHERE'S YOUR SAX?
IT'S... STILL AT THE SHOP.
WHO'S THIS, HIS GIRL-FRIEND?
HEE HEE HEE...
UH... WHAT?
SORRY... HE TOLD ME...
HEE HEE
YOU HAD...
A REAL BIG...
WH-WHAAT?!
IT'S LIKE A TREE. A GREAT BIG TREE.
AND HIS NAME'S DAI.
HEE HEE
HEE...
WH-WHAT KINDA CRAP IS THAT?! HE'S FULL OF IT, OKAY?!
HE DIDN'T EVEN SEE!
AH HA HA HA...
DON'T MISS YOUR CHANCE. HAVE HIM SHOW YOU.
COME ON.
JUST SAY, "SHOW ME."
KNOCK IT OFF!
WHAP
THIS... THIS FRIG-GIN'...!
DIDN'T YOU SAY YOU WANTED O SEE T?
HEY! I'M GONNA GET MAD!

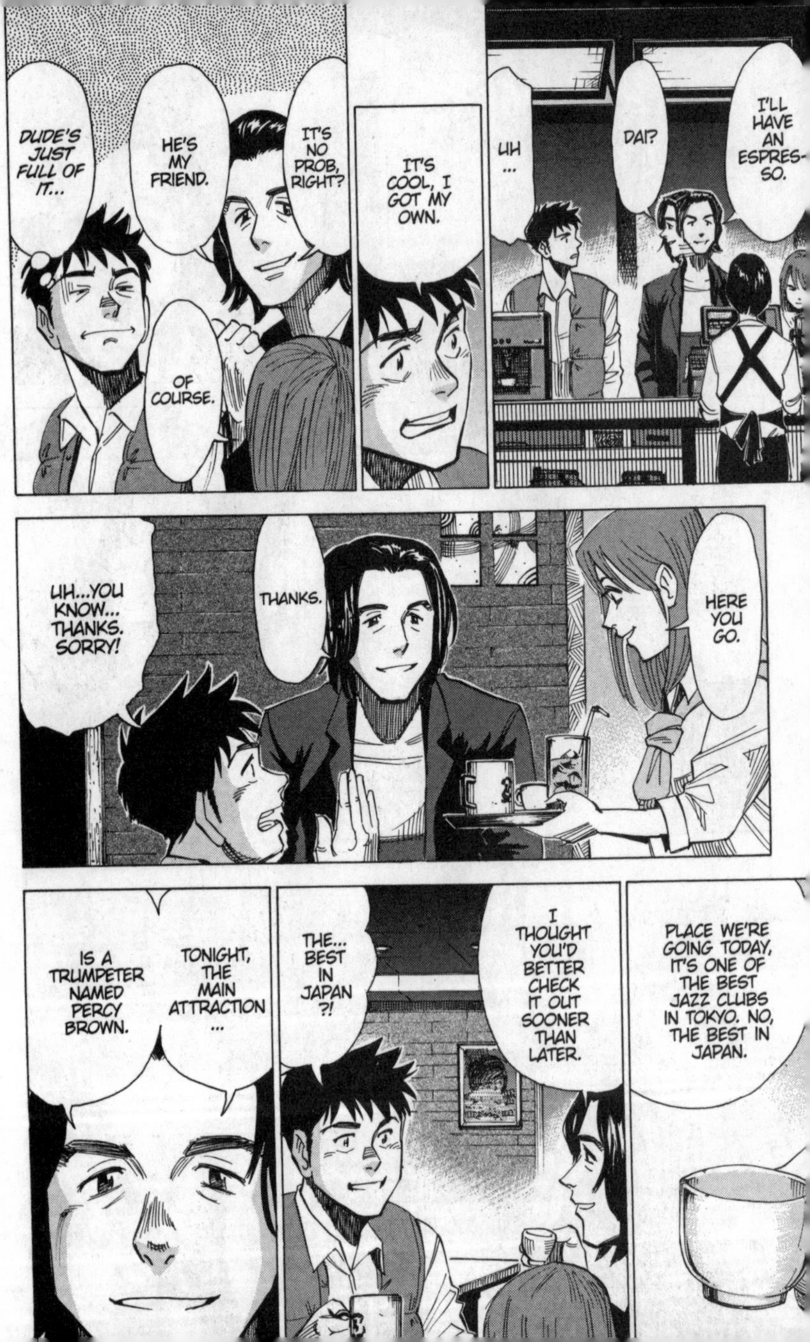
I'LL HAVE AN ESPRES-SO.
DAI?
UH ...
IT'S COOL, I GOT MY OWN.
IT'S NO PROB, RIGHT?
HE'S MY FRIEND.
OF COURSE.
DUDE'S JUST FULL OF IT...
HERE YOU GO.
THANKS.
UH...YOU KNOW... THANKS. SORRY!
PLACE WE'RE GOING TODAY, IT'S ONE OF THE BEST JAZZ CLUBS IN TOKYO. NO, THE BEST IN JAPAN.
I THOUGHT YOU'D BETTER CHECK IT OUT SOONER THAN LATER.
THE... BEST IN JAPAN ?!
TONIGHT, THE MAIN ATTRACTION ...
IS A TRUMPETER NAMED PERCY BROWN.

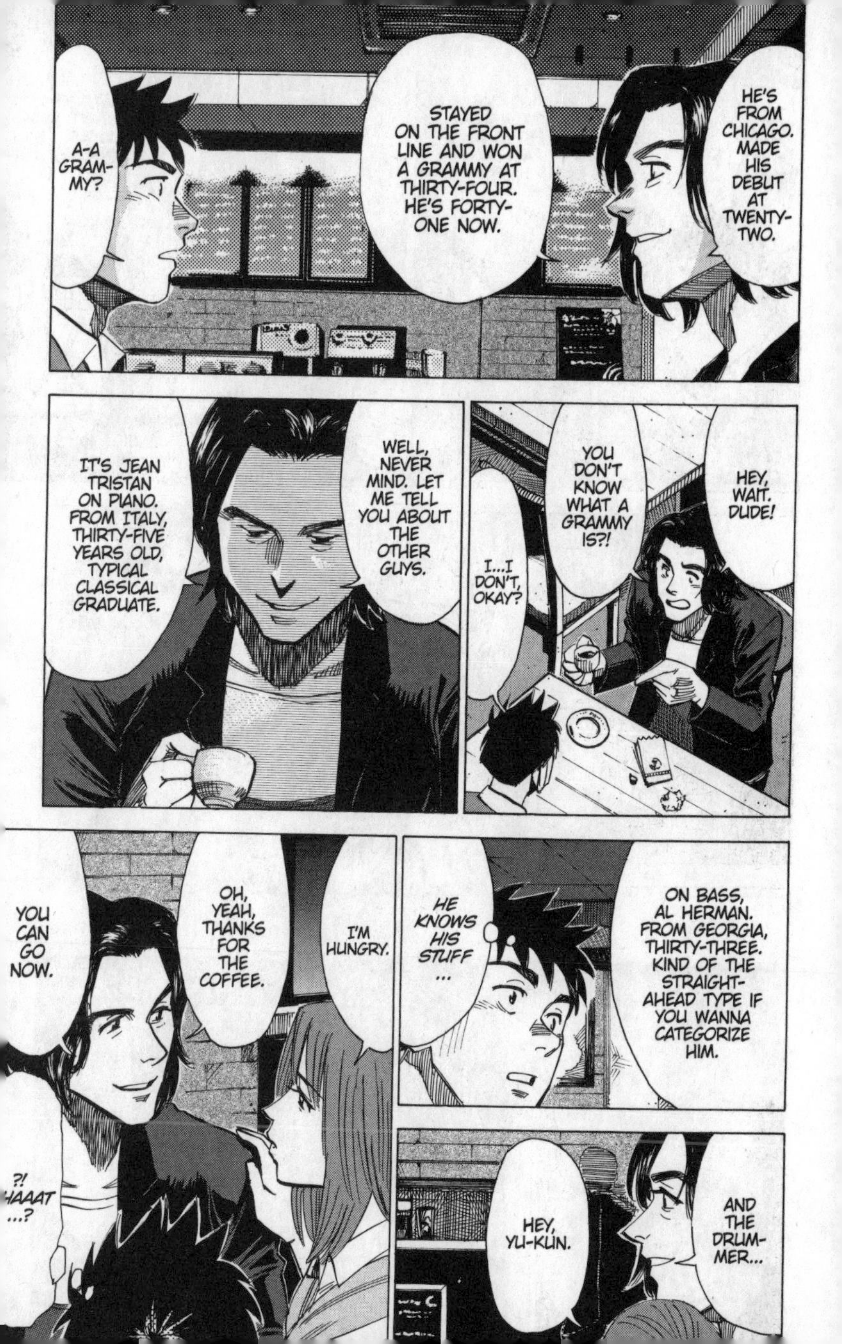
HE'S FROM CHICAGO. MADE HIS DEBUT AT TWENTY-TWO.
STAYED ON THE FRONT LINE AND WON A GRAMMY AT THIRTY-FOUR. HE'S FORTY-ONE NOW.
A-A GRAMMY?
HEY, WAIT. DUDE!
YOU DON'T KNOW WHAT A GRAMMY IS?!
I...I DON'T, OKAY?
WELL, NEVER MIND. LET ME TELL YOU ABOUT THE OTHER GUYS.
IT'S JEAN TRISTAN ON PIANO. FROM ITALY, THIRTY-FIVE YEARS OLD, TYPICAL CLASSICAL GRADUATE.
ON BASS, AL HERMAN. FROM GEORGIA, THIRTY-THREE. KIND OF THE STRAIGHT-AHEAD TYPE IF YOU WANNA CATEGORIZE HIM.
HE KNOWS HIS STUFF ...
AND THE DRUMMER...
HEY, YU-KUN.
I'M HUNGRY.
OH, YEAH, THANKS FOR THE COFFEE.
YOU CAN GO NOW.
?! HAAAT ...?

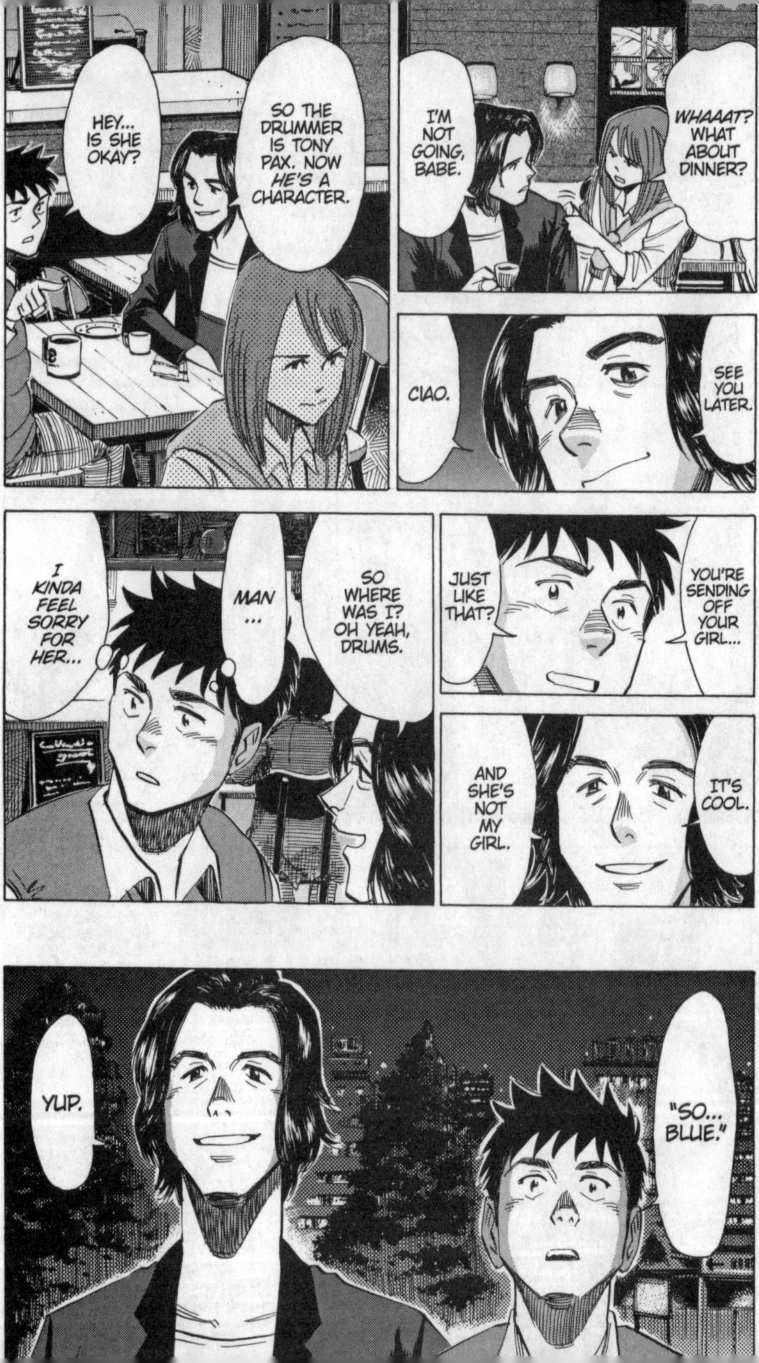
WHAAAT? WHAT ABOUT DINNER?
I'M NOT GOING, BABE.
SEE YOU LATER.
CIAO.
SO THE DRUMMER IS TONY PAX. NOW HE'S A CHARACTER.
HEY... IS SHE OKAY?
YOU'RE SENDING OFF YOUR GIRL...
JUST LIKE THAT?
IT'S COOL.
AND SHE'S NOT MY GIRL.
SO WHERE WAS I? OH YEAH, DRUMS.
MAN ...
I KINDA FEEL SORRY FOR HER...
"SO... BLUE."
YUP.

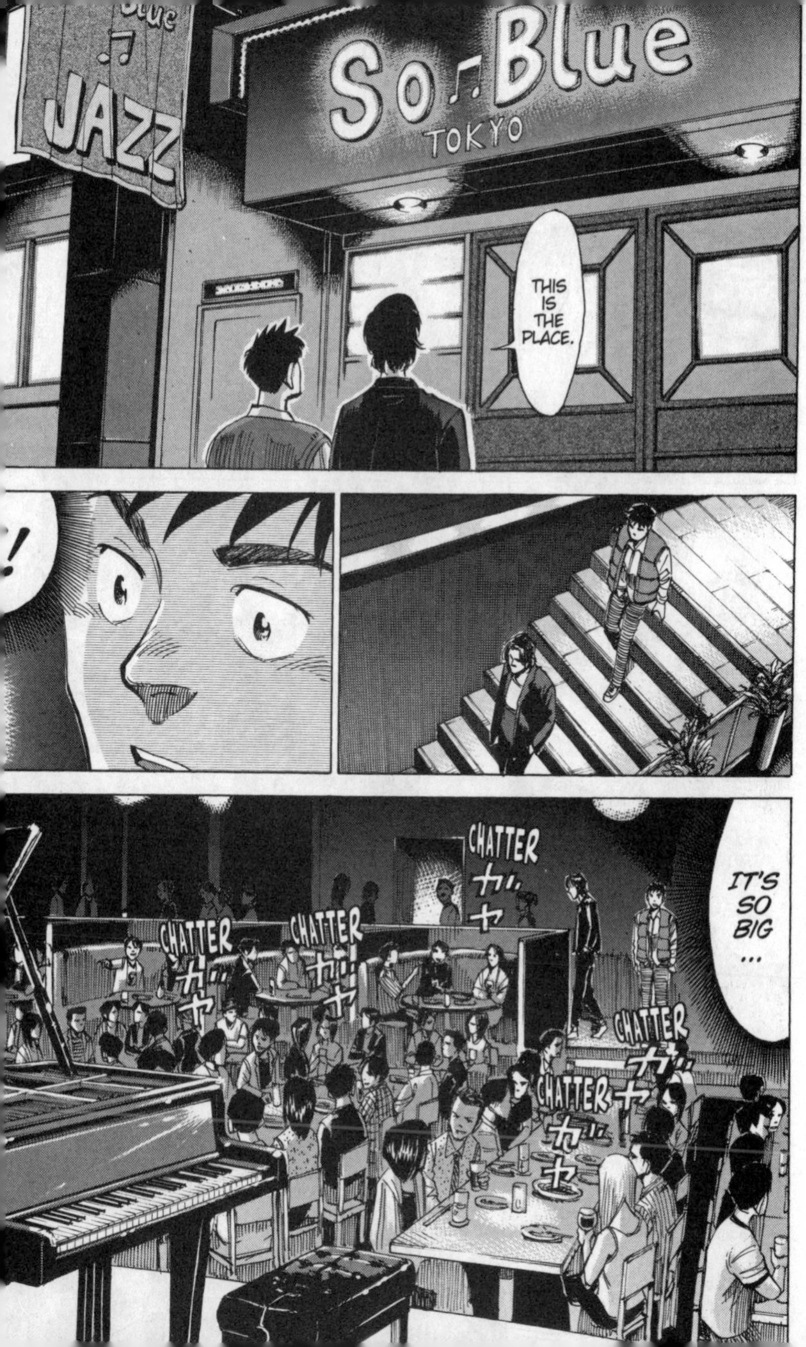
So Blue
TOKYO
JAZZ
THIS IS THE PLACE.
!
IT'S SO BIG ...
CHATTER
カヤ
CHATTER
カヤ
CHATTER
カヤ
CHATTER
カヤ
CHATTER
カヤ

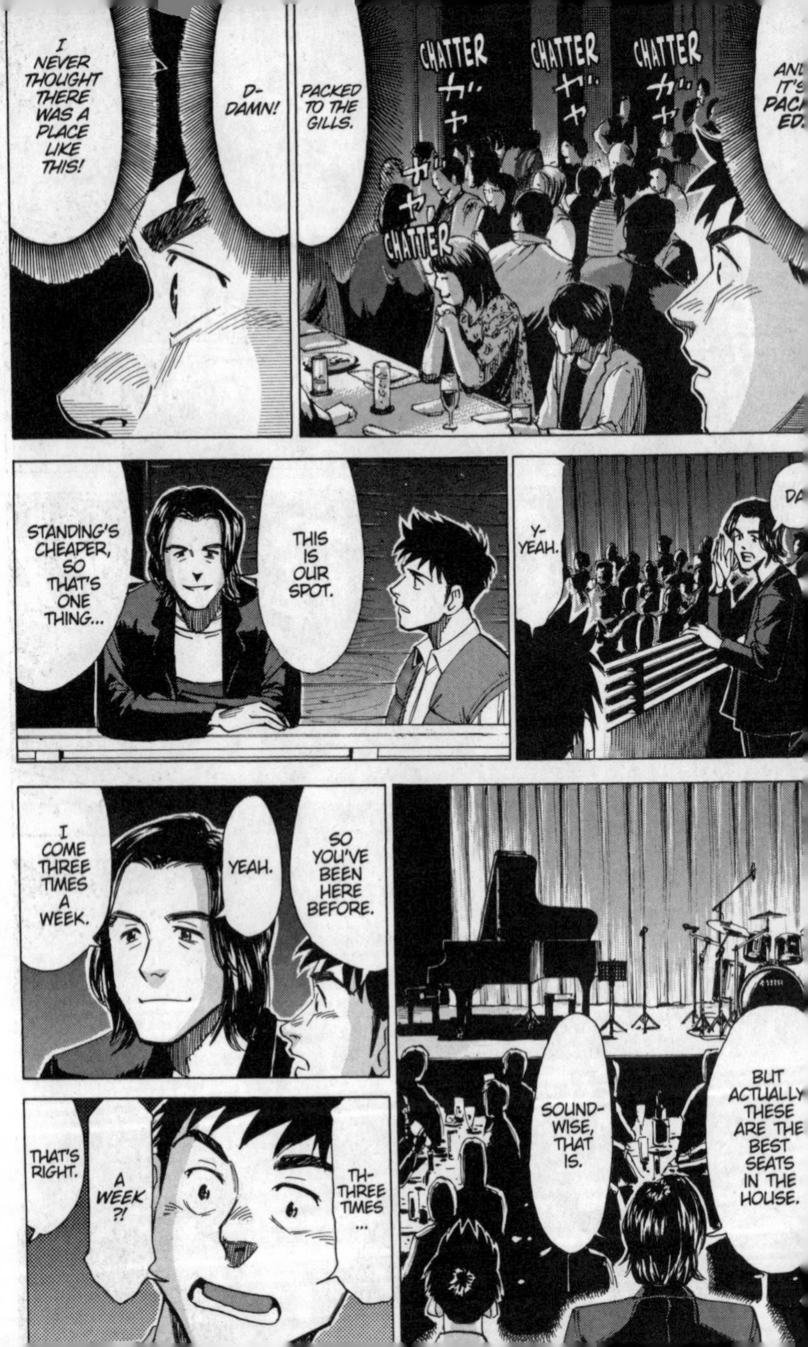
CHATTER
CHATTER
CHATTER
CHATTER
PACKED TO THE GILLS.
D-DAMN!
I NEVER THOUGHT THERE WAS A PLACE LIKE THIS!
Y-YEAH.
THIS IS OUR SPOT.
STANDING'S CHEAPER, SO THAT'S ONE THING...
BUT ACTUALLY THESE ARE THE BEST SEATS IN THE HOUSE.
SOUND-WISE, THAT IS.
SO YOU'VE BEEN HERE BEFORE.
YEAH.
I COME THREE TIMES A WEEK.
TH-THREE TIMES...
A WEEK?!
THAT'S RIGHT.

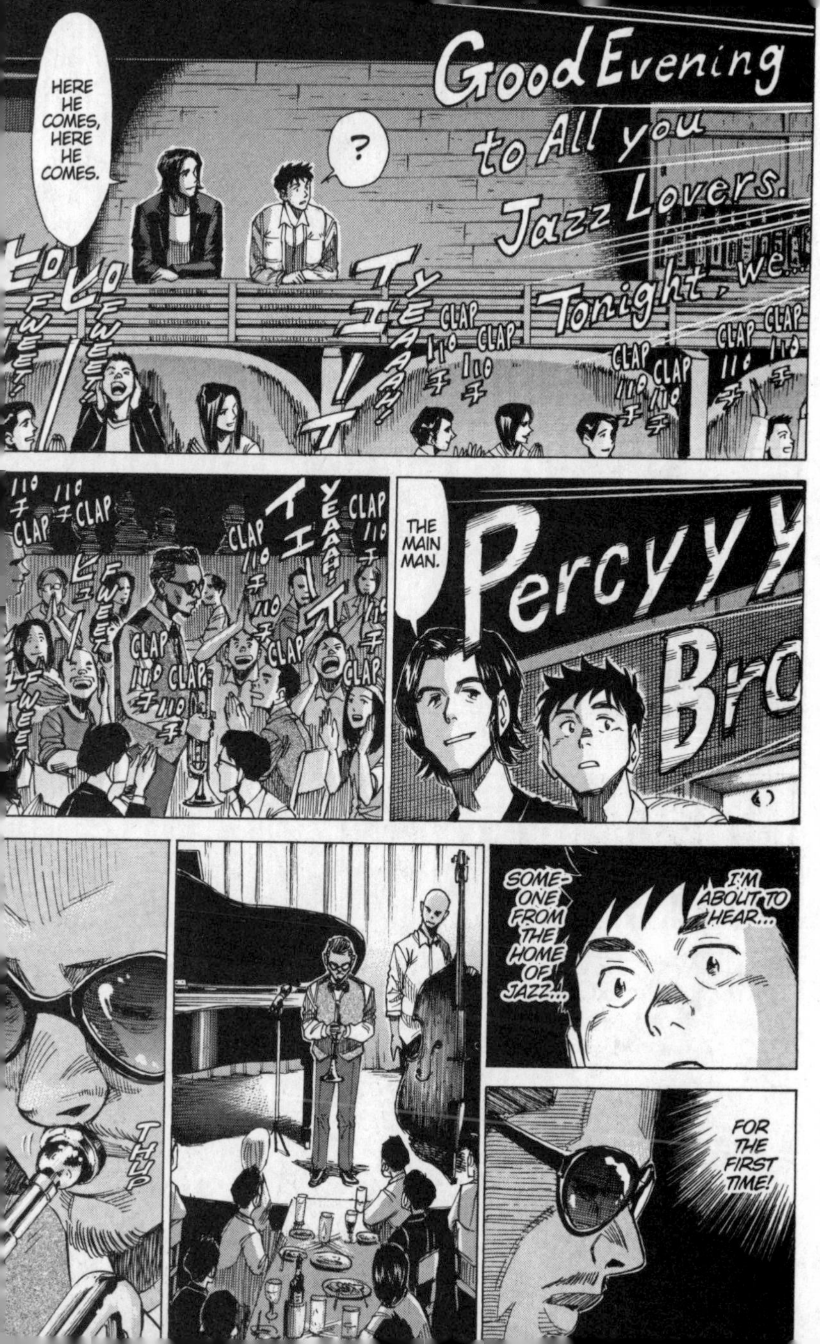

Good Evening to All you Jazz Lovers.
Tonight, we...
?
HERE HE COMES, HERE HE COMES.
YEAAAAH!
CLAP CLAP
CLAP CLAP
CLAP CLAP
FWEET!
FWEET!
Percyyy
Bro
THE MAIN MAN.
CLAP
YEAAAAH!
CLAP
CLAP
CLAP
FWEET
CLAP
CLAP
CLAP
CLAP
FWEET
I'M ABOUT TO HEAR...
SOME-ONE FROM THE HOME OF JAZZ...
FOR THE FIRST TIME!
THUP

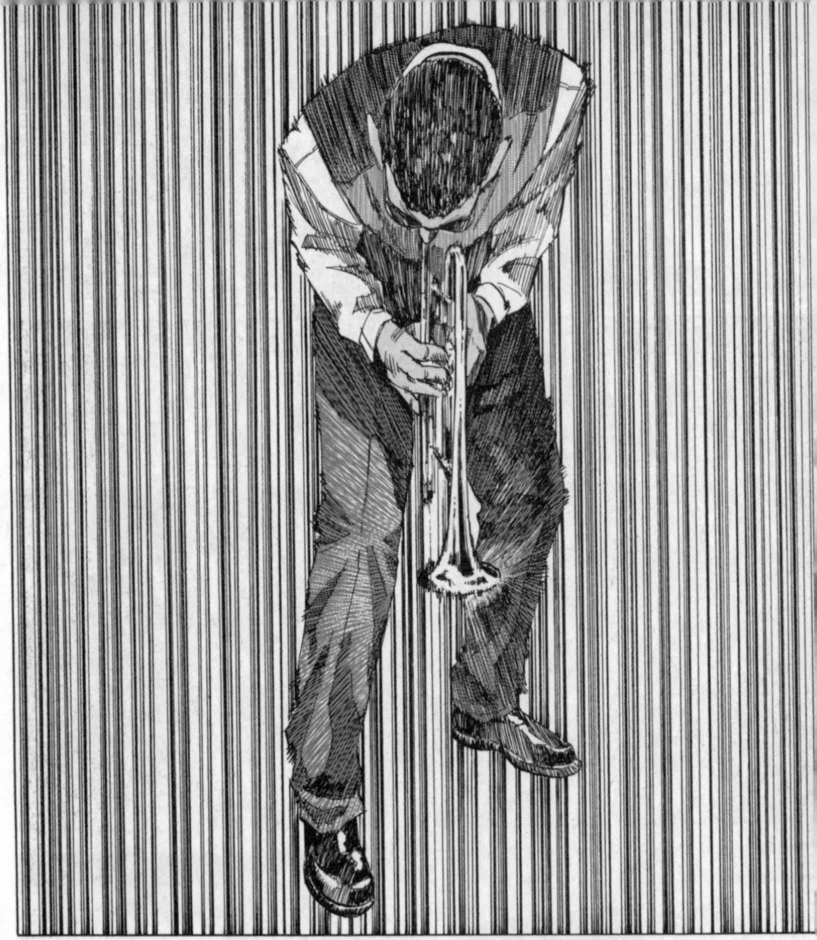

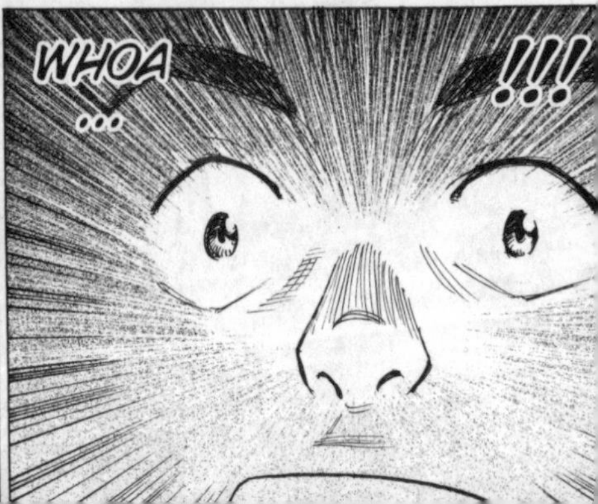
WHOA...
!!!

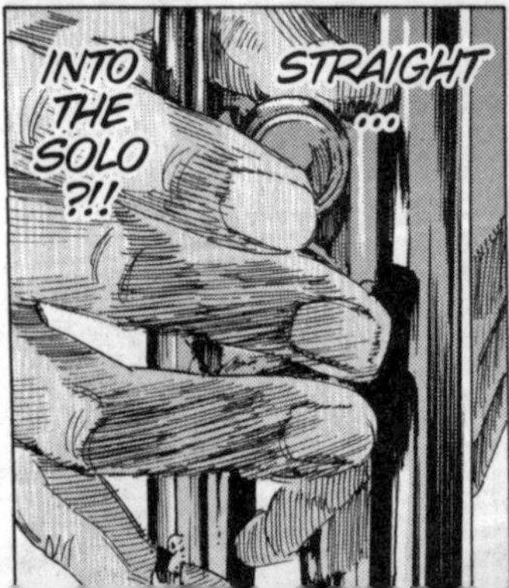
STRAIGHT...
INTO THE SOLO?!!

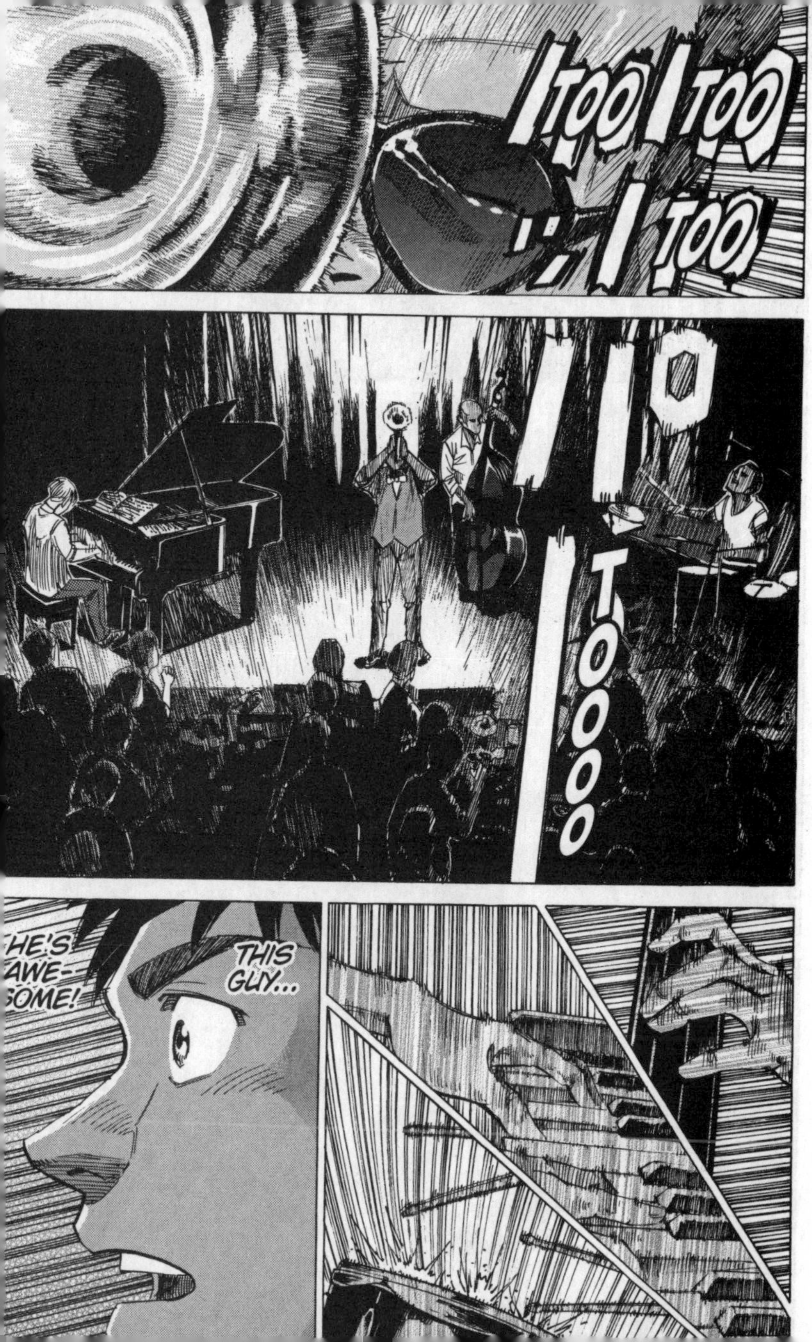
TOO TOO
TOO
TOOOOOO
THIS GUY...
HE'S AWE-SOME!

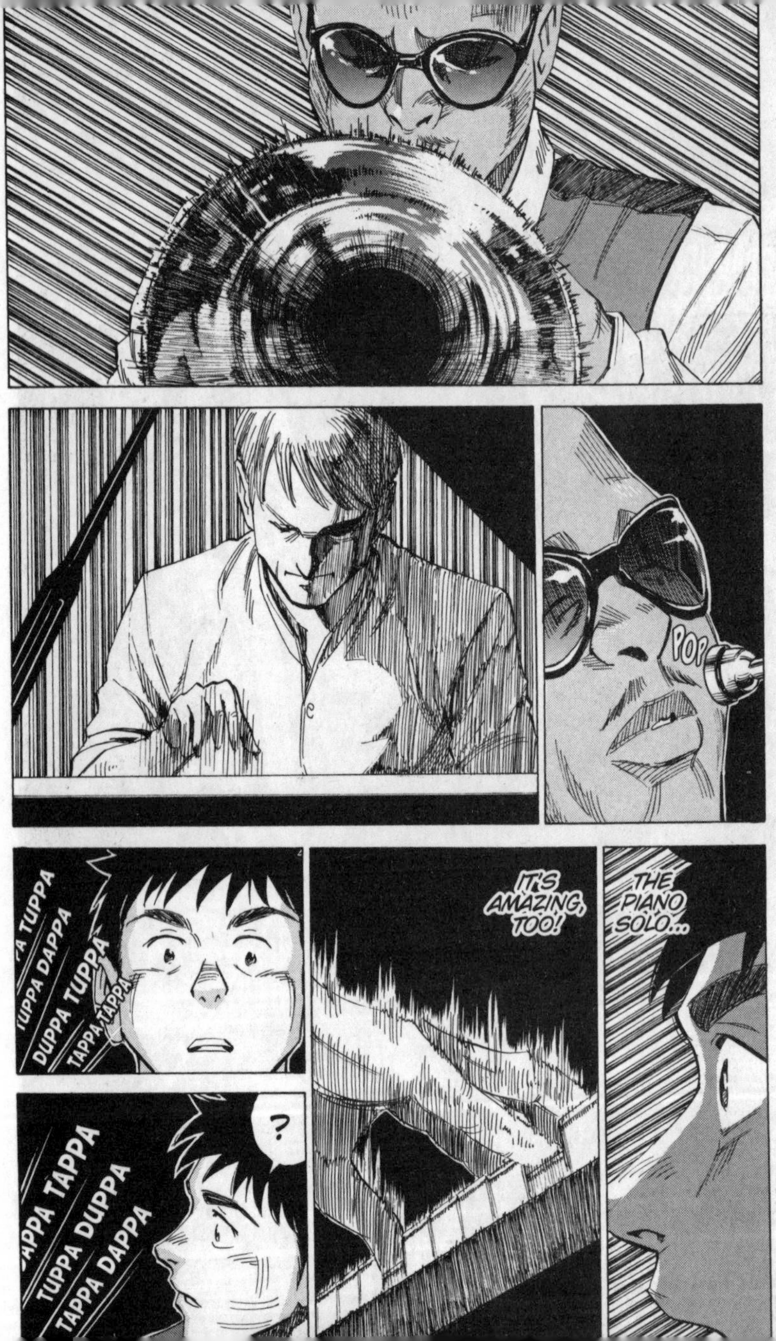
POP
THE PIANO SOLO...
IT'S AMAZING, TOO!
PA TUPPA
TUPPA DAPPA
DUPPA TUPPA
TAPPA TAPPA
?
APPA TAPPA
TUPPA DUPPA
TAPPA DAPPA

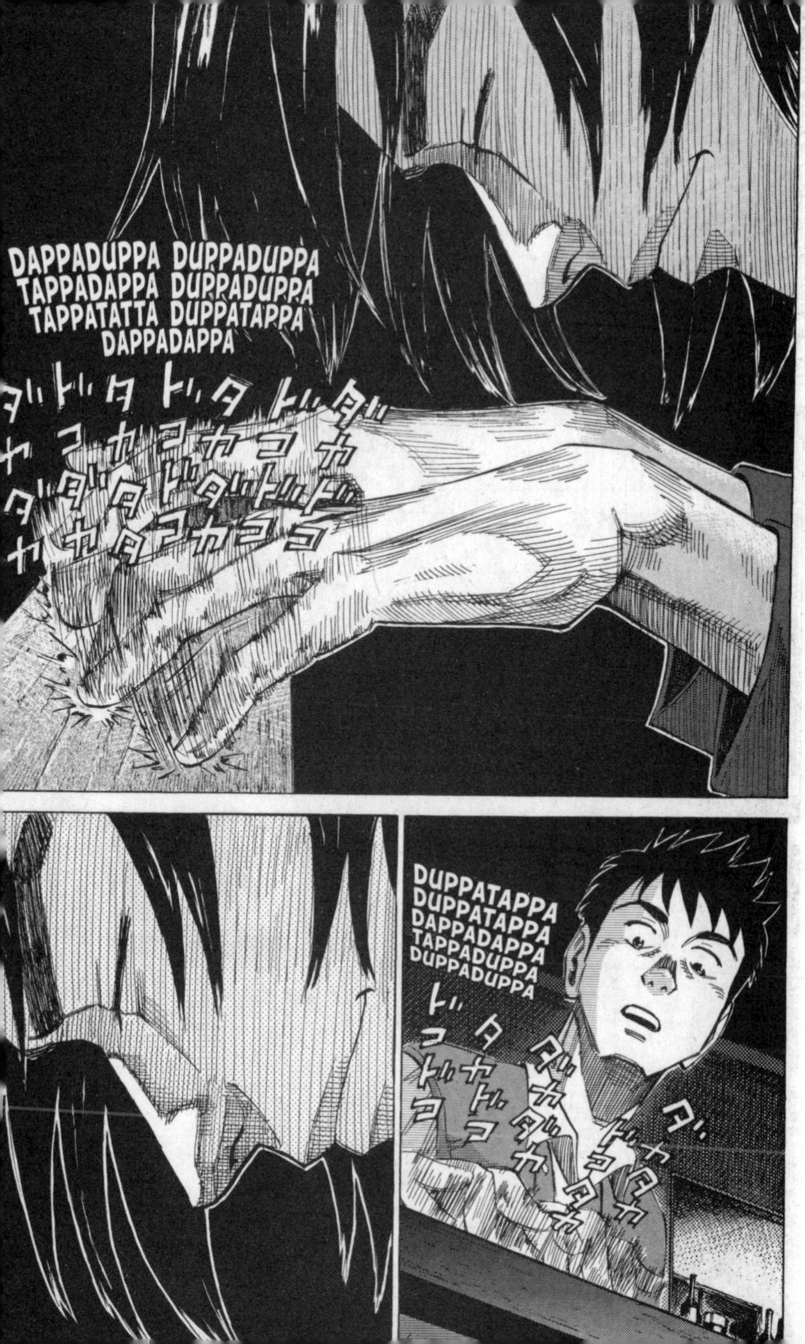
DAPPADUPPA DUPPADUPPA
TAPPADAPPA DUPPADUPPA
TAPPATATTA DUPPATAPPA
DAPPADAPPA
DUPPATAPPA
DUPPATAPPA
DAPPADAPPA
TAPPADUPPA
DUPPADUPPA

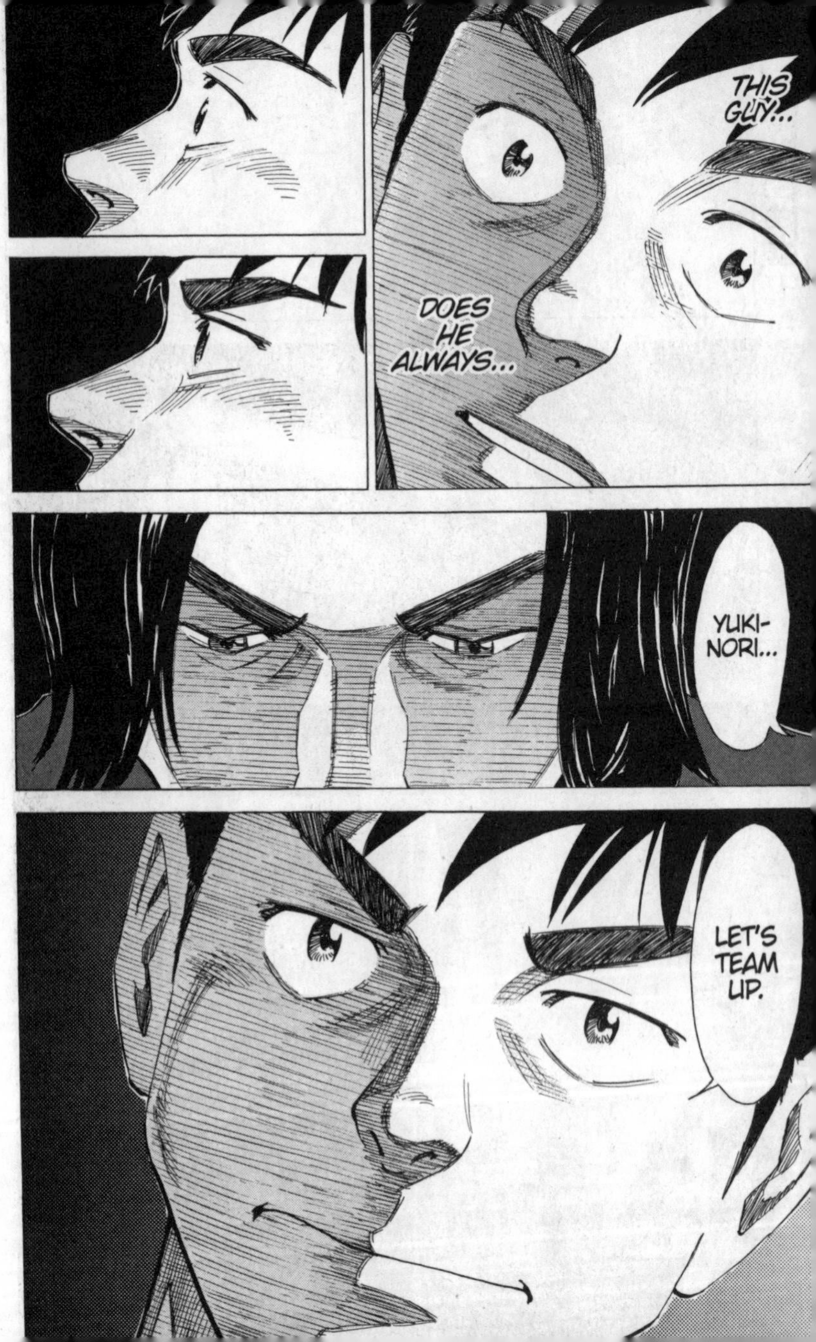
THIS GUY...
DOES HE ALWAYS...
YUKI-NORI...
LET'S TEAM UP.

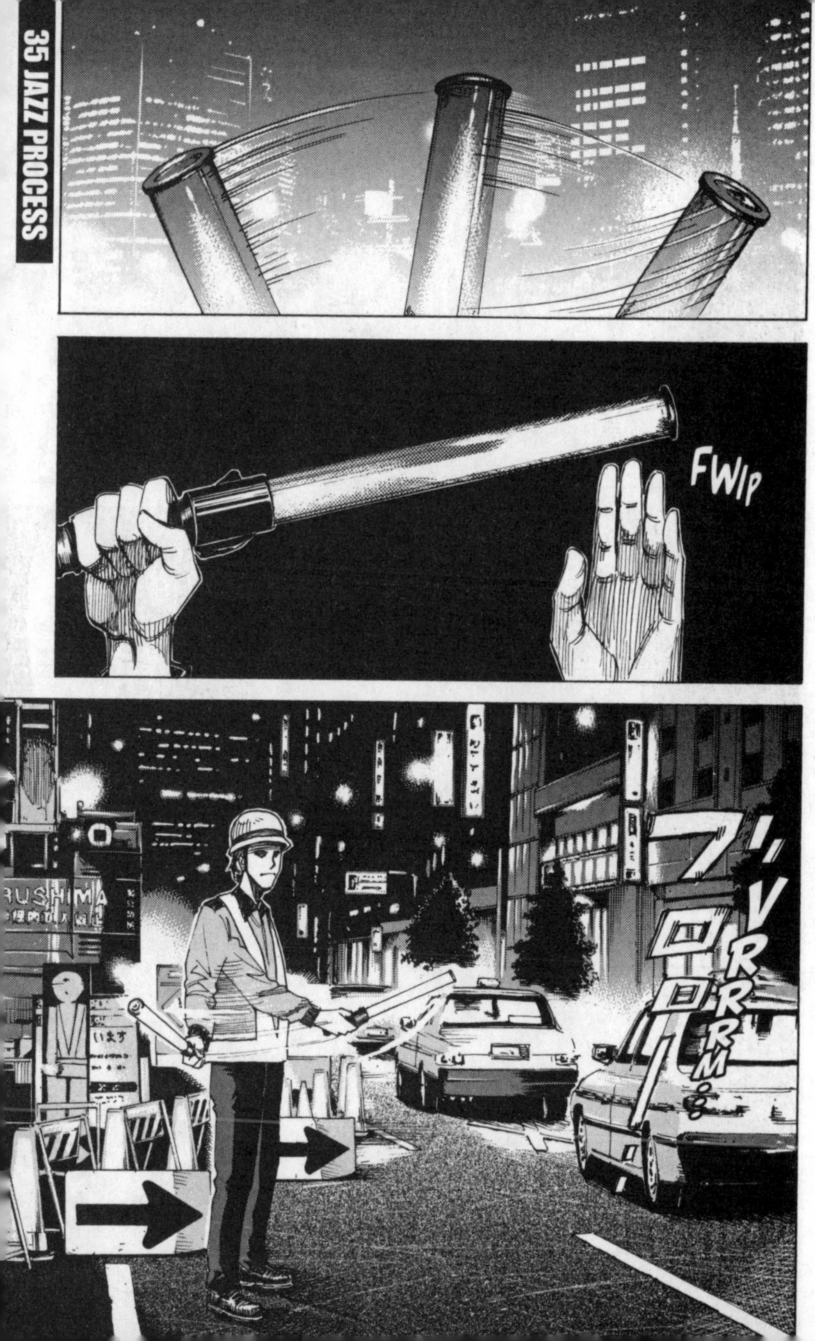
FWIP
ブロロ
VRRRRM

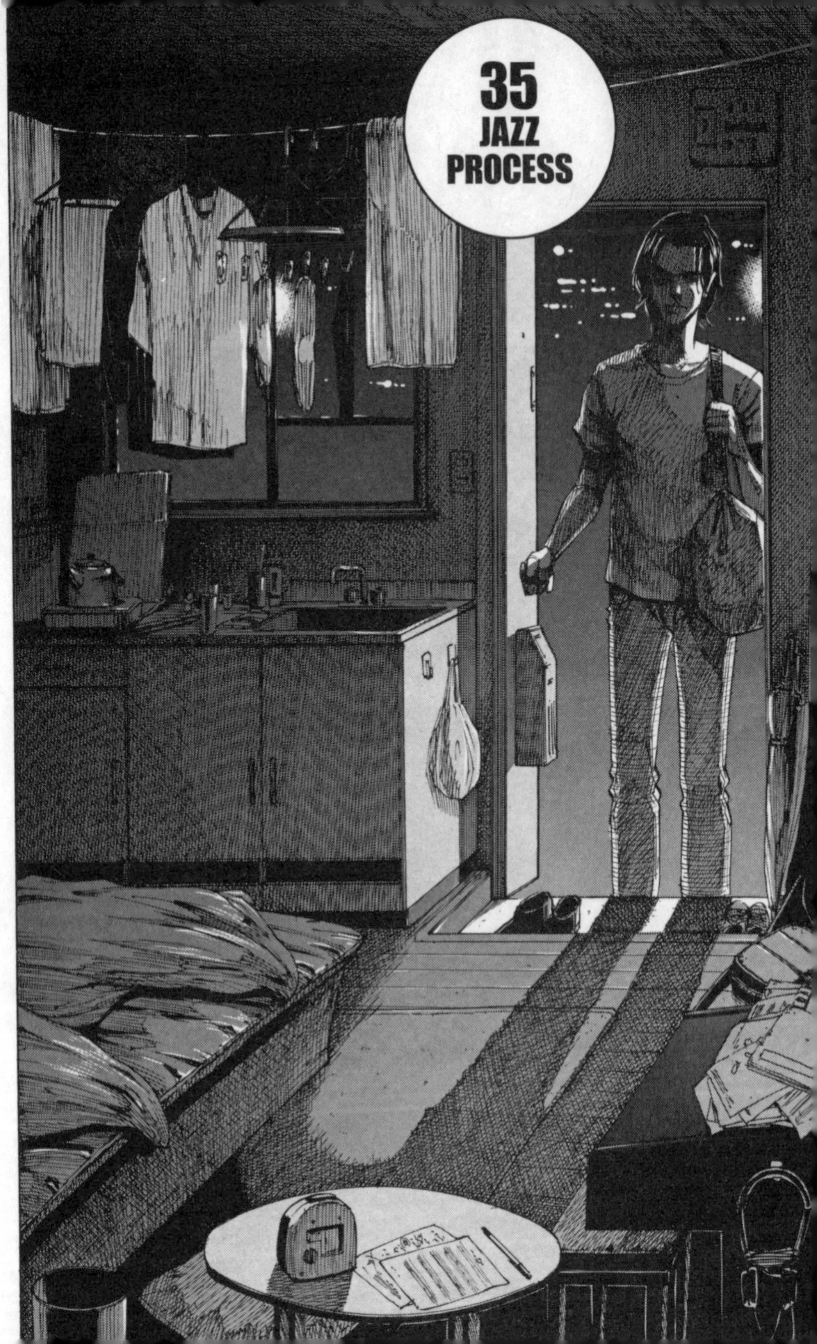
35
JAZZ
PROCESS

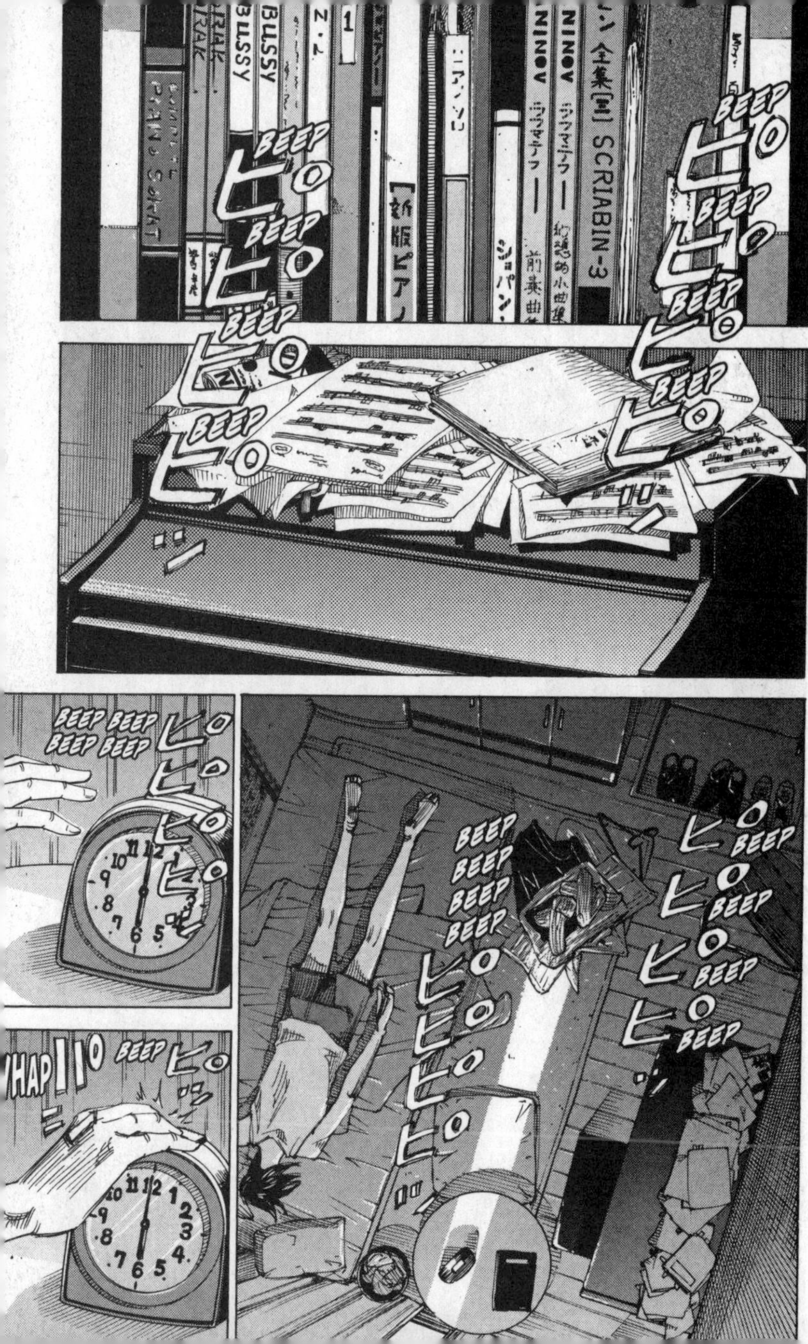

BEEP ピ
BEEP ピ
BEEP ピ
BEEP ピ
SCRIABIN-3
BEEP ピ
BEEP ピ
BEEP ピ
BEEP ピ
BEEP ピ
BEEP ピ
BEEP ピ
BEEP ピ
BEEP ピ
BEEP ピ
BEEP ピ
BEEP ピ
BEEP BEEP BEEP BEEP ピピピピ
WHAP
BEEP ピ

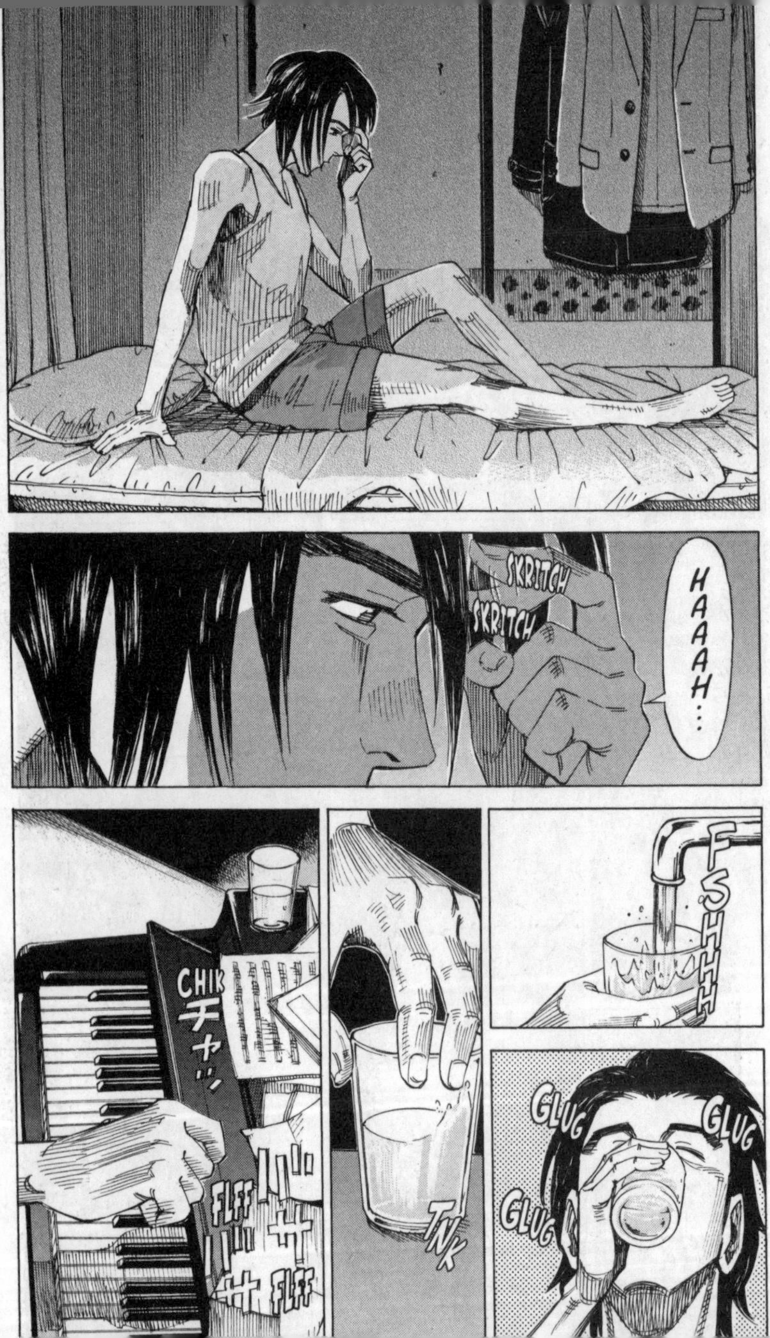
SKRITCH
SKRITCH
HAAAAH...
FSHHHH
GLUG
GLUG
GLUG
TNK
CHIK
チャッ
FLFF
FLFF

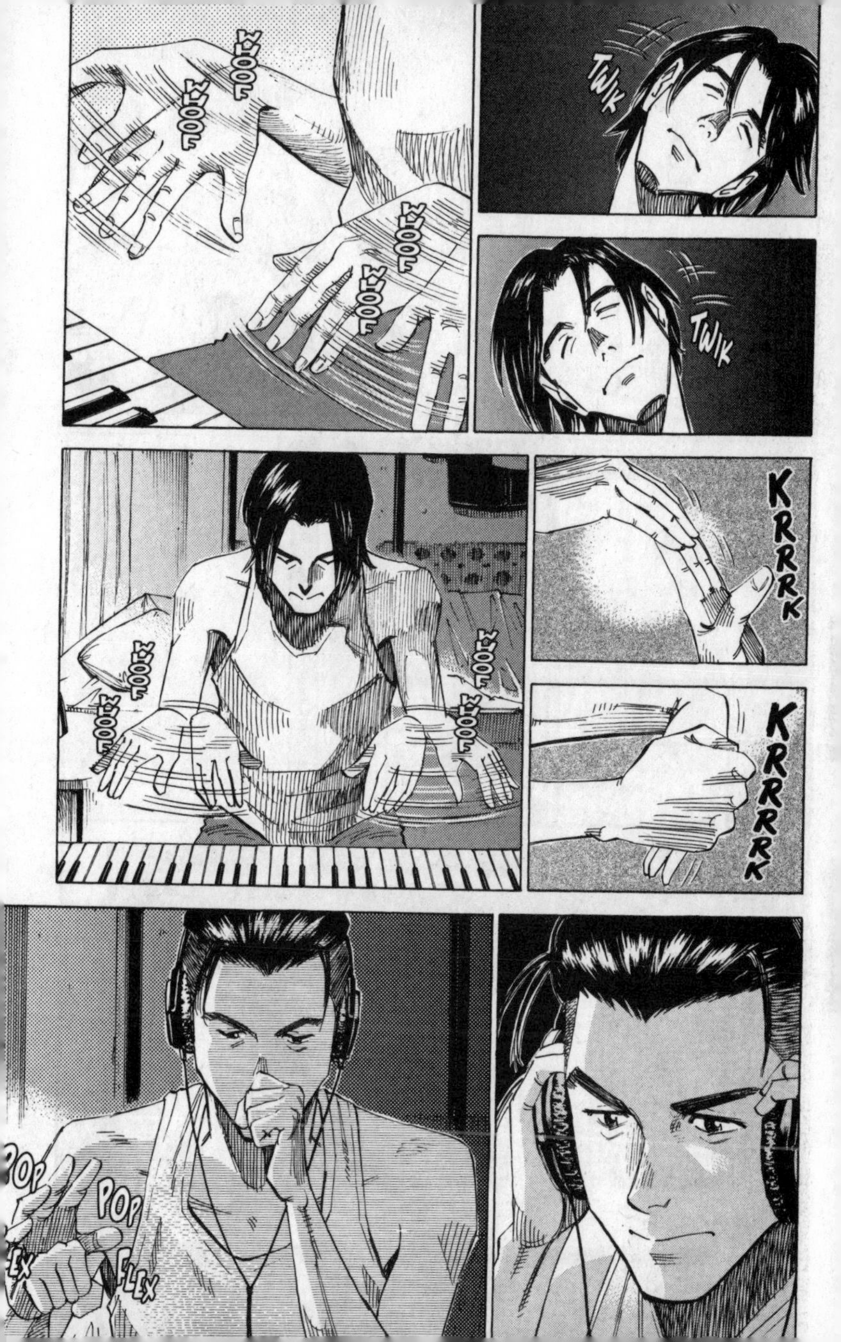
TWIK
TWIK
WHOOF
WHOOF
WHOOF
WHOOF
KRRRK
KRRRRK
WHOOF
WHOOF
WHOOF
WHOOF
POP
POP
FLEX

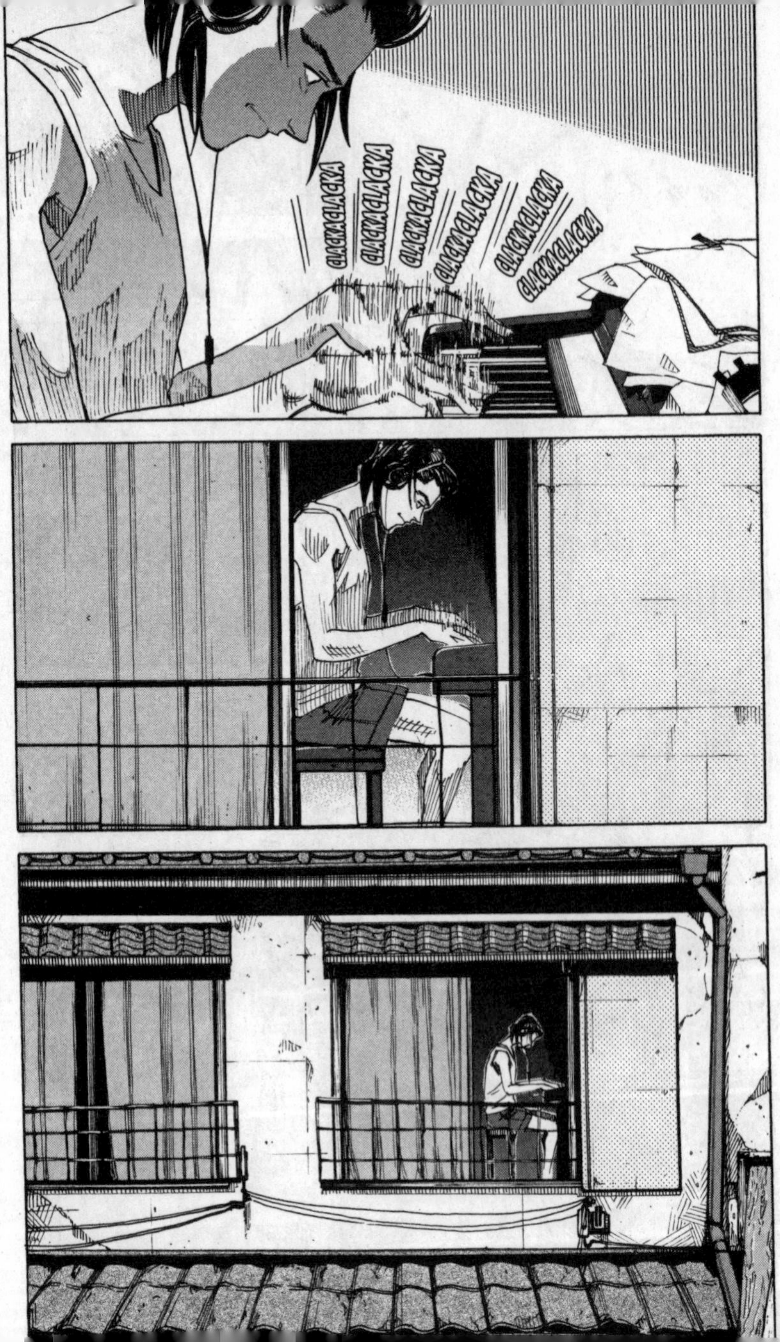
CLACKACLACKA
CLACKACLACKA
CLACKACLACKA
CLACKACLACKA
CLACKACLACKA
CLACKACLACKA

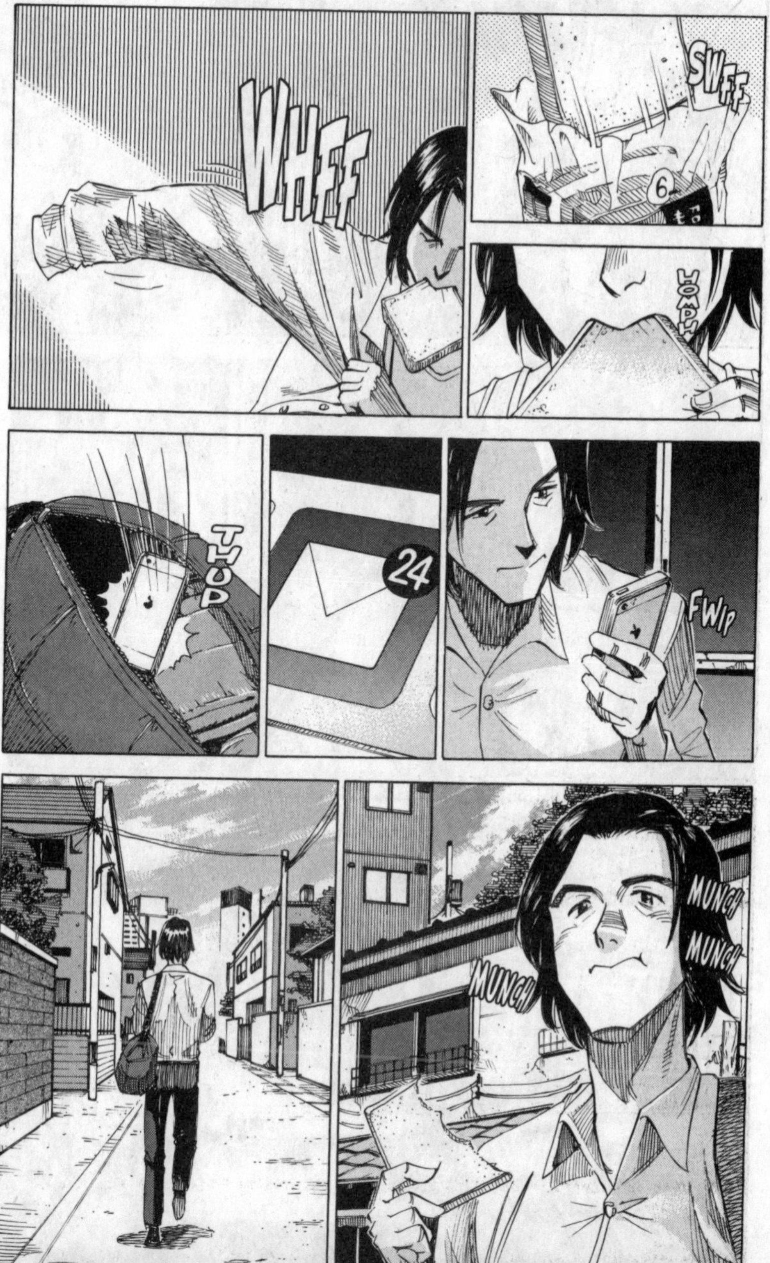
SWFF
6
HOMPH
WHFF
FWIP
24
THUD
MUNCH
MUNCH
MUNCH

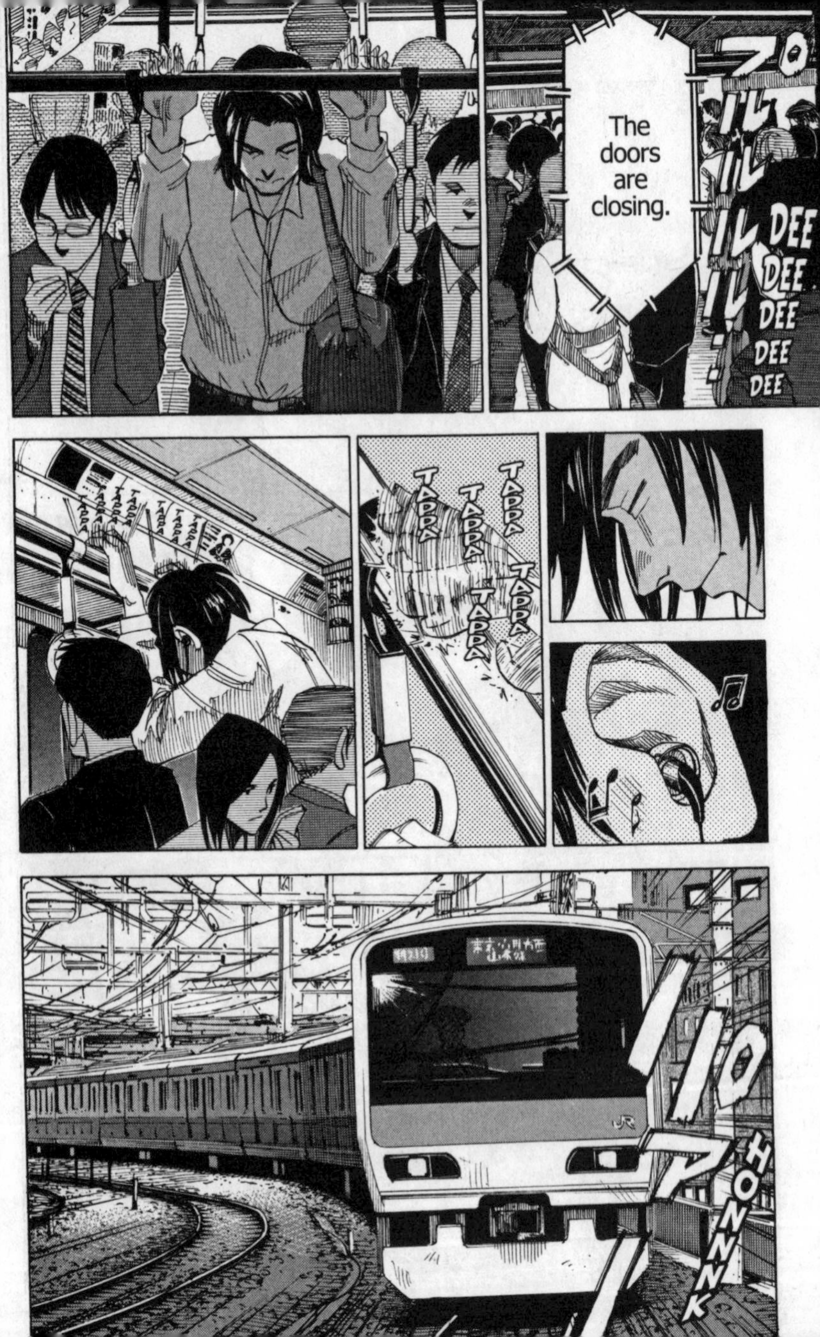

The doors are closing.
DEE DEE DEE DEE DEE
TAPPA TAPPA TAPPA TAPPA TAPPA TAPPA
HONNK

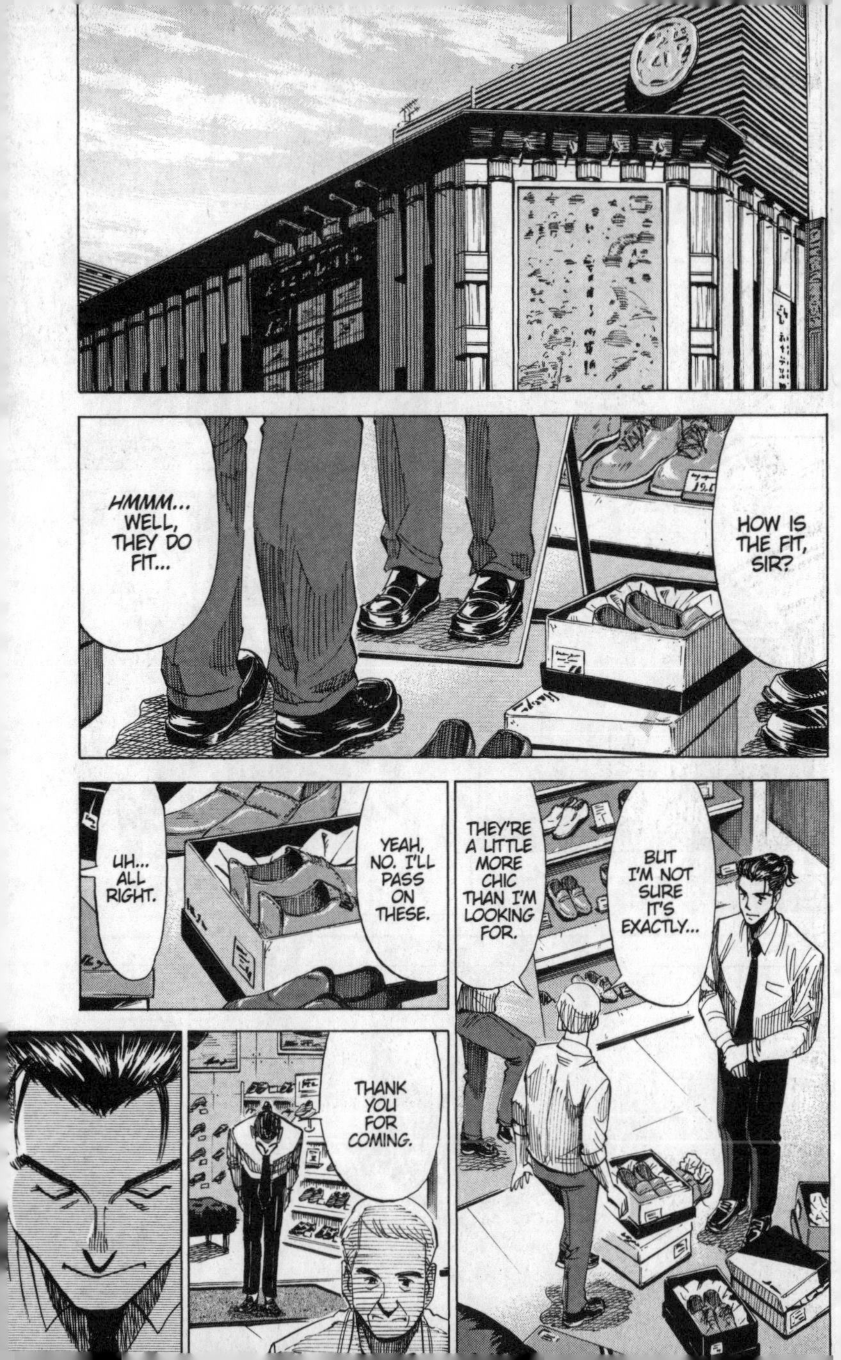
HOW IS THE FIT, SIR?
HMMM... WELL, THEY DO FIT...
BUT I'M NOT SURE IT'S EXACTLY...
THEY'RE A LITTLE MORE CHIC THAN I'M LOOKING FOR.
YEAH, NO. I'LL PASS ON THESE.
UH... ALL RIGHT.
THANK YOU FOR COMING.

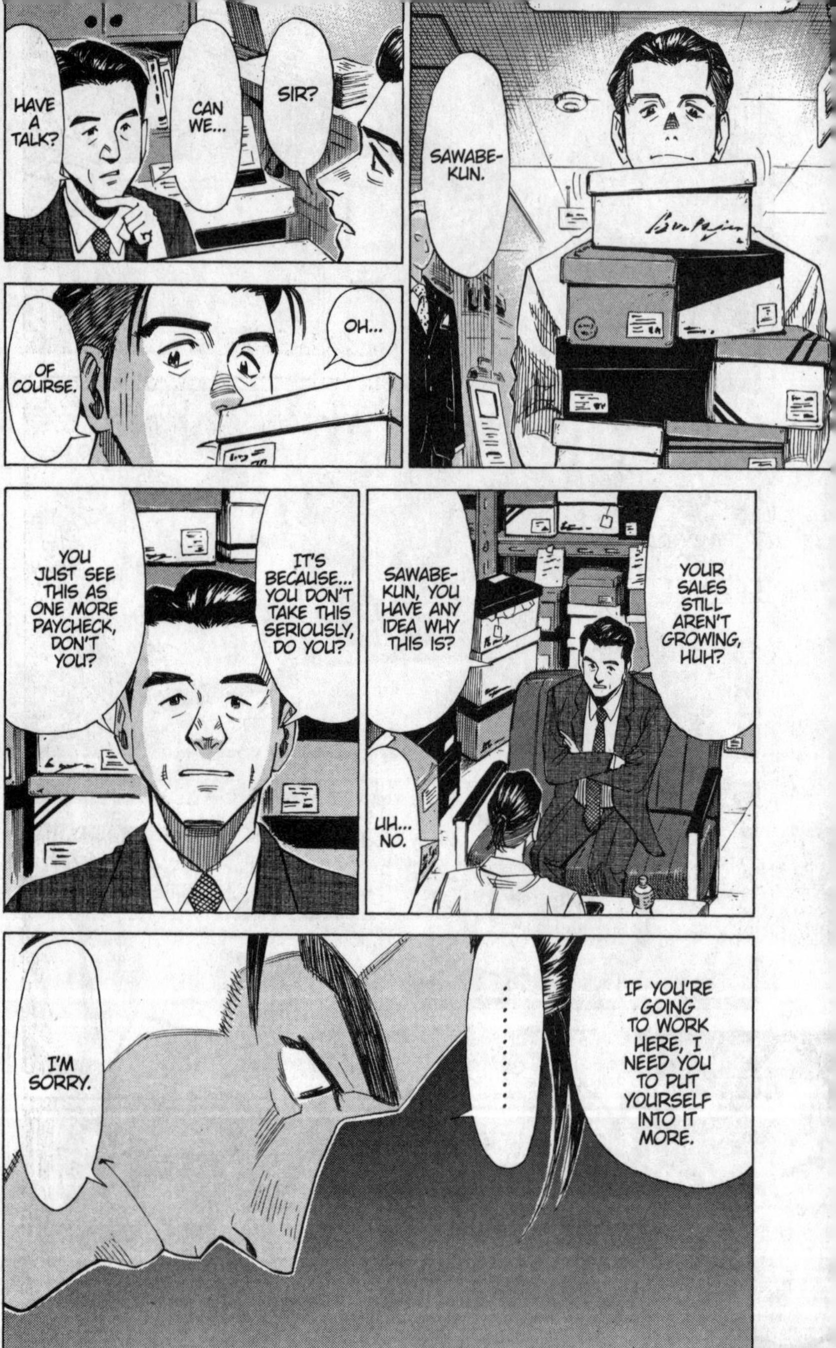
SAWABE-KUN.
SIR?
CAN WE...
HAVE A TALK?
OH...
OF COURSE.
YOUR SALES STILL AREN'T GROWING, HUH?
SAWABE-KUN, YOU HAVE ANY IDEA WHY THIS IS?
UH... NO.
IT'S BECAUSE... YOU DON'T TAKE THIS SERIOUSLY, DO YOU?
YOU JUST SEE THIS AS ONE MORE PAYCHECK, DON'T YOU?
IF YOU'RE GOING TO WORK HERE, I NEED YOU TO PUT YOURSELF INTO IT MORE.
......
I'M SORRY.

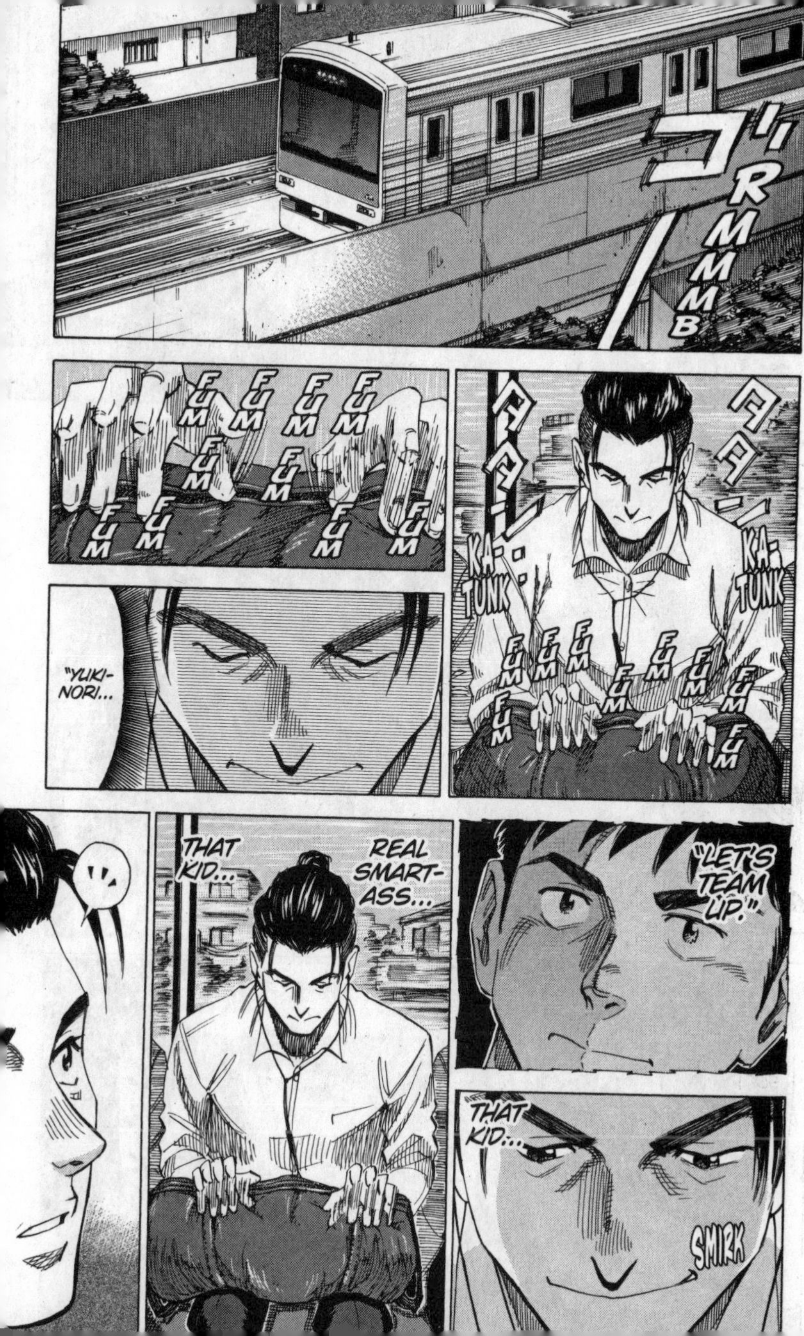

RMMMMB
KA-TUNK
KA-TUNK
FUM FUM FUM FUM FUM FUM FUM FUM FUM FUM
FUM FUM FUM FUM FUM FUM FUM FUM FUM FUM FUM FUM
"YUKI-NORI...
"LET'S TEAM UP."
THAT KID...
SMIRK
REAL SMART-ASS...
THAT KID...

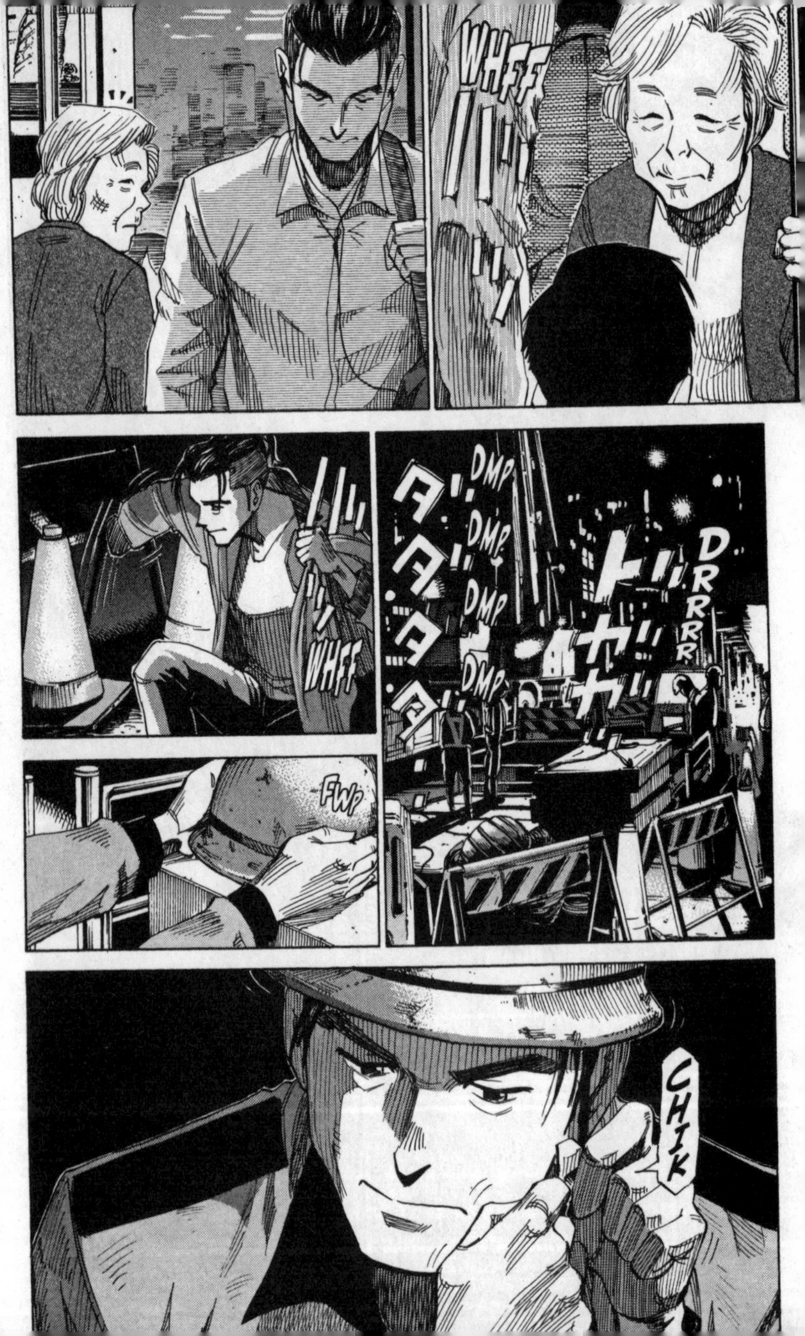

WHFF
DMP
DMP
DMP
DMP
DRRRR
WHFF
FWP
CHIK

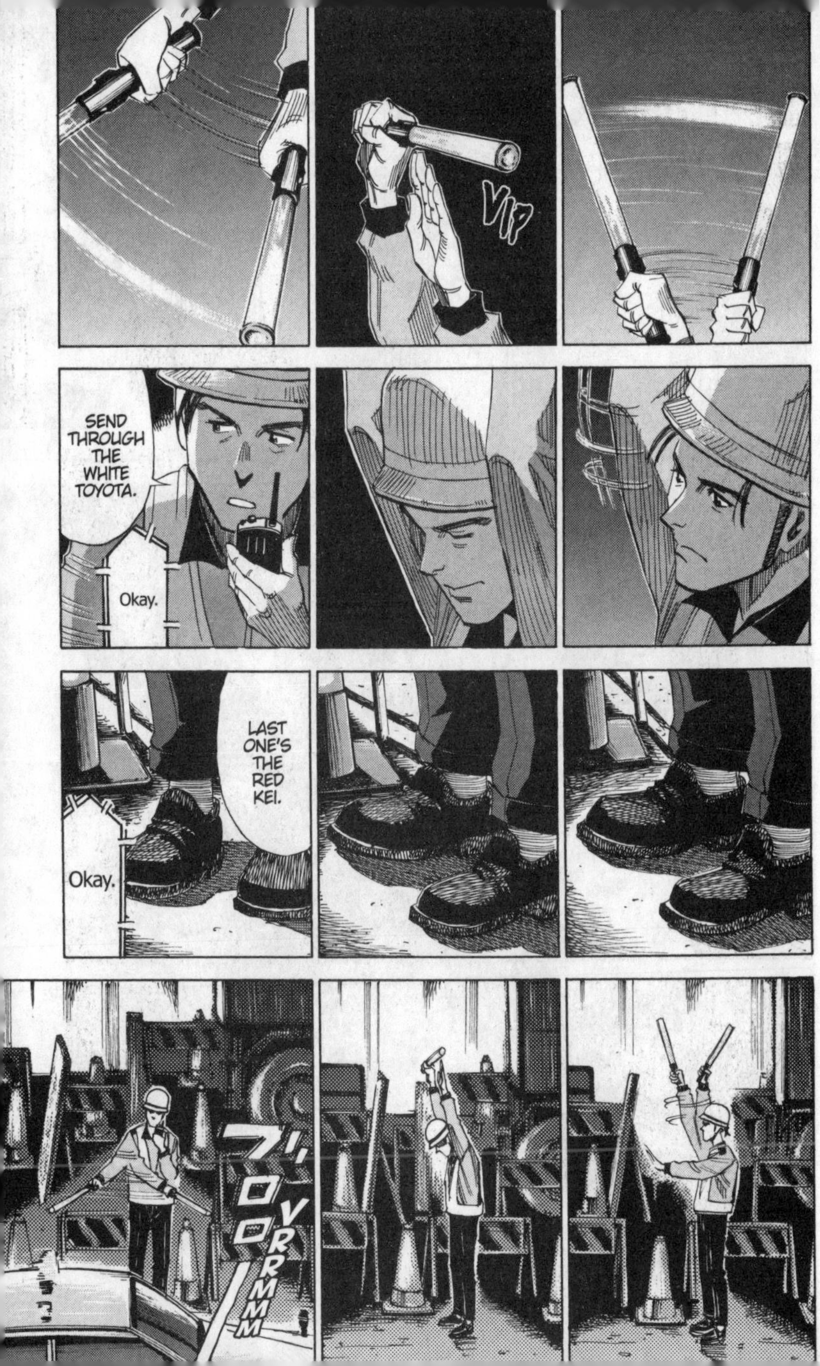
Vip
SEND THROUGH THE WHITE TOYOTA.
Okay.
LAST ONE'S THE RED KEI.
Okay.
VRRMMM

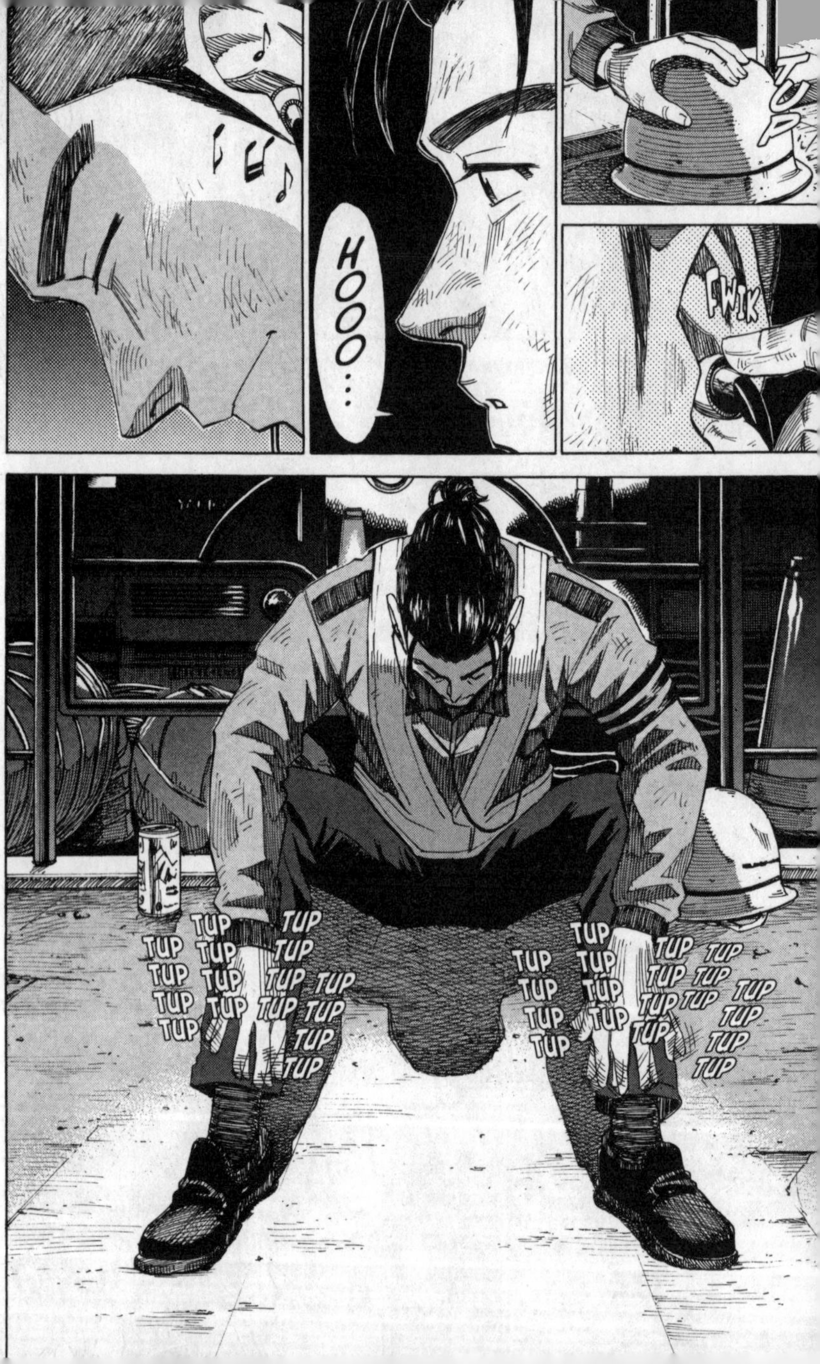
TUP
FWIK
HOOOO...
TUP TUP TUP TUP TUP TUP TUP TUP TUP TUP TUP TUP TUP TUP TUP TUP TUP TUP TUP TUP TUP
TUP TUP TUP TUP TUP TUP TUP TUP TUP TUP TUP TUP TUP TUP TUP TUP TUP TUP TUP TUP TUP TUP

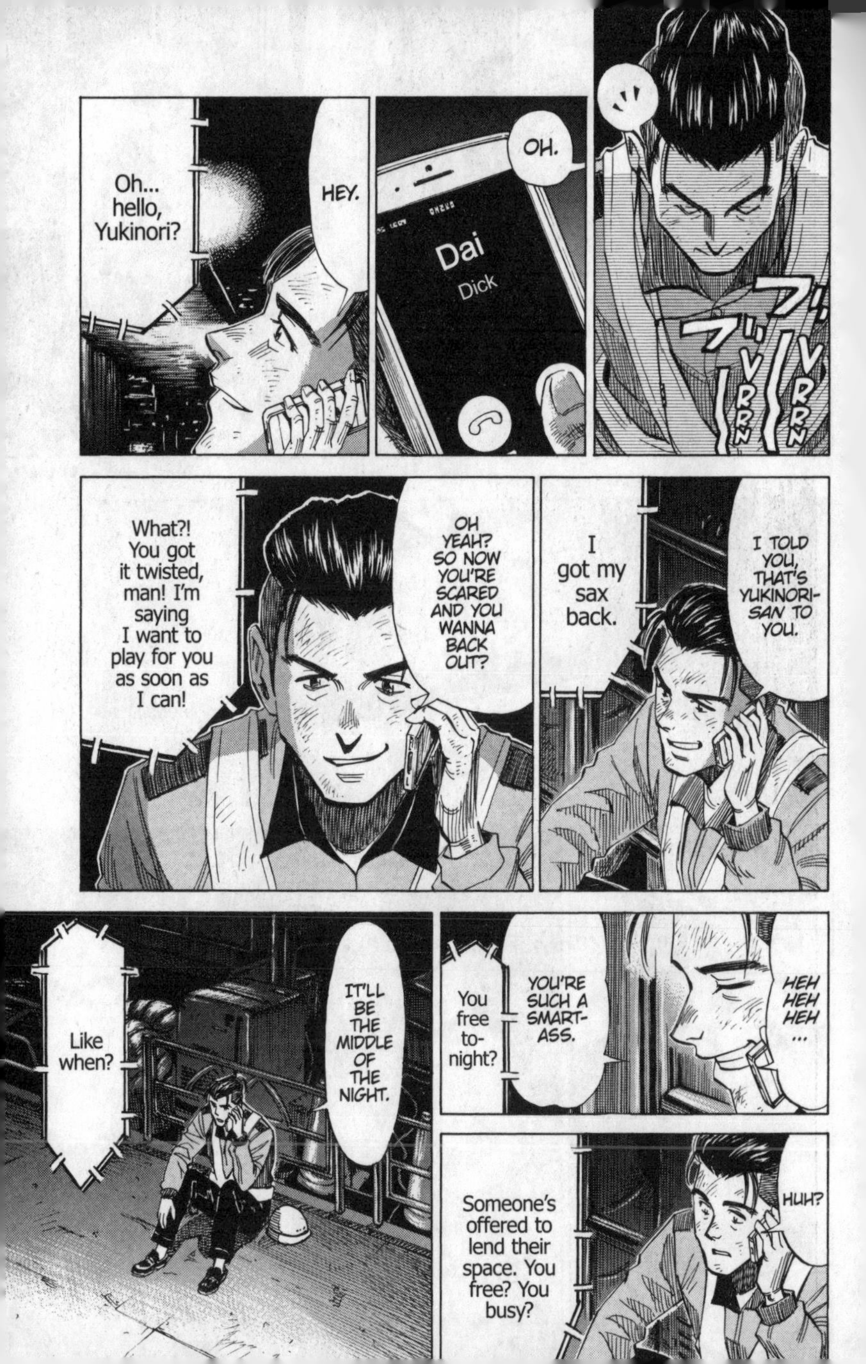
VRRN
VRRN
OH.
Dai
Dick
HEY.
Oh... hello, Yukinori?
I TOLD YOU, THAT'S YUKINORI-SAN TO YOU.
I got my sax back.
OH YEAH? SO NOW YOU'RE SCARED AND YOU WANNA BACK OUT?
What?! You got it twisted, man! I'm saying I want to play for you as soon as I can!
HEH HEH HEH ...
YOU'RE SUCH A SMART-ASS.
You free to-night?
HUH?
Someone's offered to lend their space. You free? You busy?
IT'LL BE THE MIDDLE OF THE NIGHT.
Like when?

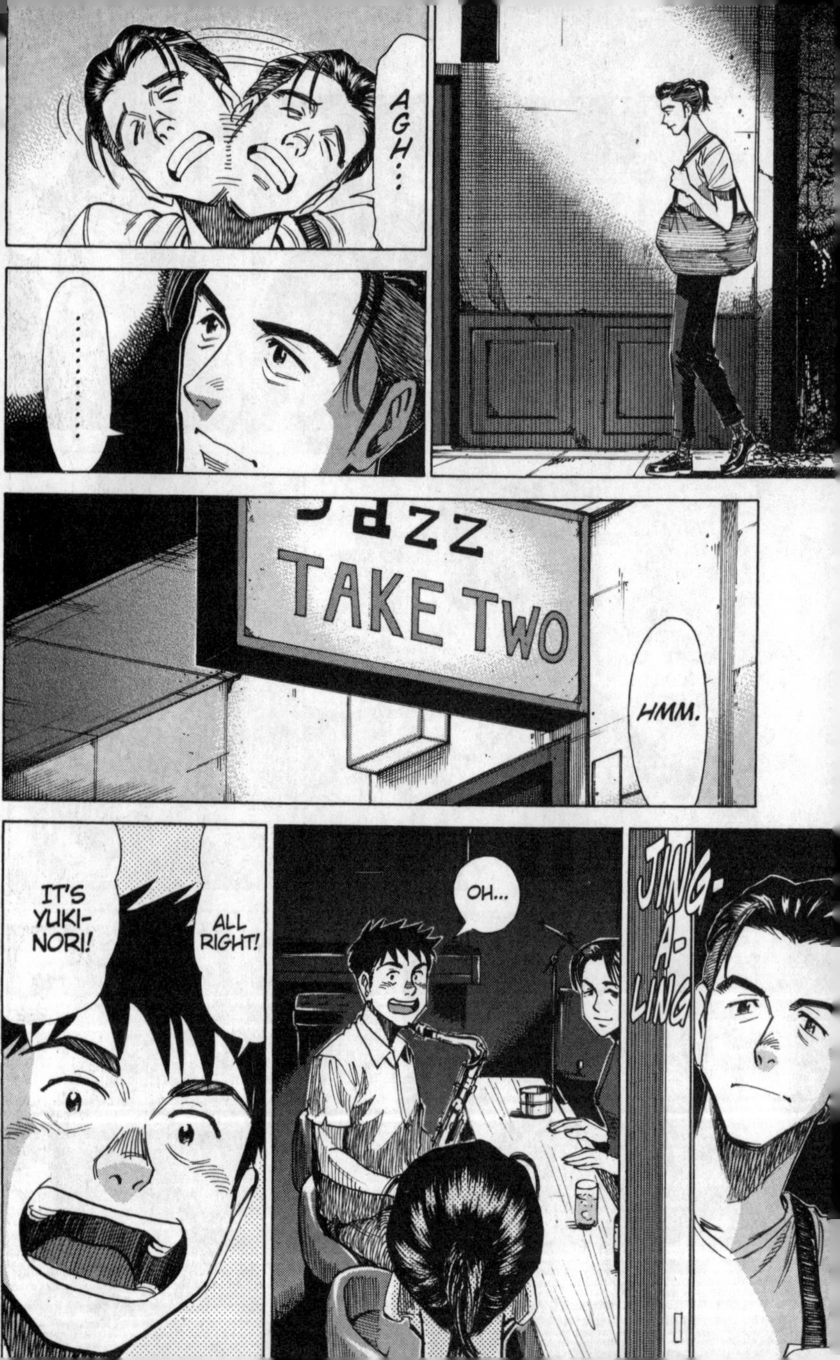
AGH...
......
TAKE TWO
HMM.
JING-A-LING
OH...
ALL RIGHT!
IT'S YUKI-NORI!

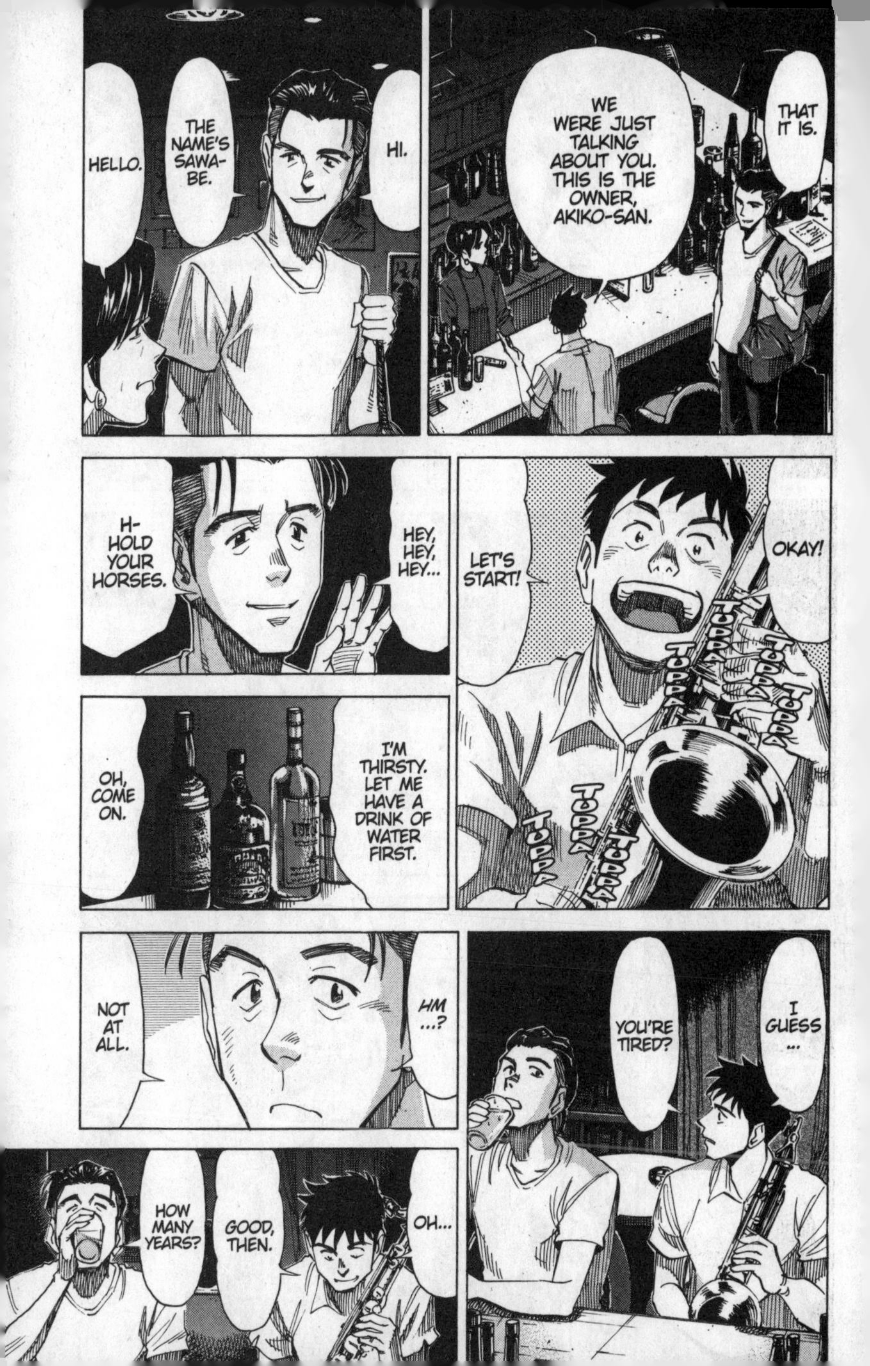
THAT IT IS.
WE WERE JUST TALKING ABOUT YOU. THIS IS THE OWNER, AKIKO-SAN.
HI.
THE NAME'S SAWA-BE.
HELLO.
OKAY!
LET'S START!
TOPPA TOPPA TOPPA
TOPPA TOPPA
TOPPA TOPPA TOPPA
HEY, HEY, HEY...
H-HOLD YOUR HORSES.
I'M THIRSTY. LET ME HAVE A DRINK OF WATER FIRST.
OH, COME ON.
I GUESS...
YOU'RE TIRED?
HM...?
NOT AT ALL.
OH...
GOOD, THEN.
HOW MANY YEARS?

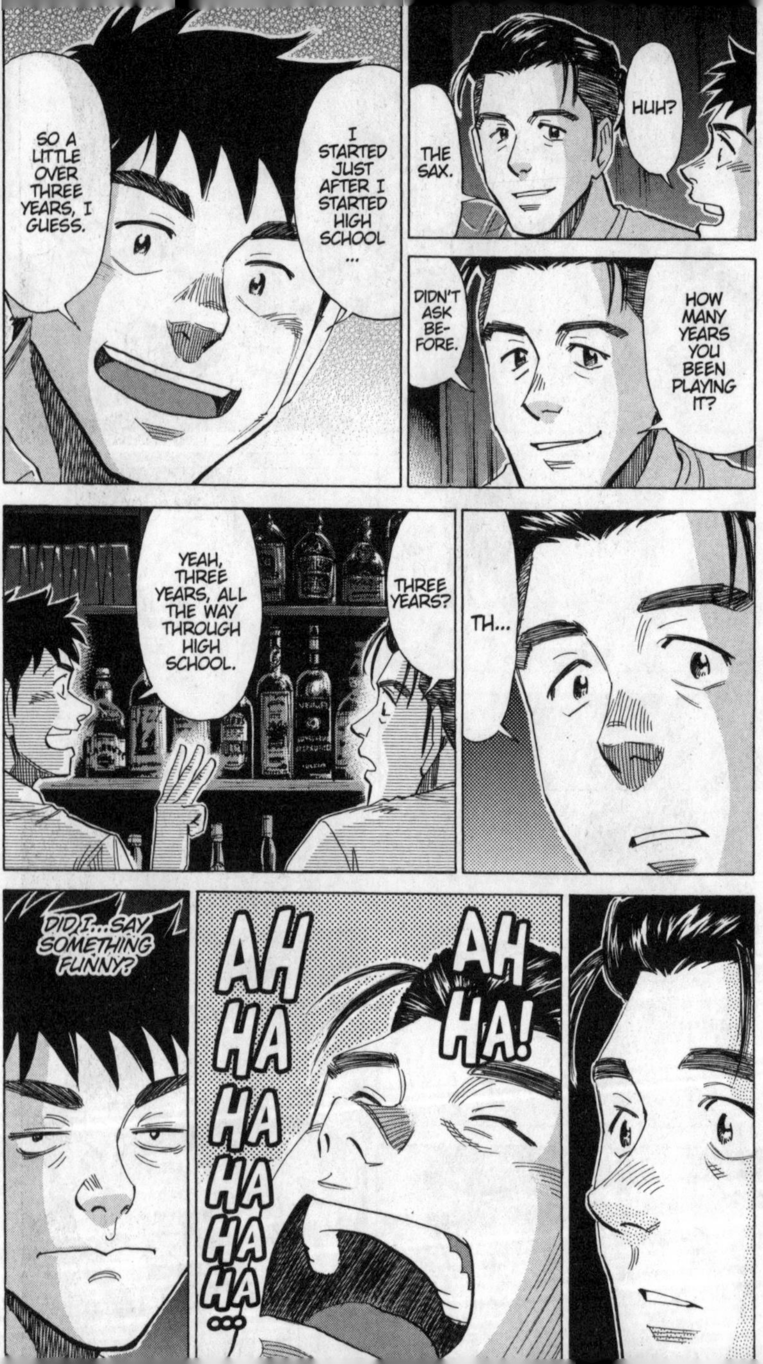
HUH?
THE SAX.
HOW MANY YEARS YOU BEEN PLAYING IT?
DIDN'T ASK BE-FORE.
I STARTED JUST AFTER I STARTED HIGH SCHOOL ...
SO A LITTLE OVER THREE YEARS, I GUESS.
TH...
THREE YEARS?
YEAH, THREE YEARS, ALL THE WAY THROUGH HIGH SCHOOL.
AH HA!
AH HA HA HA HA HA HA...
DID I...SAY SOMETHING FUNNY?

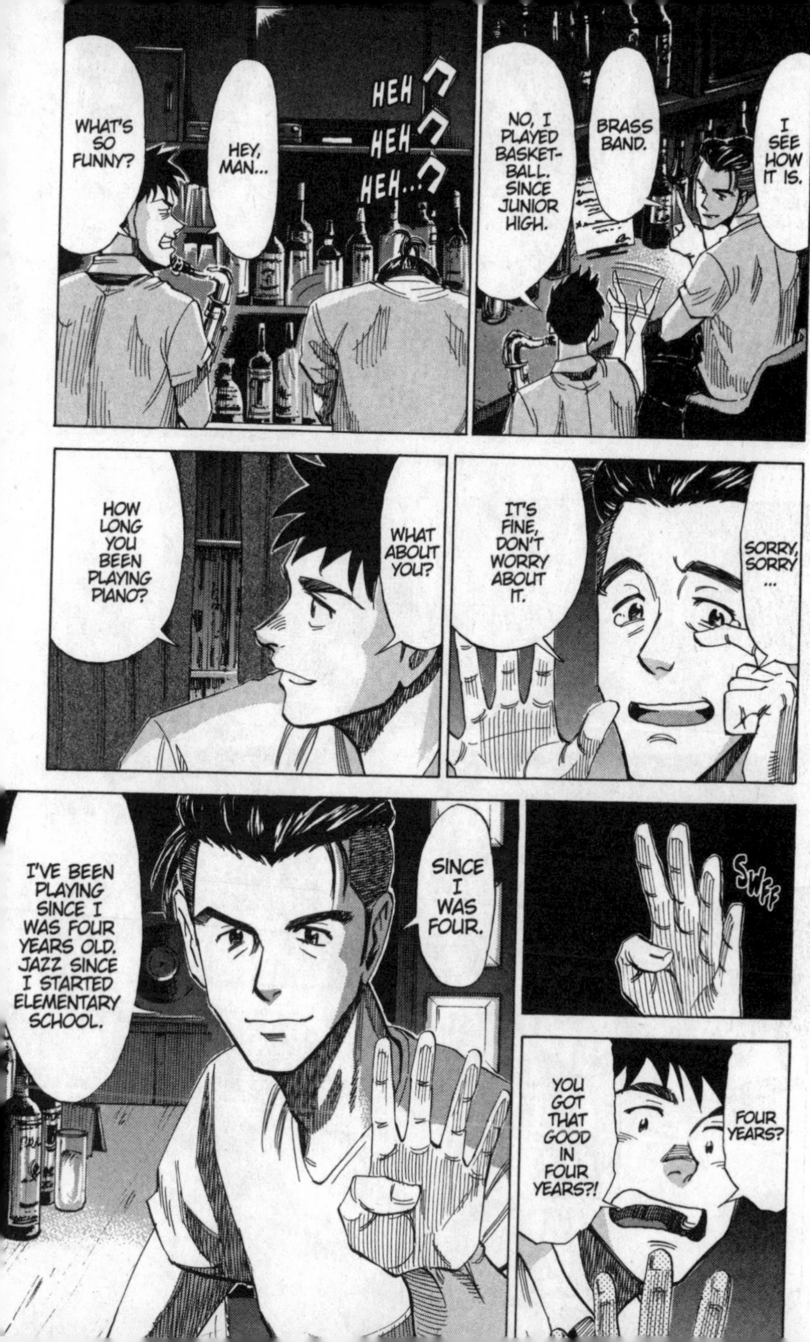
I SEE HOW IT IS.
BRASS BAND.
NO, I PLAYED BASKET-BALL. SINCE JUNIOR HIGH.
HEH HEH HEH...
HEY, MAN...
WHAT'S SO FUNNY?
SORRY, SORRY ...
IT'S FINE, DON'T WORRY ABOUT IT.
WHAT ABOUT YOU?
HOW LONG YOU BEEN PLAYING PIANO?
SINCE I WAS FOUR.
I'VE BEEN PLAYING SINCE I WAS FOUR YEARS OLD. JAZZ SINCE I STARTED ELEMENTARY SCHOOL.
SWFF
FOUR YEARS?
YOU GOT THAT GOOD IN FOUR YEARS?!

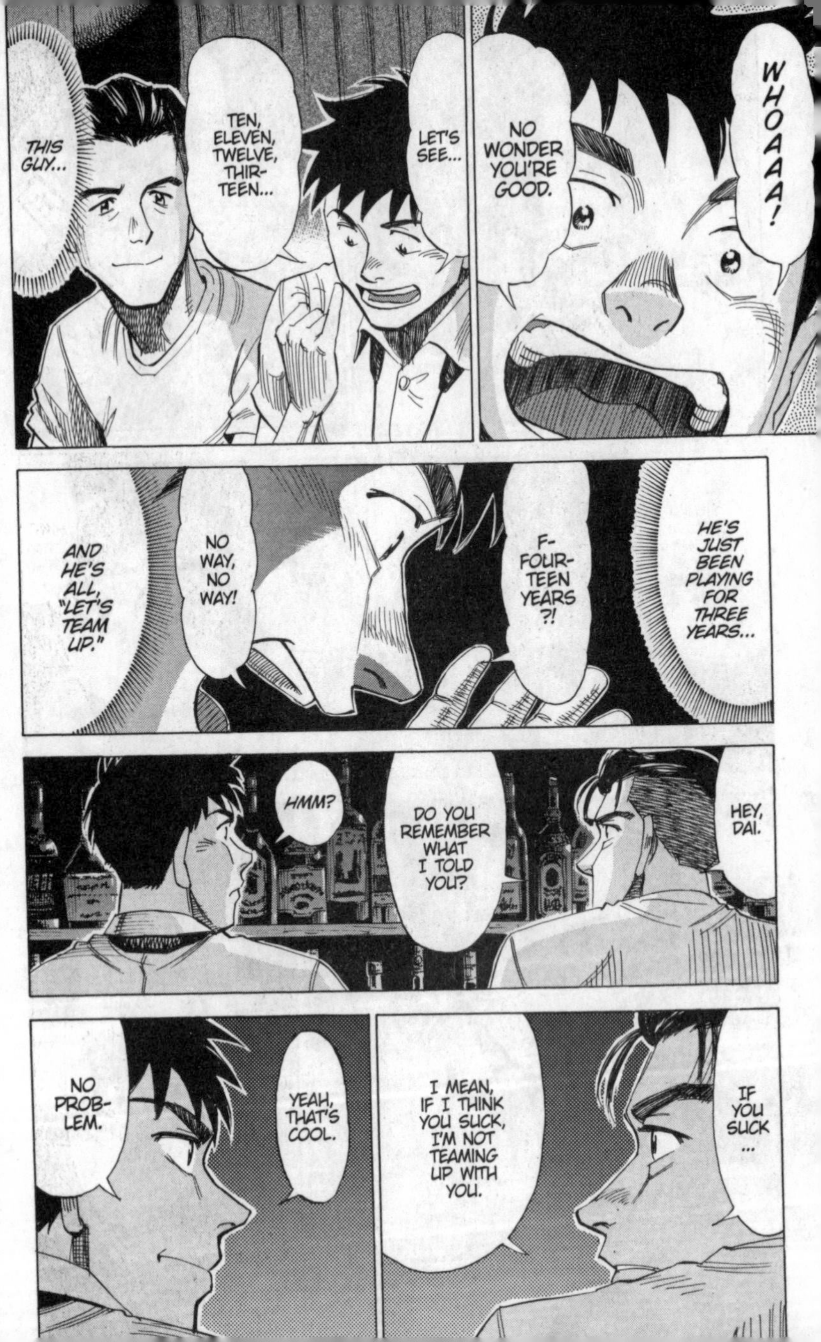
WHOAAAA!
NO WONDER YOU'RE GOOD.
LET'S SEE...
TEN, ELEVEN, TWELVE, THIR-TEEN...
THIS GUY...
HE'S JUST BEEN PLAYING FOR THREE YEARS...
F- FOUR-TEEN YEARS?!
NO WAY, NO WAY!
AND HE'S ALL, "LET'S TEAM UP."
HEY, DAI.
DO YOU REMEMBER WHAT I TOLD YOU?
HMM?
IF YOU SUCK...
I MEAN, IF I THINK YOU SUCK, I'M NOT TEAMING UP WITH YOU.
YEAH, THAT'S COOL.
NO PROB-LEM.

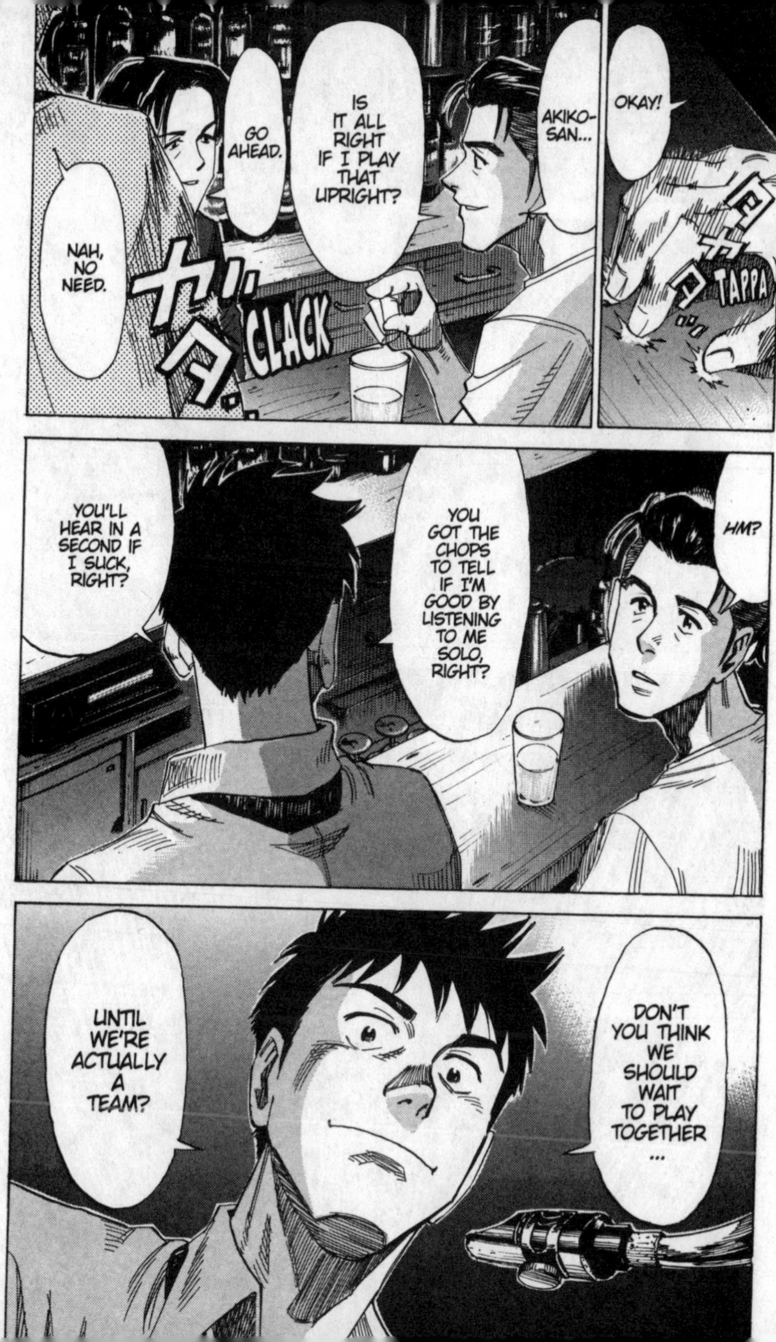
OKAY!
TAPPA
AKIKO-SAN...
IS IT ALL RIGHT IF I PLAY THAT UPRIGHT?
GO AHEAD.
NAH, NO NEED.
CLACK
HM?
YOU GOT THE CHOPS TO TELL IF I'M GOOD BY LISTENING TO ME SOLO, RIGHT?
YOU'LL HEAR IN A SECOND IF I SUCK, RIGHT?
DON'T YOU THINK WE SHOULD WAIT TO PLAY TOGETHER ...
UNTIL WE'RE ACTUALLY A TEAM?

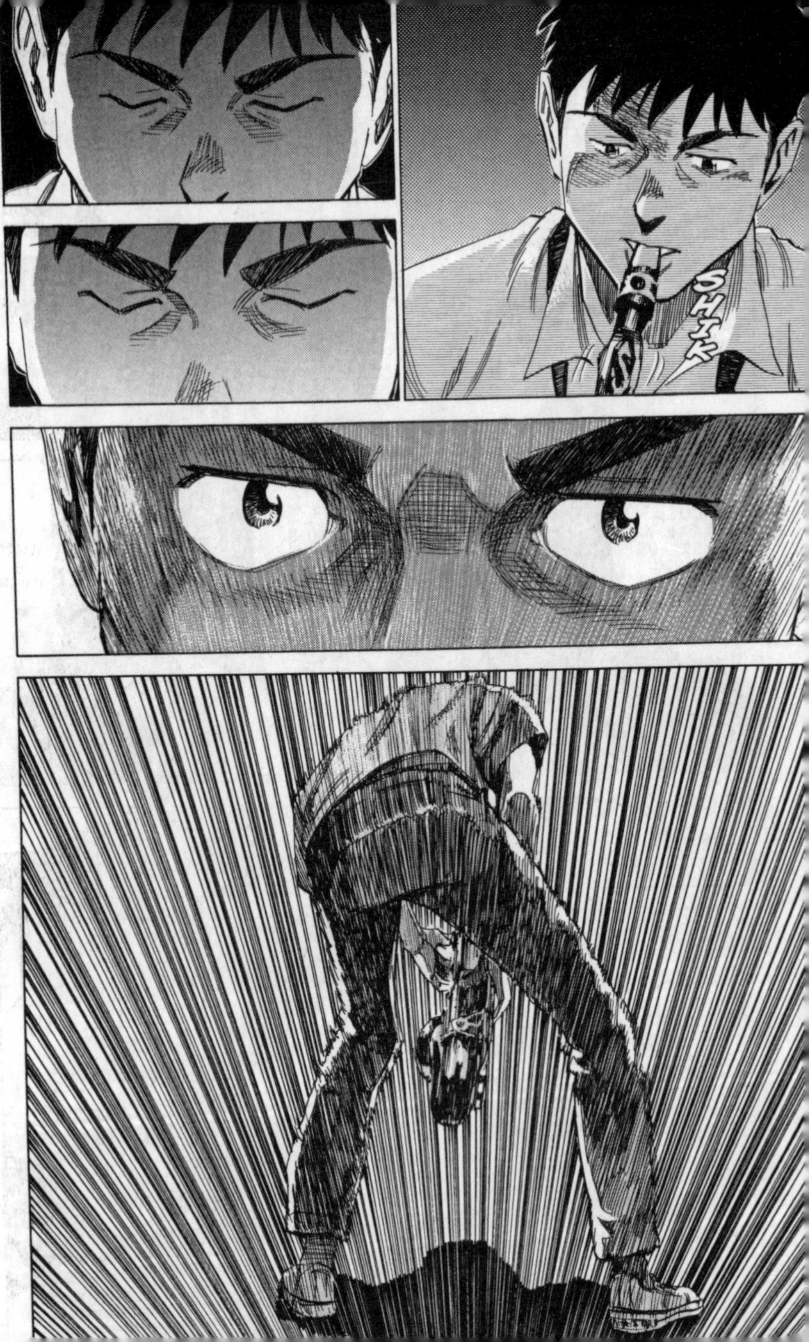
SHIK

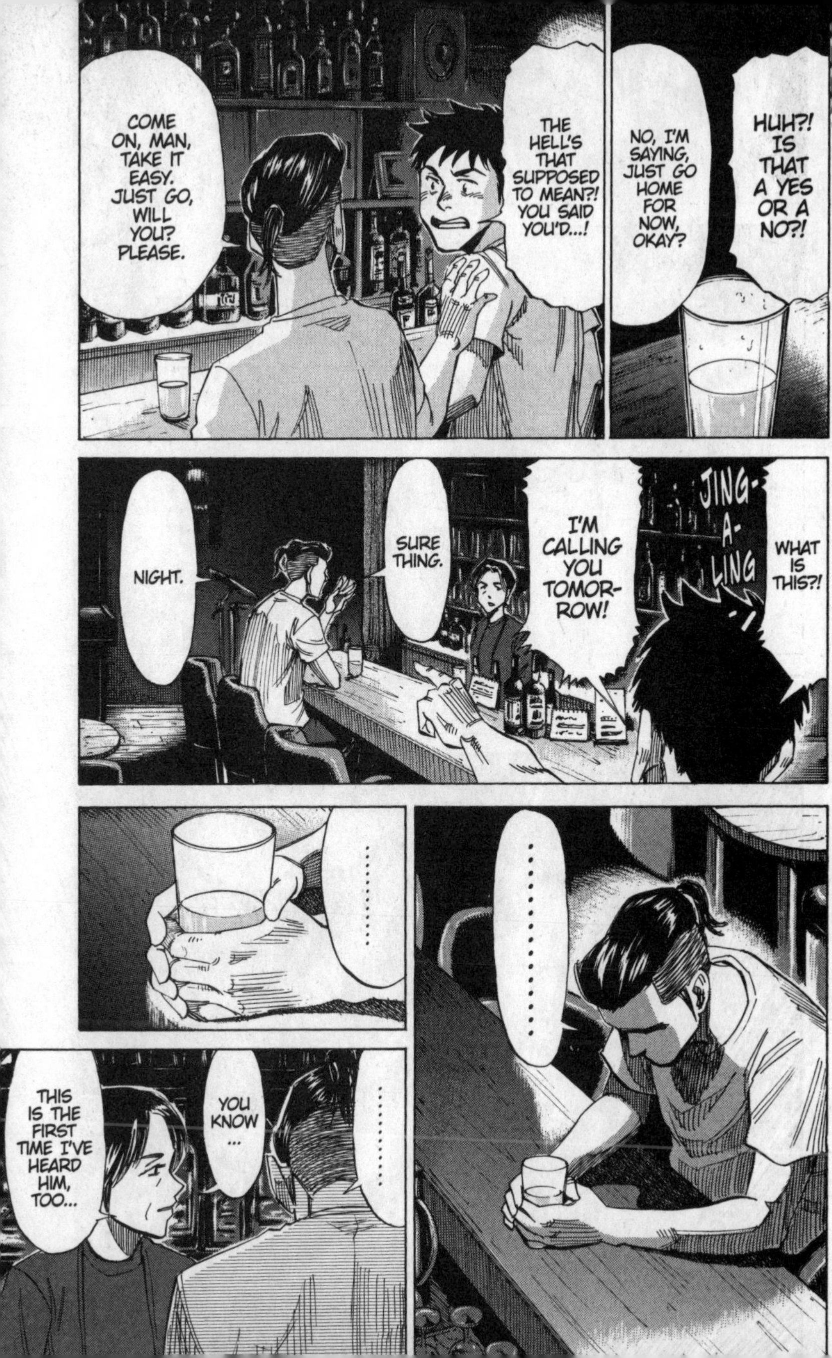
HUH?! IS THAT A YES OR A NO?!
NO, I'M SAYING, JUST GO HOME FOR NOW, OKAY?
THE HELL'S THAT SUPPOSED TO MEAN?! YOU SAID YOU'D...!
COME ON, MAN, TAKE IT EASY. JUST GO, WILL YOU? PLEASE.
WHAT IS THIS?!
JING-A-LING
I'M CALLING YOU TOMORROW!
SURE THING.
NIGHT.
......
......
......
YOU KNOW ...
THIS IS THE FIRST TIME I'VE HEARD HIM, TOO...

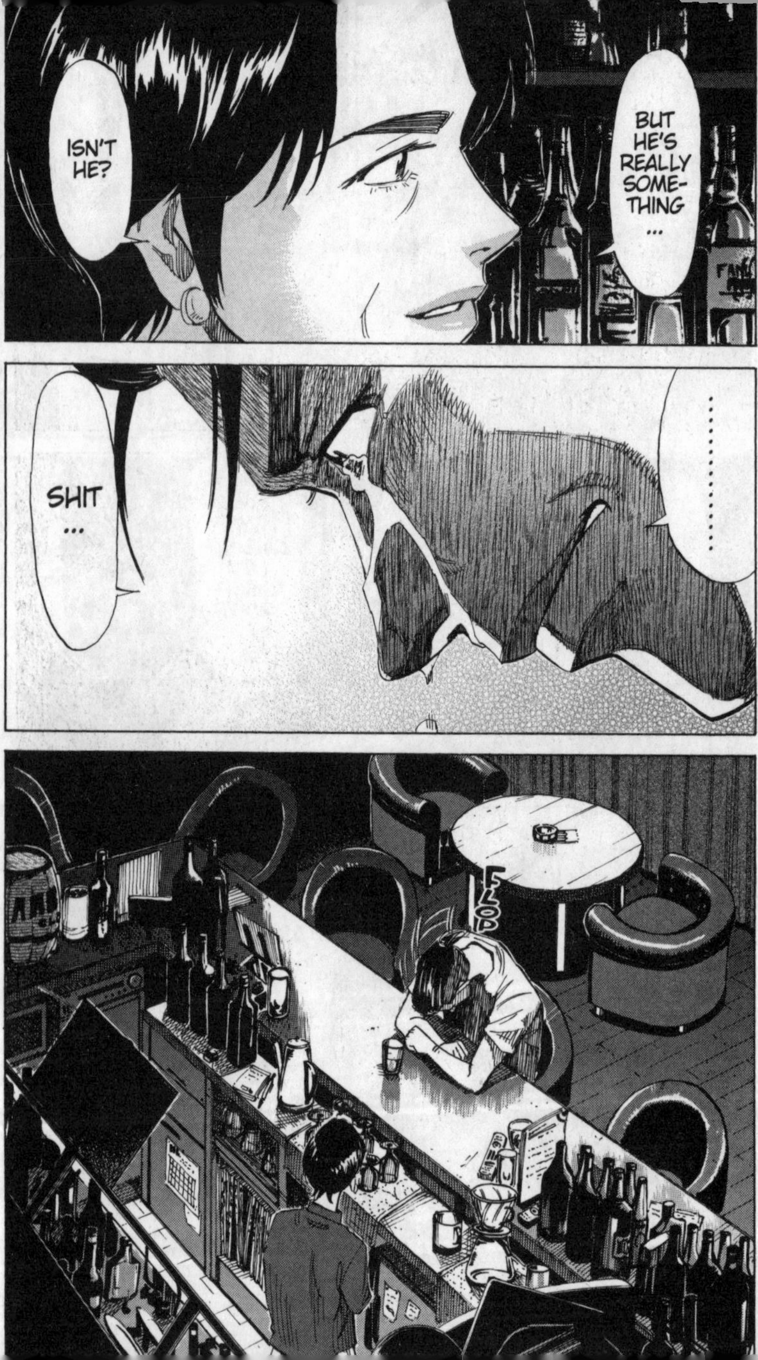
BUT HE'S REALLY SOMETHING ...
ISN'T HE?
......
SHIT ...
FLOP

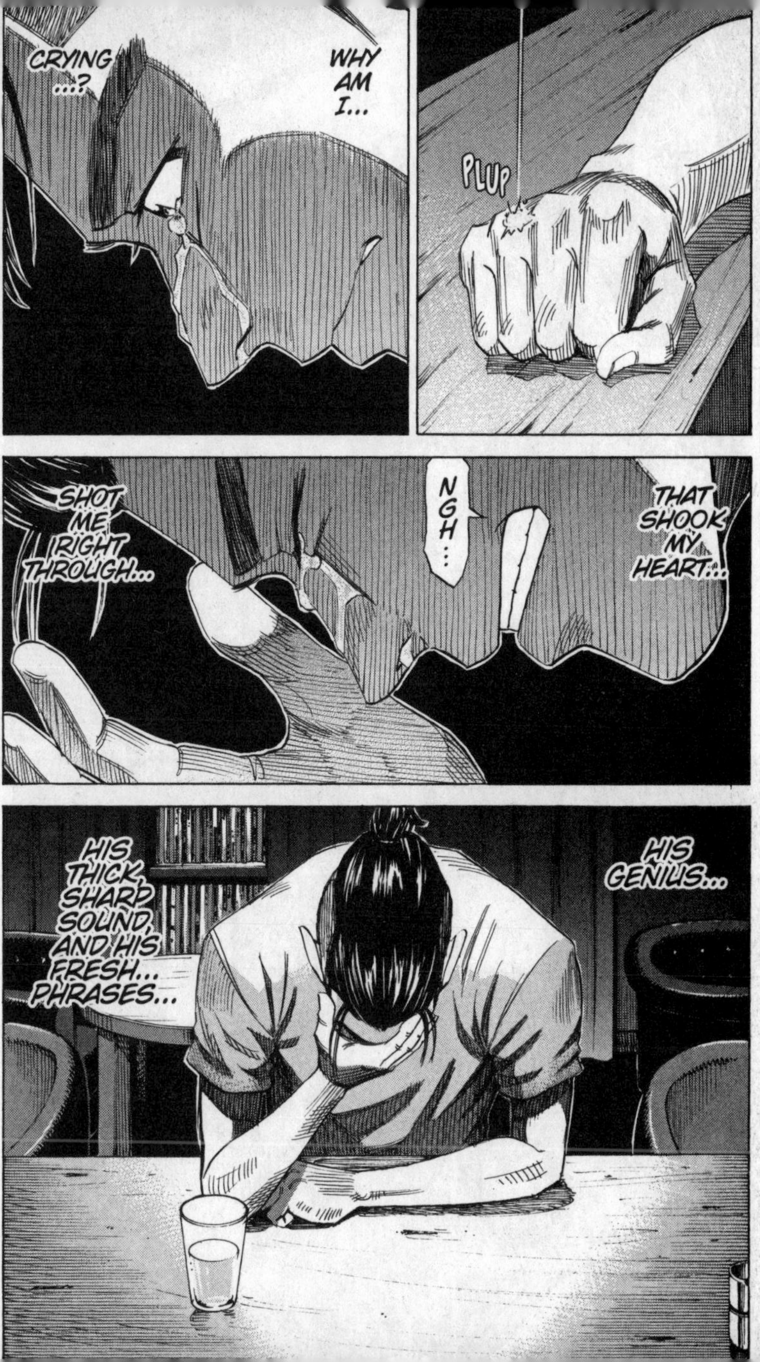
PLUP
WHY AM I...
CRYING ...?
THAT SHOOK MY HEART...
NGH...
SHOT ME RIGHT THROUGH...
HIS GENIUS...
HIS THICK, SHARP SOUND, AND HIS FRESH... PHRASES...

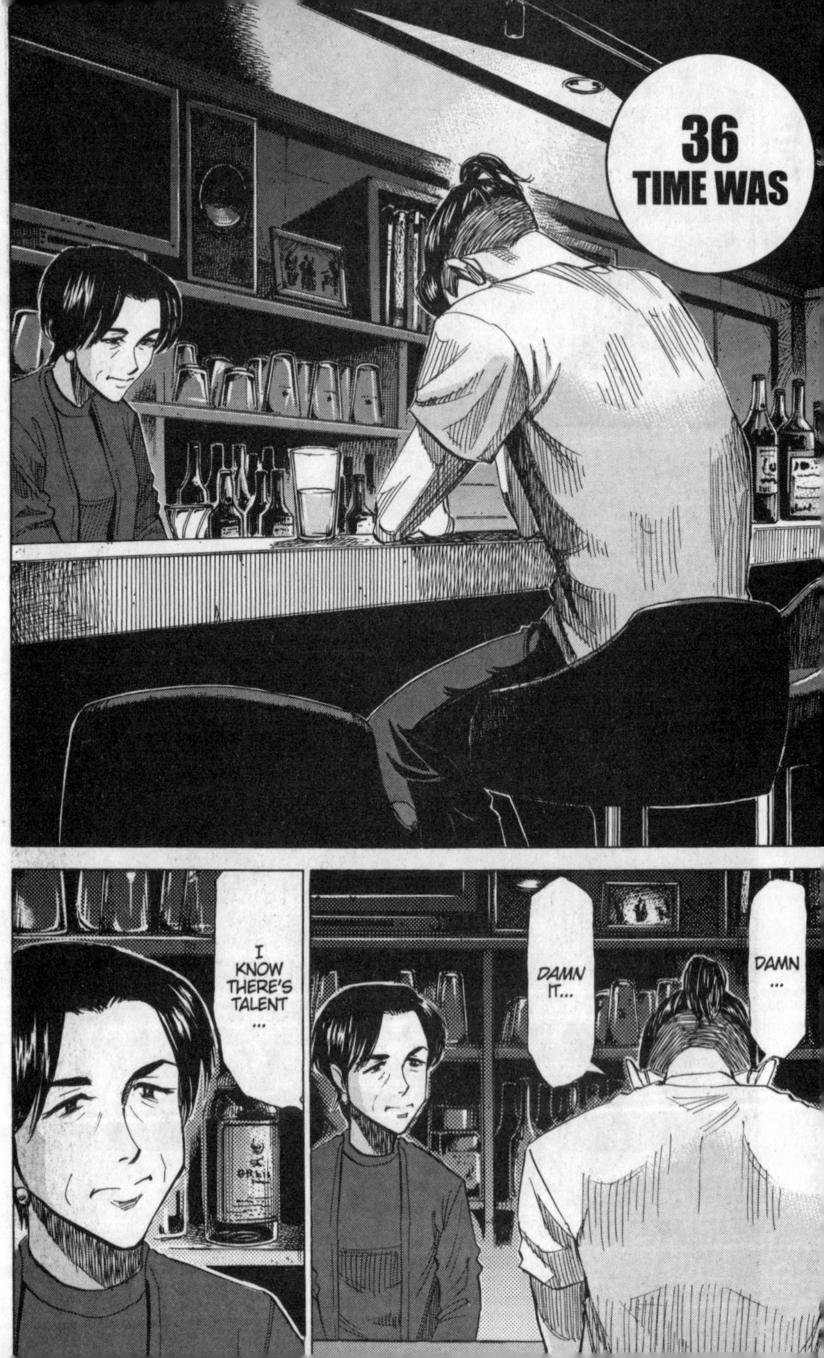
36
TIME WAS
DAMN ...
DAMN IT...
I KNOW THERE'S TALENT ...

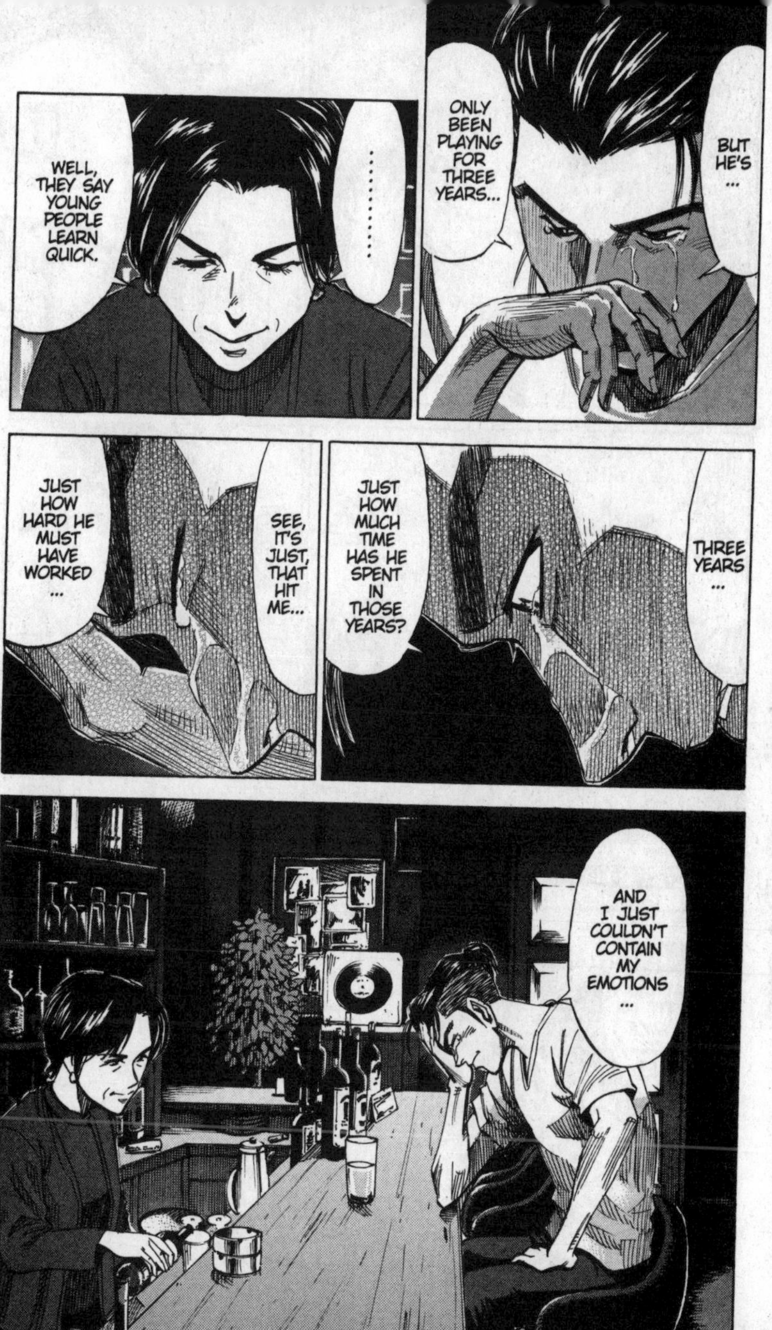
BUT HE'S ...
ONLY BEEN PLAYING FOR THREE YEARS...
....
WELL, THEY SAY YOUNG PEOPLE LEARN QUICK.
THREE YEARS ...
JUST HOW MUCH TIME HAS HE SPENT IN THOSE YEARS?
SEE, IT'S JUST, THAT HIT ME...
JUST HOW HARD HE MUST HAVE WORKED ...
AND I JUST COULDN'T CONTAIN MY EMOTIONS ...

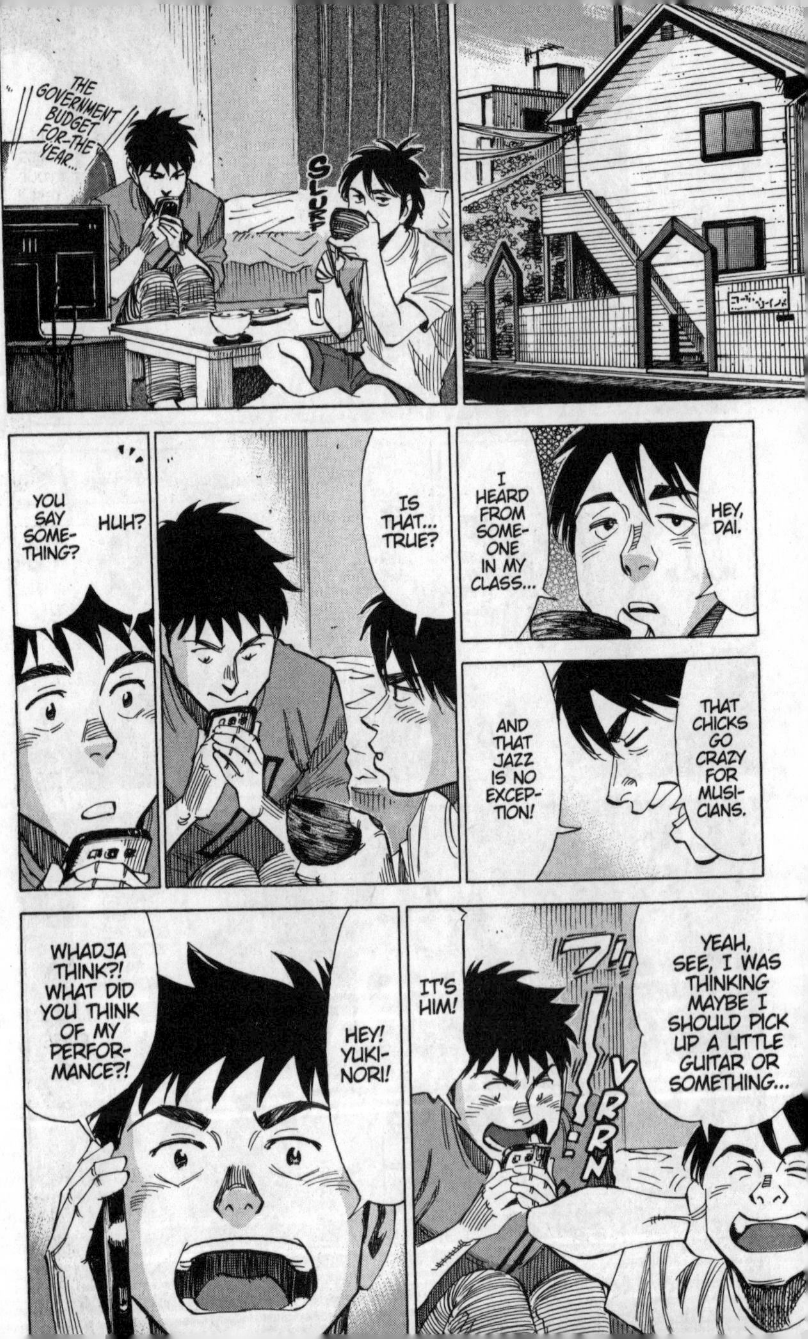
THE GOVERNMENT BUDGET FOR THE YEAR...
SLURP
HEY, DAI.
I HEARD FROM SOMEONE IN MY CLASS...
THAT CHICKS GO CRAZY FOR MUSICIANS.
AND THAT JAZZ IS NO EXCEPTION!
IS THAT... TRUE?
HUH?
YOU SAY SOMETHING?
YEAH, SEE, I WAS THINKING MAYBE I SHOULD PICK UP A LITTLE GUITAR OR SOMETHING...
VRRN
IT'S HIM!
HEY! YUKI-NORI!
WHADJA THINK?! WHAT DID YOU THINK OF MY PERFORMANCE?!

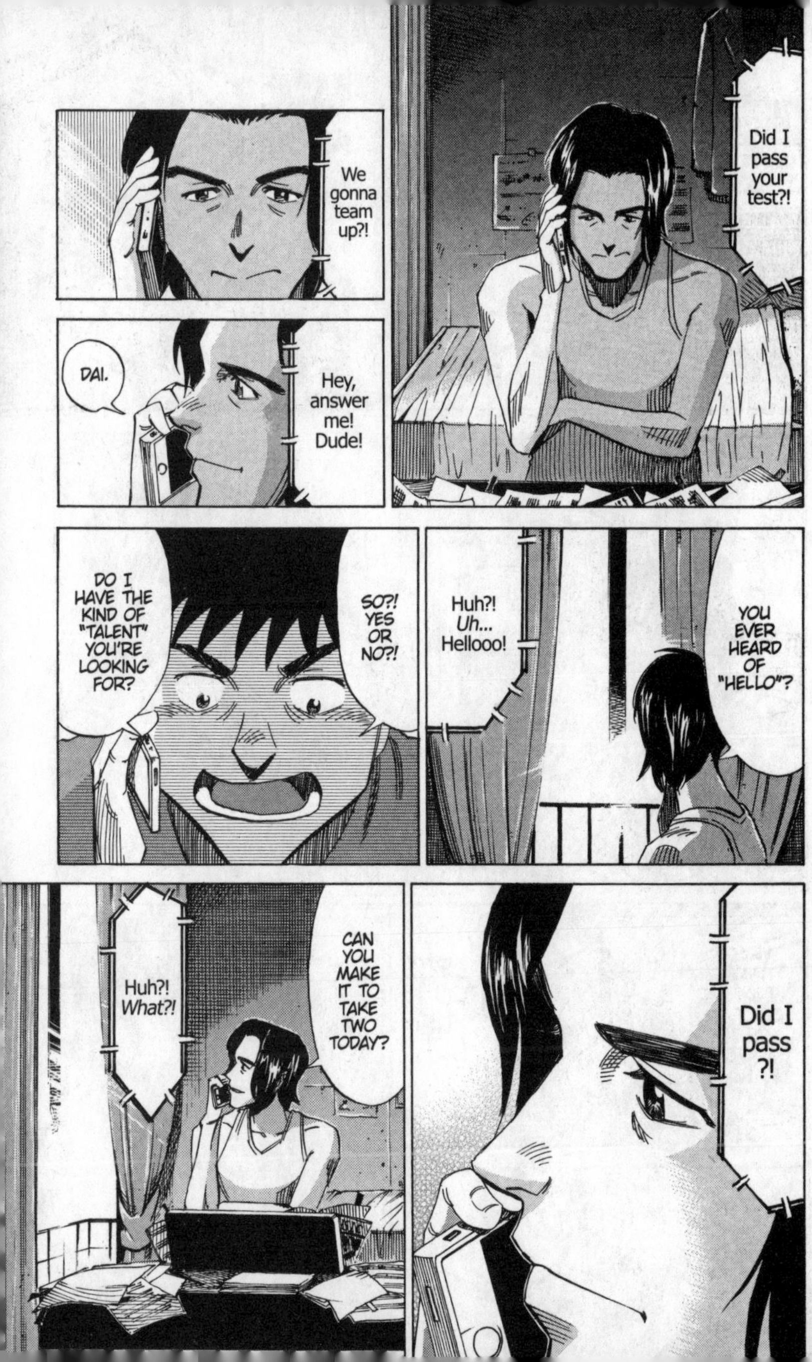
Did I pass your test?!
We gonna team up?!
Hey, answer me! Dude!
DAI.
YOU EVER HEARD OF "HELLO"?
Huh?! *Uh...* Hellooo!
SO?! YES OR NO?!
DO I HAVE THE KIND OF "TALENT" YOU'RE LOOKING FOR?
Did I pass ?!
CAN YOU MAKE IT TO TAKE TWO TODAY?
Huh?! *What?!*

MIYA-MOTO DAI.

YOU PASS.

UH...

LET'S DO IT, YUKI-NORI!

OKAY.

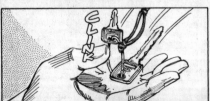

CLINK

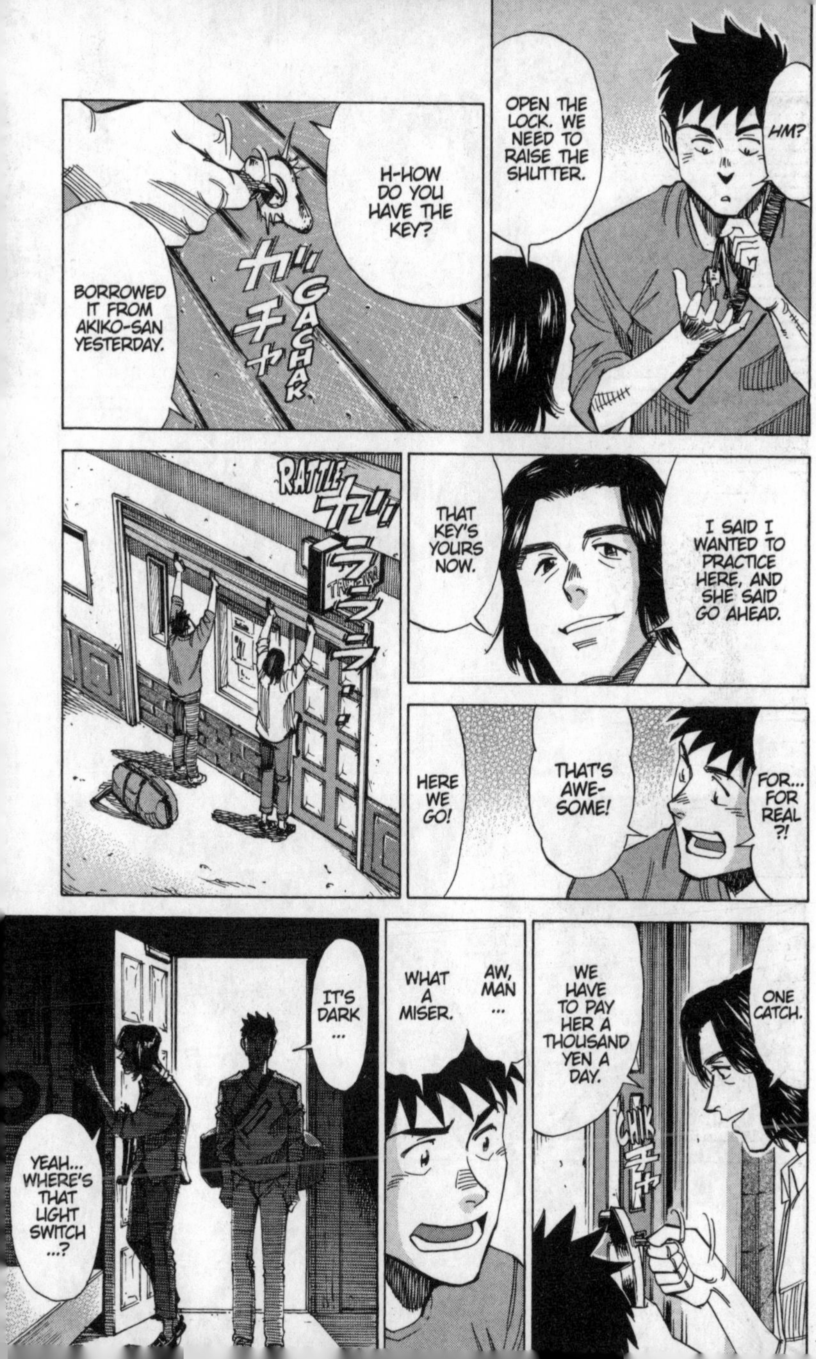
HM?
OPEN THE LOCK. WE NEED TO RAISE THE SHUTTER.
H-HOW DO YOU HAVE THE KEY?
GACHAK
BORROWED IT FROM AKIKO-SAN YESTERDAY.
I SAID I WANTED TO PRACTICE HERE, AND SHE SAID GO AHEAD.
THAT KEY'S YOURS NOW.
FOR... FOR REAL?!
THAT'S AWE-SOME!
HERE WE GO!
RATTLE
ONE CATCH.
WE HAVE TO PAY HER A THOUSAND YEN A DAY.
CHIK
AW, MAN ...
WHAT A MISER.
IT'S DARK ...
YEAH... WHERE'S THAT LIGHT SWITCH ...?

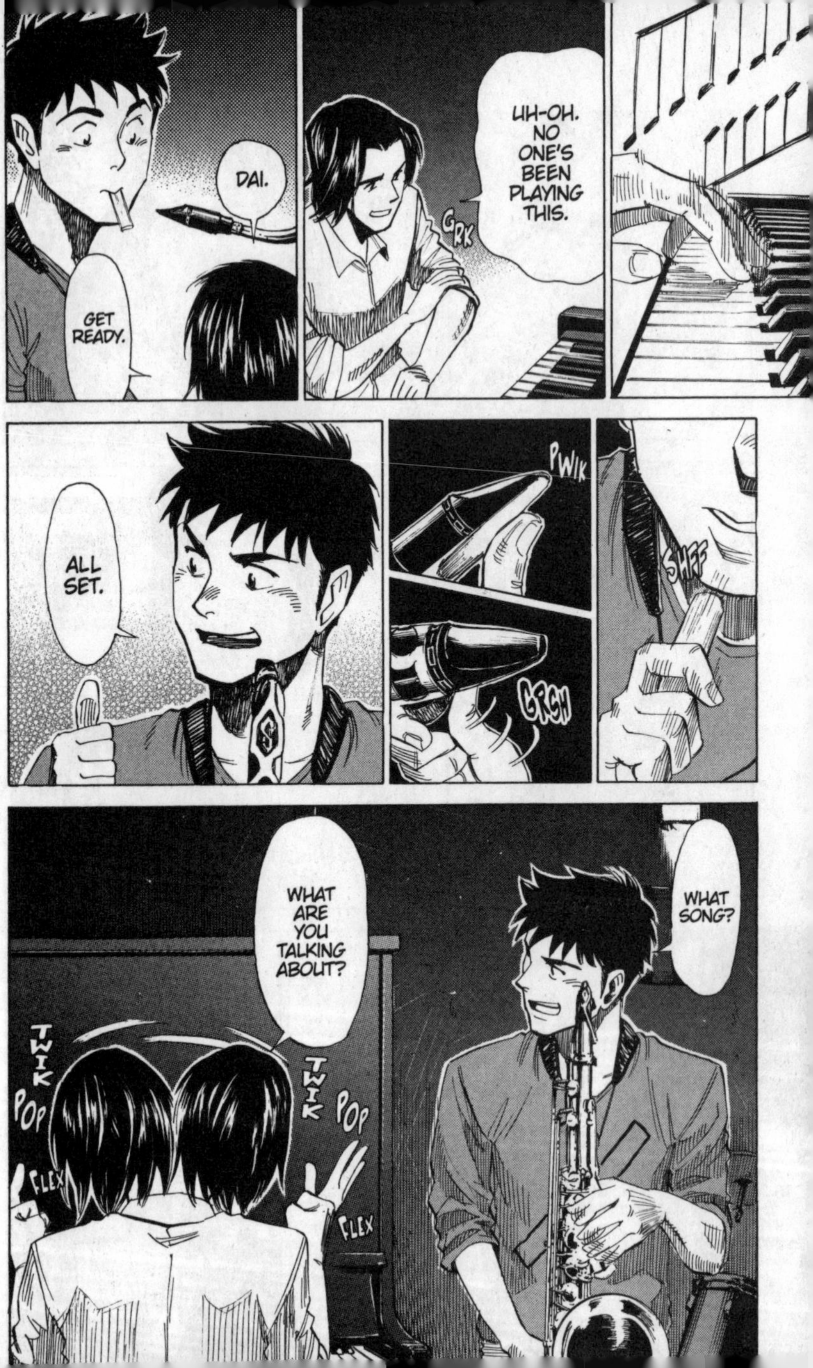
GRK
UH-OH. NO ONE'S BEEN PLAYING THIS.
DAI.
GET READY.
SHFF
PWIK
GRSH
ALL SET.
WHAT SONG?
WHAT ARE YOU TALKING ABOUT?
TWIK
POP
TWIK
POP
FLEX
FLEX

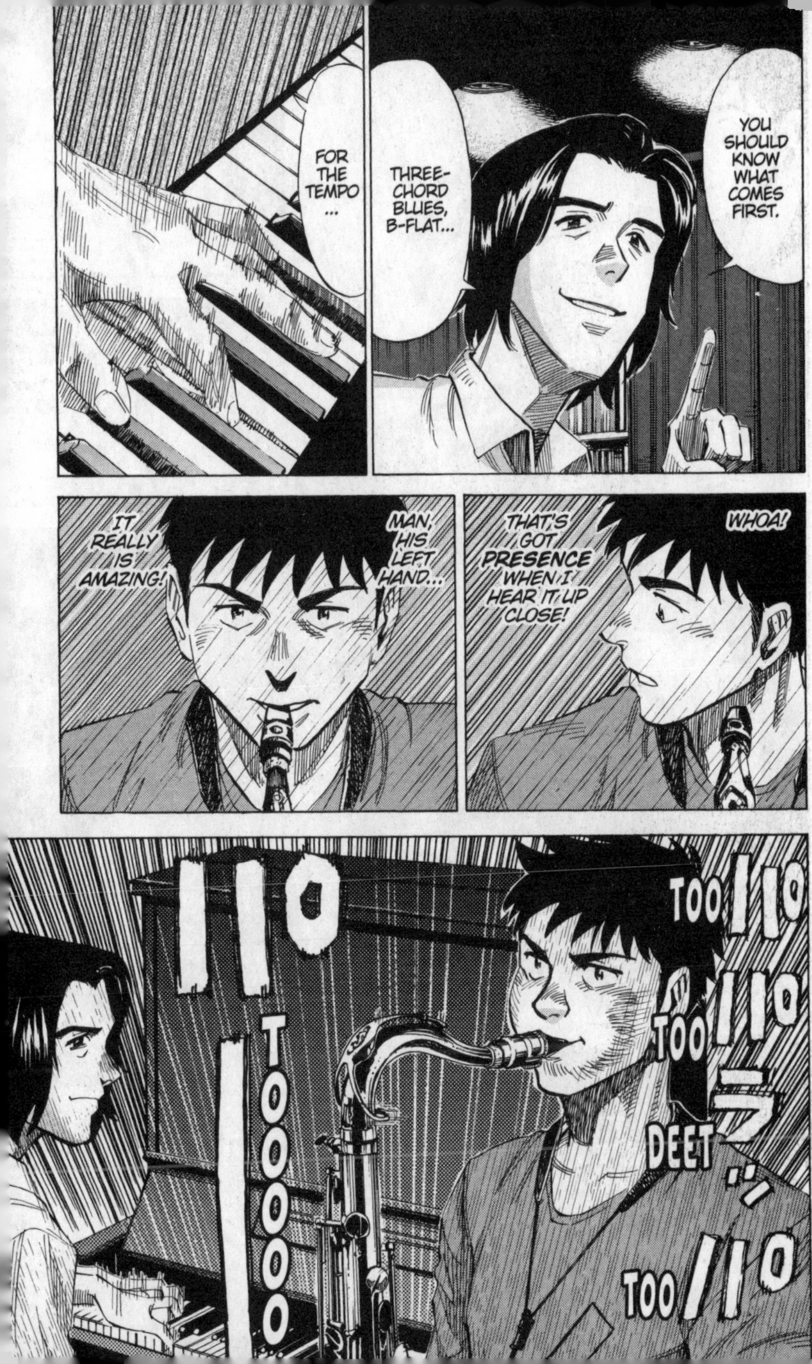
YOU SHOULD KNOW WHAT COMES FIRST.
THREE-CHORD BLUES, B-FLAT...
FOR THE TEMPO ...
WHOA!
THAT'S GOT PRESENCE WHEN I HEAR IT UP CLOSE!
MAN, HIS LEFT HAND...
IT REALLY IS AMAZING!
TOO
TOO
DEET
TOO
TOOOOO

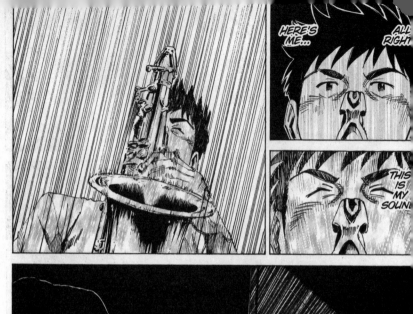

HERE'S ME... ALL RIGHT

THIS IS MY SOUND

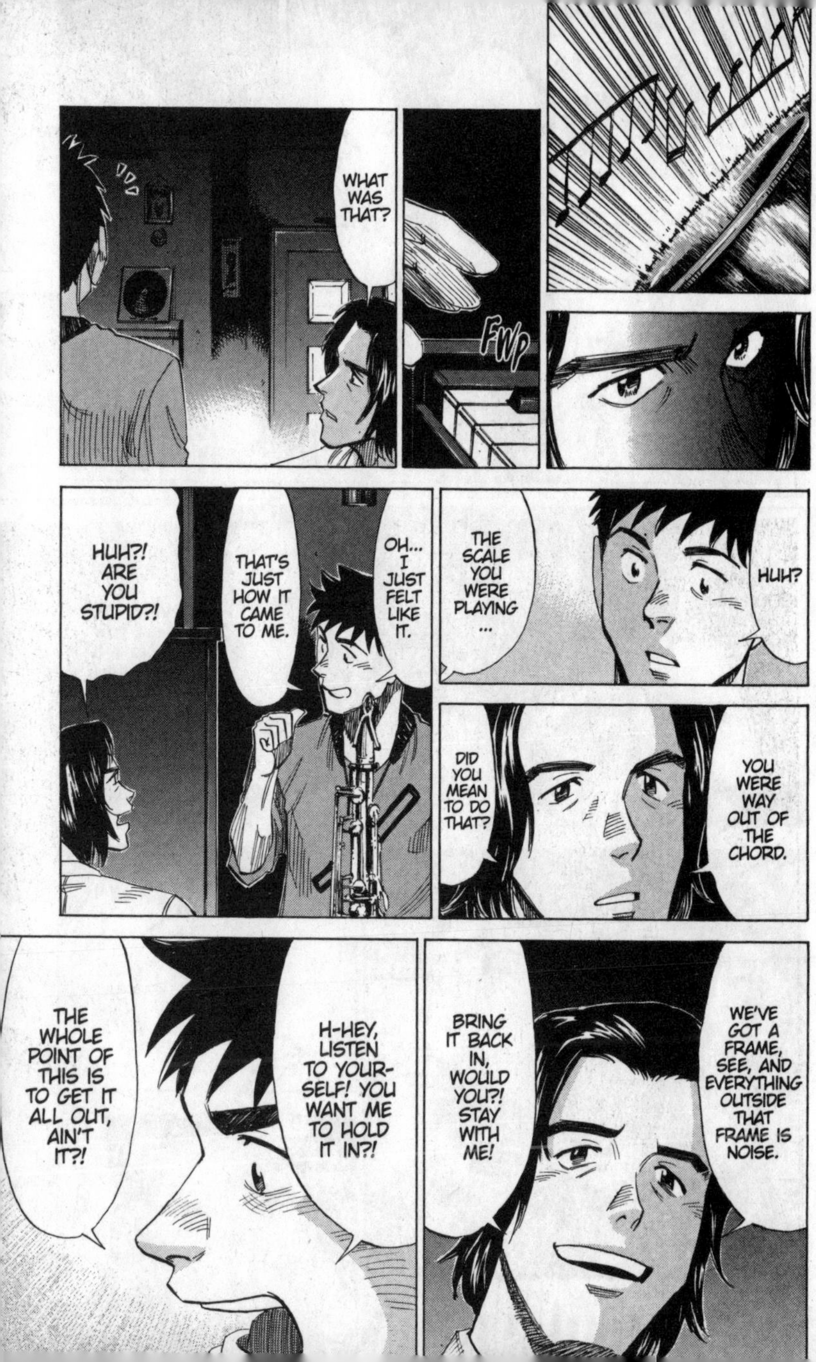
FWP
WHAT WAS THAT?
HUH?
THE SCALE YOU WERE PLAYING ...
YOU WERE WAY OUT OF THE CHORD.
DID YOU MEAN TO DO THAT?
OH... I JUST FELT LIKE IT.
THAT'S JUST HOW IT CAME TO ME.
HUH?! ARE YOU STUPID?!
WE'VE GOT A FRAME, SEE, AND EVERYTHING OUTSIDE THAT FRAME IS NOISE.
BRING IT BACK IN, WOULD YOU?! STAY WITH ME!
H-HEY, LISTEN TO YOURSELF! YOU WANT ME TO HOLD IT IN?!
THE WHOLE POINT OF THIS IS TO GET IT ALL OUT, AIN'T IT?!

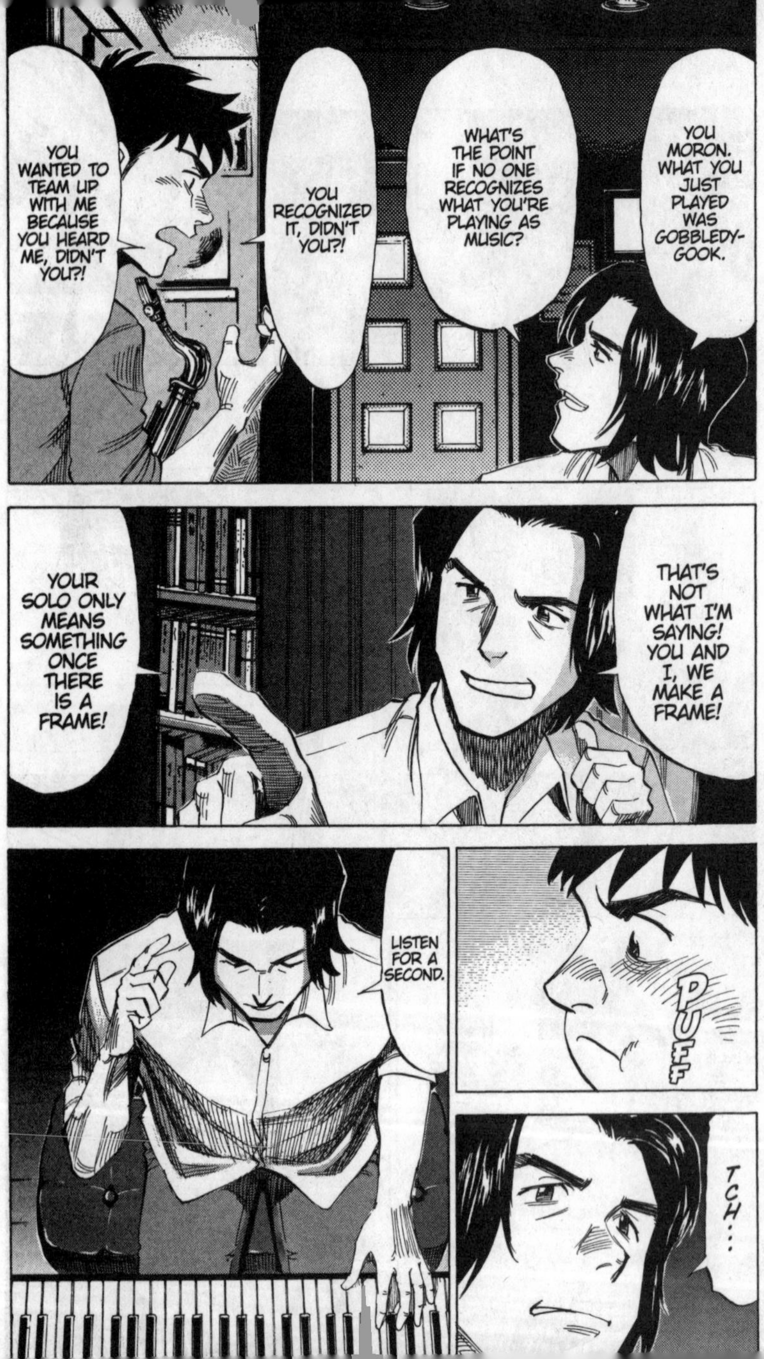
YOU MORON. WHAT YOU JUST PLAYED WAS GOBBLEDY-GOOK.
WHAT'S THE POINT IF NO ONE RECOGNIZES WHAT YOU'RE PLAYING AS MUSIC?
YOU RECOGNIZED IT, DIDN'T YOU?!
YOU WANTED TO TEAM UP WITH ME BECAUSE YOU HEARD ME, DIDN'T YOU?!
THAT'S NOT WHAT I'M SAYING! YOU AND I, WE MAKE A FRAME!
YOUR SOLO ONLY MEANS SOMETHING ONCE THERE IS A FRAME!
PUFF
TCH...
LISTEN FOR A SECOND.

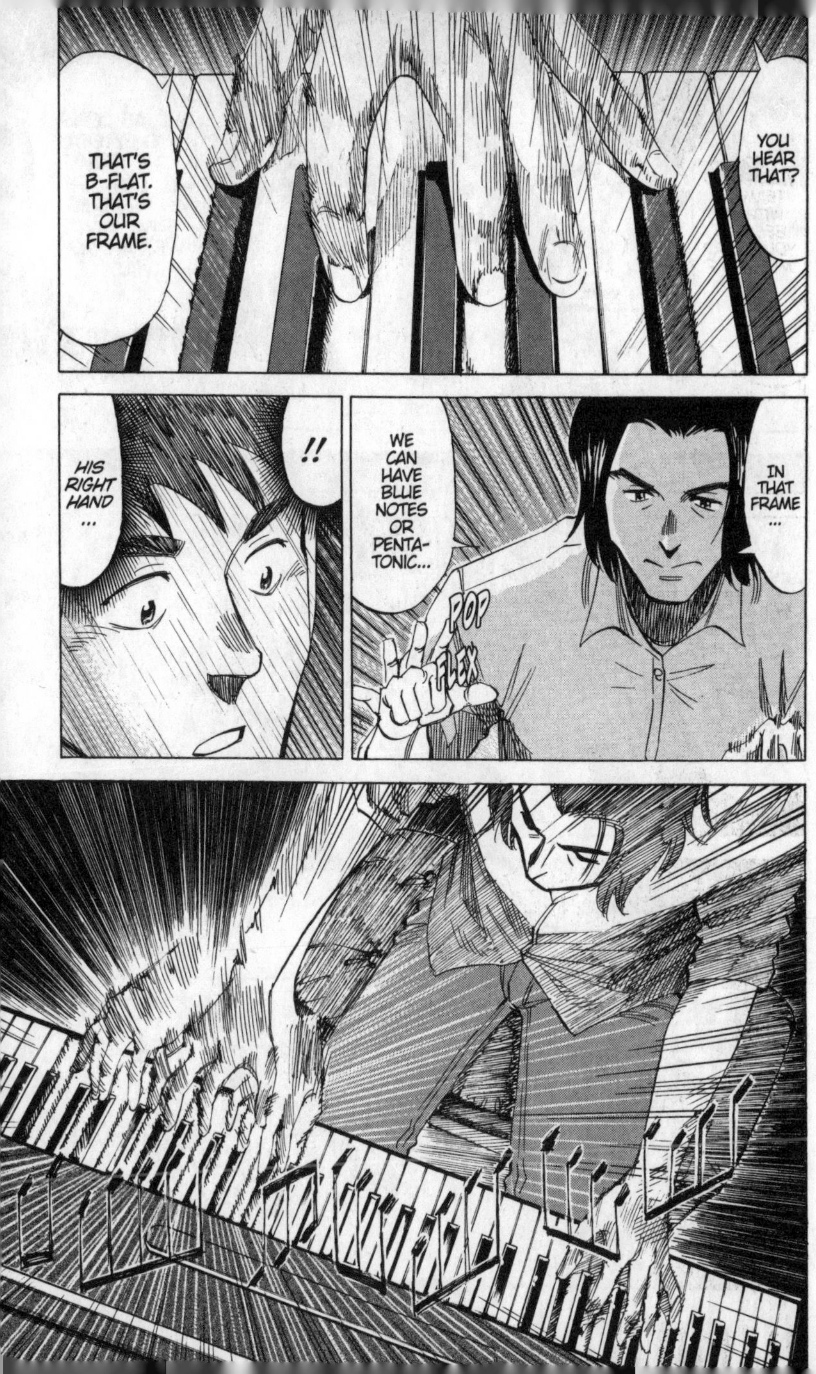
YOU HEAR THAT?
THAT'S B-FLAT. THAT'S OUR FRAME.
IN THAT FRAME...
WE CAN HAVE BLUE NOTES OR PENTA-TONIC...
POP
FLEX
!!
HIS RIGHT HAND...

AND AS LONG AS THEY STAY IN THE FRAME, WE CAN GET AS INSPIRED AS WE WANT! WE CAN GO WILD!

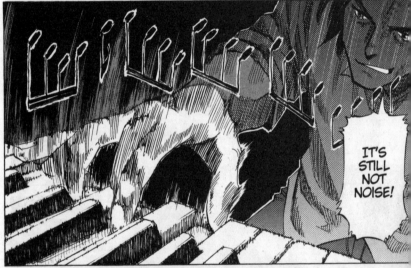

IT'S STILL NOT NOISE!

HE'S AWE-SOME...

WHOA...

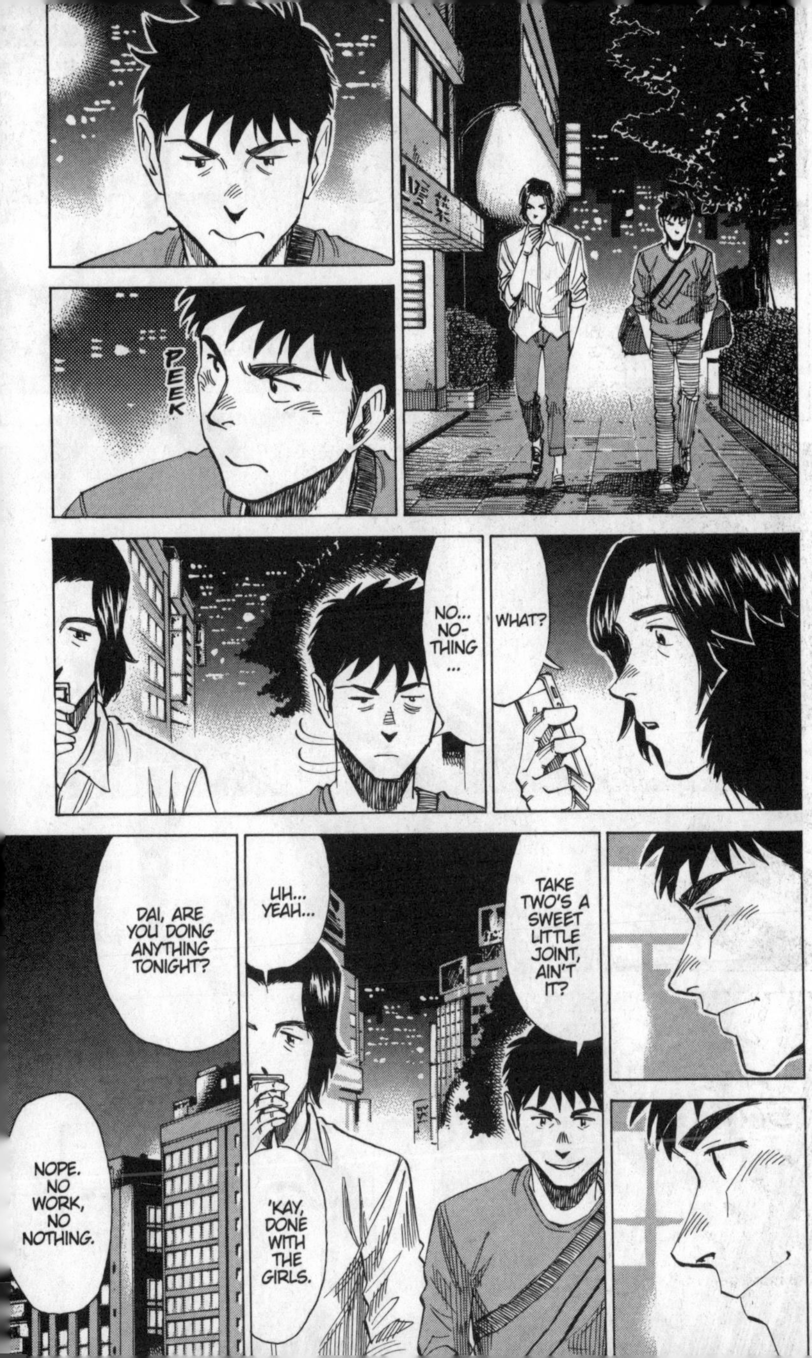
PEEK
WHAT?
NO... NO-THING ...
TAKE TWO'S A SWEET LITTLE JOINT, AIN'T IT?
UH... YEAH...
'KAY, DONE WITH THE GIRLS.
DAI, ARE YOU DOING ANYTHING TONIGHT?
NOPE. NO WORK, NO NOTHING.

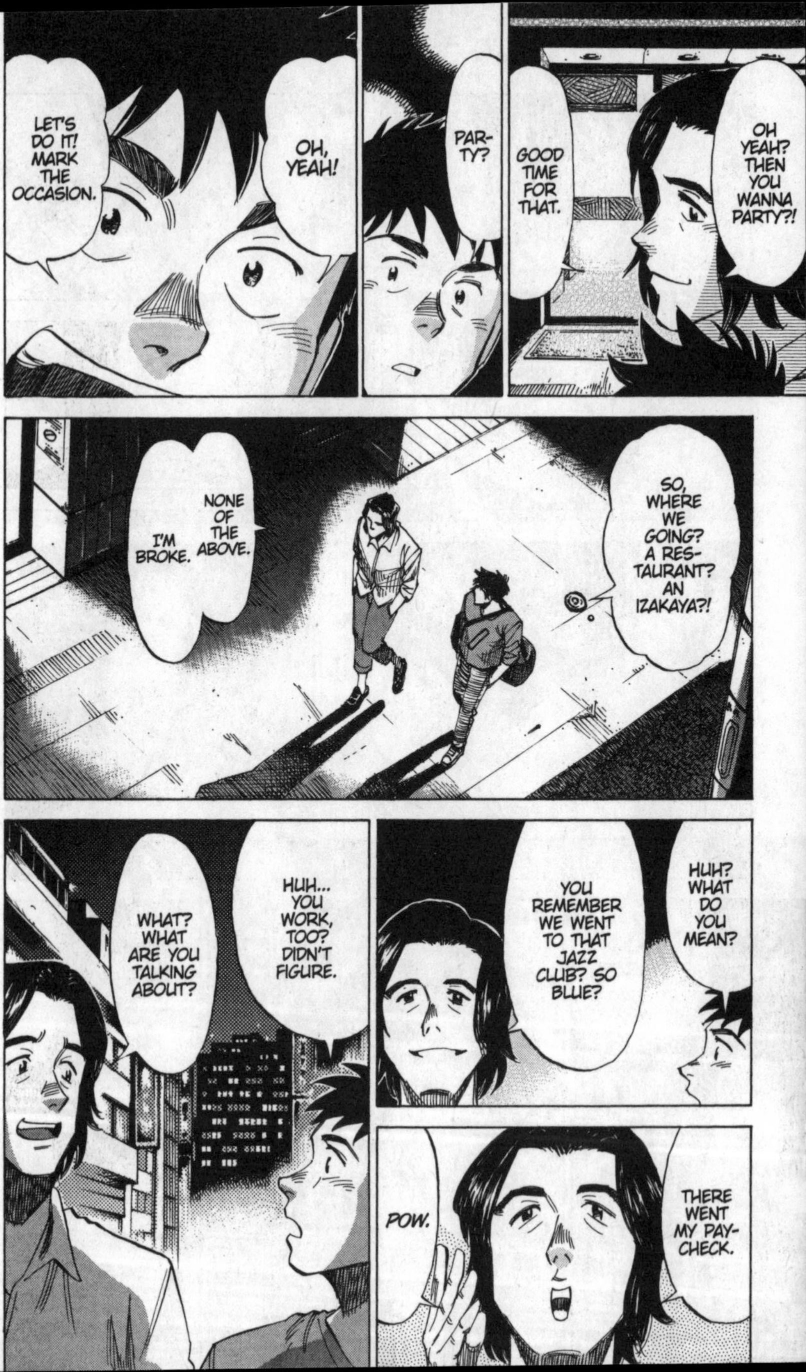
OH YEAH? THEN YOU WANNA PARTY?!
GOOD TIME FOR THAT.
PARTY?
OH, YEAH!
LET'S DO IT! MARK THE OCCASION.
SO, WHERE WE GOING? A RESTAURANT? AN IZAKAYA?!
NONE OF THE ABOVE.
I'M BROKE.
HUH? WHAT DO YOU MEAN?
YOU REMEMBER WE WENT TO THAT JAZZ CLUB? SO BLUE?
THERE WENT MY PAYCHECK.
POW.
HUH... YOU WORK, TOO? DIDN'T FIGURE.
WHAT? WHAT ARE YOU TALKING ABOUT?

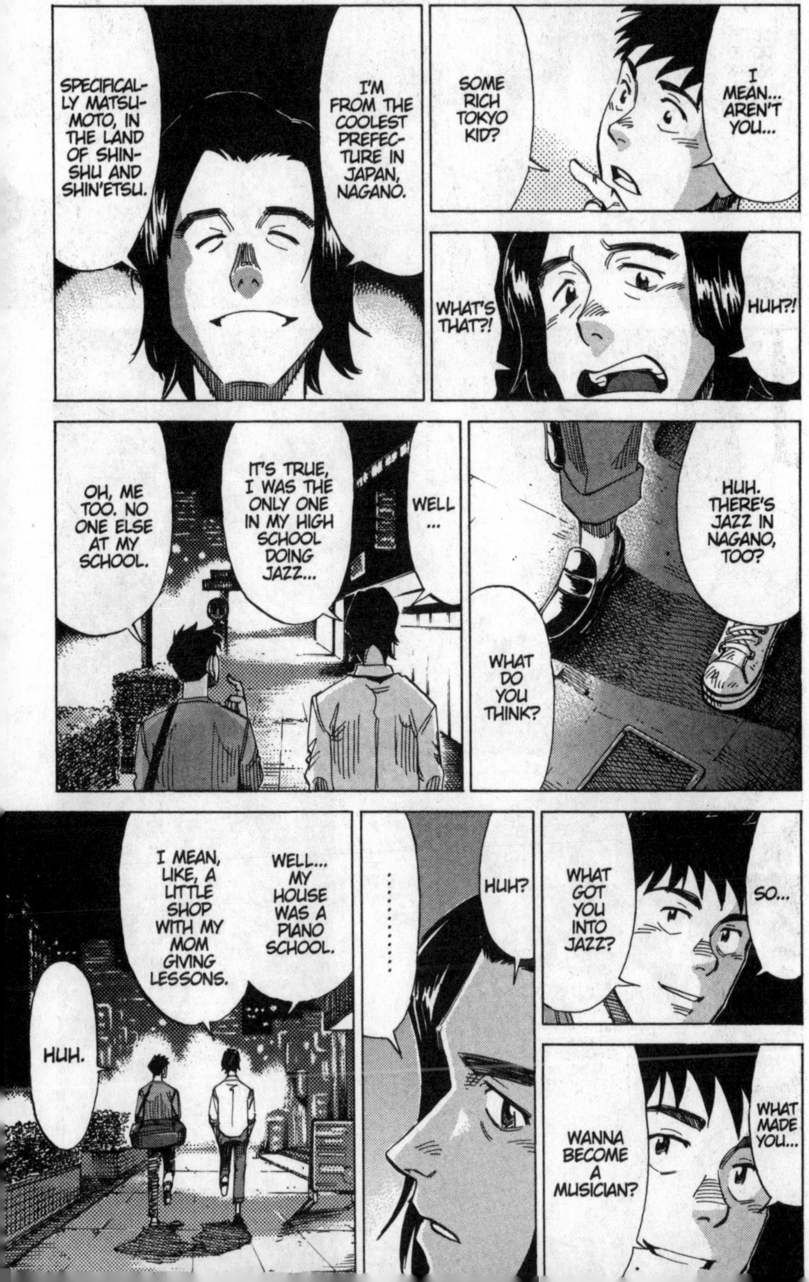
I MEAN... AREN'T YOU...
SOME RICH TOKYO KID?
HUH?!
WHAT'S THAT?!
I'M FROM THE COOLEST PREFECTURE IN JAPAN, NAGANO.
SPECIFICALLY MATSUMOTO, IN THE LAND OF SHINSHU AND SHIN'ETSU.
HUH. THERE'S JAZZ IN NAGANO, TOO?
WHAT DO YOU THINK?
WELL ...
IT'S TRUE, I WAS THE ONLY ONE IN MY HIGH SCHOOL DOING JAZZ...
OH, ME TOO. NO ONE ELSE AT MY SCHOOL.
SO...
WHAT GOT YOU INTO JAZZ?
WHAT MADE YOU...
WANNA BECOME A MUSICIAN?
HUH?
......
WELL... MY HOUSE WAS A PIANO SCHOOL.
I MEAN, LIKE, A LITTLE SHOP WITH MY MOM GIVING LESSONS.
HUH.

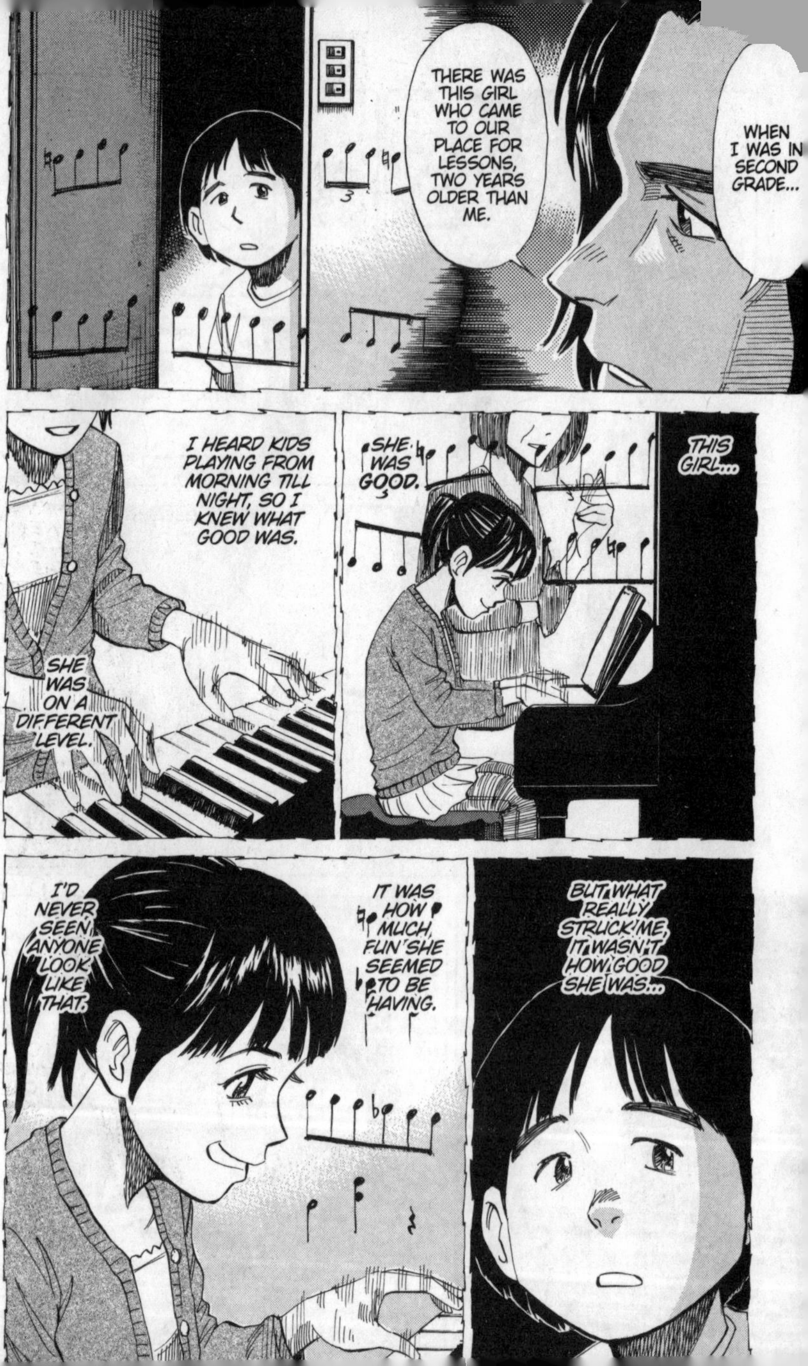
WHEN I WAS IN SECOND GRADE...
THERE WAS THIS GIRL WHO CAME TO OUR PLACE FOR LESSONS, TWO YEARS OLDER THAN ME.
THIS GIRL...
SHE WAS GOOD.
I HEARD KIDS PLAYING FROM MORNING TILL NIGHT, SO I KNEW WHAT GOOD WAS.
SHE WAS ON A DIFFERENT LEVEL.
BUT WHAT REALLY STRUCK ME, IT WASN'T HOW GOOD SHE WAS...
IT WAS HOW MUCH FUN SHE SEEMED TO BE HAVING.
I'D NEVER SEEN ANYONE LOOK LIKE THAT.

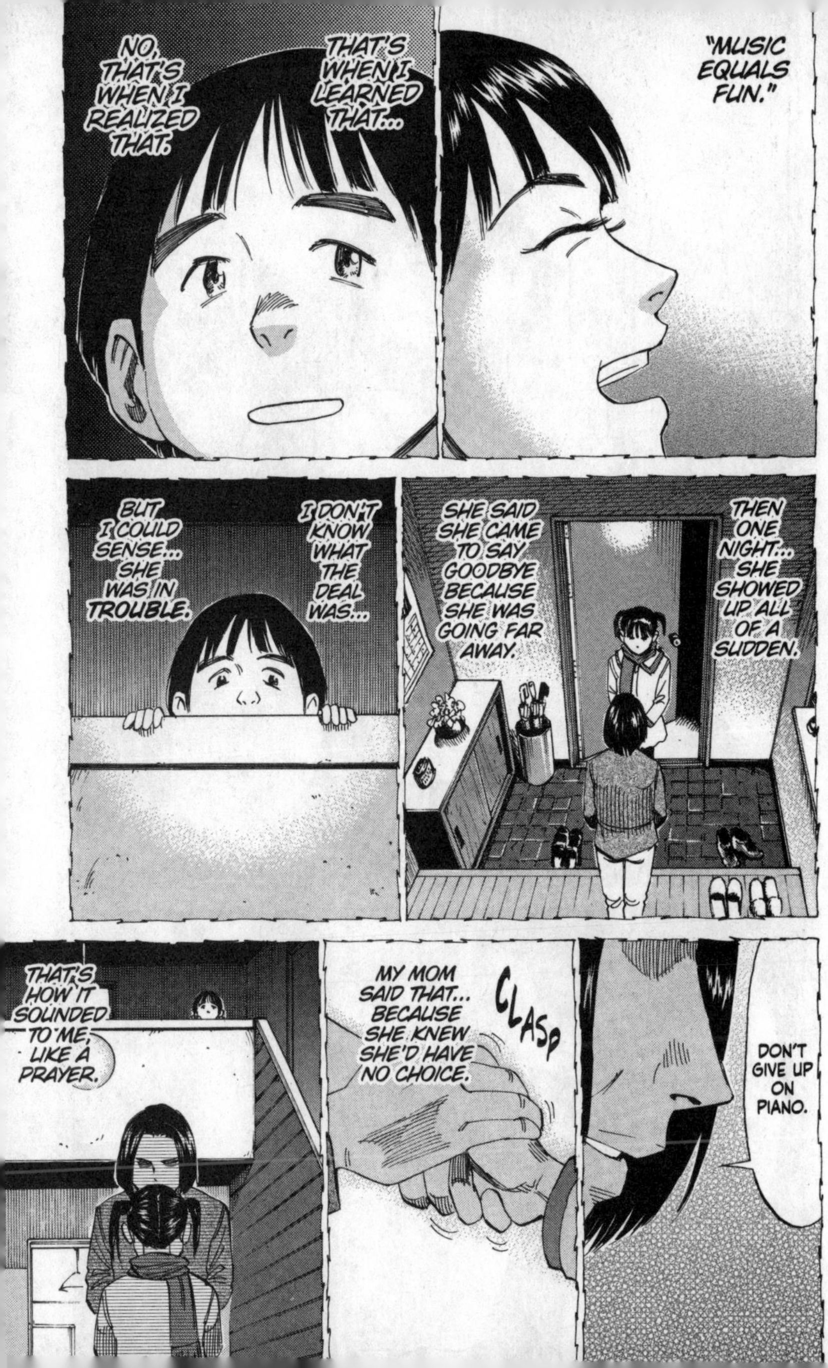
"MUSIC EQUALS FUN."
THAT'S WHEN I LEARNED THAT...
NO, THAT'S WHEN I REALIZED THAT.
THEN ONE NIGHT... SHE SHOWED UP ALL OF A SUDDEN.
SHE SAID SHE CAME TO SAY GOODBYE BECAUSE SHE WAS GOING FAR AWAY.
I DON'T KNOW WHAT THE DEAL WAS...
BUT I COULD SENSE... SHE WAS IN TROUBLE.
DON'T GIVE UP ON PIANO.
CLASP
MY MOM SAID THAT... BECAUSE SHE KNEW SHE'D HAVE NO CHOICE.
THAT'S HOW IT SOUNDED TO ME, LIKE A PRAYER.

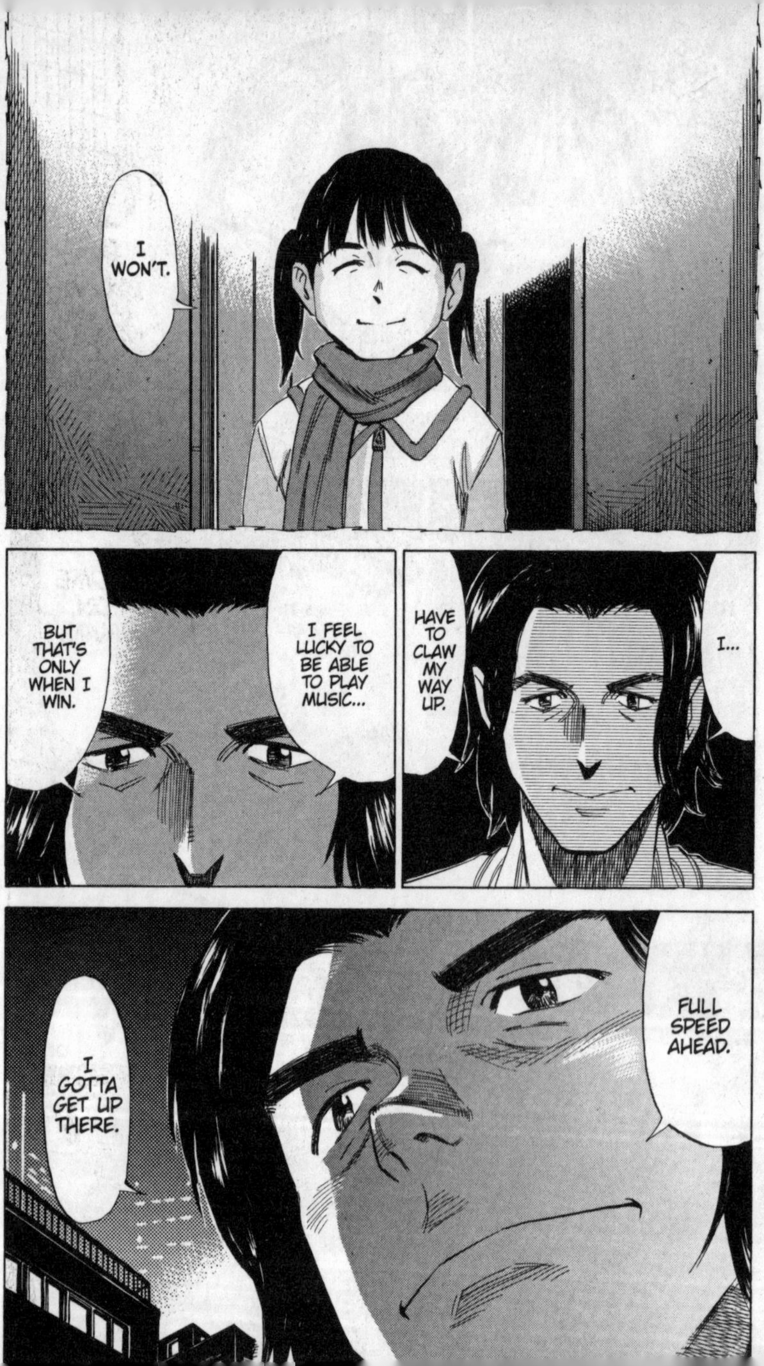
I WON'T.
I...
HAVE TO CLAW MY WAY UP.
I FEEL LUCKY TO BE ABLE TO PLAY MUSIC...
BUT THAT'S ONLY WHEN I WIN.
FULL SPEED AHEAD.
I GOTTA GET UP THERE.

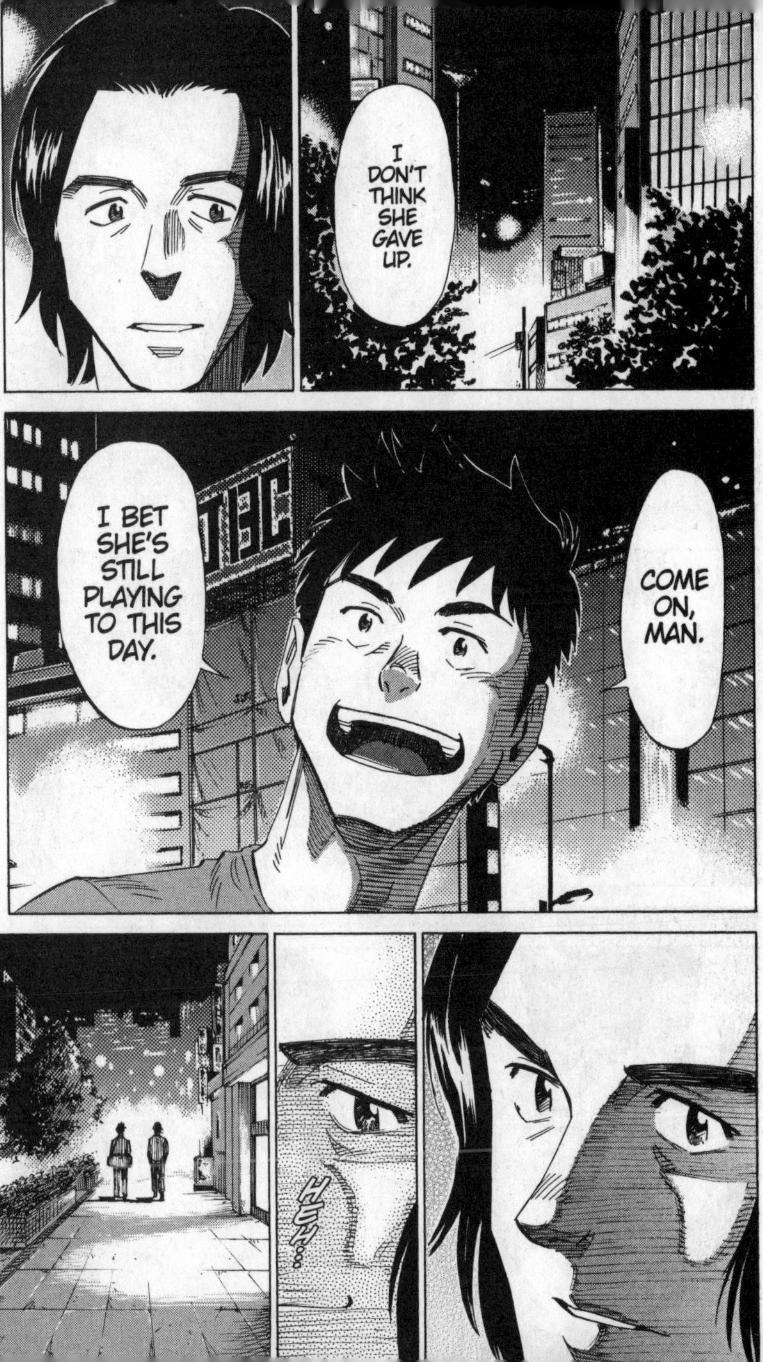
I DON'T THINK SHE GAVE UP.
COME ON, MAN.
I BET SHE'S STILL PLAYING TO THIS DAY.
HEH...

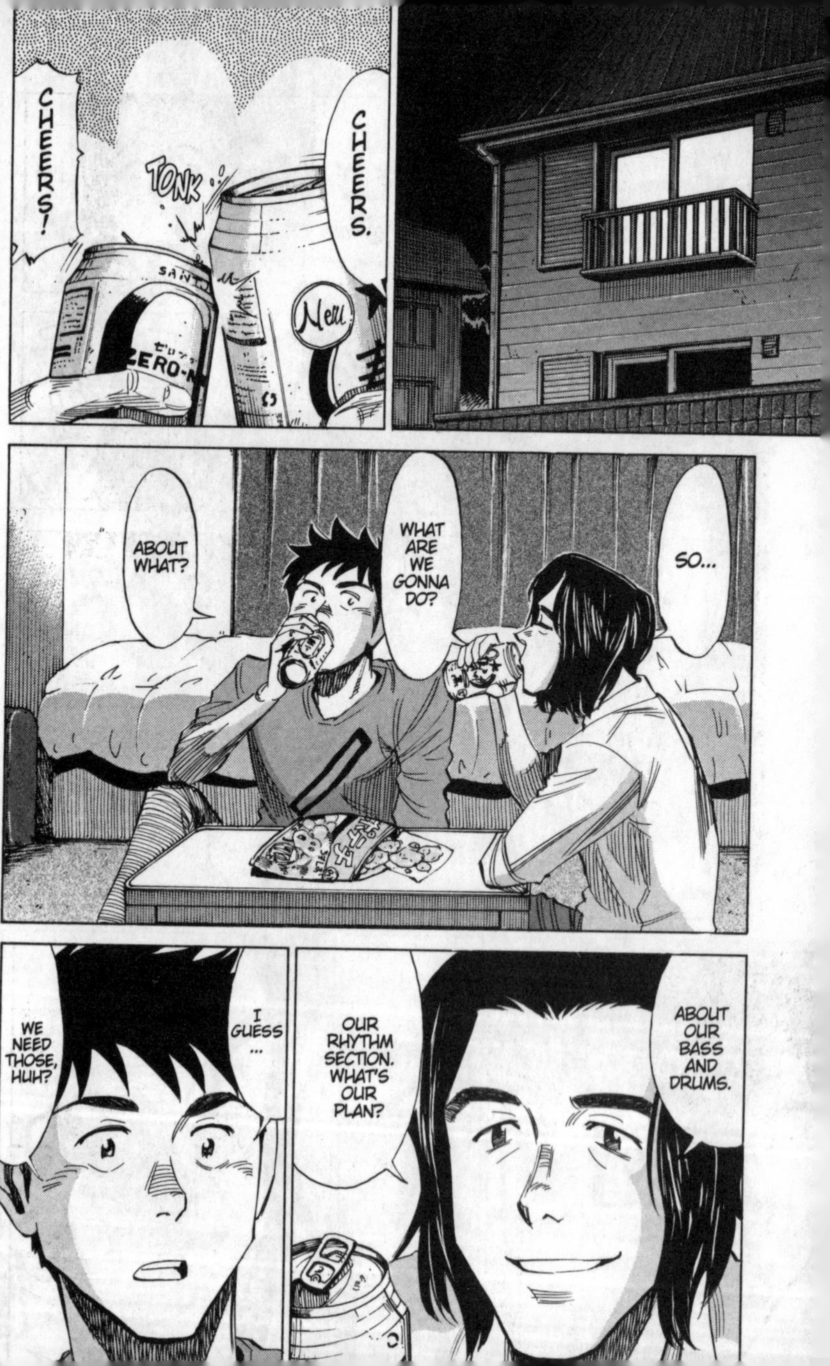
CHEERS.
TONK
CHEERS!
SO...
WHAT ARE WE GONNA DO?
ABOUT WHAT?
ABOUT OUR BASS AND DRUMS.
OUR RHYTHM SECTION. WHAT'S OUR PLAN?
I GUESS ...
WE NEED THOSE, HUH?

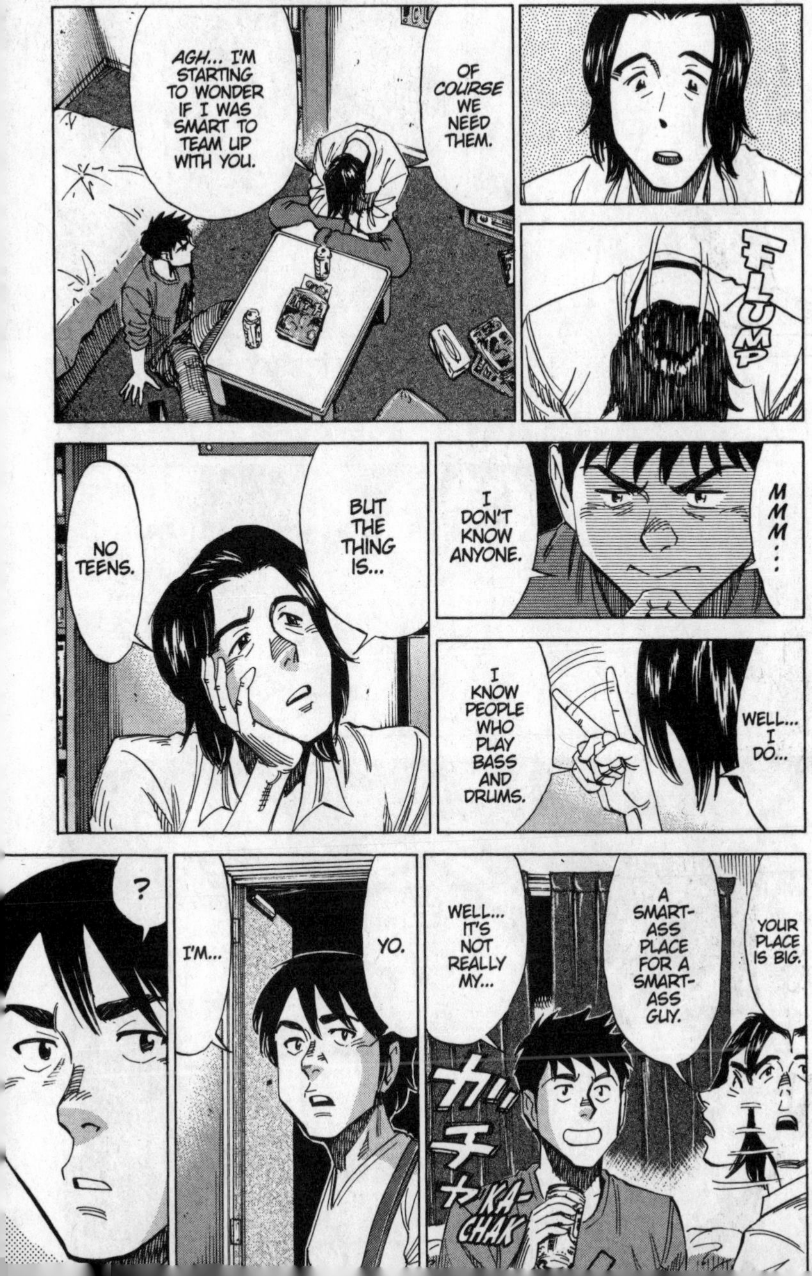
FLUMP
OF COURSE WE NEED THEM.
AGH... I'M STARTING TO WONDER IF I WAS SMART TO TEAM UP WITH YOU.
MMM...
I DON'T KNOW ANYONE.
WELL... I DO...
I KNOW PEOPLE WHO PLAY BASS AND DRUMS.
BUT THE THING IS...
NO TEENS.
YOUR PLACE IS BIG.
A SMART-ASS PLACE FOR A SMART-ASS GUY.
WELL... IT'S NOT REALLY MY...
カチャ
KA-CHAK
YO.
I'M...
?

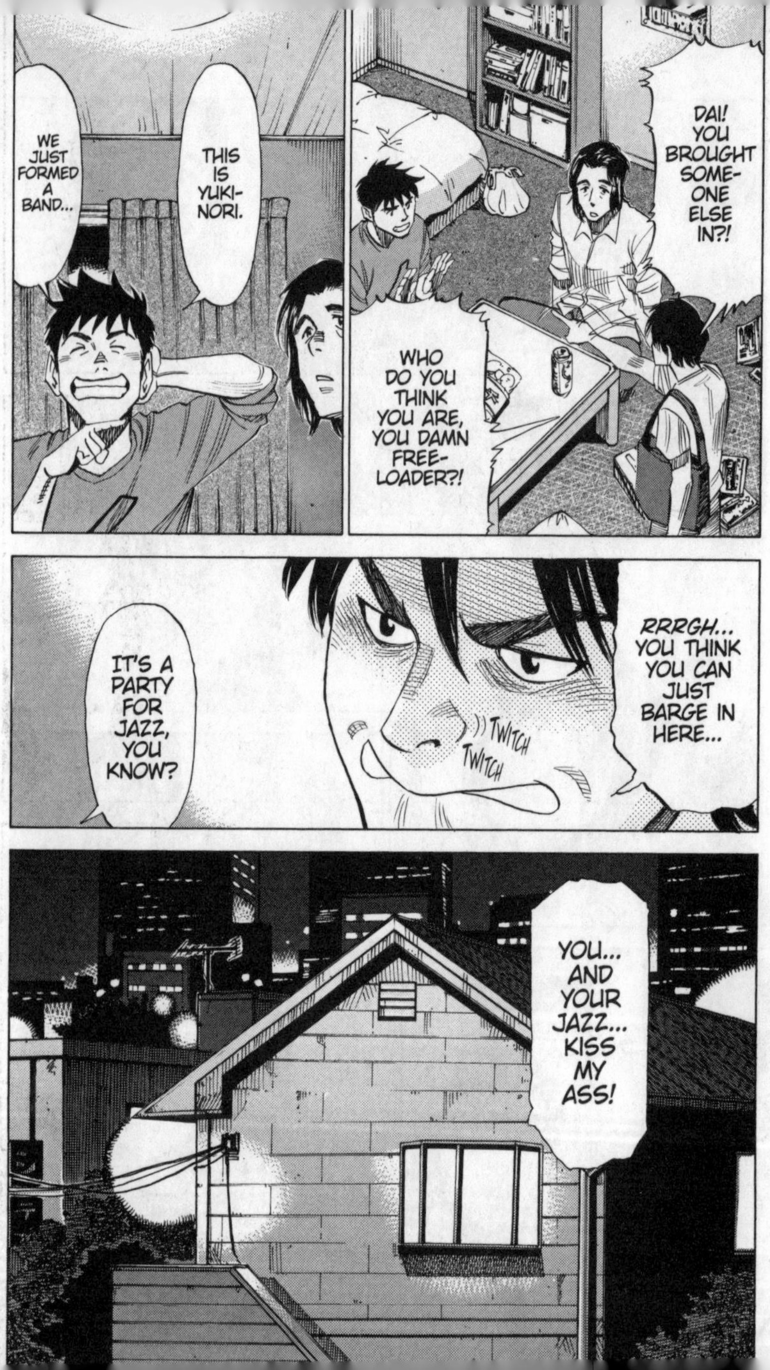
DAI! YOU BROUGHT SOME-ONE ELSE IN?!
WHO DO YOU THINK YOU ARE, YOU DAMN FREE-LOADER?!
THIS IS YUKI-NORI.
WE JUST FORMED A BAND...
RRRGH... YOU THINK YOU CAN JUST BARGE IN HERE...
TWITCH
TWITCH
IT'S A PARTY FOR JAZZ, YOU KNOW?
YOU... AND YOUR JAZZ... KISS MY ASS!

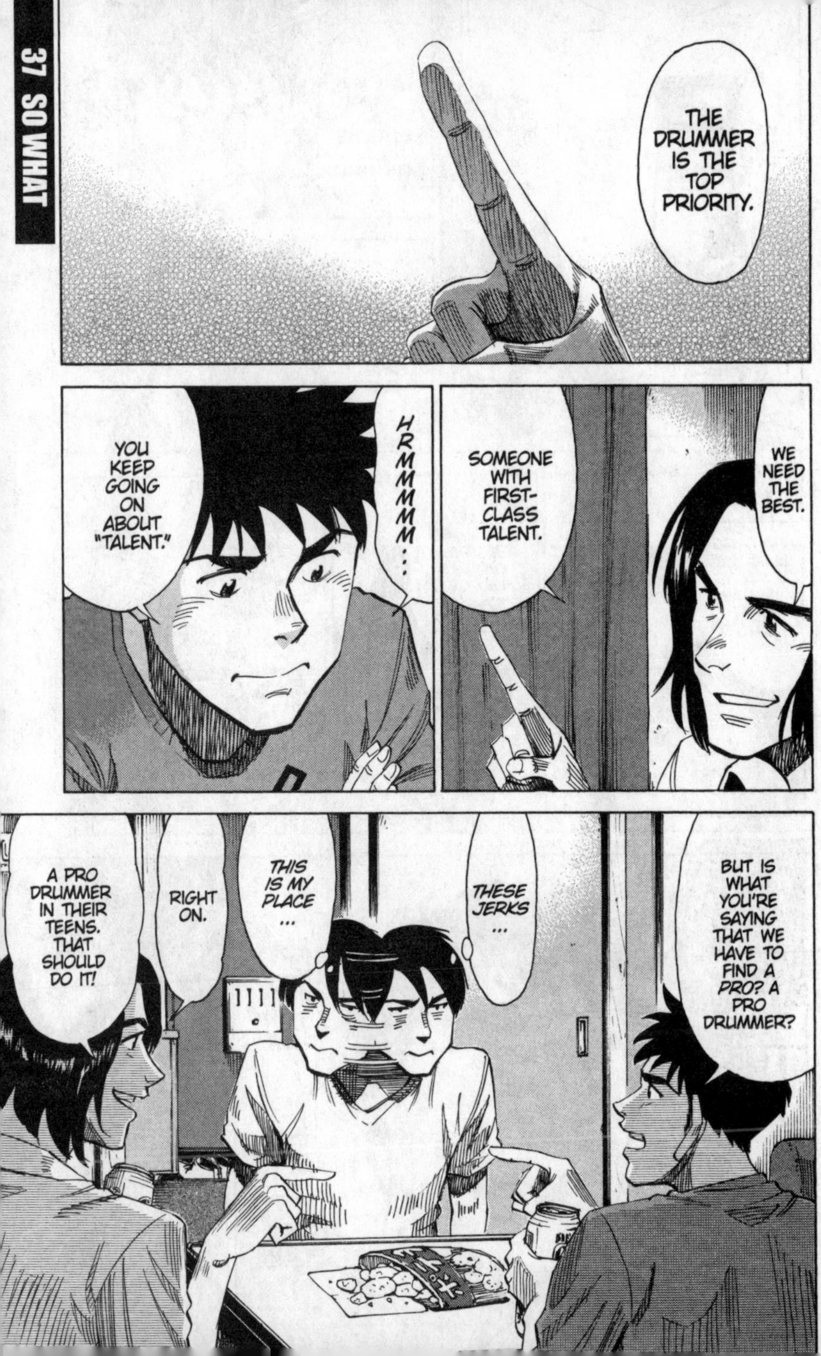
THE DRUMMER IS THE TOP PRIORITY.
WE NEED THE BEST.
SOMEONE WITH FIRST-CLASS TALENT.
HRMMMMM...
YOU KEEP GOING ON ABOUT "TALENT."
BUT IS WHAT YOU'RE SAYING THAT WE HAVE TO FIND A *PRO*? A PRO DRUMMER?
THESE JERKS ...
THIS IS MY PLACE ...
RIGHT ON.
A PRO DRUMMER IN THEIR TEENS. THAT SHOULD DO IT!

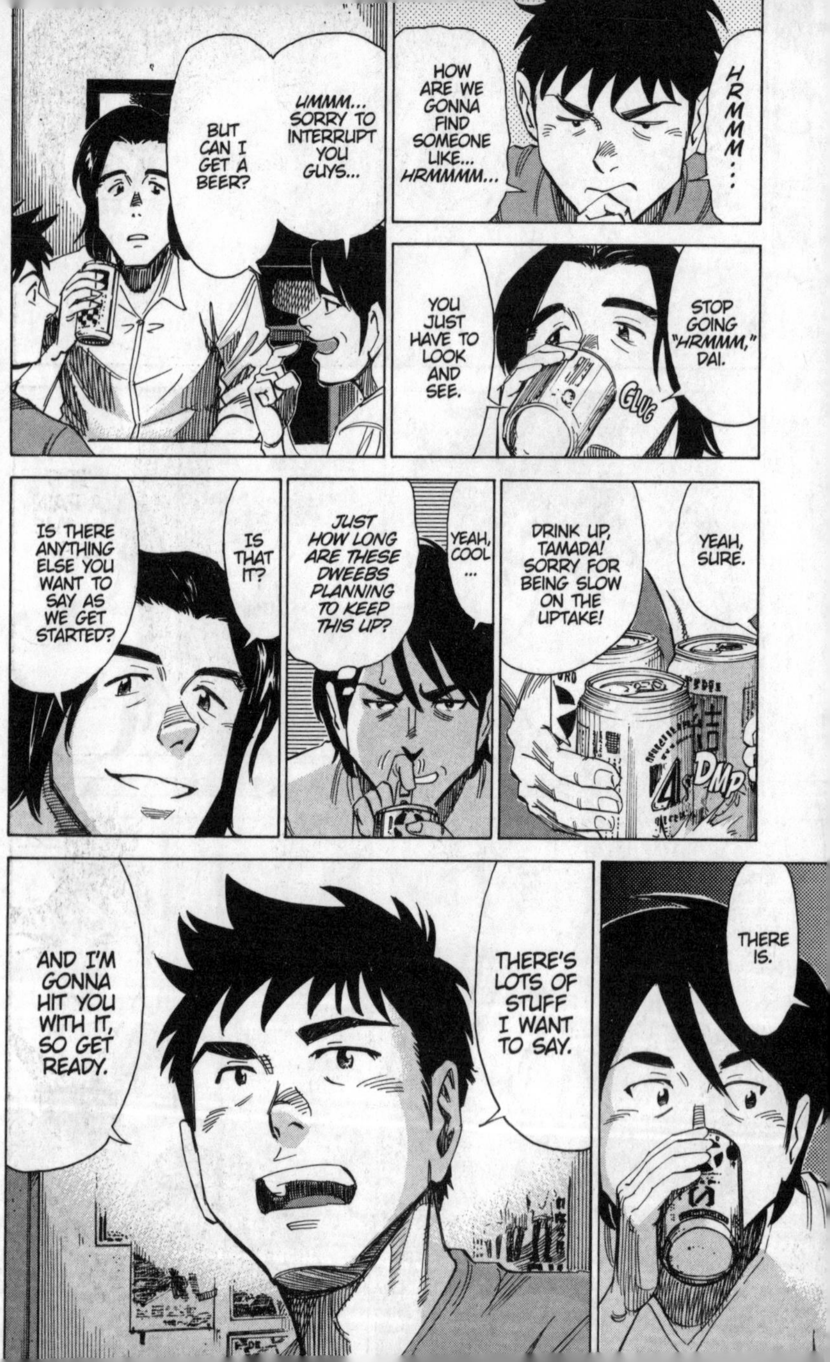
HRMMM...
HOW ARE WE GONNA FIND SOMEONE LIKE... HRMMMM...
STOP GOING "HRMMM," DAI.
YOU JUST HAVE TO LOOK AND SEE.
GLUG
UMMM... SORRY TO INTERRUPT YOU GUYS...
BUT CAN I GET A BEER?
YEAH, SURE.
DRINK UP, TAMADA! SORRY FOR BEING SLOW ON THE UPTAKE!
DMP
YEAH, COOL ...
JUST HOW LONG ARE THESE DWEEBS PLANNING TO KEEP THIS UP?
IS THAT IT?
IS THERE ANYTHING ELSE YOU WANT TO SAY AS WE GET STARTED?
THERE IS.
THERE'S LOTS OF STUFF I WANT TO SAY.
AND I'M GONNA HIT YOU WITH IT, SO GET READY.

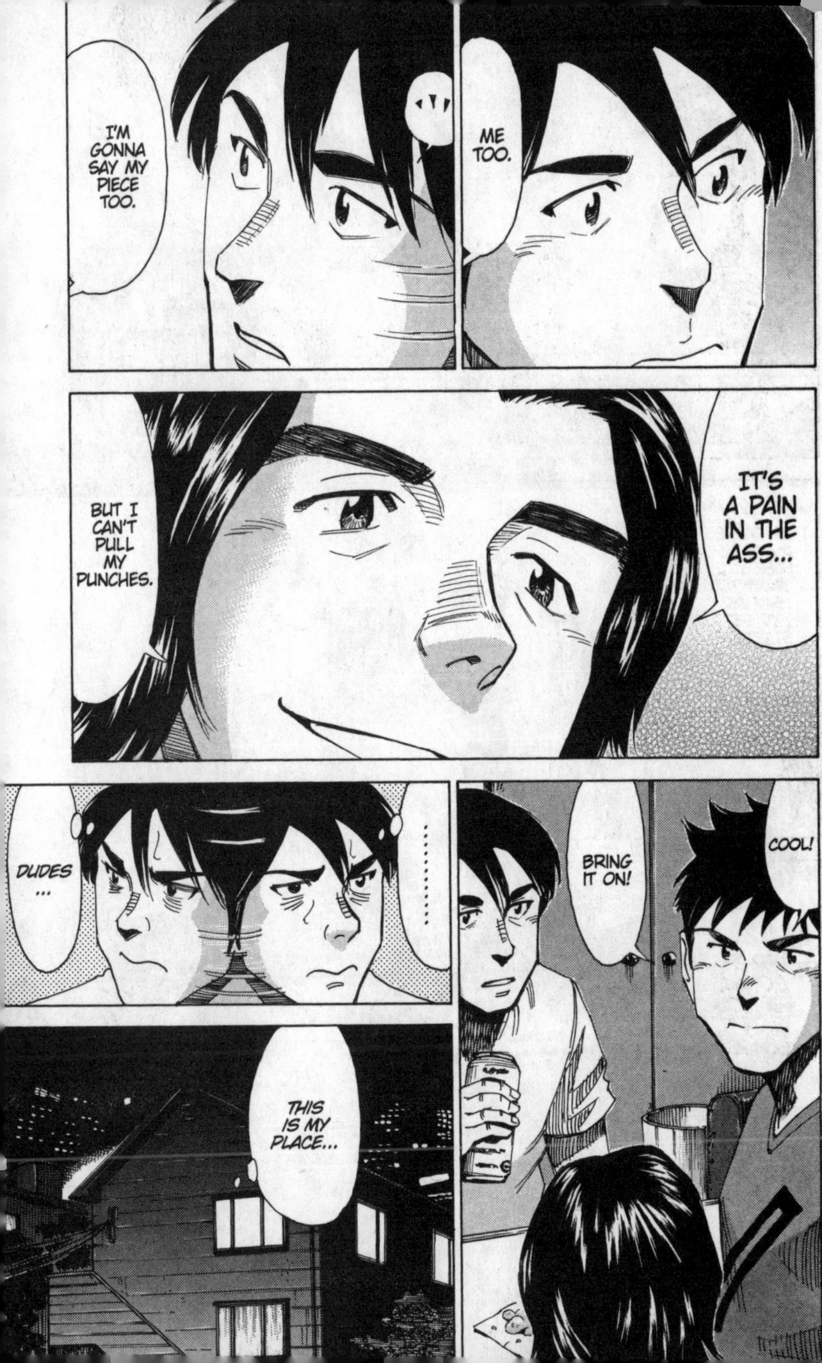
ME TOO.
I'M GONNA SAY MY PIECE TOO.
IT'S A PAIN IN THE ASS...
BUT I CAN'T PULL MY PUNCHES.
COOL!
BRING IT ON!
......
DUDES ...
THIS IS MY PLACE...

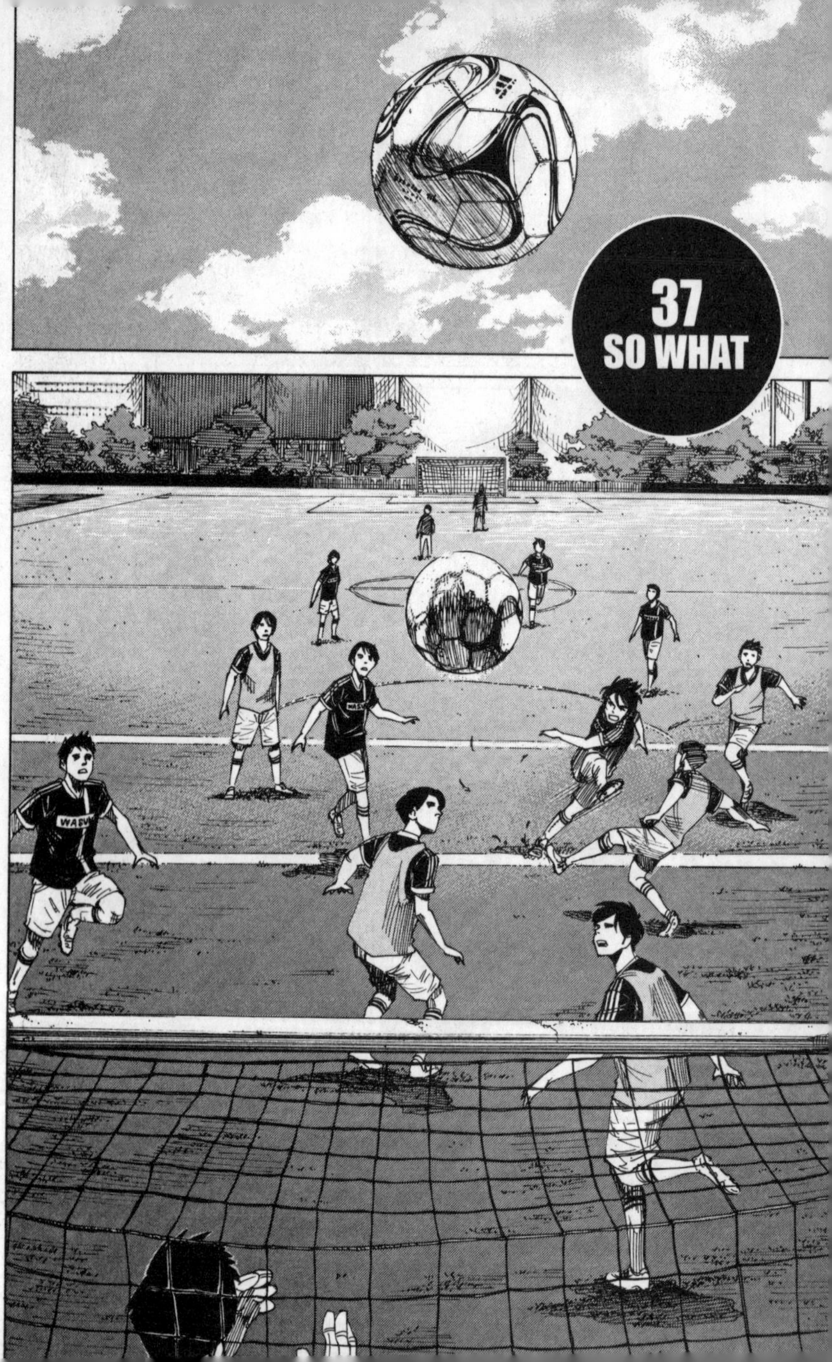
37
SO WHAT

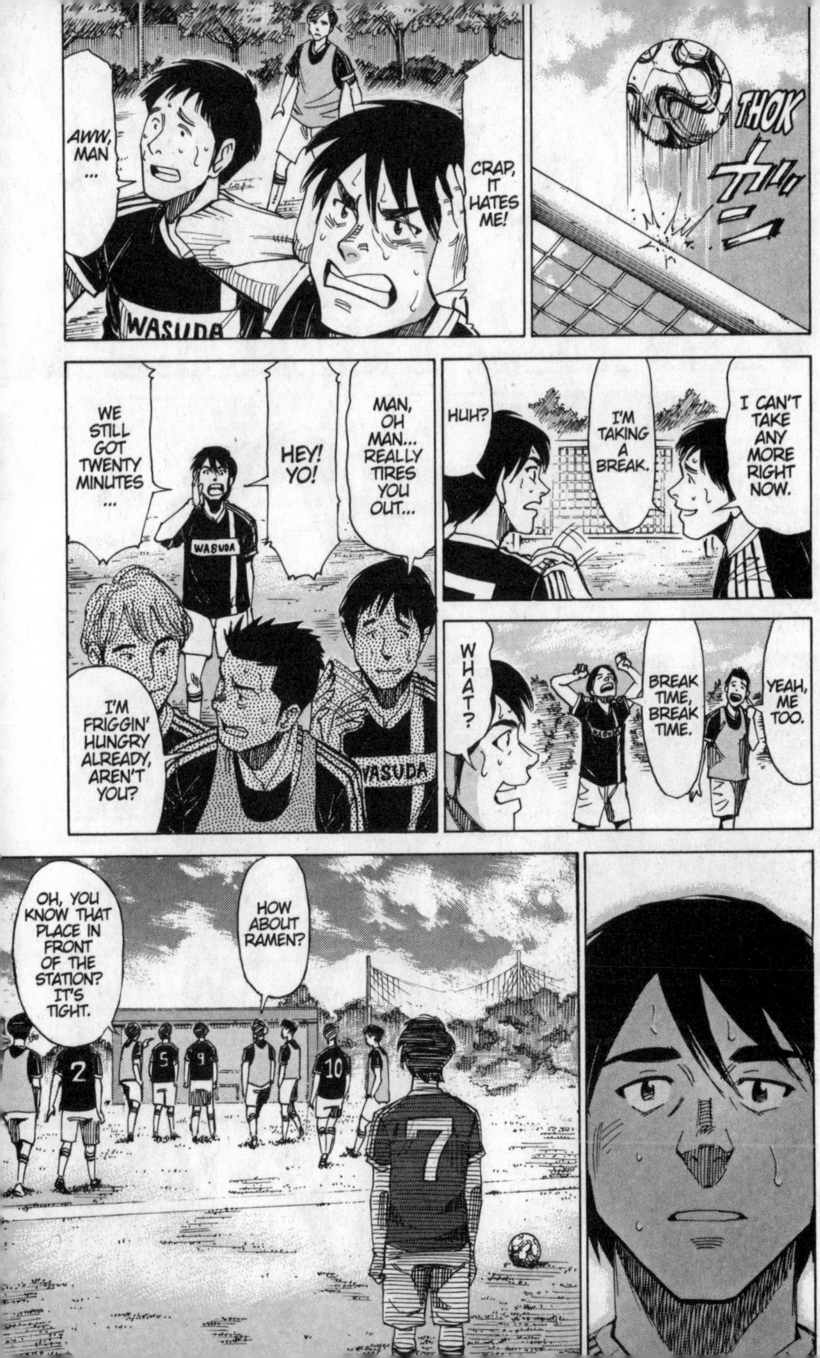
THOK
CRAP, IT HATES ME!
AWW, MAN ...
I CAN'T TAKE ANY MORE RIGHT NOW.
I'M TAKING A BREAK.
HUH?
YEAH, ME TOO.
BREAK TIME, BREAK TIME.
WHAT?
MAN, OH MAN... REALLY TIRES YOU OUT...
HEY! YO!
WE STILL GOT TWENTY MINUTES ...
I'M FRIGGIN' HUNGRY ALREADY, AREN'T YOU?
HOW ABOUT RAMEN?
OH, YOU KNOW THAT PLACE IN FRONT OF THE STATION? IT'S TIGHT.

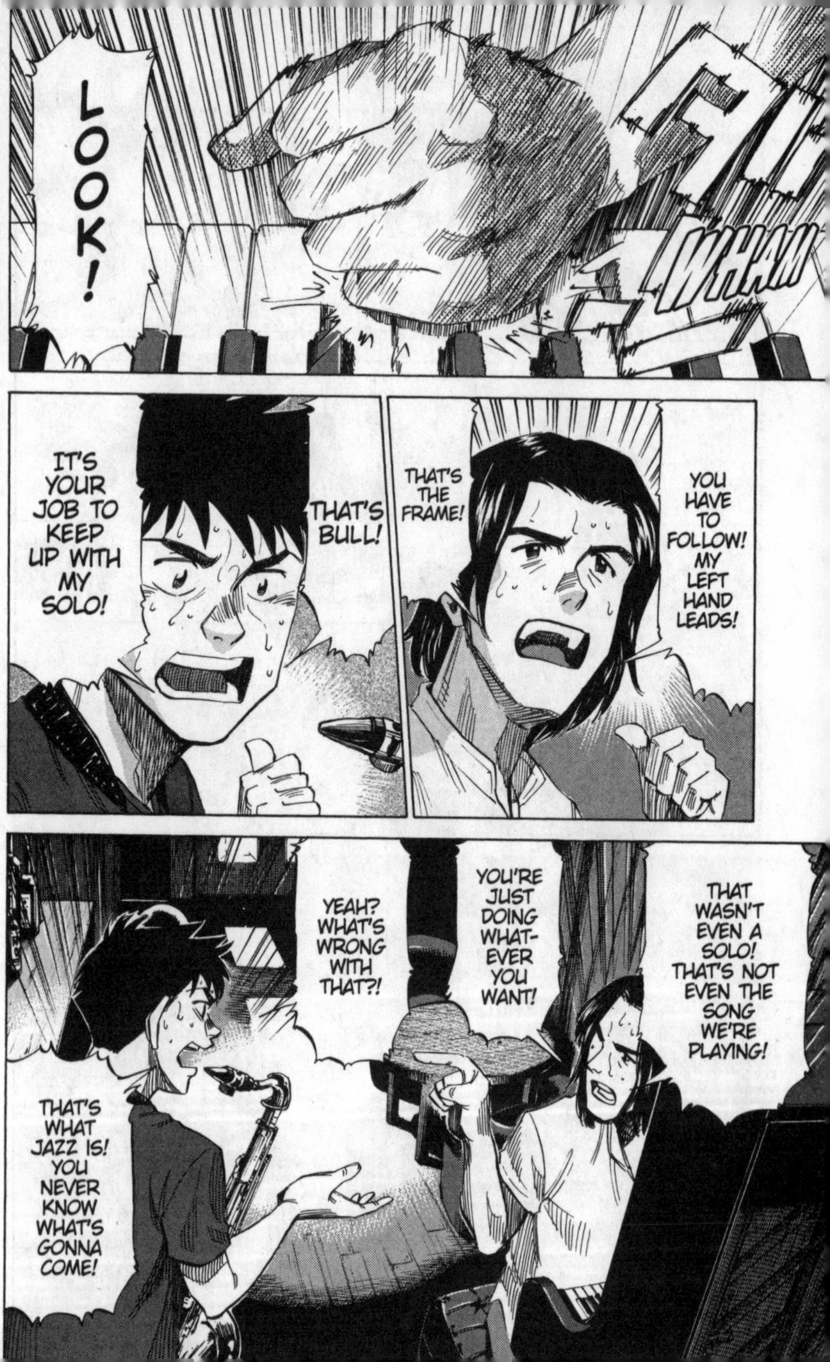
WHAM
LOOK!
YOU HAVE TO FOLLOW! MY LEFT HAND LEADS!
THAT'S THE FRAME!
THAT'S BULL!
IT'S YOUR JOB TO KEEP UP WITH MY SOLO!
THAT WASN'T EVEN A SOLO! THAT'S NOT EVEN THE SONG WE'RE PLAYING!
YOU'RE JUST DOING WHAT-EVER YOU WANT!
YEAH? WHAT'S WRONG WITH THAT?!
THAT'S WHAT JAZZ IS! YOU NEVER KNOW WHAT'S GONNA COME!

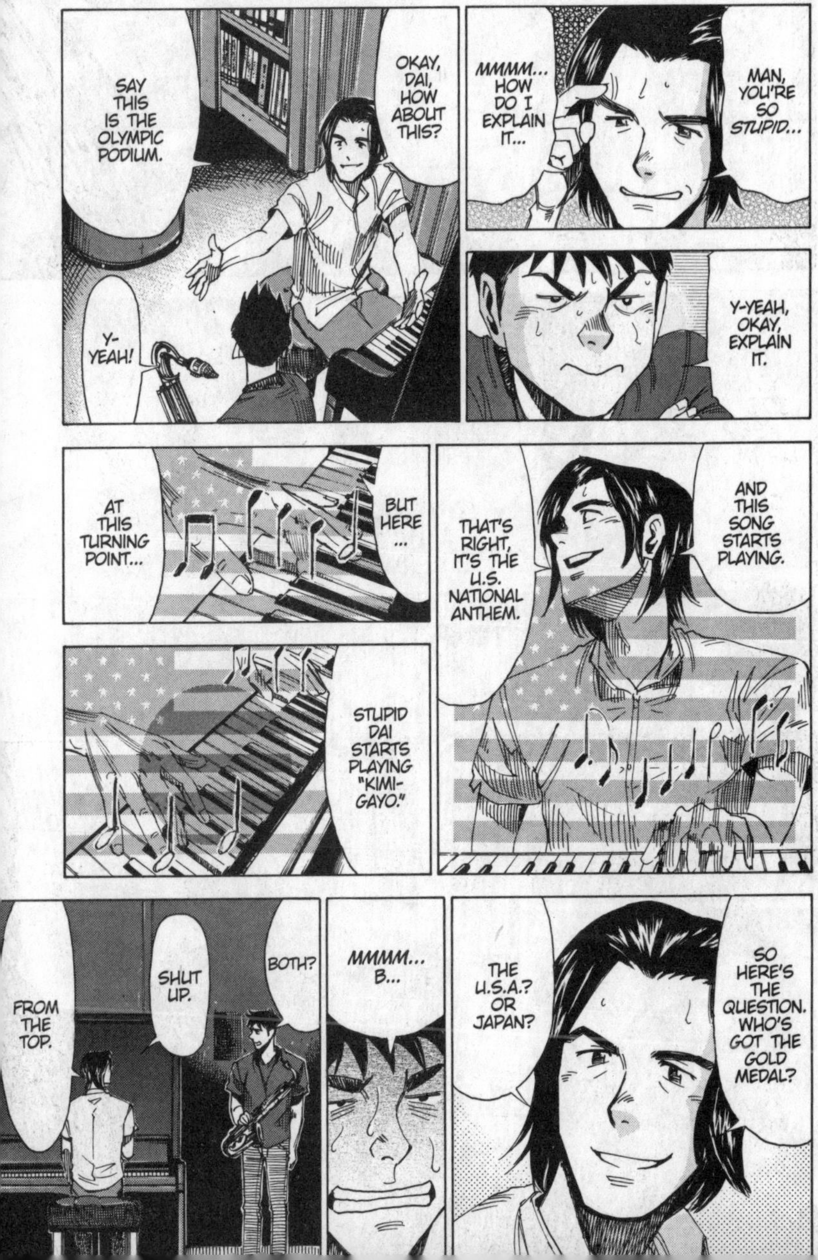
MAN, YOU'RE SO STUPID...
MMMM... HOW DO I EXPLAIN IT...
Y-YEAH, OKAY, EXPLAIN IT.
OKAY, DAI, HOW ABOUT THIS?
SAY THIS IS THE OLYMPIC PODIUM.
Y-YEAH!
AND THIS SONG STARTS PLAYING.
THAT'S RIGHT, IT'S THE U.S. NATIONAL ANTHEM.
BUT HERE...
AT THIS TURNING POINT...
STUPID DAI STARTS PLAYING "KIMI-GAYO."
SO HERE'S THE QUESTION. WHO'S GOT THE GOLD MEDAL?
THE U.S.A.? OR JAPAN?
MMMM... B...
BOTH?
SHUT UP.
FROM THE TOP.

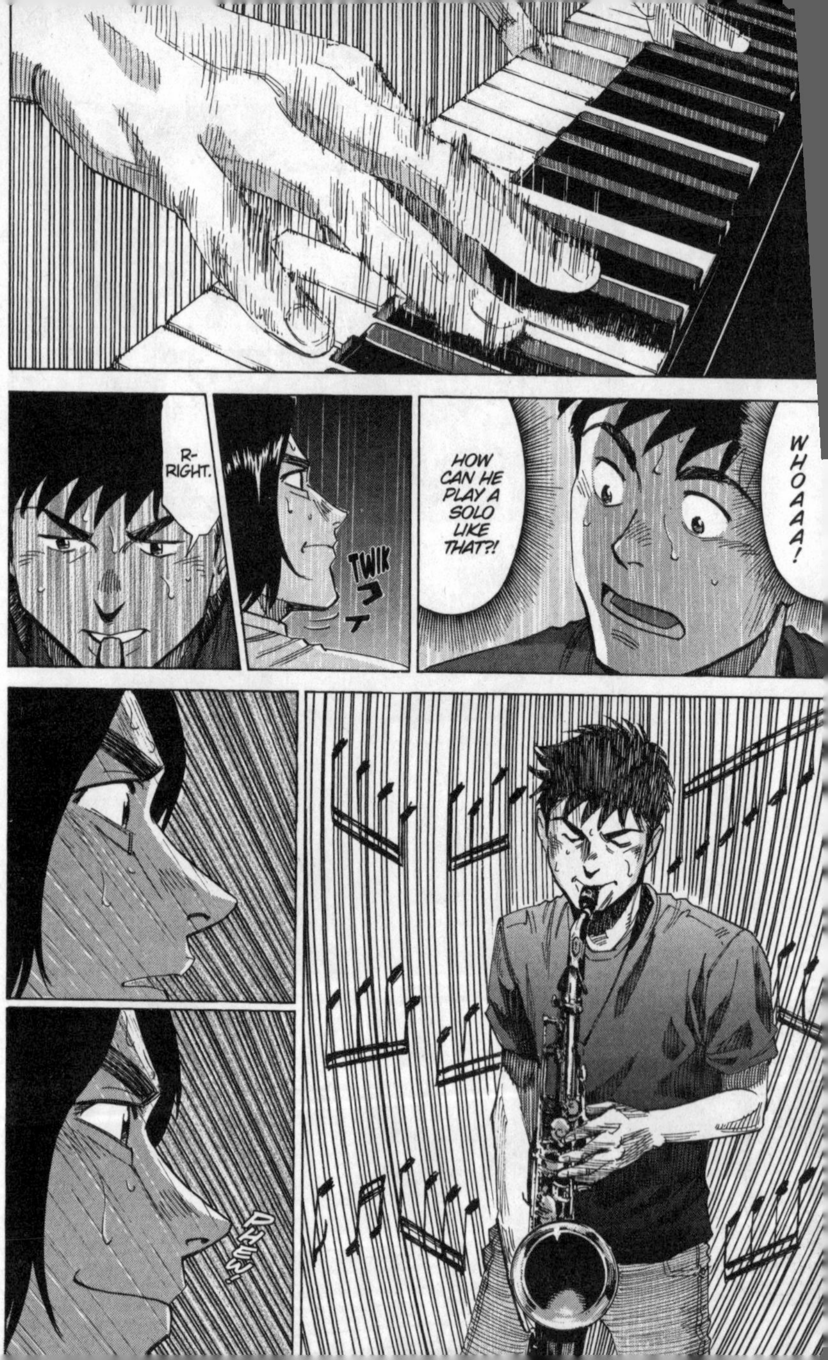
WHOAAA!
HOW CAN HE PLAY A SOLO LIKE THAT?!
TWIK
R-RIGHT.
PHEW!

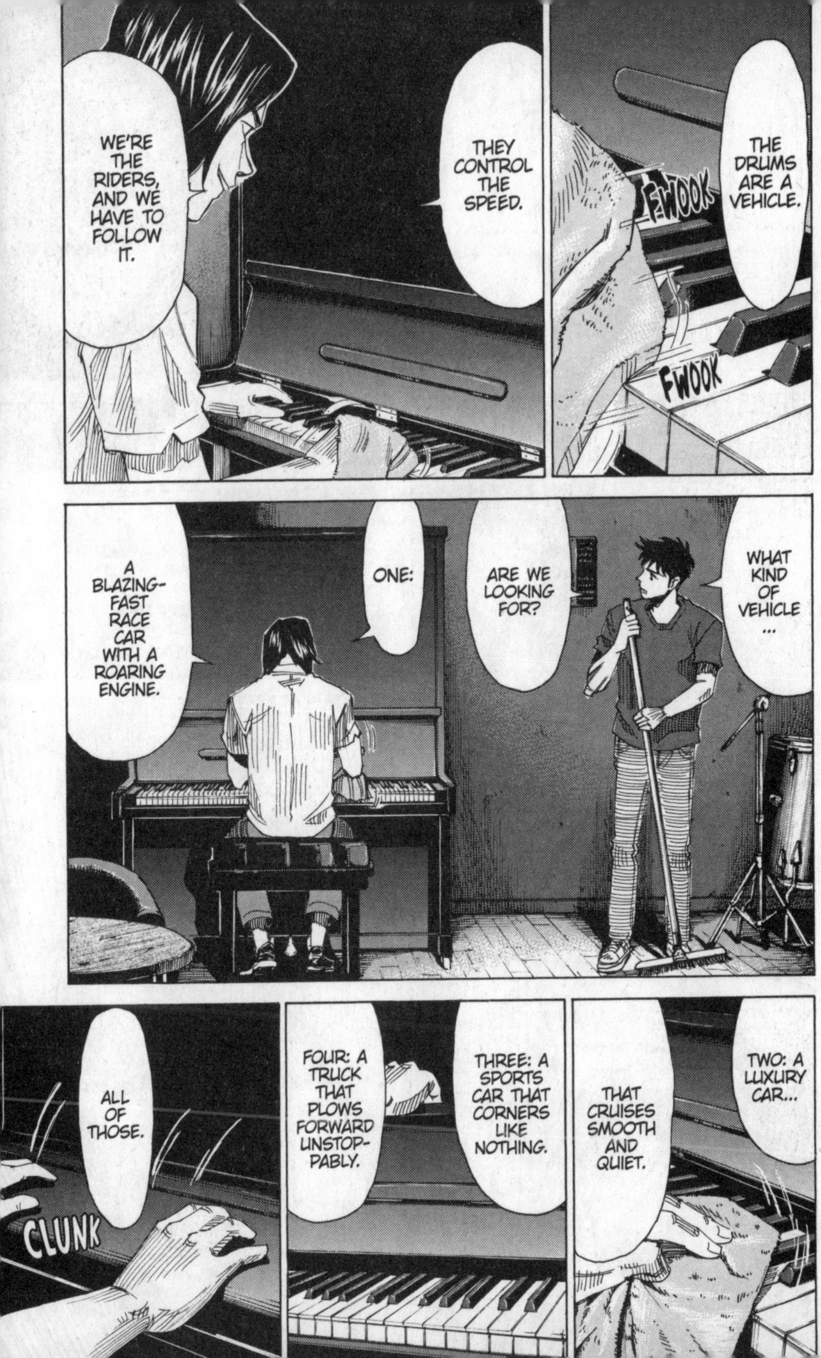
THE DRUMS ARE A VEHICLE.
FWOOK
FWOOK
THEY CONTROL THE SPEED.
WE'RE THE RIDERS, AND WE HAVE TO FOLLOW IT.
WHAT KIND OF VEHICLE ...
ARE WE LOOKING FOR?
ONE:
A BLAZING-FAST RACE CAR WITH A ROARING ENGINE.
TWO: A LUXURY CAR...
THAT CRUISES SMOOTH AND QUIET.
THREE: A SPORTS CAR THAT CORNERS LIKE NOTHING.
FOUR: A TRUCK THAT PLOWS FORWARD UNSTOPPABLY.
ALL OF THOSE.
CLUNK

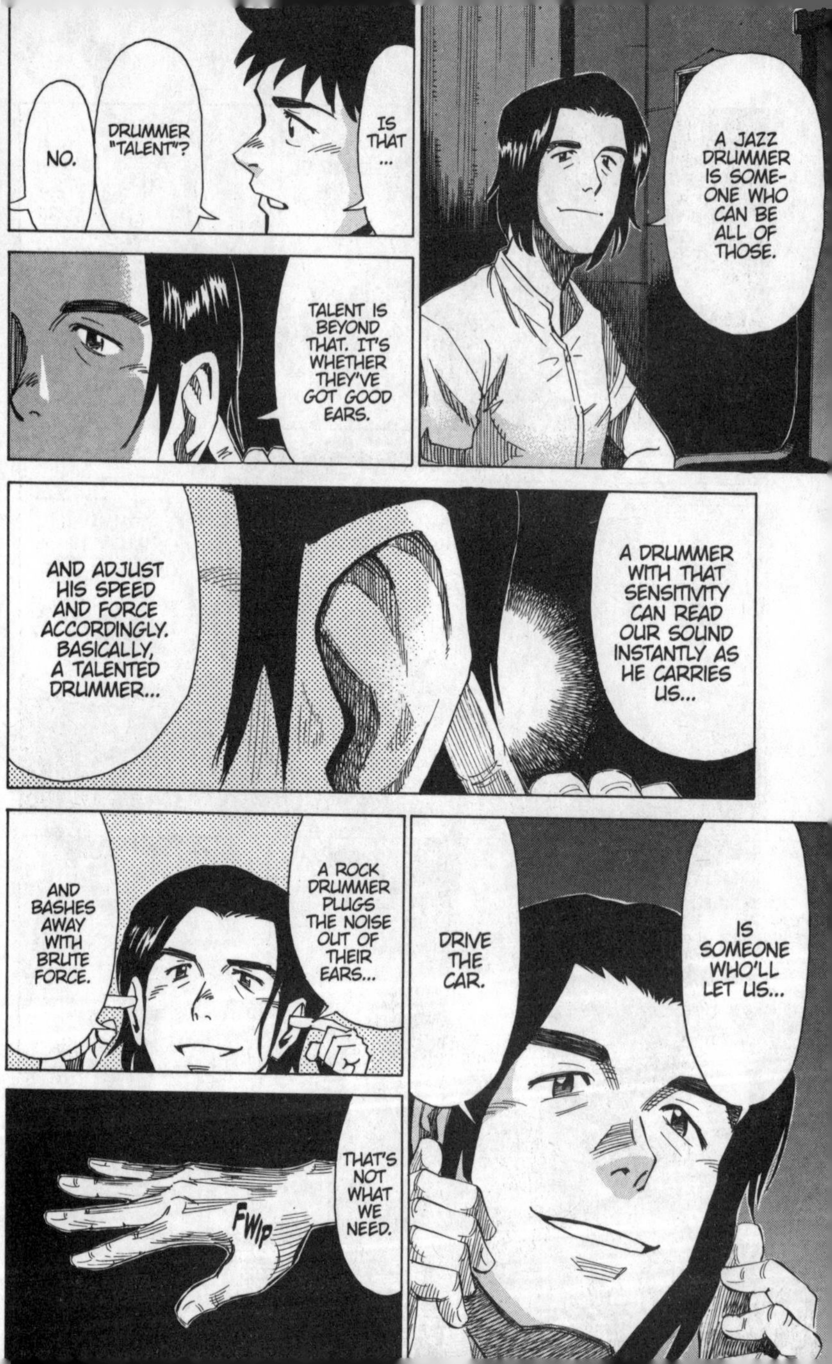
A JAZZ DRUMMER IS SOMEONE WHO CAN BE ALL OF THOSE.
IS THAT ...
DRUMMER "TALENT"?
NO.
TALENT IS BEYOND THAT. IT'S WHETHER THEY'VE GOT GOOD EARS.
A DRUMMER WITH THAT SENSITIVITY CAN READ OUR SOUND INSTANTLY AS HE CARRIES US...
AND ADJUST HIS SPEED AND FORCE ACCORDINGLY. BASICALLY, A TALENTED DRUMMER...
IS SOMEONE WHO'LL LET US...
DRIVE THE CAR.
A ROCK DRUMMER PLUGS THE NOISE OUT OF THEIR EARS...
AND BASHES AWAY WITH BRUTE FORCE.
THAT'S NOT WHAT WE NEED.
FWIP

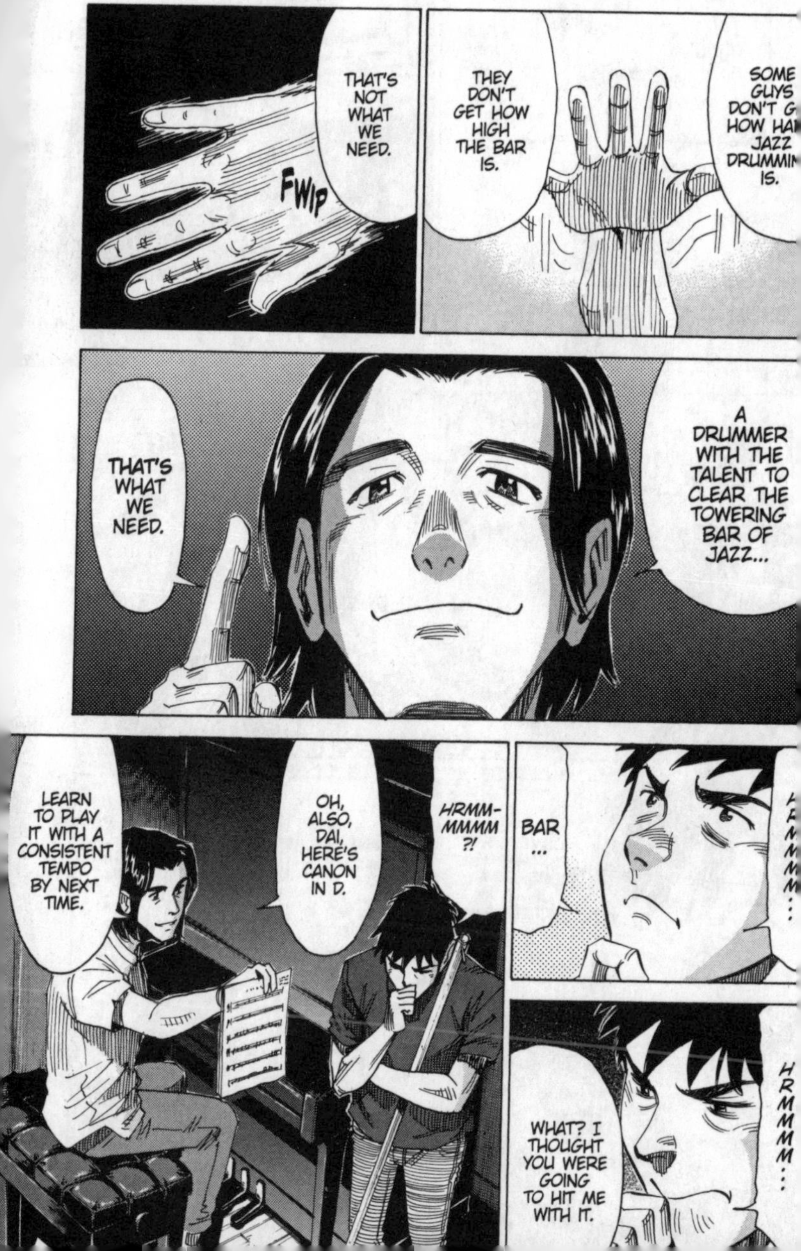
SOME GUYS DON'T G HOW HA JAZZ DRUMMIN IS.
THEY DON'T GET HOW HIGH THE BAR IS.
THAT'S NOT WHAT WE NEED.
FWIP
A DRUMMER WITH THE TALENT TO CLEAR THE TOWERING BAR OF JAZZ...
THAT'S WHAT WE NEED.
HRMMMMM...
BAR ...
HRMMMMM...
WHAT? I THOUGHT YOU WERE GOING TO HIT ME WITH IT.
HRMM-MMMM?!
OH, ALSO, DAI, HERE'S CANON IN D.
LEARN TO PLAY IT WITH A CONSISTENT TEMPO BY NEXT TIME.

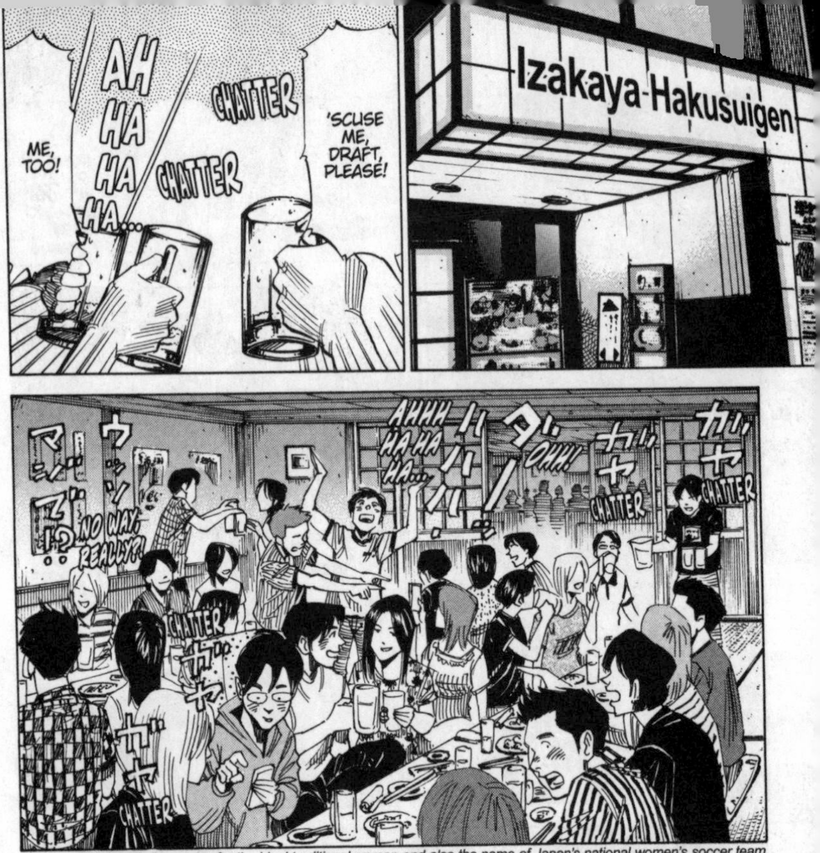
Izakaya Hakusuigen
'SCUSE ME, DRAFT, PLEASE!
CHATTER
CHATTER
AH HA HA HA HA...
ME, TOO!
CHATTER
CHATTER
OHH!
AHHH HA HA HA HA...
NO WAY, REALLY?!
CHATTER
CHATTER

*"Nadeshiko" is a term for the ideal traditional woman and also the name of Japan's national women's soccer team.

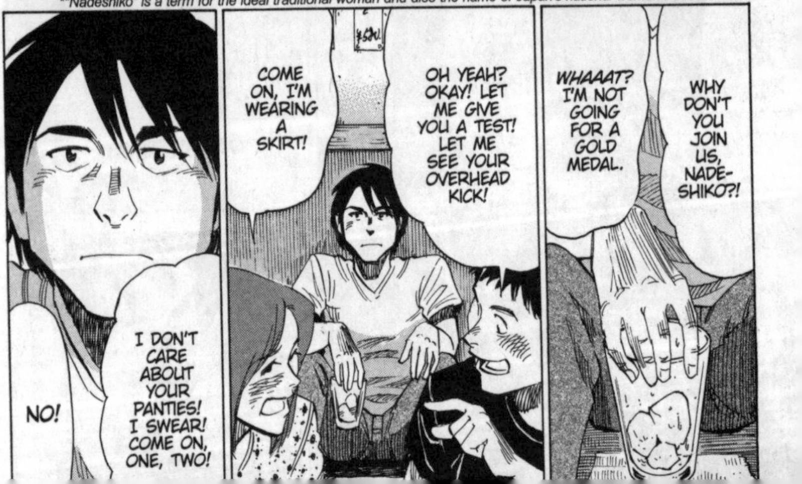
WHY DON'T YOU JOIN US, NADESHIKO?!
WHAAAT? I'M NOT GOING FOR A GOLD MEDAL.
OH YEAH? OKAY! LET ME GIVE YOU A TEST! LET ME SEE YOUR OVERHEAD KICK!
COME ON, I'M WEARING A SKIRT!
I DON'T CARE ABOUT YOUR PANTIES! I SWEAR! COME ON, ONE, TWO!
NO!

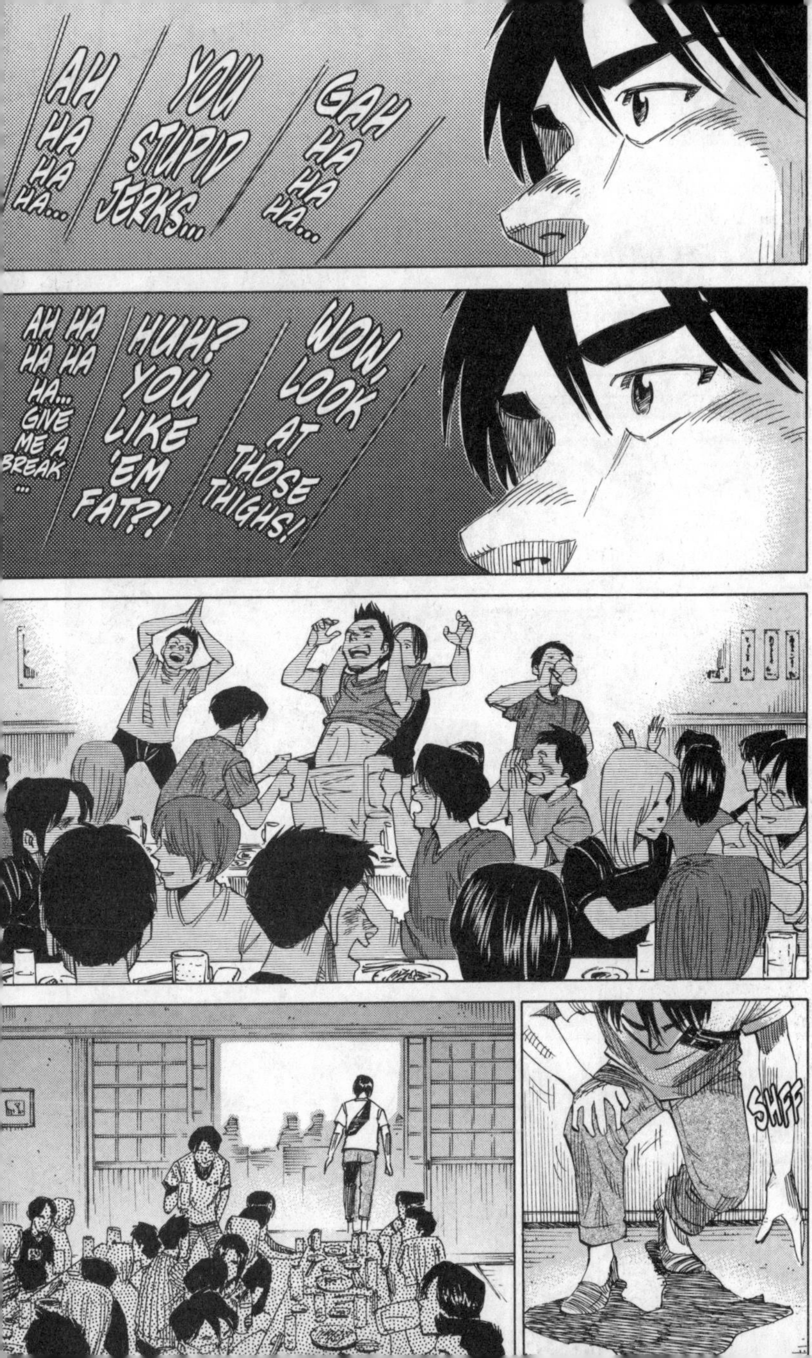
GAH HA HA HA...
YOU STUPID JERKS...
AH HA HA HA...
WOW, LOOK AT THOSE THIGHS!
HUH? YOU LIKE 'EM FAT?!
AH HA HA HA HA... GIVE ME A BREAK...
SHFF

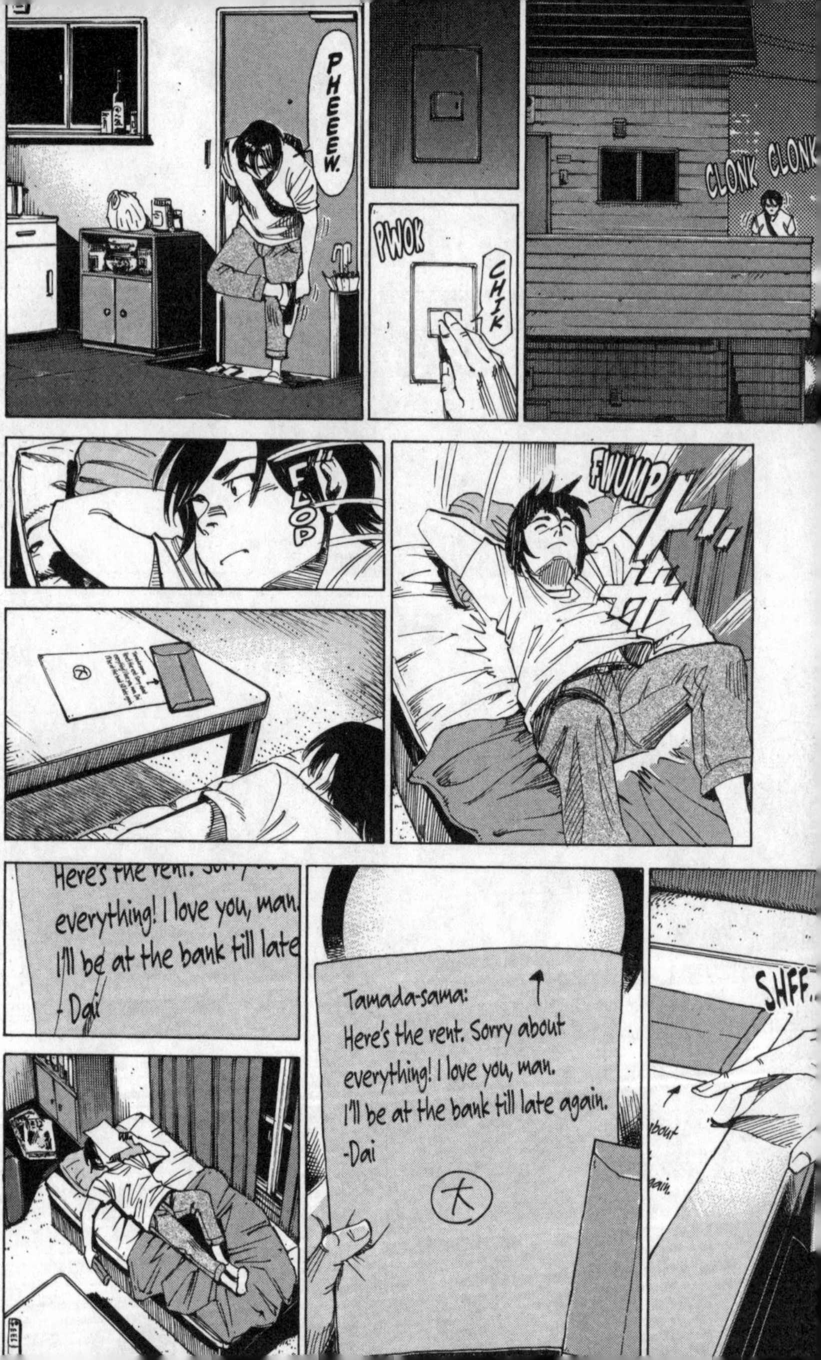
CLONK CLONK
PWOK
CHIK
PHEEEEW.
FWUMP
FLOP
SHFF...
Tamada-sama:
Here's the rent. Sorry about
everything! I love you, man.
I'll be at the bank till late again.
-Dai
Here's the rent.
everything! I love you, man.
I'll be at the bank till late
-Dai

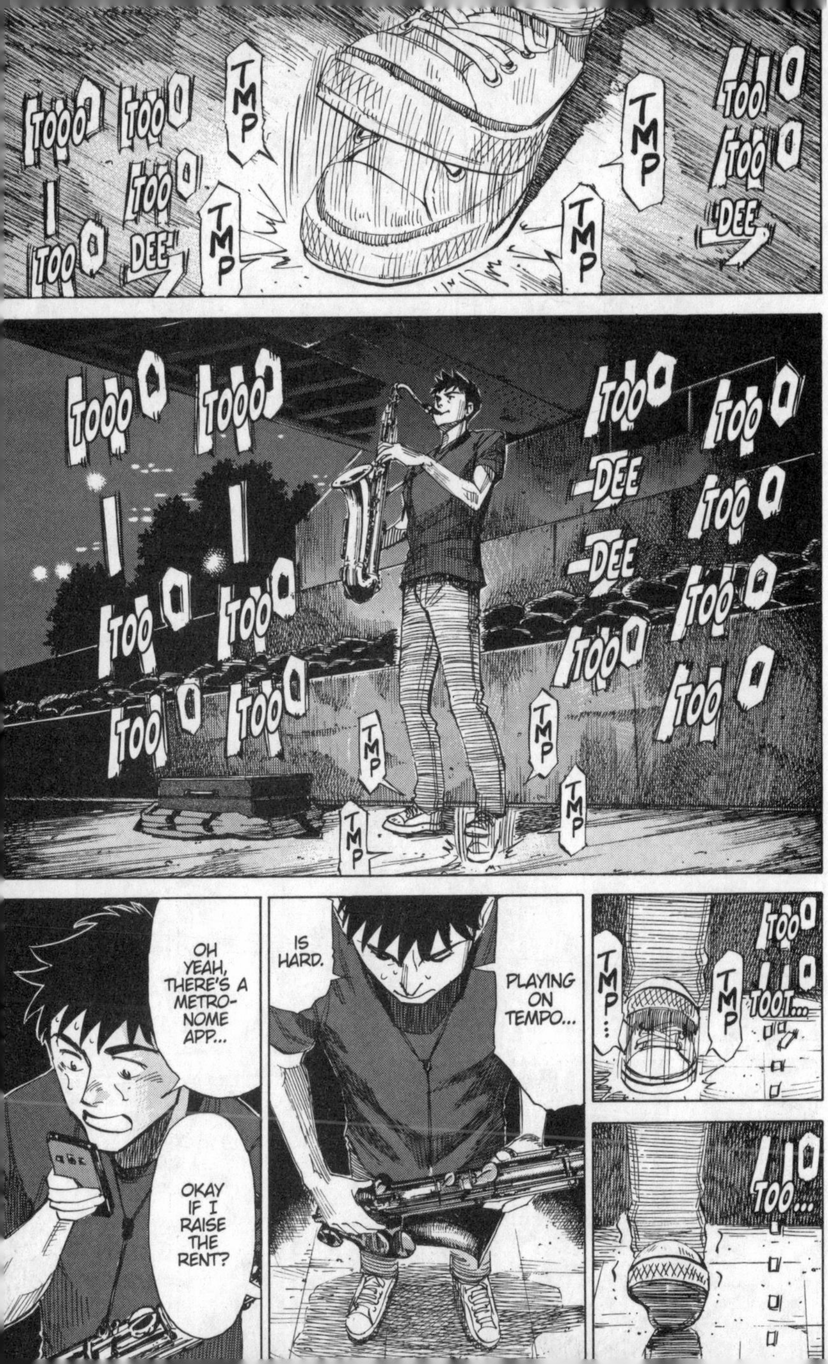
TOO
TOO
DEE
TMP
TMP
TMP
TMP
TOOO
TOO
TOO
DEE
TOO
TOO
TOO
TOO
TOO
TOO
DEE
DEE
TOO
TMP
TMP
TMP
TMP
TOOO
TOOO
TOO
TOO
TOO
TOO
TOO
TOOT...
TMP
TMP...
TOO...
PLAYING ON TEMPO...
IS HARD.
OH YEAH, THERE'S A METRO-NOME APP...
OKAY IF I RAISE THE RENT?

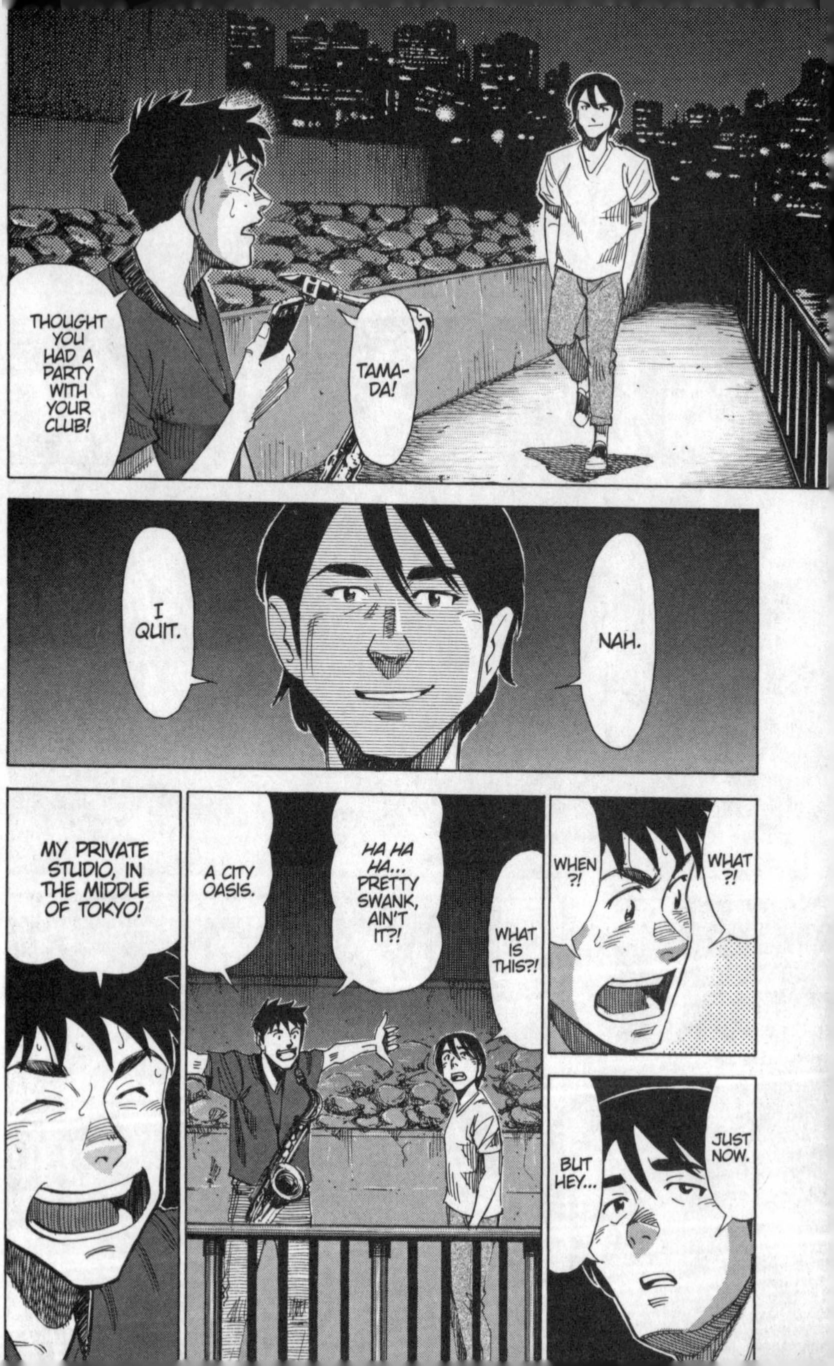
TAMA-DA!
THOUGHT YOU HAD A PARTY WITH YOUR CLUB!
NAH.
I QUIT.
WHAT?!
WHEN?!
JUST NOW.
BUT HEY...
WHAT IS THIS?!
HA HA HA... PRETTY SWANK, AIN'T IT?!
A CITY OASIS.
MY PRIVATE STUDIO, IN THE MIDDLE OF TOKYO!

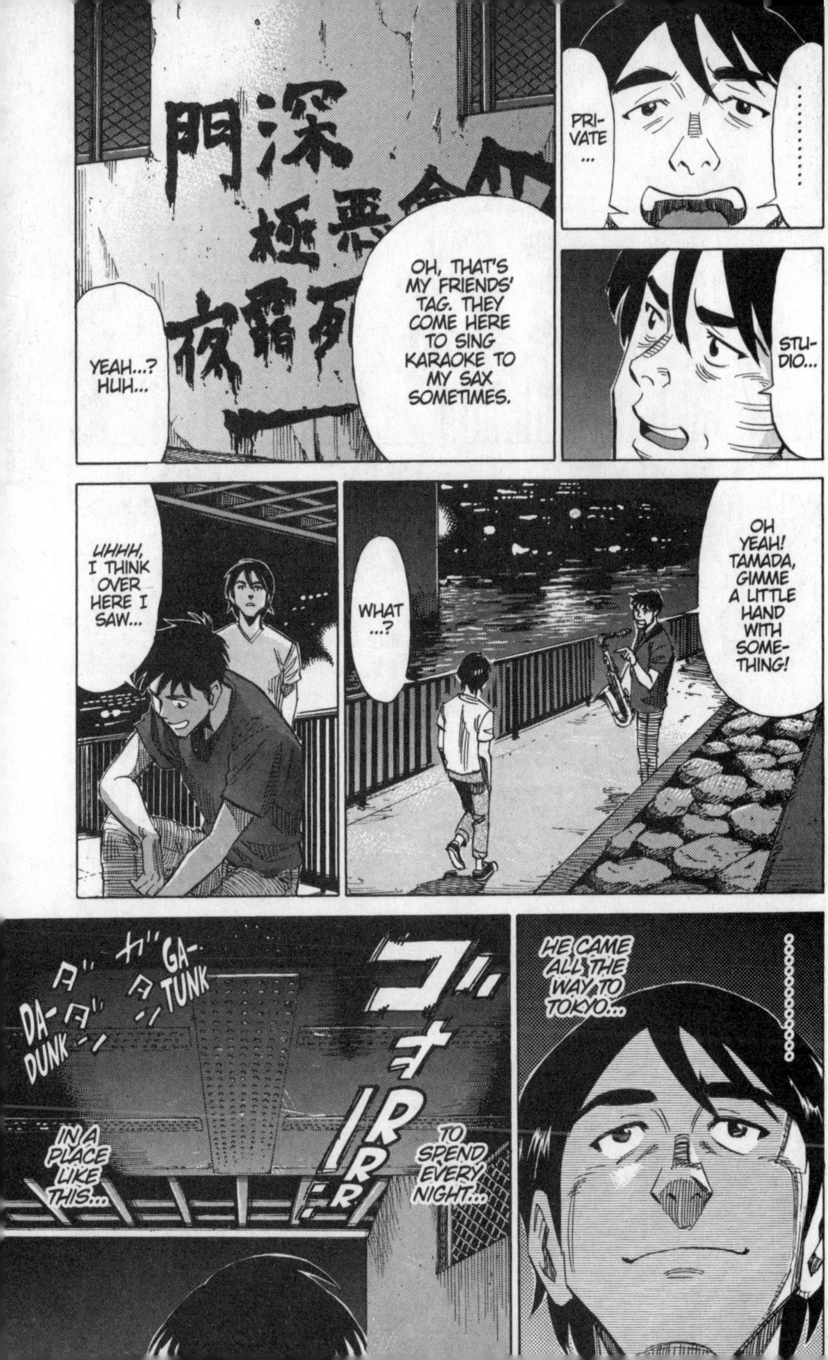
PRI-VATE ...
....
STU-DIO...
OH, THAT'S MY FRIENDS' TAG. THEY COME HERE TO SING KARAOKE TO MY SAX SOMETIMES.
YEAH...? HUH...
OH YEAH! TAMADA, GIMME A LITTLE HAND WITH SOME-THING!
WHAT ...?
UHHH, I THINK OVER HERE I SAW...
HE CAME ALL THE WAY TO TOKYO...
....
TO SPEND EVERY NIGHT...
RRR
GA-TUNK
DA-DUNK
IN A PLACE LIKE THIS...

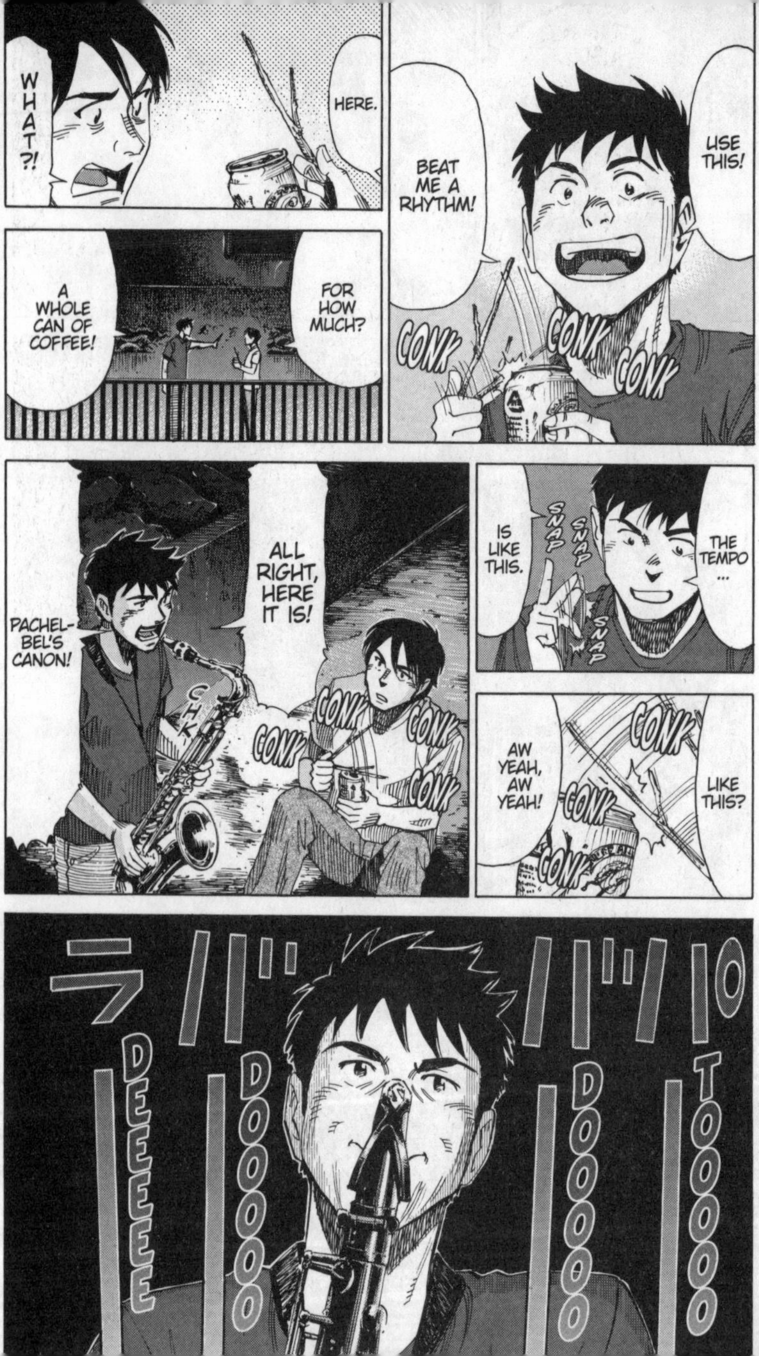
USE THIS!
BEAT ME A RHYTHM!
CONK
CONK
CONK
HERE.
WHAT?!
FOR HOW MUCH?
A WHOLE CAN OF COFFEE!
THE TEMPO ...
IS LIKE THIS.
SNAP
SNAP
SNAP
LIKE THIS?
CONK
CONK
CONK
AW YEAH, AW YEAH!
ALL RIGHT, HERE IT IS!
PACHELBEL'S CANON!
CHK
CONK
CONK
CONK
CONK
TOOOOOO
DOOOOOO
DOOOOOO
DEEEEEE

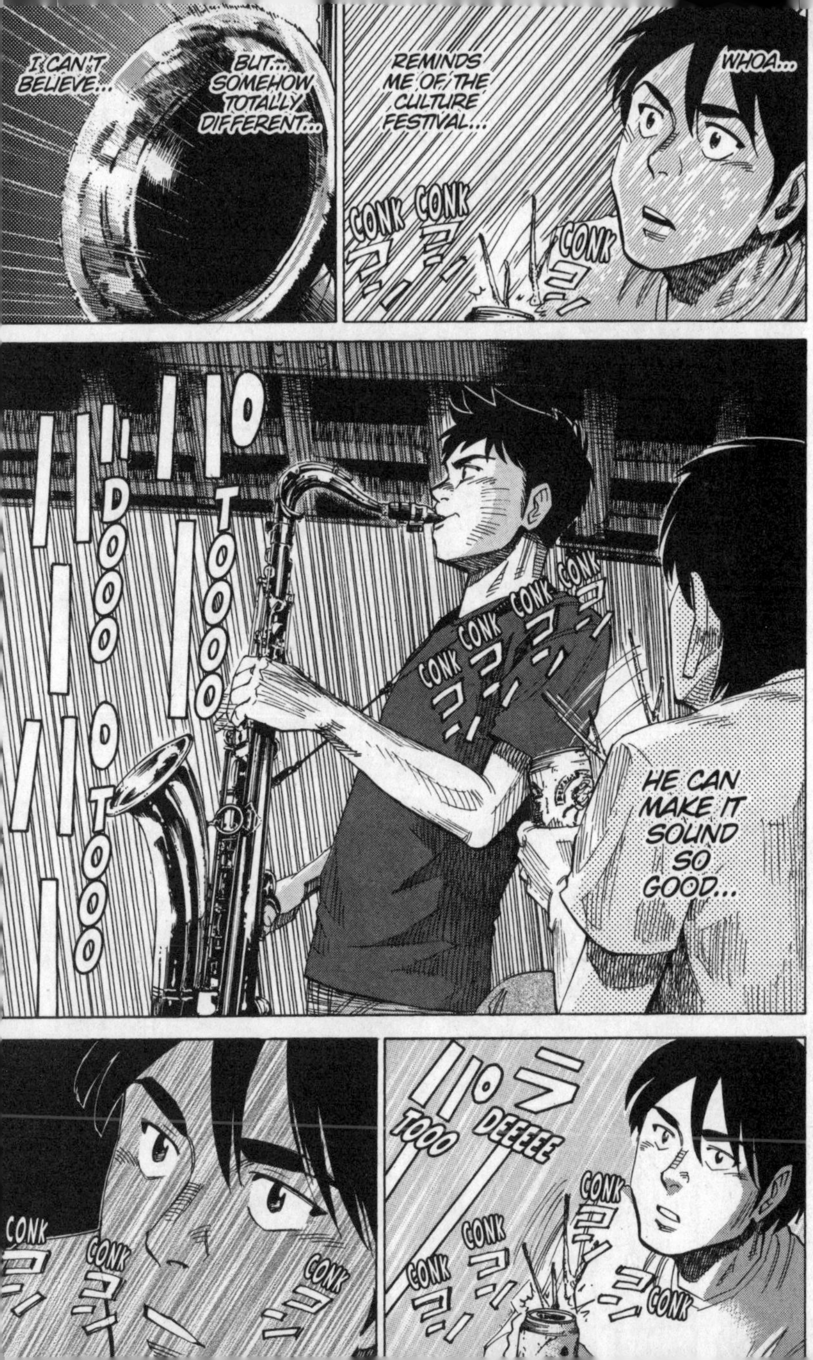
WHOA...
REMINDS ME OF THE CULTURE FESTIVAL...
CONK CONK
CONK
BUT... SOMEHOW TOTALLY DIFFERENT...
I CAN'T BELIEVE...
TOOOOO
DOOOOO
TOOOO
CONK
CONK
CONK
CONK
HE CAN MAKE IT SOUND SO GOOD...
DEEEEEE
TOOO
CONK
CONK
CONK
CONK
CONK
CONK
CONK

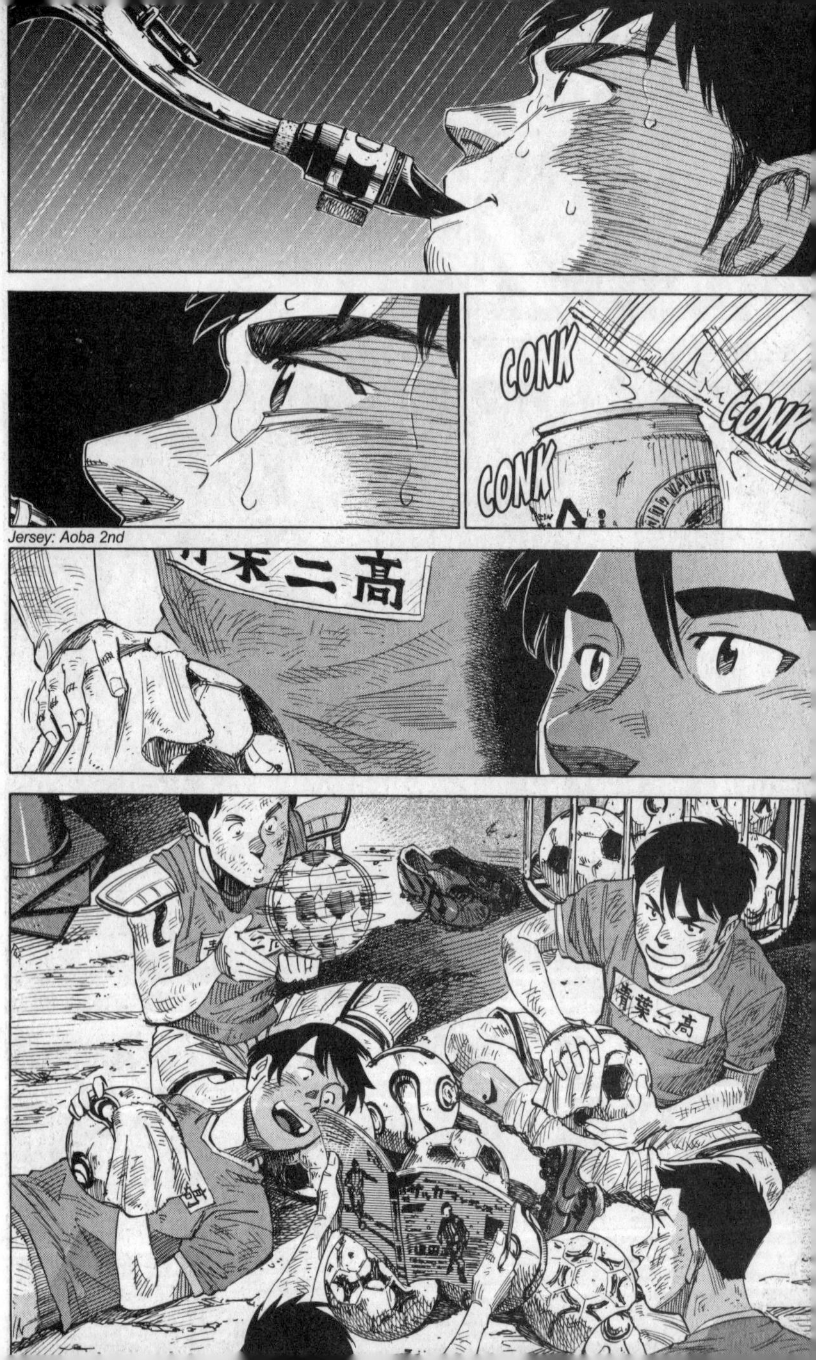
CONK
CONK
CONK
Jersey: Aoba 2nd
青葉二高

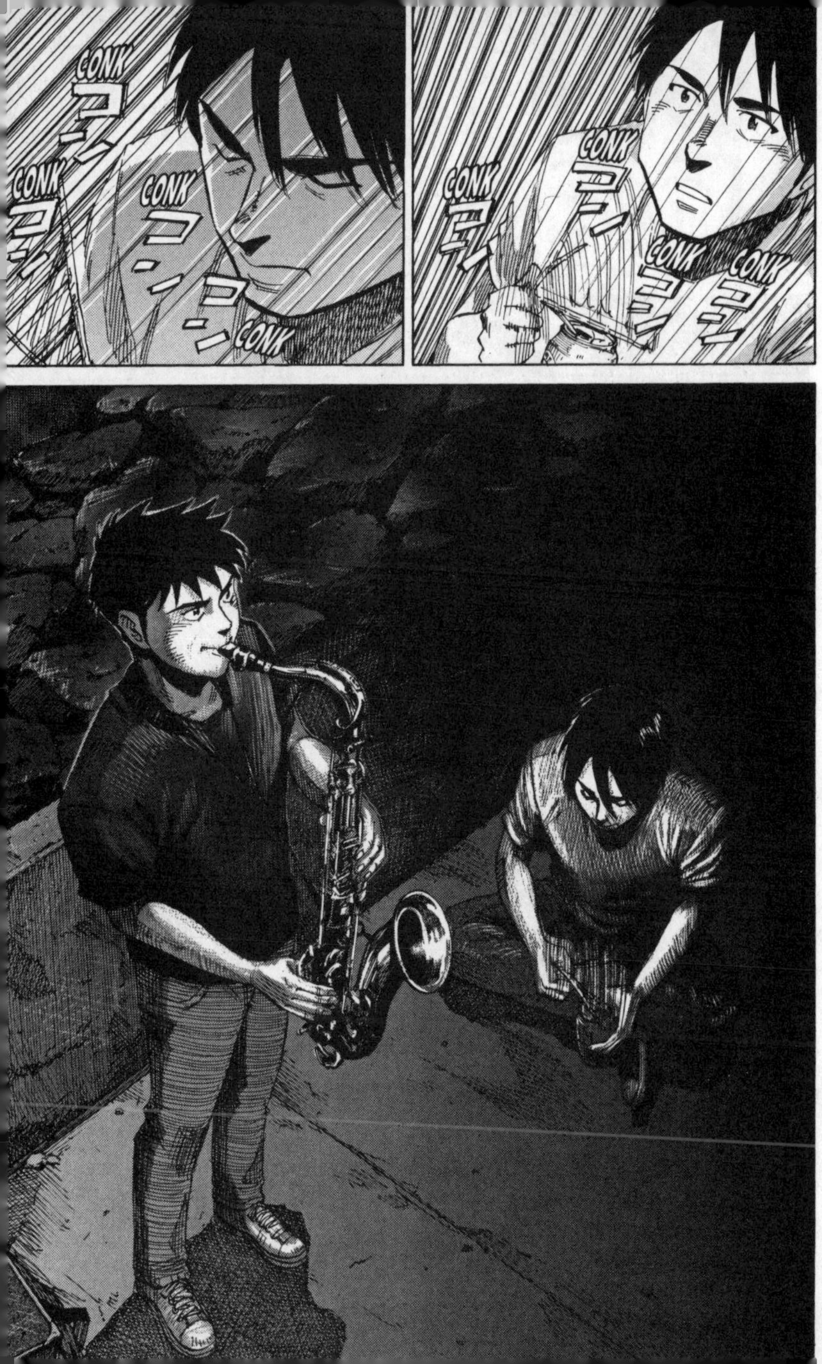
CONK
コーン
CONK
コーン
CONK
コーン
CONK
コーン
CONK
コーン
CONK
コーン
CONK
コーン
CONK
コーン

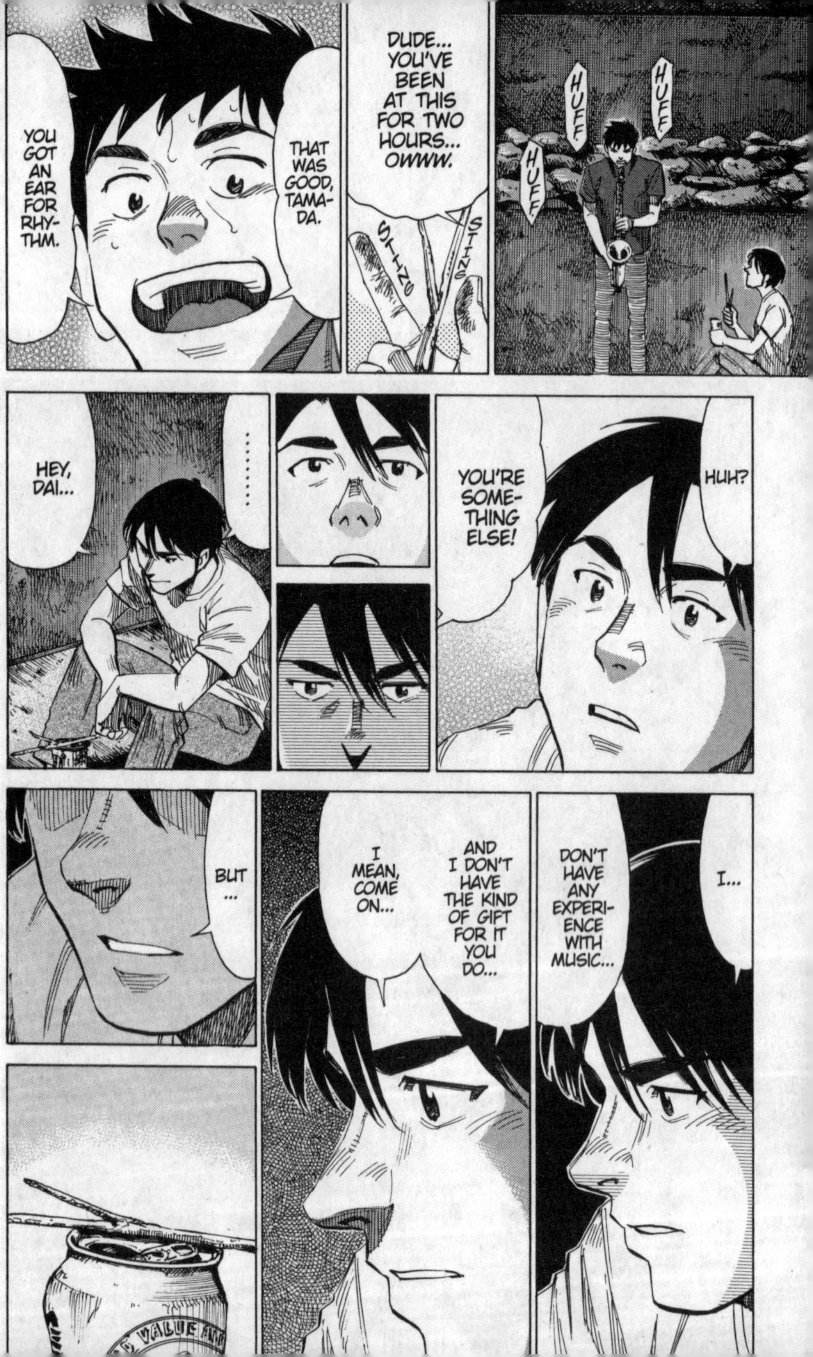
HUFF
HUFF
HUFF
DUDE... YOU'VE BEEN AT THIS FOR TWO HOURS... OWWW.
STING
STING
THAT WAS GOOD, TAMADA.
YOU GOT AN EAR FOR RHYTHM.
HUH?
YOU'RE SOMETHING ELSE!
......
HEY, DAI...
I...
DON'T HAVE ANY EXPERIENCE WITH MUSIC...
AND I DON'T HAVE THE KIND OF GIFT FOR IT YOU DO...
I MEAN, COME ON...
BUT ...

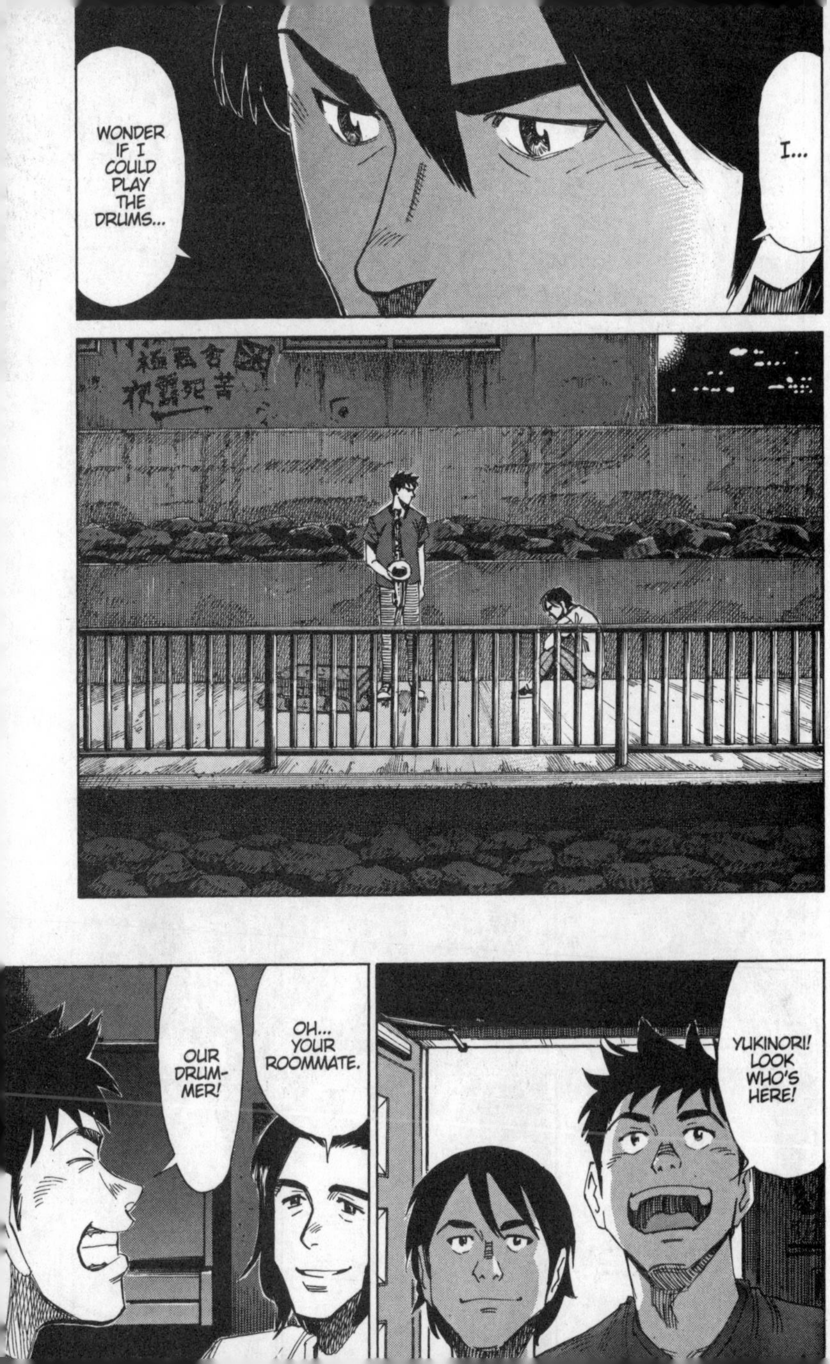
I...
WONDER IF I COULD PLAY THE DRUMS...
YUKINORI! LOOK WHO'S HERE!
OH... YOUR ROOMMATE.
OUR DRUMMER!

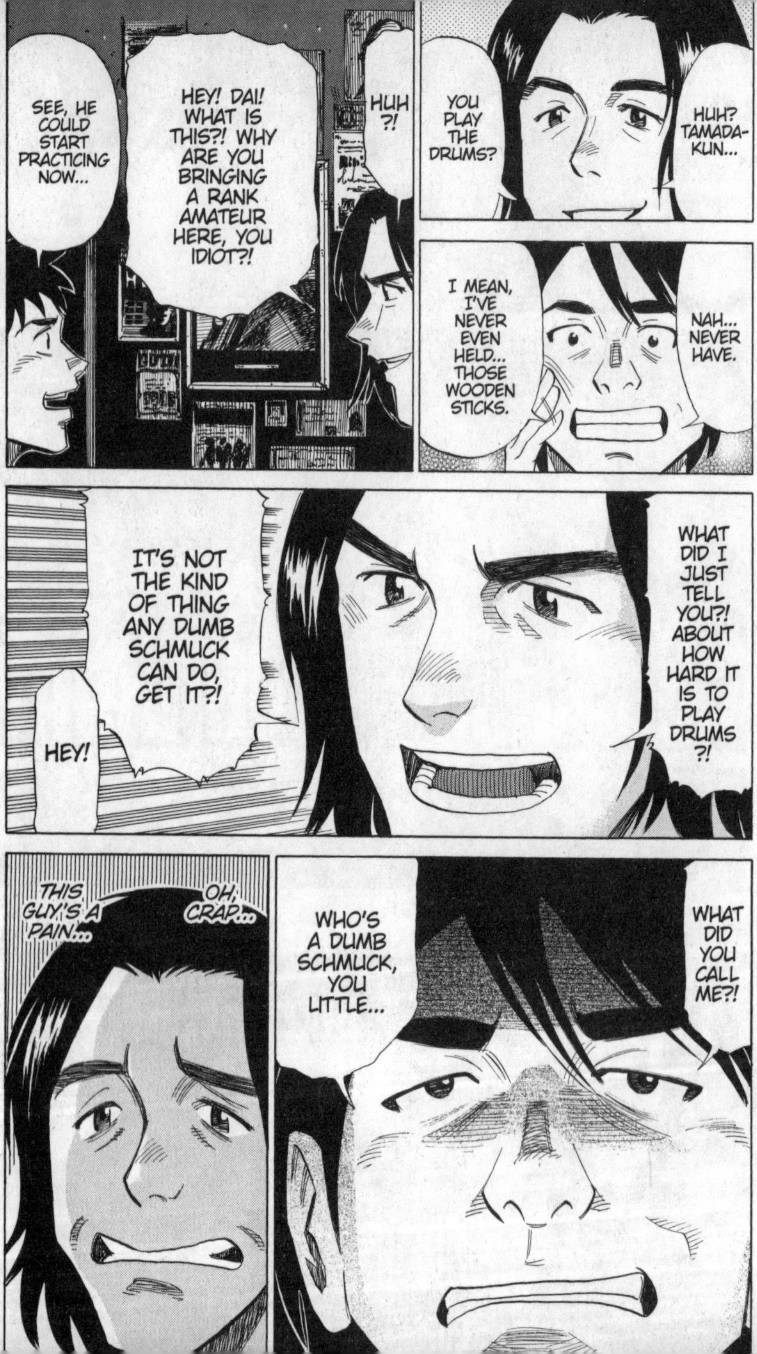
HUH? TAMADA-KUN...
YOU PLAY THE DRUMS?
NAH... NEVER HAVE.
I MEAN, I'VE NEVER EVEN HELD... THOSE WOODEN STICKS.
HUH?!
HEY! DAI! WHAT IS THIS?! WHY ARE YOU BRINGING A RANK AMATEUR HERE, YOU IDIOT?!
SEE, HE COULD START PRACTICING NOW...
WHAT DID I JUST TELL YOU?! ABOUT HOW HARD IT IS TO PLAY DRUMS?!
IT'S NOT THE KIND OF THING ANY DUMB SCHMUCK CAN DO, GET IT?!
HEY!
WHAT DID YOU CALL ME?!
WHO'S A DUMB SCHMUCK, YOU LITTLE...
OH, CRAP...
THIS GUY'S A PAIN...

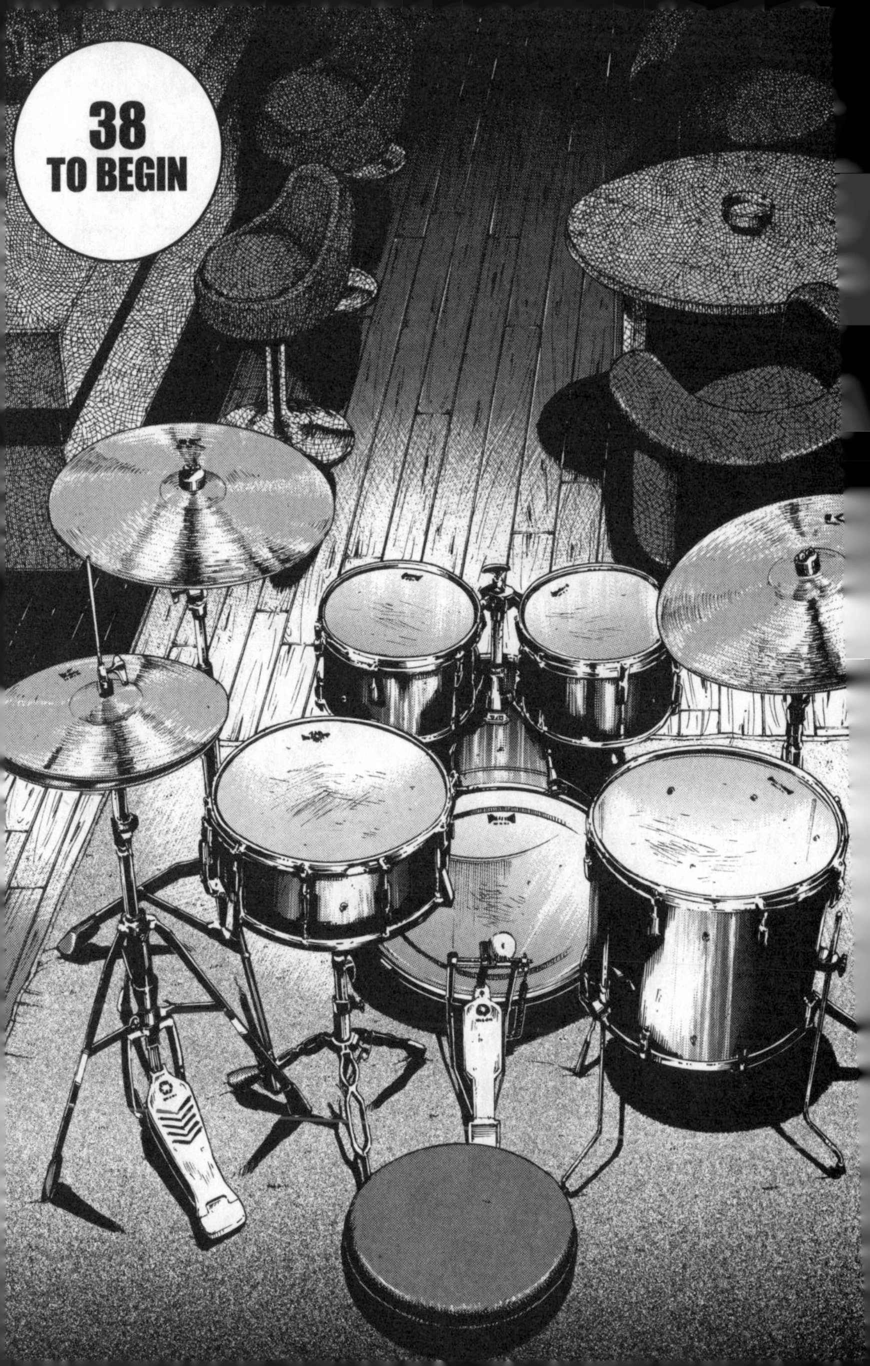
38
TO BEGIN

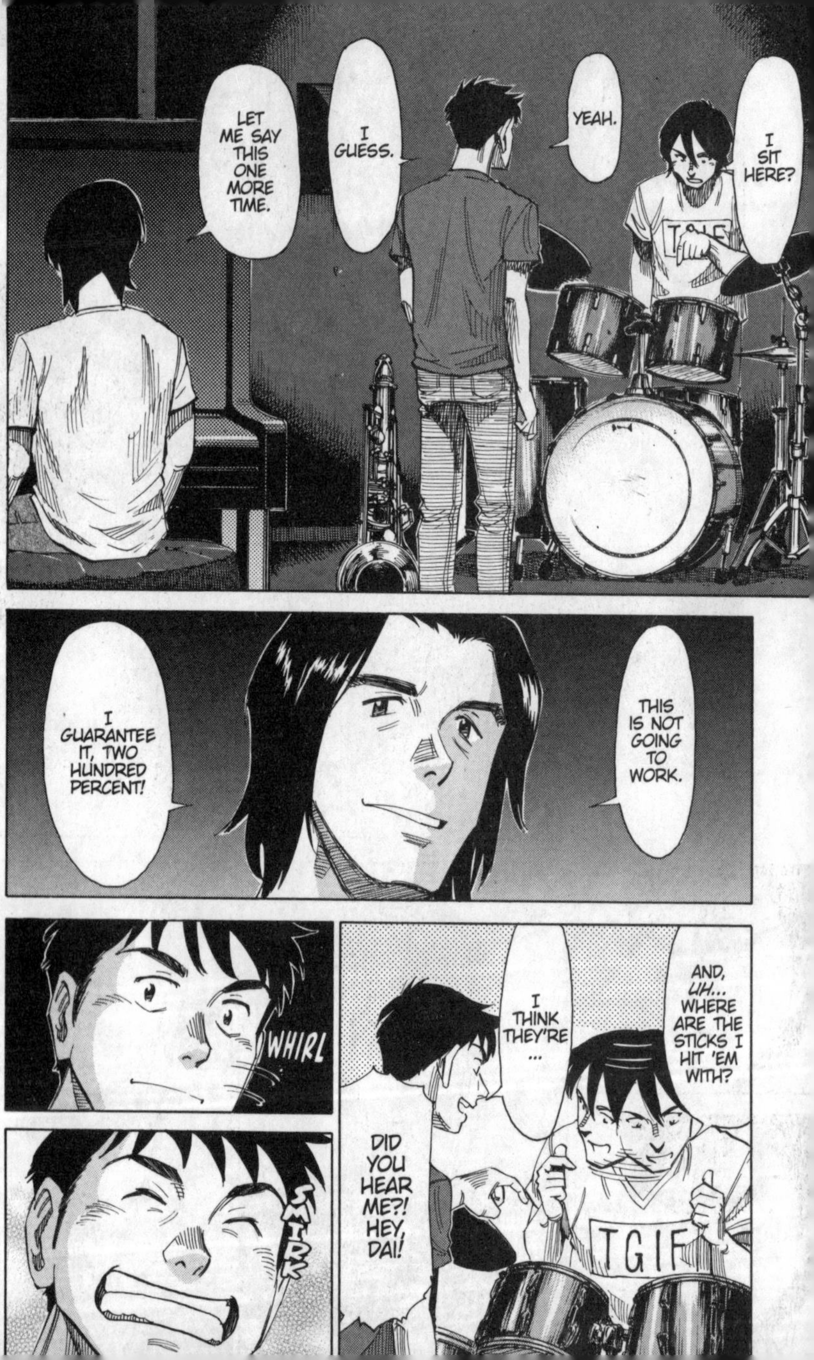
I SIT HERE?
YEAH.
I GUESS.
LET ME SAY THIS ONE MORE TIME.
THIS IS NOT GOING TO WORK.
I GUARANTEE IT, TWO HUNDRED PERCENT!
AND, UH... WHERE ARE THE STICKS I HIT 'EM WITH?
I THINK THEY'RE ...
TGIF
DID YOU HEAR ME?! HEY, DAI!
WHIRL
SMIRK

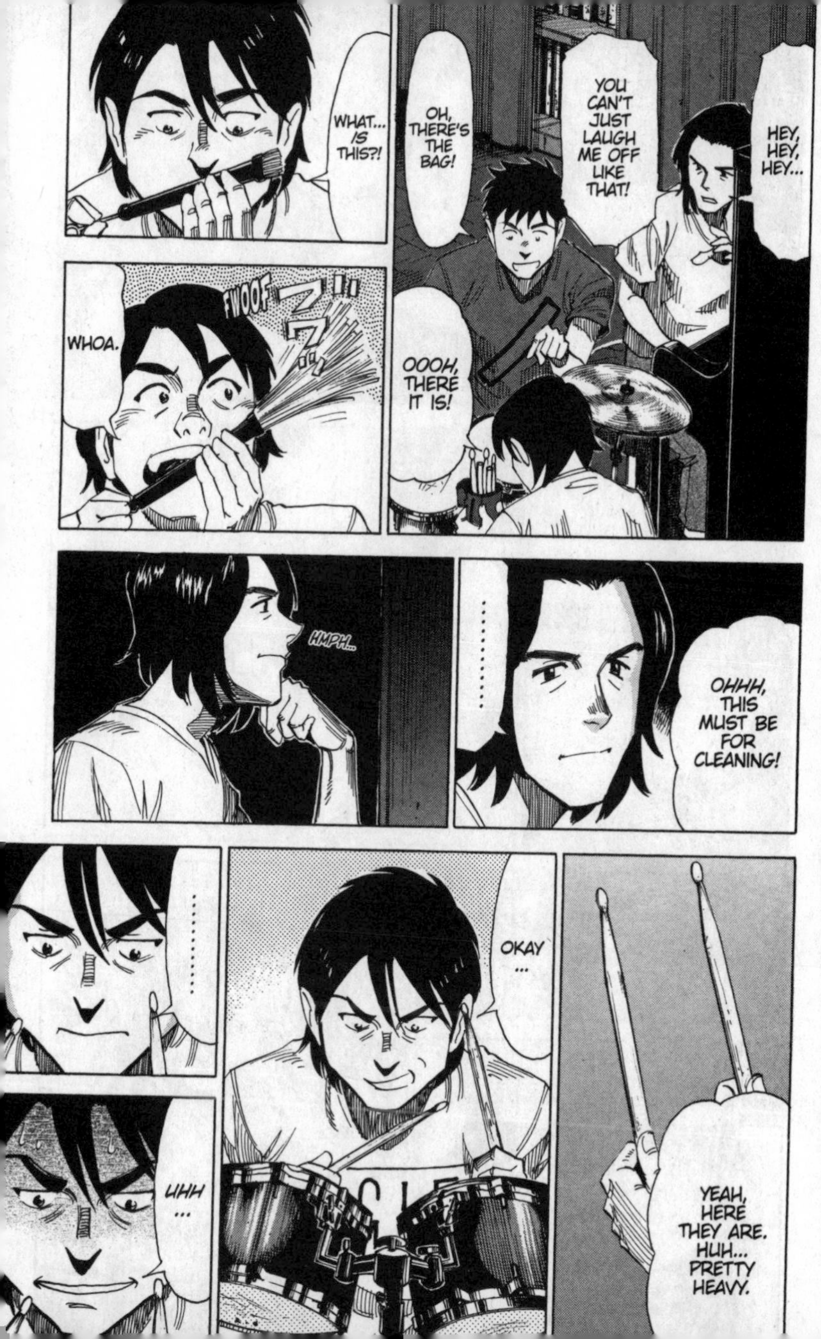
HEY, HEY, HEY...
YOU CAN'T JUST LAUGH ME OFF LIKE THAT!
OH, THERE'S THE BAG!
OOOH, THERE IT IS!
WHAT... IS THIS?!
FWOOF
WHOA.
......
OHHH, THIS MUST BE FOR CLEANING!
HMPH...
YEAH, HERE THEY ARE. HUH... PRETTY HEAVY.
OKAY ...
......
UHH ...

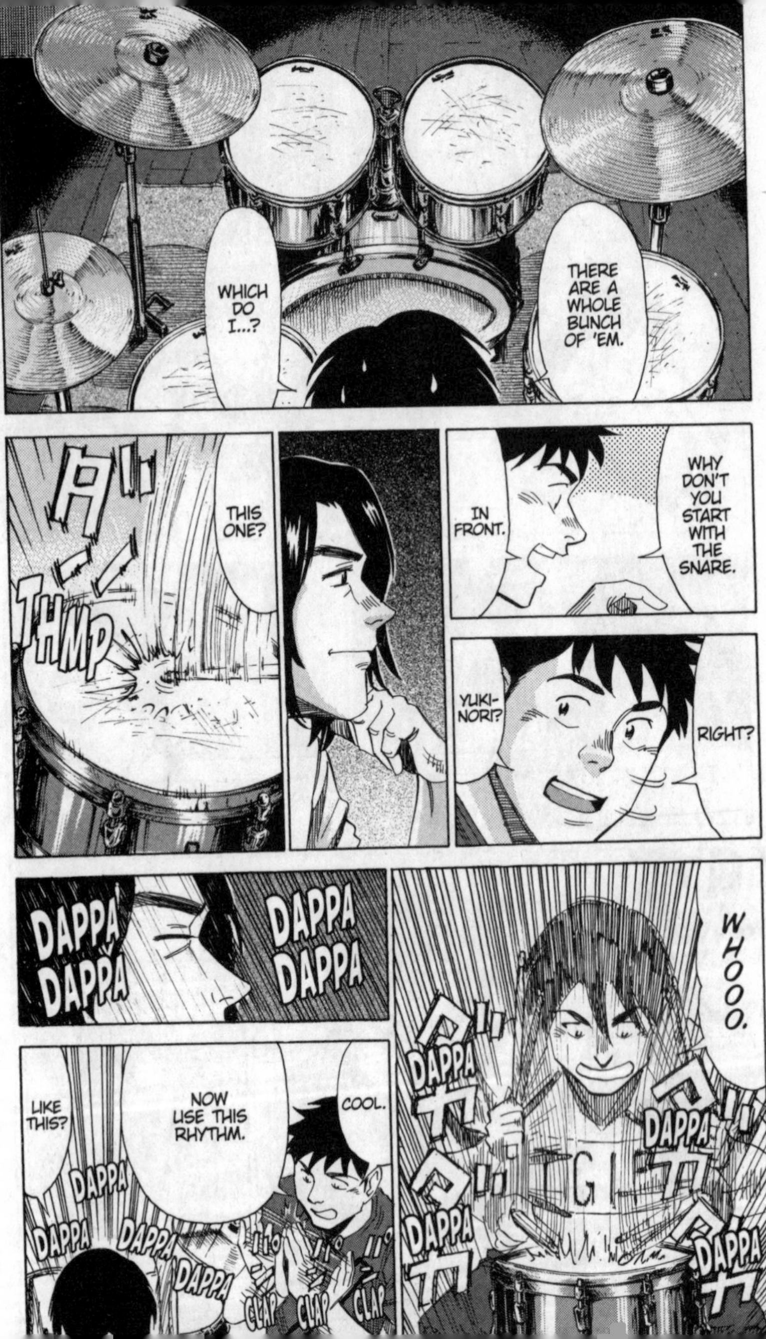
THERE ARE A WHOLE BUNCH OF 'EM.
WHICH DO I...?
WHY DON'T YOU START WITH THE SNARE.
IN FRONT.
RIGHT?
YUKI-NORI?
THIS ONE?
THMP
WHOOOO.
DAPPA
DAPPA
DAPPA
DAPPA
DAPPA DAPPA
DAPPA DAPPA
COOL.
NOW USE THIS RHYTHM.
LIKE THIS?
DAPPA
DAPPA
DAPPA
DAPPA
CLAP
CLAP
CLAP

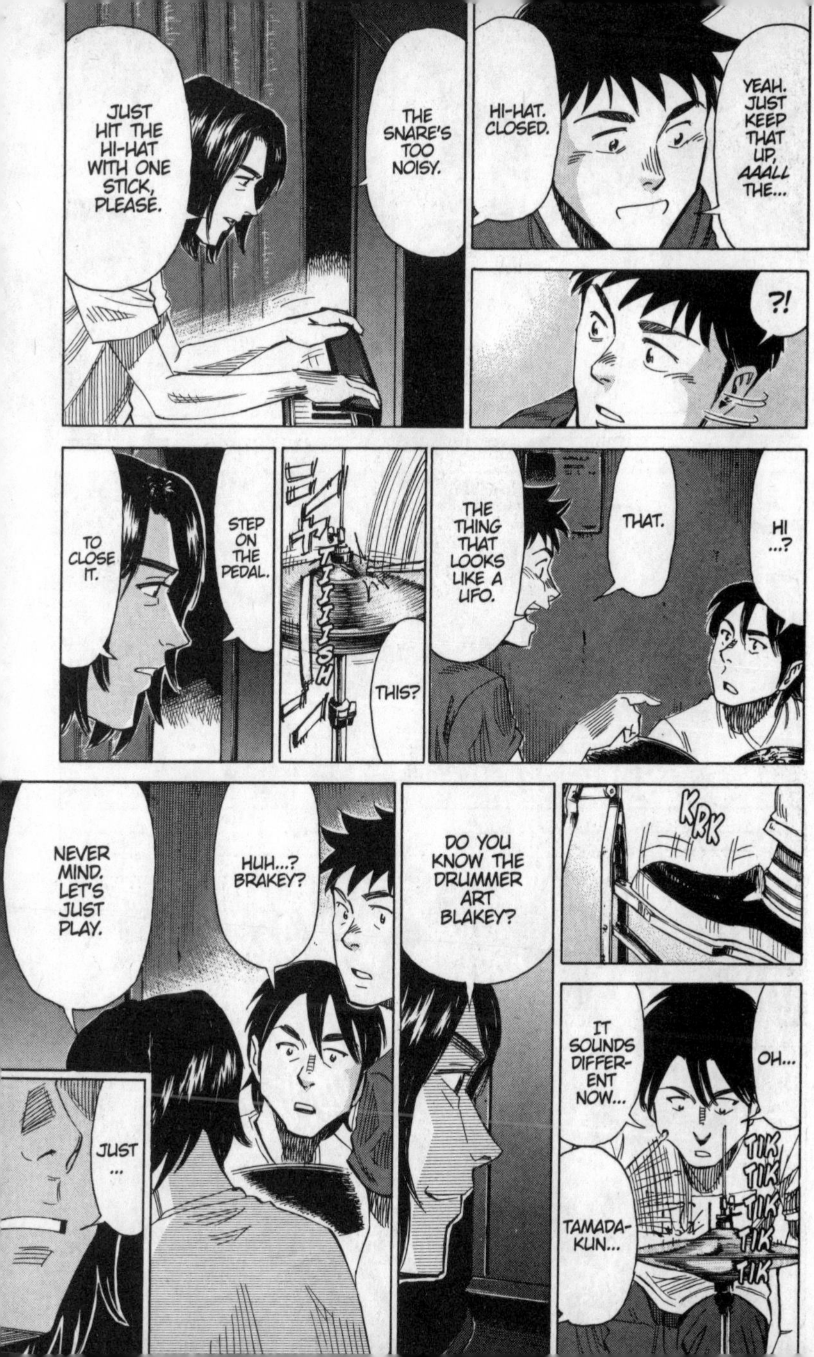
YEAH. JUST KEEP THAT UP, AAALL THE...
HI-HAT. CLOSED.
?!
THE SNARE'S TOO NOISY.
JUST HIT THE HI-HAT WITH ONE STICK, PLEASE.
HI ...?
THAT.
THE THING THAT LOOKS LIKE A UFO.
TIIIIISH
THIS?
STEP ON THE PEDAL.
TO CLOSE IT.
KRK
OH...
IT SOUNDS DIFFER-ENT NOW...
TAMADA-KUN...
TIK TIK TIK TIK TIK
DO YOU KNOW THE DRUMMER ART BLAKEY?
HUH...? BRAKEY?
NEVER MIND. LET'S JUST PLAY.
JUST ...

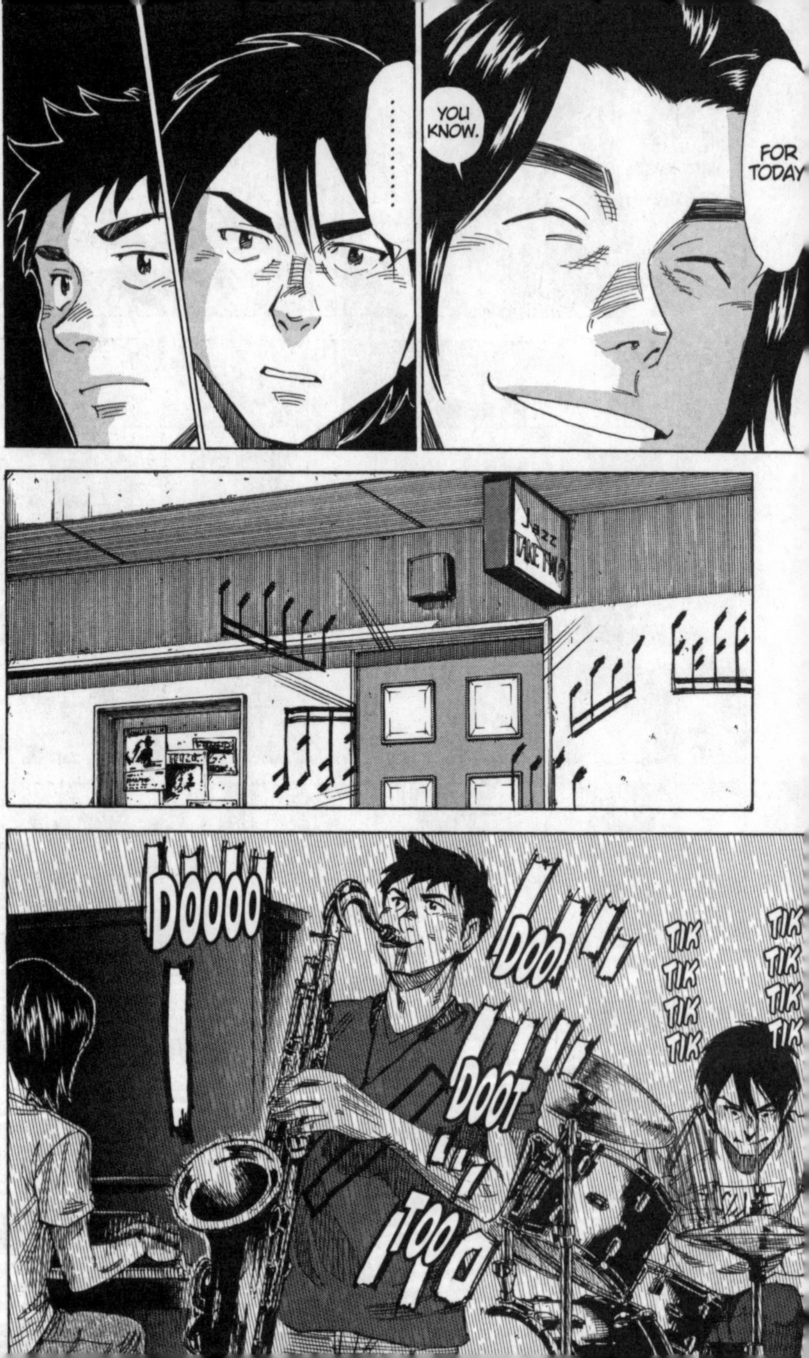
FOR TODAY
YOU KNOW.
......
Jazz
TAKE TWO
TIK TIK TIK TIK
TIK TIK TIK TIK
DOO
DOOOO
DOOT
TOO

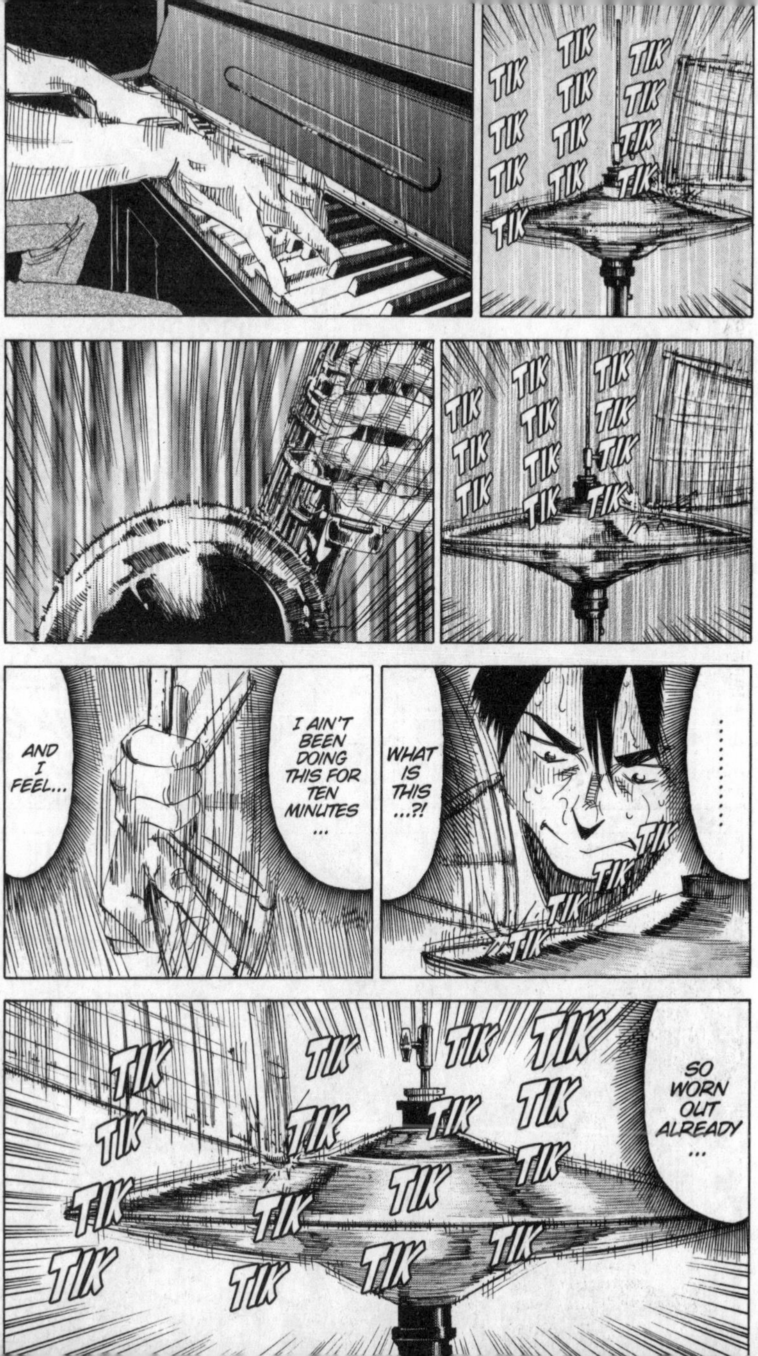
TIK TIK TIK TIK TIK TIK TIK TIK TIK TIK TIK TIK TIK
TIK TIK TIK TIK TIK TIK TIK TIK TIK TIK TIK TIK
......
WHAT IS THIS ...?!
TIK TIK TIK TIK
I AIN'T BEEN DOING THIS FOR TEN MINUTES ...
AND I FEEL...
SO WORN OUT ALREADY ...
TIK TIK TIK TIK TIK TIK TIK TIK TIK TIK TIK TIK TIK TIK TIK TIK TIK

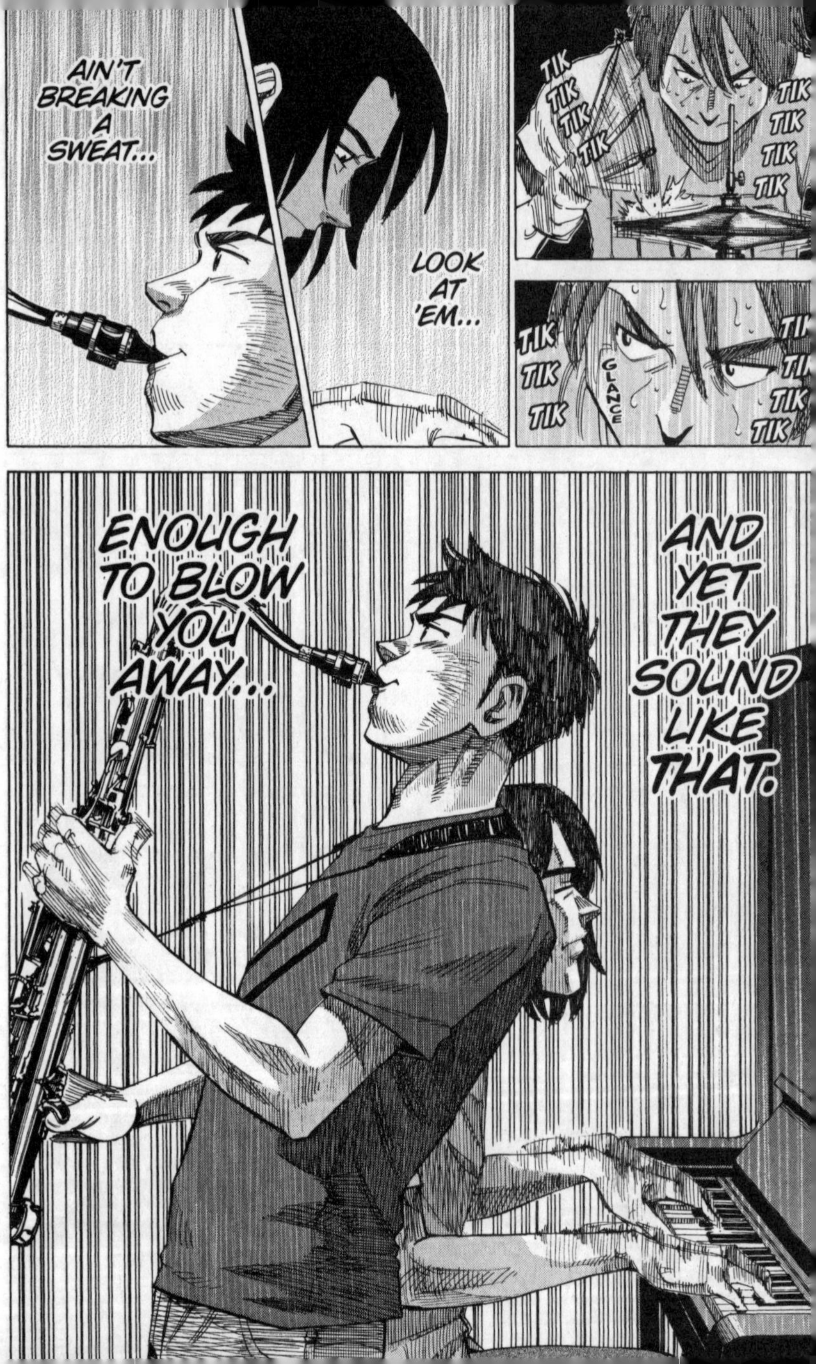
TIK TIK TIK TIK
TIK TIK TIK TIK
TIK TIK TIK TIK
GLANCE
TIK TIK TIK
AIN'T BREAKING A SWEAT...
LOOK AT 'EM...
AND YET THEY SOUND LIKE THAT.
ENOUGH TO BLOW YOU AWAY...

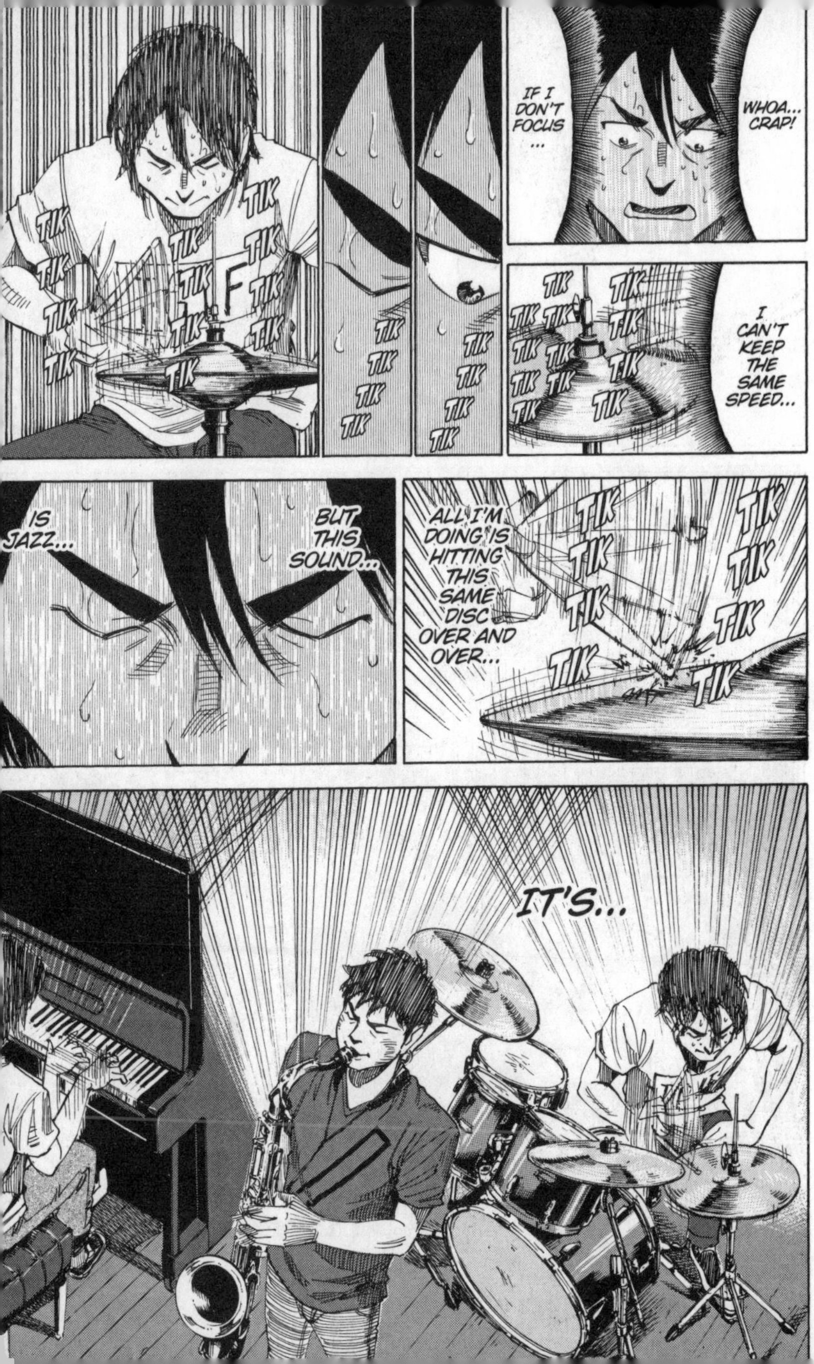
WHOA... CRAP!
IF I DON'T FOCUS ...
I CAN'T KEEP THE SAME SPEED...
TIK TIK TIK TIK TIK TIK TIK TIK TIK TIK TIK TIK TIK
TIK TIK TIK TIK TIK
TIK TIK TIK TIK
TIK TIK TIK TIK TIK TIK TIK TIK TIK TIK TIK TIK
ALL I'M DOING IS HITTING THIS SAME DISC OVER AND OVER...
TIK TIK TIK TIK TIK TIK TIK TIK
BUT THIS SOUND...
IS JAZZ...
IT'S...

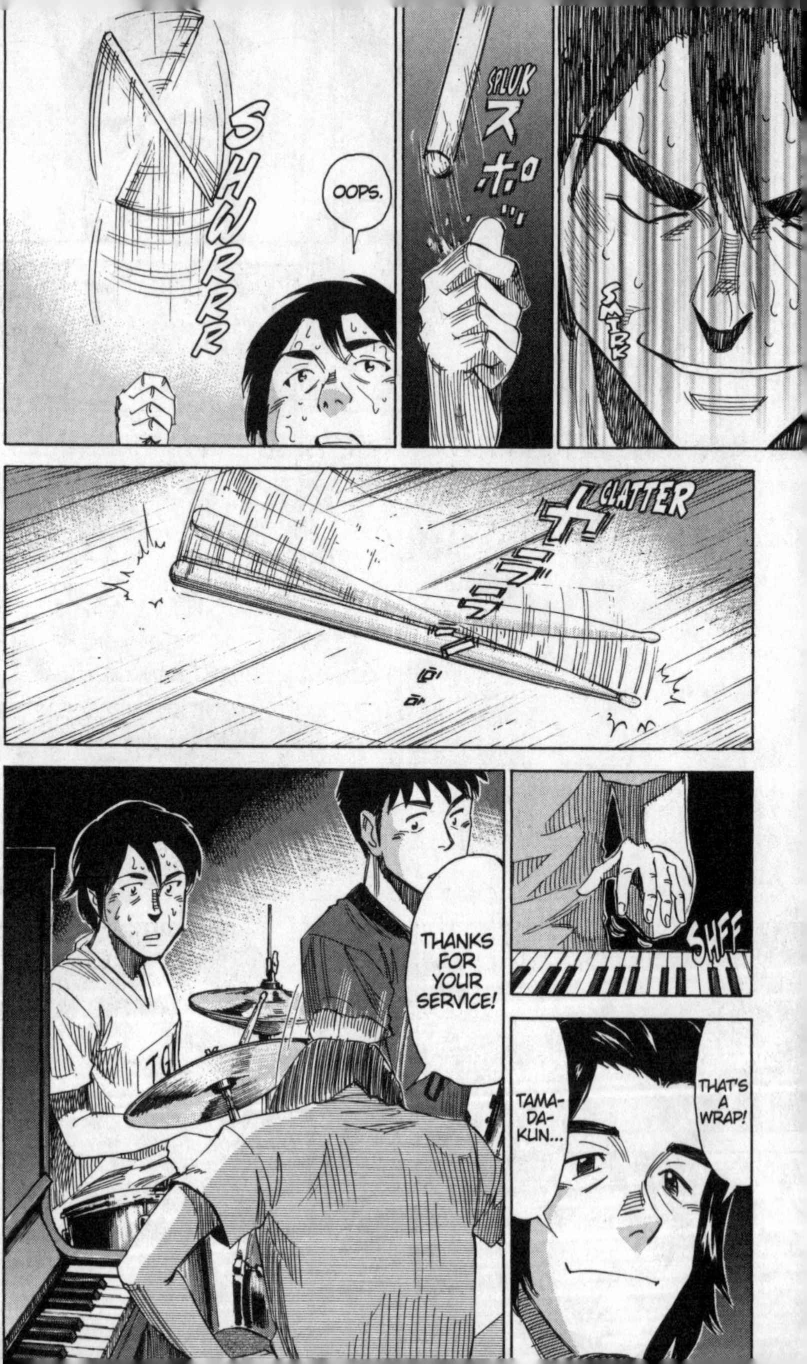
SMIRK
SPLUK
スポッ
OOPS.
SHWRRR
CLATTER
SHFF
THAT'S A WRAP!
TAMA-DA-KUN...
THANKS FOR YOUR SERVICE!

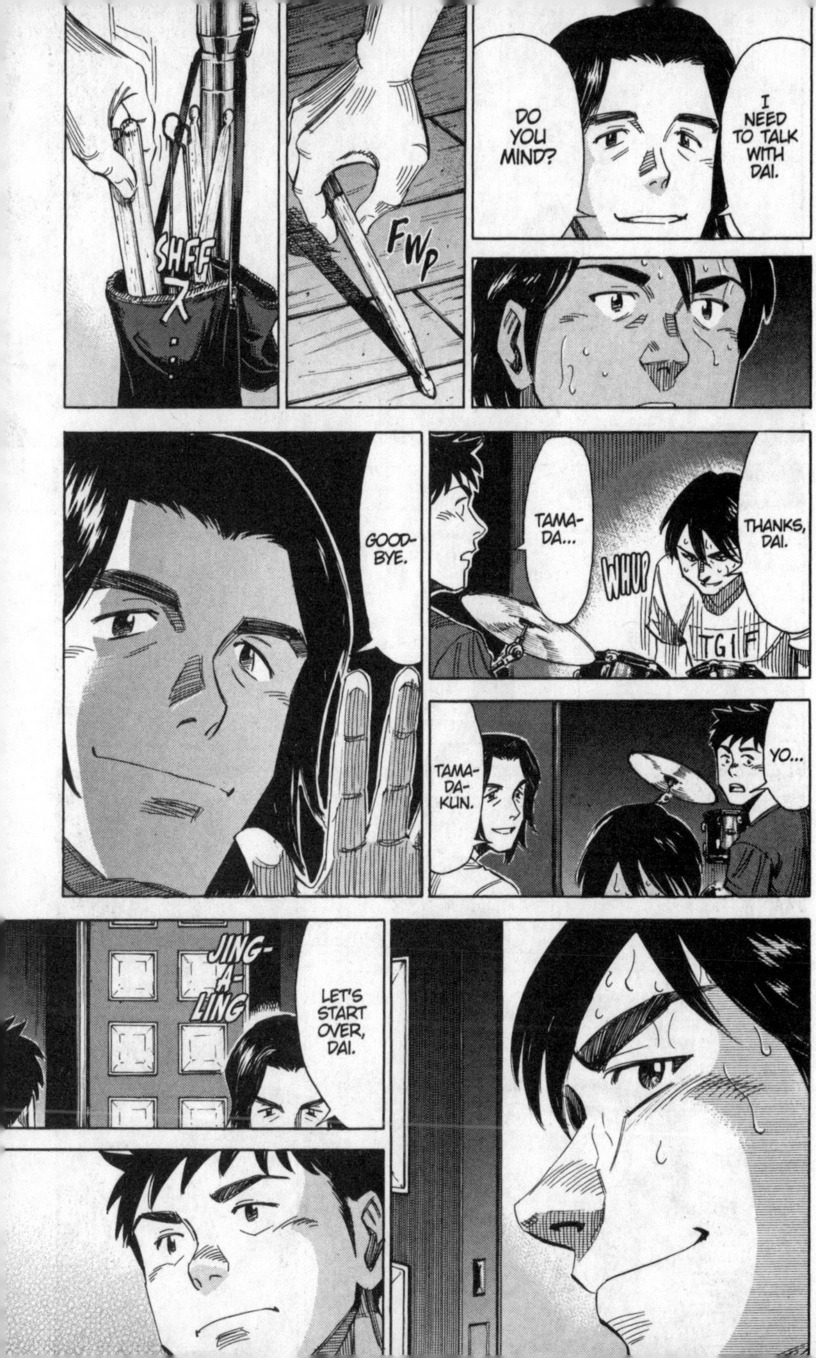
I NEED TO TALK WITH DAI.
DO YOU MIND?
FWP
SHFF
ス
THANKS, DAI.
WHUP
TAMA-DA...
YO...
TAMA-DA-KUN.
GOOD-BYE.
LET'S START OVER, DAI.
JING-A-LING

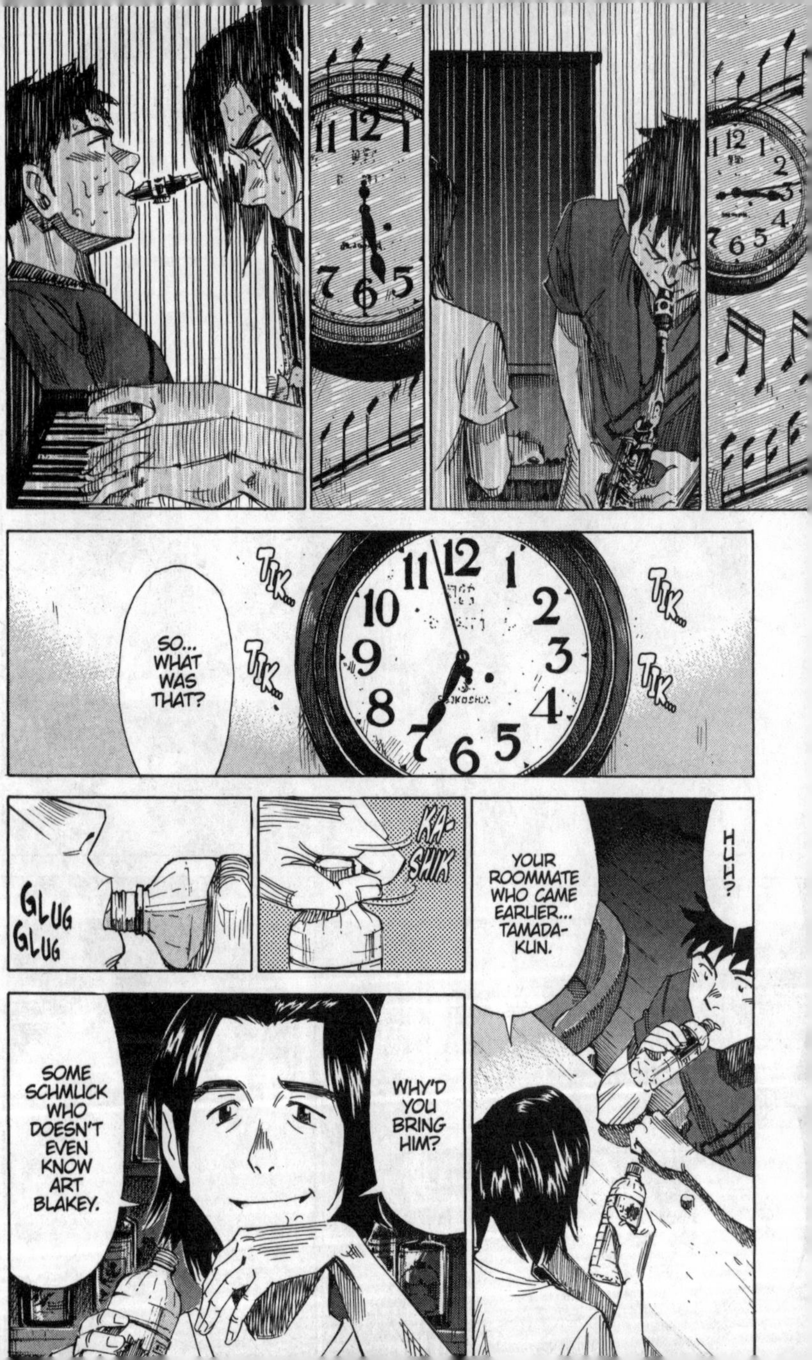
TIK...
TIK...
TIK...
TIK...
SO... WHAT WAS THAT?
HUH?
YOUR ROOMMATE WHO CAME EARLIER... TAMADA-KUN.
KA-SHIK
GLUG GLUG
WHY'D YOU BRING HIM?
SOME SCHMUCK WHO DOESN'T EVEN KNOW ART BLAKEY.

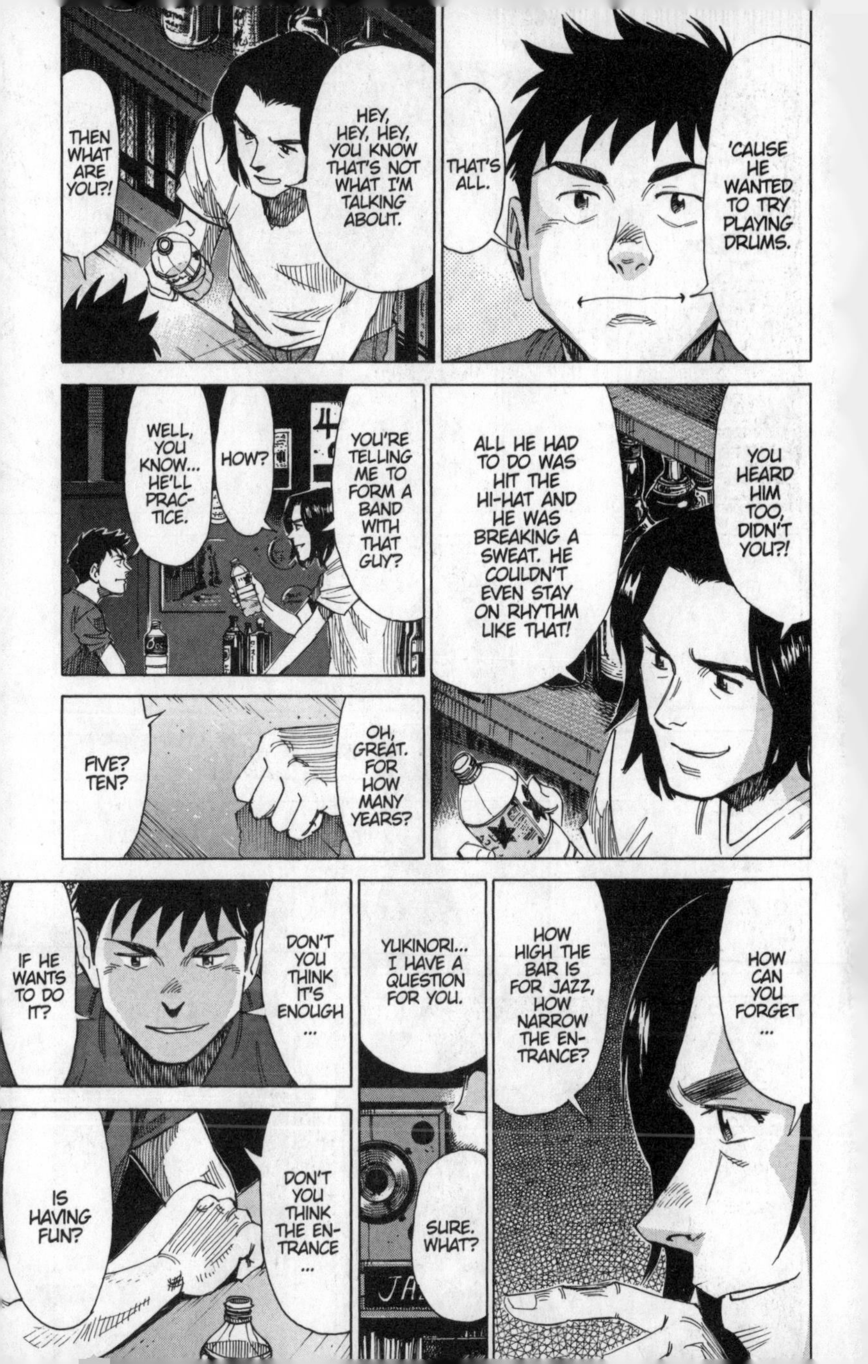
'CAUSE HE WANTED TO TRY PLAYING DRUMS.
THAT'S ALL.
HEY, HEY, HEY, YOU KNOW THAT'S NOT WHAT I'M TALKING ABOUT.
THEN WHAT ARE YOU?!
YOU HEARD HIM TOO, DIDN'T YOU?!
ALL HE HAD TO DO WAS HIT THE HI-HAT AND HE WAS BREAKING A SWEAT. HE COULDN'T EVEN STAY ON RHYTHM LIKE THAT!
YOU'RE TELLING ME TO FORM A BAND WITH THAT GUY?
HOW?
WELL, YOU KNOW... HE'LL PRAC-TICE.
OH, GREAT. FOR HOW MANY YEARS?
FIVE? TEN?
HOW CAN YOU FORGET...
HOW HIGH THE BAR IS FOR JAZZ, HOW NARROW THE EN-TRANCE?
YUKINORI... I HAVE A QUESTION FOR YOU.
SURE. WHAT?
DON'T YOU THINK IT'S ENOUGH...
IF HE WANTS TO DO IT?
DON'T YOU THINK THE EN-TRANCE...
IS HAVING FUN?

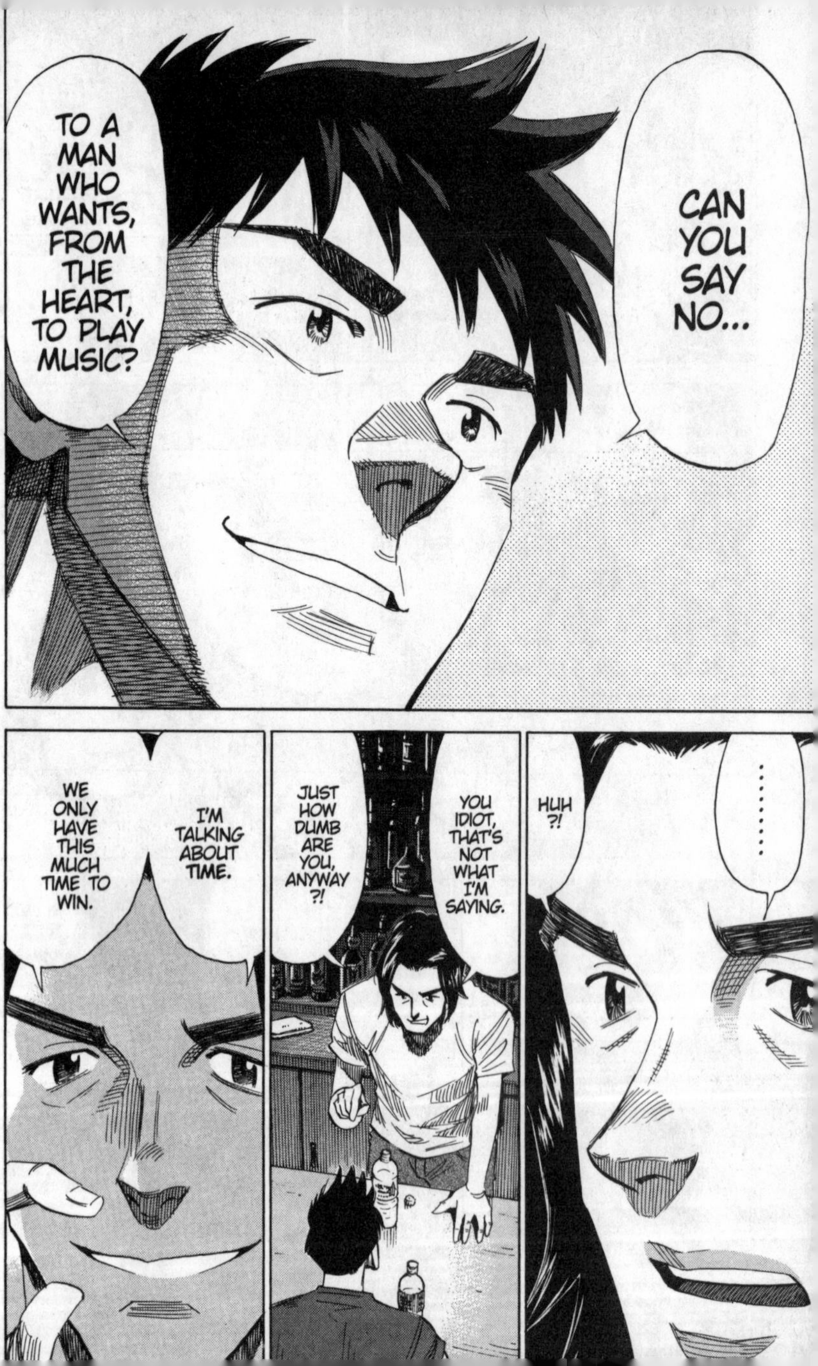
CAN YOU SAY NO...
TO A MAN WHO WANTS, FROM THE HEART, TO PLAY MUSIC?
......
HUH ?!
YOU IDIOT, THAT'S NOT WHAT I'M SAYING.
JUST HOW DUMB ARE YOU, ANYWAY ?!
I'M TALKING ABOUT TIME.
WE ONLY HAVE THIS MUCH TIME TO WIN.

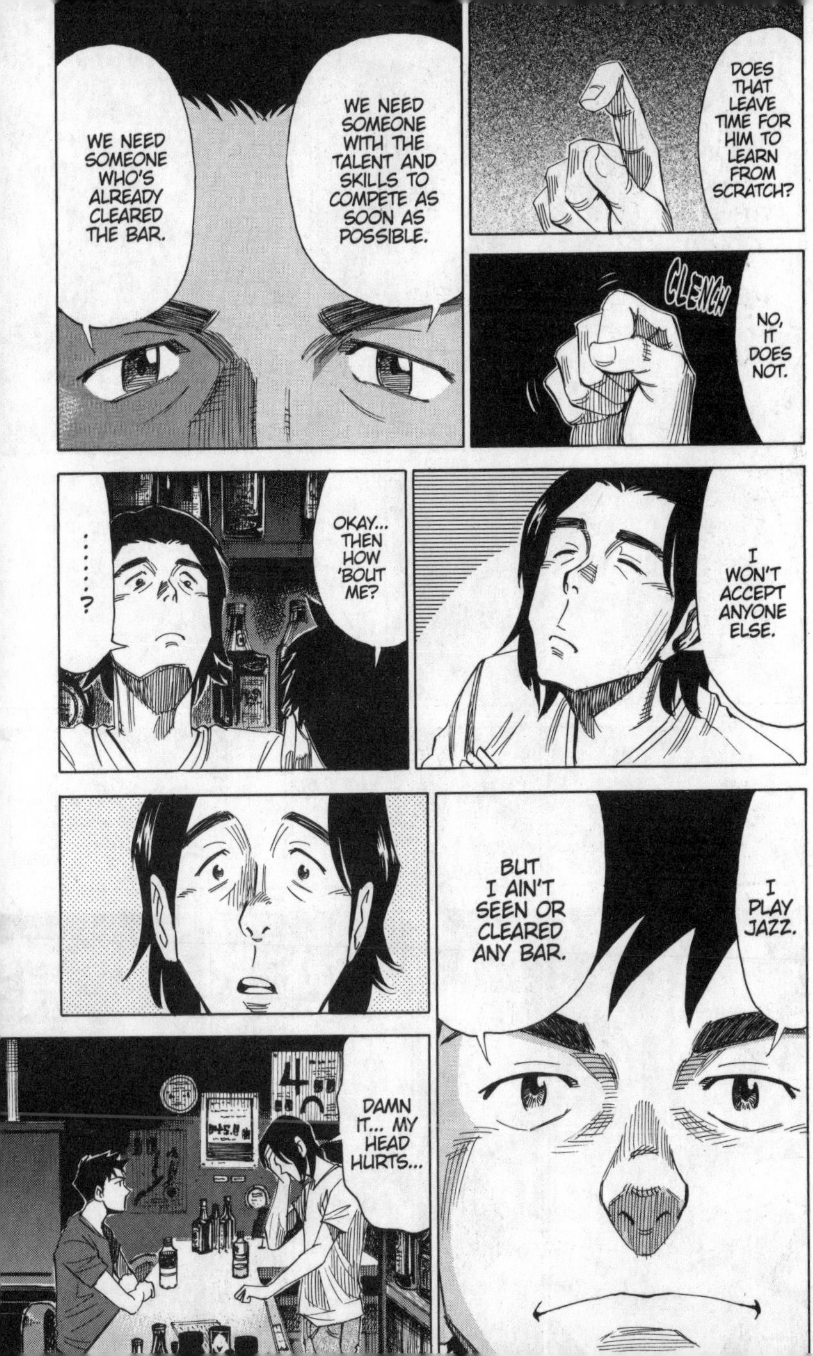
DOES THAT LEAVE TIME FOR HIM TO LEARN FROM SCRATCH?
CLENCH
NO, IT DOES NOT.
WE NEED SOMEONE WITH THE TALENT AND SKILLS TO COMPETE AS SOON AS POSSIBLE.
WE NEED SOMEONE WHO'S ALREADY CLEARED THE BAR.
I WON'T ACCEPT ANYONE ELSE.
OKAY... THEN HOW 'BOUT ME?
......?
I PLAY JAZZ.
BUT I AIN'T SEEN OR CLEARED ANY BAR.
DAMN IT... MY HEAD HURTS...

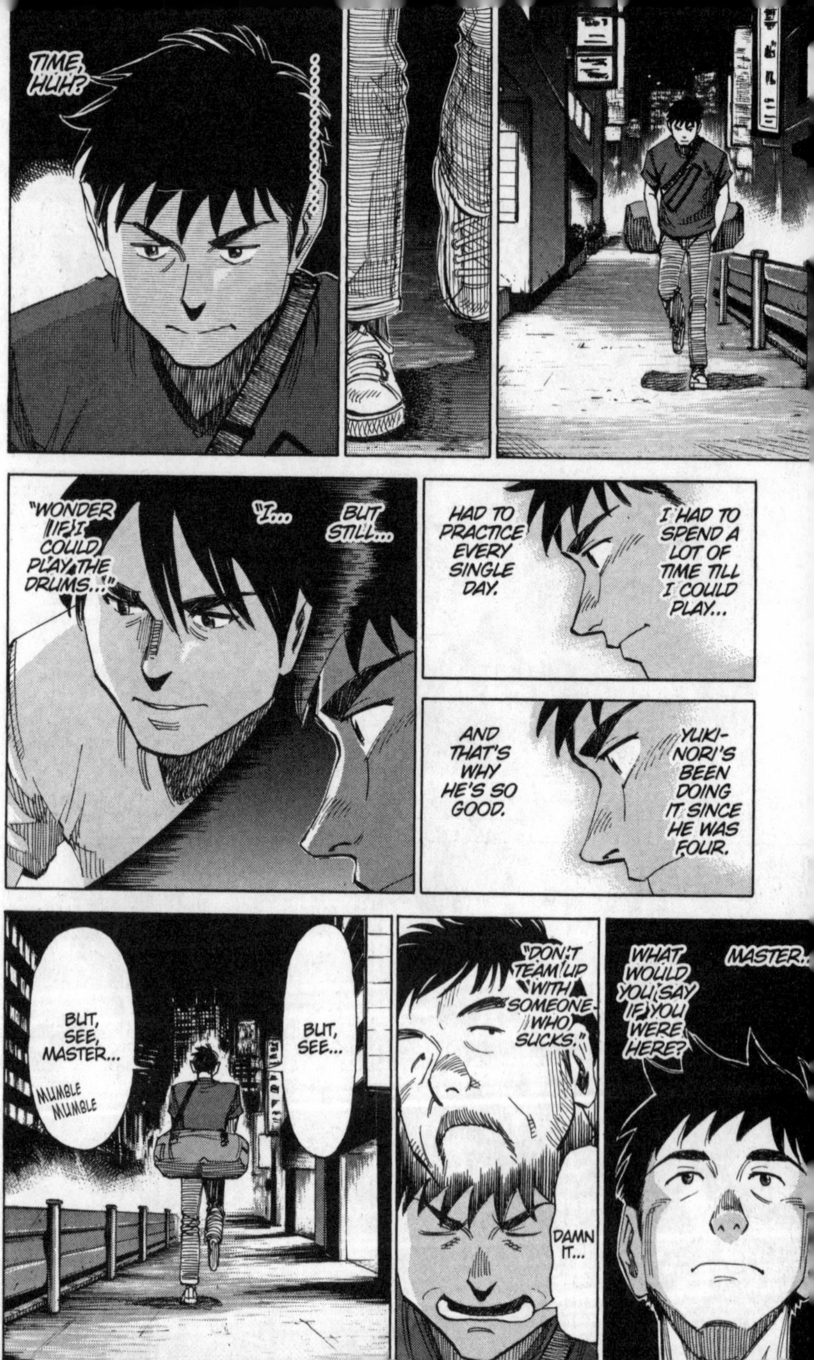
TIME, HUH?
I HAD TO SPEND A LOT OF TIME TILL I COULD PLAY...
HAD TO PRACTICE EVERY SINGLE DAY.
YUKI-NORI'S BEEN DOING IT SINCE HE WAS FOUR.
AND THAT'S WHY HE'S SO GOOD.
BUT STILL...
"I...
"WONDER IF I COULD PLAY THE DRUMS..."
MASTER...
WHAT WOULD YOU SAY IF YOU WERE HERE?
"DON'T TEAM UP WITH SOMEONE WHO SUCKS."
DAMN IT...
BUT, SEE...
BUT, SEE, MASTER...
MUMBLE MUMBLE

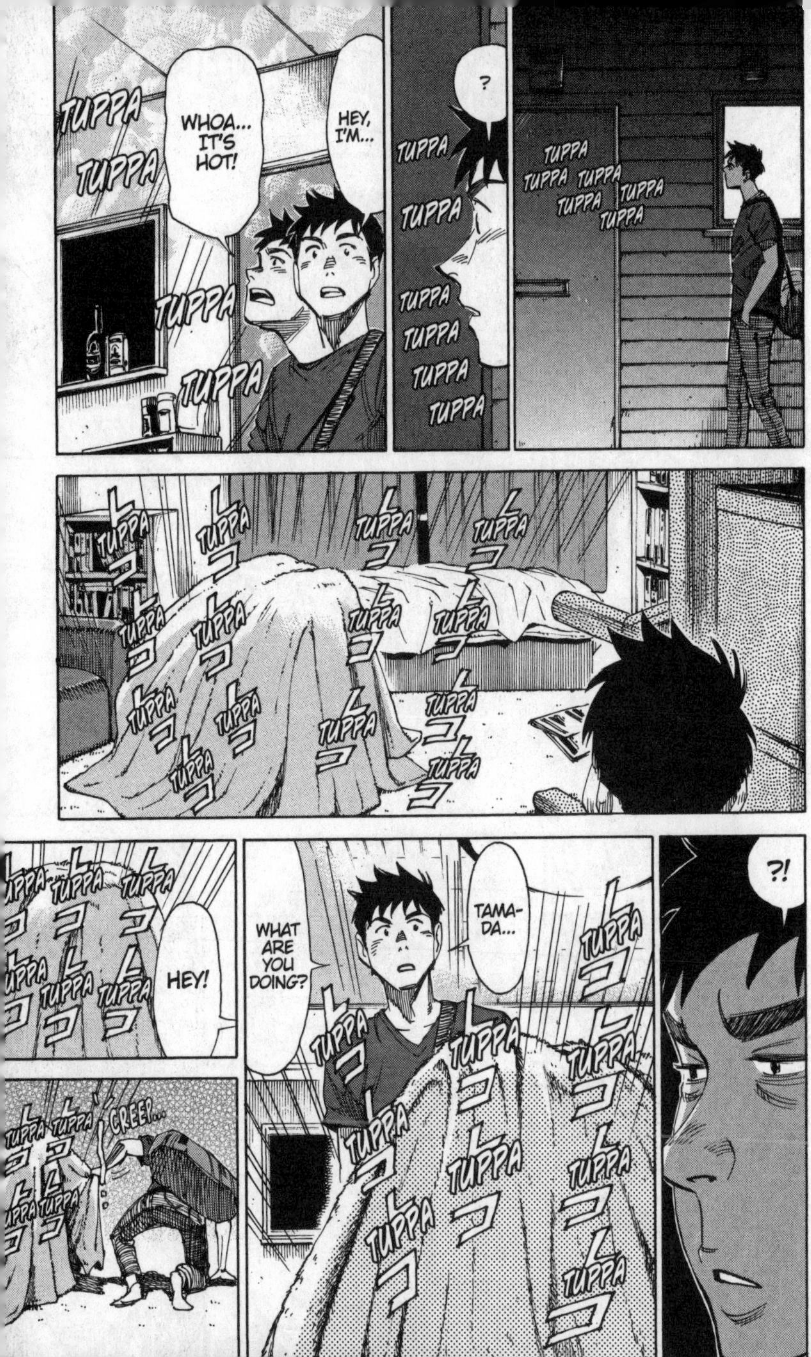
TUPPA TUPPA TUPPA TUPPA TUPPA TUPPA
?
TUPPA TUPPA TUPPA TUPPA TUPPA TUPPA
HEY, I'M...
WHOA... IT'S HOT!
TUPPA TUPPA TUPPA TUPPA
TUPPA TUPPA TUPPA TUPPA TUPPA TUPPA TUPPA TUPPA TUPPA TUPPA TUPPA TUPPA TUPPA TUPPA
?!
TUPPA TUPPA TUPPA TUPPA TUPPA
TAMA-DA...
WHAT ARE YOU DOING?
TUPPA TUPPA TUPPA TUPPA TUPPA TUPPA
HEY!
TUPPA TUPPA TUPPA TUPPA TUPPA TUPPA TUPPA
CREEP...
TUPPA TUPPA TUPPA

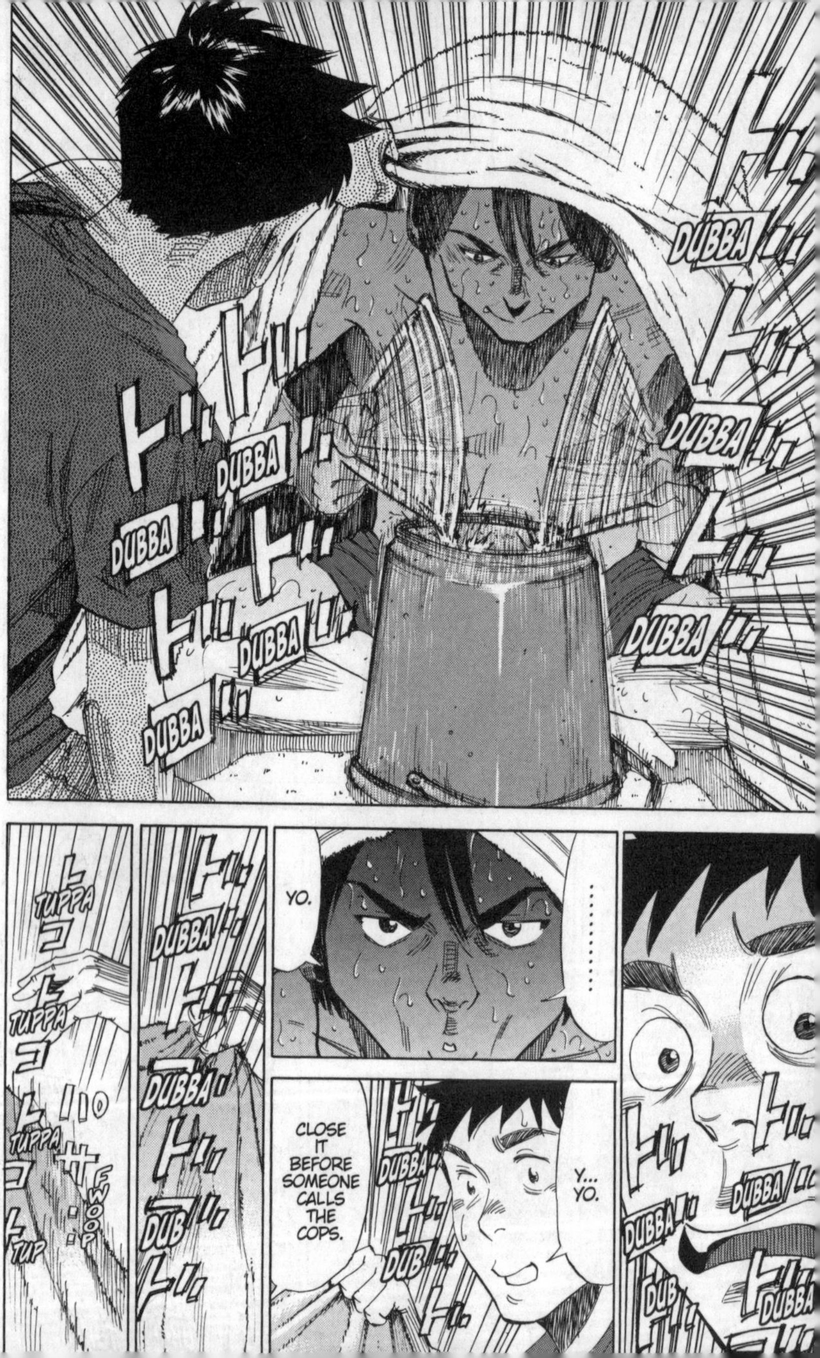

DUBBA
DUBBA
DUBBA
DUBBA
DUBBA
DUBBA
DUBBA
DUBBA
DUBBA
DUB
DUBBA
......
YO.
Y... YO.
CLOSE IT BEFORE SOMEONE CALLS THE COPS.
DUBBA
DUB
DUBBA
DUBBA
DUBBA
DUB
TUPPA
TUPPA
TUPPA
FWOOP
TUP

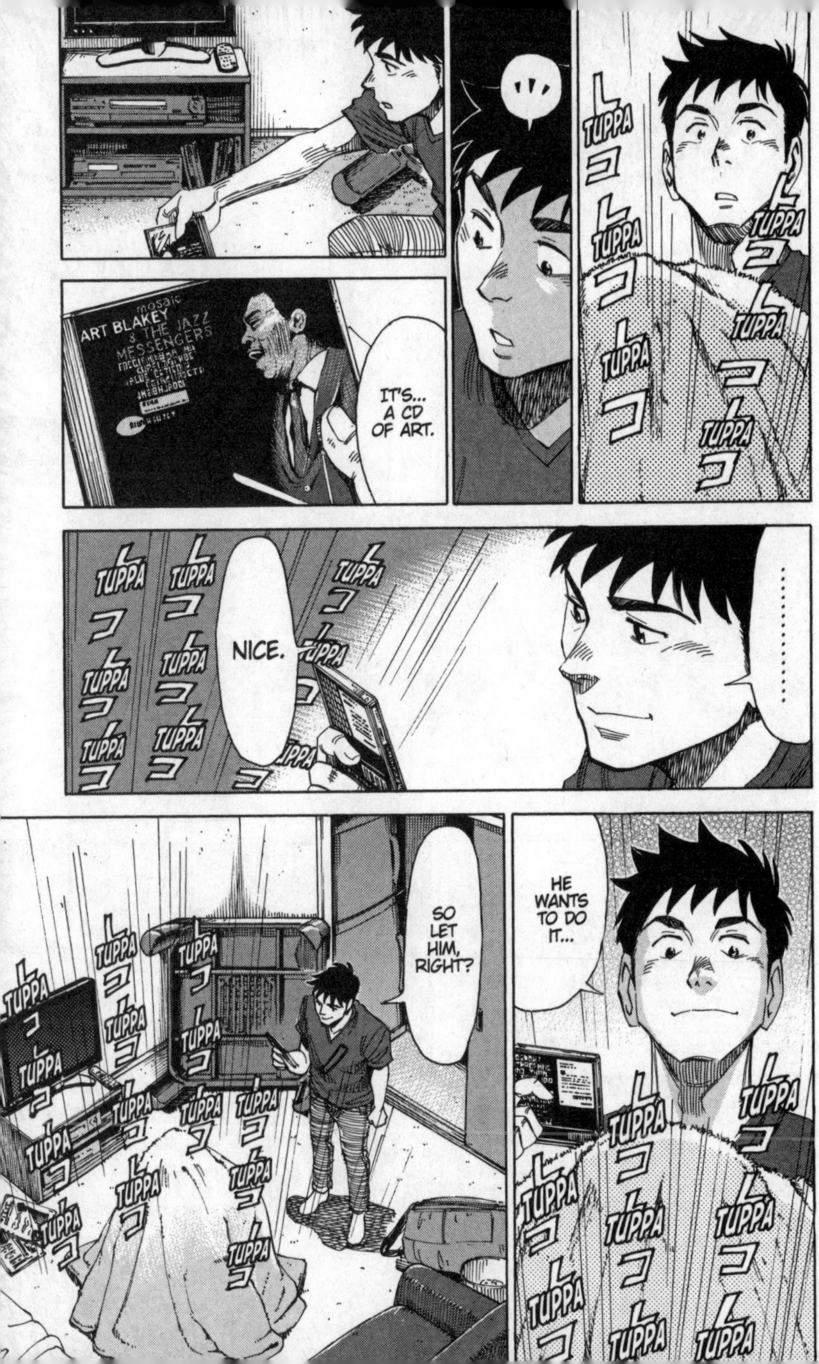
TUPPA
TUPPA
TUPPA
TUPPA
TUPPA
TUPPA
...!
mosaic
ART BLAKEY & THE JAZZ MESSENGERS
IT'S... A CD OF ART.
TUPPA
TUPPA
TUPPA
TUPPA
TUPPA
TUPPA
TUPPA
......
NICE.
TUPPA
TUPPA
TUPPA
TUPPA
TUPPA
TUPPA
HE WANTS TO DO IT...
TUPPA
TUPPA
TUPPA
TUPPA
TUPPA
TUPPA
TUPPA
TUPPA
SO LET HIM, RIGHT?

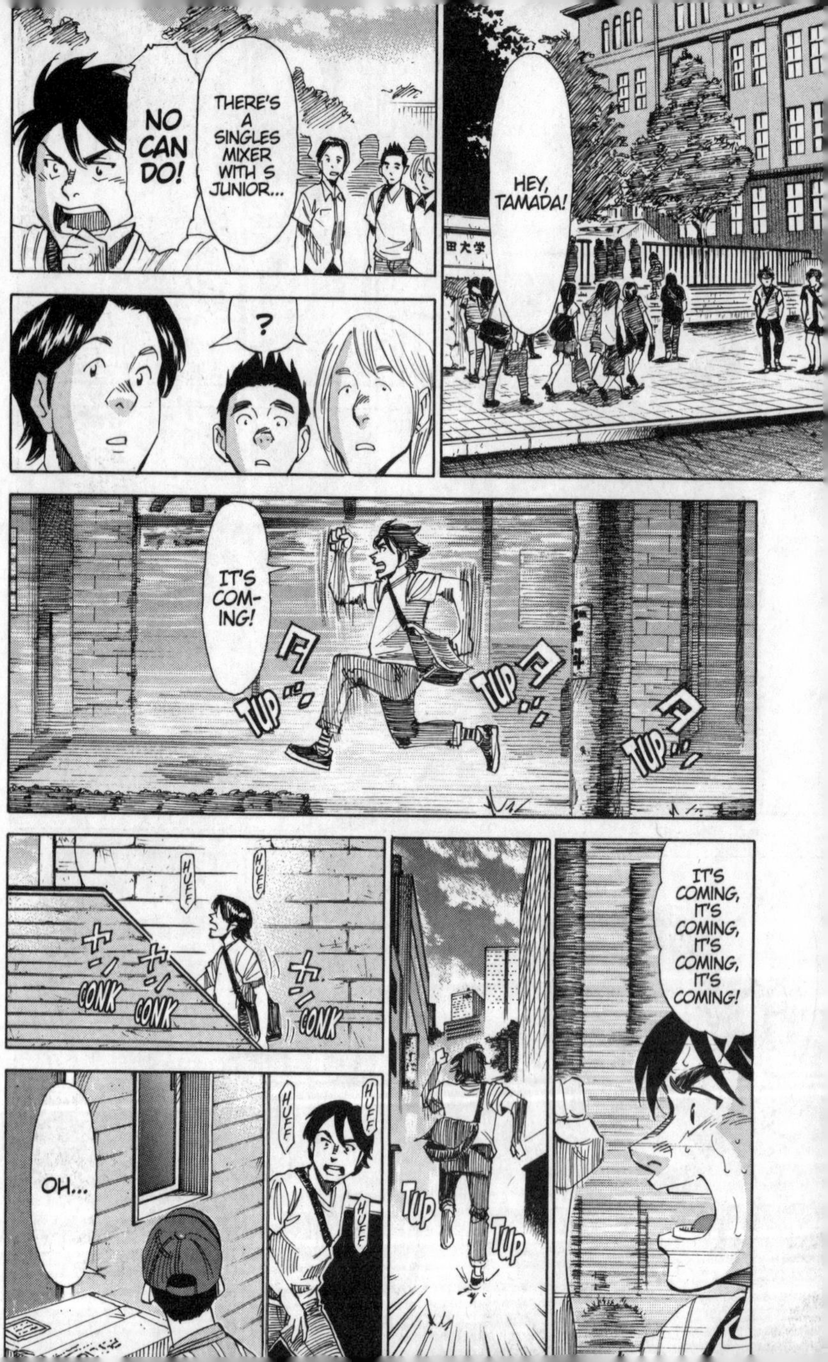
HEY, TAMADA!
THERE'S A SINGLES MIXER WITH S JUNIOR...
NO CAN DO!
?
IT'S COMING!
TUP
TUP
TUP
IT'S COMING, IT'S COMING, IT'S COMING, IT'S COMING!
TUP
TUP
HUFF
HUFF
CONK
CONK
CONK
HUFF
HUFF
HUFF
OH...

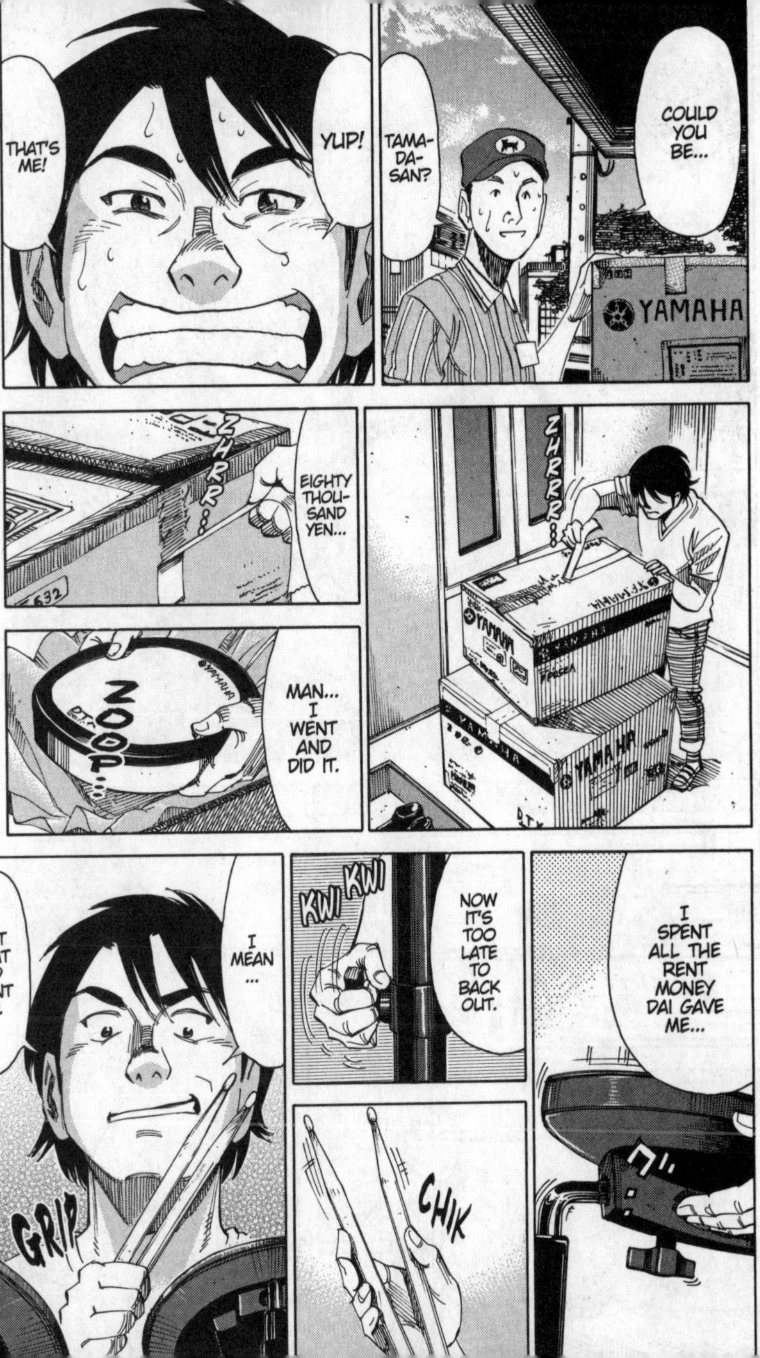
COULD YOU BE...
TAMA-DA-SAN?
YAMAHA
YUP!
THAT'S ME!
ZHRRR...
ZHRR...
EIGHTY THOUSAND YEN...
ZOOP...
MAN... I WENT AND DID IT.
I SPENT ALL THE RENT MONEY DAI GAVE ME...
KWI KWI
NOW IT'S TOO LATE TO BACK OUT.
CHIK
I MEAN...
NOT THAT I'D WANT TO.
GRIP

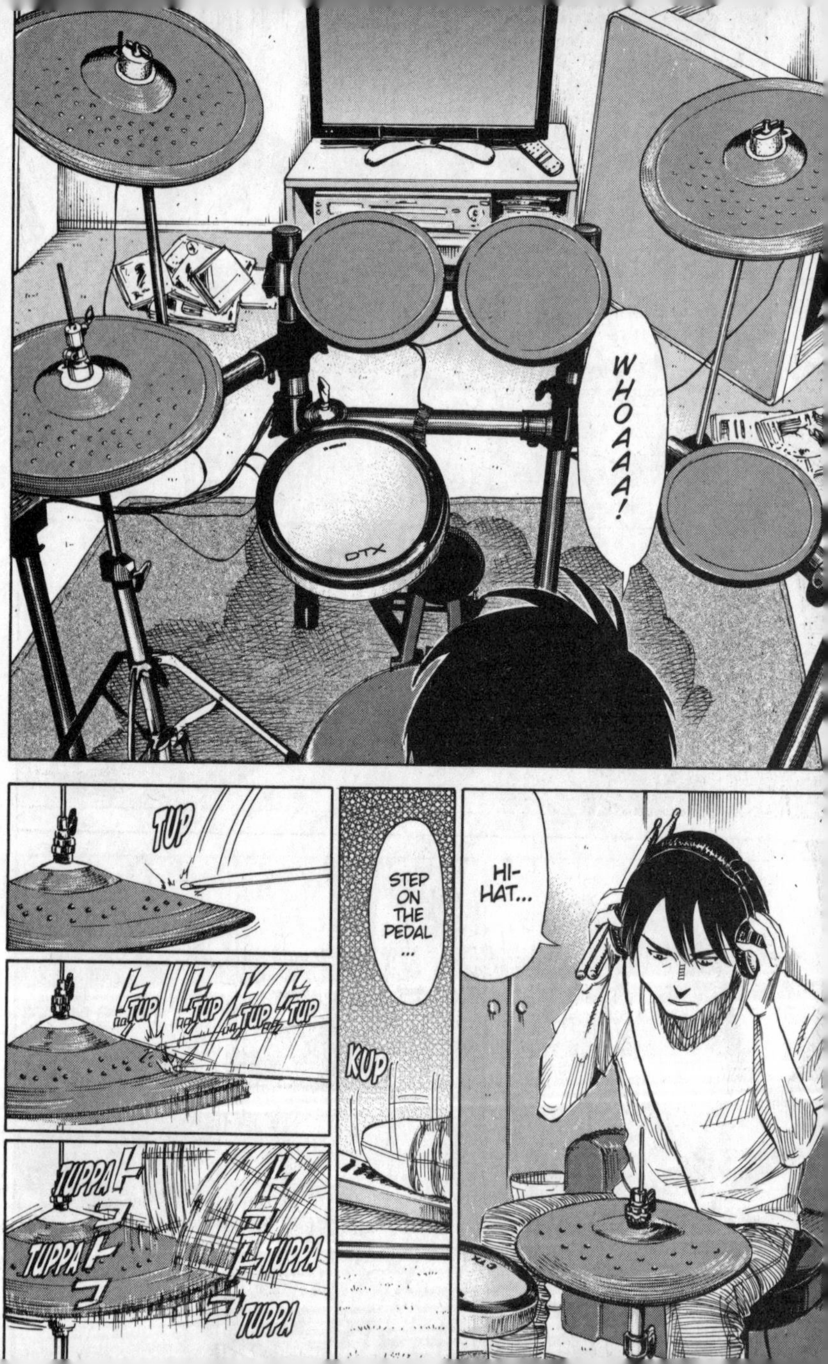
WHOAAA!
HI-HAT...
STEP ON THE PEDAL ...
KUP
TUP
TUP TUP TUP TUP
TUPPA TUPPA TUPPA TUPPA

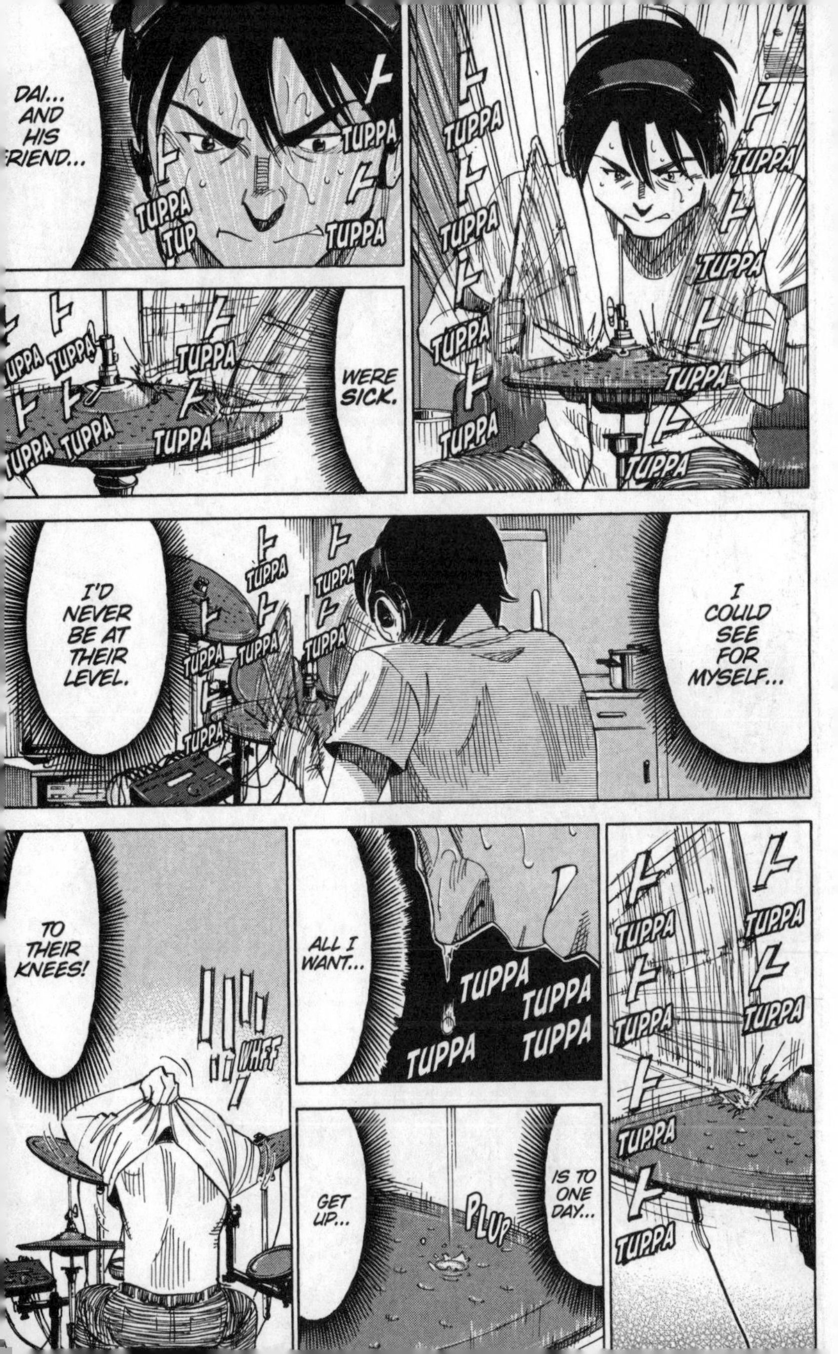

ト TUPPA ト TUPPA ト TUPPA
TUPPA ト TUPPA ト TUPPA
TUPPA ト TUPPA
DAI... AND HIS FRIEND...
ト TUPPA ト TUPPA TUP TUPPA
ト TUPPA TUPPA ト TUPPA TUPPA TUPPA TUPPA
WERE SICK.
I COULD SEE FOR MYSELF...
I'D NEVER BE AT THEIR LEVEL.
ト TUPPA ト TUPPA ト TUPPA ト TUPPA
ト TUPPA ト TUPPA ト TUPPA ト TUPPA ト TUPPA
ALL I WANT...
TUPPA TUPPA TUPPA TUPPA
IS TO ONE DAY...
GET UP...
PLUP
TO THEIR KNEES!
WHFF

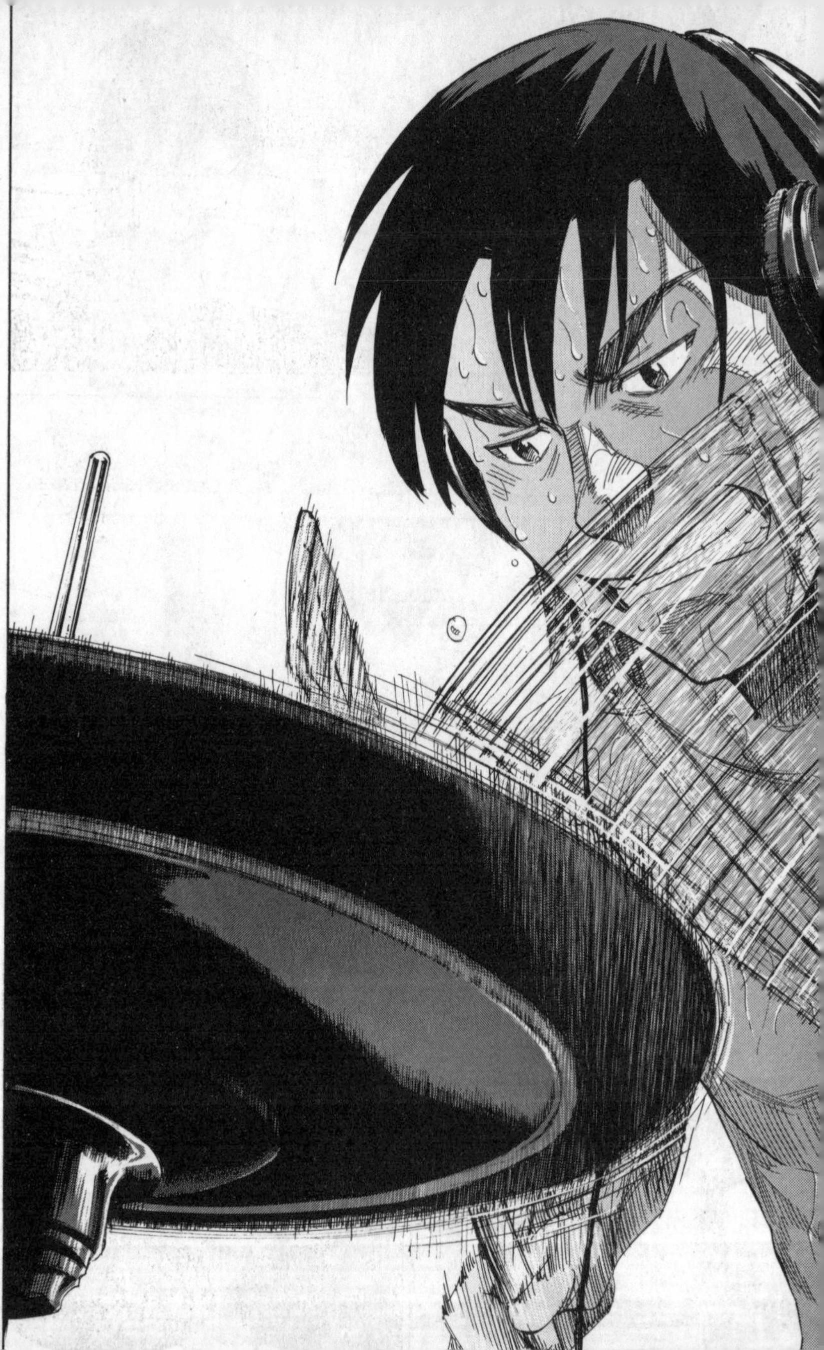

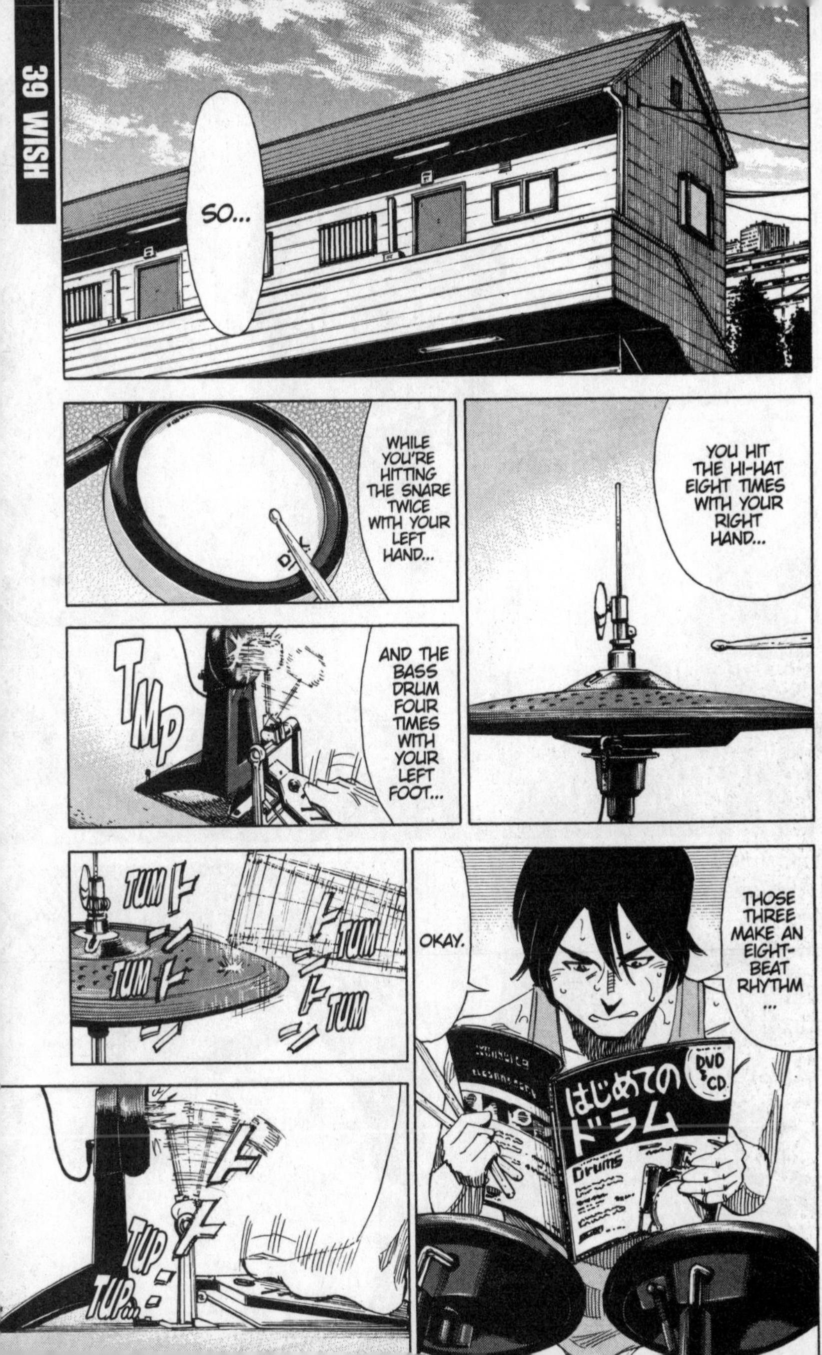
SO...
YOU HIT THE HI-HAT EIGHT TIMES WITH YOUR RIGHT HAND...
WHILE YOU'RE HITTING THE SNARE TWICE WITH YOUR LEFT HAND...
AND THE BASS DRUM FOUR TIMES WITH YOUR LEFT FOOT...
TMP
THOSE THREE MAKE AN EIGHT-BEAT RHYTHM ...
OKAY.
DVD & CD
はじめてのドラム
Drums
TUM
TUM
TUM
TUM
TUP
TUP...

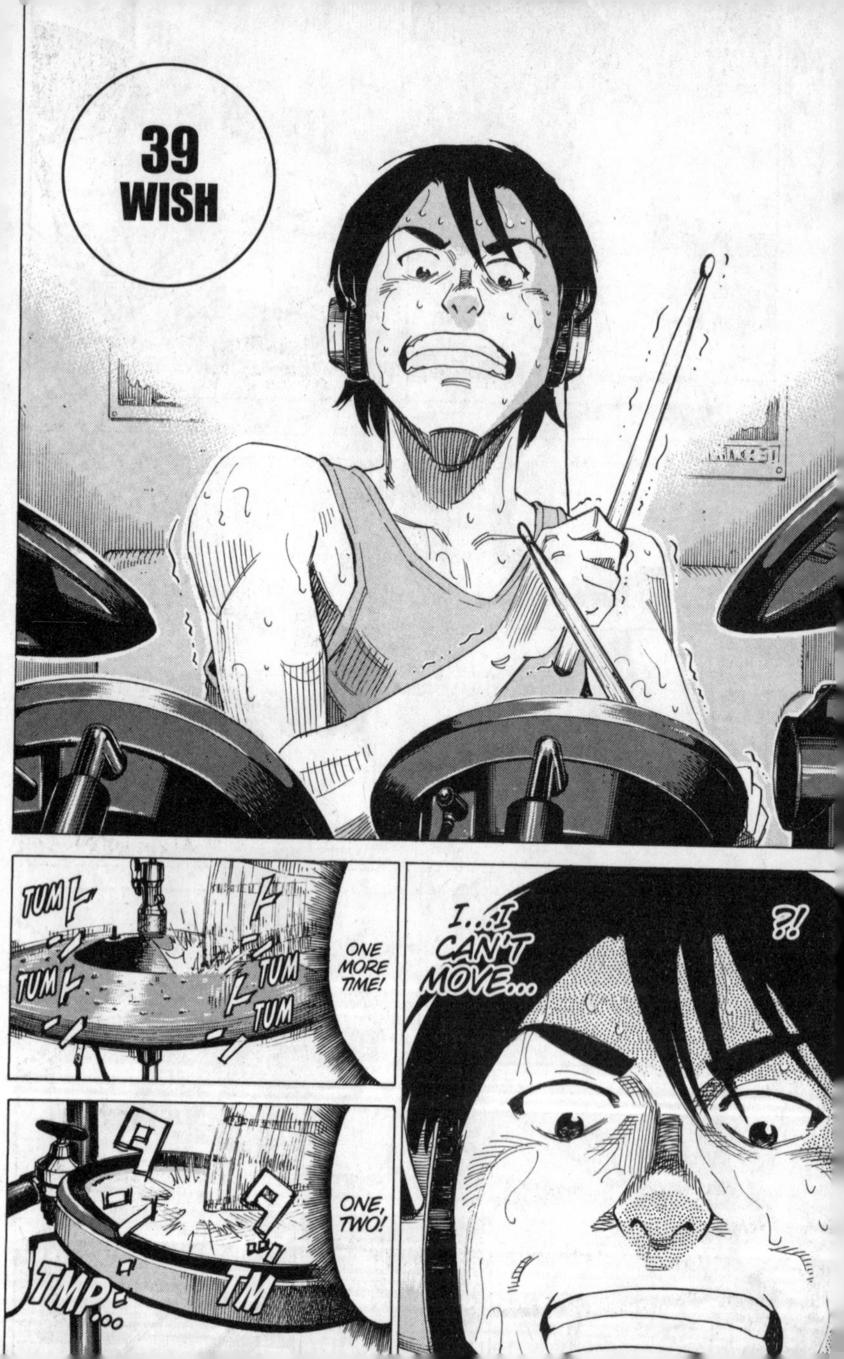
39
WISH
?!
I...I CAN'T MOVE...
ONE MORE TIME!
TUM
TUM
TUM
TUM
ONE, TWO!
TM
TMP...

WHY DO I FREEZE LIKE THAT?

NGH...

RRK

TUM TUM TUM TUM TUM

ONE MORE TIME, ONE MORE TIME!

GUH... DAMN IT!

UGH...

TUP TUP...

TP TP...

DTX

TUP

TUP...

TUP...

TUM TUM TUM TUM

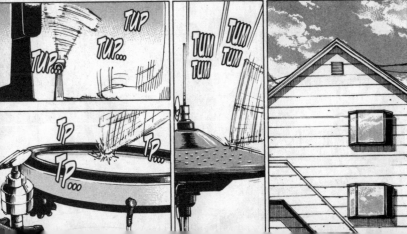

TP TP...

TP...

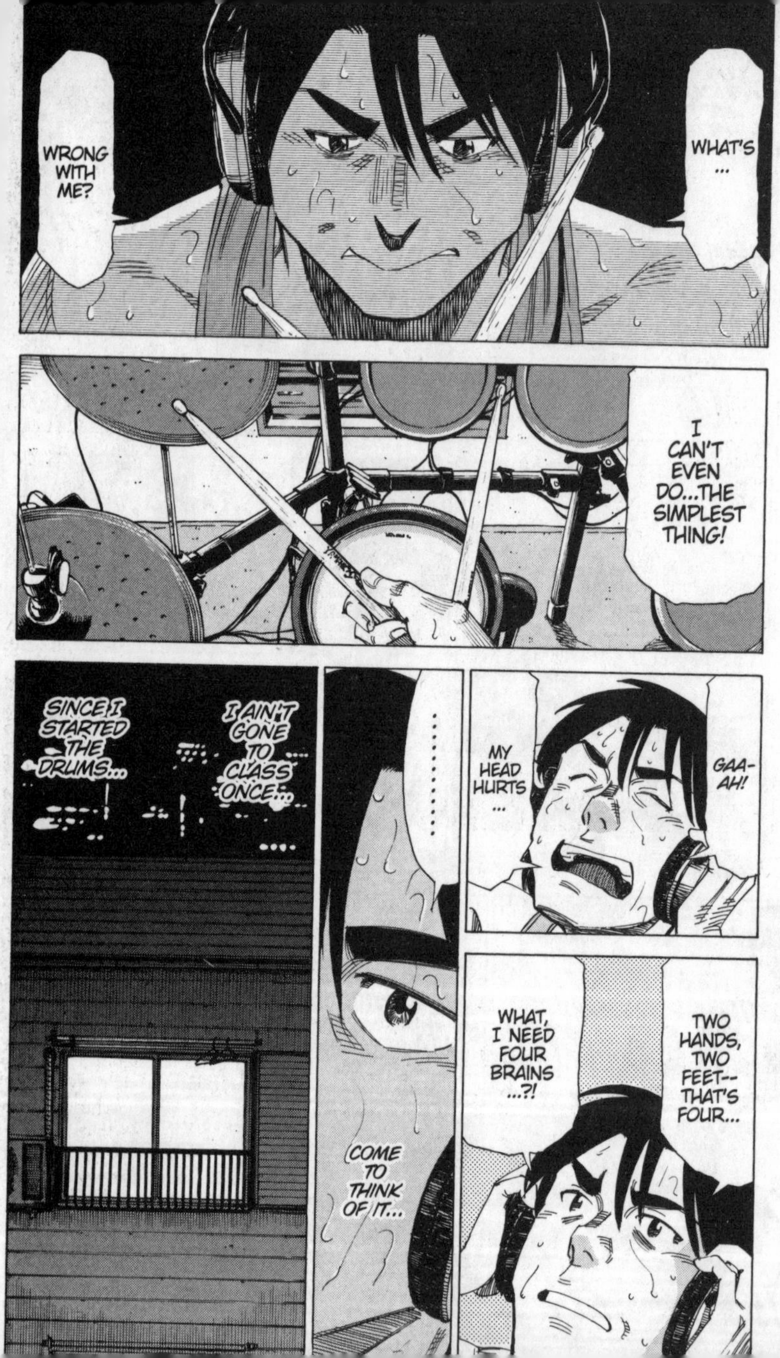
WHAT'S ...
WRONG WITH ME?
I CAN'T EVEN DO...THE SIMPLEST THING!
GAAH!
MY HEAD HURTS ...
TWO HANDS, TWO FEET-- THAT'S FOUR...
WHAT, I NEED FOUR BRAINS ...?!
......
COME TO THINK OF IT...
I AIN'T GONE TO CLASS ONCE...
SINCE I STARTED THE DRUMS...

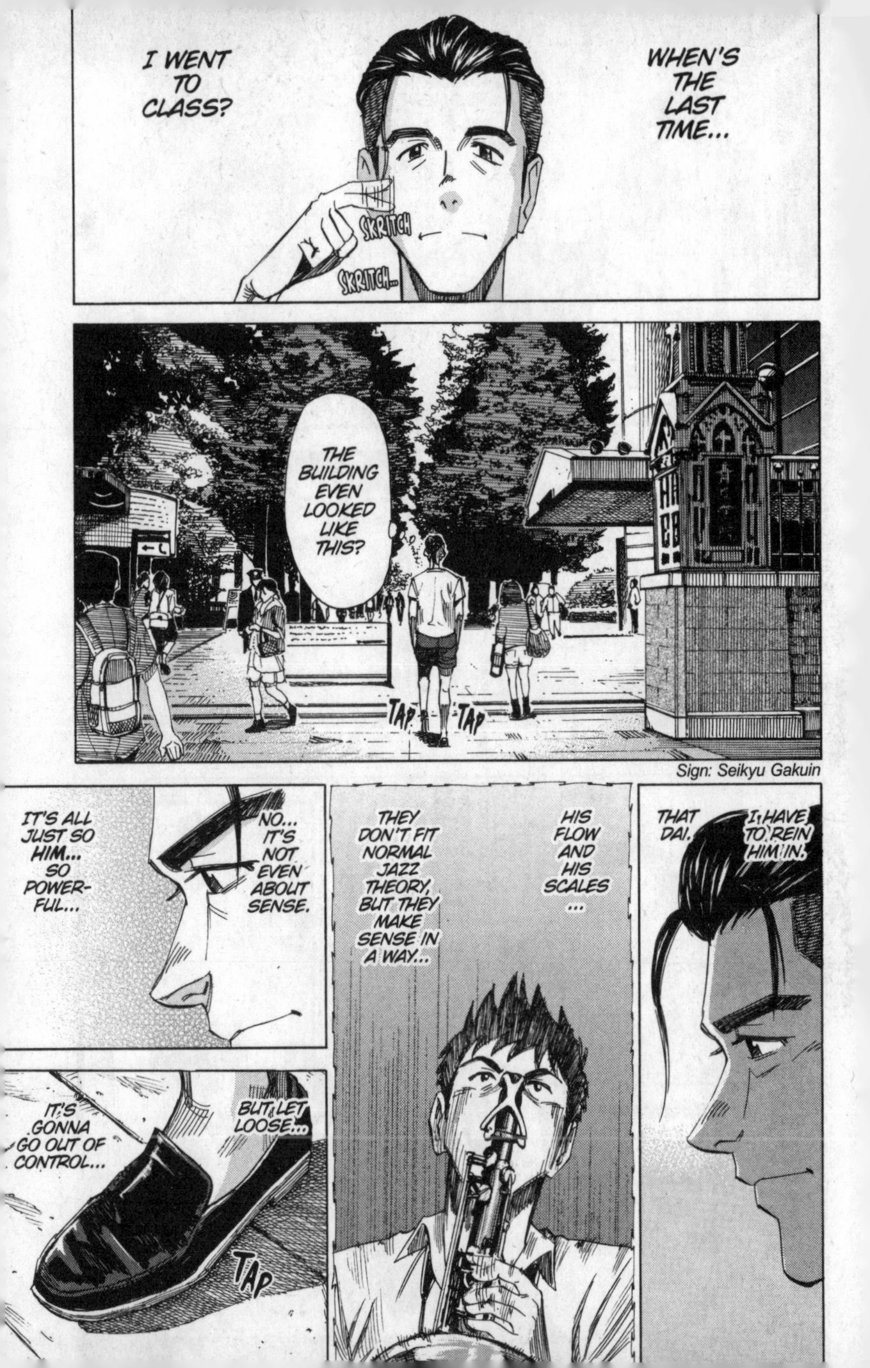
WHEN'S THE LAST TIME...
I WENT TO CLASS?
SKRITCH
SKRITCH...
THE BUILDING EVEN LOOKED LIKE THIS?
TAP TAP
I HAVE TO REIN HIM IN.
THAT DAI.
HIS FLOW AND HIS SCALES...
THEY DON'T FIT NORMAL JAZZ THEORY, BUT THEY MAKE SENSE IN A WAY...
NO... IT'S NOT EVEN ABOUT SENSE.
IT'S ALL JUST SO HIM... SO POWERFUL...
BUT LET LOOSE...
IT'S GONNA GO OUT OF CONTROL...
TAP
Sign: Seikyu Gakuin

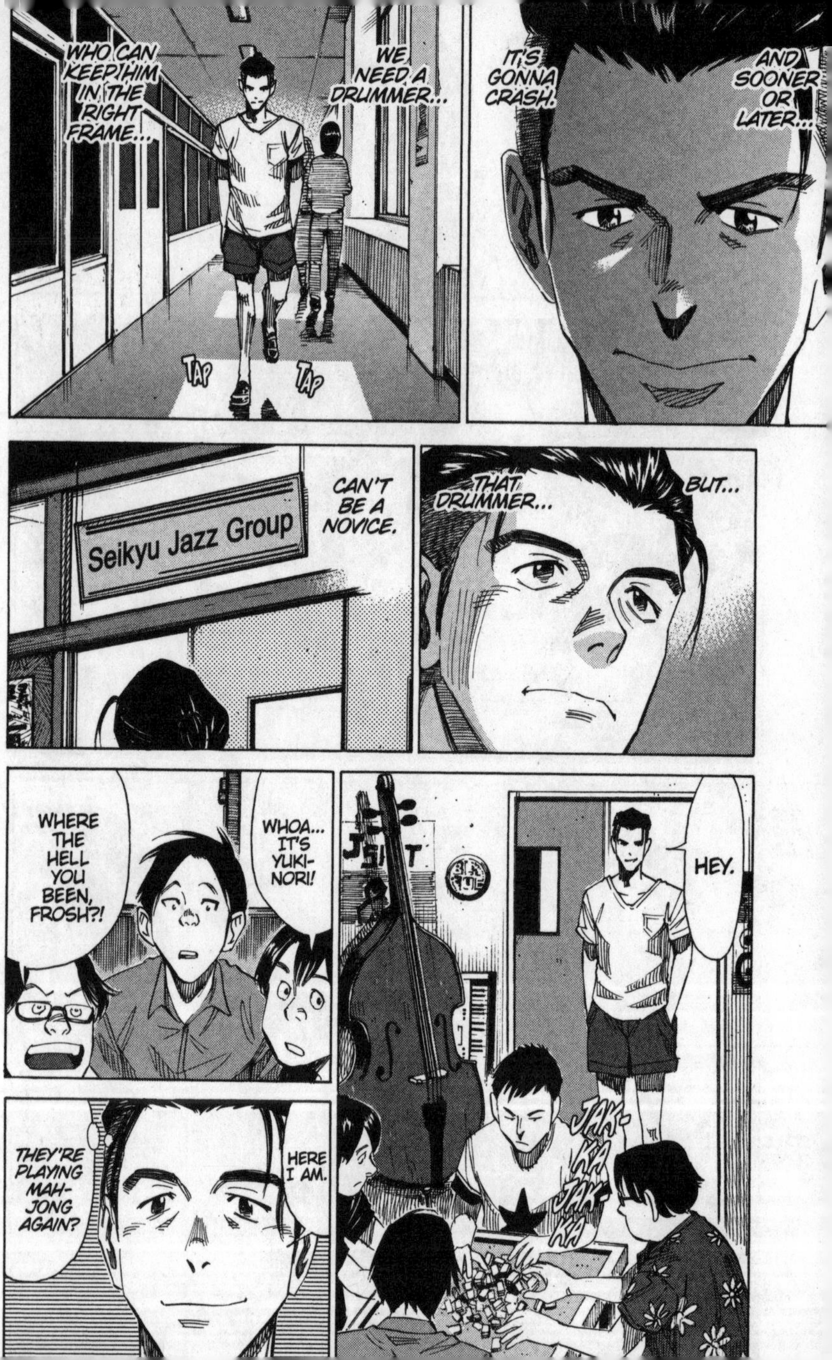
AND SOONER OR LATER...
IT'S GONNA CRASH.
WE NEED A DRUMMER...
WHO CAN KEEP HIM IN THE RIGHT FRAME...
TAP
TAP
BUT...
THAT DRUMMER...
CAN'T BE A NOVICE.
Seikyu Jazz Group
HEY.
JAK-KA JAK-KA
WHOA... IT'S YUKI-NORI!
WHERE THE HELL YOU BEEN, FROSH?!
HERE I AM.
THEY'RE PLAYING MAH-JONG AGAIN?

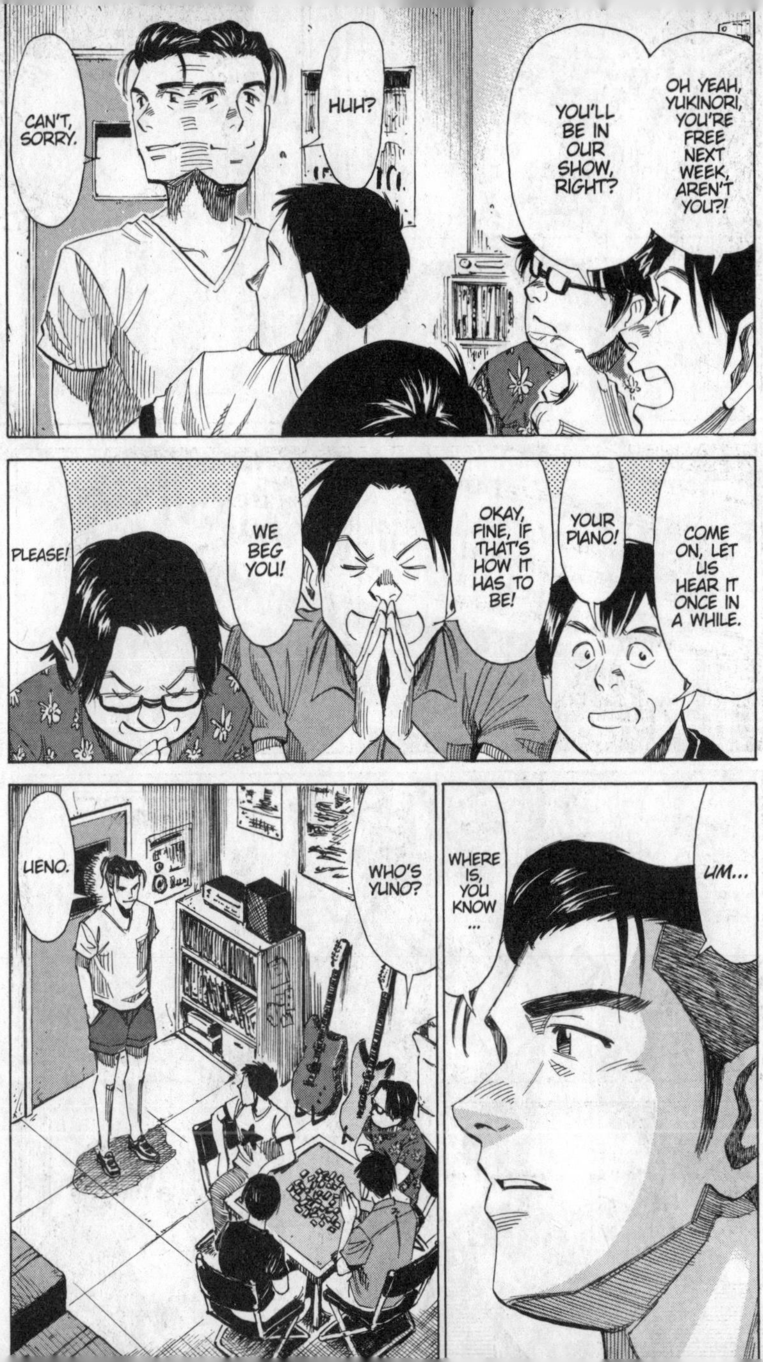
OH YEAH, YUKINORI, YOU'RE FREE NEXT WEEK, AREN'T YOU?!
YOU'LL BE IN OUR SHOW, RIGHT?
HUH?
CAN'T, SORRY.
COME ON, LET US HEAR IT ONCE IN A WHILE.
YOUR PIANO!
OKAY, FINE, IF THAT'S HOW IT HAS TO BE!
WE BEG YOU!
PLEASE!
UM...
WHERE IS, YOU KNOW ...
WHO'S YUNO?
UENO.

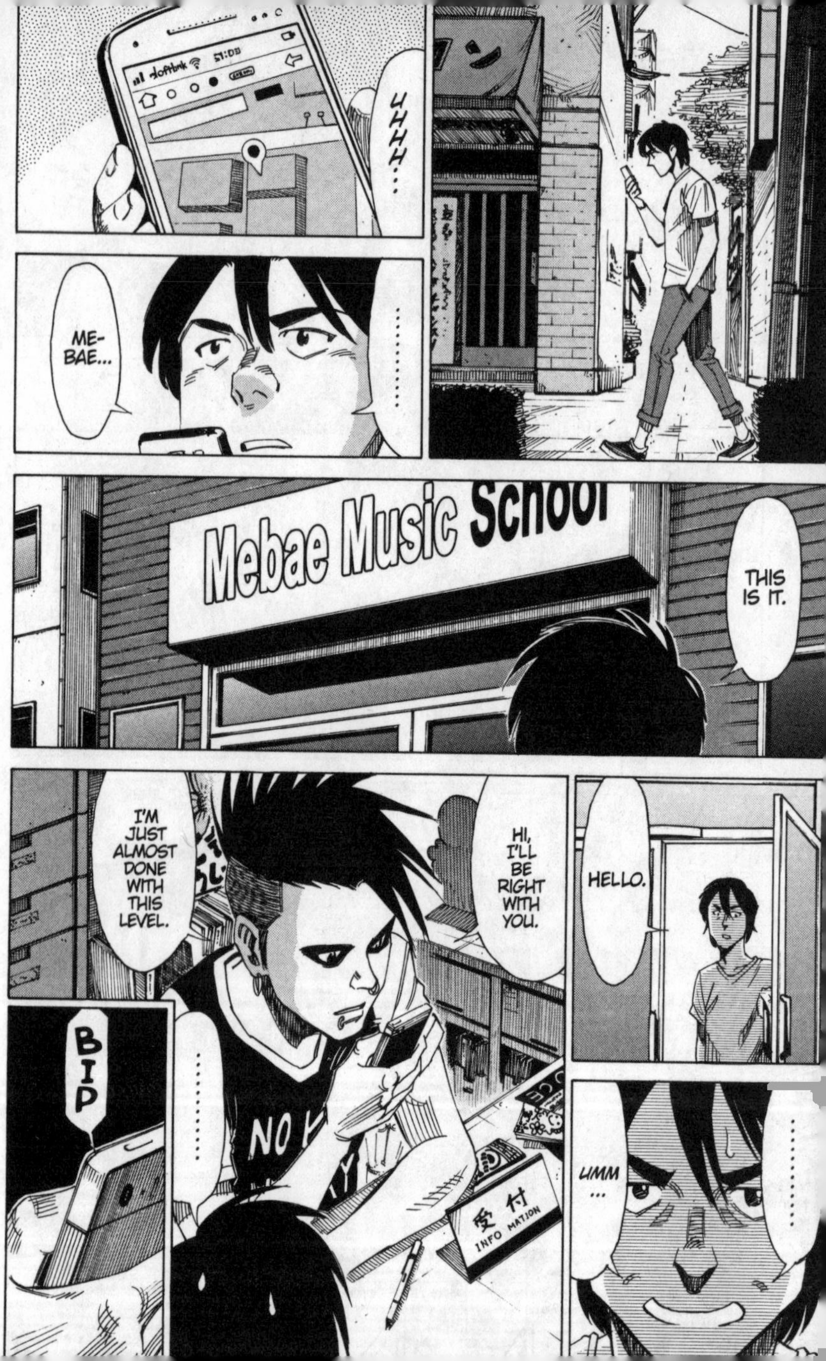
UHHHH...
......
ME-BAE...
Mebae Music School
THIS IS IT.
HELLO.
......
UMM...
HI, I'LL BE RIGHT WITH YOU.
I'M JUST ALMOST DONE WITH THIS LEVEL.
......
受付
INFO MATION
BIP

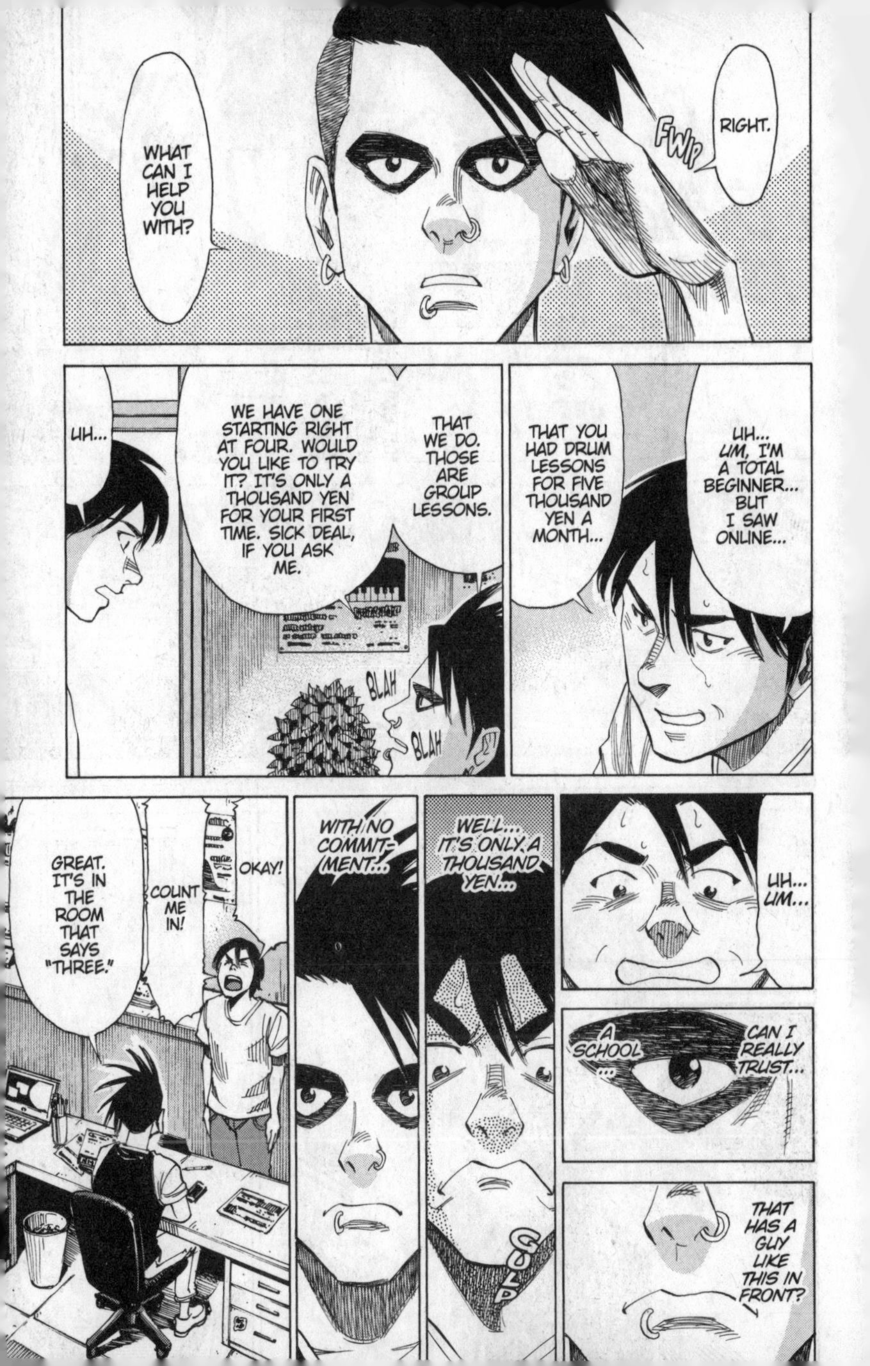
RIGHT.
FWIP
WHAT CAN I HELP YOU WITH?
UH... UM, I'M A TOTAL BEGINNER... BUT I SAW ONLINE...
THAT YOU HAD DRUM LESSONS FOR FIVE THOUSAND YEN A MONTH...
THAT WE DO. THOSE ARE GROUP LESSONS.
WE HAVE ONE STARTING RIGHT AT FOUR. WOULD YOU LIKE TO TRY IT? IT'S ONLY A THOUSAND YEN FOR YOUR FIRST TIME. SICK DEAL, IF YOU ASK ME.
BLAH
BLAH
UH...
UH... UM...
CAN I REALLY TRUST...
A SCHOOL...
THAT HAS A GUY LIKE THIS IN FRONT?
WELL... IT'S ONLY A THOUSAND YEN...
GULP
WITH NO COMMIT-MENT...
OKAY!
COUNT ME IN!
GREAT. IT'S IN THE ROOM THAT SAYS "THREE."

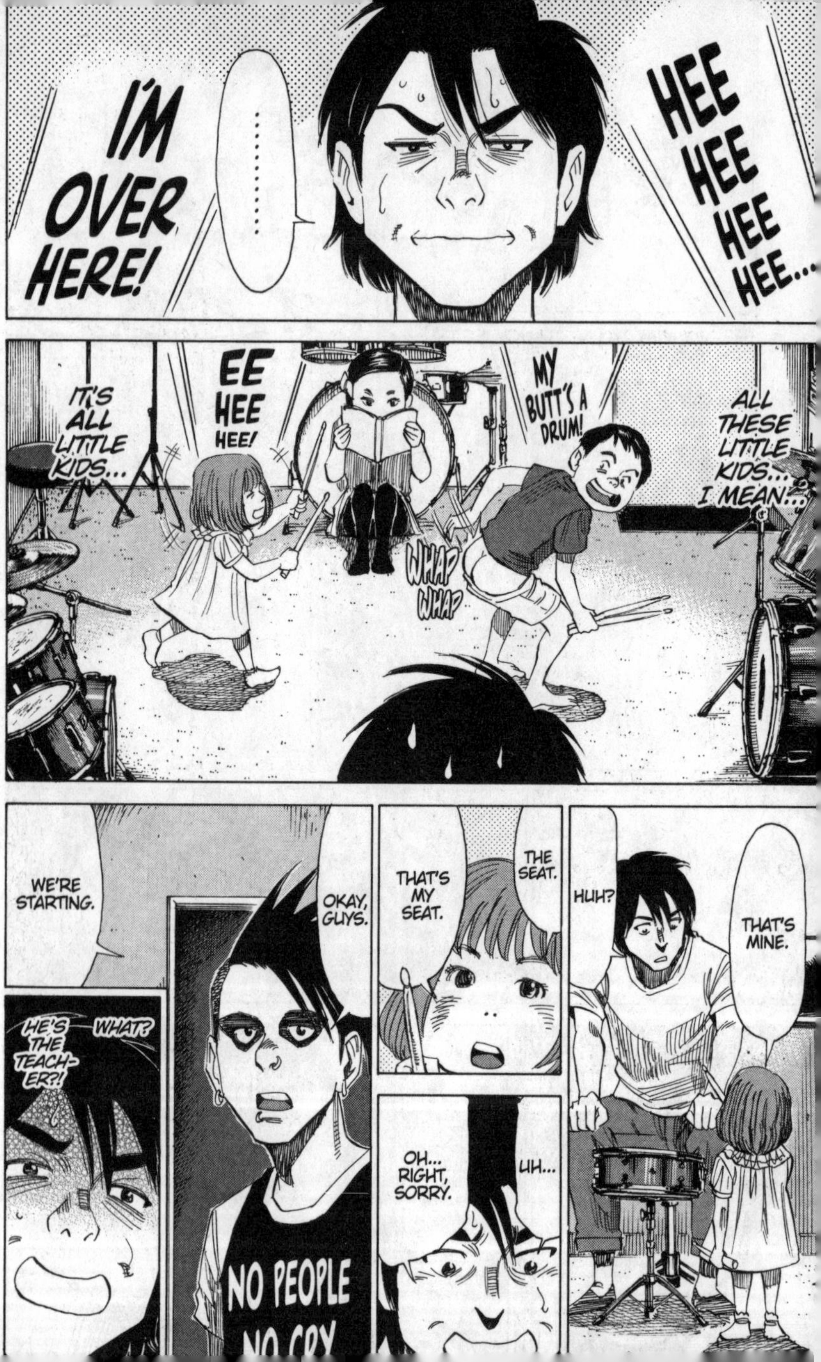
HEE HEE HEE HEE...
......
I'M OVER HERE!
ALL THESE LITTLE KIDS... I MEAN...
MY BUTT'S A DRUM!
WHAP WHAP
EE HEE HEE!
IT'S ALL LITTLE KIDS...
THAT'S MINE.
HUH?
THE SEAT.
THAT'S MY SEAT.
UH...
OH... RIGHT, SORRY.
OKAY, GUYS.
WE'RE STARTING.
NO PEOPLE
WHAT?
HE'S THE TEACHER?!

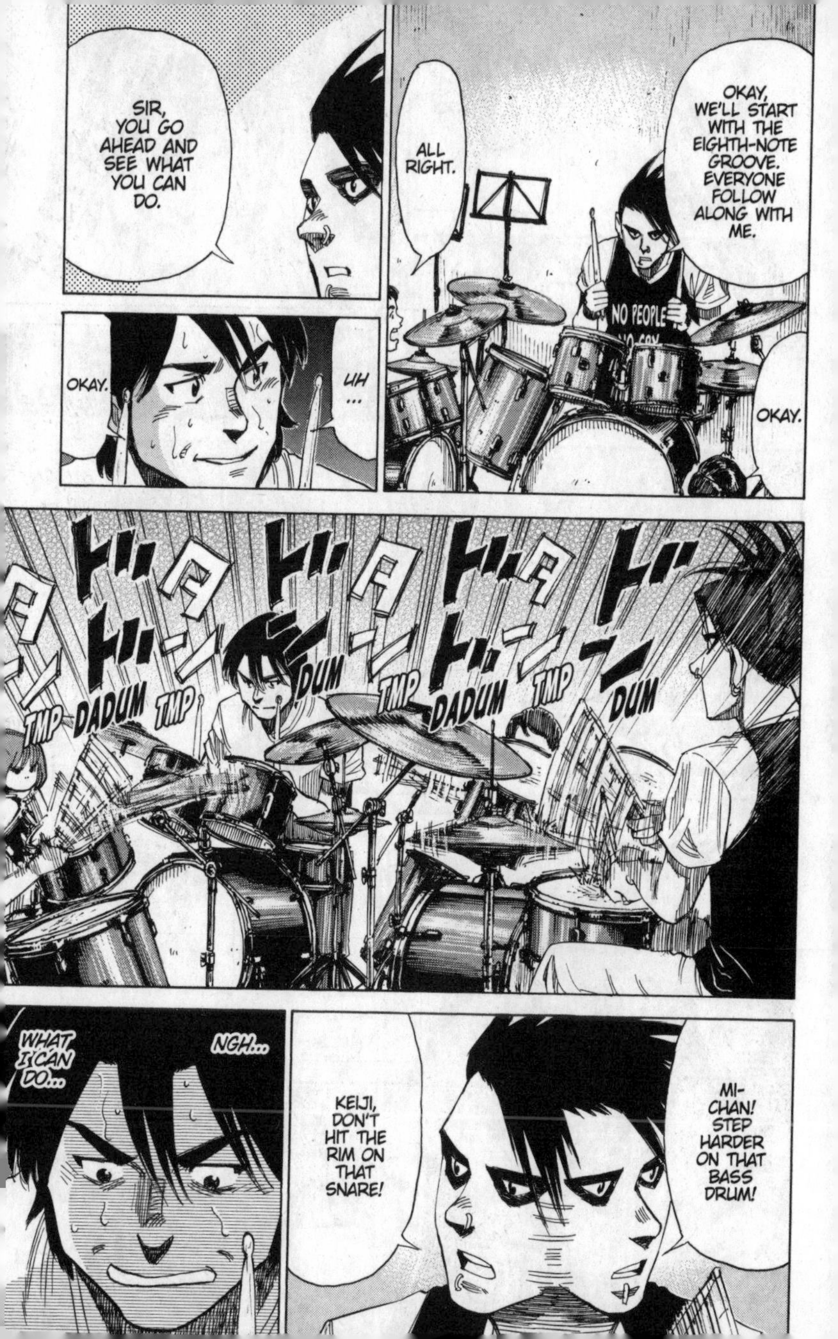
OKAY, WE'LL START WITH THE EIGHTH-NOTE GROOVE. EVERYONE FOLLOW ALONG WITH ME.
ALL RIGHT.
NO PEOPLE
OKAY.
SIR, YOU GO AHEAD AND SEE WHAT YOU CAN DO.
UH ...
OKAY.
DUM
TMP
DADUM
TMP
DUM
TMP
DADUM
TMP
MI-CHAN! STEP HARDER ON THAT BASS DRUM!
KEIJI, DON'T HIT THE RIM ON THAT SNARE!
NGH...
WHAT I CAN DO...

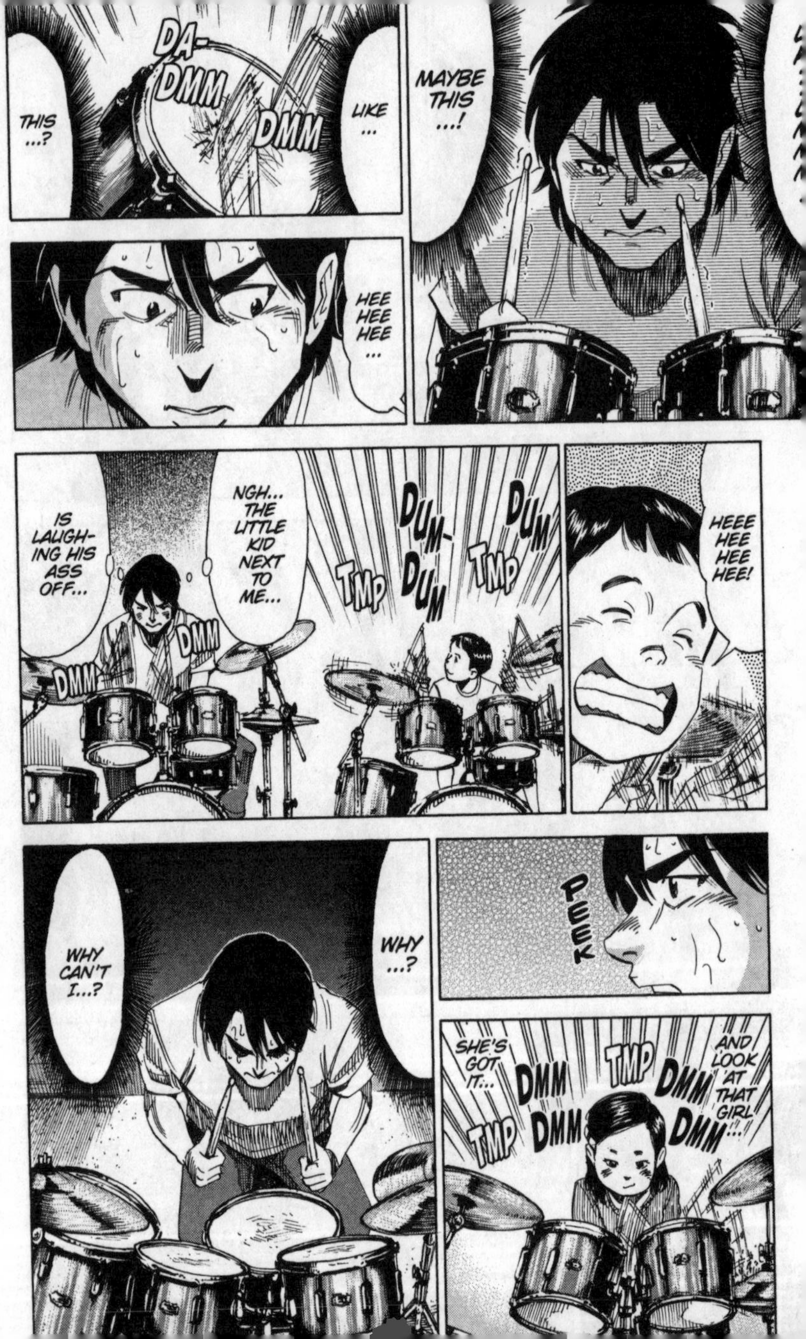
MAYBE THIS ...!
LIKE ...
DMM
DA-DMM
THIS ...?
HEE HEE HEE ...
HEEE HEE HEE HEE!
DUM
DUM-DUM
TMP
TMP
NGH... THE LITTLE KID NEXT TO ME...
IS LAUGHING HIS ASS OFF...
DMM
DMM
PEEK
AND LOOK AT THAT GIRL!!...
DMM
DMM
TMP
DMM
DMM
TMP
SHE'S GOT IT...
WHY ...?
WHY CAN'T I...?

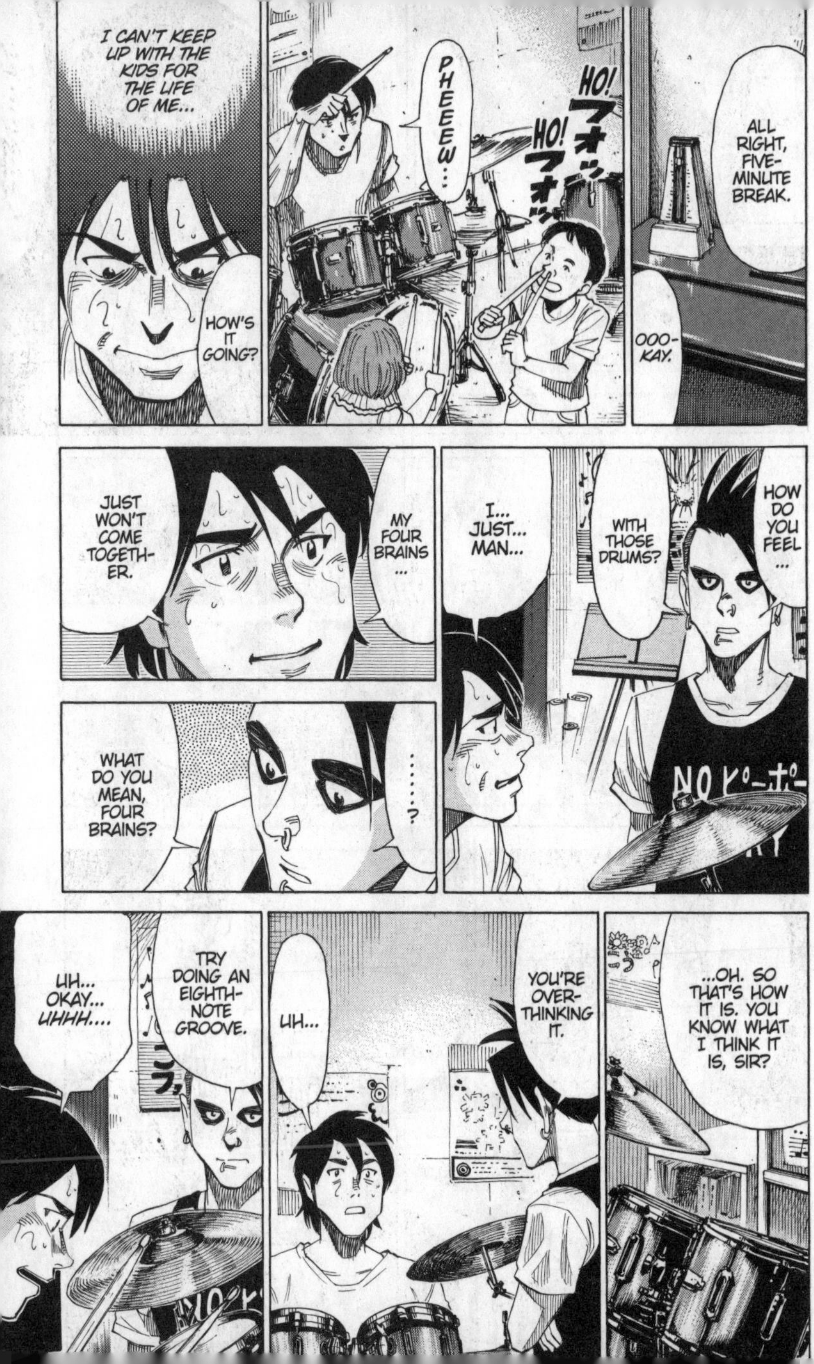
ALL RIGHT, FIVE-MINUTE BREAK.
OOO-KAY.
HO! フォッ
HO! フォッ
PHEEEW...
I CAN'T KEEP UP WITH THE KIDS FOR THE LIFE OF ME...
HOW'S IT GOING?
HOW DO YOU FEEL ...
WITH THOSE DRUMS?
I... JUST... MAN...
MY FOUR BRAINS ...
JUST WON'T COME TOGETH-ER.
......?
WHAT DO YOU MEAN, FOUR BRAINS?
...OH. SO THAT'S HOW IT IS. YOU KNOW WHAT I THINK IT IS, SIR?
YOU'RE OVER-THINKING IT.
UH...
TRY DOING AN EIGHTH-NOTE GROOVE.
UH... OKAY... UHHH....

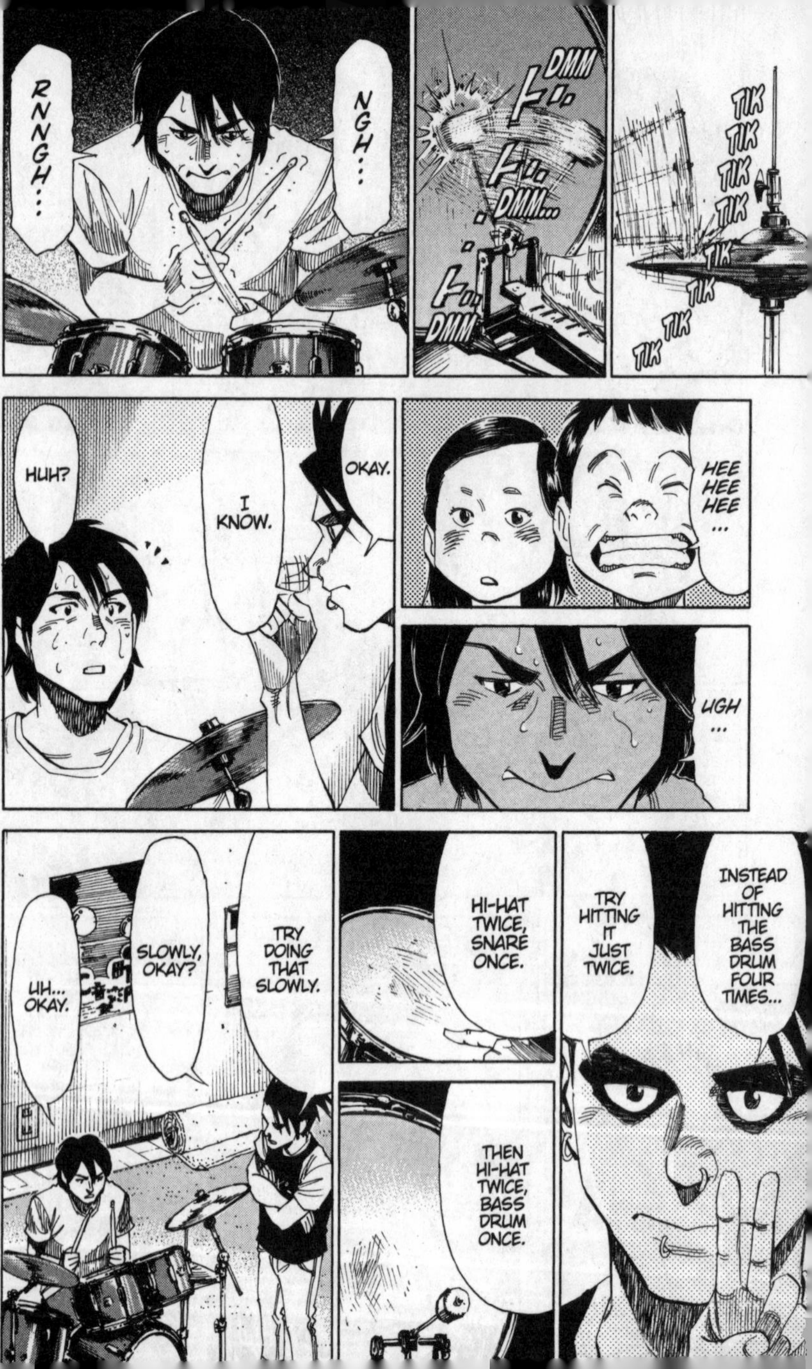
TIK TIK TIK TIK TIK TIK TIK TIK
ド DMM
ド DMM...
ド DMM
NGH...
RNNGH...
HEE HEE HEE...
UGH...
OKAY.
I KNOW.
HUH?
INSTEAD OF HITTING THE BASS DRUM FOUR TIMES...
TRY HITTING IT JUST TWICE.
HI-HAT TWICE, SNARE ONCE.
THEN HI-HAT TWICE, BASS DRUM ONCE.
TRY DOING THAT SLOWLY.
SLOWLY, OKAY?
UH... OKAY.

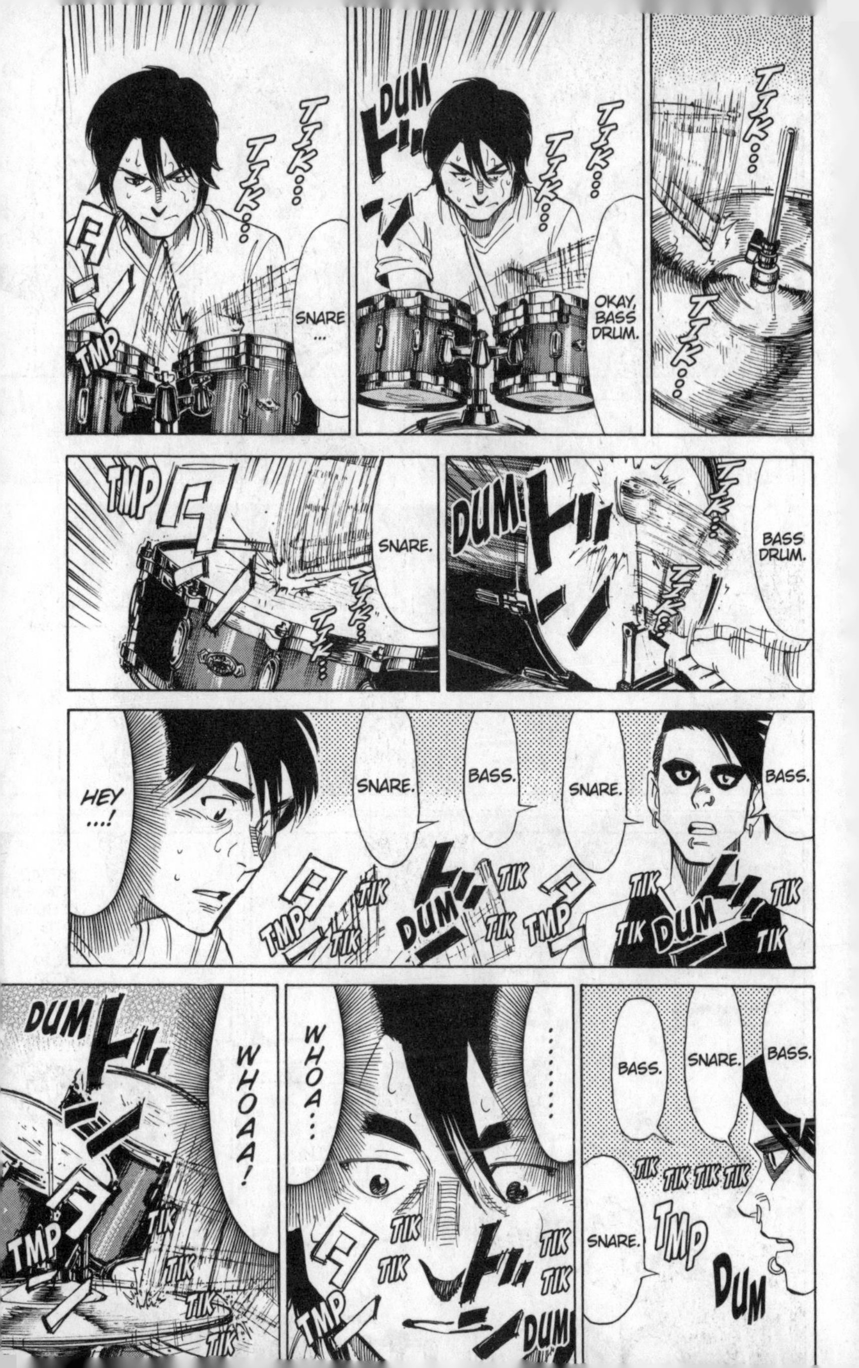
TIK... TIK...
TIK... TIK...
DUM
OKAY, BASS DRUM.
TIK... TIK...
SNARE...
TMP
BASS DRUM.
TIK... TIK...
DUM
SNARE.
TIK... TIK...
TMP
BASS.
SNARE.
BASS.
SNARE.
TIK TIK DUM TIK TIK
TMP TIK TIK DUM TIK TIK
TMP TIK TIK
HEY ...!
BASS.
SNARE.
BASS.
SNARE.
TIK TIK TIK TIK
TMP
DUM
......
WHOA...
TIK TIK TIK TIK TIK
TMP
DUM
WHOAA!
DUM
TMP
TIK TIK TIK TIK

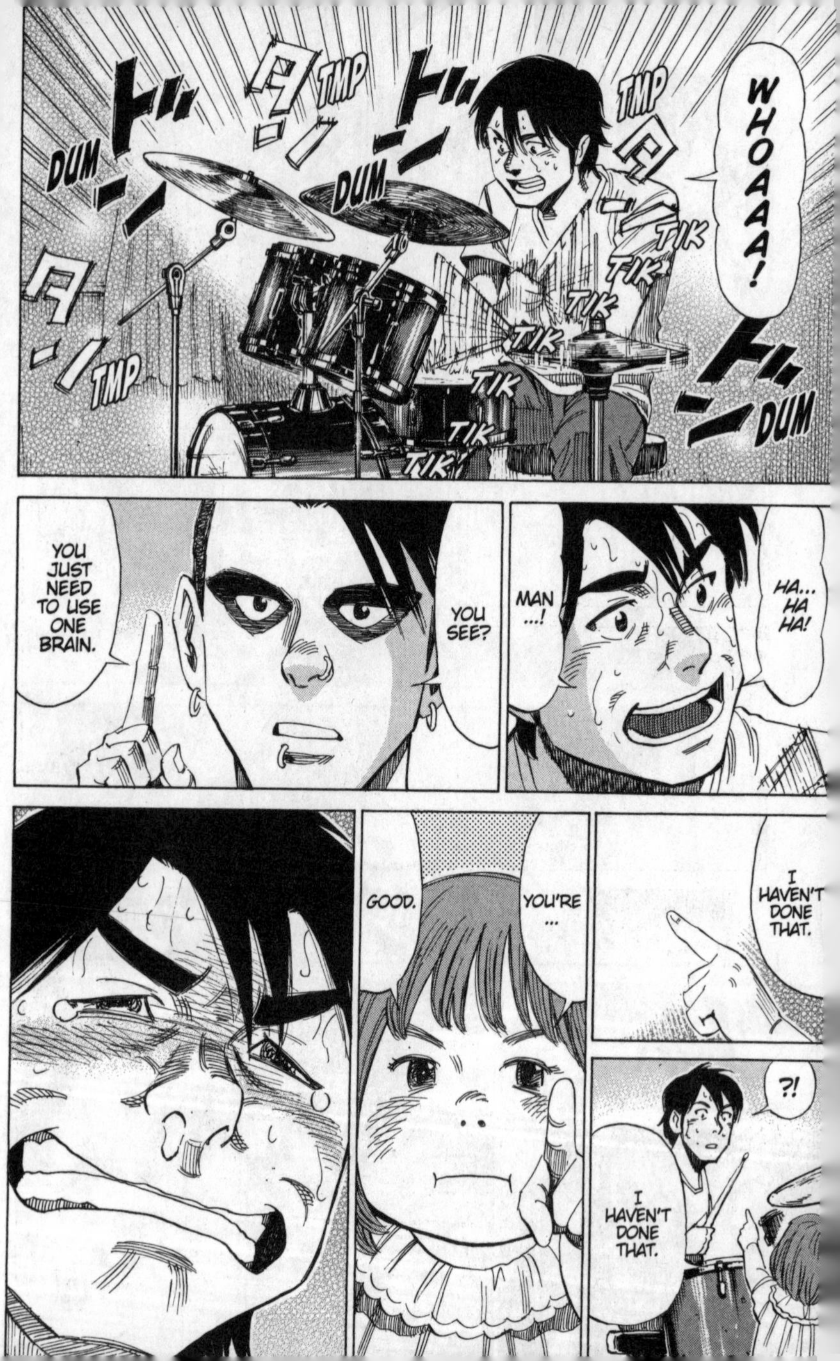
WHOAAAA!
TMP
DUM
TIK TIK TIK TIK TIK TIK TIK
TMP
DUM
DUM
TMP
HA... HA HA!
MAN ...!
YOU SEE?
YOU JUST NEED TO USE ONE BRAIN.
I HAVEN'T DONE THAT.
?!
I HAVEN'T DONE THAT.
YOU'RE ...
GOOD.

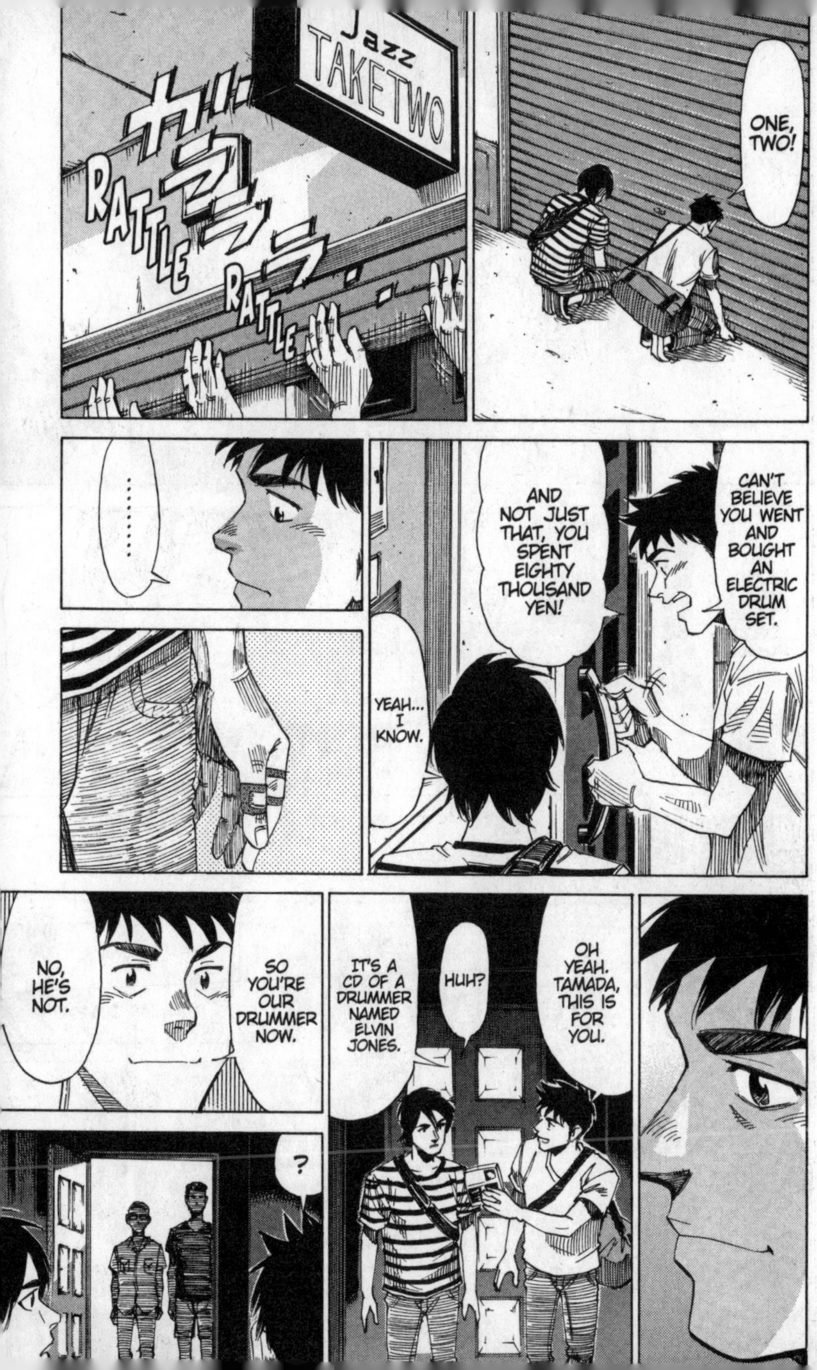
ONE, TWO!
Jazz TAKETWO
RATTLE
RATTLE
CAN'T BELIEVE YOU WENT AND BOUGHT AN ELECTRIC DRUM SET.
AND NOT JUST THAT, YOU SPENT EIGHTY THOUSAND YEN!
YEAH... I KNOW.
......
OH YEAH. TAMADA, THIS IS FOR YOU.
HUH?
IT'S A CD OF A DRUMMER NAMED ELVIN JONES.
SO YOU'RE OUR DRUMMER NOW.
NO, HE'S NOT.
?

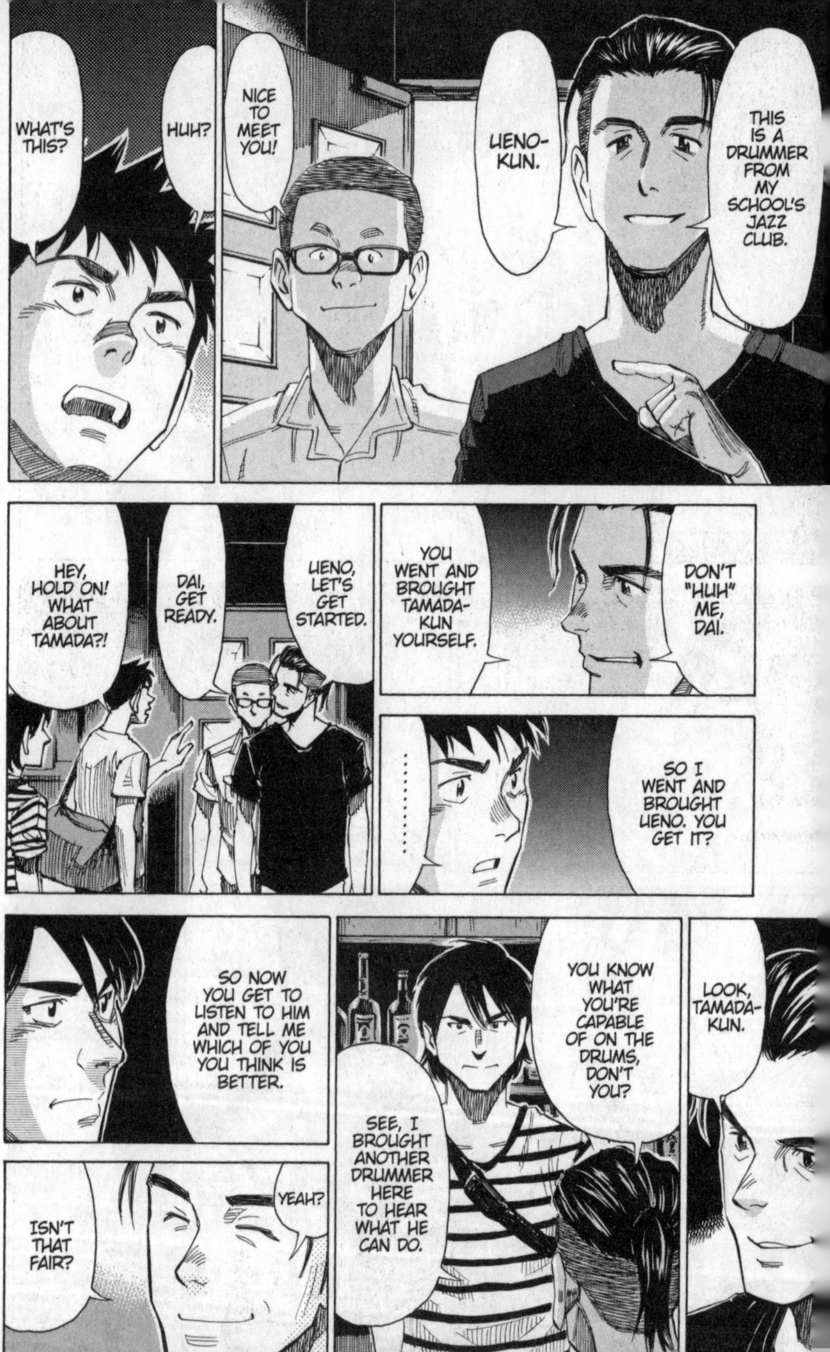
THIS IS A DRUMMER FROM MY SCHOOL'S JAZZ CLUB.
UENO-KUN.
NICE TO MEET YOU!
HUH?
WHAT'S THIS?
DON'T "HUH" ME, DAI.
YOU WENT AND BROUGHT TAMADA-KUN YOURSELF.
SO I WENT AND BROUGHT UENO. YOU GET IT?
......
UENO, LET'S GET STARTED.
DAI, GET READY.
HEY, HOLD ON! WHAT ABOUT TAMADA?!
LOOK, TAMADA-KUN.
YOU KNOW WHAT YOU'RE CAPABLE OF ON THE DRUMS, DON'T YOU?
SEE, I BROUGHT ANOTHER DRUMMER HERE TO HEAR WHAT HE CAN DO.
SO NOW YOU GET TO LISTEN TO HIM AND TELL ME WHICH OF YOU YOU THINK IS BETTER.
YEAH?
ISN'T THAT FAIR?

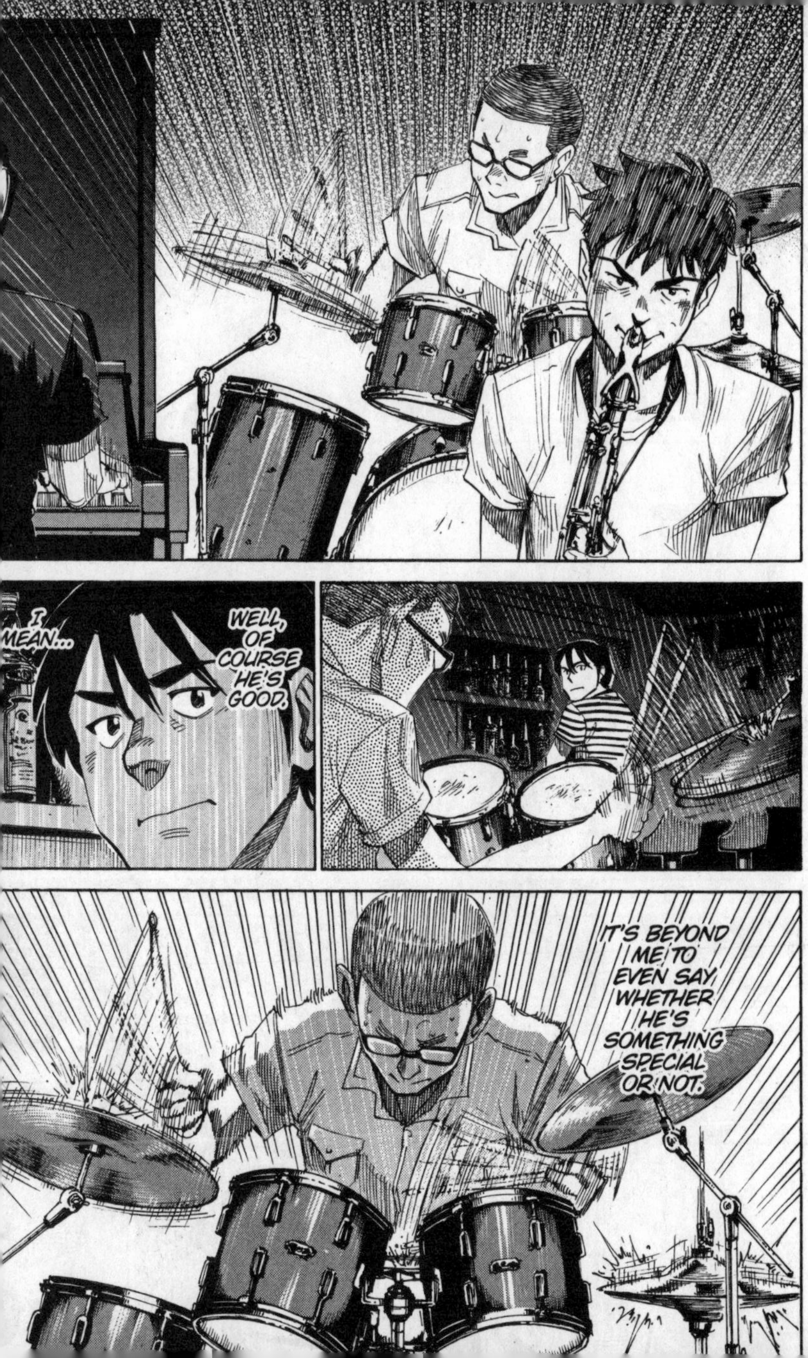
WELL, OF COURSE HE'S GOOD.
I MEAN...
IT'S BEYOND ME TO EVEN SAY WHETHER HE'S SOMETHING SPECIAL OR NOT.

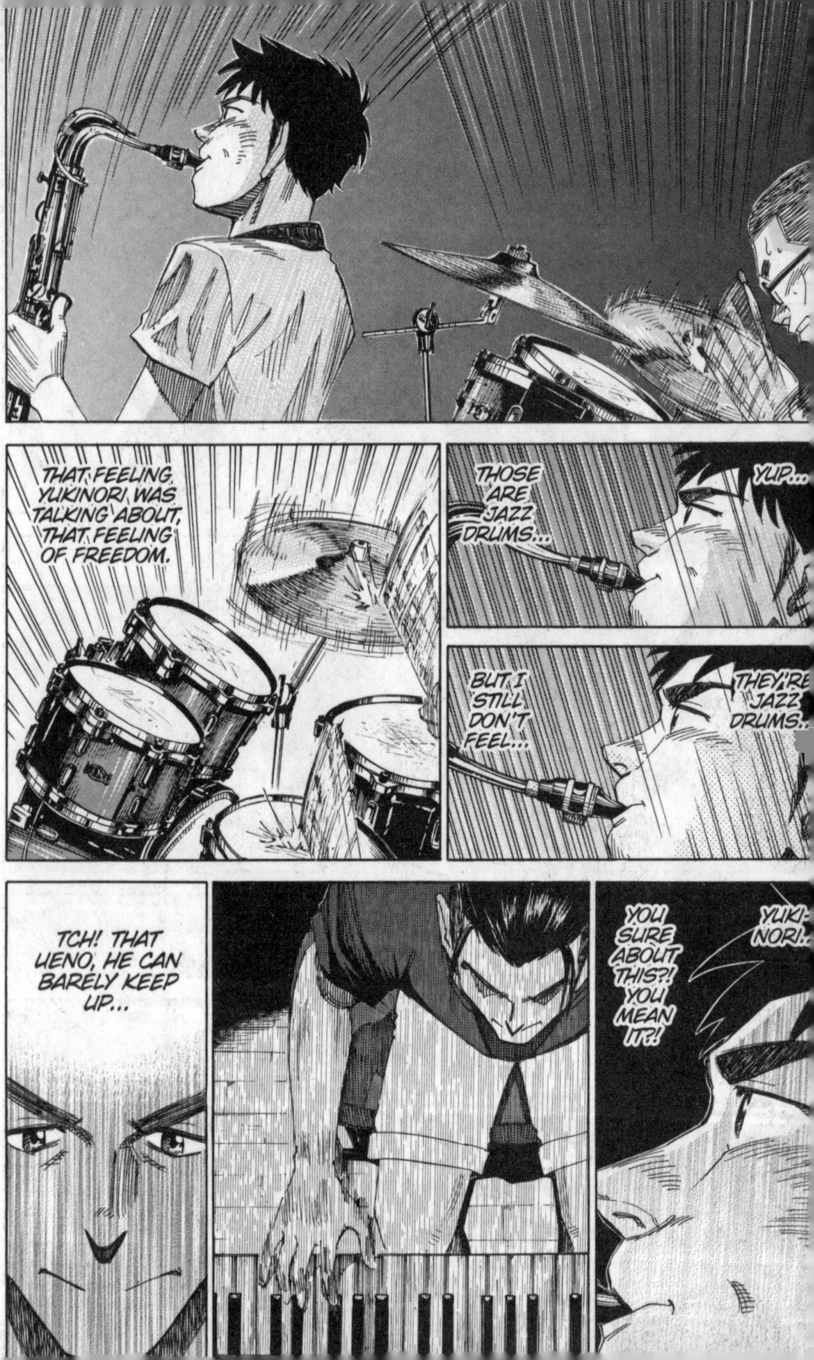

YUP...
THOSE ARE JAZZ DRUMS...
THEY'RE JAZZ DRUMS...
BUT I STILL DON'T FEEL...
THAT FEELING YUKINORI WAS TALKING ABOUT, THAT FEELING OF FREEDOM.
YUKI-NORI...
YOU SURE ABOUT THIS?! YOU MEAN IT?!
TCH! THAT UENO, HE CAN BARELY KEEP UP...

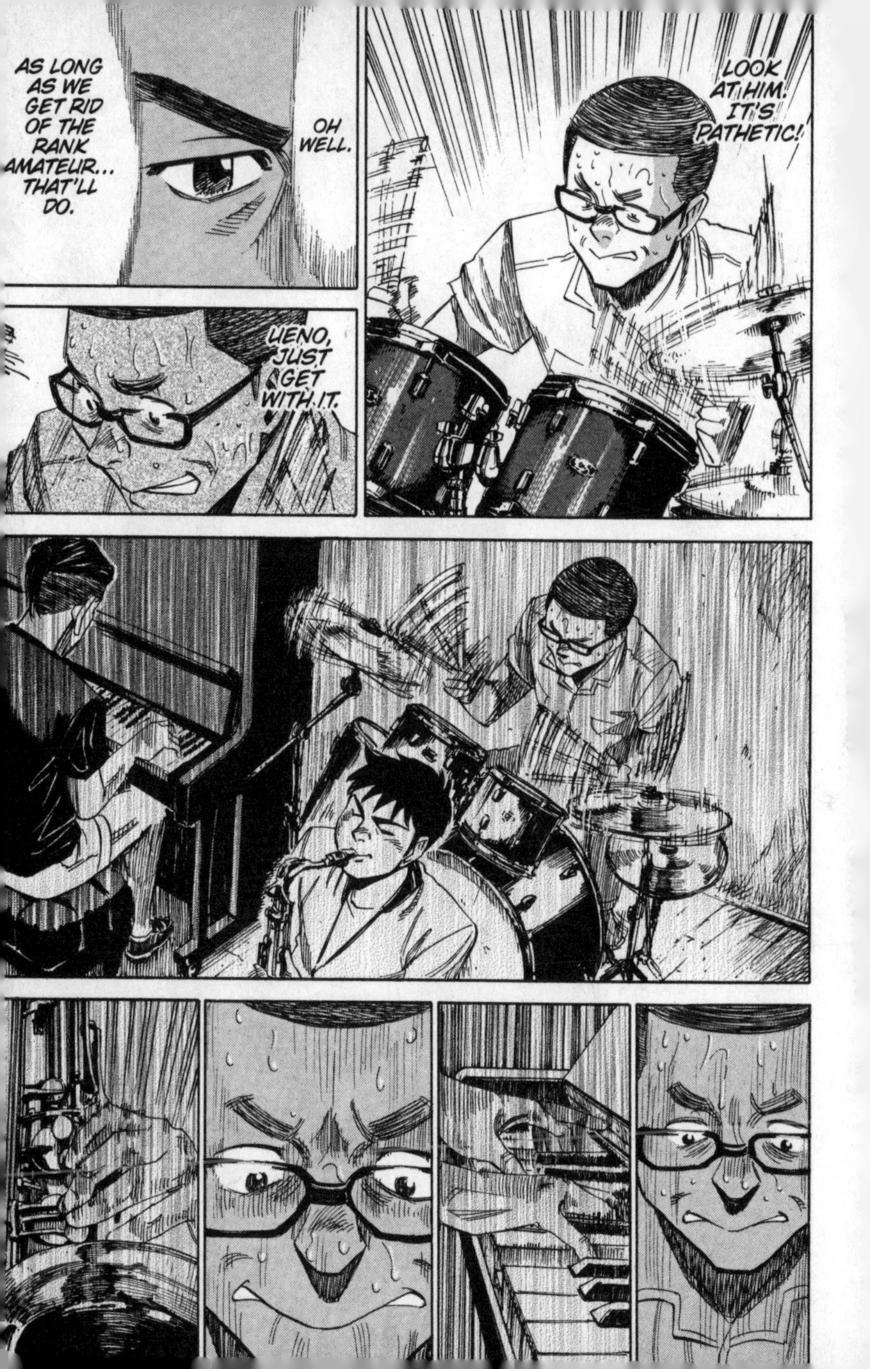
LOOK AT HIM. IT'S PATHETIC!
OH WELL.
AS LONG AS WE GET RID OF THE RANK AMATEUR... THAT'LL DO.
UENO, JUST GET WITH IT.

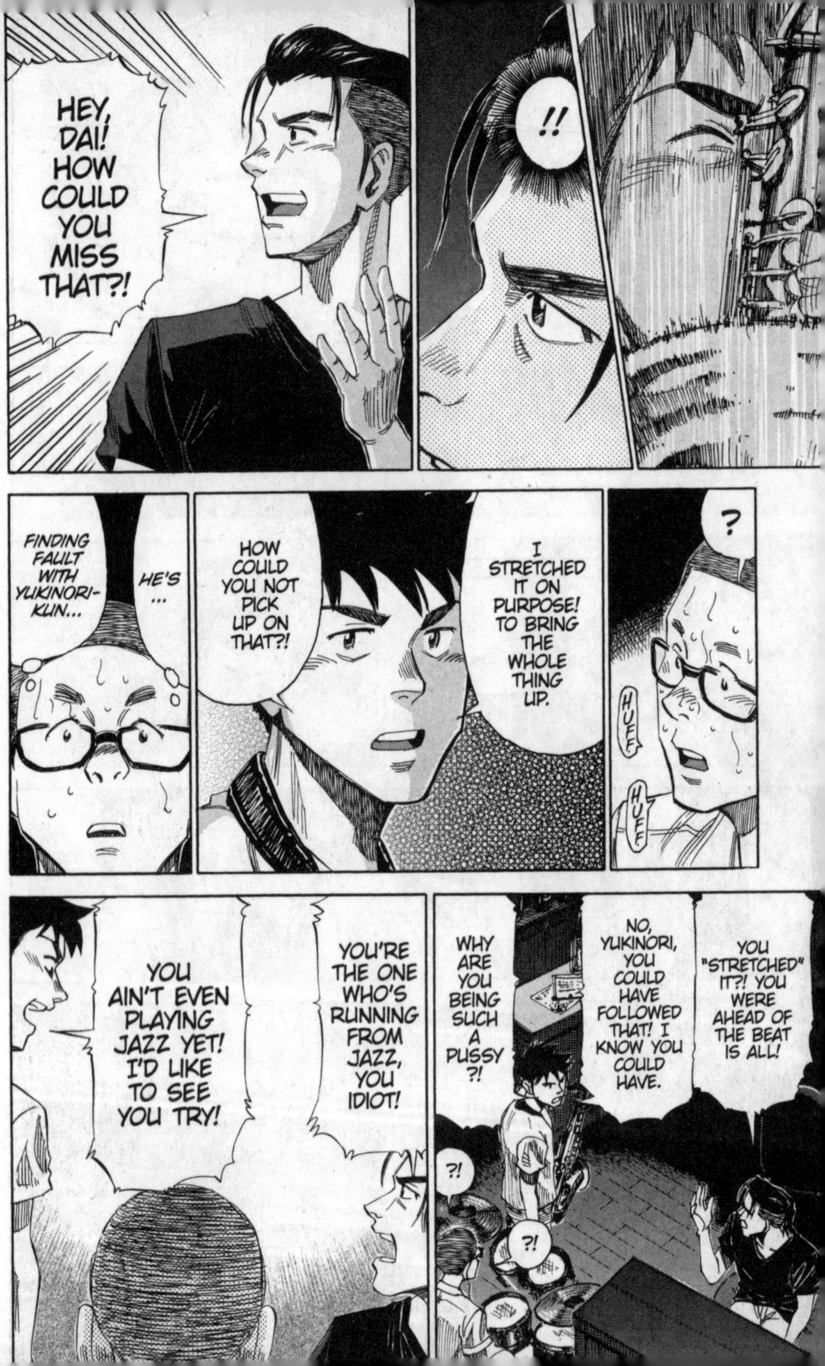
!!
HEY, DAI! HOW COULD YOU MISS THAT?!
?
HUFF.
HUFF.
I STRETCHED IT ON PURPOSE! TO BRING THE WHOLE THING UP.
HOW COULD YOU NOT PICK UP ON THAT?!
HE'S...
FINDING FAULT WITH YUKINORI-KUN...
YOU "STRETCHED" IT?! YOU WERE AHEAD OF THE BEAT IS ALL!
NO, YUKINORI, YOU COULD HAVE FOLLOWED THAT! I KNOW YOU COULD HAVE.
WHY ARE YOU BEING SUCH A PUSSY?!
?!
?!
YOU'RE THE ONE WHO'S RUNNING FROM JAZZ, YOU IDIOT!
YOU AIN'T EVEN PLAYING JAZZ YET! I'D LIKE TO SEE YOU TRY!

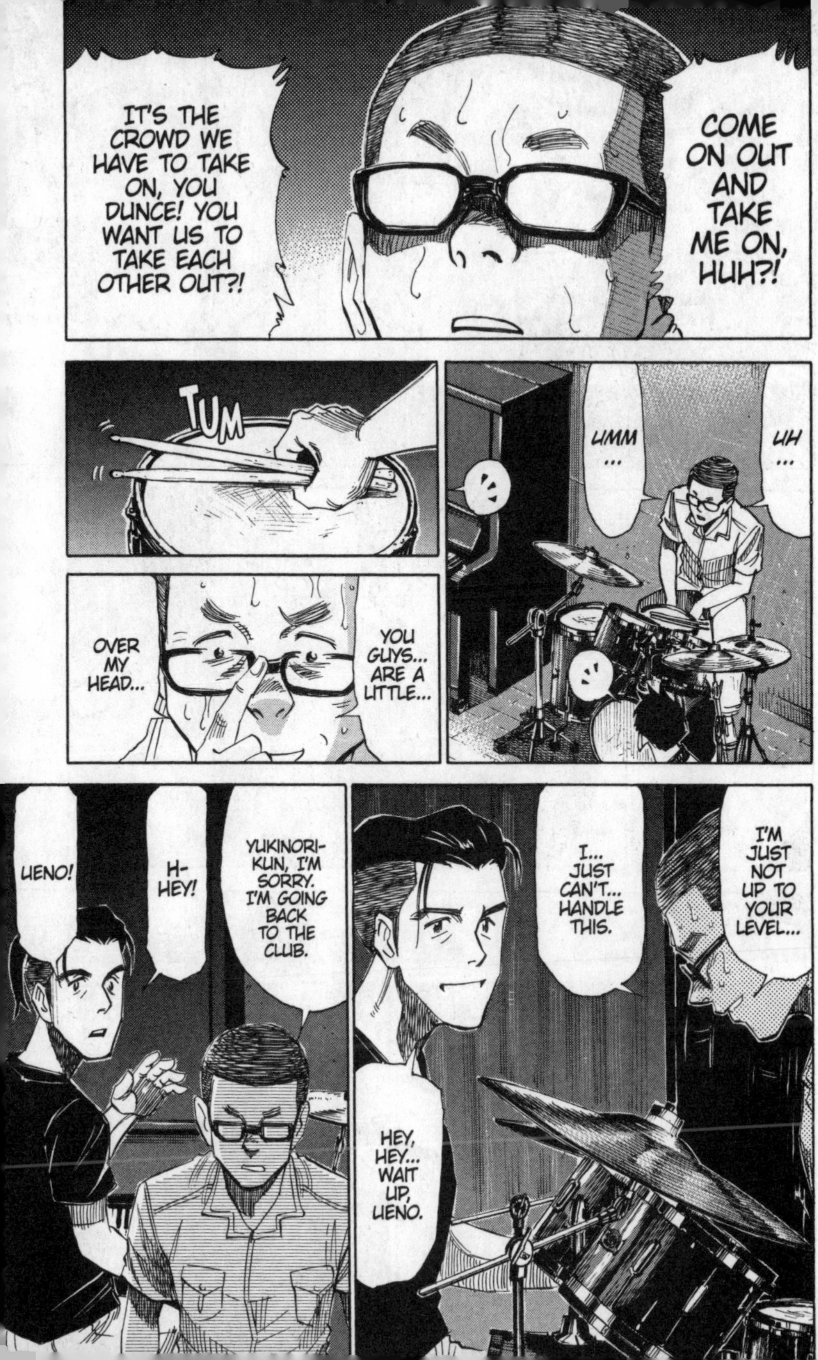
COME ON OUT AND TAKE ME ON, HUH?!
IT'S THE CROWD WE HAVE TO TAKE ON, YOU DUNCE! YOU WANT US TO TAKE EACH OTHER OUT?!
UH...
UMM...
TUM
YOU GUYS... ARE A LITTLE...
OVER MY HEAD...
I'M JUST NOT UP TO YOUR LEVEL...
I... JUST CAN'T... HANDLE THIS.
HEY, HEY... WAIT UP, UENO.
YUKINORI-KUN, I'M SORRY. I'M GOING BACK TO THE CLUB.
H-HEY!
UENO!

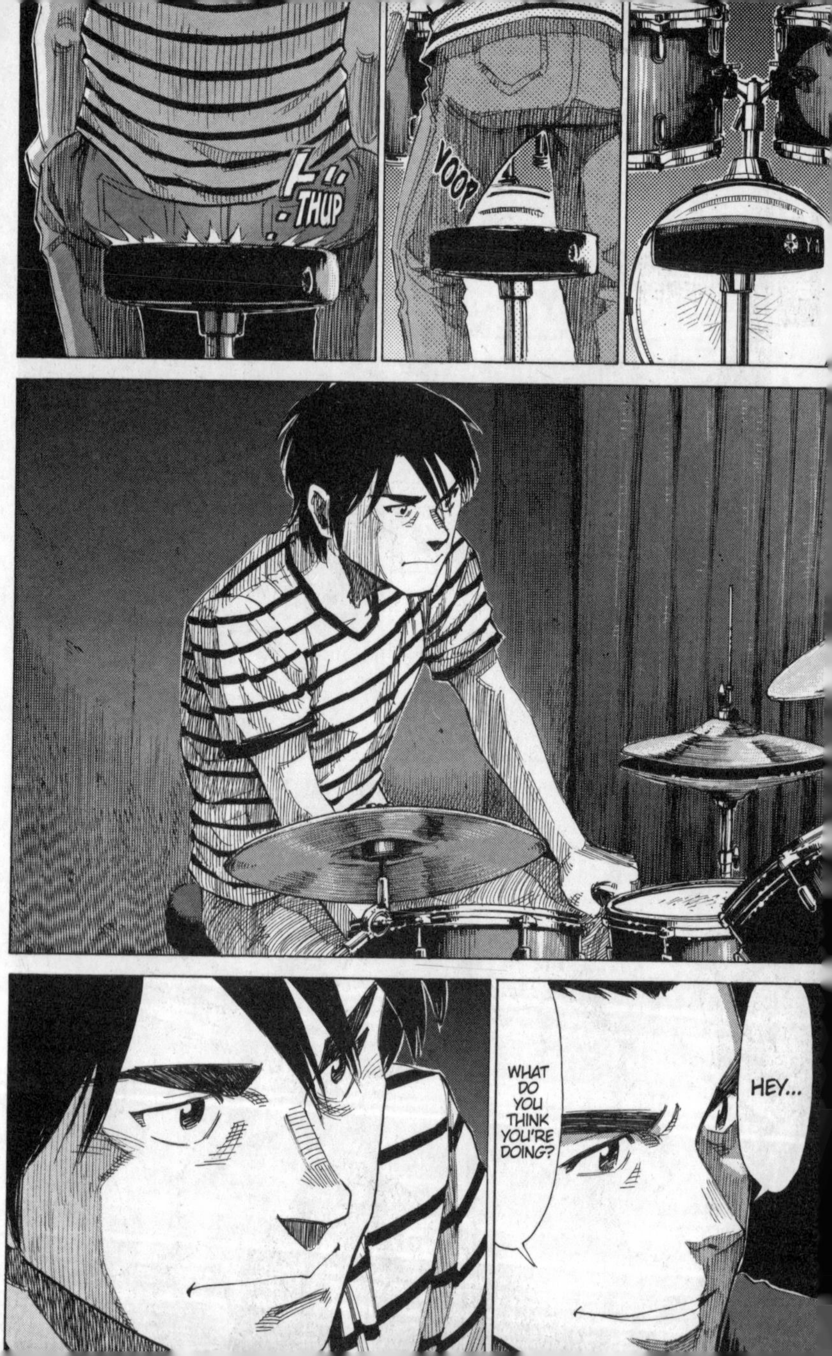
VOOP
ト..
THUP
HEY...
WHAT DO YOU THINK YOU'RE DOING?

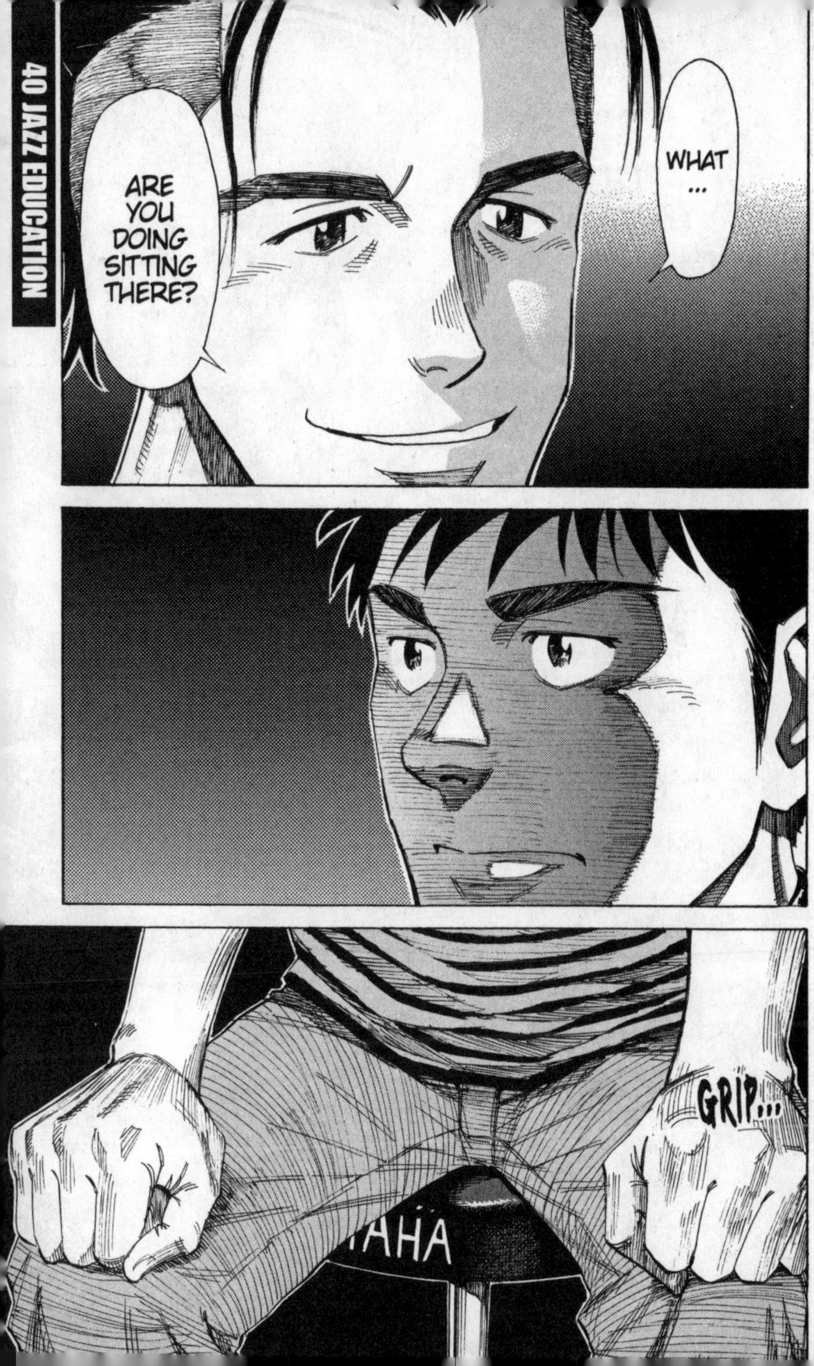
WHAT ...
ARE YOU DOING SITTING THERE?
GRIP...

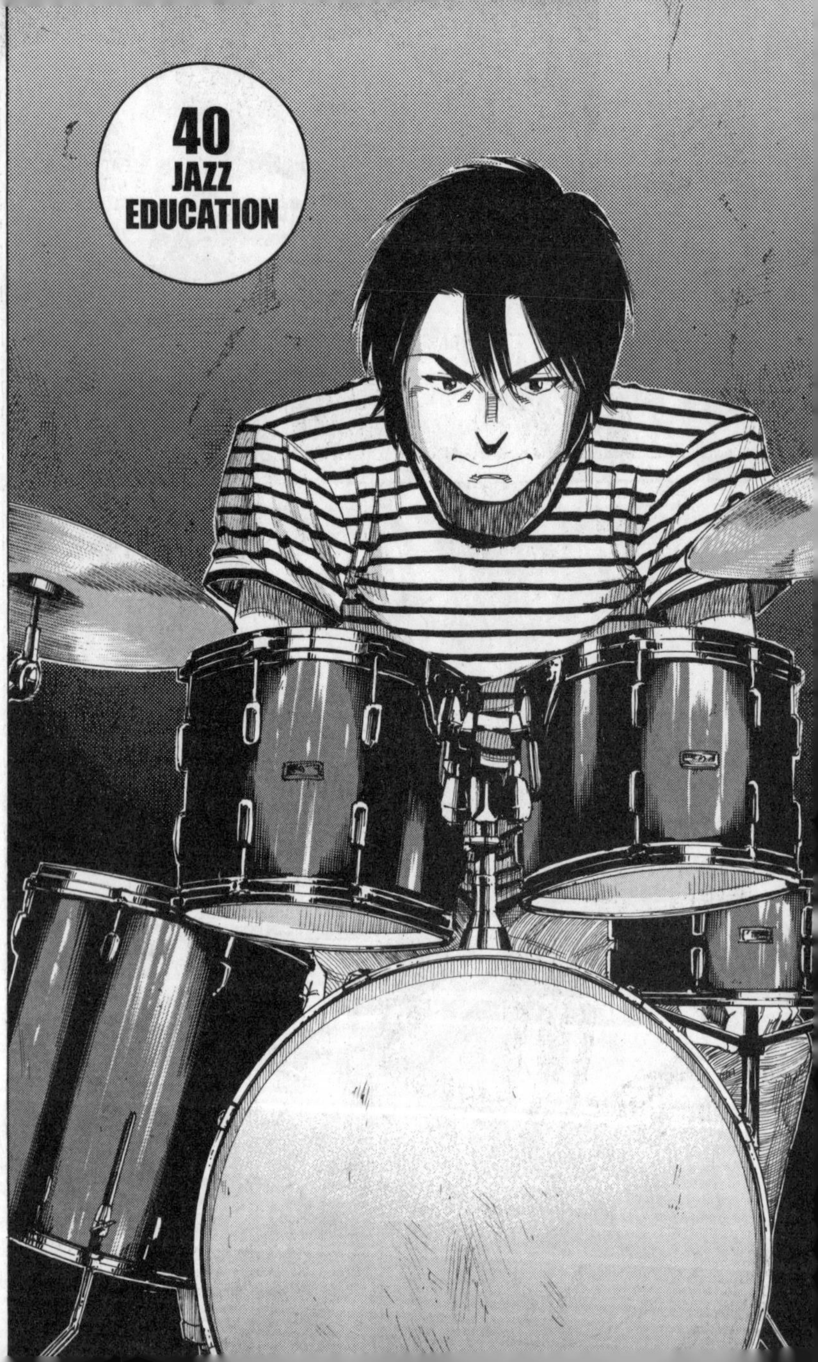
40
JAZZ
EDUCATION

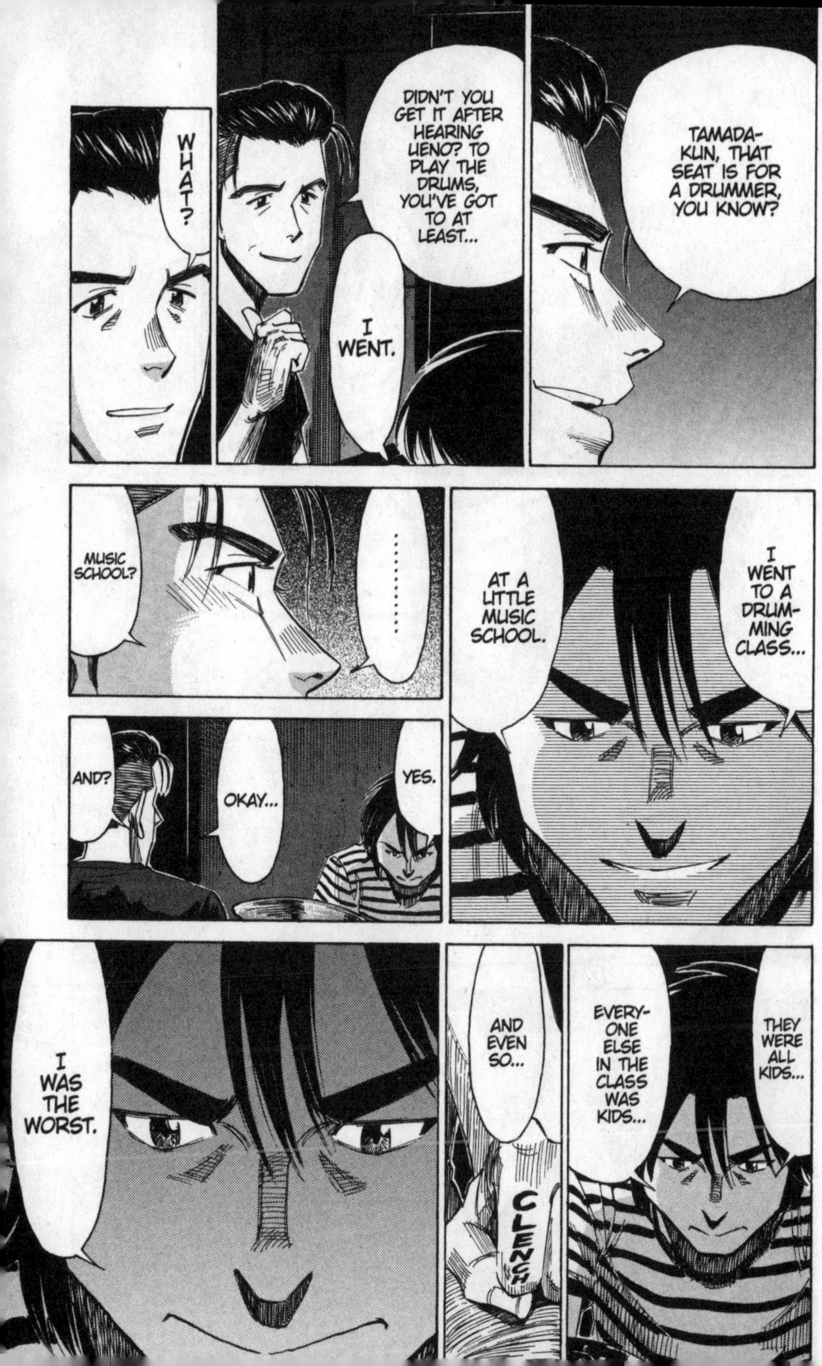
TAMADA-KUN, THAT SEAT IS FOR A DRUMMER, YOU KNOW?
DIDN'T YOU GET IT AFTER HEARING UENO? TO PLAY THE DRUMS, YOU'VE GOT TO AT LEAST...
I WENT.
WHAT?
I WENT TO A DRUMMING CLASS...
AT A LITTLE MUSIC SCHOOL.
......
MUSIC SCHOOL?
YES.
OKAY...
AND?
THEY WERE ALL KIDS...
EVERYONE ELSE IN THE CLASS WAS KIDS...
AND EVEN SO...
CLENCH
I WAS THE WORST.

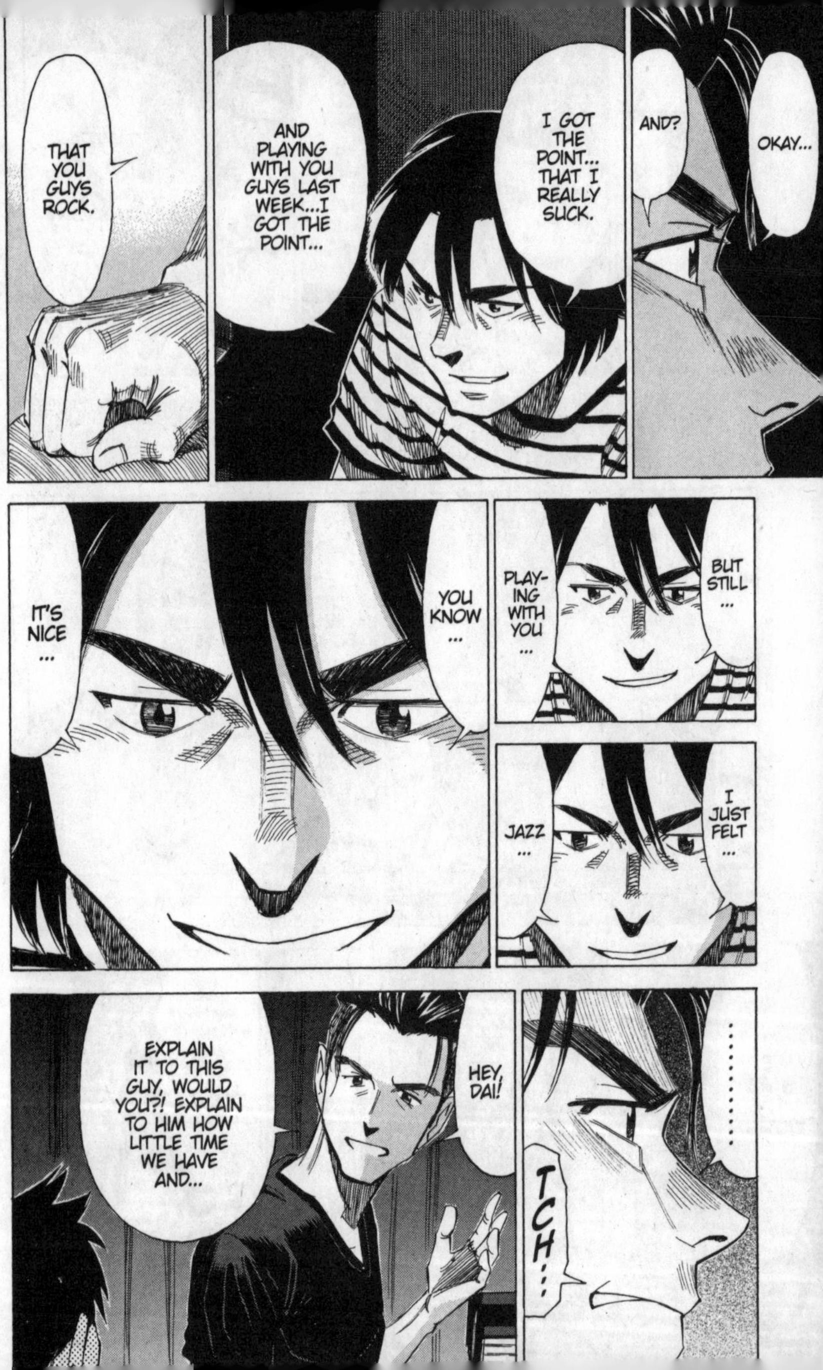
OKAY...
AND?
I GOT THE POINT... THAT I REALLY SUCK.
AND PLAYING WITH YOU GUYS LAST WEEK...I GOT THE POINT...
THAT YOU GUYS ROCK.
BUT STILL ...
PLAYING WITH YOU ...
I JUST FELT ...
JAZZ ...
YOU KNOW ...
IT'S NICE ...
....
TCH...
HEY, DAI!
EXPLAIN IT TO THIS GUY, WOULD YOU?! EXPLAIN TO HIM HOW LITTLE TIME WE HAVE AND...

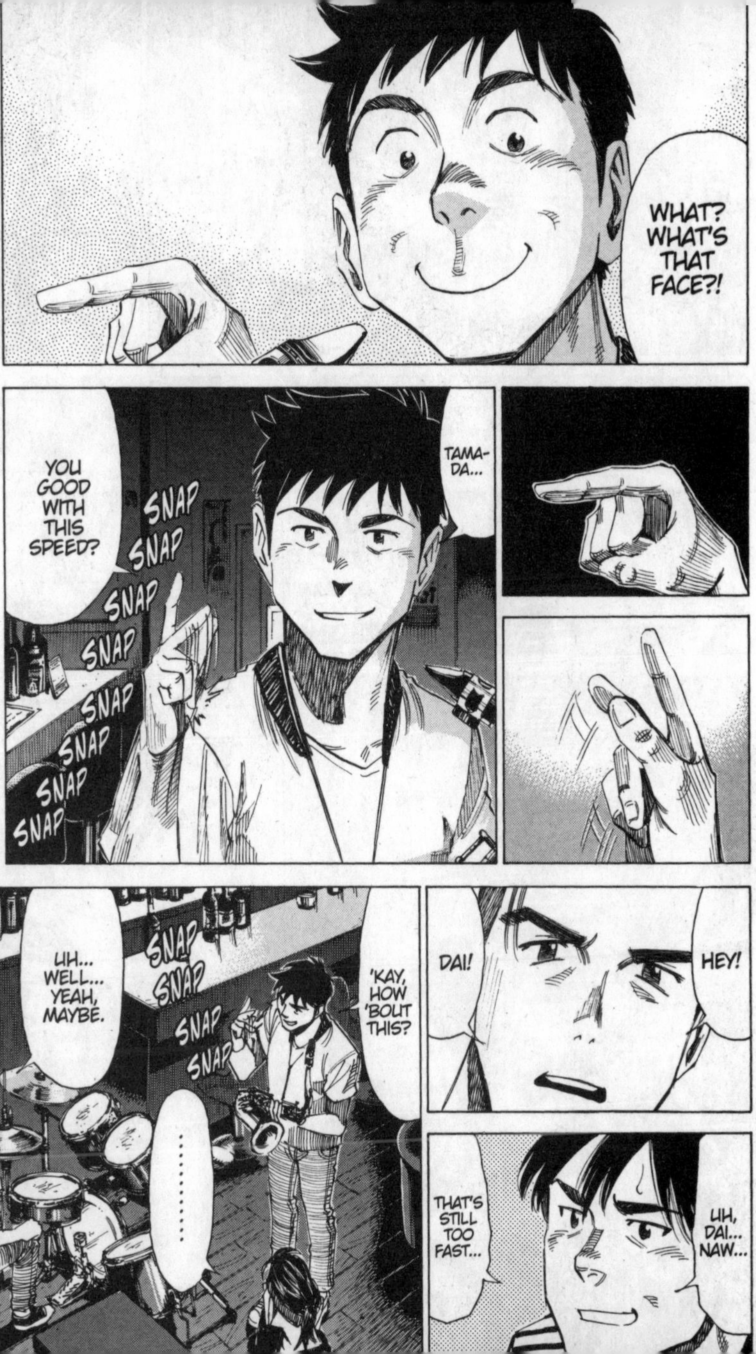
WHAT? WHAT'S THAT FACE?!
TAMA-DA...
YOU GOOD WITH THIS SPEED?
SNAP SNAP SNAP SNAP SNAP SNAP SNAP SNAP
HEY!
DAI!
UH, DAI... NAW...
THAT'S STILL TOO FAST...
'KAY, HOW 'BOUT THIS?
SNAP SNAP SNAP SNAP
UH... WELL... YEAH, MAYBE.
......

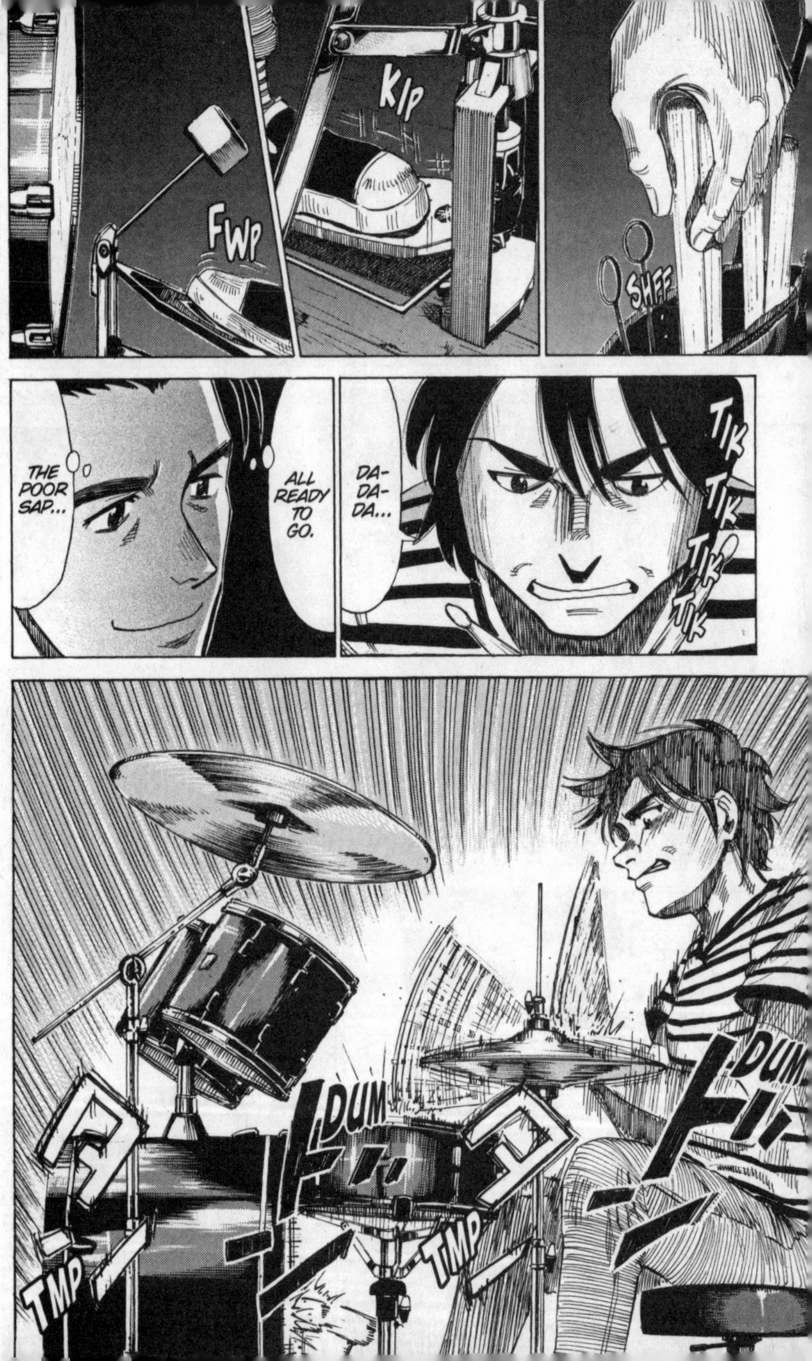
SHFF
KIP
FWP
DA-
DA-
DA...
TIK TIK TIK TIK TIK
ALL READY TO GO.
THE POOR SAP...
DUM
TMP
DUM
TMP

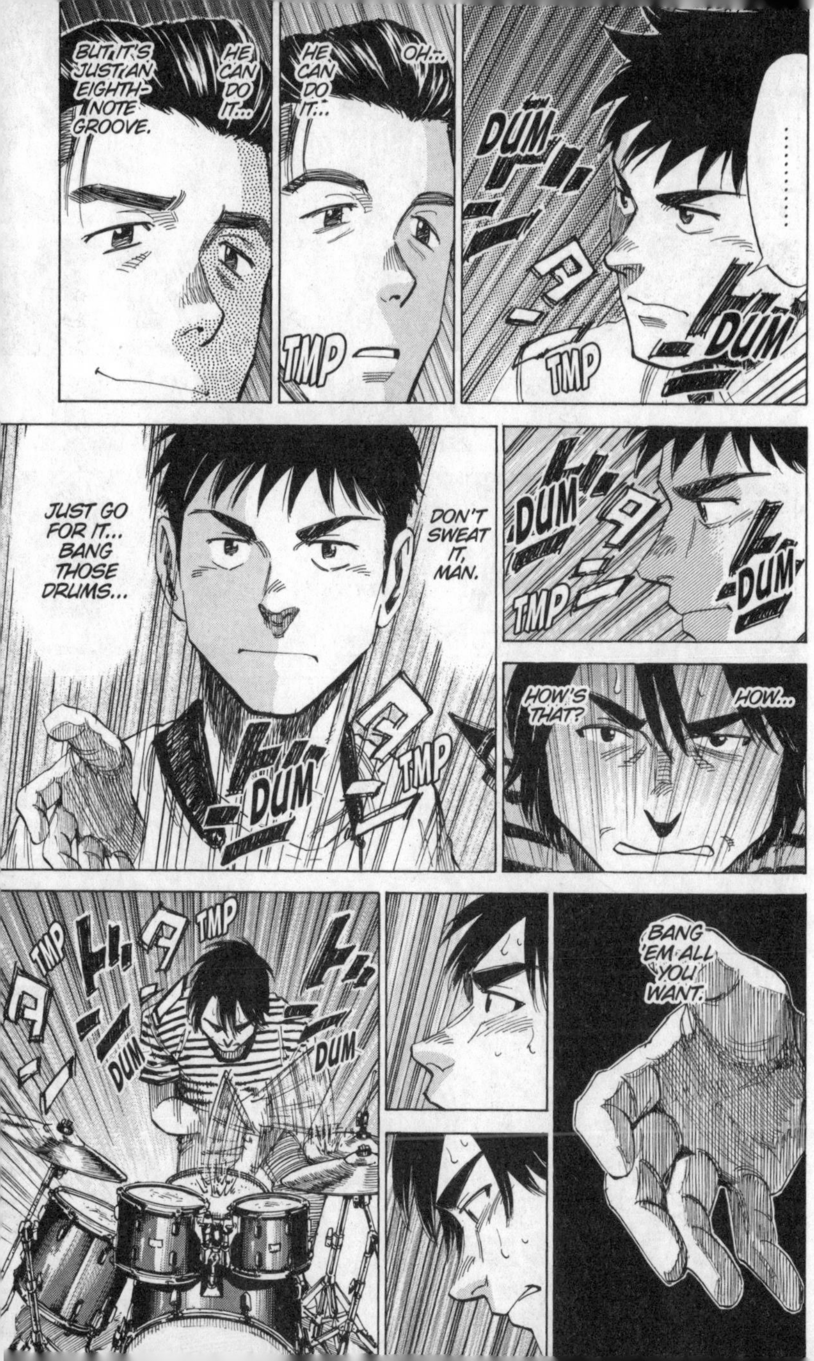
......
DUM
TMP
DUM
OH...
HE CAN DO IT...
TMP
HE CAN DO IT...
BUT IT'S JUST AN EIGHTH-NOTE GROOVE.
DUM
DUM
TMP
HOW...
HOW'S THAT?
DON'T SWEAT IT, MAN.
JUST GO FOR IT... BANG THOSE DRUMS...
TMP
DUM
BANG 'EM ALL YOU WANT.
TMP
TMP
DUM
DUM

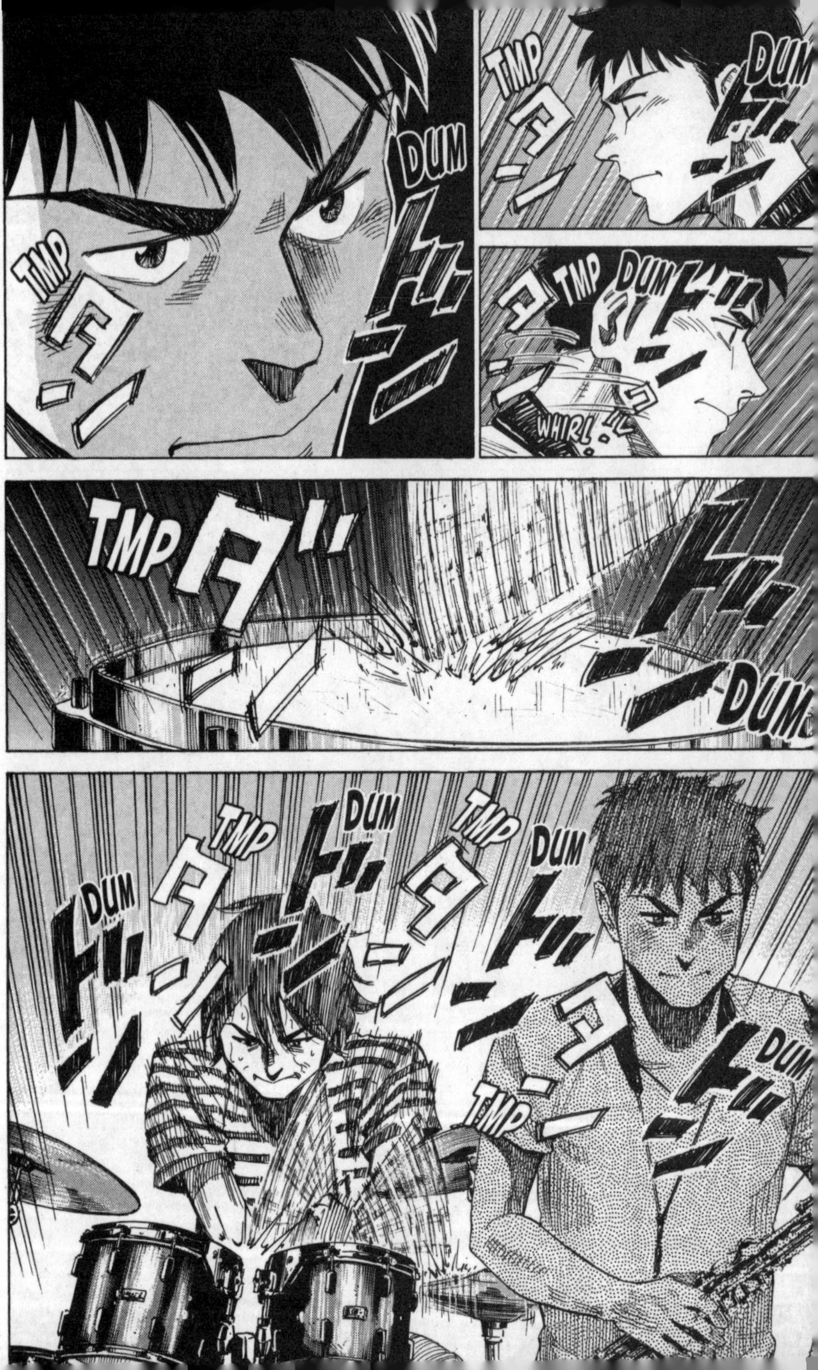

DUM
TMP
DUM
TMP
WHIRL
DUM
TMP
DUM
TMP
DUM
TMP
DUM
TMP
DUM
DUM
TMP

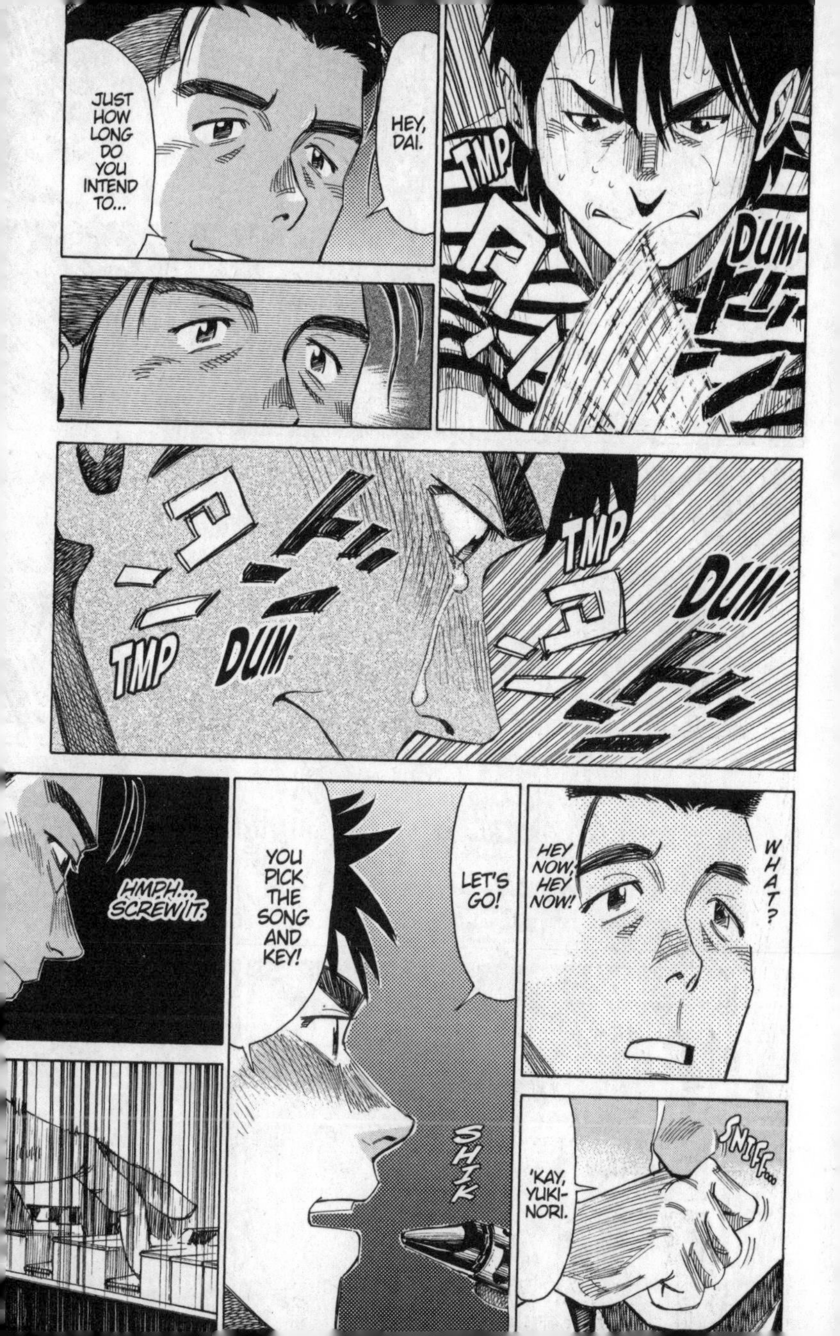
TMP
DUM
HEY, DAI.
JUST HOW LONG DO YOU INTEND TO...
TMP
DUM
TMP
DUM
WHAT?
HEY NOW, HEY NOW!
SNIFF...
'KAY, YUKI-NORI.
LET'S GO!
YOU PICK THE SONG AND KEY!
SHIK
HMPH... SCREW IT.

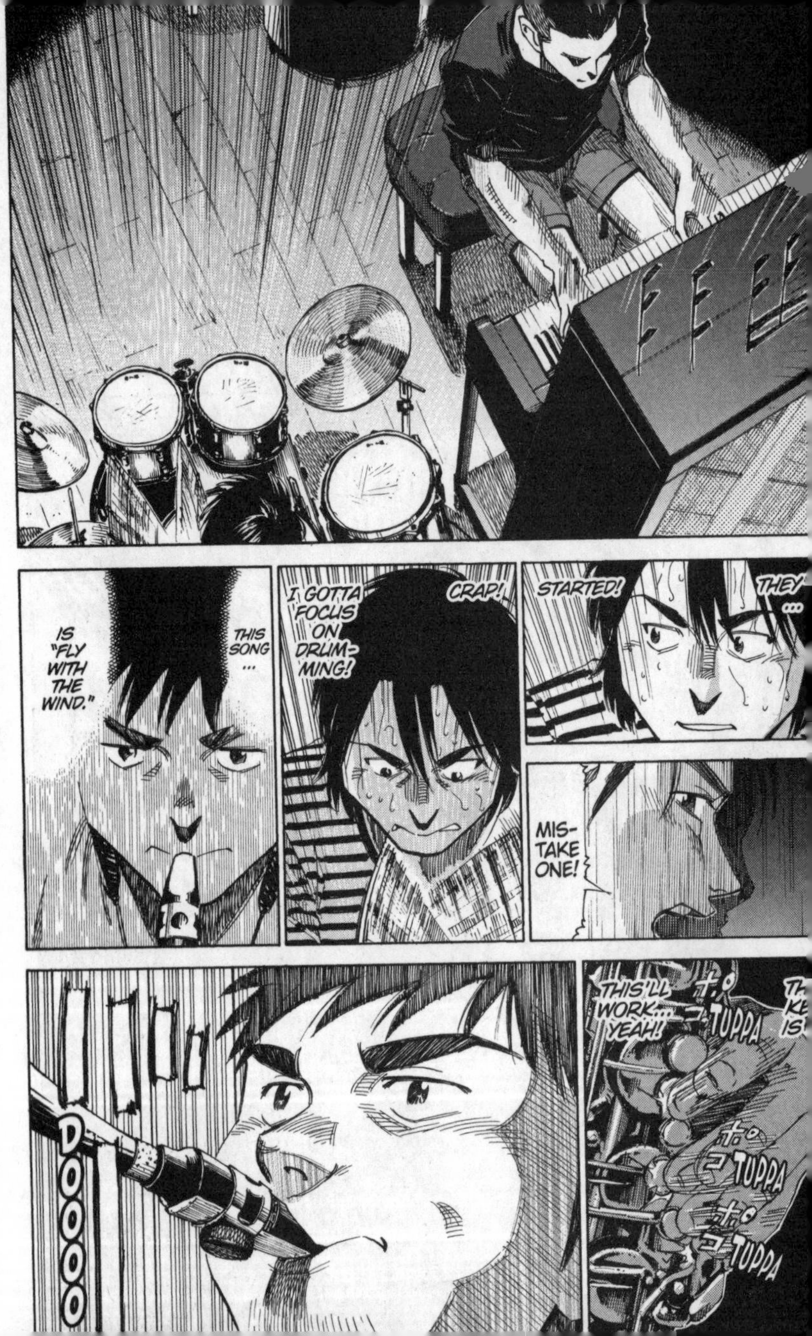
THEY' ...
STARTED!
MIS-TAKE ONE!
CRAP!
I GOTTA FOCUS ON DRUM-MING!
THIS SONG ...
IS "FLY WITH THE WIND."
THIS'LL WORK... YEAH!
TUPPA
TUPPA
TUPPA
DOOOOO

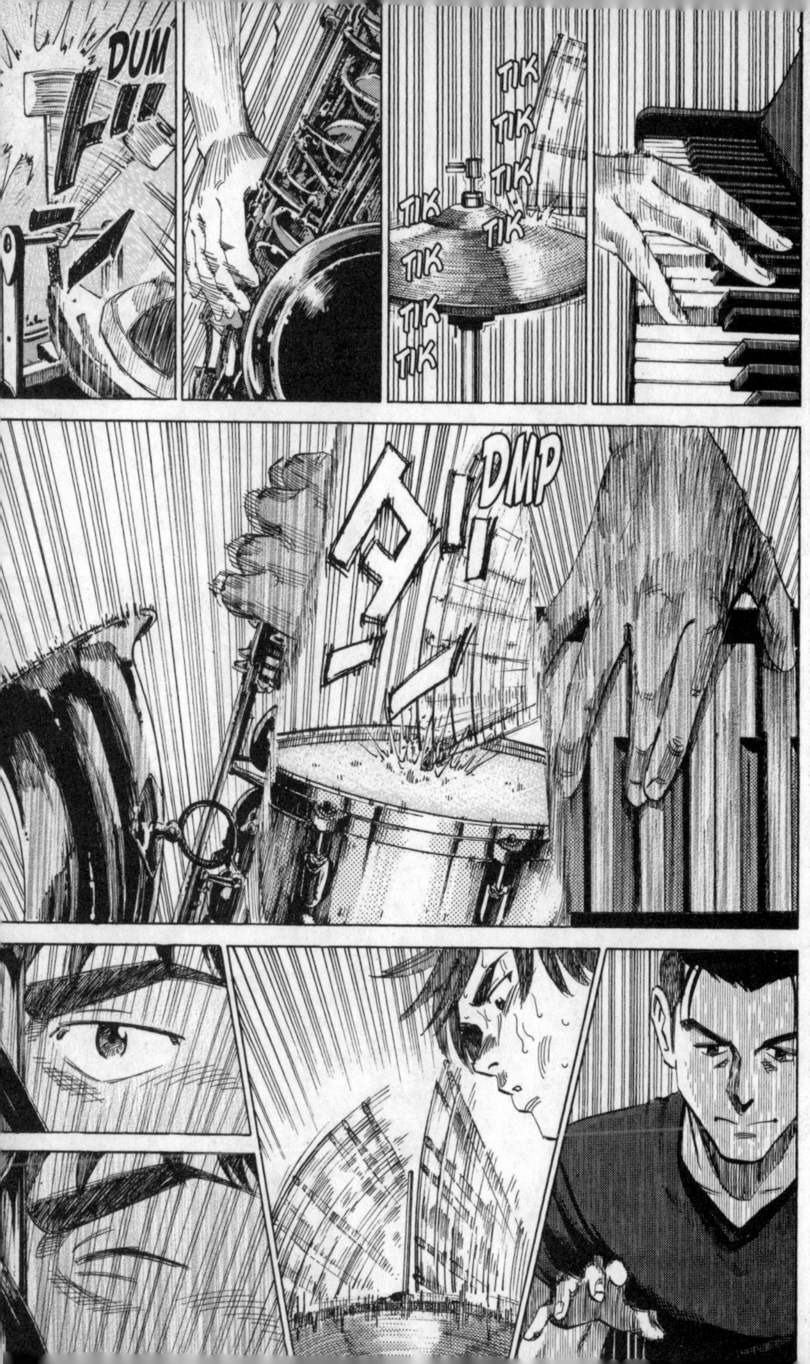
TIK TIK TIK TIK
TIK TIK TIK TIK
DUM
DMP

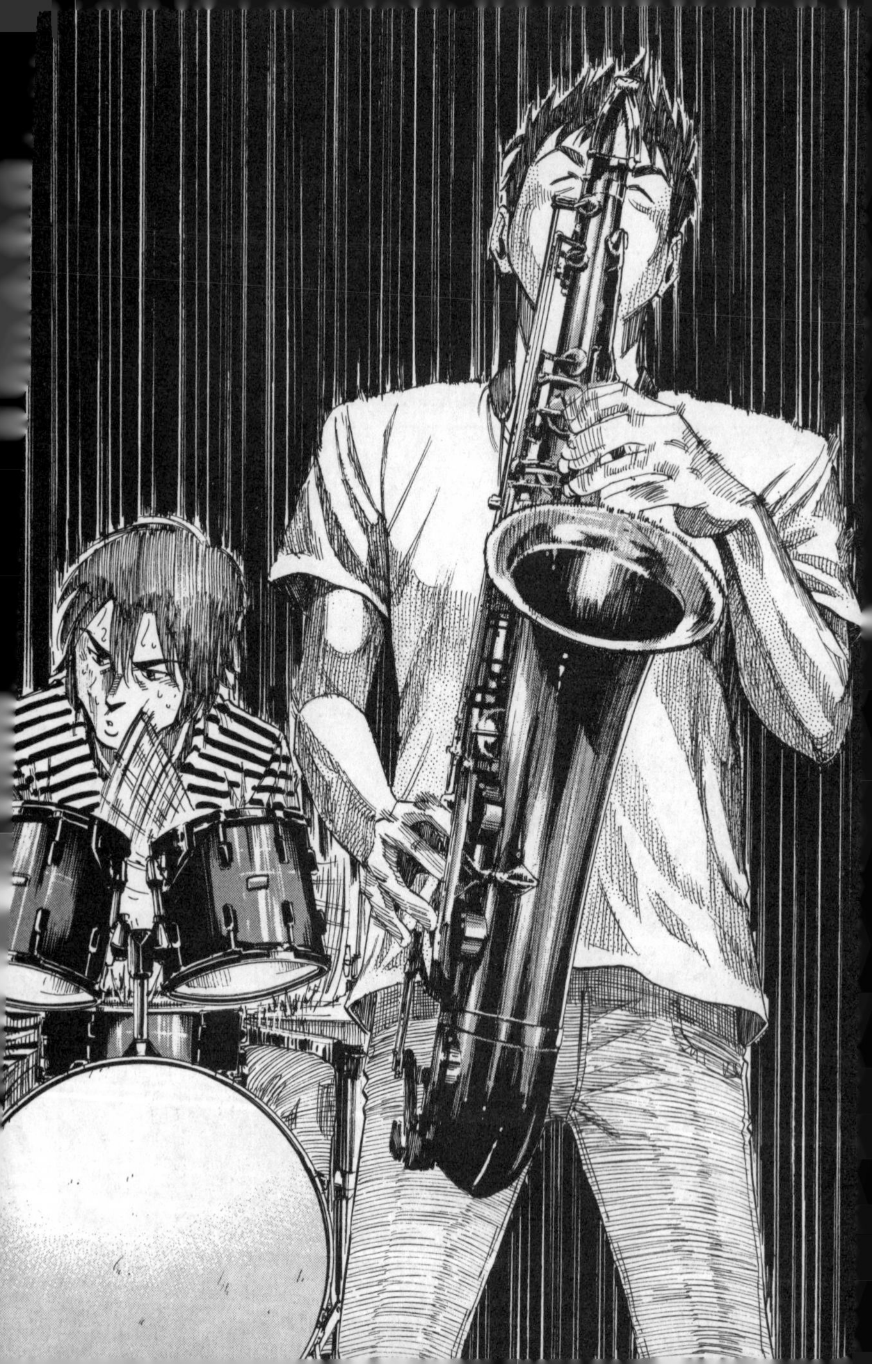

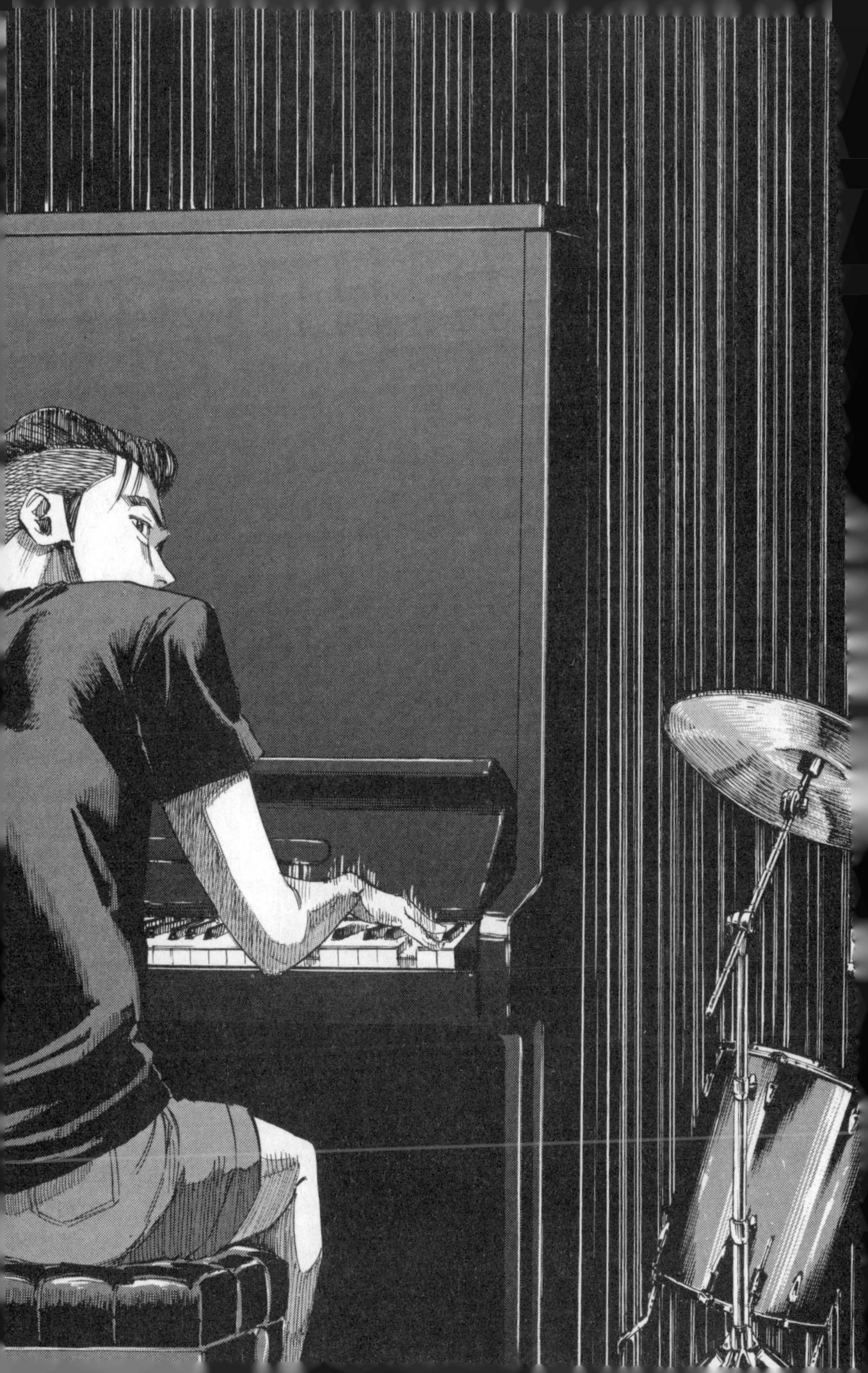

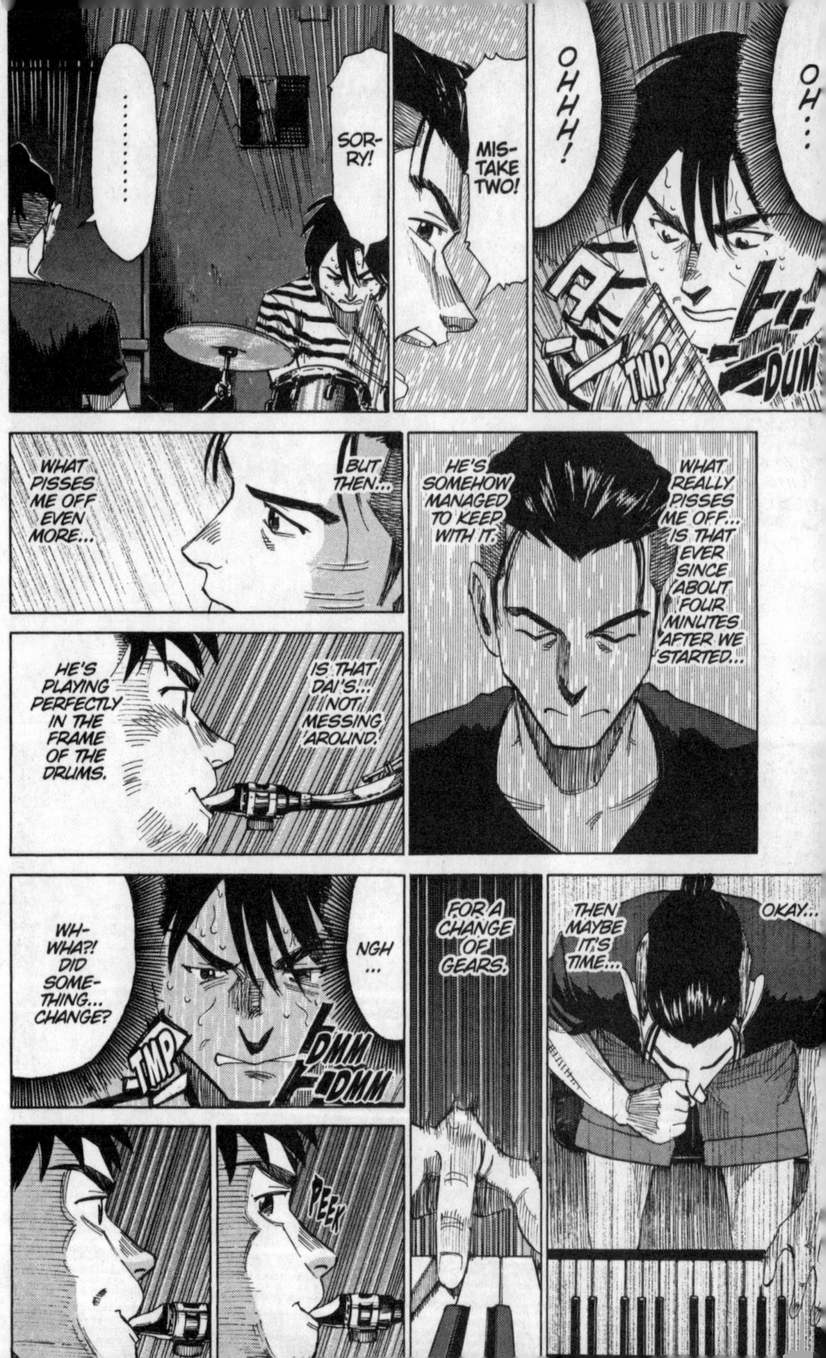
OH...
OHHH!
DUM
TMP
MIS-TAKE TWO!
SOR-RY!
......
WHAT REALLY PISSES ME OFF... IS THAT EVER SINCE ABOUT FOUR MINUTES AFTER WE STARTED...
HE'S SOMEHOW MANAGED TO KEEP WITH IT.
BUT THEN...
WHAT PISSES ME OFF EVEN MORE...
IS THAT DAI'S... NOT MESSING AROUND.
HE'S PLAYING PERFECTLY IN THE FRAME OF THE DRUMS.
OKAY...
THEN MAYBE IT'S TIME...
FOR A CHANGE OF GEARS.
NGH ...
WH-WHA?! DID SOME-THING... CHANGE?
DMM
DMM
TMP
PEEK

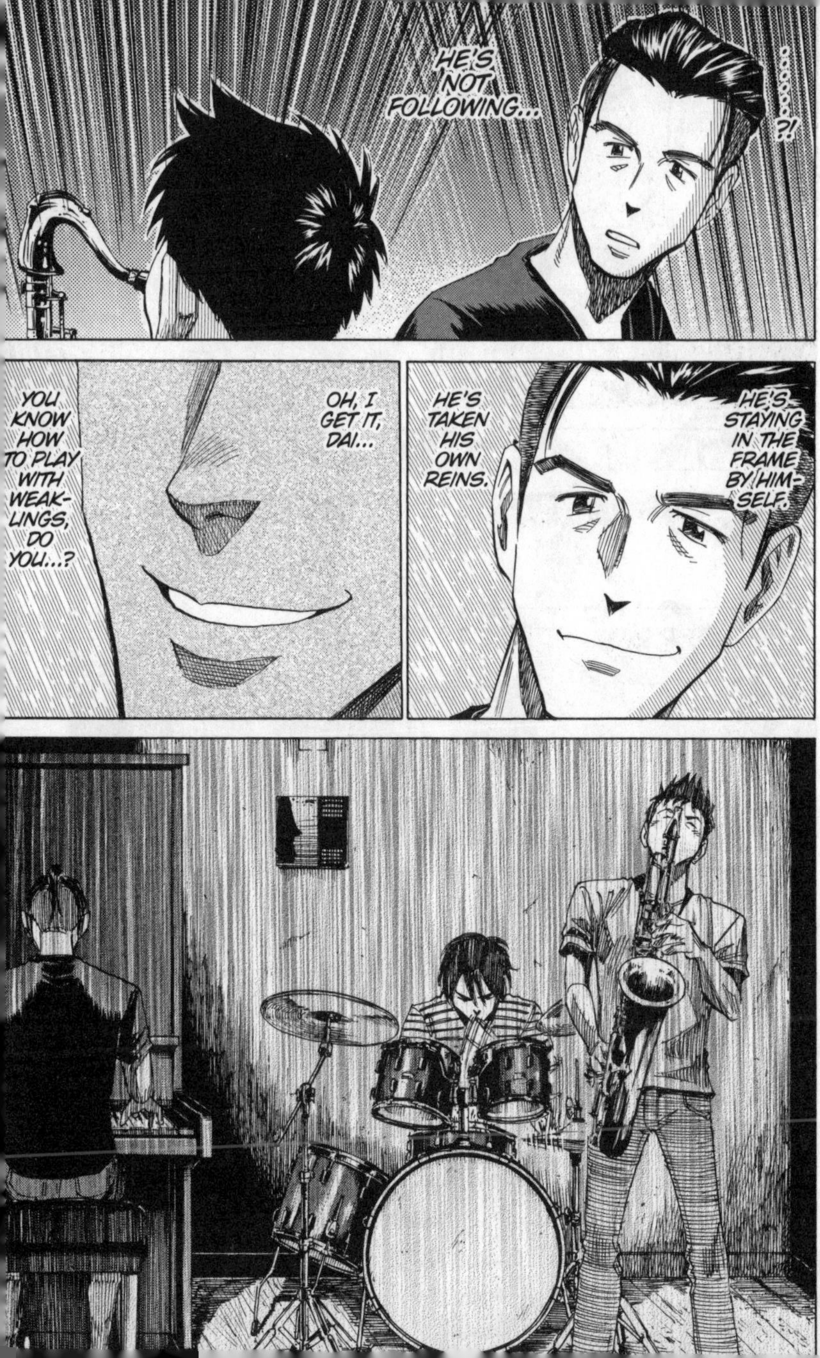
......?!
HE'S NOT FOLLOWING...
HE'S STAYING IN THE FRAME BY HIMSELF.
HE'S TAKEN HIS OWN REINS.
OH, I GET IT, DAI...
YOU KNOW HOW TO PLAY WITH WEAKLINGS, DO YOU...?

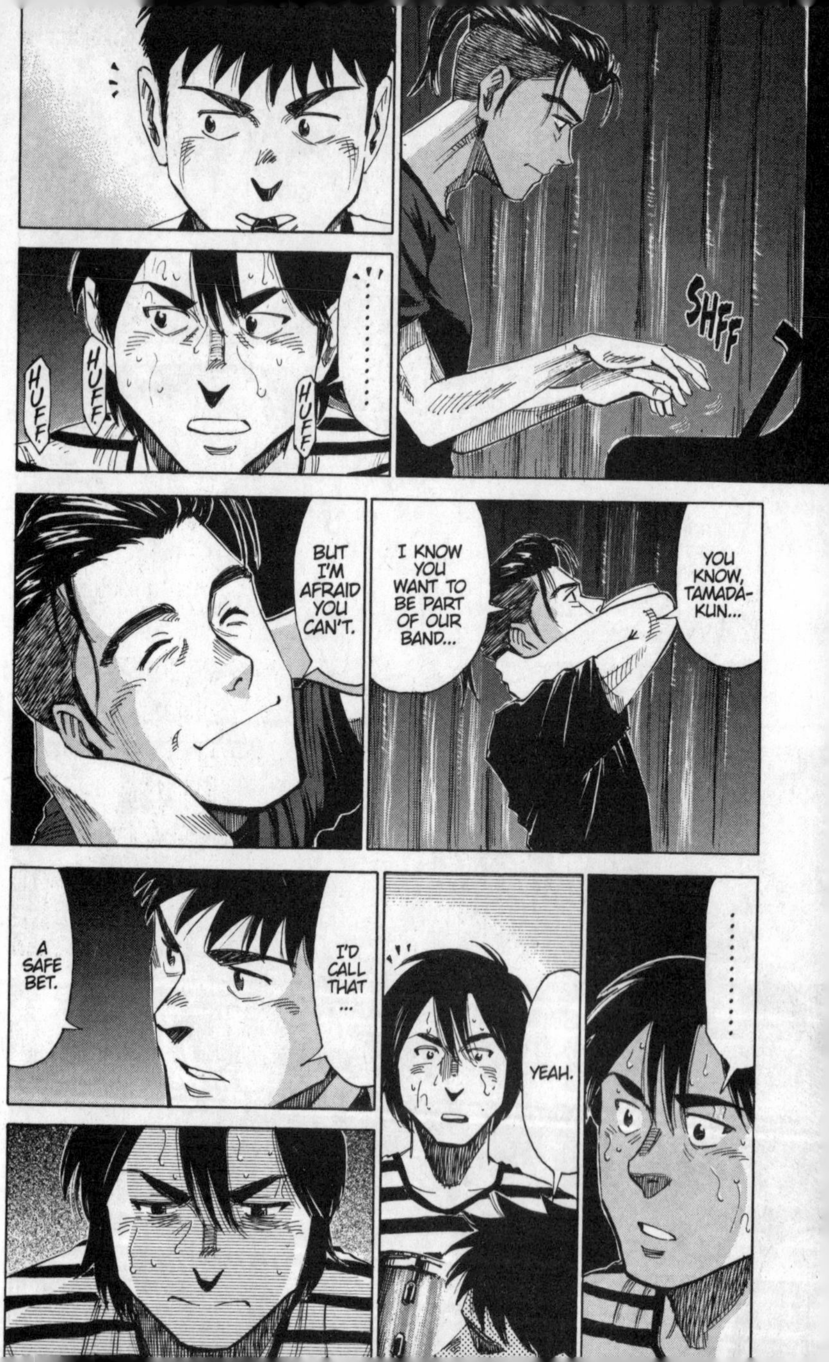
SHFF
......
HUFF
HUFF
HUFF
YOU KNOW, TAMADA-KUN...
I KNOW YOU WANT TO BE PART OF OUR BAND...
BUT I'M AFRAID YOU CAN'T.
......
YEAH.
I'D CALL THAT ...
A SAFE BET.

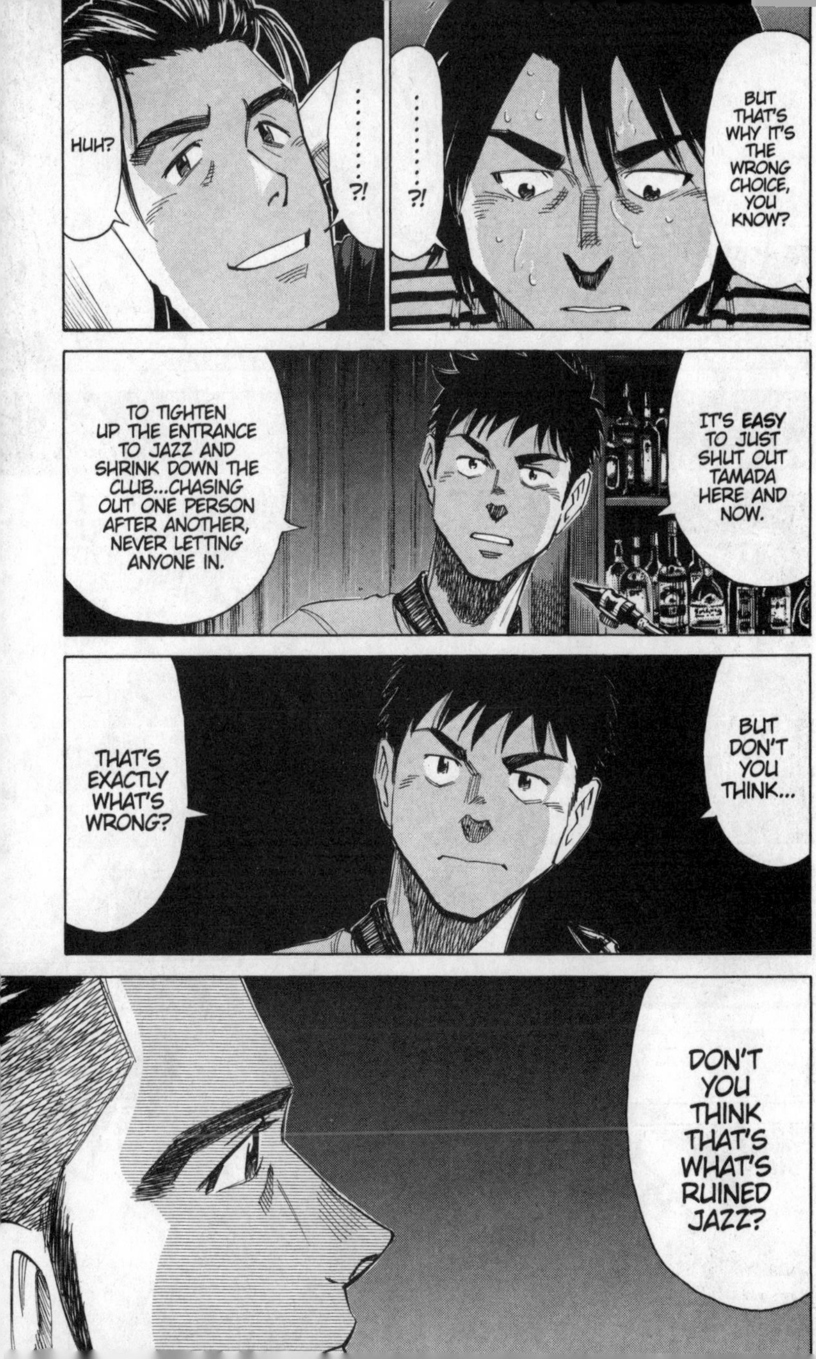
BUT THAT'S WHY IT'S THE WRONG CHOICE, YOU KNOW?
......?!
......?!
HUH?
IT'S EASY TO JUST SHUT OUT TAMADA HERE AND NOW.
TO TIGHTEN UP THE ENTRANCE TO JAZZ AND SHRINK DOWN THE CLUB...CHASING OUT ONE PERSON AFTER ANOTHER, NEVER LETTING ANYONE IN.
BUT DON'T YOU THINK...
THAT'S EXACTLY WHAT'S WRONG?
DON'T YOU THINK THAT'S WHAT'S RUINED JAZZ?

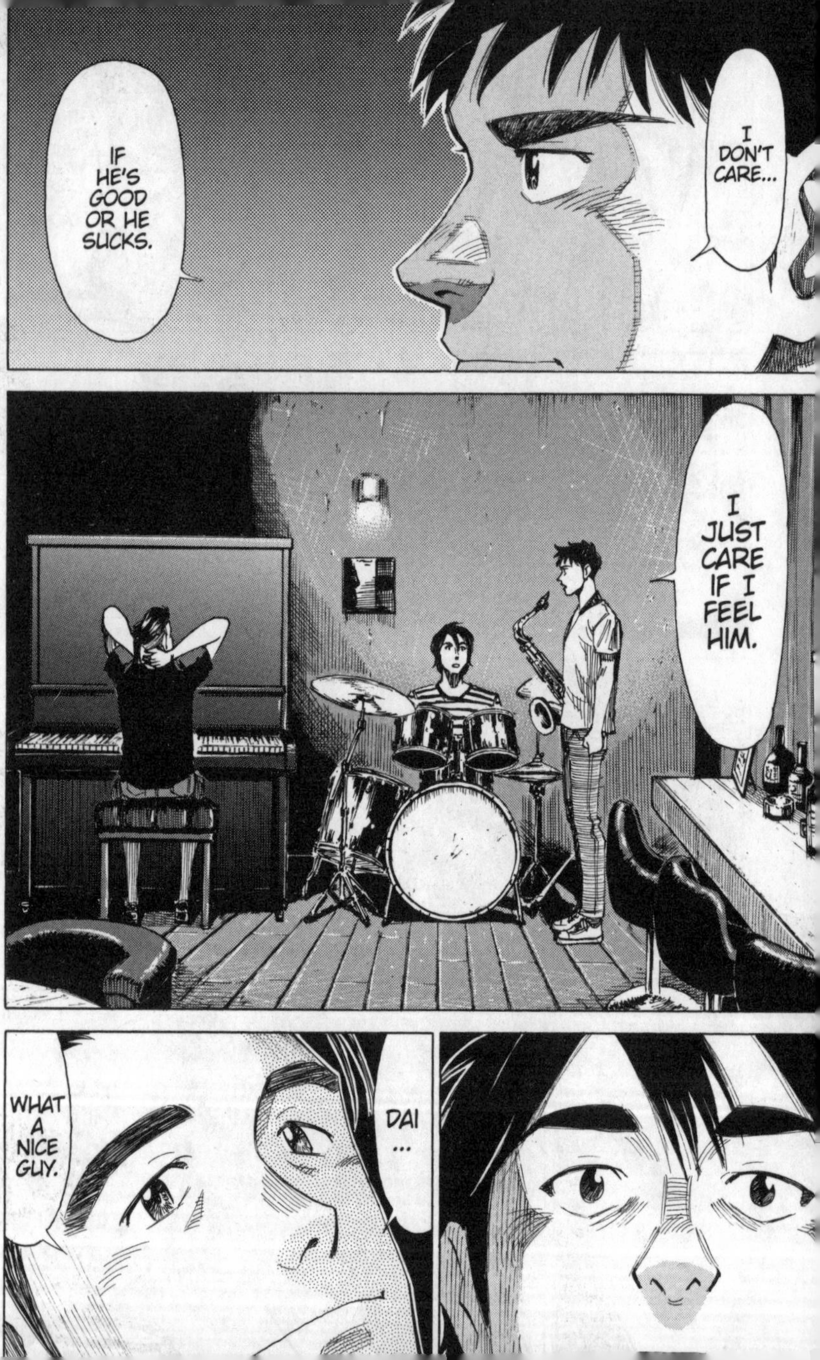
I DON'T CARE...
IF HE'S GOOD OR HE SUCKS.
I JUST CARE IF I FEEL HIM.
DAI ...
WHAT A NICE GUY.

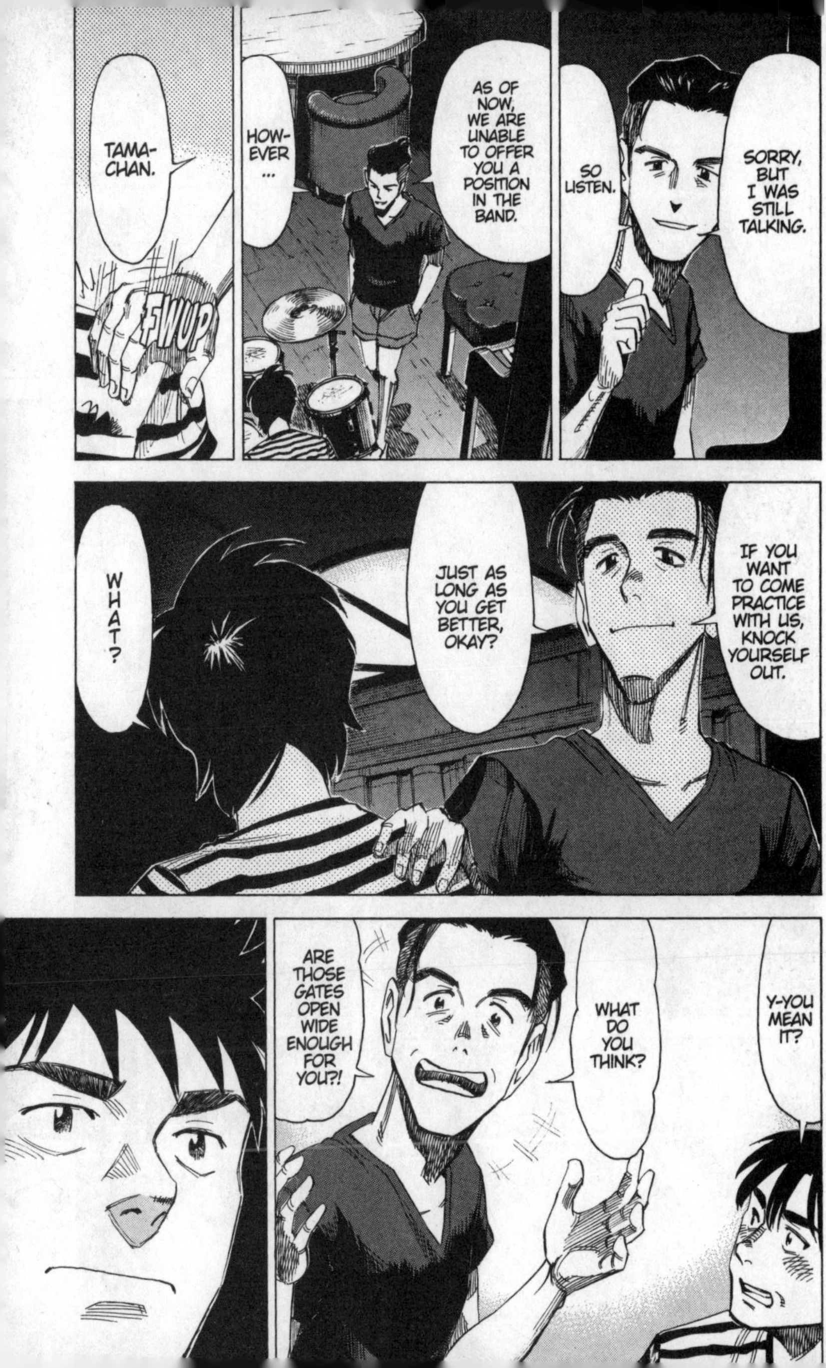
SORRY, BUT I WAS STILL TALKING.
SO LISTEN.
AS OF NOW, WE ARE UNABLE TO OFFER YOU A POSITION IN THE BAND.
HOW-EVER ...
TAMA-CHAN.
FWUP
IF YOU WANT TO COME PRACTICE WITH US, KNOCK YOURSELF OUT.
JUST AS LONG AS YOU GET BETTER, OKAY?
WHAT?
Y-YOU MEAN IT?
WHAT DO YOU THINK?
ARE THOSE GATES OPEN WIDE ENOUGH FOR YOU?!

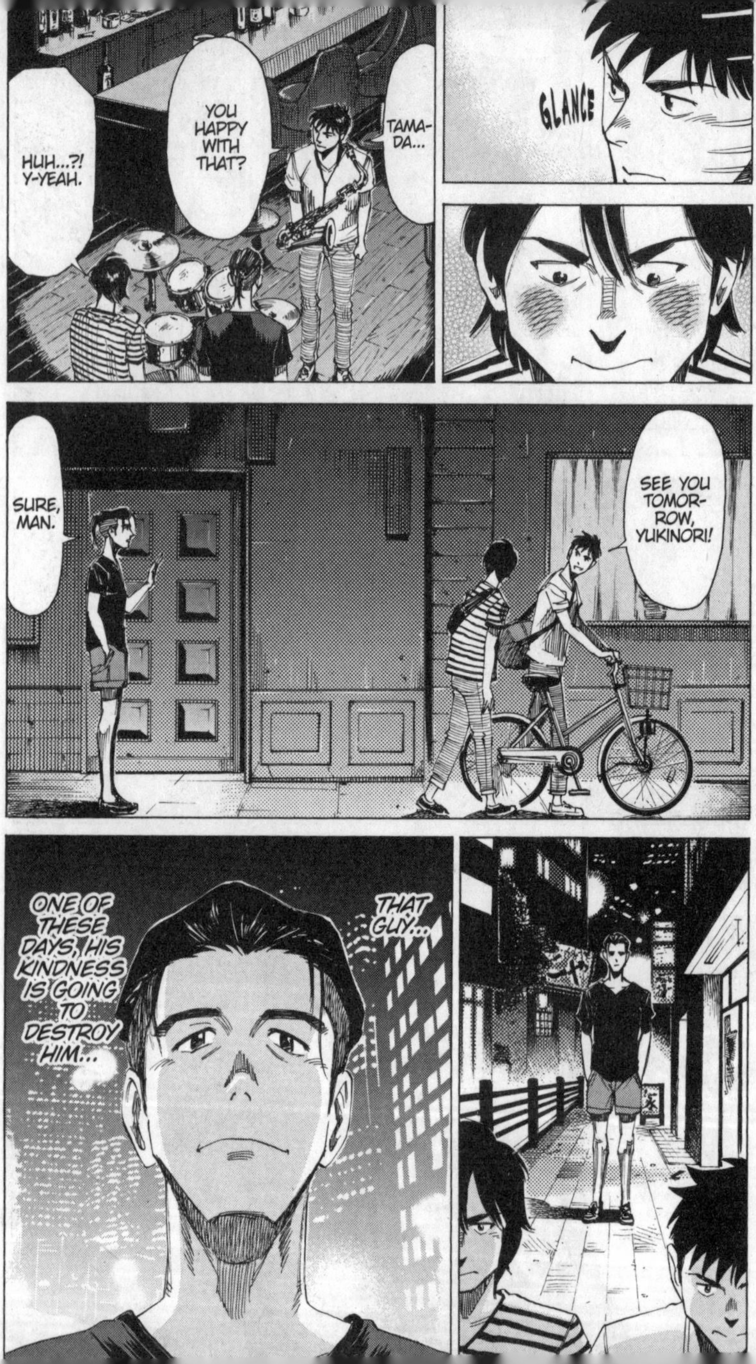
GLANCE
TAMA-DA...
YOU HAPPY WITH THAT?
HUH...?! Y-YEAH.
SEE YOU TOMORROW, YUKINORI!
SURE, MAN.
THAT GUY...
ONE OF THESE DAYS, HIS KINDNESS IS GOING TO DESTROY HIM...

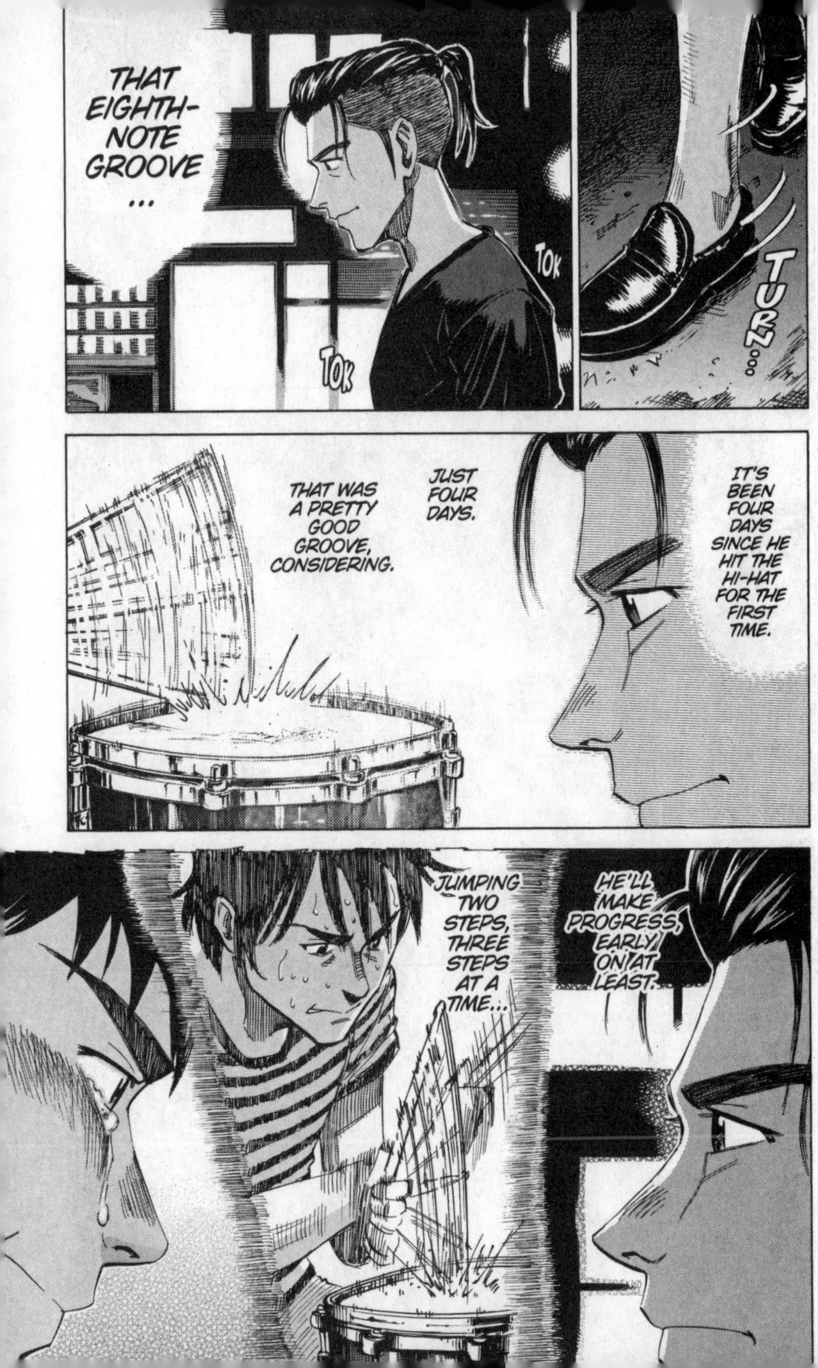
TURN...
THAT EIGHTH-NOTE GROOVE ...
TOK
TOK
IT'S BEEN FOUR DAYS SINCE HE HIT THE HI-HAT FOR THE FIRST TIME.
JUST FOUR DAYS.
THAT WAS A PRETTY GOOD GROOVE, CONSIDERING.
HE'LL MAKE PROGRESS, EARLY ON AT LEAST.
JUMPING TWO STEPS, THREE STEPS AT A TIME...

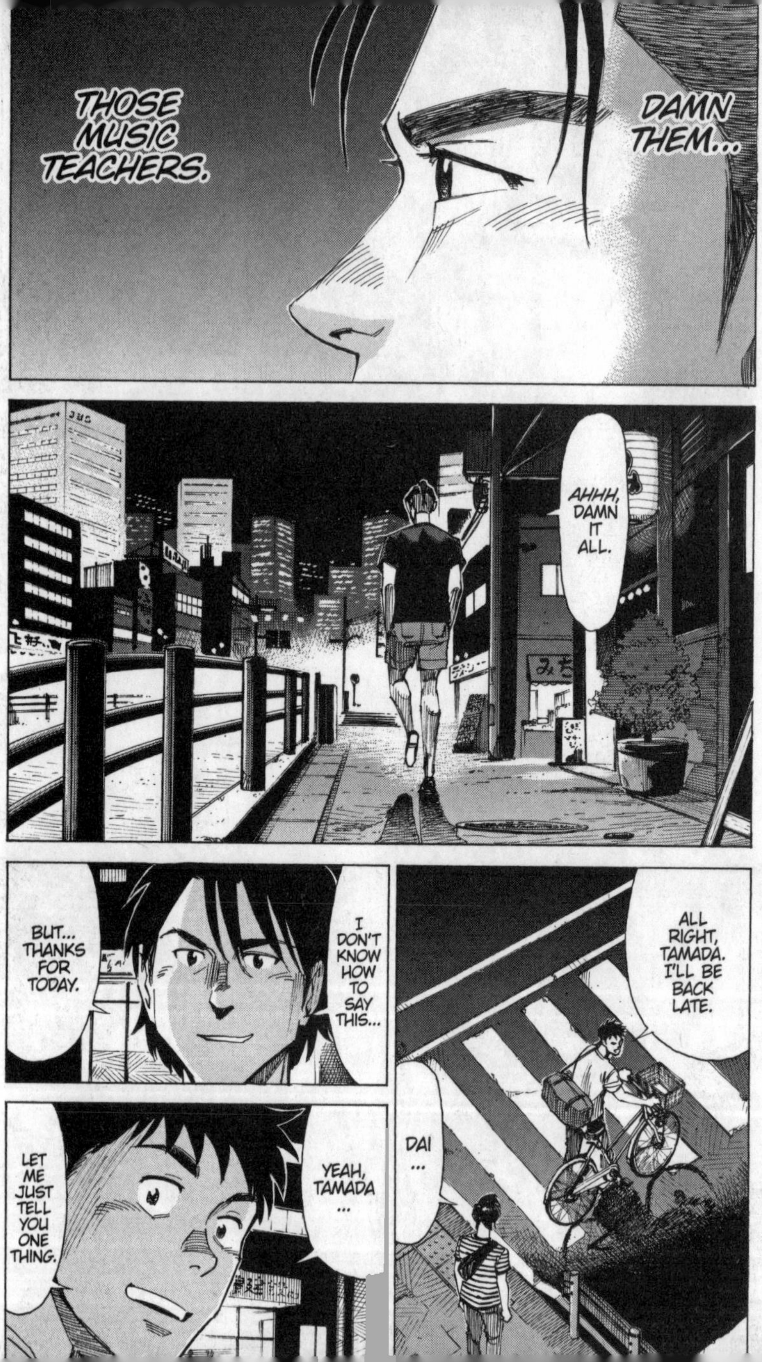
DAMN THEM...
THOSE MUSIC TEACHERS.
AHHH, DAMN IT ALL.
ALL RIGHT, TAMADA. I'LL BE BACK LATE.
DAI ...
I DON'T KNOW HOW TO SAY THIS...
BUT... THANKS FOR TODAY.
YEAH, TAMADA ...
LET ME JUST TELL YOU ONE THING.

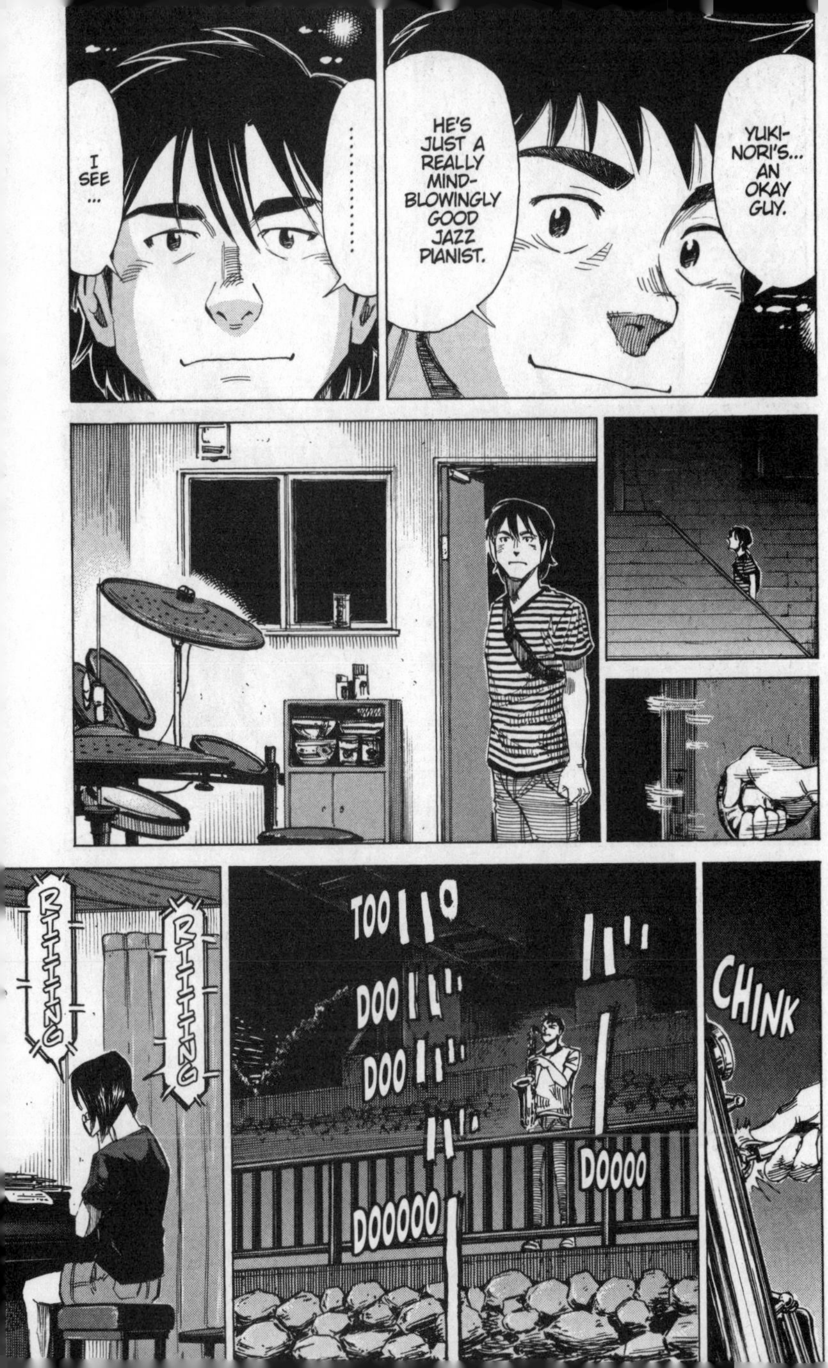
YUKI-NORI'S... AN OKAY GUY.
HE'S JUST A REALLY MIND-BLOWINGLY GOOD JAZZ PIANIST.
......
I SEE ...
CHINK
TOO
DOO
DOO
DOOOO
DOOOOO
RIIIING
RIIIING

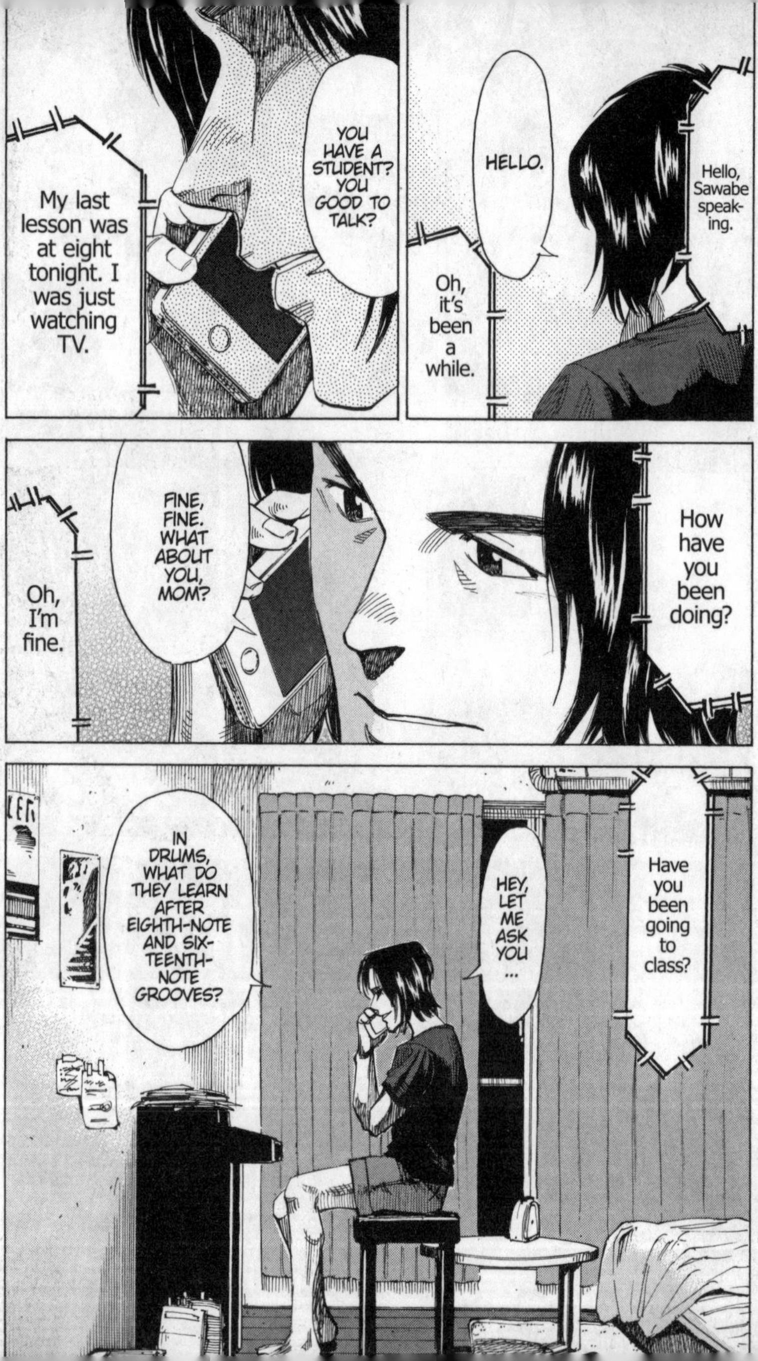
Hello, Sawabe speaking.
HELLO.
Oh, it's been a while.
YOU HAVE A STUDENT? YOU GOOD TO TALK?
My last lesson was at eight tonight. I was just watching TV.
How have you been doing?
FINE, FINE. WHAT ABOUT YOU, MOM?
Oh, I'm fine.
Have you been going to class?
HEY, LET ME ASK YOU ...
IN DRUMS, WHAT DO THEY LEARN AFTER EIGHTH-NOTE AND SIXTEENTH-NOTE GROOVES?

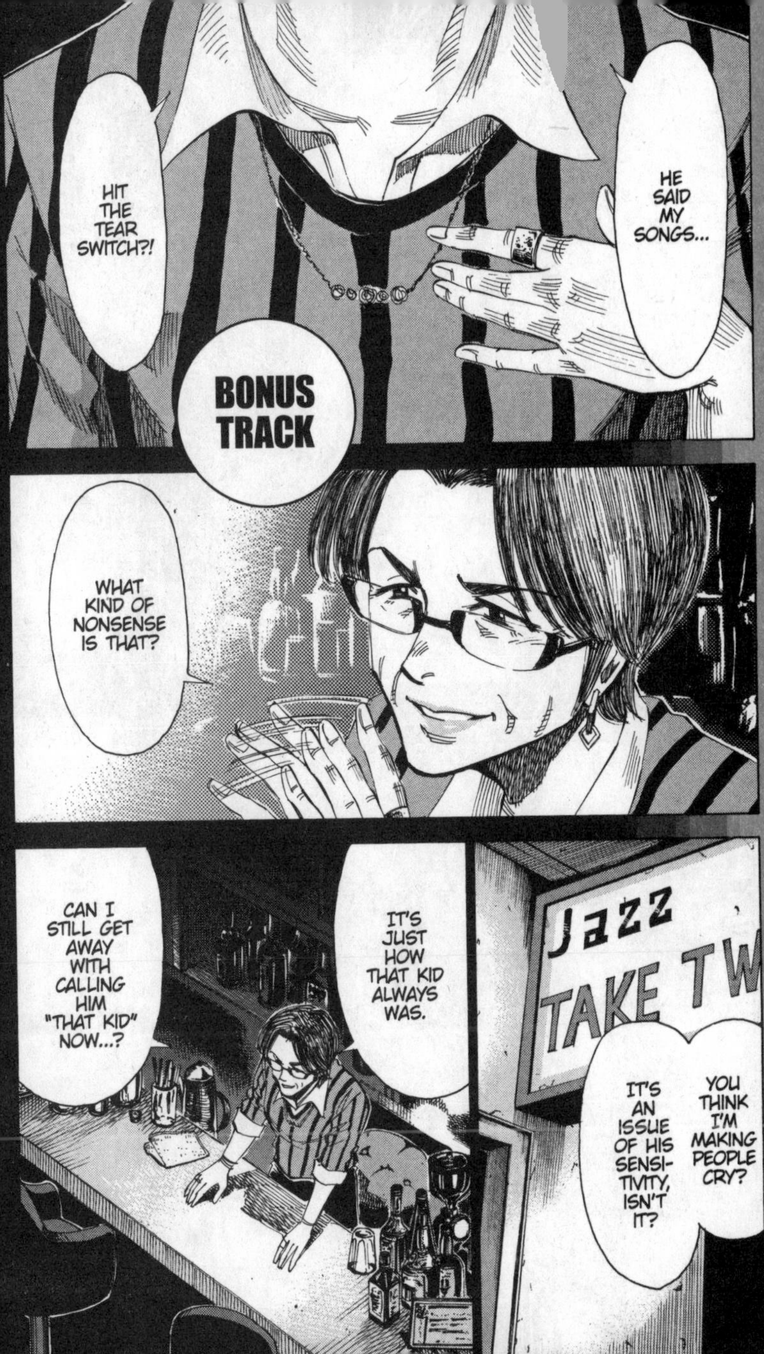
HE SAID MY SONGS...
HIT THE TEAR SWITCH?!
BONUS TRACK
WHAT KIND OF NONSENSE IS THAT?
YOU THINK I'M MAKING PEOPLE CRY?
IT'S AN ISSUE OF HIS SENSI-TIVITY, ISN'T IT?
Jazz
TAKE TW
IT'S JUST HOW THAT KID ALWAYS WAS.
CAN I STILL GET AWAY WITH CALLING HIM "THAT KID" NOW...?

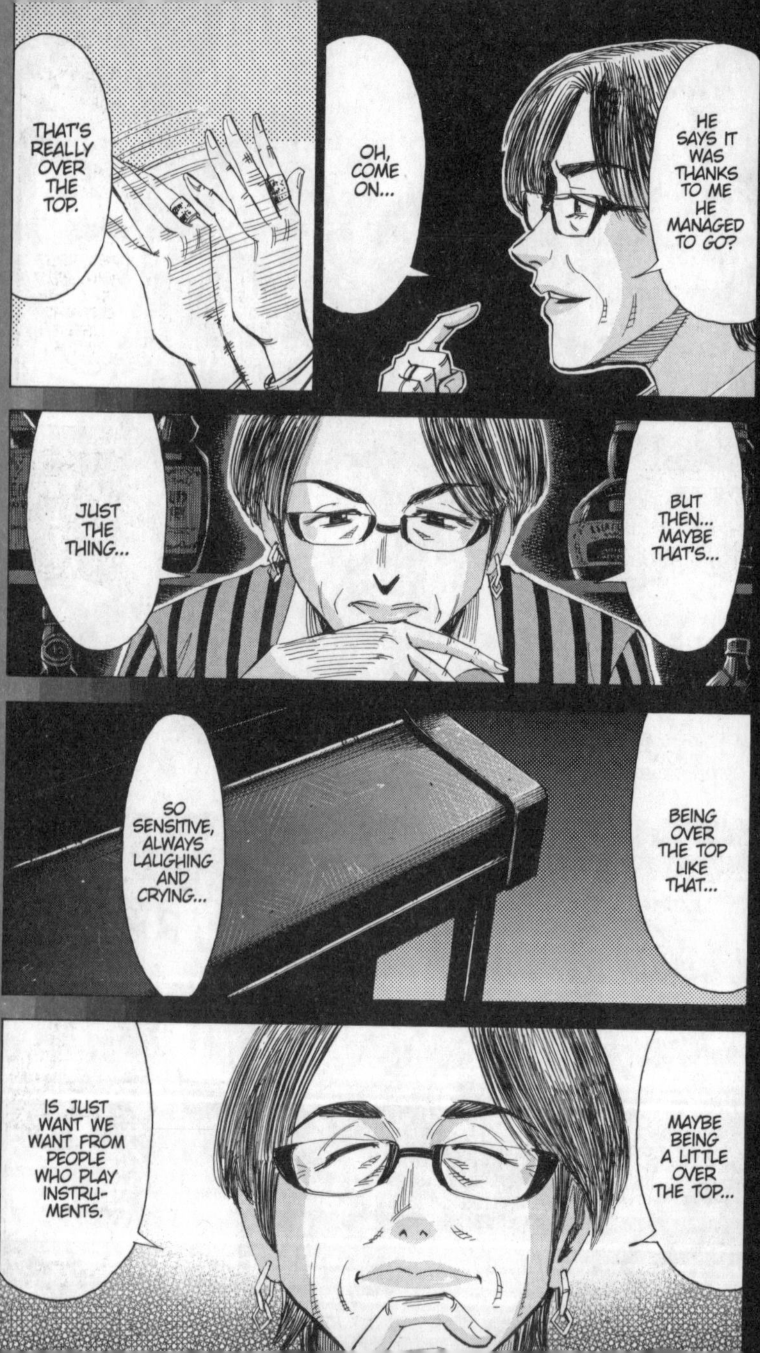
HE SAYS IT WAS THANKS TO ME HE MANAGED TO GO?
OH, COME ON...
THAT'S REALLY OVER THE TOP.
BUT THEN... MAYBE THAT'S...
JUST THE THING...
BEING OVER THE TOP LIKE THAT...
SO SENSITIVE, ALWAYS LAUGHING AND CRYING...
MAYBE BEING A LITTLE OVER THE TOP...
IS JUST WANT WE WANT FROM PEOPLE WHO PLAY INSTRU-MENTS.

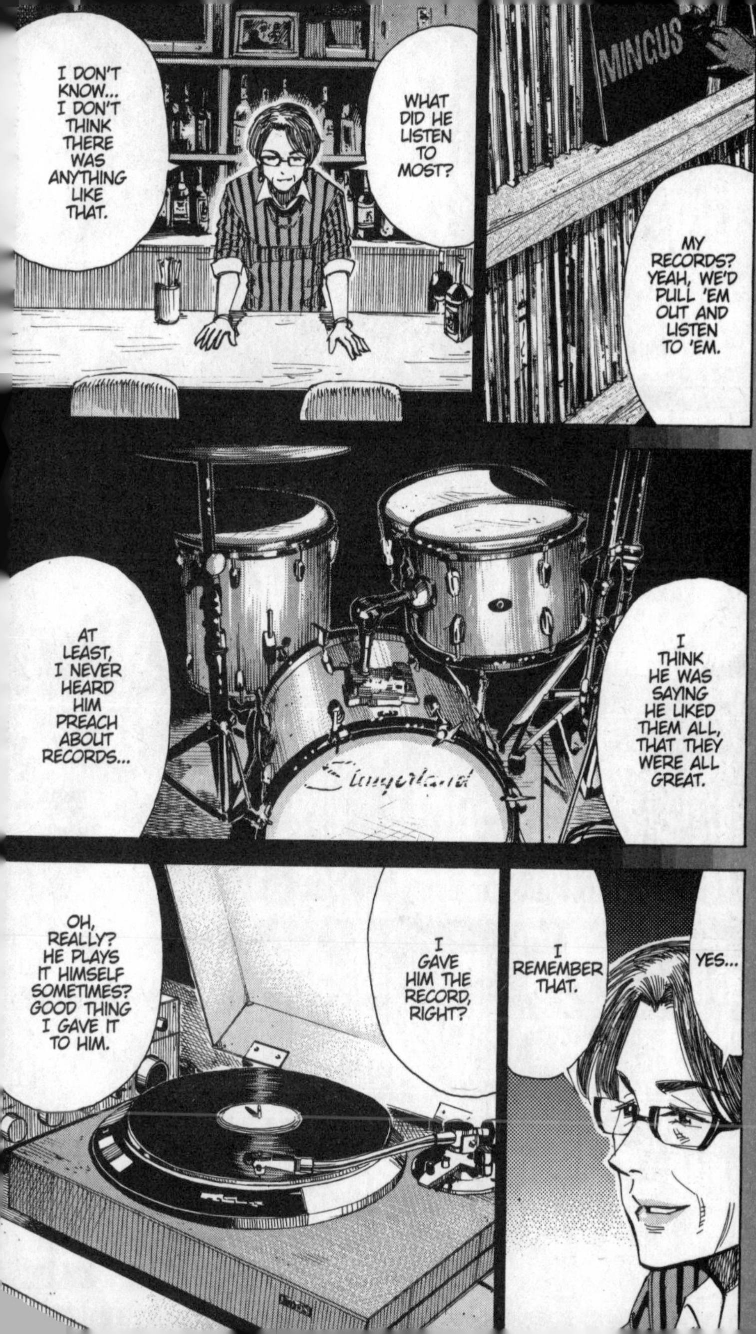

MINGUS
MY RECORDS? YEAH, WE'D PULL 'EM OUT AND LISTEN TO 'EM.
WHAT DID HE LISTEN TO MOST?
I DON'T KNOW... I DON'T THINK THERE WAS ANYTHING LIKE THAT.
AT LEAST, I NEVER HEARD HIM PREACH ABOUT RECORDS...
I THINK HE WAS SAYING HE LIKED THEM ALL, THAT THEY WERE ALL GREAT.
YES...
I REMEMBER THAT.
I GAVE HIM THE RECORD, RIGHT?
OH, REALLY? HE PLAYS IT HIMSELF SOMETIMES? GOOD THING I GAVE IT TO HIM.

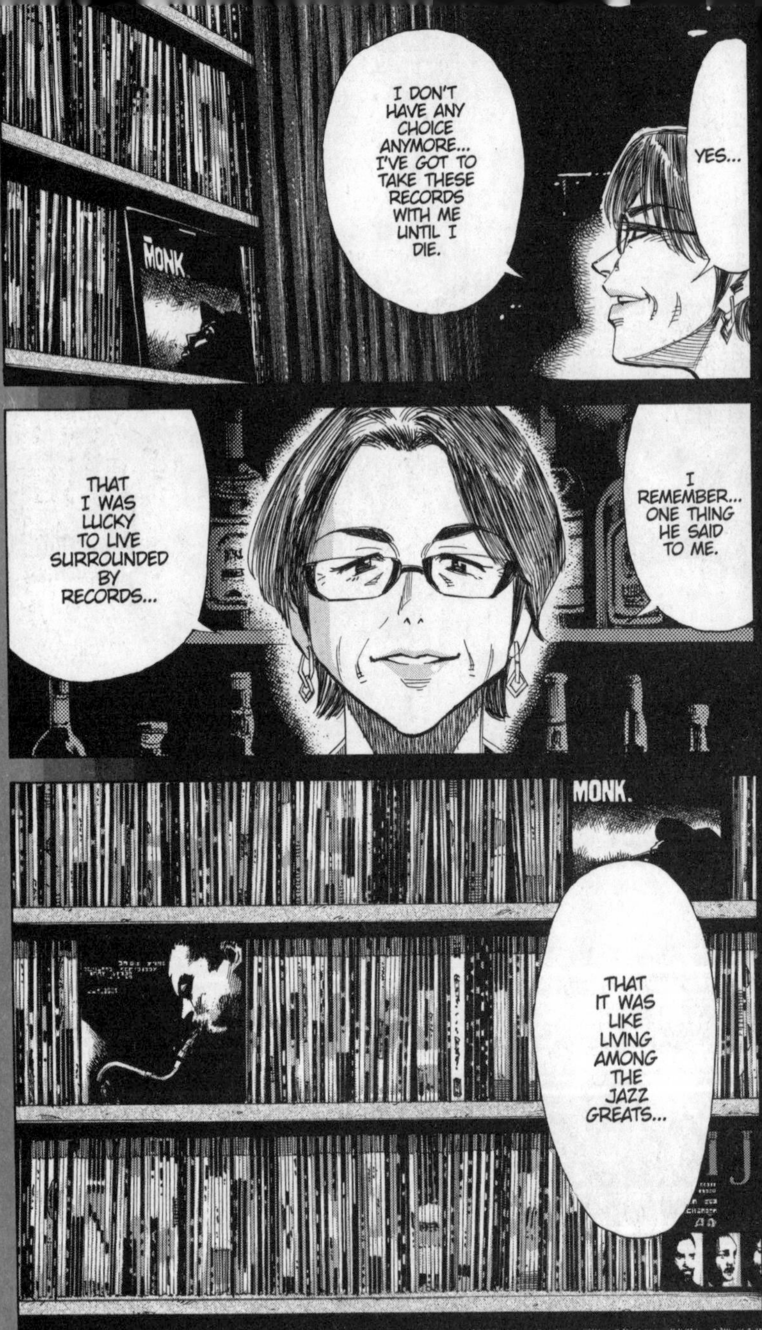
YES...
I DON'T HAVE ANY CHOICE ANYMORE... I'VE GOT TO TAKE THESE RECORDS WITH ME UNTIL I DIE.
MONK.
I REMEMBER... ONE THING HE SAID TO ME.
THAT I WAS LUCKY TO LIVE SURROUNDED BY RECORDS...
MONK.
THAT IT WAS LIKE LIVING AMONG THE JAZZ GREATS...

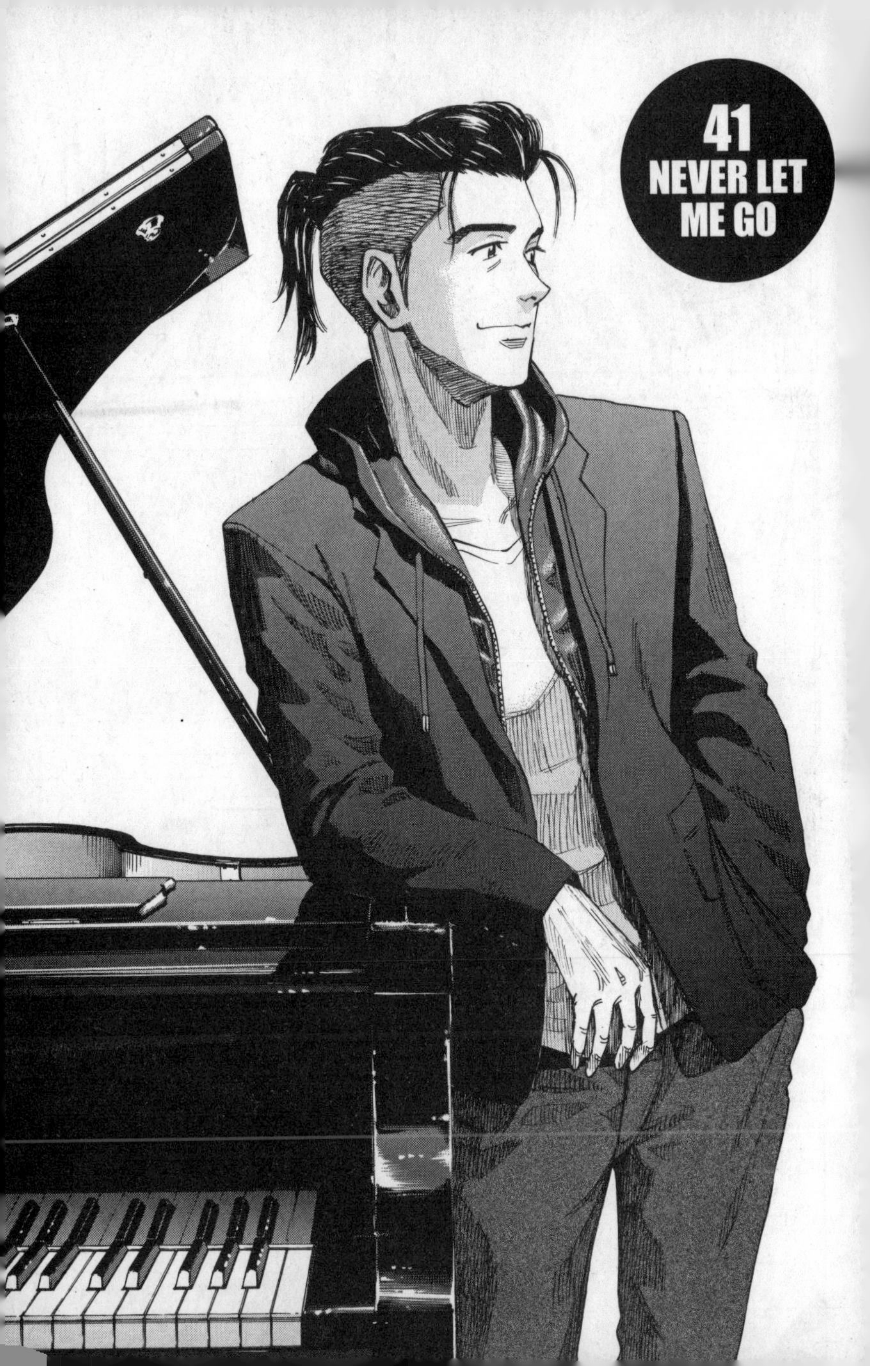
41
NEVER LET ME GO

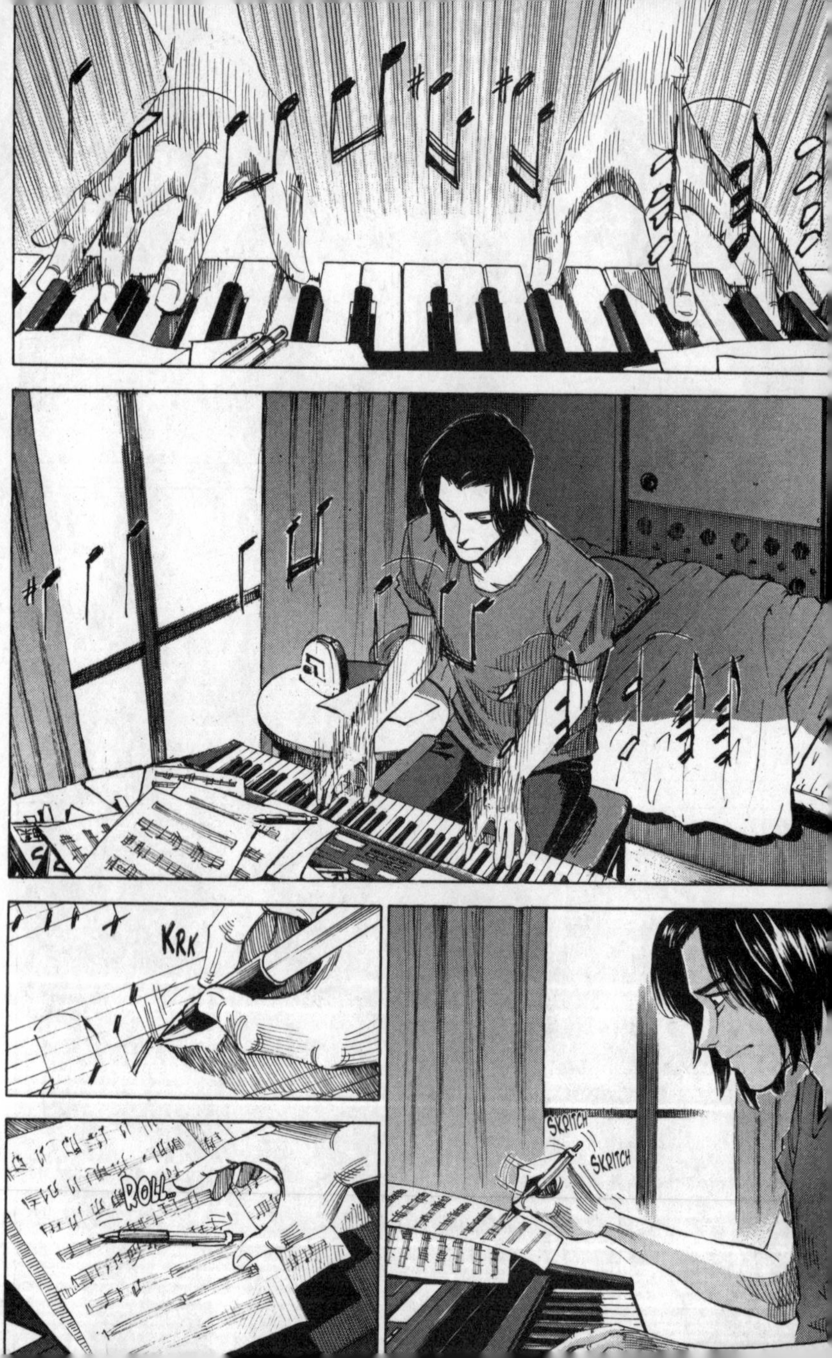
SKRITCH
SKRITCH
KRK
ROLL...

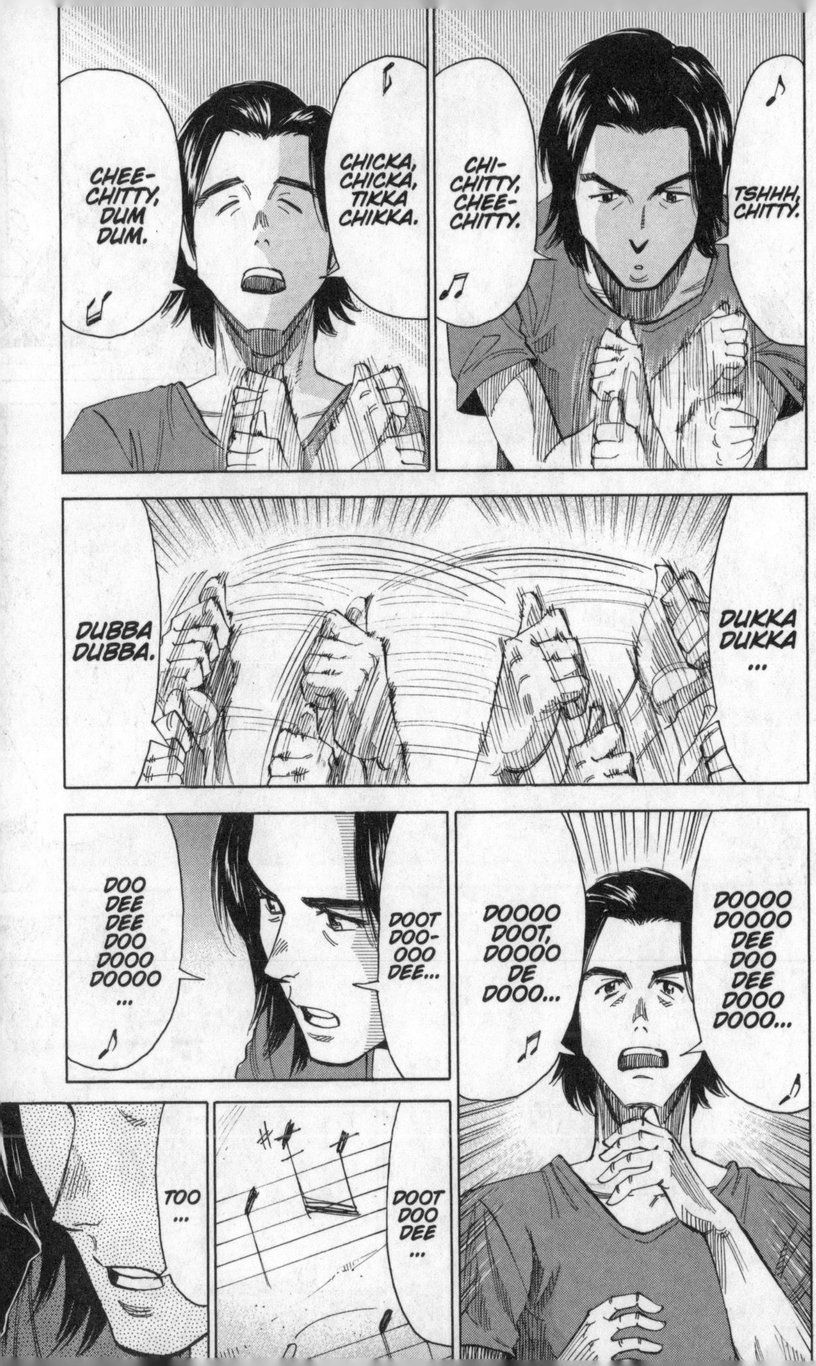
TSHHH, CHITTY.
CHI-CHITTY, CHEE-CHITTY.
CHICKA, CHICKA, TIKKA CHIKKA.
CHEE-CHITTY, DUM DUM.
DUKKA DUKKA ...
DUBBA DUBBA.
DOOOO DOOOO DEE DOO DEE DOOO DOOO...
DOOOO DOOT, DOOOO DE DOOO...
DOOT DOO-OOO DEE...
DOO DEE DEE DOO DOOO DOOOO ...
DOOT DOO DEE ...
TOO ...

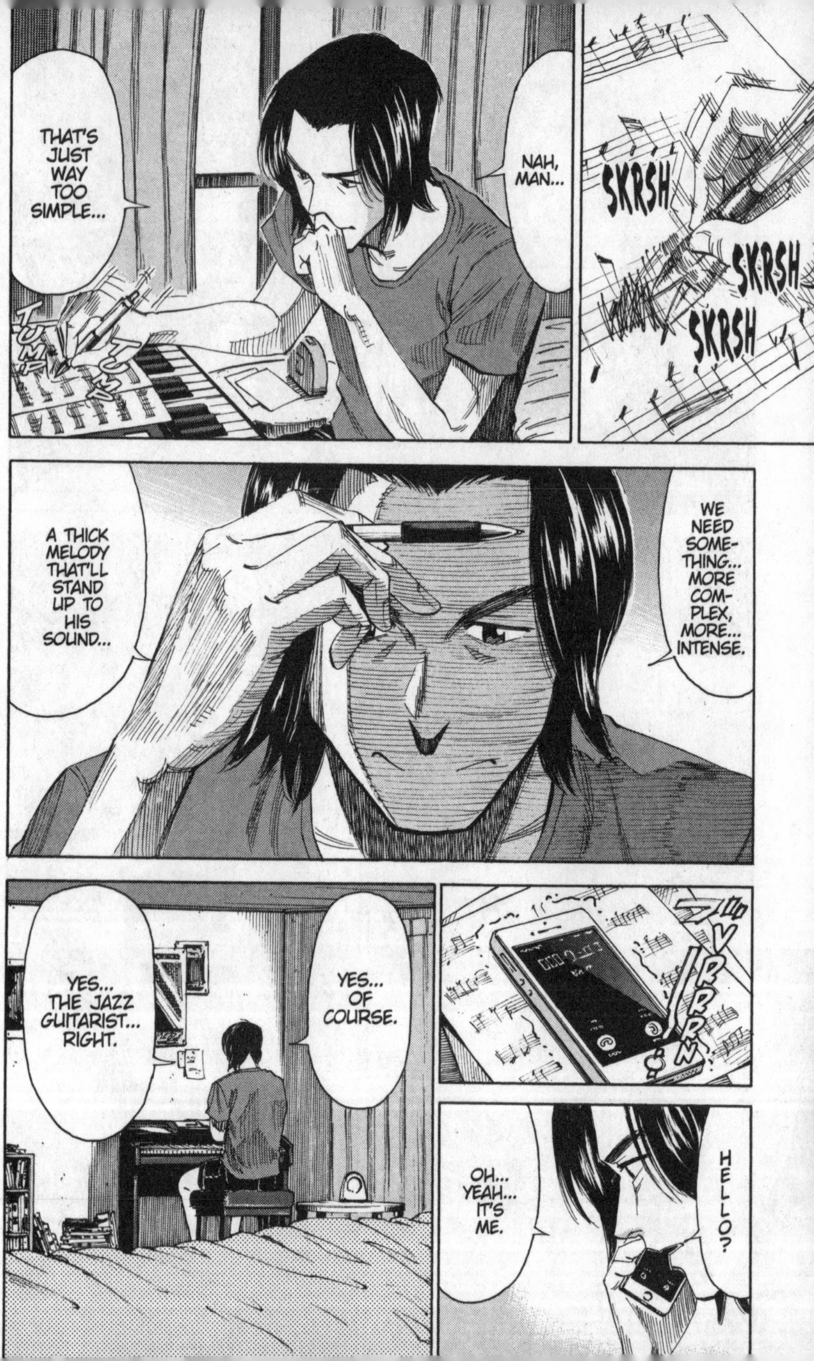
SKRSH
SKRSH
SKRSH
NAH, MAN...
THAT'S JUST WAY TOO SIMPLE...
TUMP
TUMP
WE NEED SOMETHING... MORE COMPLEX, MORE... INTENSE.
A THICK MELODY THAT'LL STAND UP TO HIS SOUND...
VRRRRN
HELLO?
OH... YEAH... IT'S ME.
YES... OF COURSE.
YES... THE JAZZ GUITARIST... RIGHT.

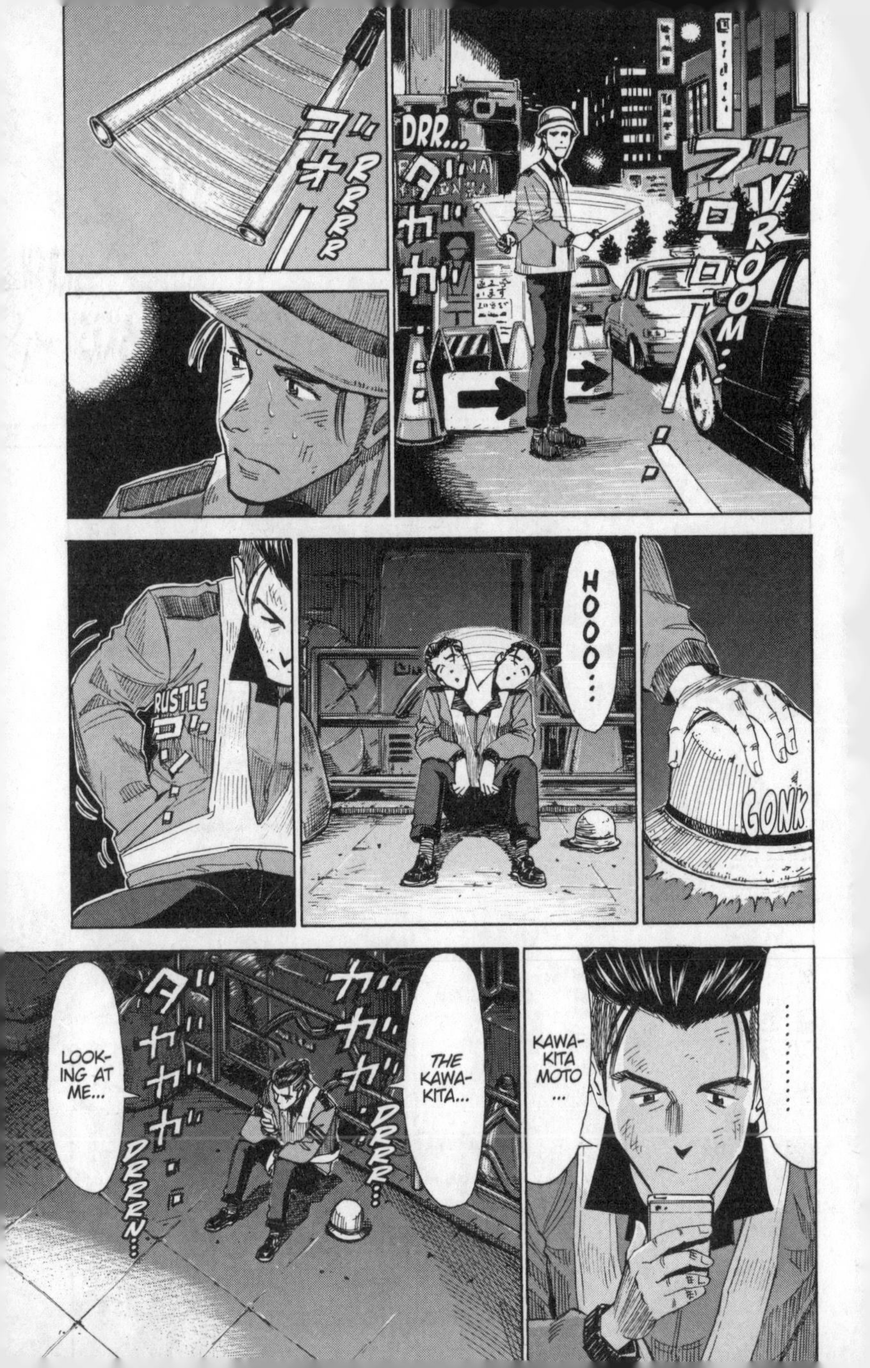

DRR...
ダカダカ
ブロロロ
VROOM...
ゴォー
RRRRR
GONK
HOOO...
RUSTLE
ゴソ
......
KAWA-KITA MOTO ...
THE KAWA-KITA...
DRRR...
LOOKING AT ME...
DRRRN...

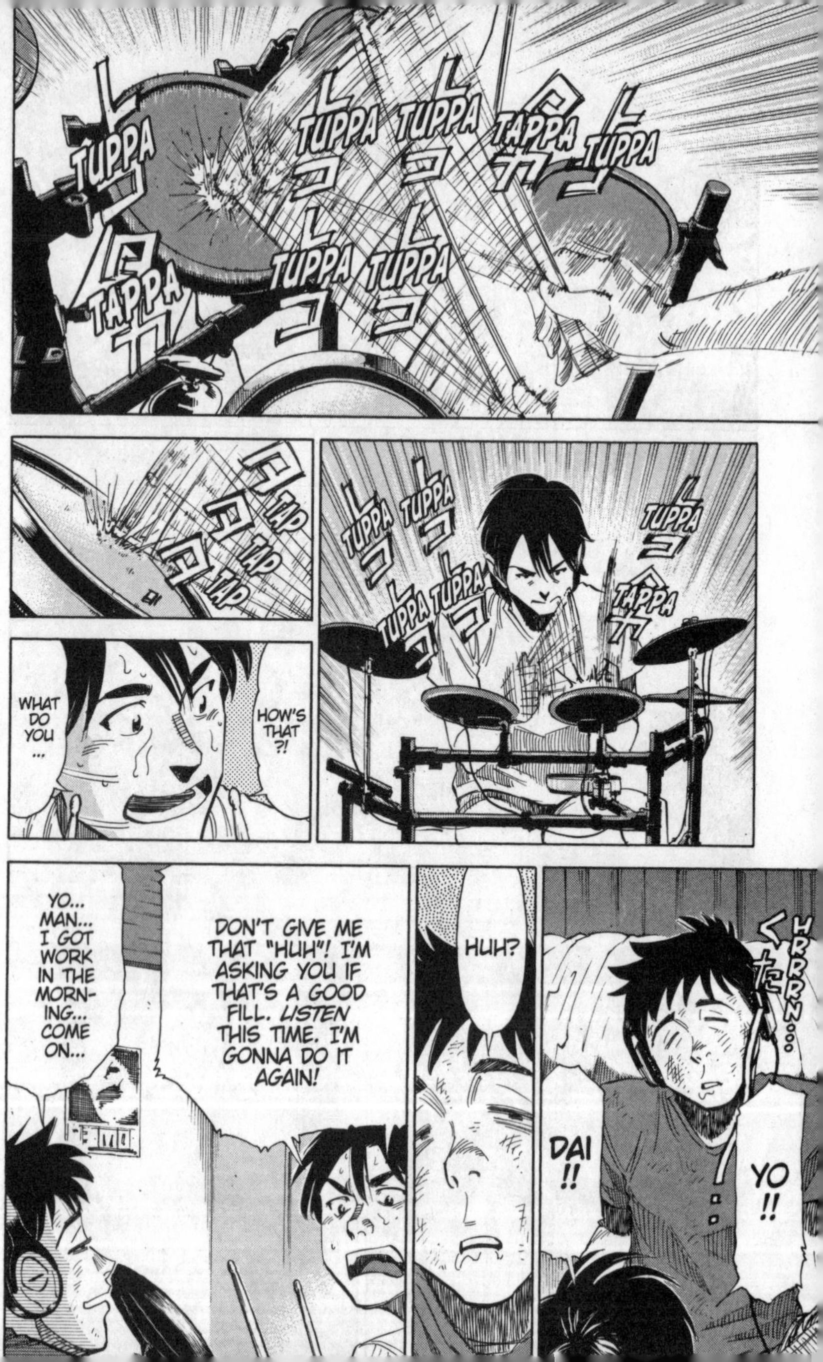

TUPPA
TAPPA
TUPPA
TUPPA
TUPPA
TUPPA
TUPPA
TAPPA
TUPPA
TAPPA
TUPPA
TUPPA
TUPPA
TUPPA
TAP
TAP
TAP
HOW'S THAT ?!
WHAT DO YOU ...
HRRRN...
YO !!
DAI !!
HUH?
DON'T GIVE ME THAT "HUH"! I'M ASKING YOU IF THAT'S A GOOD FILL. *LISTEN* THIS TIME. I'M GONNA DO IT AGAIN!
YO... MAN... I GOT WORK IN THE MORN-ING... COME ON...

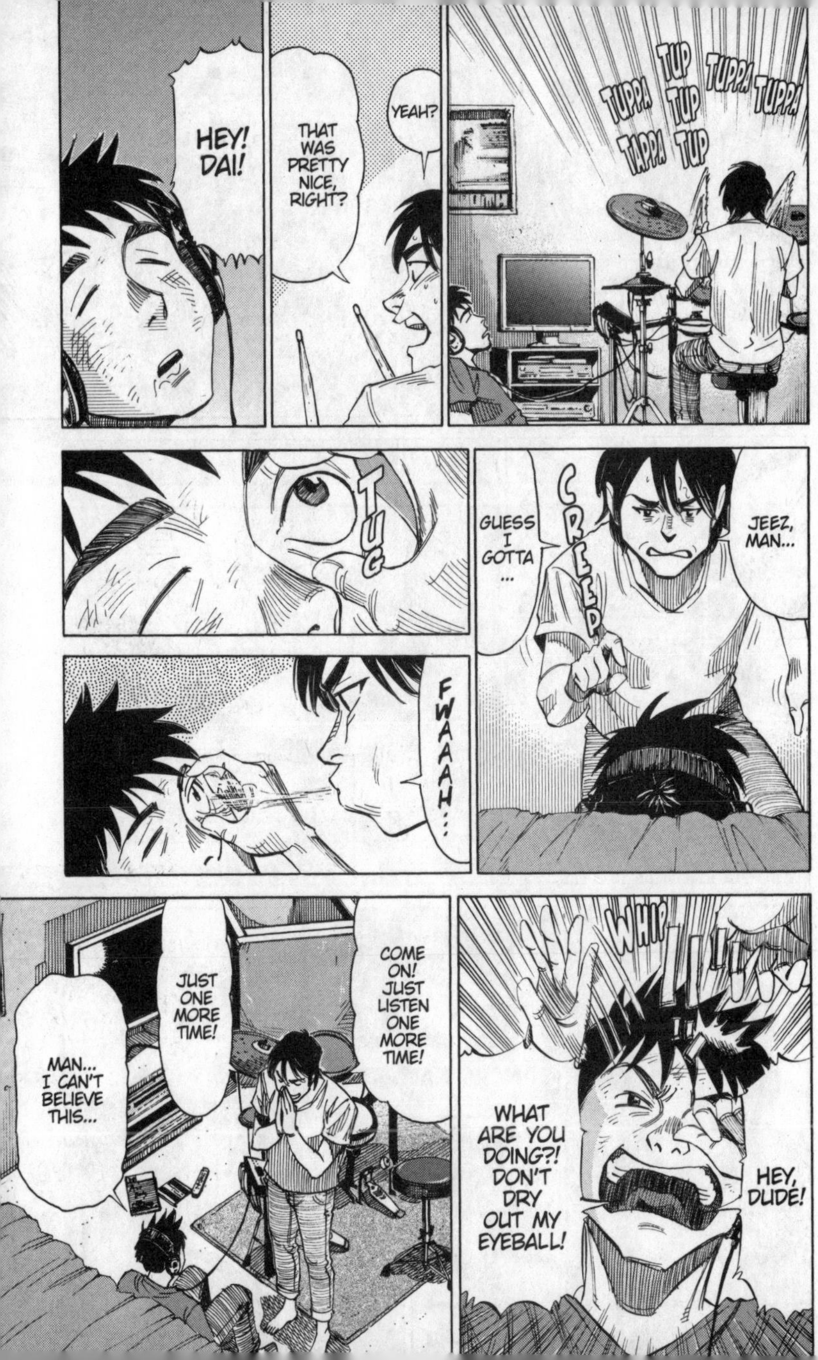

TUPPA TUPPA
TUPPA
TUP TUP TUP
TAPPA
YEAH?
THAT WAS PRETTY NICE, RIGHT?
HEY! DAI!
JEEZ, MAN...
CREEP
GUESS I GOTTA ...
TUG
FWAAAH...
WHIP
HEY, DUDE!
WHAT ARE YOU DOING?! DON'T DRY OUT MY EYEBALL!
COME ON! JUST LISTEN ONE MORE TIME!
JUST ONE MORE TIME!
MAN... I CAN'T BELIEVE THIS...

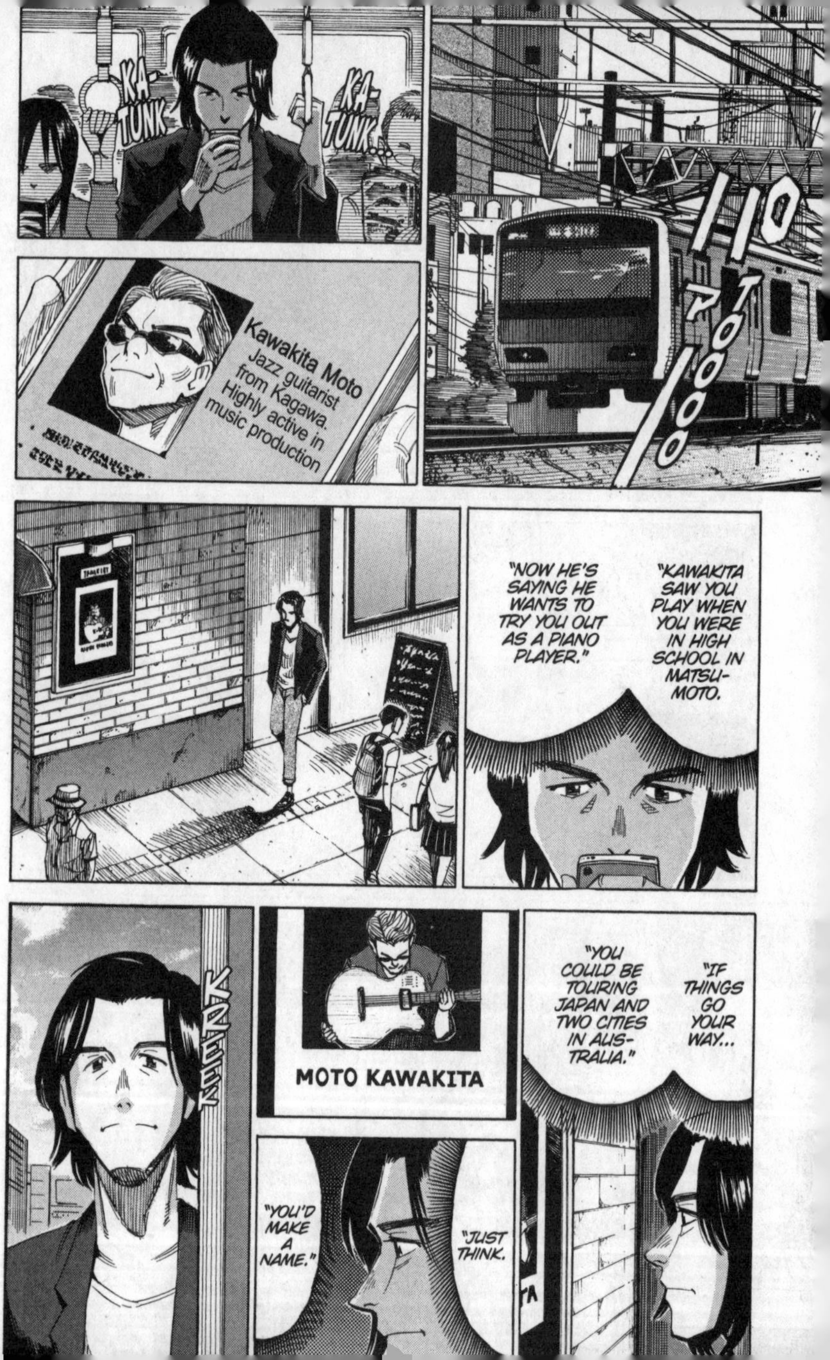
KA-TUNK
KA-TUNK...
Kawakita Moto
Jazz guitarist from Kagawa. Highly active in music production
"KAWAKITA SAW YOU PLAY WHEN YOU WERE IN HIGH SCHOOL IN MATSU-MOTO.
"NOW HE'S SAYING HE WANTS TO TRY YOU OUT AS A PIANO PLAYER."
"IF THINGS GO YOUR WAY...
"YOU COULD BE TOURING JAPAN AND TWO CITIES IN AUS-TRALIA."
MOTO KAWAKITA
"JUST THINK.
"YOU'D MAKE A NAME."

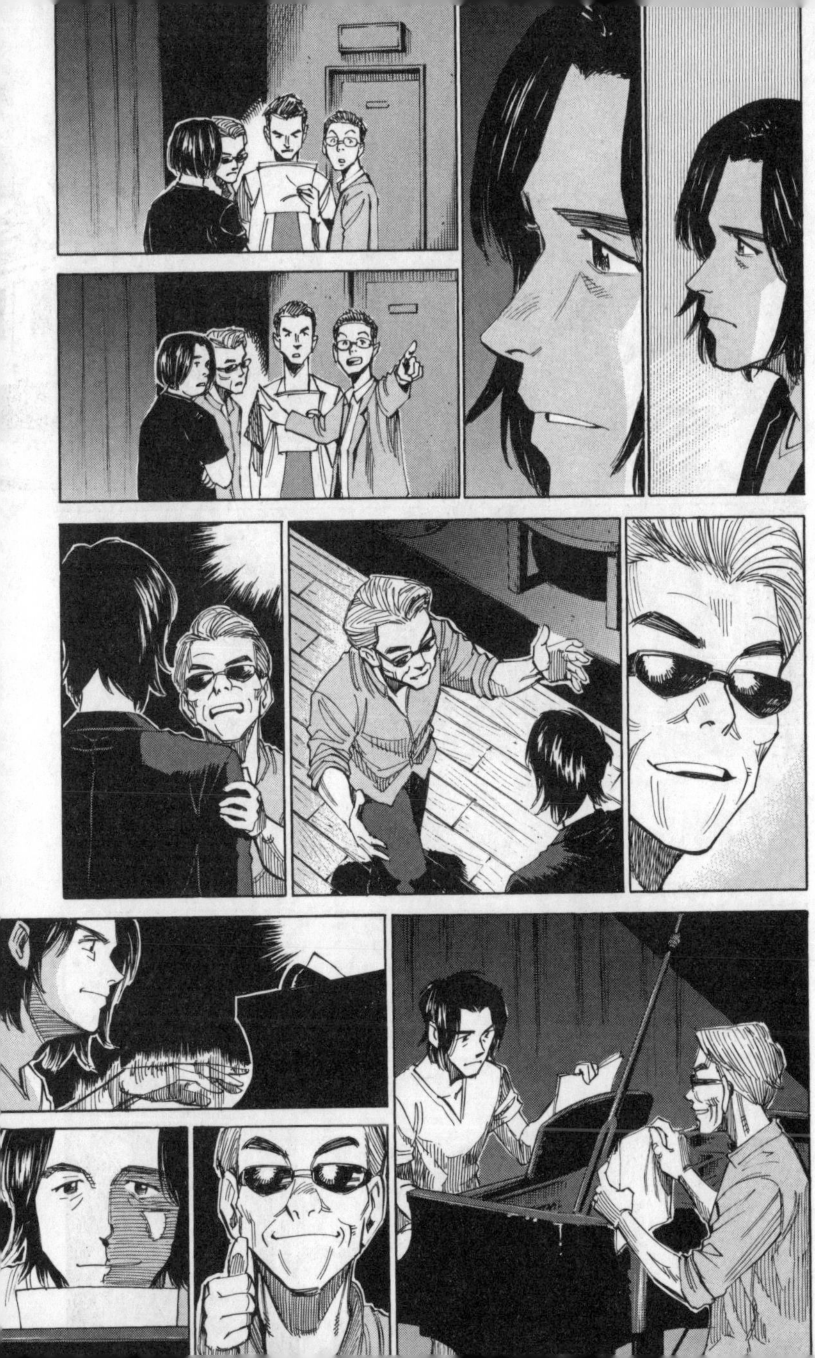

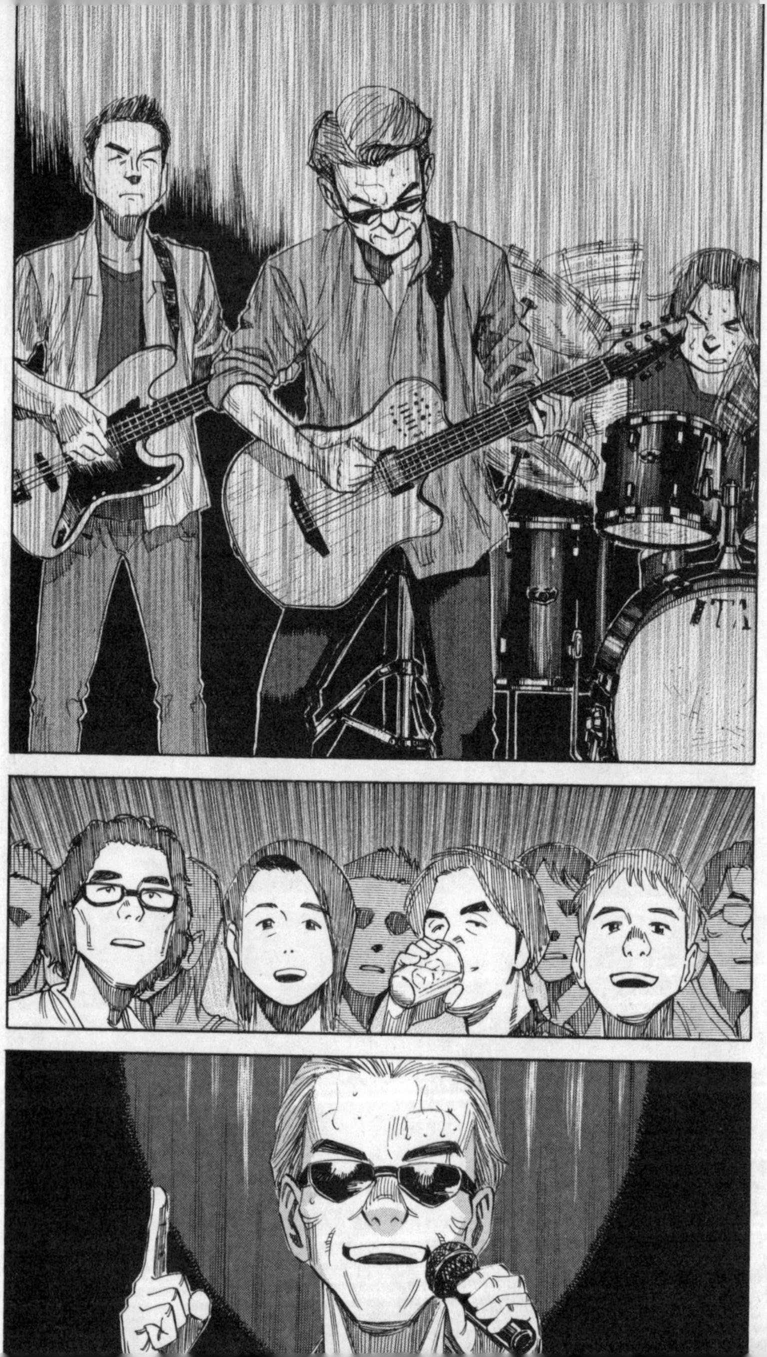

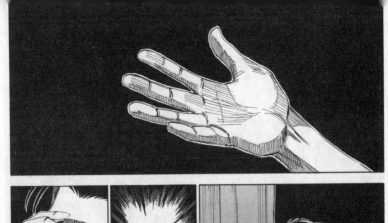

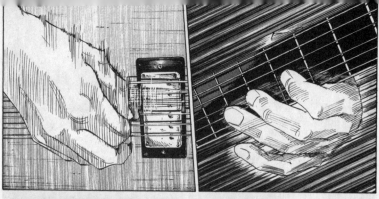

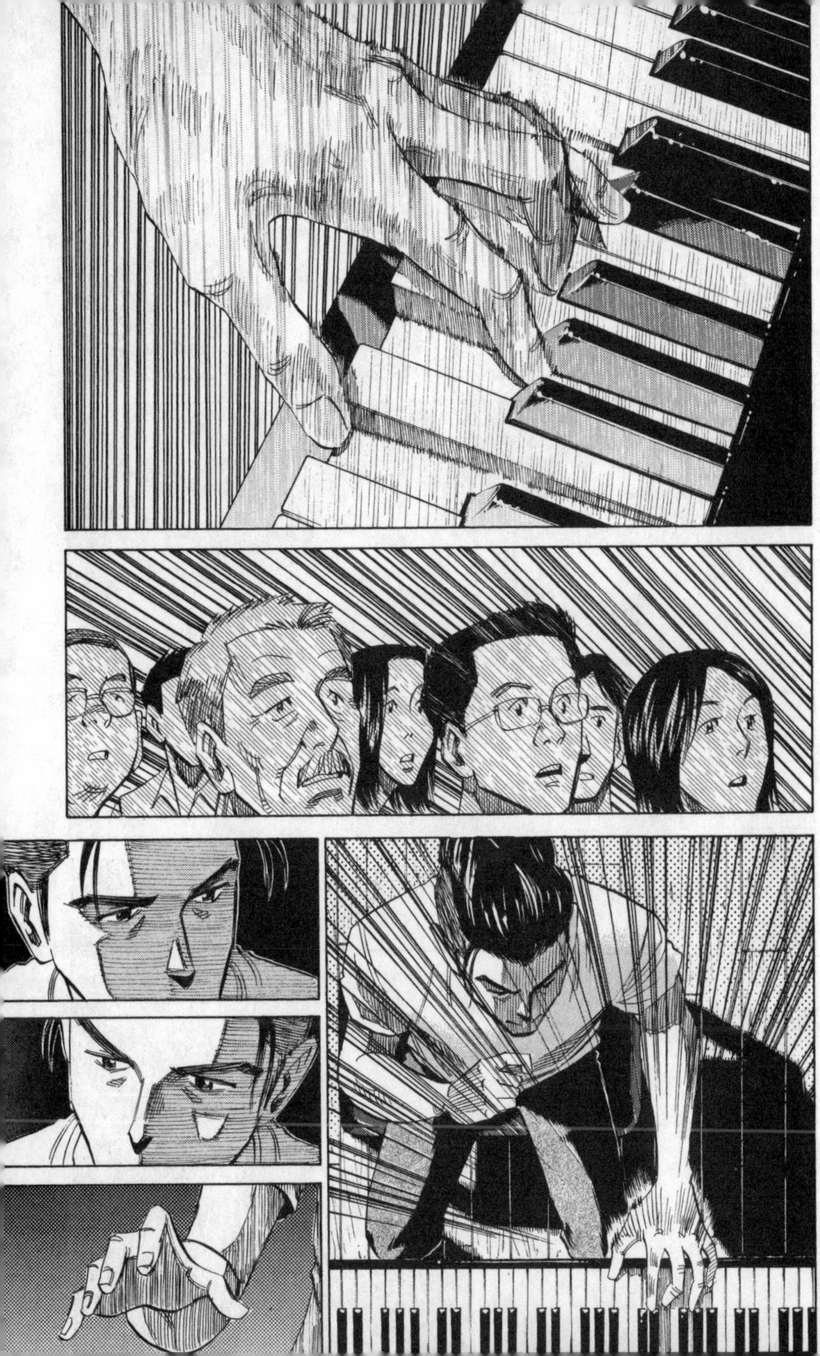

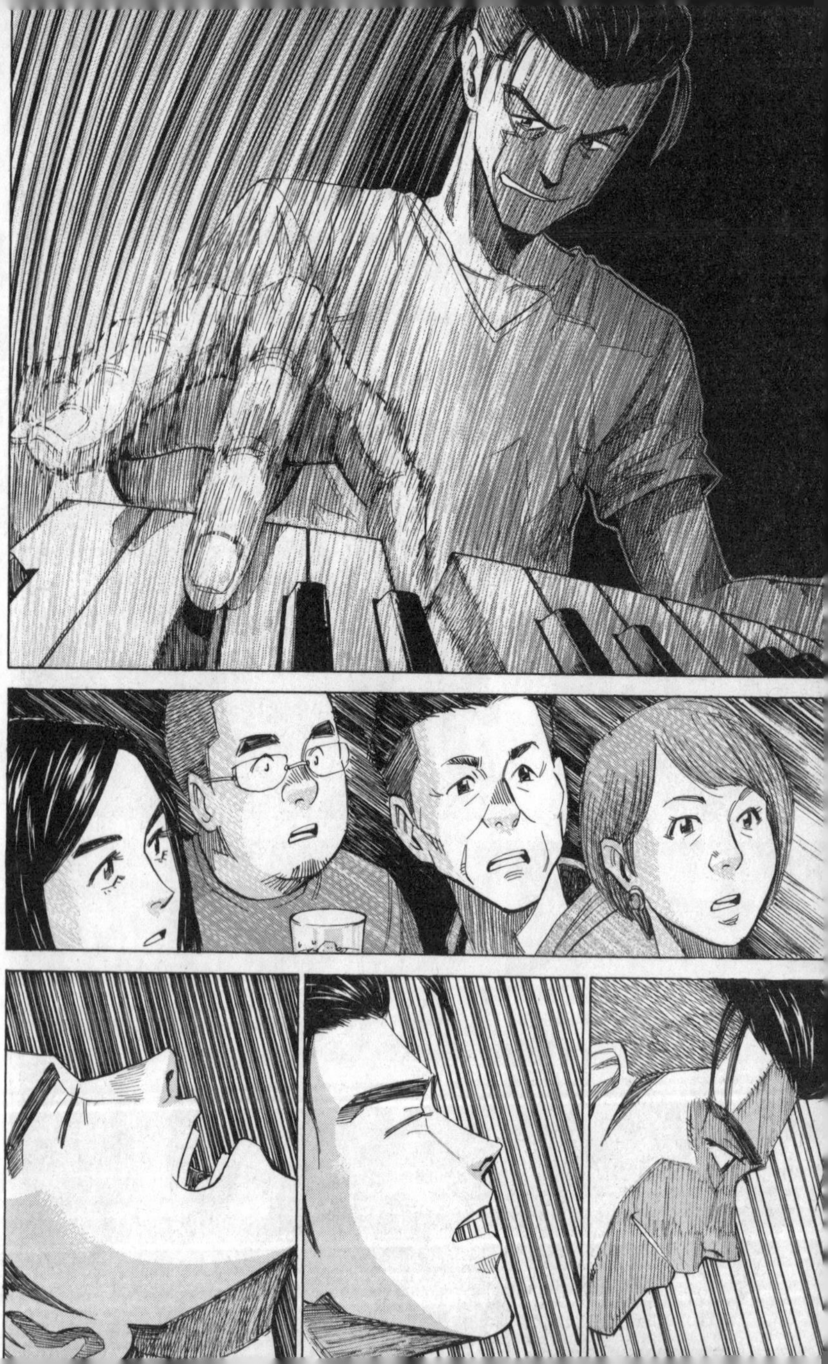

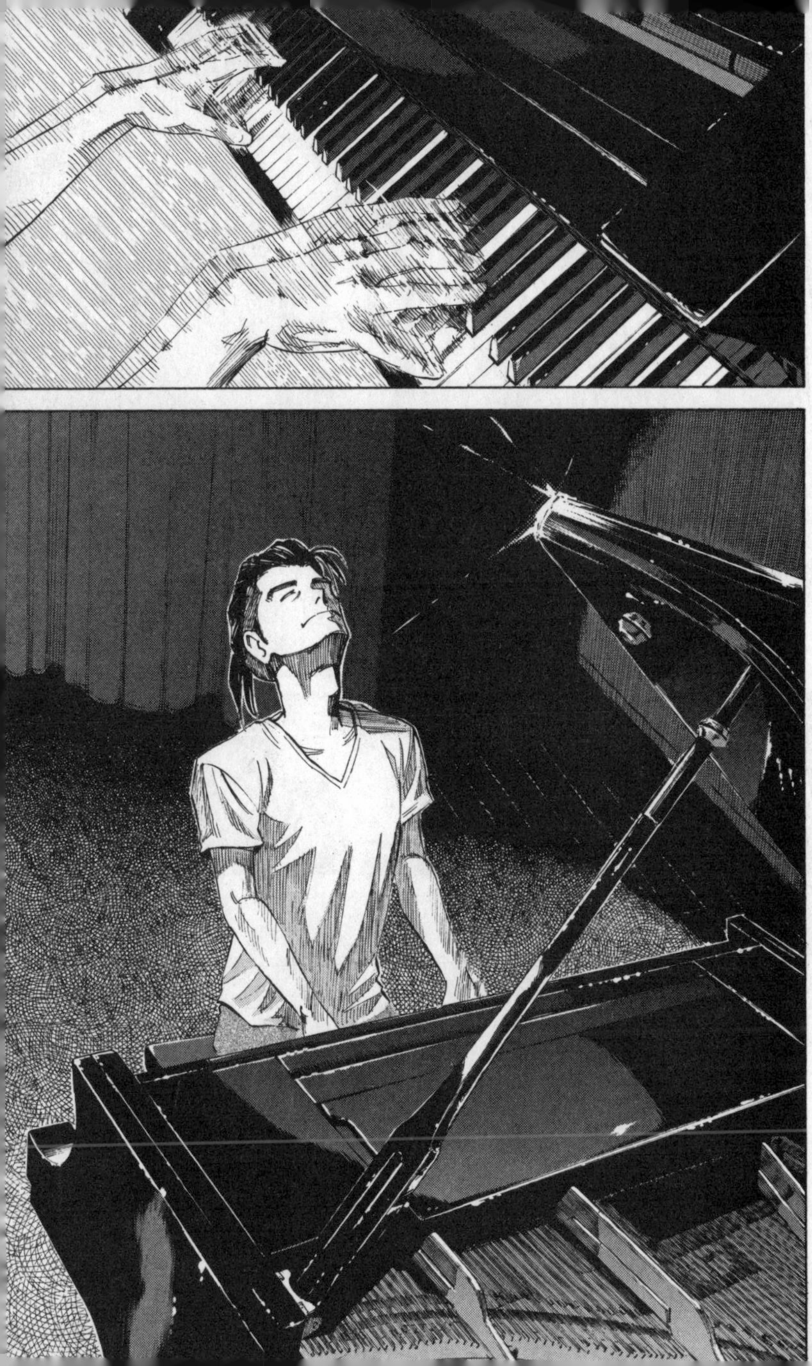

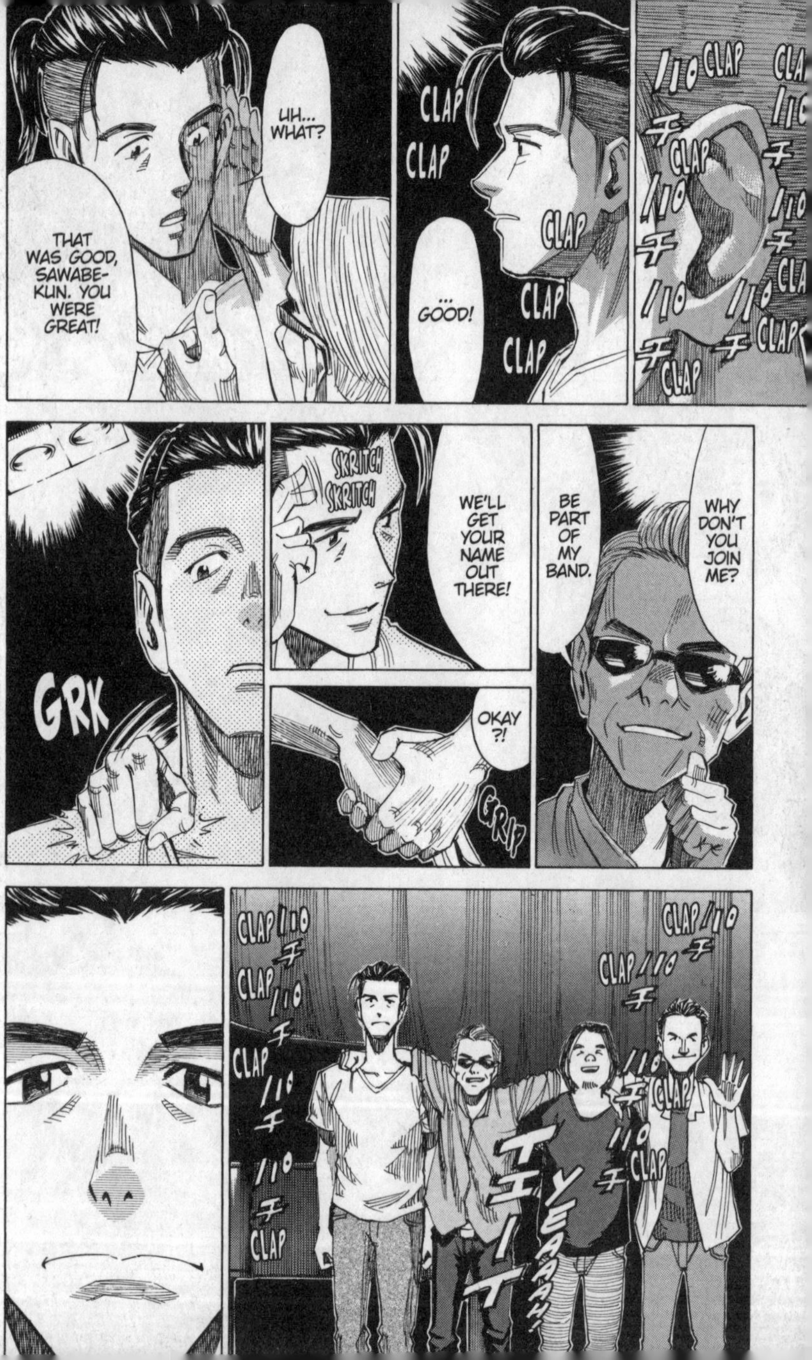

CLAP
CLAP
CLAP
CLAP
CLAP
CLAP
CLAP
CLAP
CLAP
CLAP
CLAP
CLAP
...GOOD!
UH... WHAT?
THAT WAS GOOD, SAWABE-KUN. YOU WERE GREAT!
WHY DON'T YOU JOIN ME?
BE PART OF MY BAND.
WE'LL GET YOUR NAME OUT THERE!
SKRITCH
SKRITCH
OKAY ?!
GRIP
GRK
CLAP
CLAP
CLAP
CLAP
CLAP
CLAP
CLAP
YEAAAH!

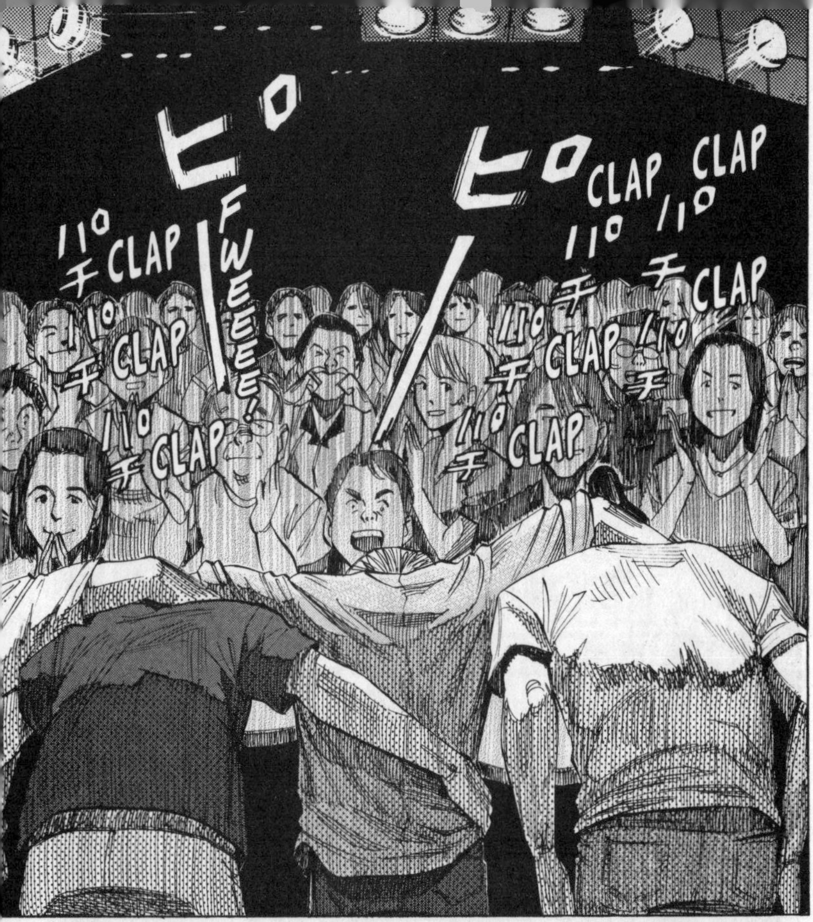
FWEEEE!
CLAP CLAP
CLAP
CLAP
CLAP
CLAP
CLAP
CLAP
CLAP
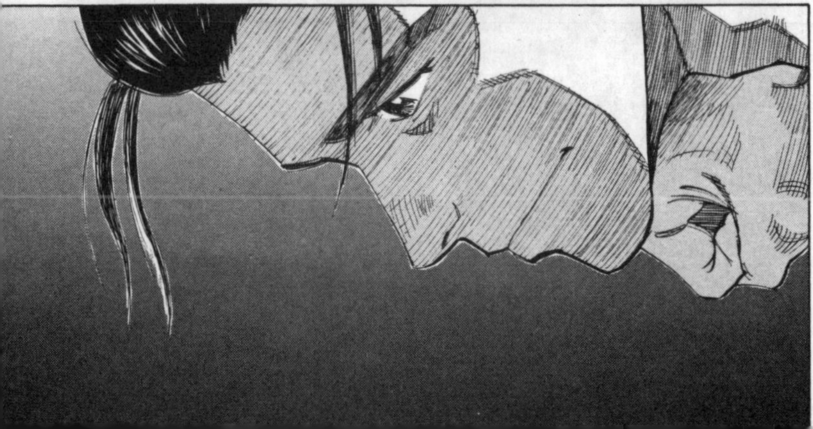

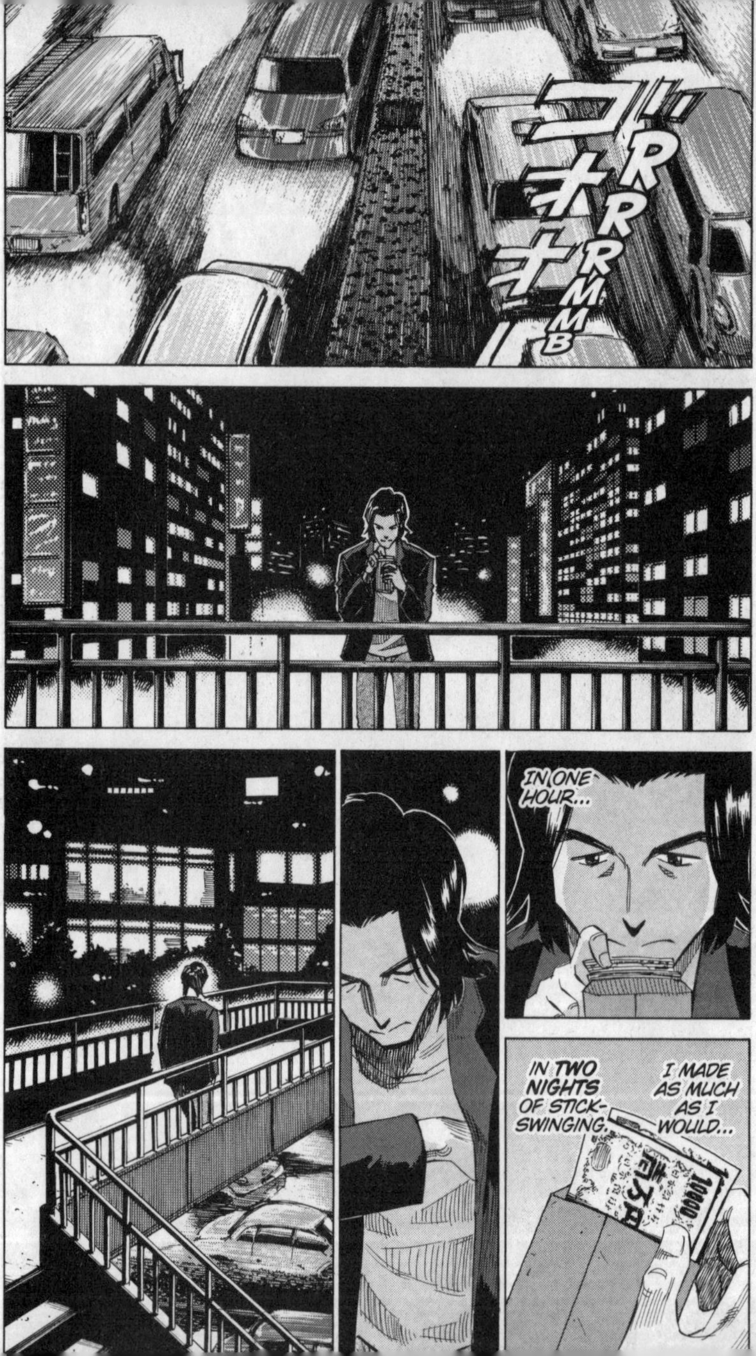
ゴオオ
RRRMMB
IN ONE HOUR...
I MADE AS MUCH AS I WOULD...
IN TWO NIGHTS OF STICK-SWINGING.

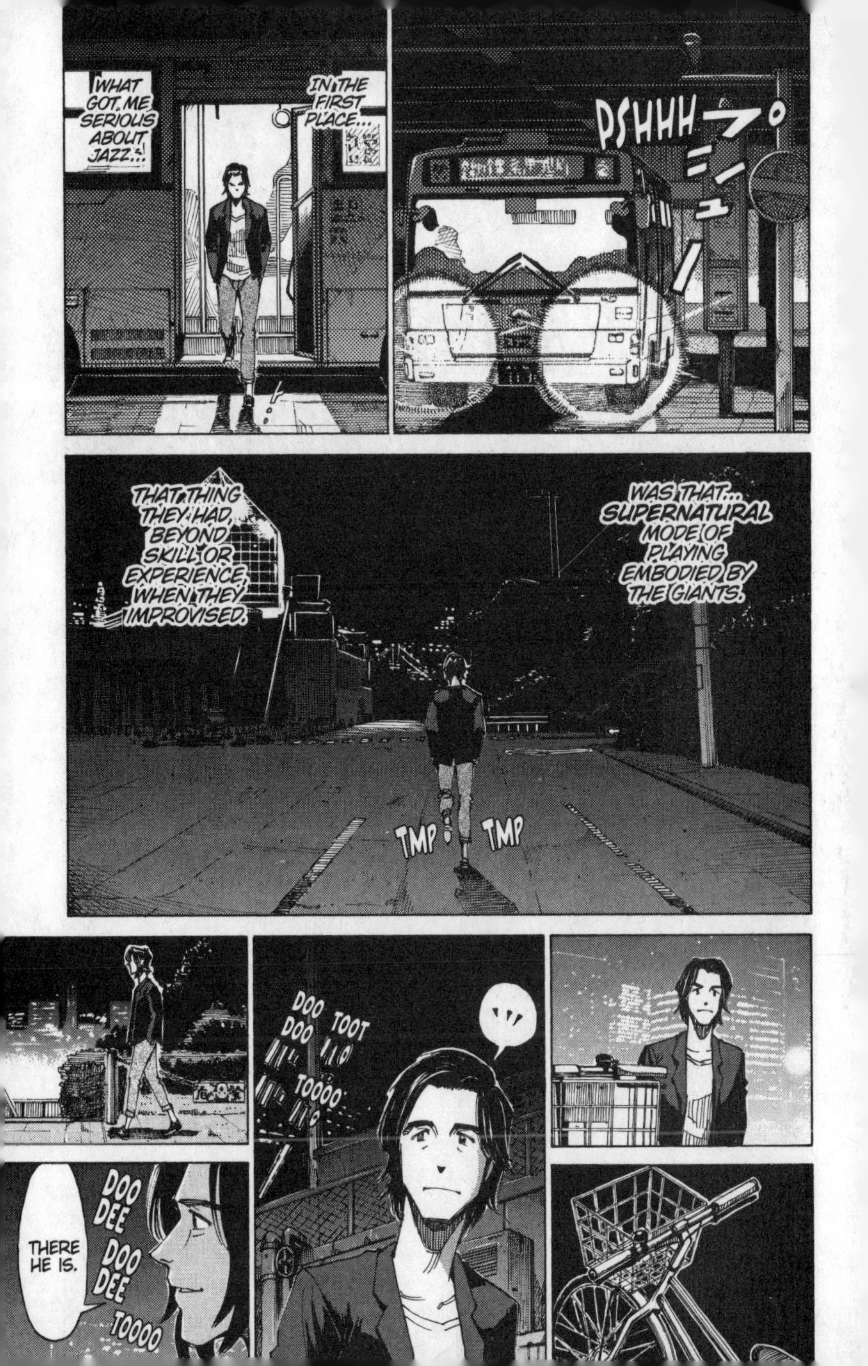
PSHHH
IN THE FIRST PLACE...
WHAT GOT ME SERIOUS ABOUT JAZZ...!
WAS THAT... SUPERNATURAL MODE OF PLAYING EMBODIED BY THE GIANTS.
THAT THING THEY HAD, BEYOND SKILL OR EXPERIENCE, WHEN THEY IMPROVISED.
TMP TMP
!
DOO DOO TOOT TOOOO
DOO DEE DOO DEE TOOOO
THERE HE IS.

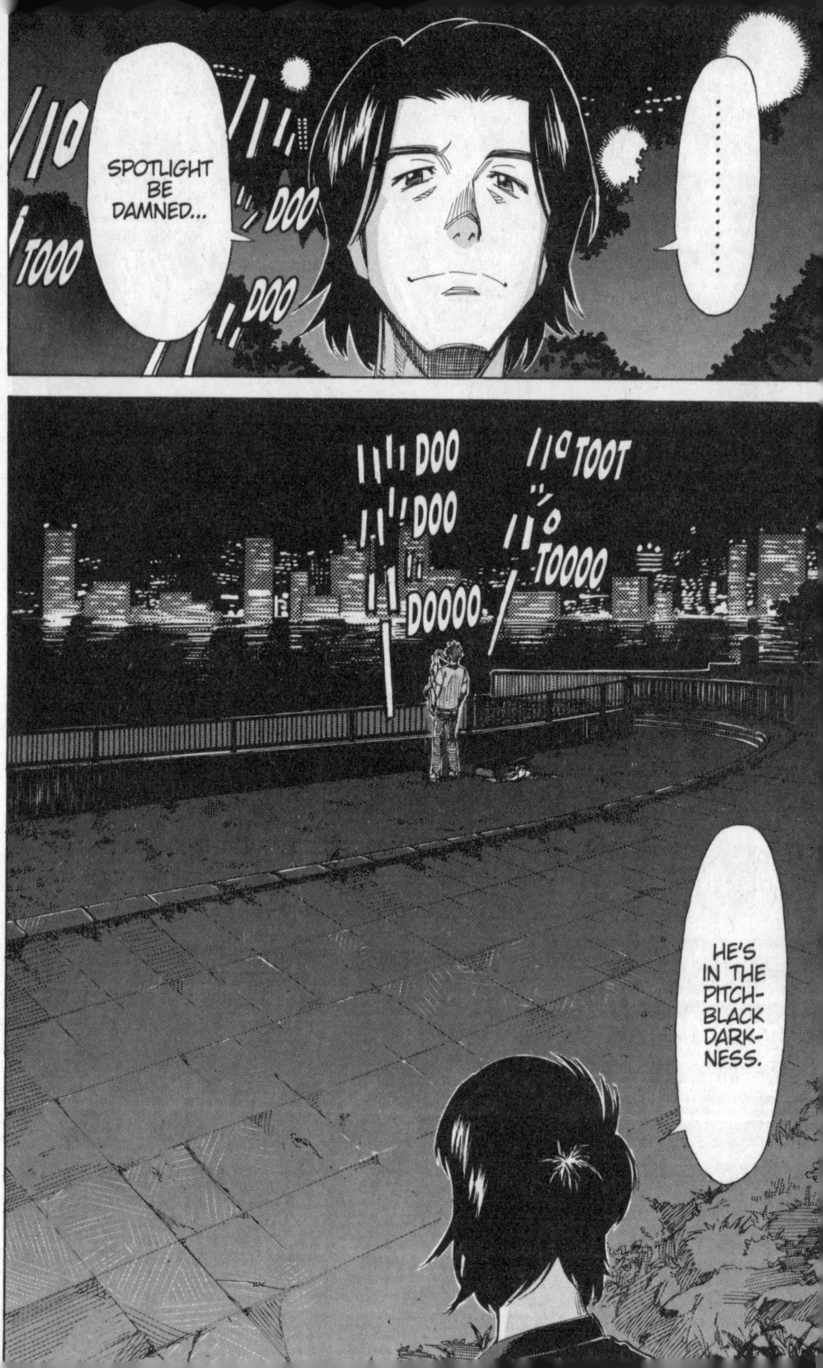
......
DOO
DOO
SPOTLIGHT BE DAMNED...
TOOO
TOOT
TOOOO
DOO
DOO
DOOOO
HE'S IN THE PITCH-BLACK DARKNESS.

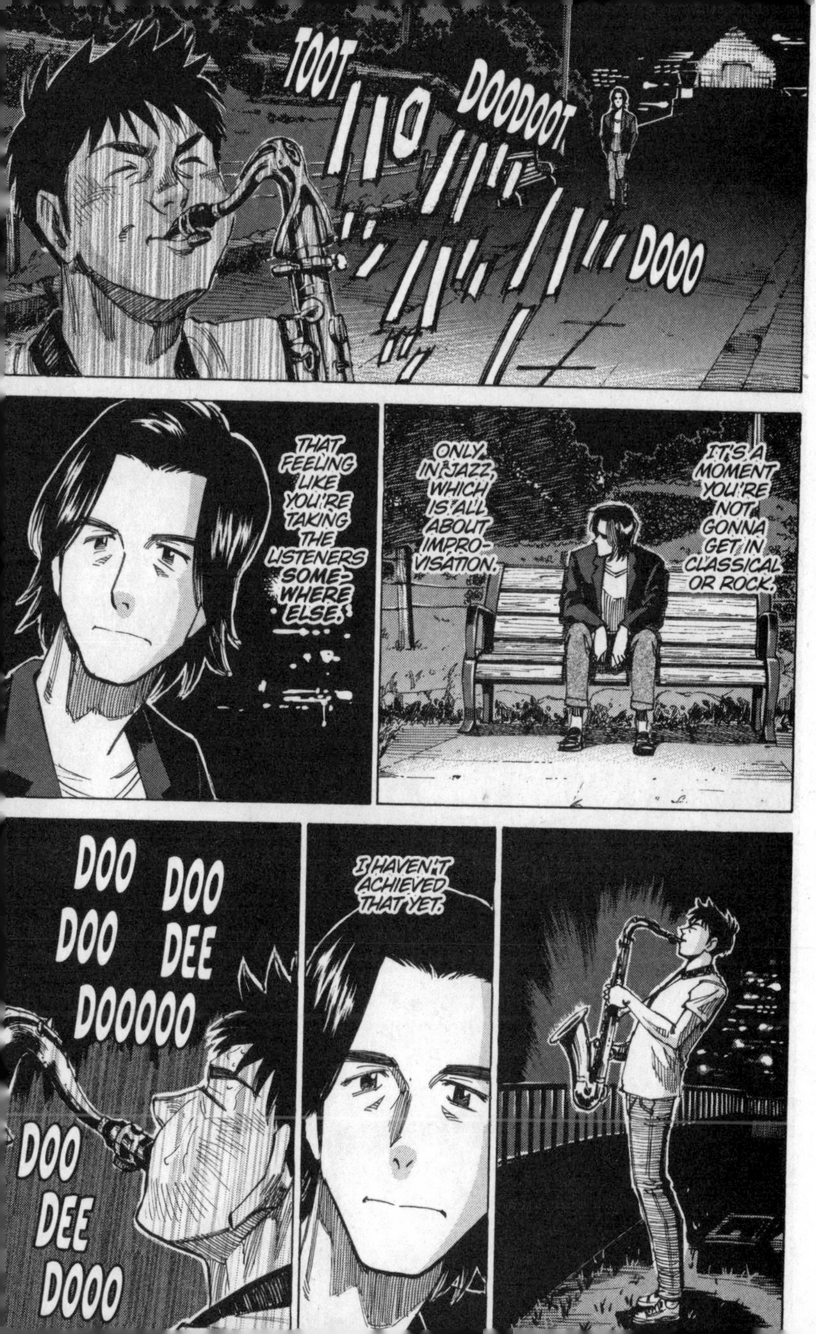
TOOT
DOODOOT
DOOO
IT'S A MOMENT YOU'RE NOT GONNA GET IN CLASSICAL OR ROCK.
ONLY IN JAZZ, WHICH IS ALL ABOUT IMPRO-VISATION.
THAT FEELING LIKE YOU'RE TAKING THE LISTENERS SOME-WHERE ELSE.
I HAVEN'T ACHIEVED THAT YET.
DOO DEE
DOO DOO DOOOOO
DOO DEE DOOO

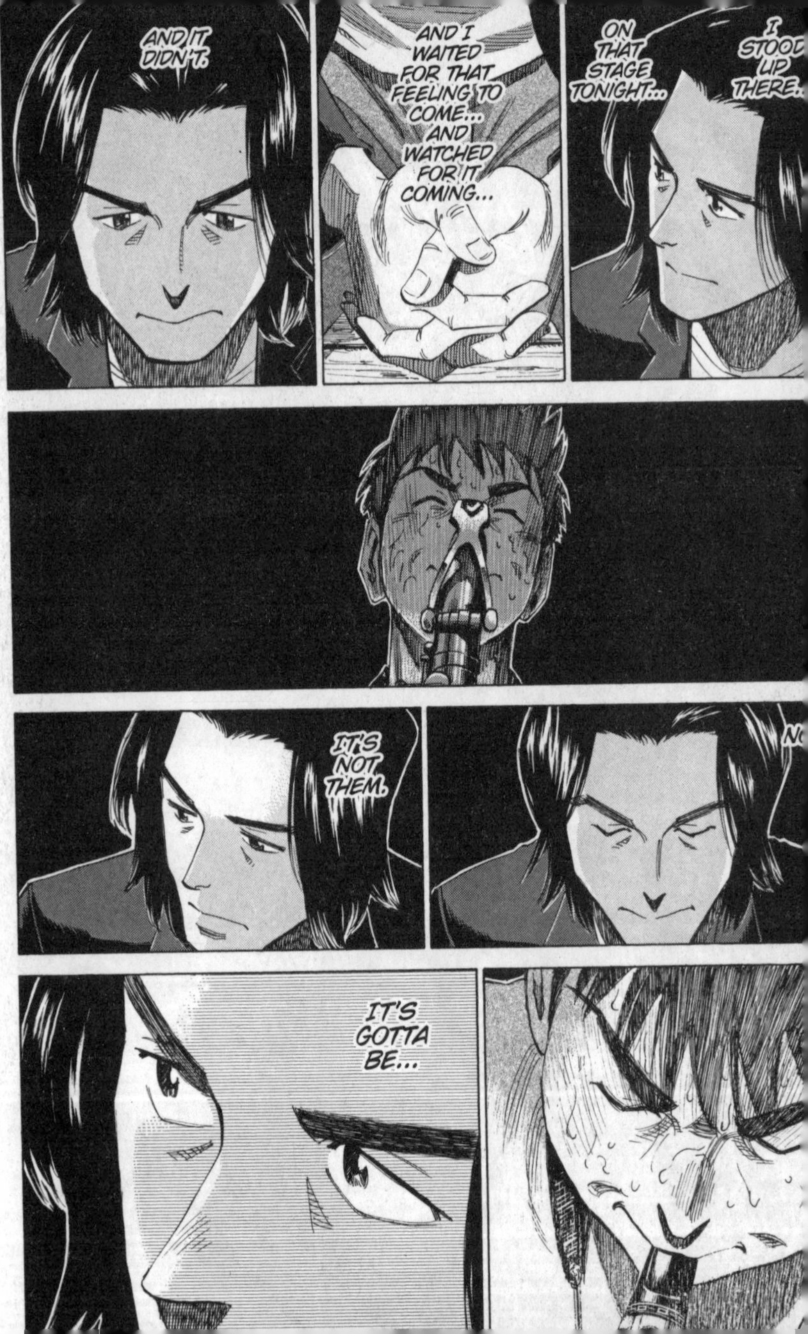
I STOOD UP THERE...
ON THAT STAGE TONIGHT...
AND I WAITED FOR THAT FEELING TO COME... AND WATCHED FOR IT COMING...
AND IT DIDN'T.
IT'S NOT THEM.
IT'S GOTTA BE...

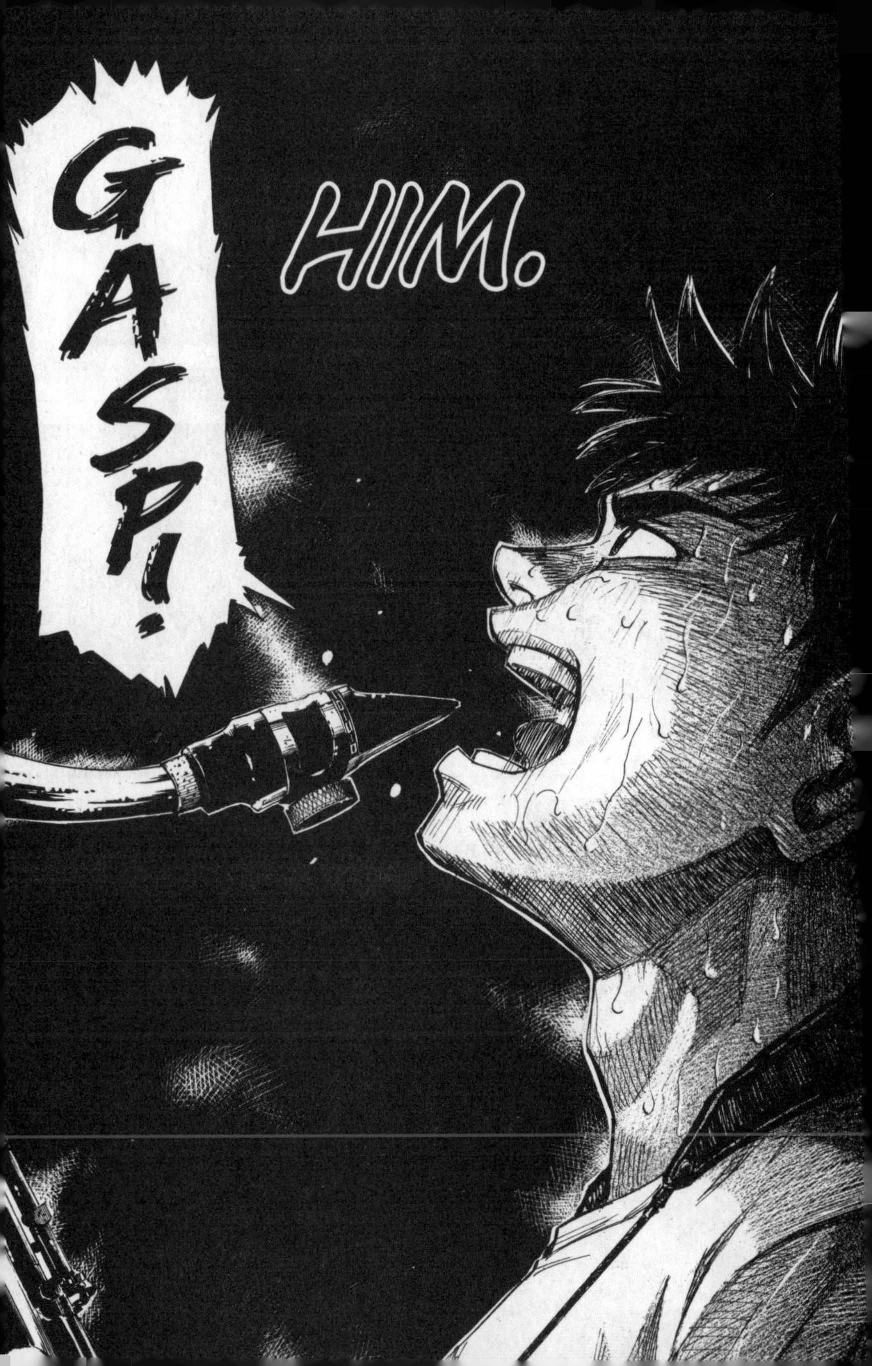
HIM.
GASP!

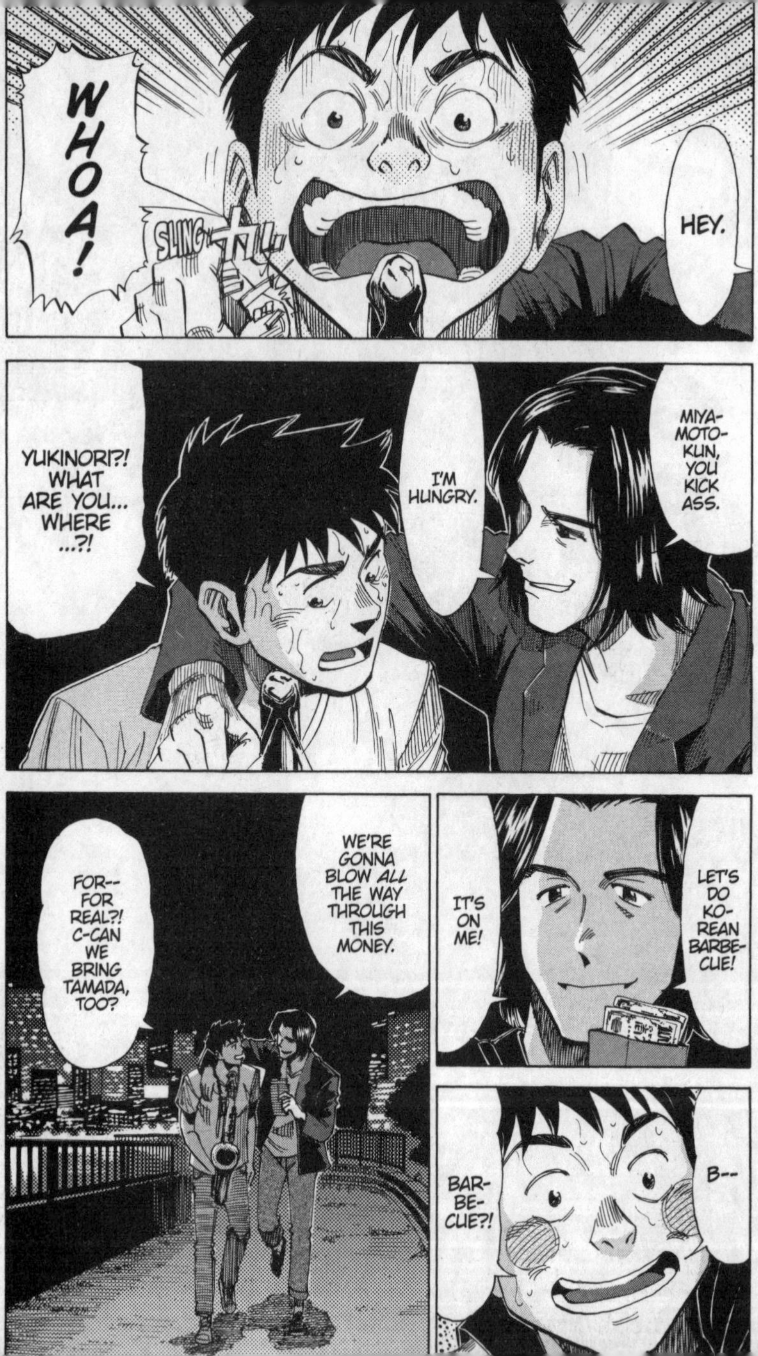
HEY.
WHOA!
SLING
MIYA-MOTO-KUN, YOU KICK ASS.
I'M HUNGRY.
YUKINORI?! WHAT ARE YOU... WHERE ...?!
LET'S DO KO-REAN BARBE-CUE!
IT'S ON ME!
B--
BAR-BE-CUE?!
WE'RE GONNA BLOW *ALL* THE WAY THROUGH THIS MONEY.
FOR-- FOR REAL?! C-CAN WE BRING TAMADA, TOO?

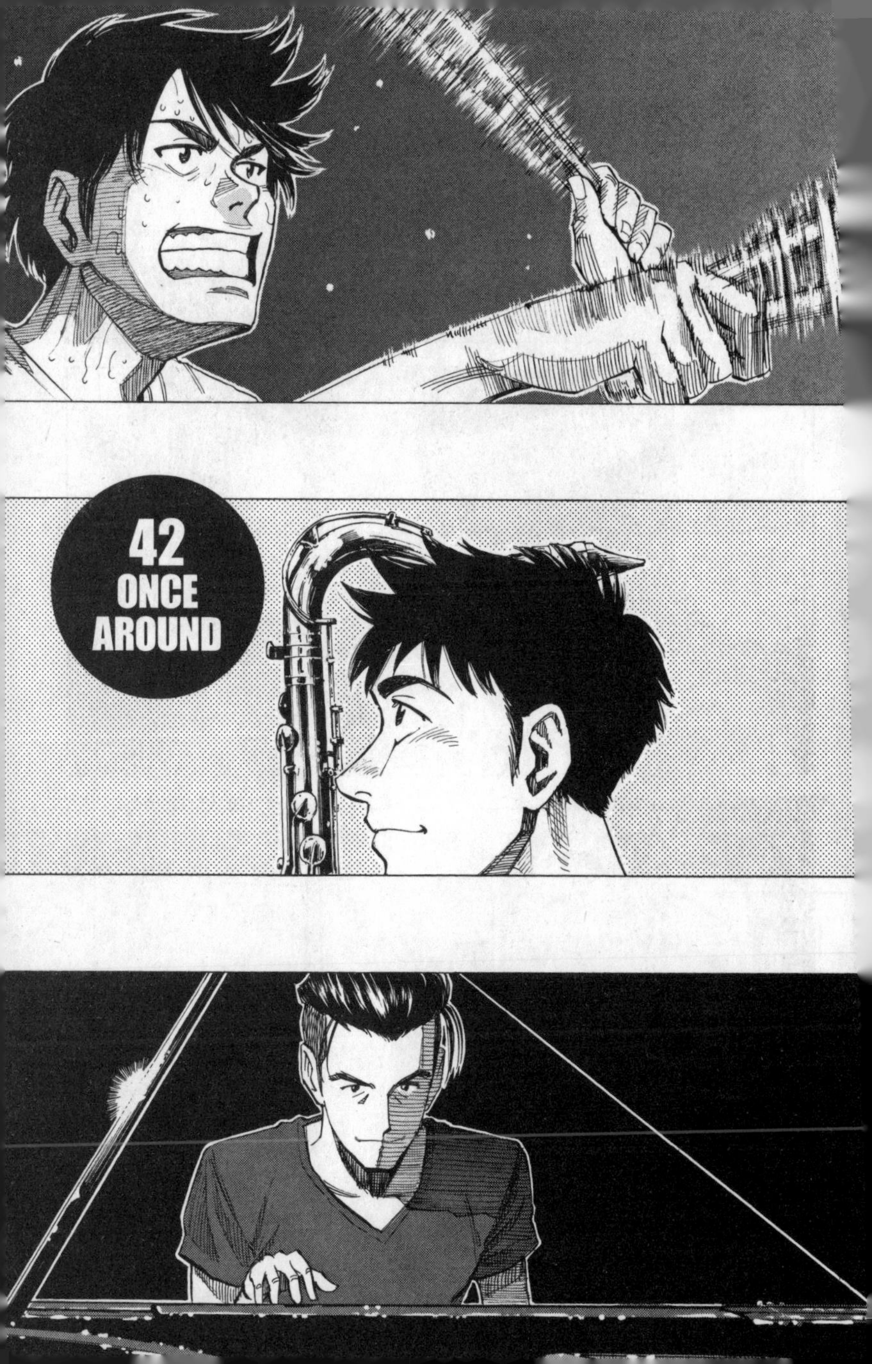
42
ONCE
AROUND

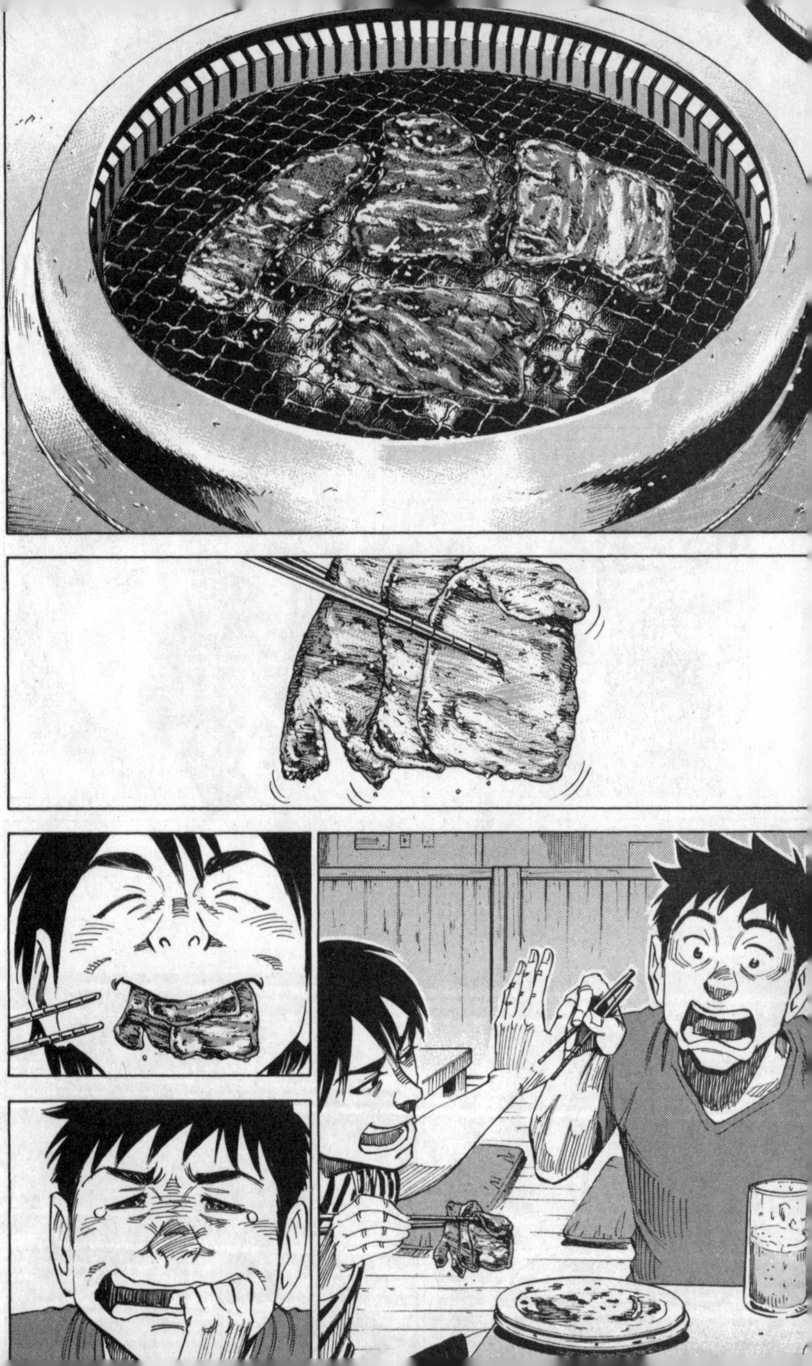

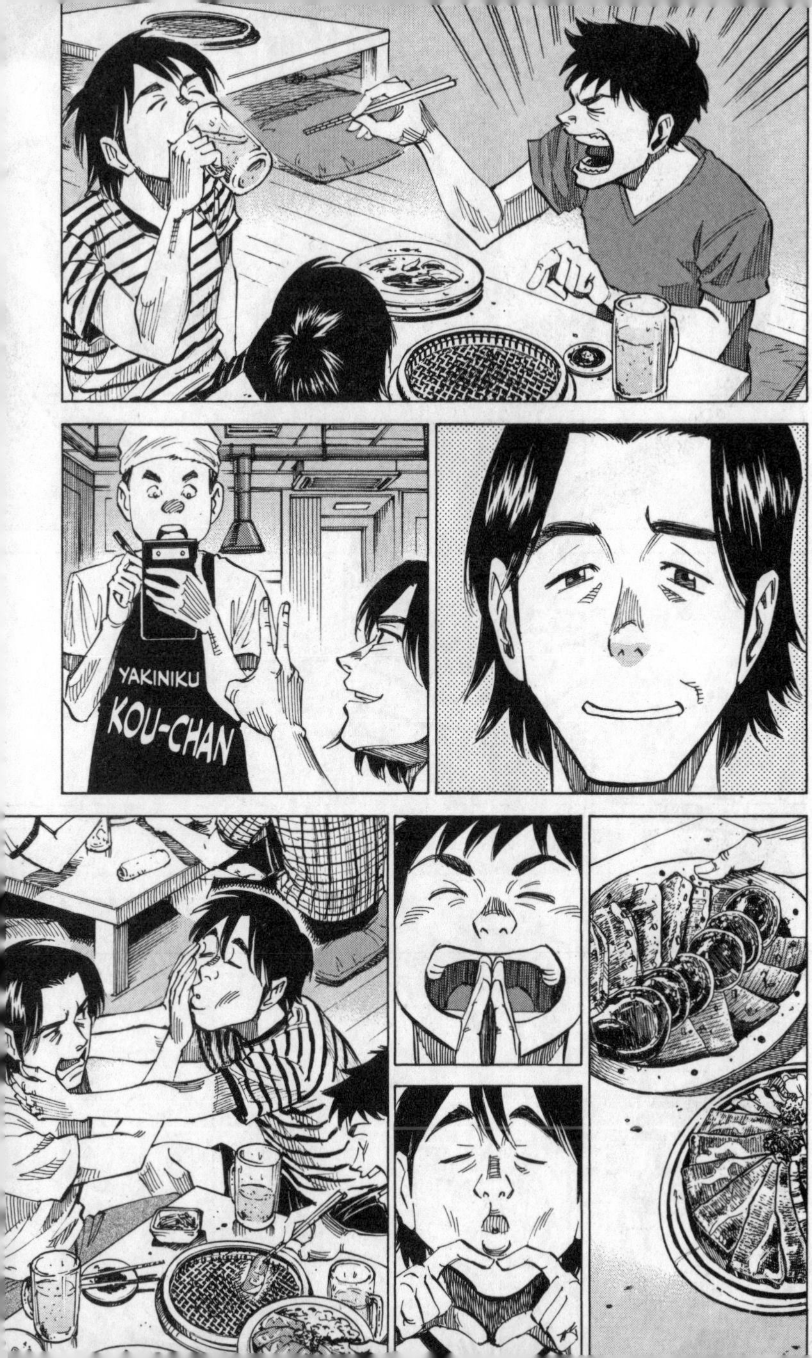
YAKINIKU
KOU-CHAN

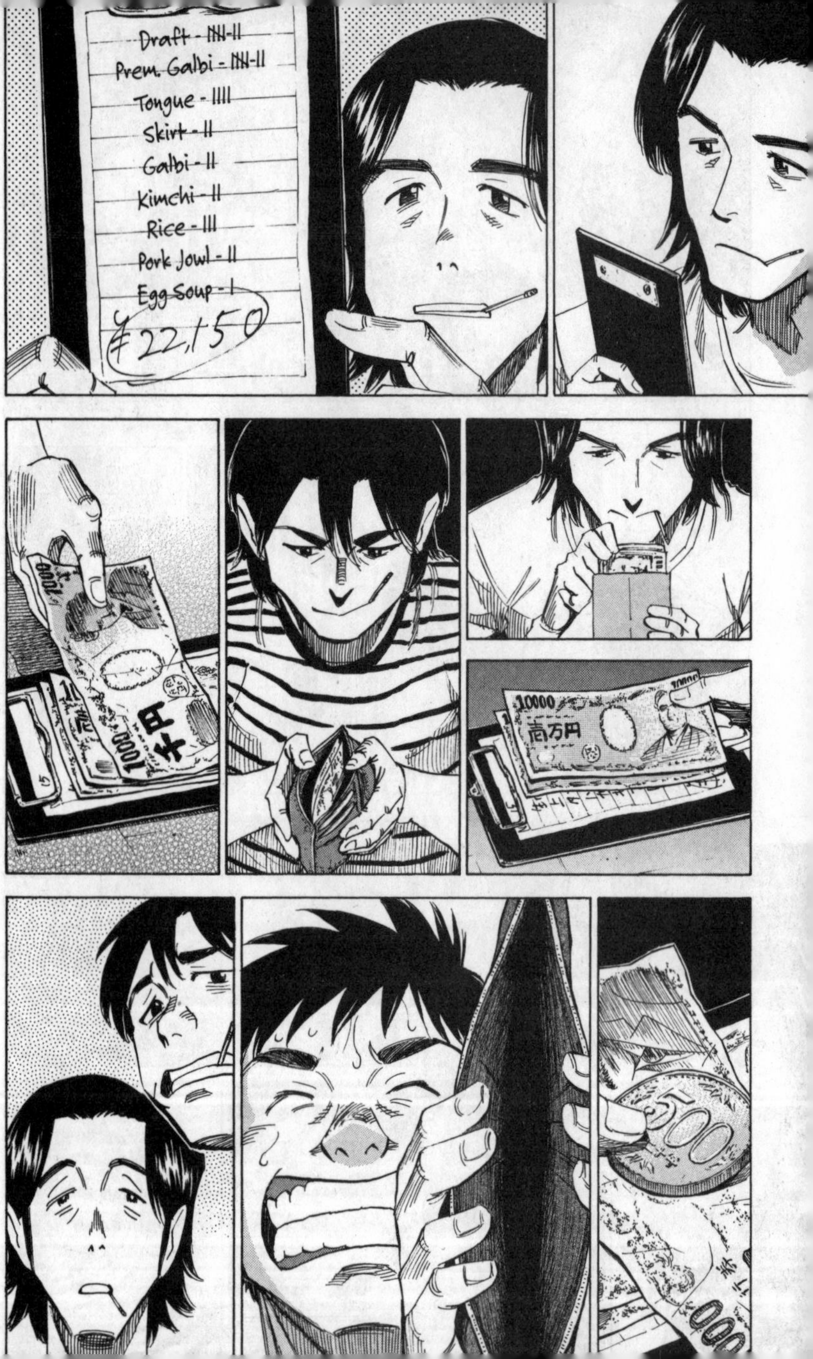
Draft - ||||-||
Prem. Galbi - ||||-||
Tongue - ||||
Skirt - ||
Galbi - ||
Kimchi - ||
Rice - |||
Pork Jowl - ||
Egg Soup - |
¥22,150

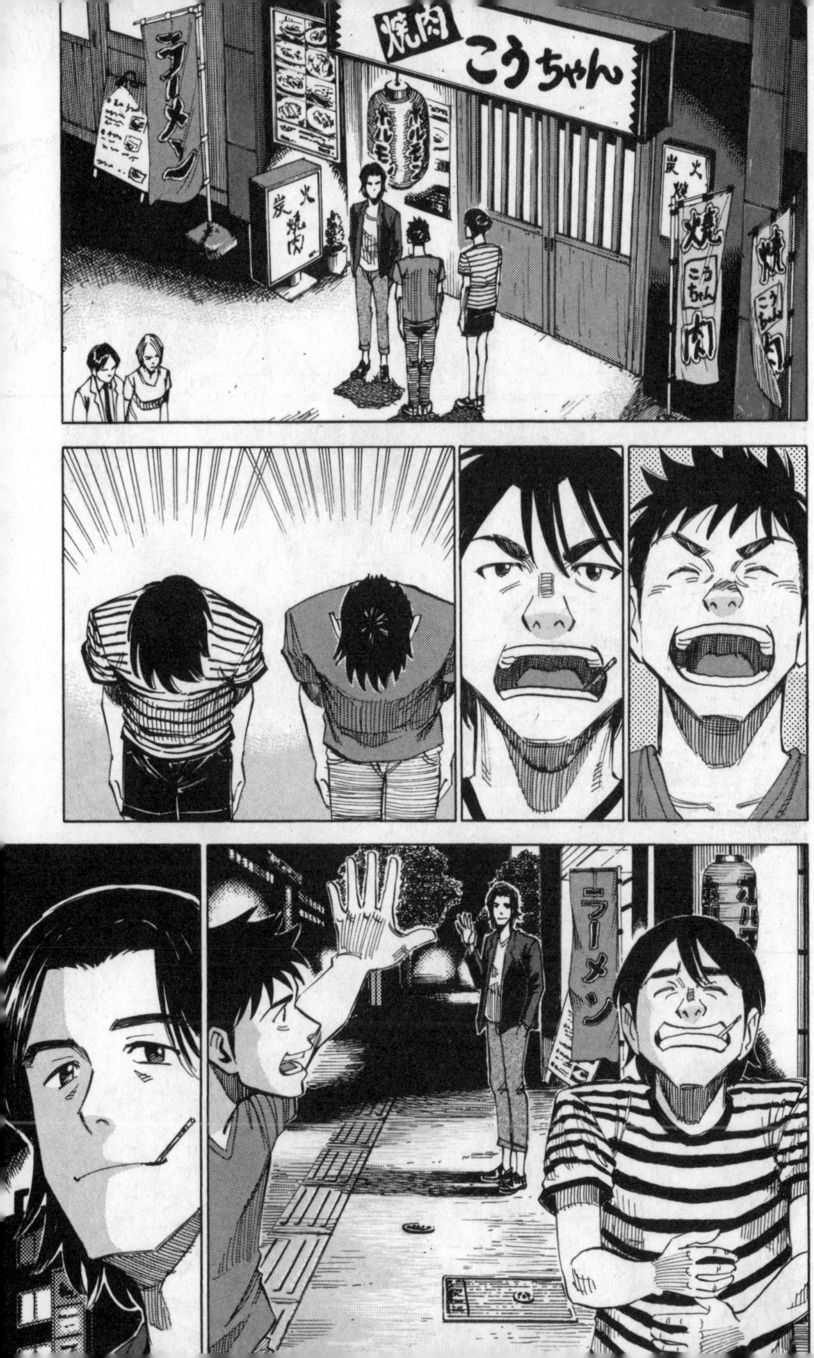
焼肉
こうちゃん
炭火焼
焼肉
こうちゃん
ホルモン
炭火焼肉
ラーメン
ラーメン

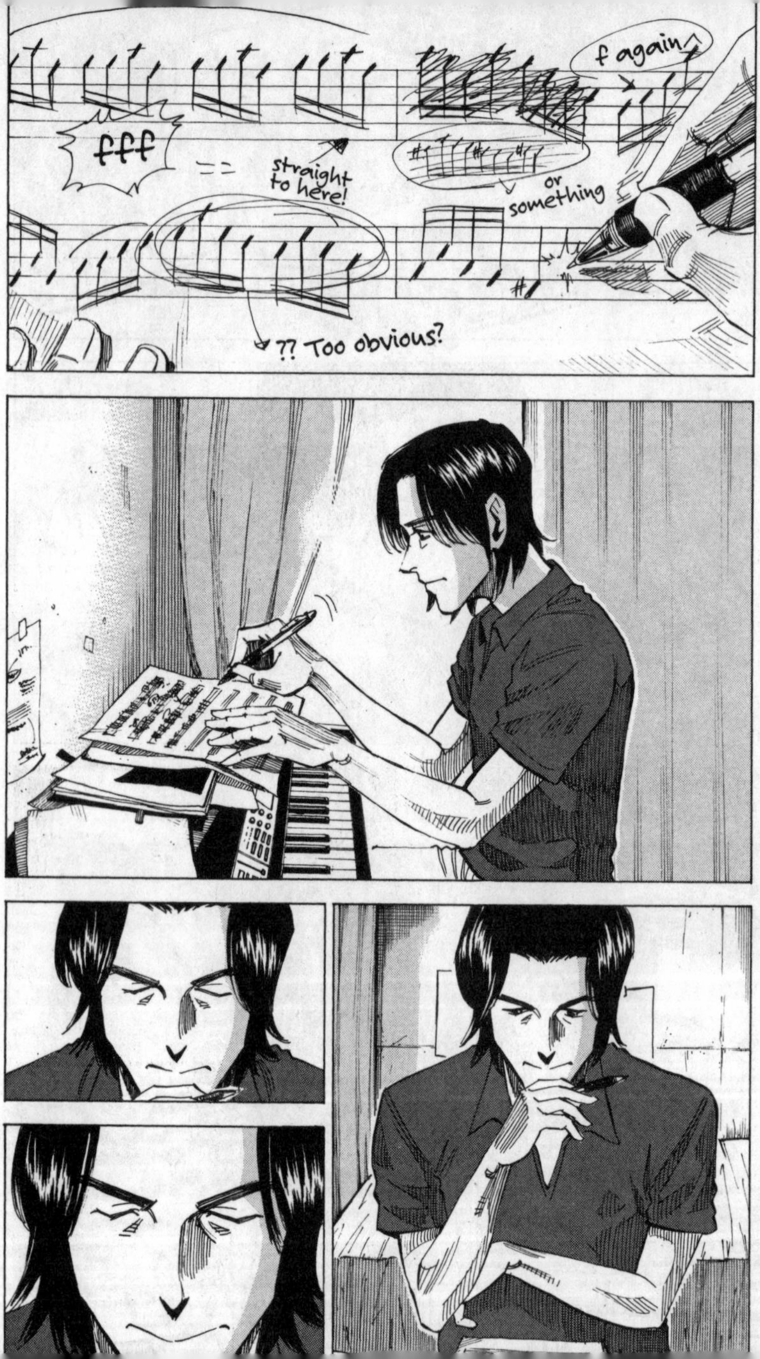
f again
or something
straight to here!
fff
?? Too obvious?

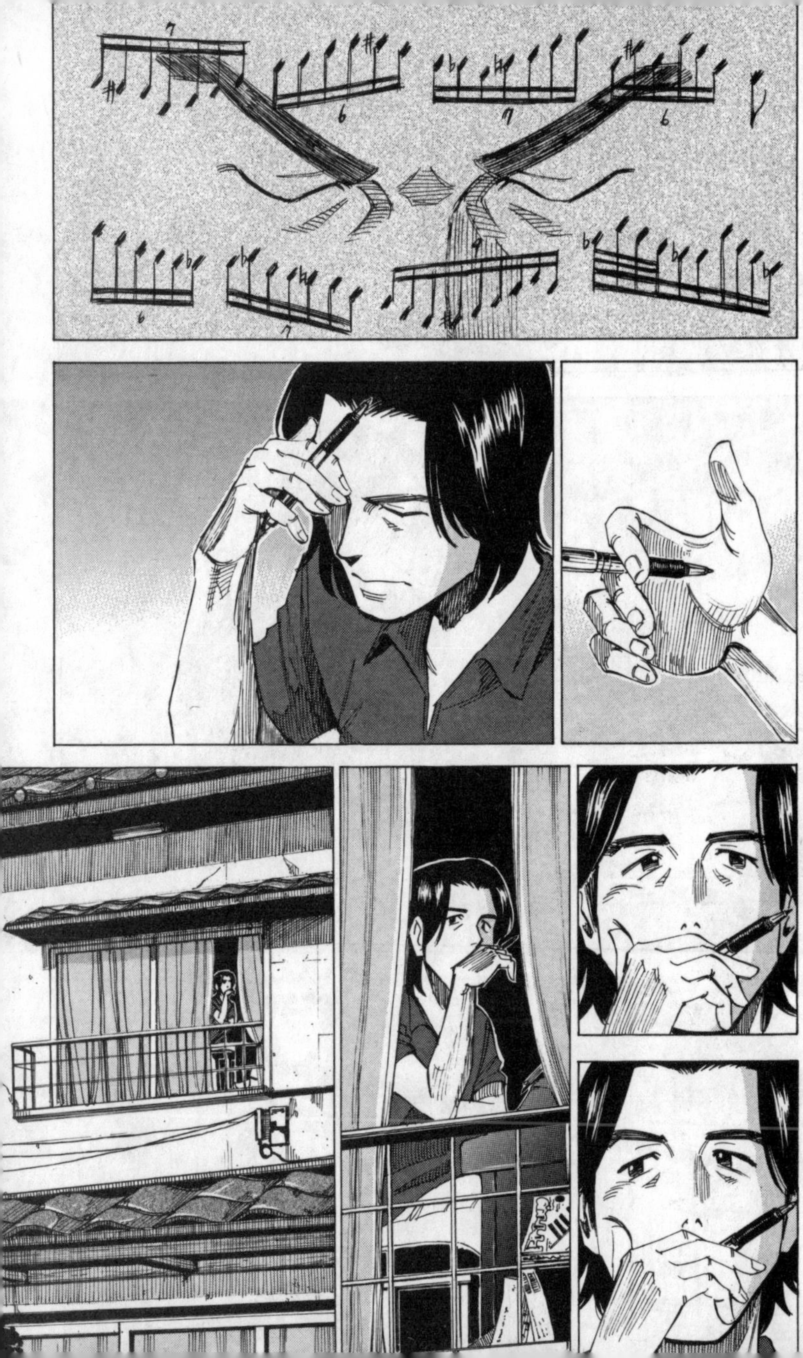

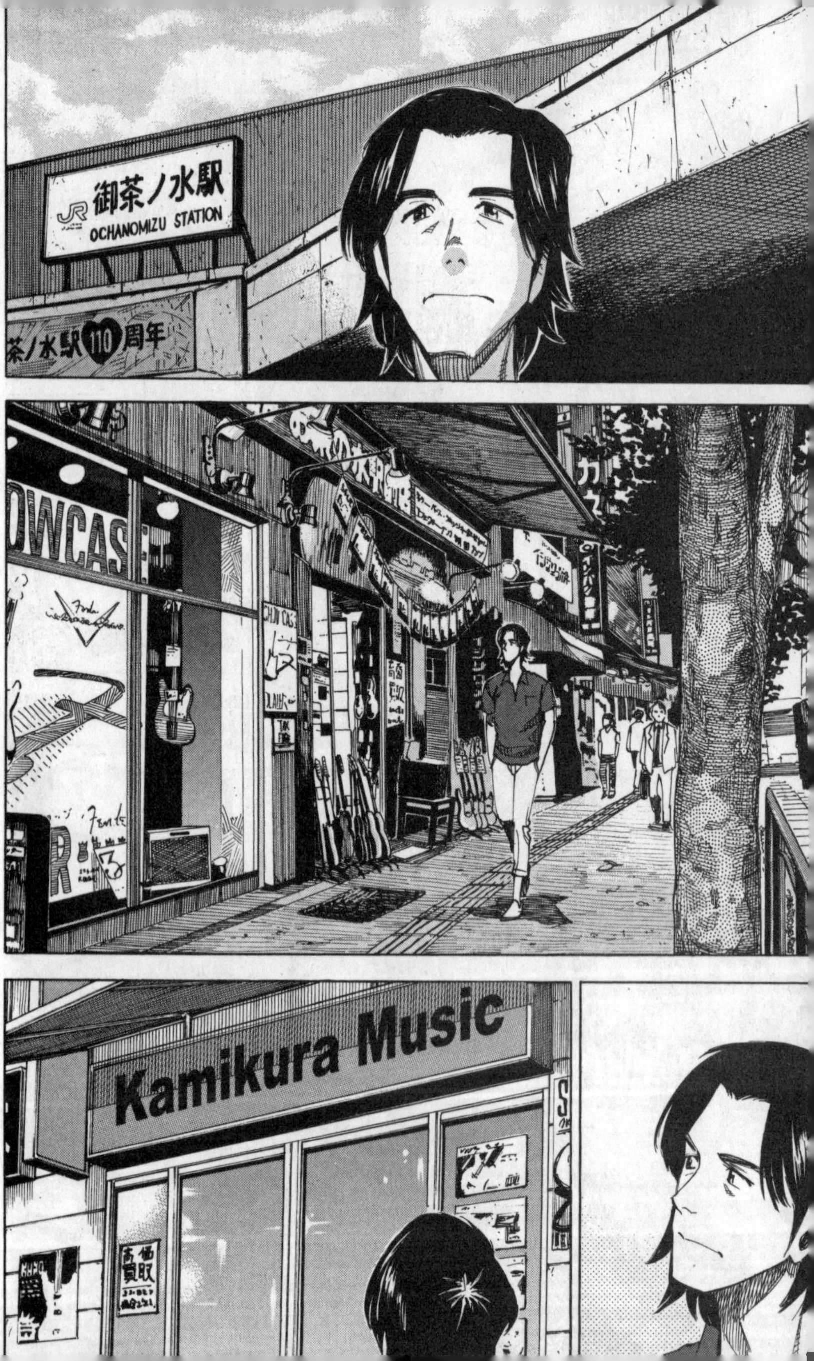
御茶ノ水駅
OCHANOMIZU STATION
茶ノ水駅110周年
Kamikura Music
高価買取

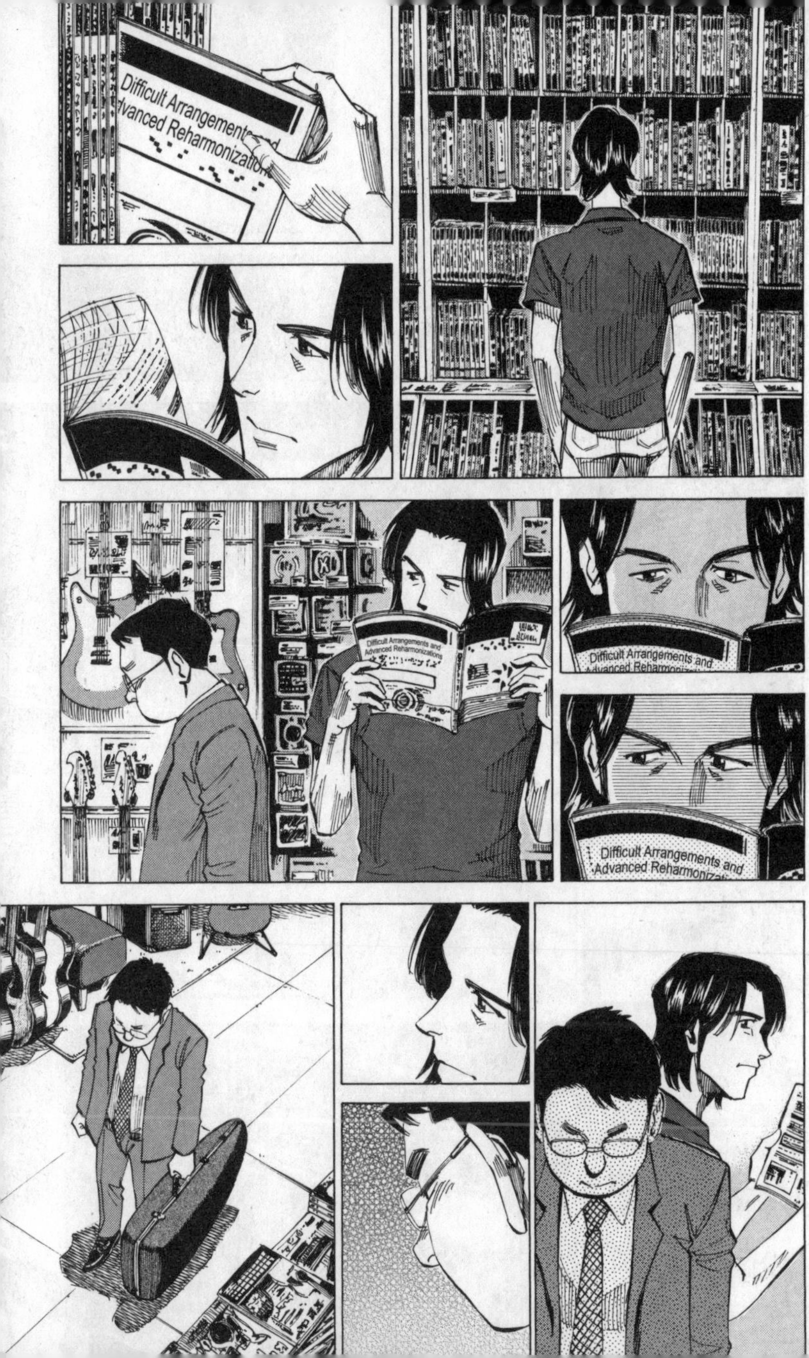

Difficult Arrangements
Difficult Arrangements and
Difficult Arrangements and
Difficult Arrangements and
Advanced Reharmonizations

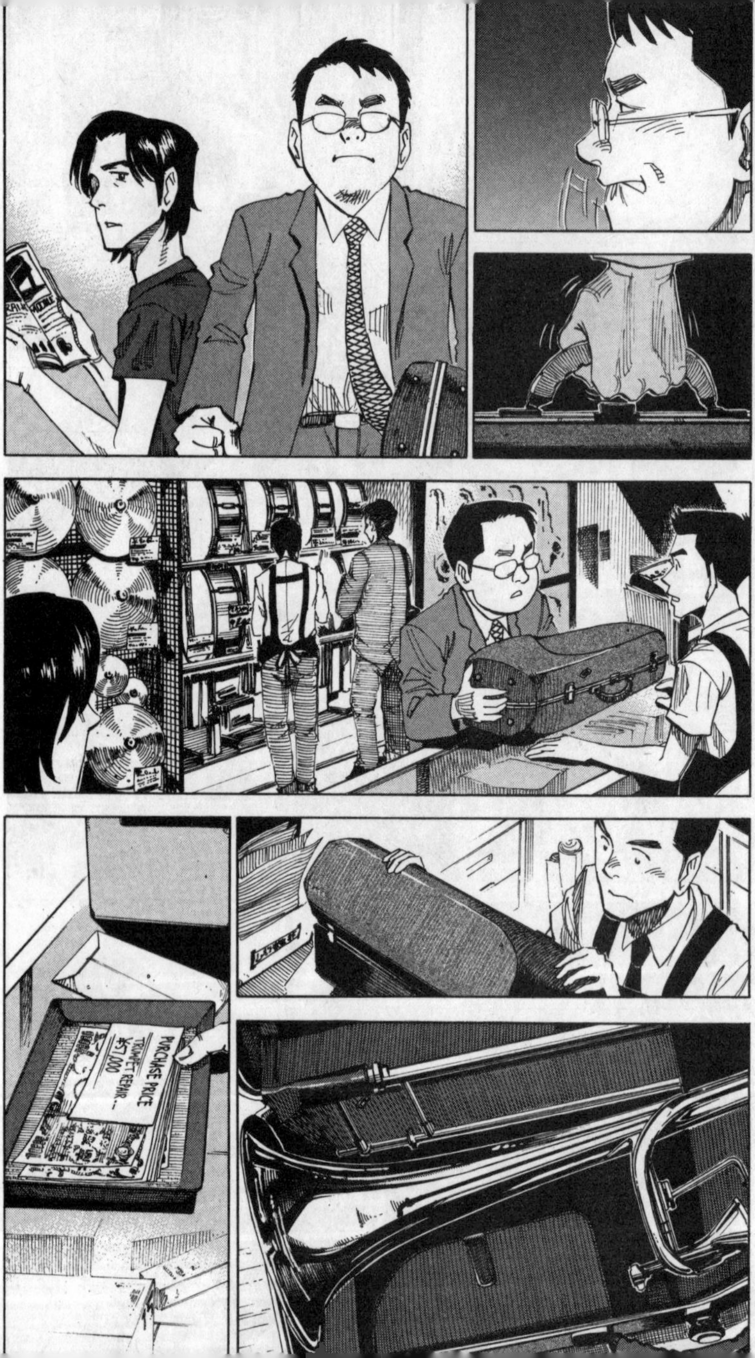
PURCHASE PRICE
TRUMPET REPAIR...
約7,000

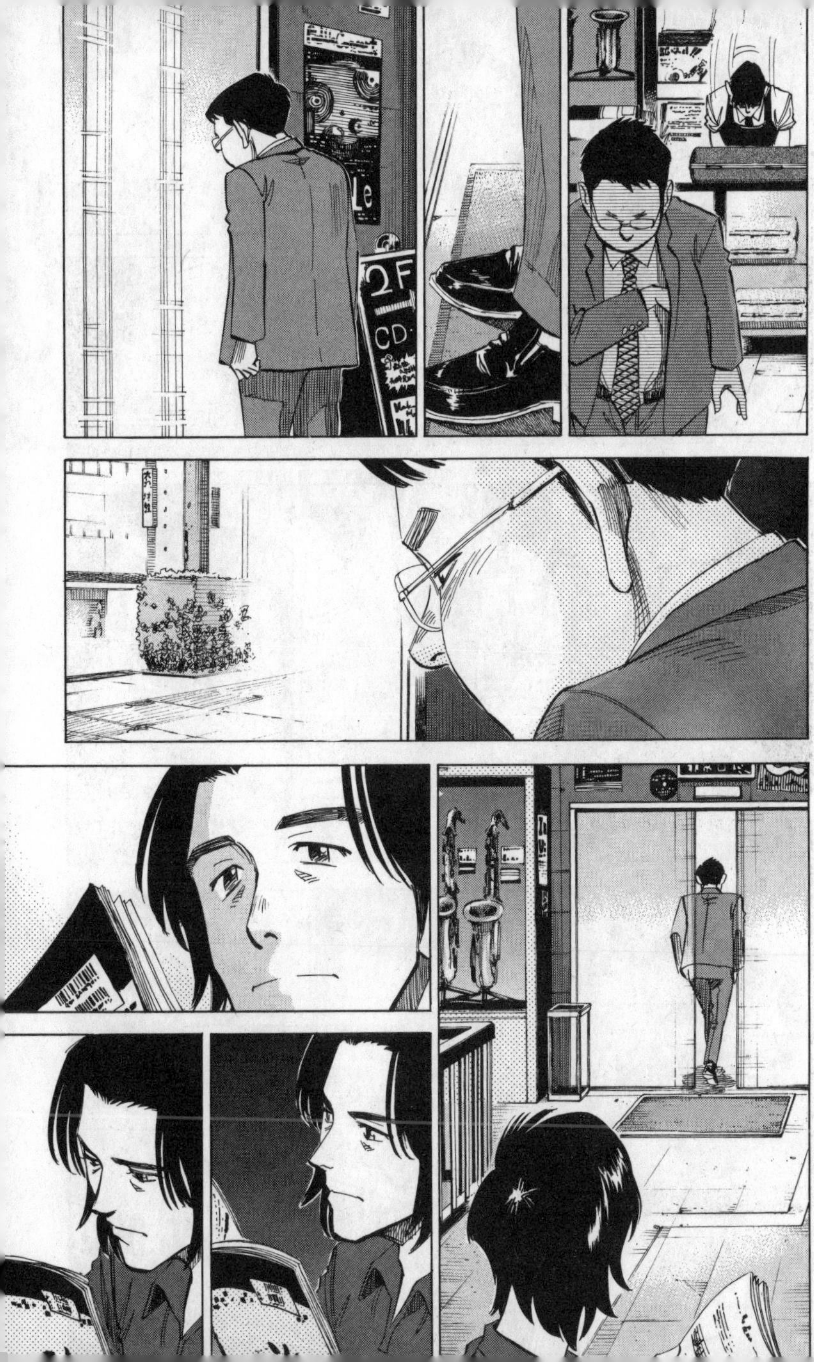
Le
2F
CD

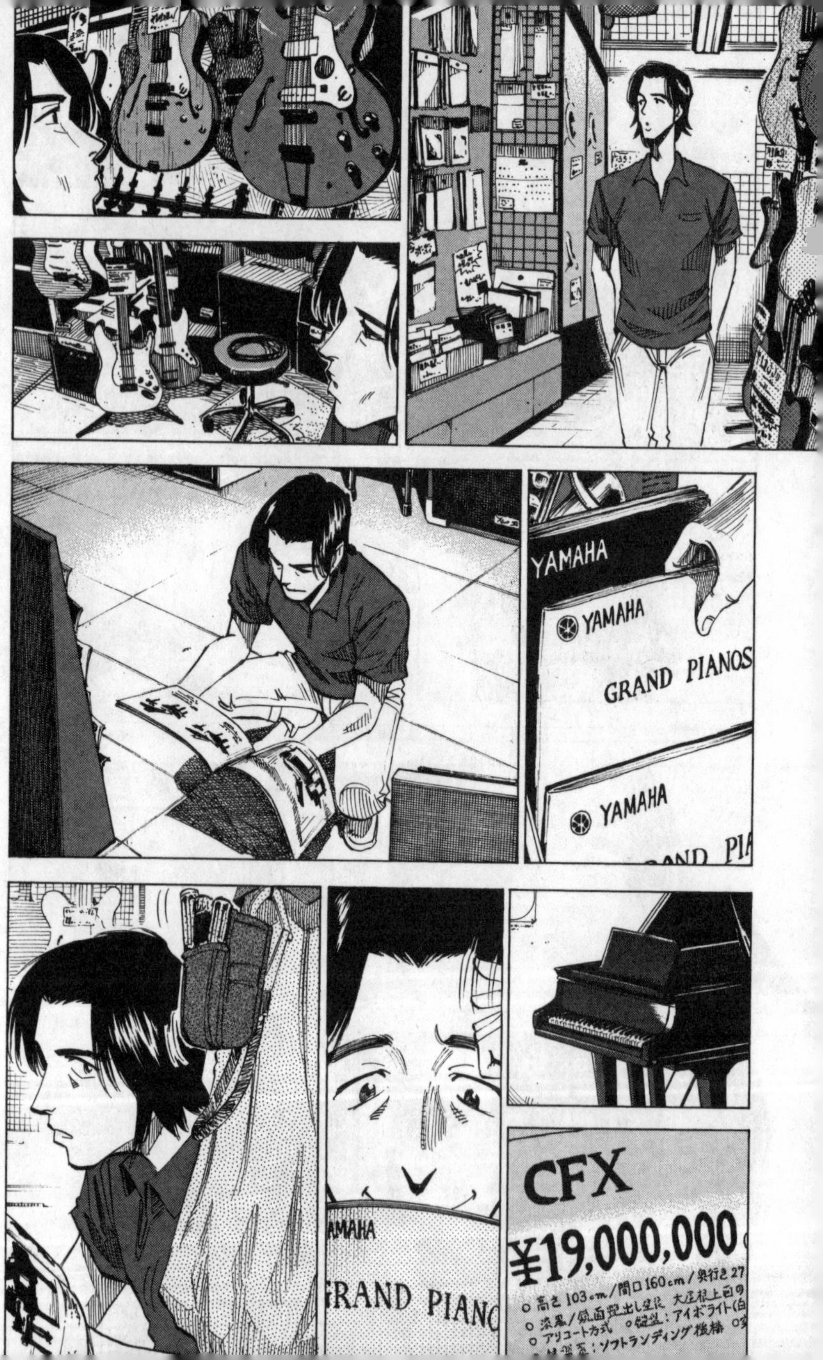

YAMAHA
YAMAHA
GRAND PIANOS
YAMAHA
CFX
¥19,000,000
○高さ103cm/間口160cm/奥行き27
○漆黒/鏡面艶出し塗装 大屋根上面の
○アリコート方式 ○鍵盤：アイボライト(白
ソフトランディング機構
YAMAHA
GRAND PIANO

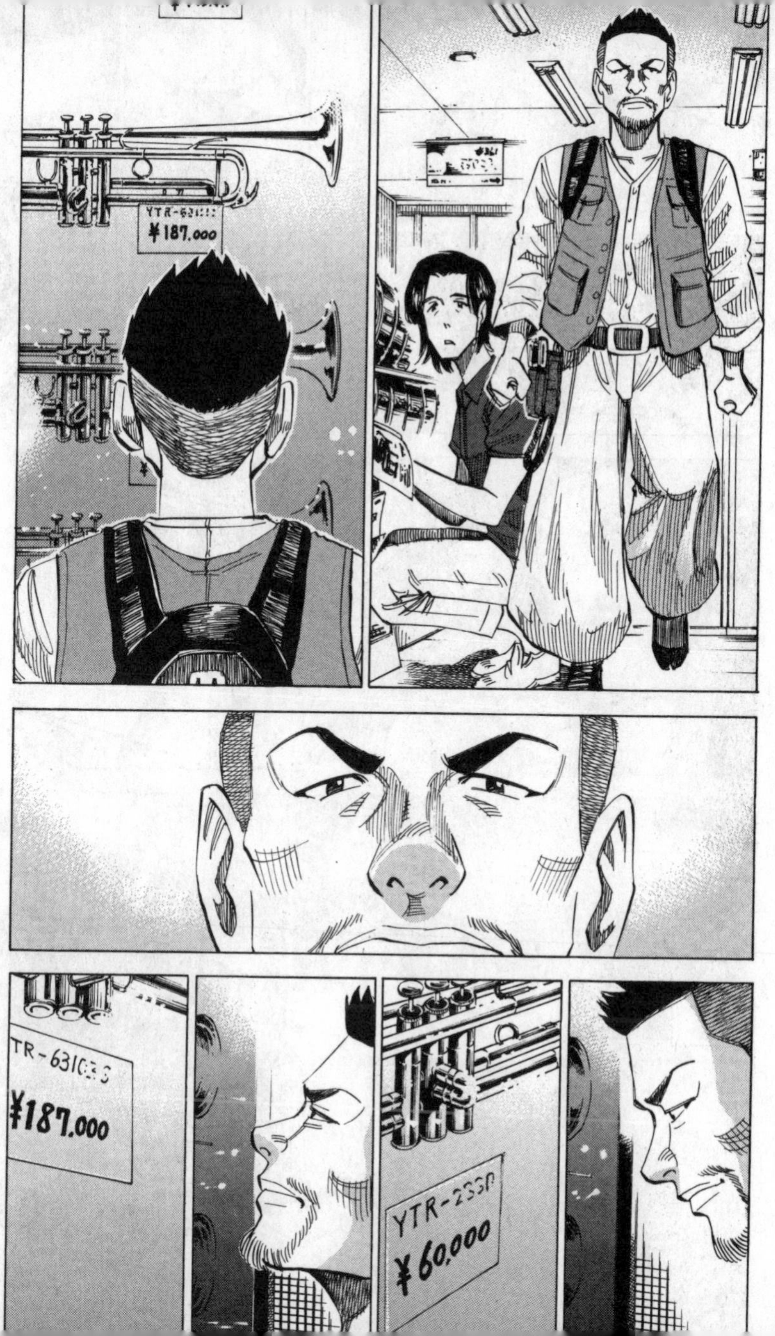
¥187.000
¥60,000
¥187.000

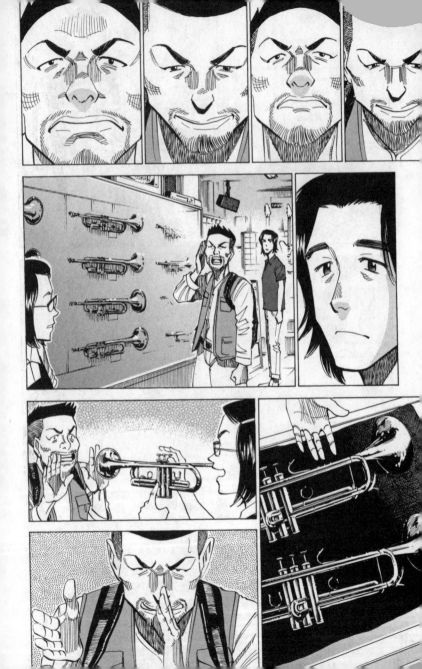

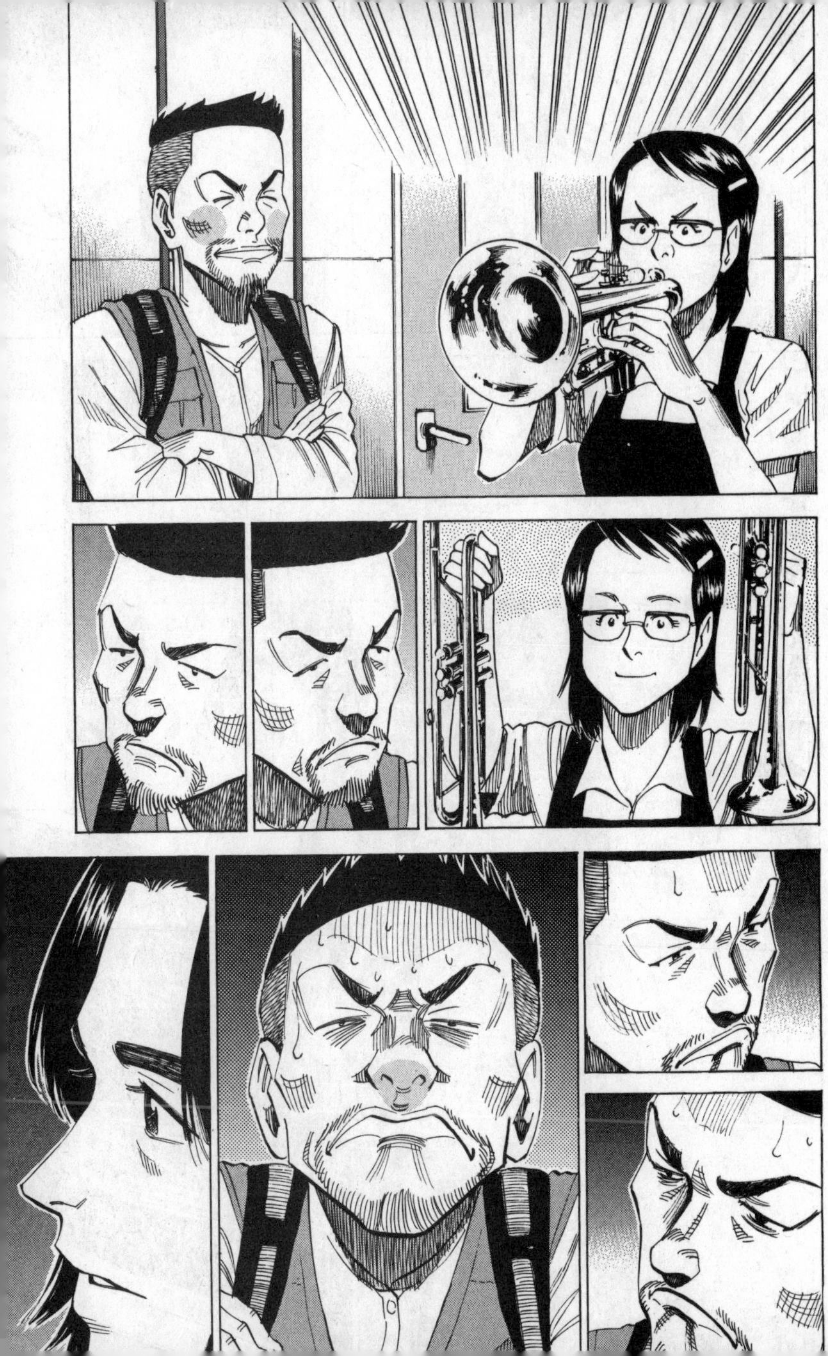

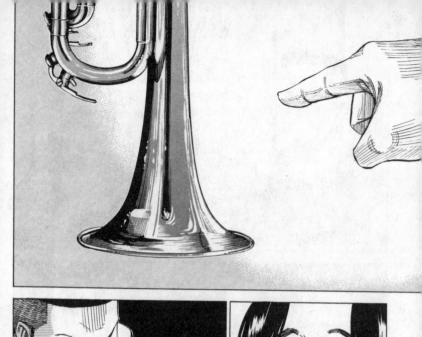

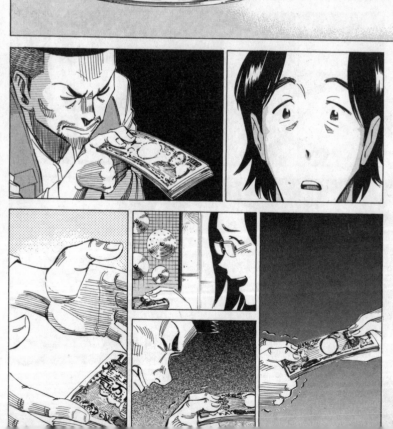

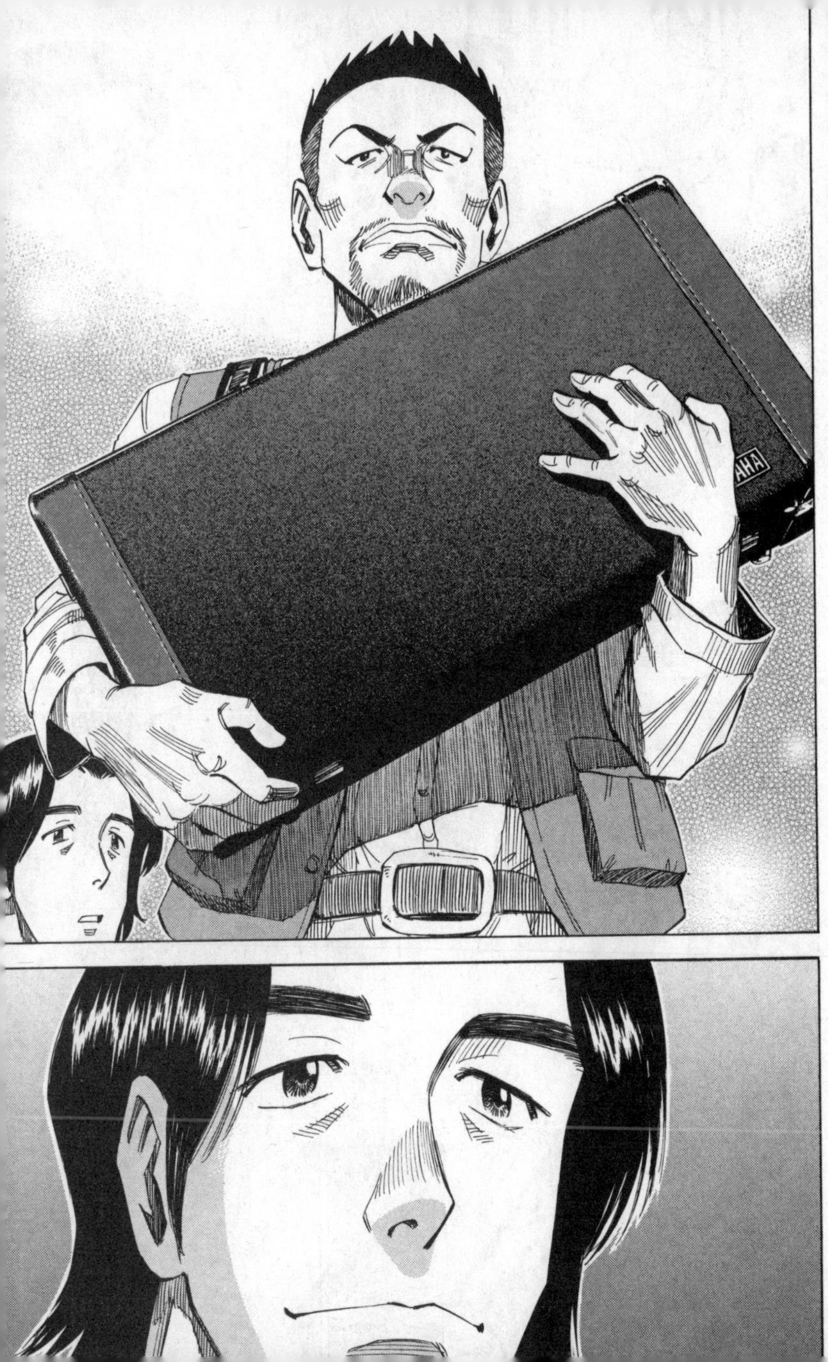

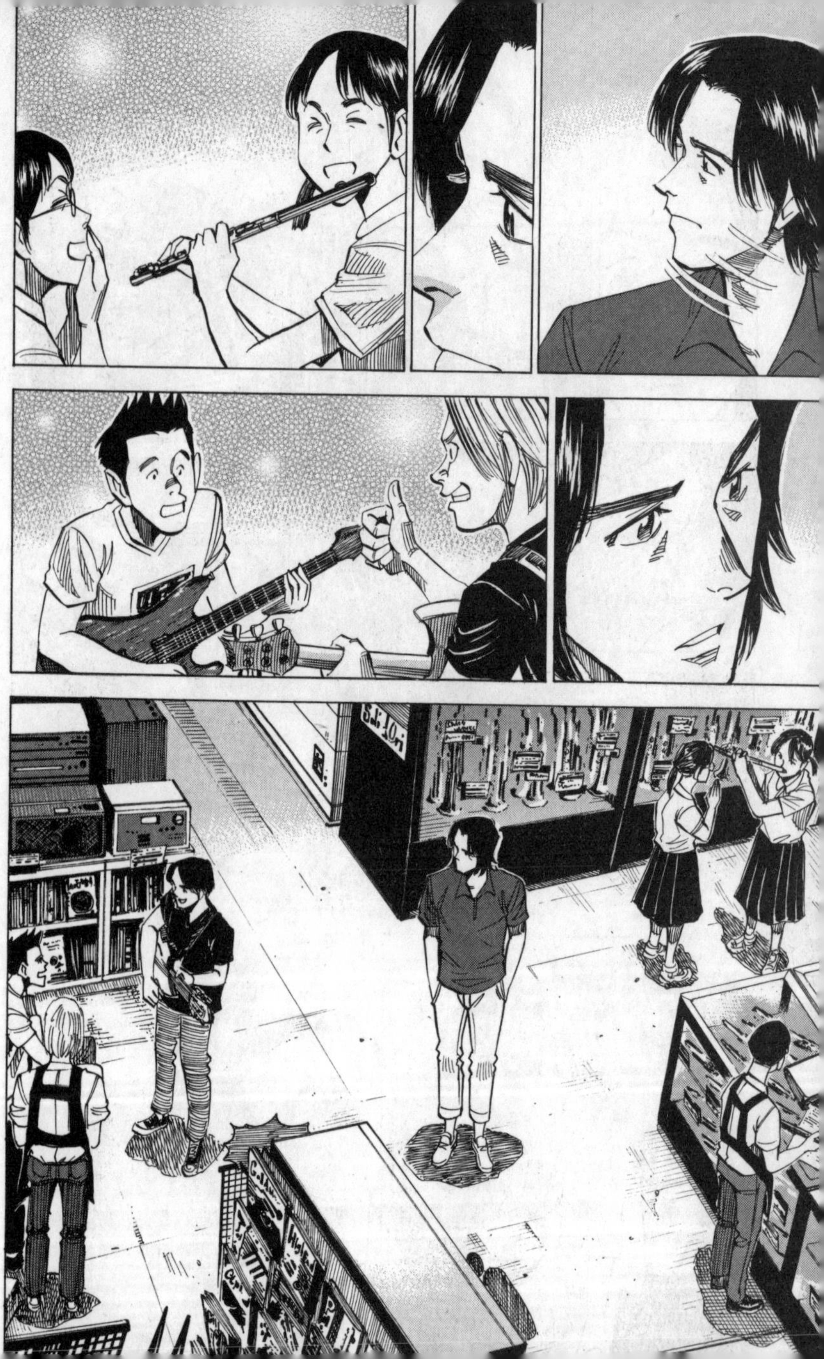

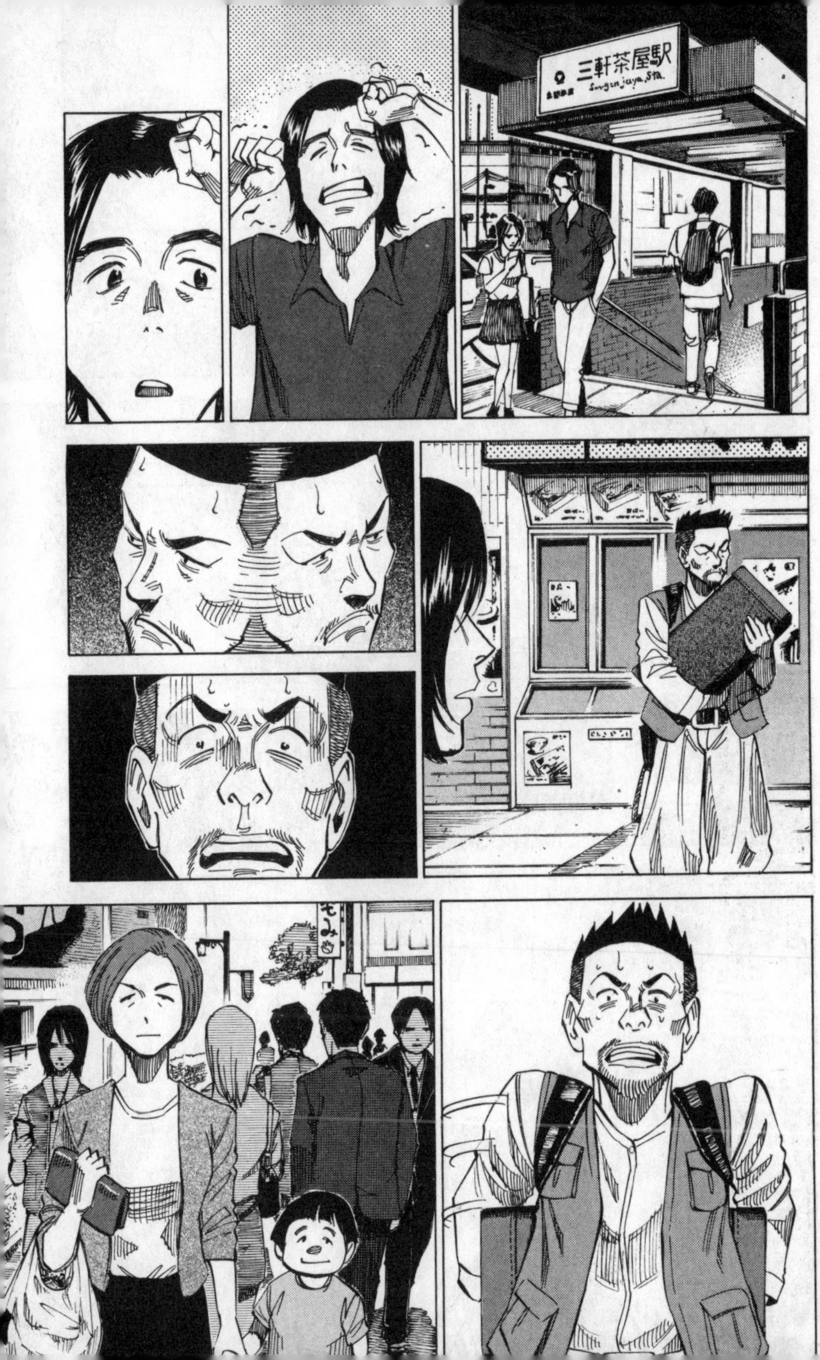
三軒茶屋駅
Sangenjaya Sta.

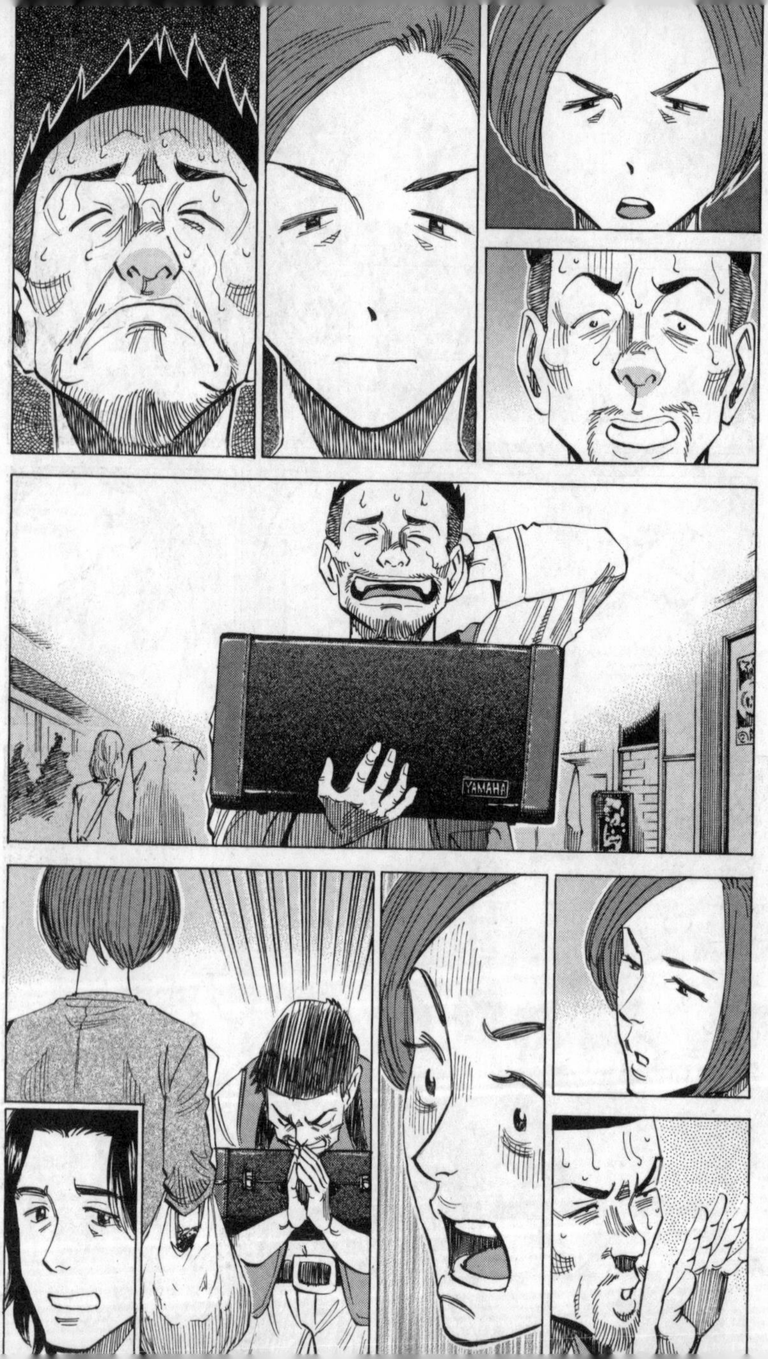
YAMAHA

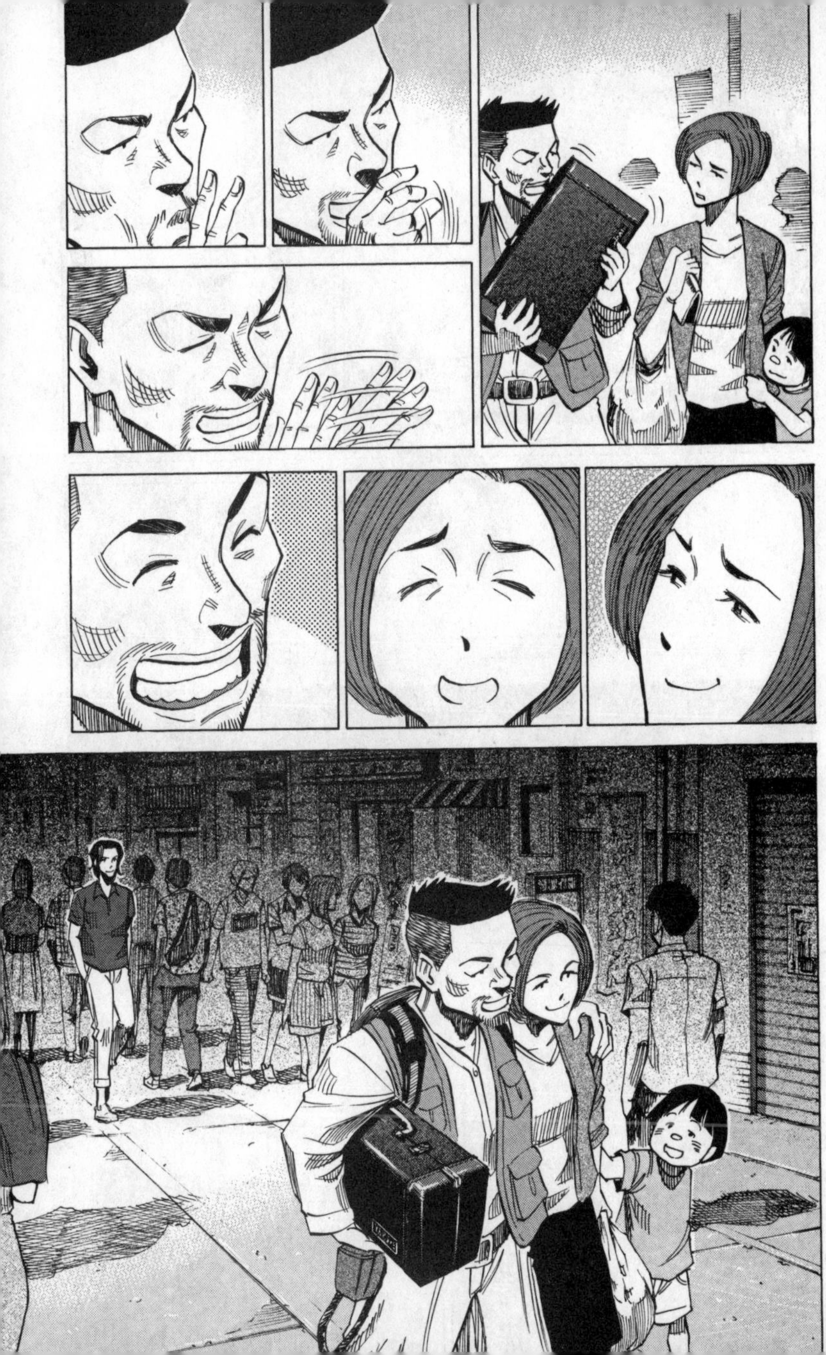

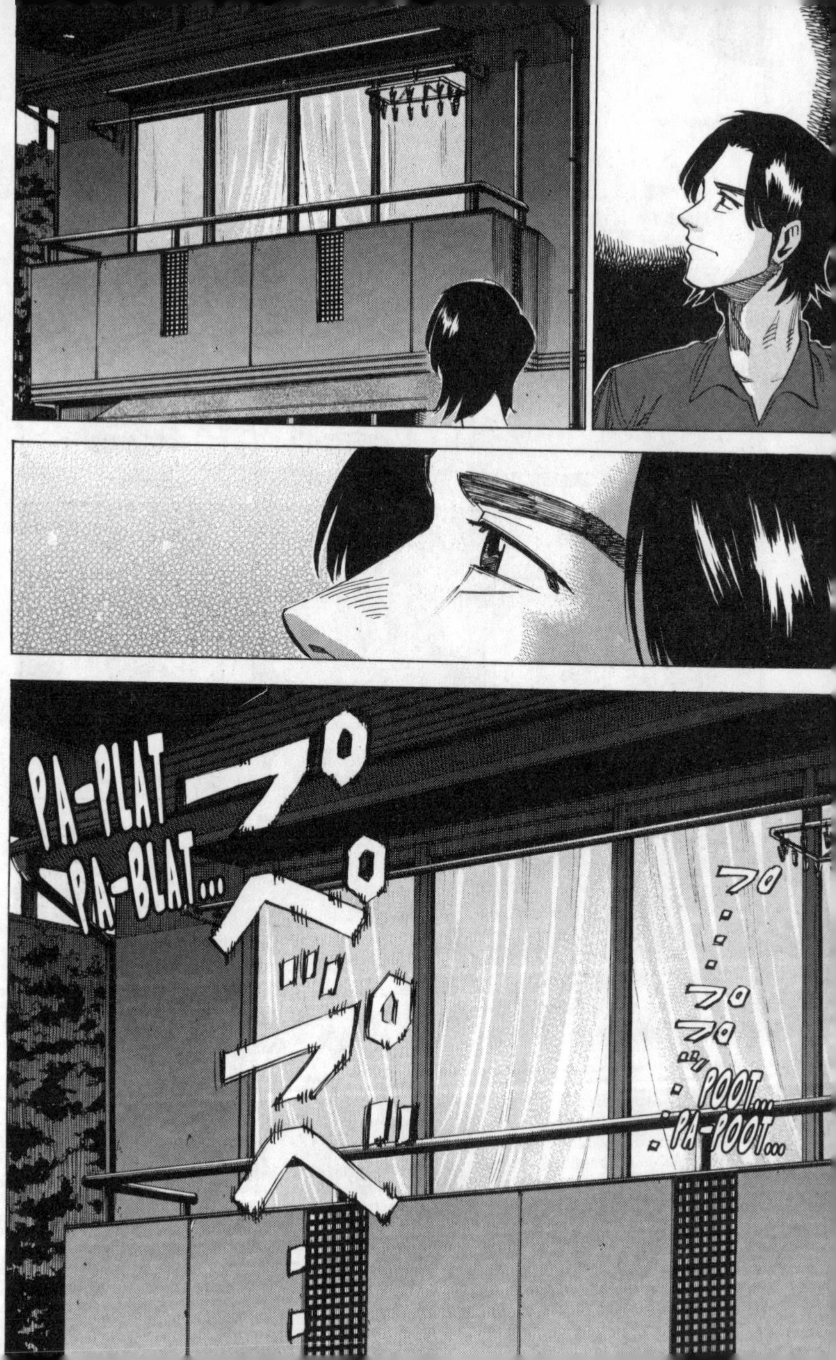

PA-PLAT
PA-BLAT...
POOT...
PA-POOT...

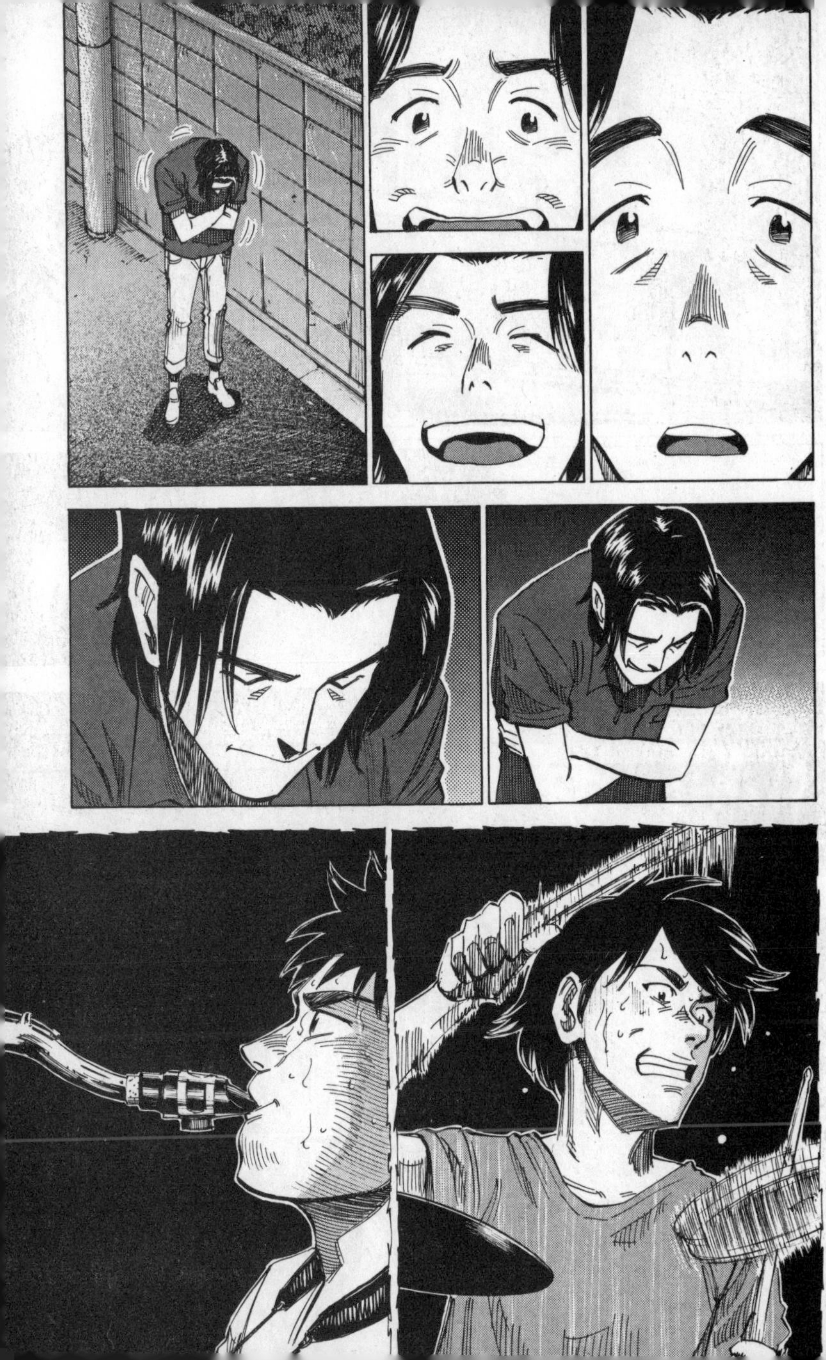

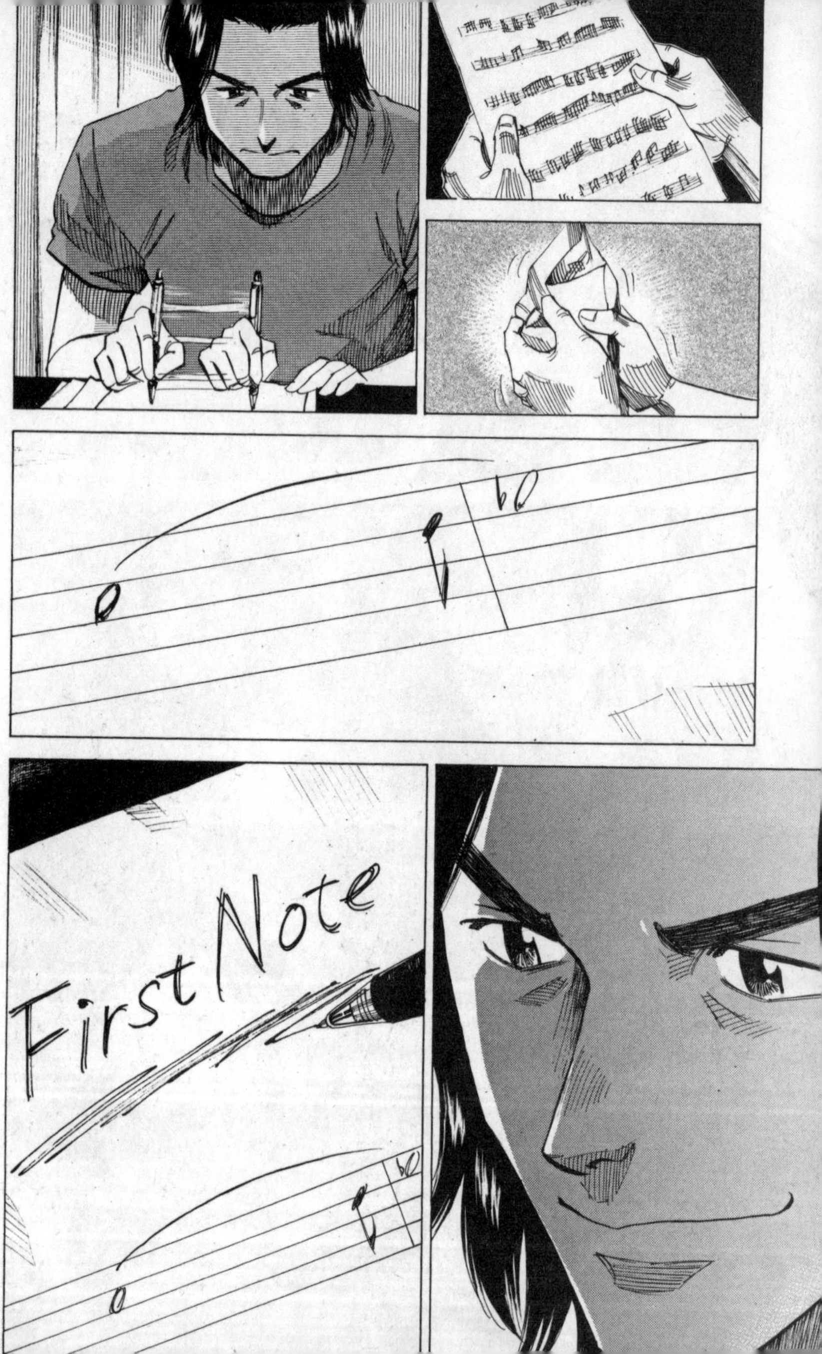
First Note

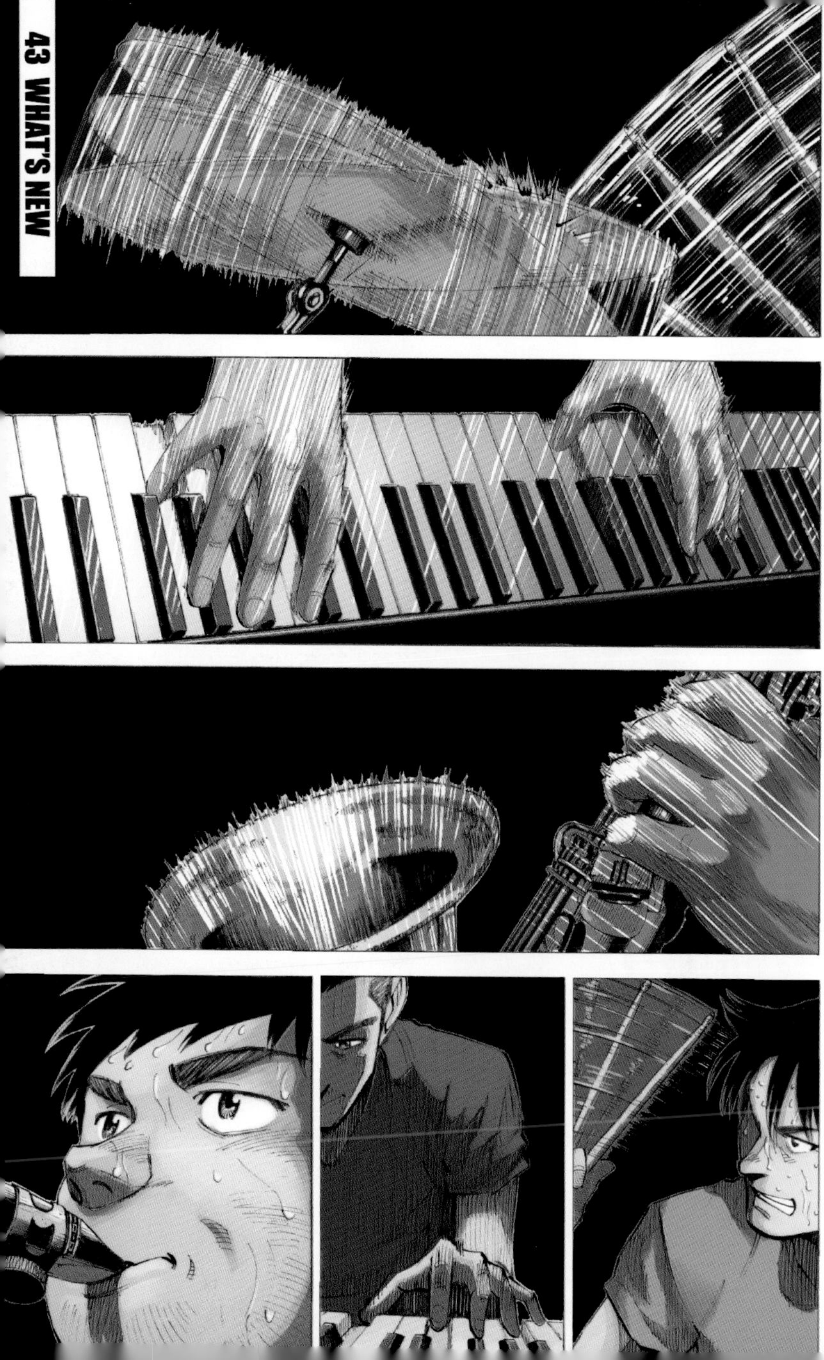
43 WHAT'S NEW

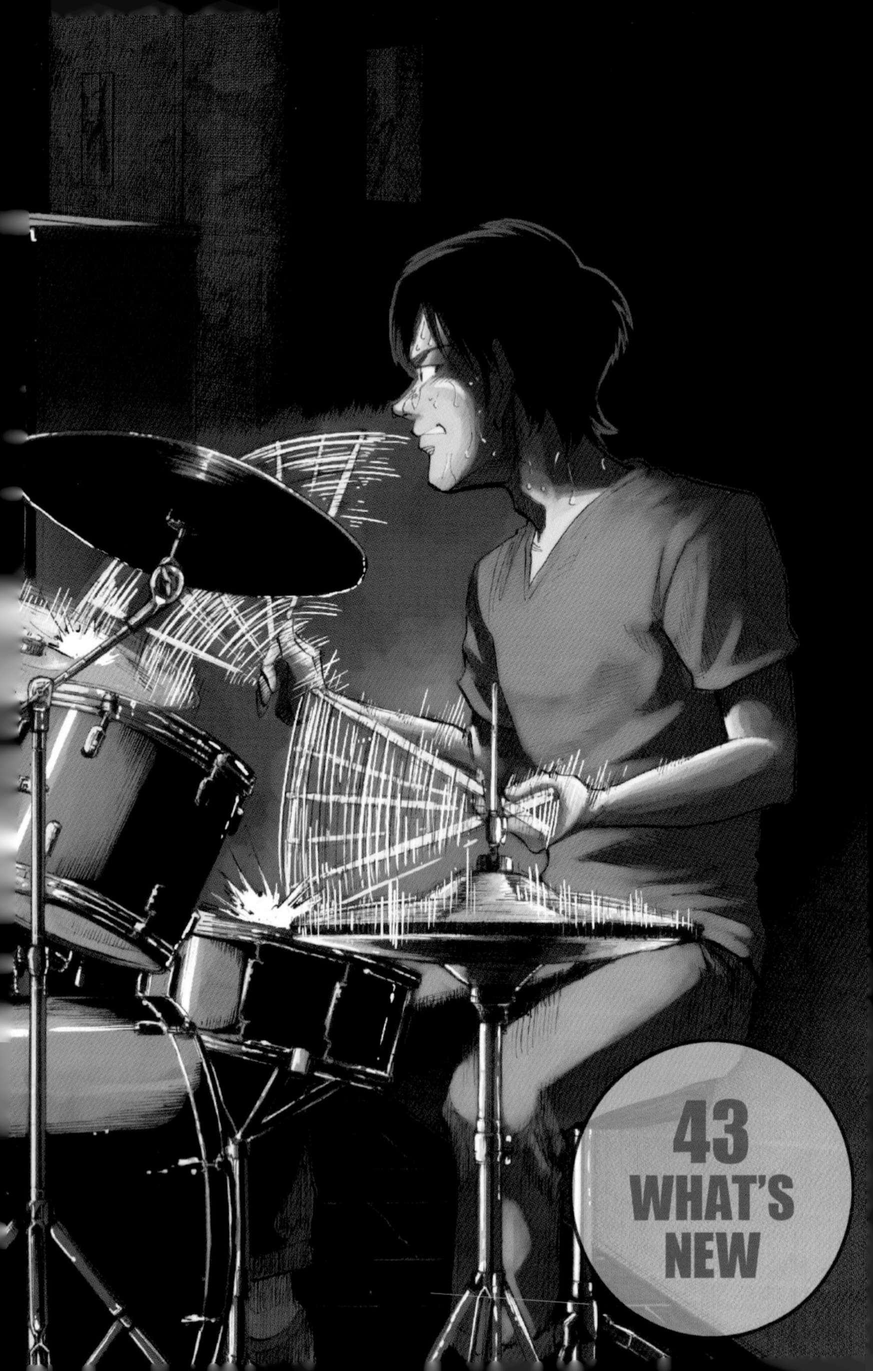
43
WHAT'S
NEW

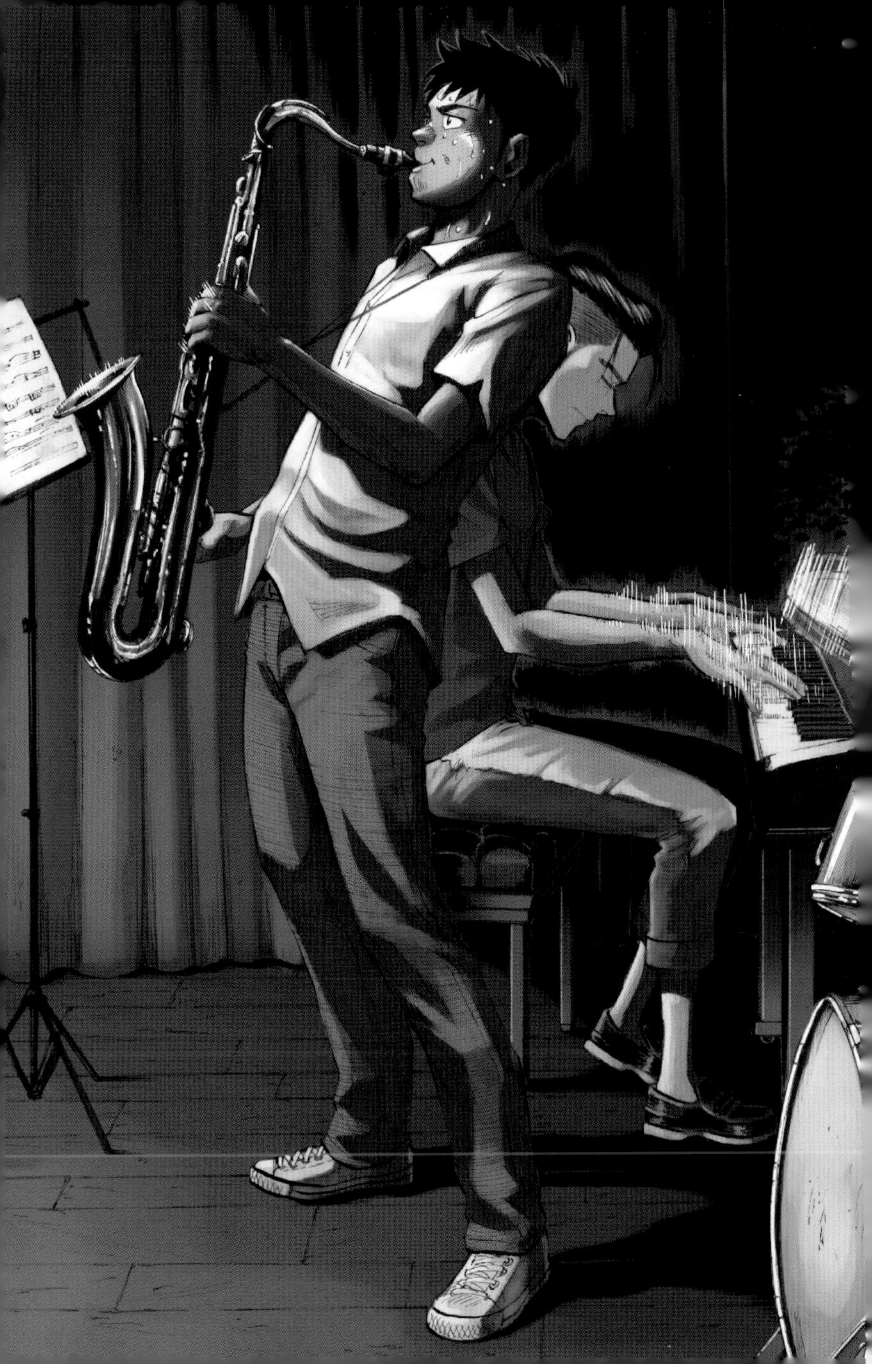

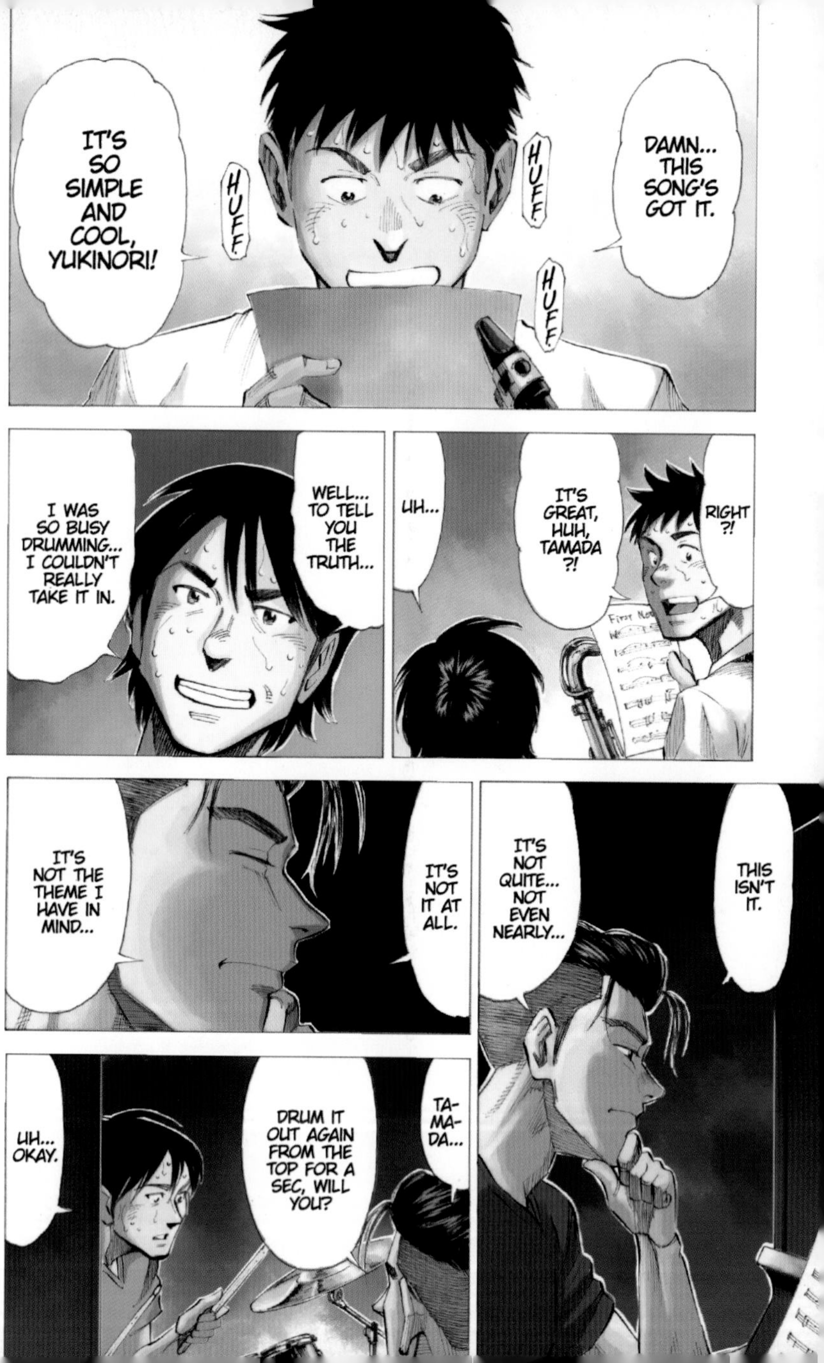
DAMN... THIS SONG'S GOT IT.
HUFF.
HUFF.
HUFF.
IT'S SO SIMPLE AND COOL, YUKINORI!
RIGHT?!
IT'S GREAT, HUH, TAMADA?!
UH...
WELL... TO TELL YOU THE TRUTH...
I WAS SO BUSY DRUMMING... I COULDN'T REALLY TAKE IT IN.
THIS ISN'T IT.
IT'S NOT QUITE... NOT EVEN NEARLY...
IT'S NOT IT AT ALL.
IT'S NOT THE THEME I HAVE IN MIND...
TA-MA-DA...
DRUM IT OUT AGAIN FROM THE TOP FOR A SEC, WILL YOU?
UH... OKAY.

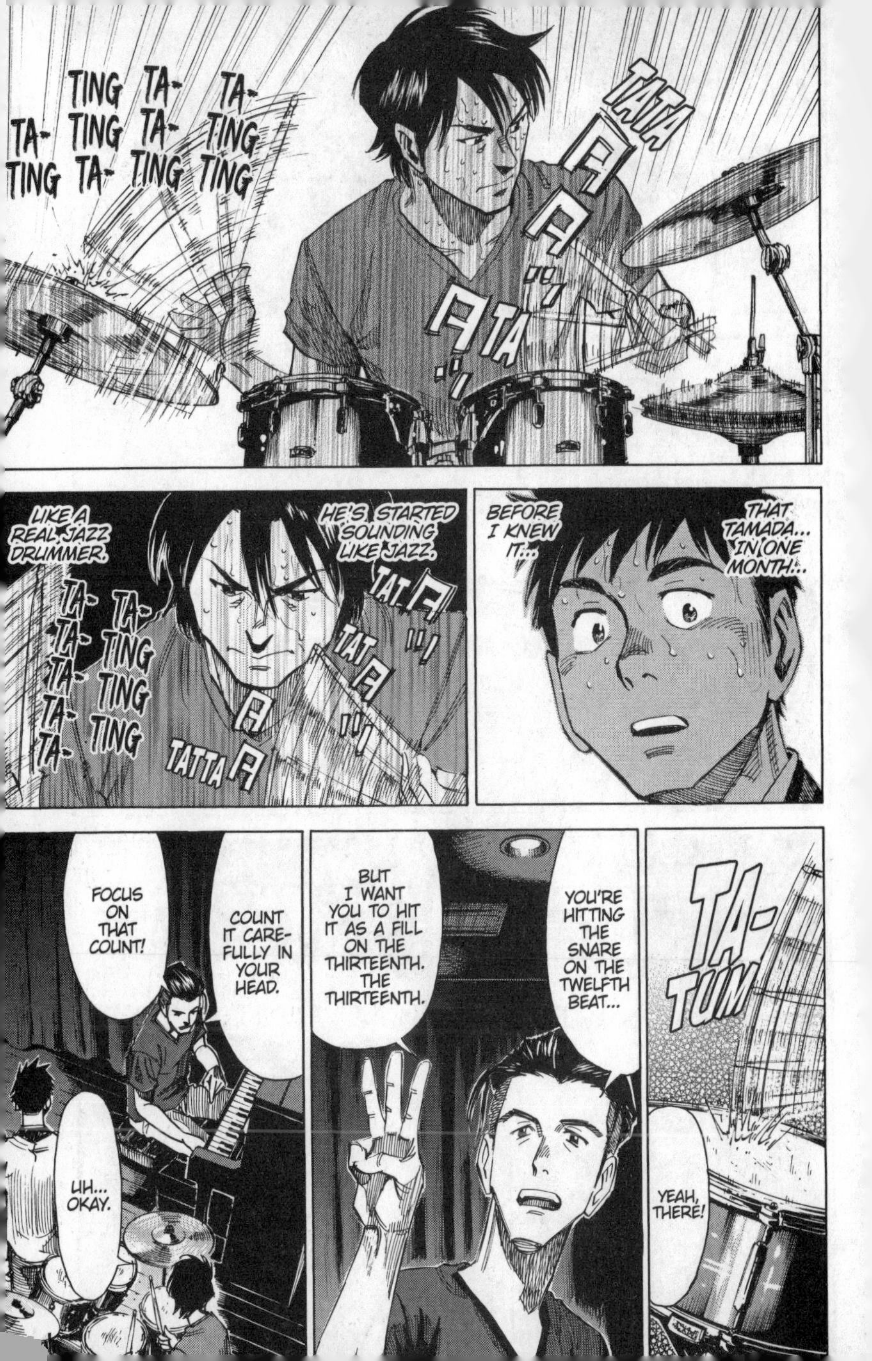
TATA
A
A
TA
TING TA- TA-
TA- TING TA- TING
TING TA- TING TING
THAT TAMADA... IN ONE MONTH...
BEFORE I KNEW IT...
HE'S STARTED SOUNDING LIKE JAZZ.
TAT A
TAT A
TATTA A
LIKE A REAL JAZZ DRUMMER.
TA- TA-
TA- TING
TA- TING
TA- TING
TA-
TA-TUM
YEAH, THERE!
YOU'RE HITTING THE SNARE ON THE TWELFTH BEAT...
BUT I WANT YOU TO HIT IT AS A FILL ON THE THIRTEENTH. THE THIRTEENTH.
COUNT IT CAREFULLY IN YOUR HEAD.
FOCUS ON THAT COUNT!
UH... OKAY.

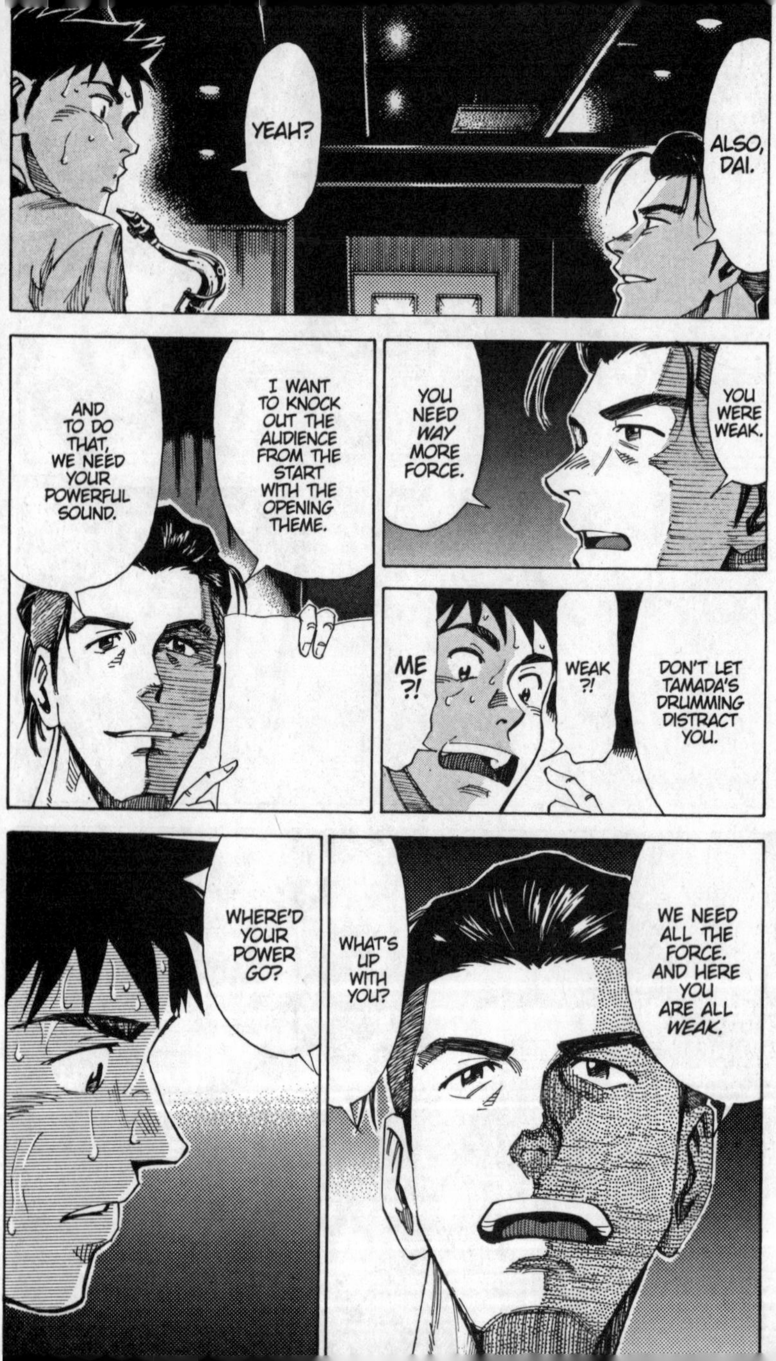
ALSO, DAI.
YEAH?
YOU WERE WEAK.
YOU NEED *WAY* MORE FORCE.
DON'T LET TAMADA'S DRUMMING DISTRACT YOU.
WEAK ?!
ME ?!
I WANT TO KNOCK OUT THE AUDIENCE FROM THE START WITH THE OPENING THEME.
AND TO DO THAT, WE NEED YOUR POWERFUL SOUND.
WE NEED ALL THE FORCE. AND HERE YOU ARE ALL *WEAK.*
WHAT'S UP WITH YOU?
WHERE'D YOUR POWER GO?

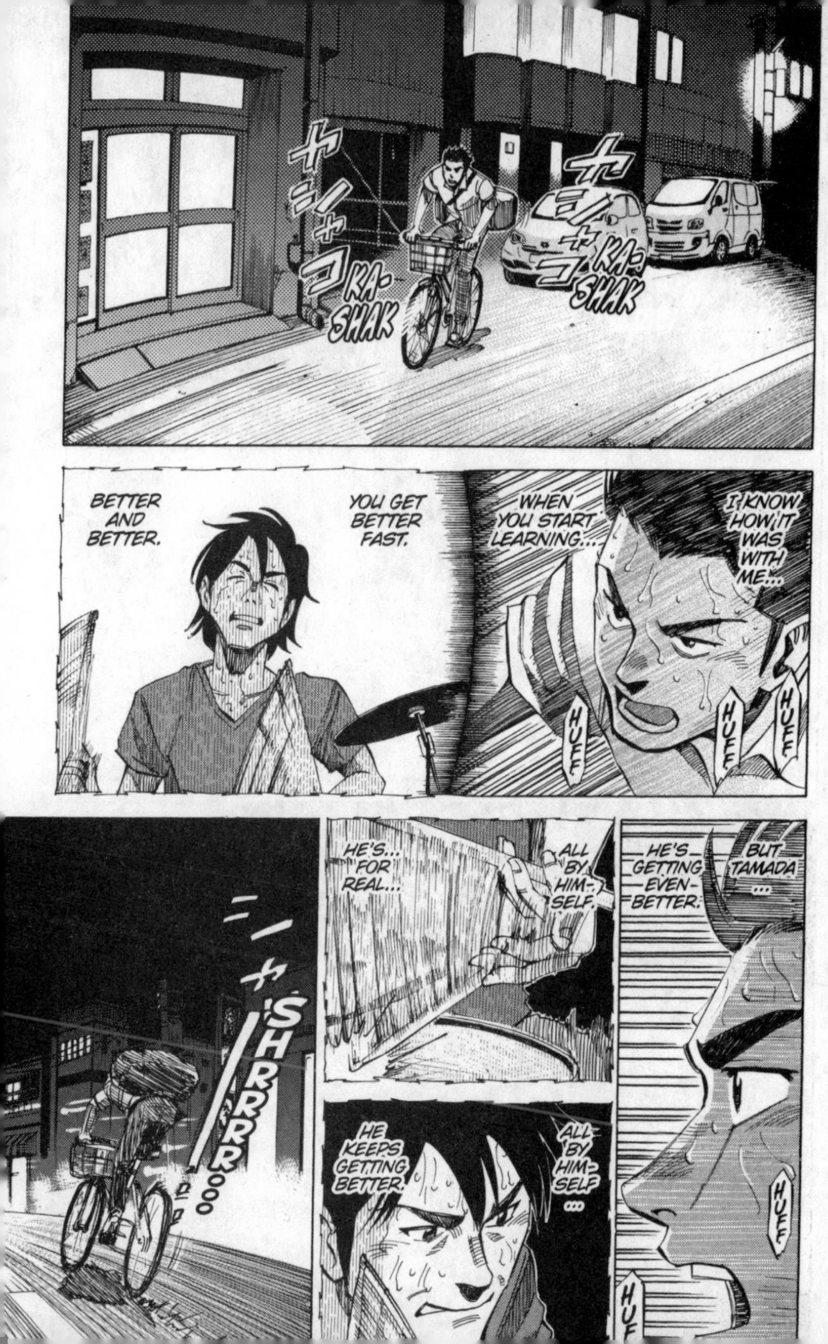
KA-SHAK
KA-SHAK
I KNOW HOW IT WAS WITH ME...
WHEN YOU START LEARNING...
HUFF
HUFF
HUFF
YOU GET BETTER FAST.
BETTER AND BETTER.
BUT TAMADA...
HE'S GETTING EVEN BETTER.
HUFF
HUF
ALL BY HIMSELF.
HE'S... FOR REAL...
ALL BY HIMSELF...
HE KEEPS GETTING BETTER.
SHRRRRooo

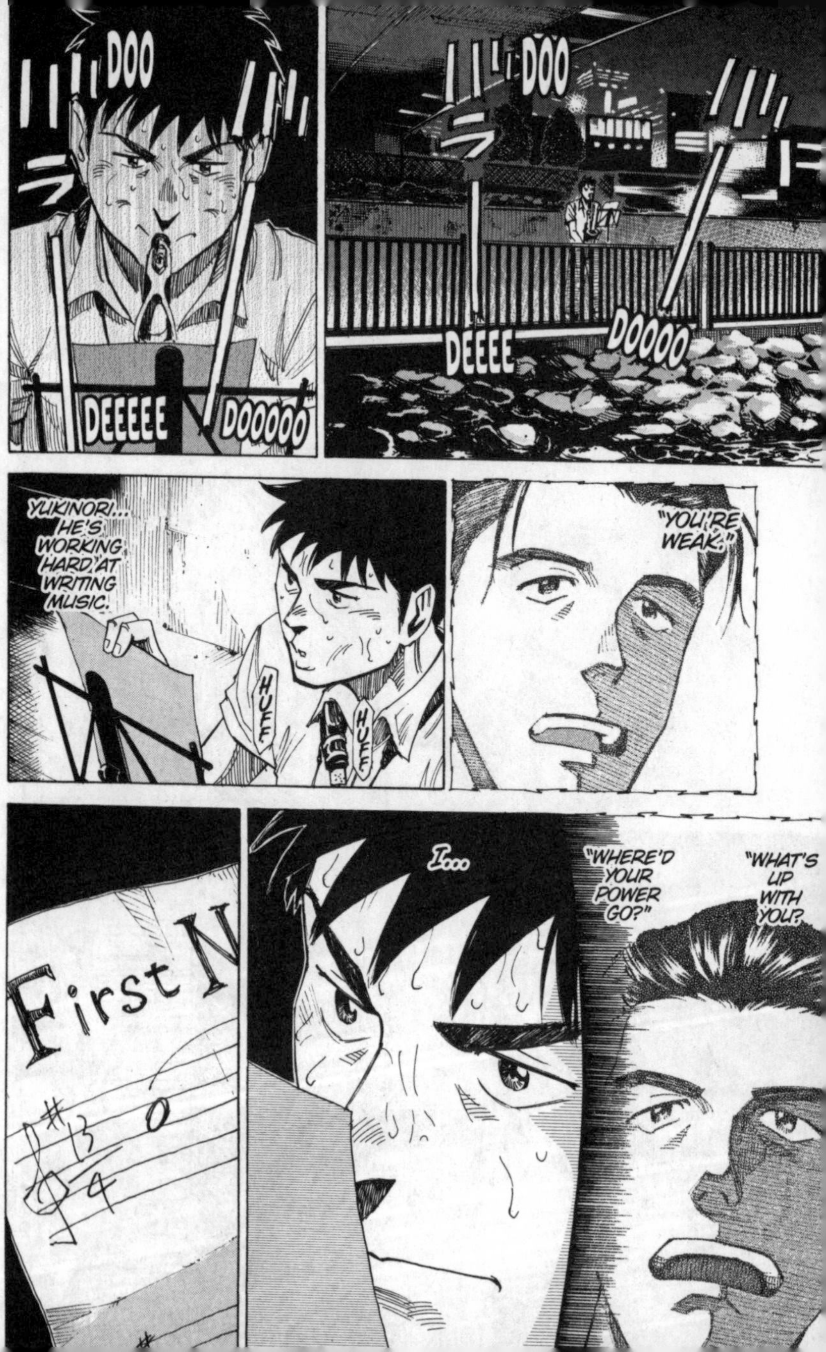
DOO
DOOOO
DEEEE
DOO
DOOOOO
DEEEEE
"YOU'RE WEAK."
YUKINORI... HE'S WORKING HARD AT WRITING MUSIC.
HUFF
HUFF
"WHAT'S UP WITH YOU?"
"WHERE'D YOUR POWER GO?"
I...
First N

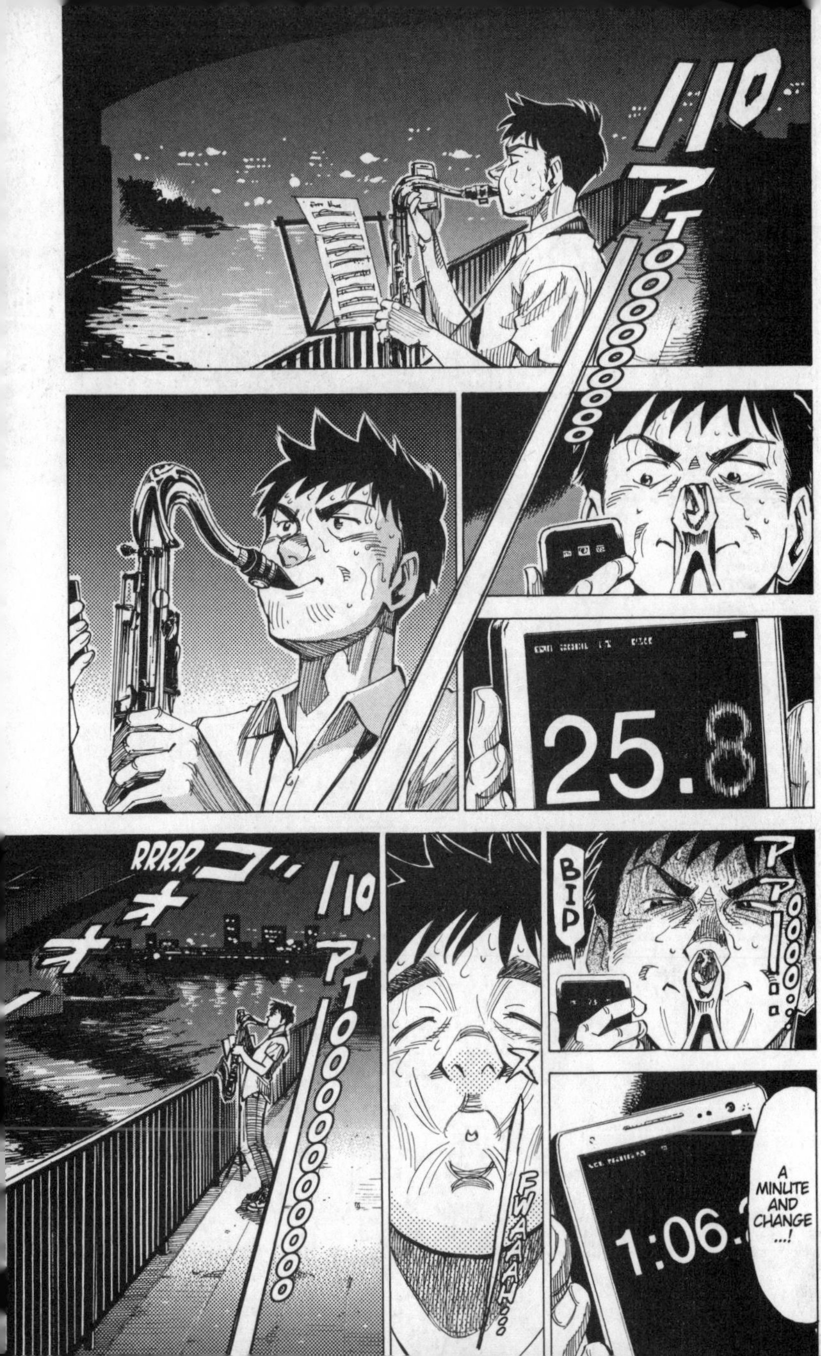

TOOOOOOOOOOOOO
25.8
BIP
Toooo...
A MINUTE AND CHANGE ...!
1:06.
FWAAAAH...
RRRR
TOOOOOOOOOOOOOOOO

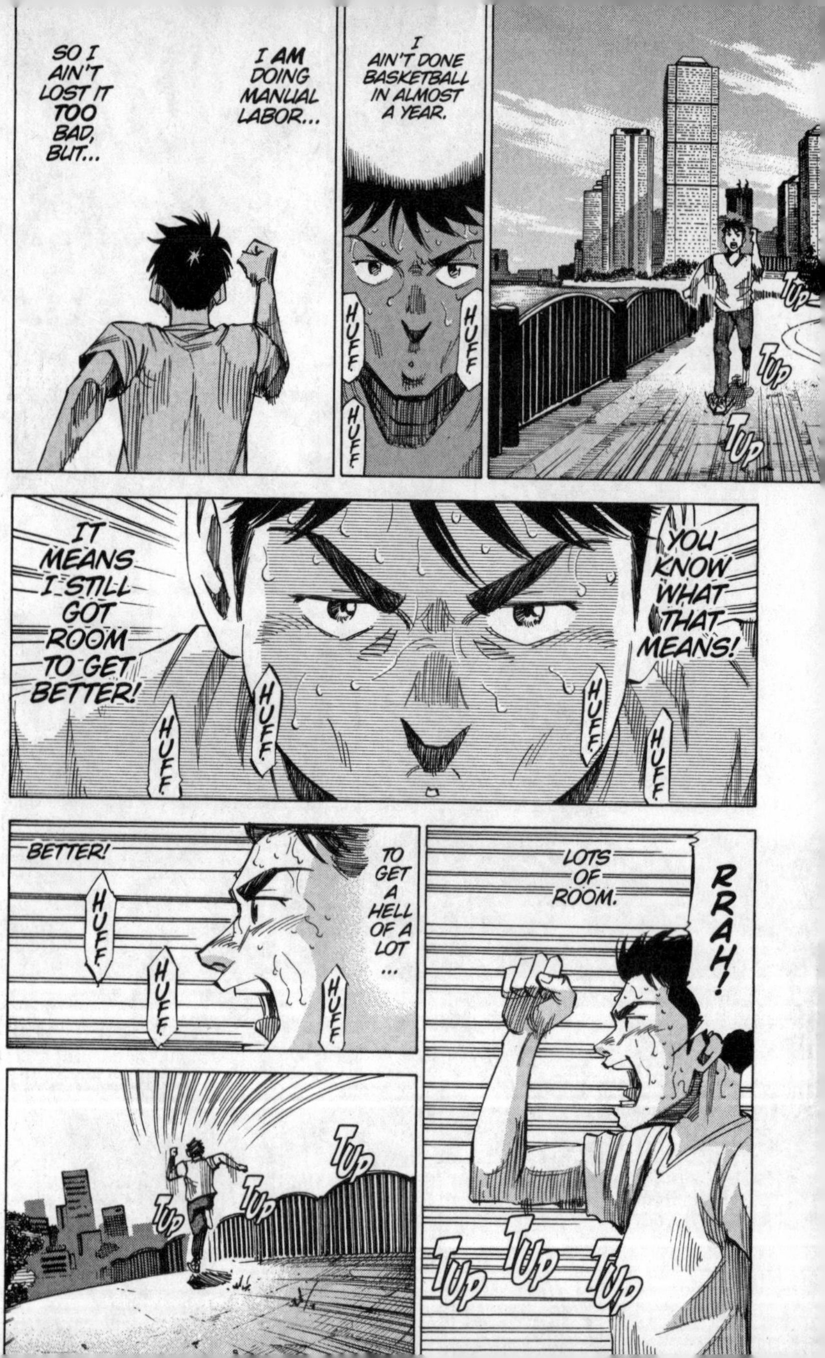
TUP
TUP
TUP
I AIN'T DONE BASKETBALL IN ALMOST A YEAR.
HUFF
HUFF
HUFF
I AM DOING MANUAL LABOR...
SO I AIN'T LOST IT TOO BAD, BUT...
YOU KNOW WHAT THAT MEANS!
HUFF
HUFF
HUFF
IT MEANS I STILL GOT ROOM TO GET BETTER!
HUFF
LOTS OF ROOM.
RRAH!
TUP
TUP
TUP
TO GET A HELL OF A LOT...
BETTER!
HUFF
HUFF
HUFF
TUP
TUP
TUP

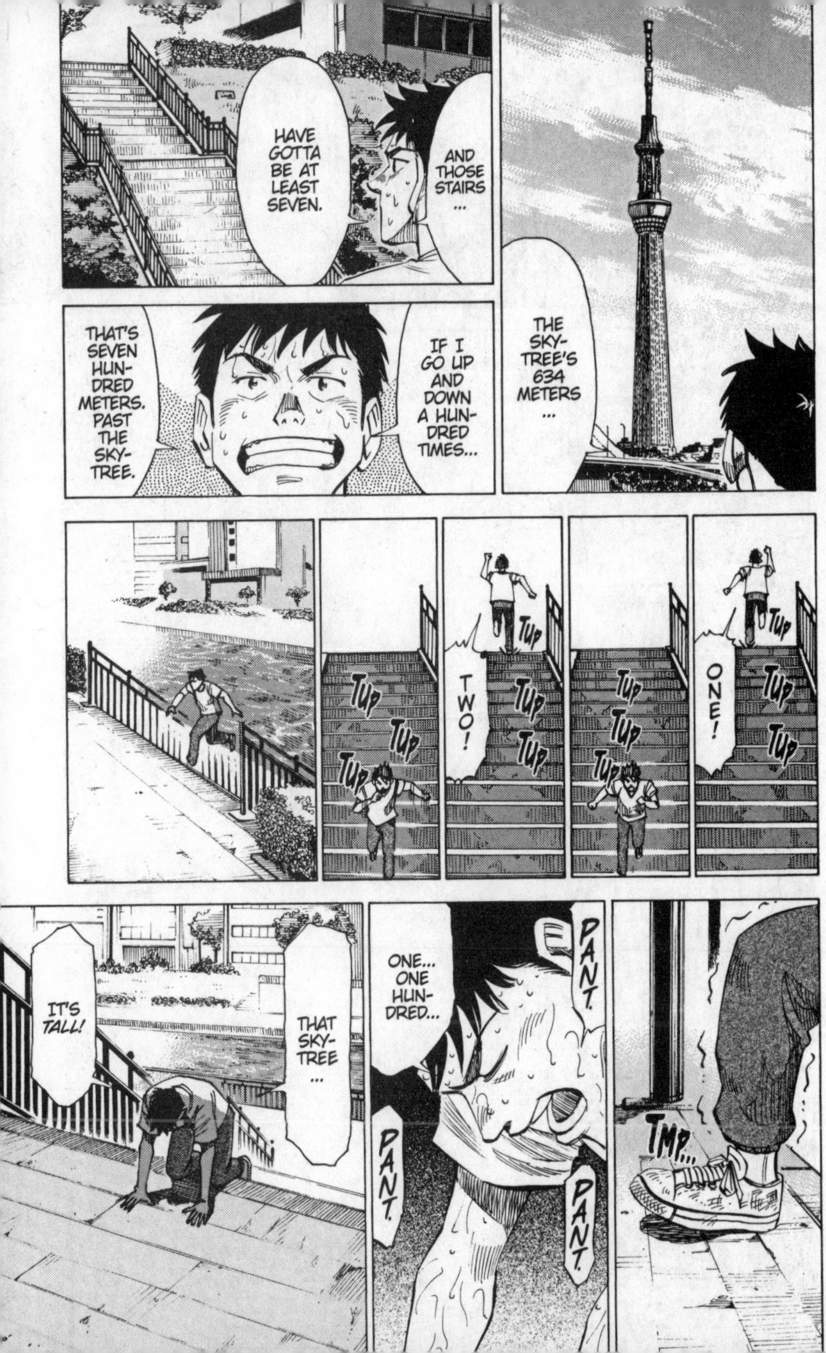
THE SKY-TREE'S 634 METERS ...
AND THOSE STAIRS ...
HAVE GOTTA BE AT LEAST SEVEN.
IF I GO UP AND DOWN A HUNDRED TIMES...
THAT'S SEVEN HUNDRED METERS. PAST THE SKY-TREE.
ONE!
TUP
TUP
TUP
TUP
TUP
TUP
TUP
TWO!
TUP
TUP
TUP
TUP
TUP
TUP
TMP...
PANT.
ONE... ONE HUNDRED...
PANT.
PANT.
THAT SKY-TREE ...
IT'S TALL!

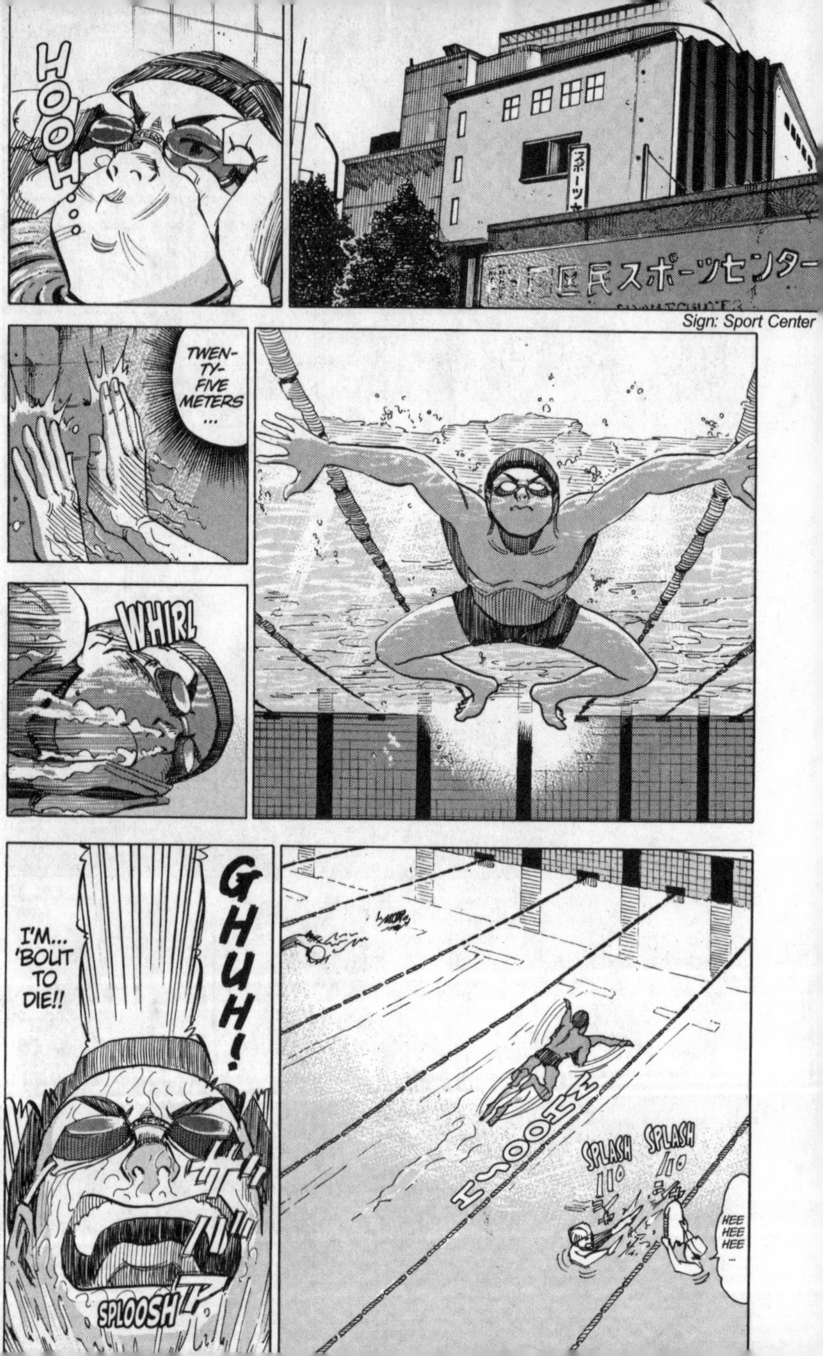

Sign: Sport Center
HOOH...
TWENTY-FIVE METERS...
WHIRL
SPLASH
SPLASH
HEE HEE HEE...
GHUH!
I'M... 'BOUT TO DIE!!
SPLOOSH

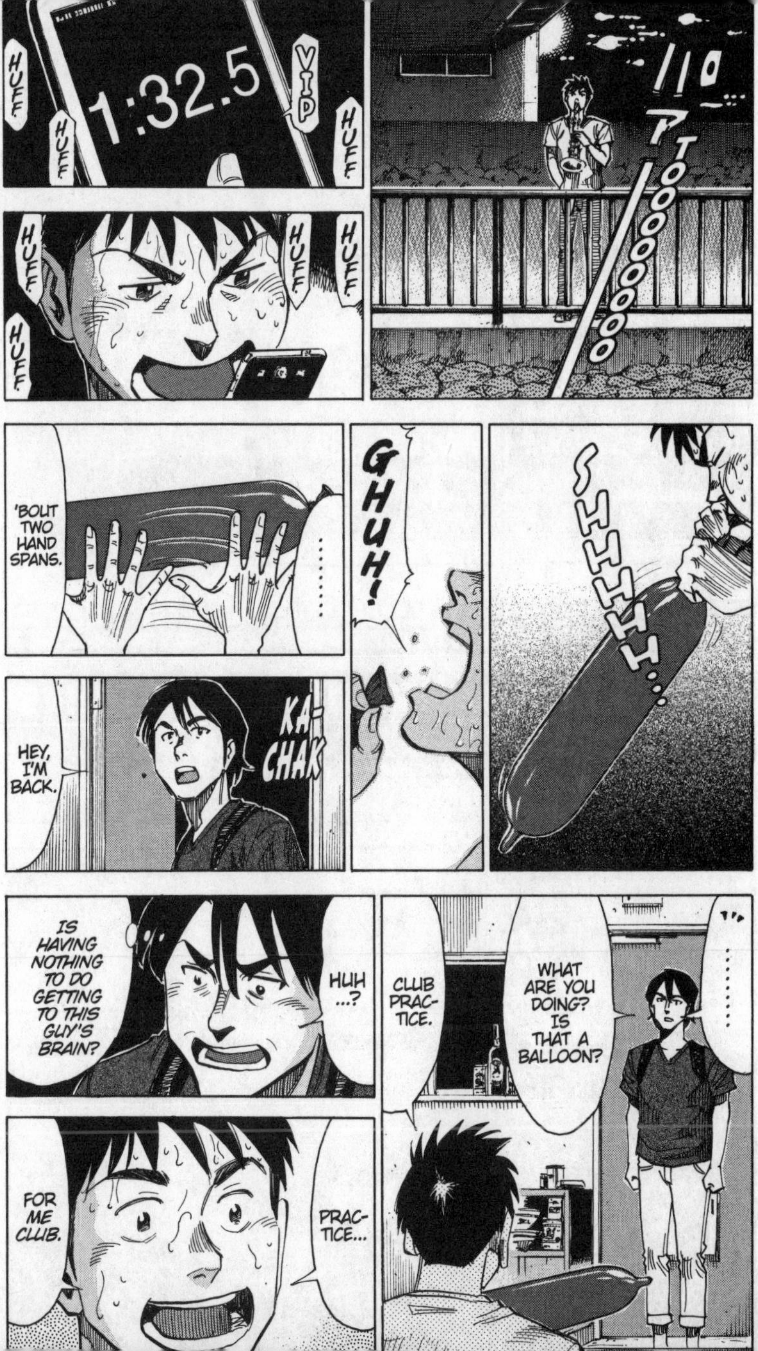
PTOOOOOOOOOO
HUFF
VIP
1:32.5
HUFF
HUFF
HUFF
HUFF
HUFF
HUFF
SHHHHHH...
GHUH!
......
'BOUT TWO HAND SPANS.
KA-CHAK
HEY, I'M BACK.
......
WHAT ARE YOU DOING? IS THAT A BALLOON?
CLUB PRACTICE.
HUH ...?
IS HAVING NOTHING TO DO GETTING TO THIS GUY'S BRAIN?
PRACTICE...
FOR ME CLUB.

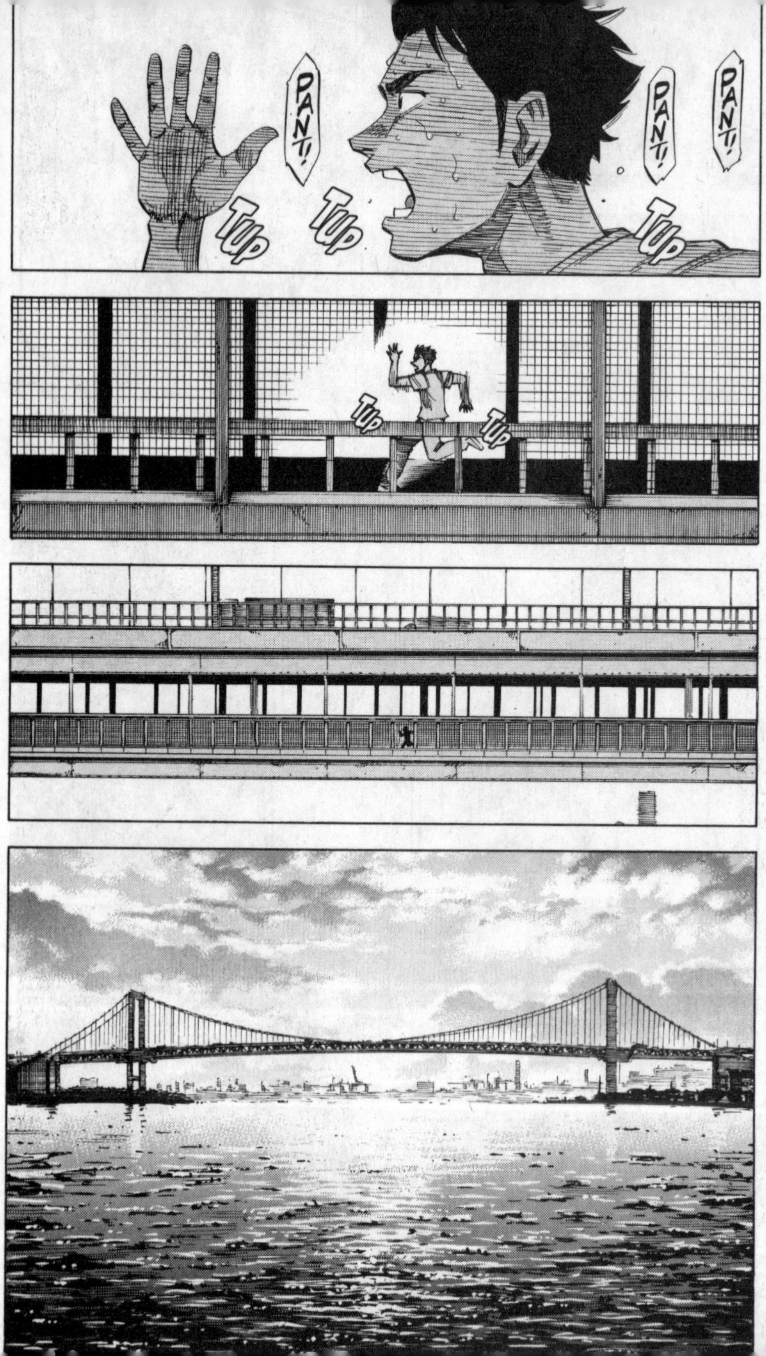
PANT!!
PANT!!
TUP
PANT!!
TUP
TUP
TUP
TUP

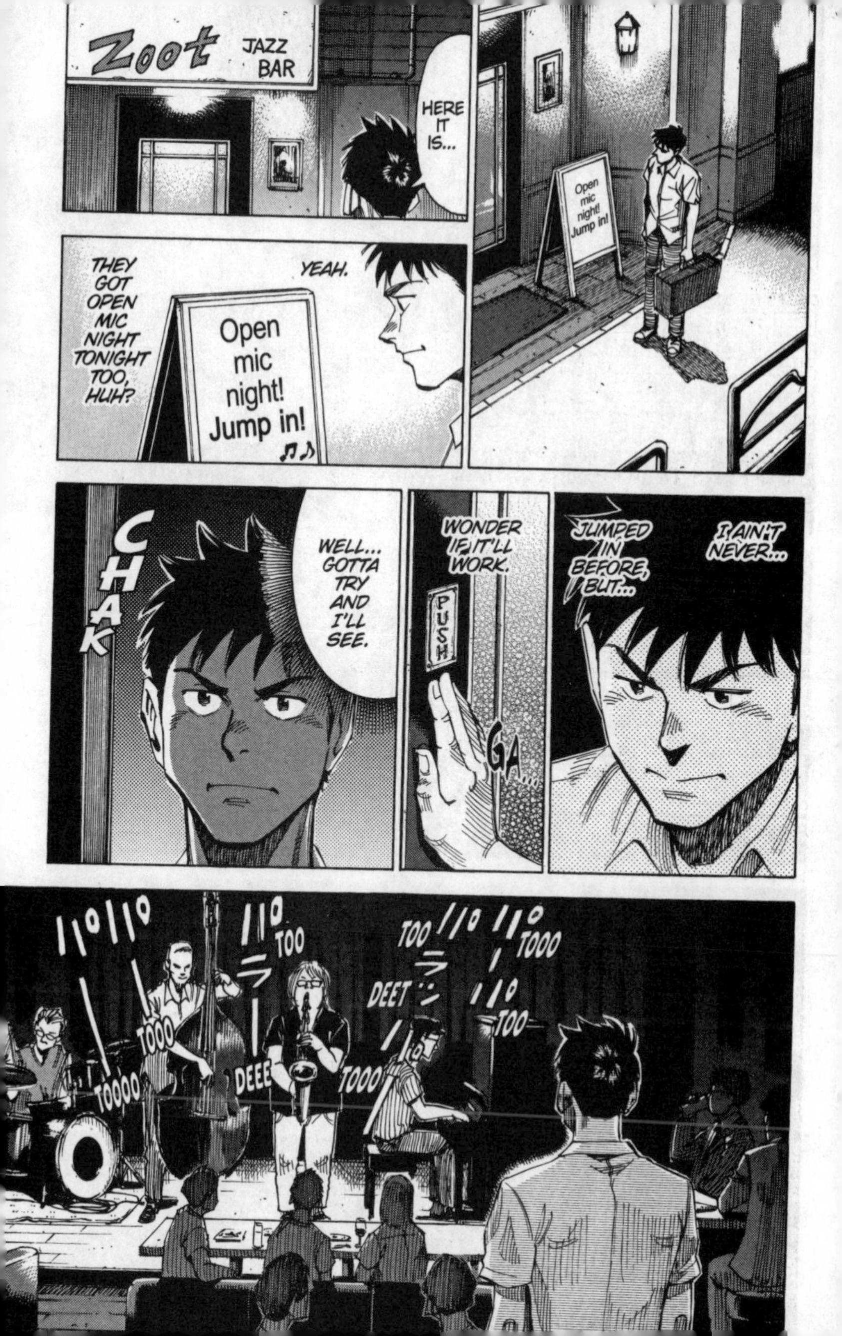
Open mic night! Jump in!
Zoot
JAZZ BAR
HERE IT IS...
THEY GOT OPEN MIC NIGHT TONIGHT TOO, HUH?
YEAH.
Open mic night! Jump in!
I AIN'T NEVER...
JUMPED IN BEFORE, BUT...
WONDER IF IT'LL WORK.
PUSH
GA...
WELL... GOTTA TRY AND I'LL SEE.
CHAK
TOOO
TOO
TOO
DEET
TOO
TOOO
DEEE
TOOO
TOOOO

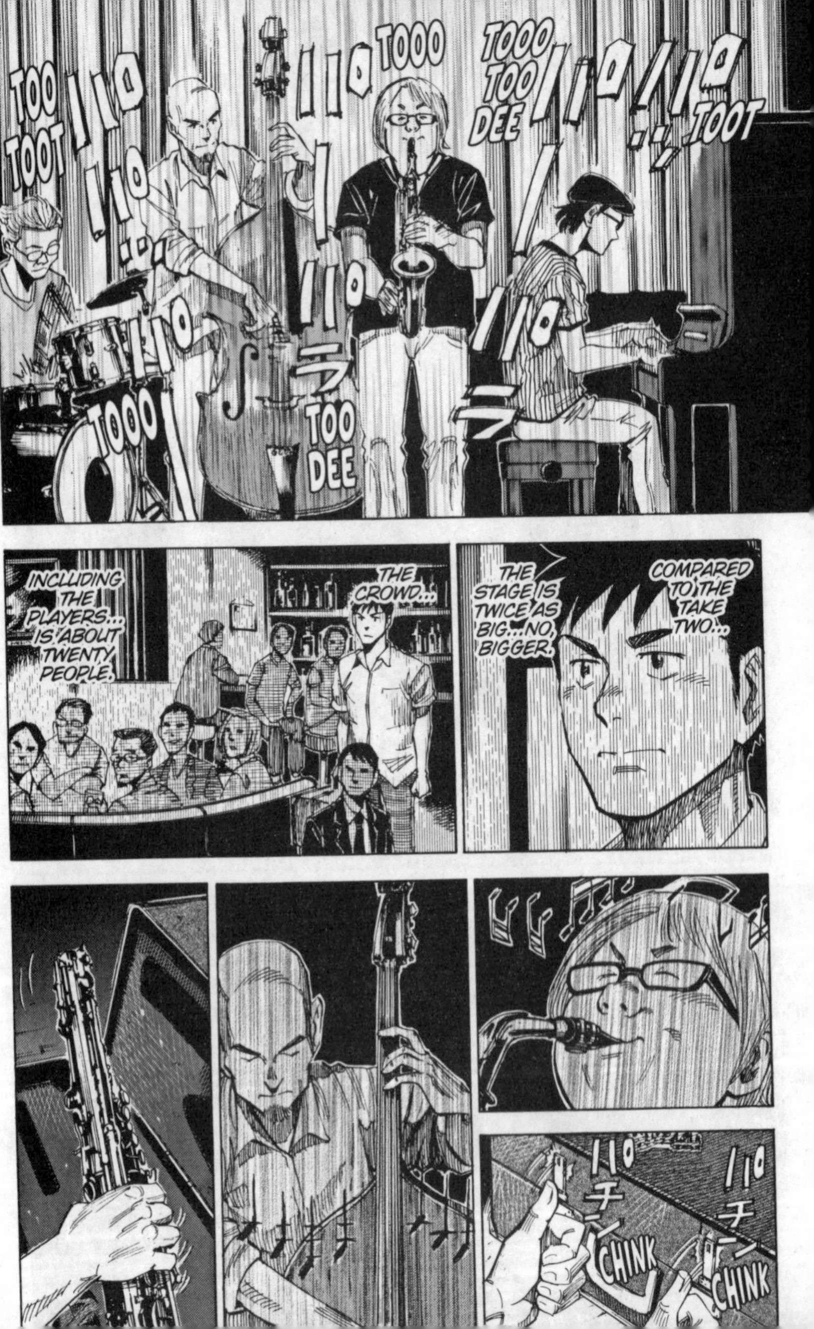

TOOO TOO DEE
TOOT
TOOO
TOO TOOT
TOO DEE
TOOO
COMPARED TO THE TAKE TWO...
THE STAGE IS TWICE AS BIG... NO, BIGGER.
THE CROWD...
INCLUDING THE PLAYERS... IS ABOUT TWENTY PEOPLE.
CHINK
CHINK

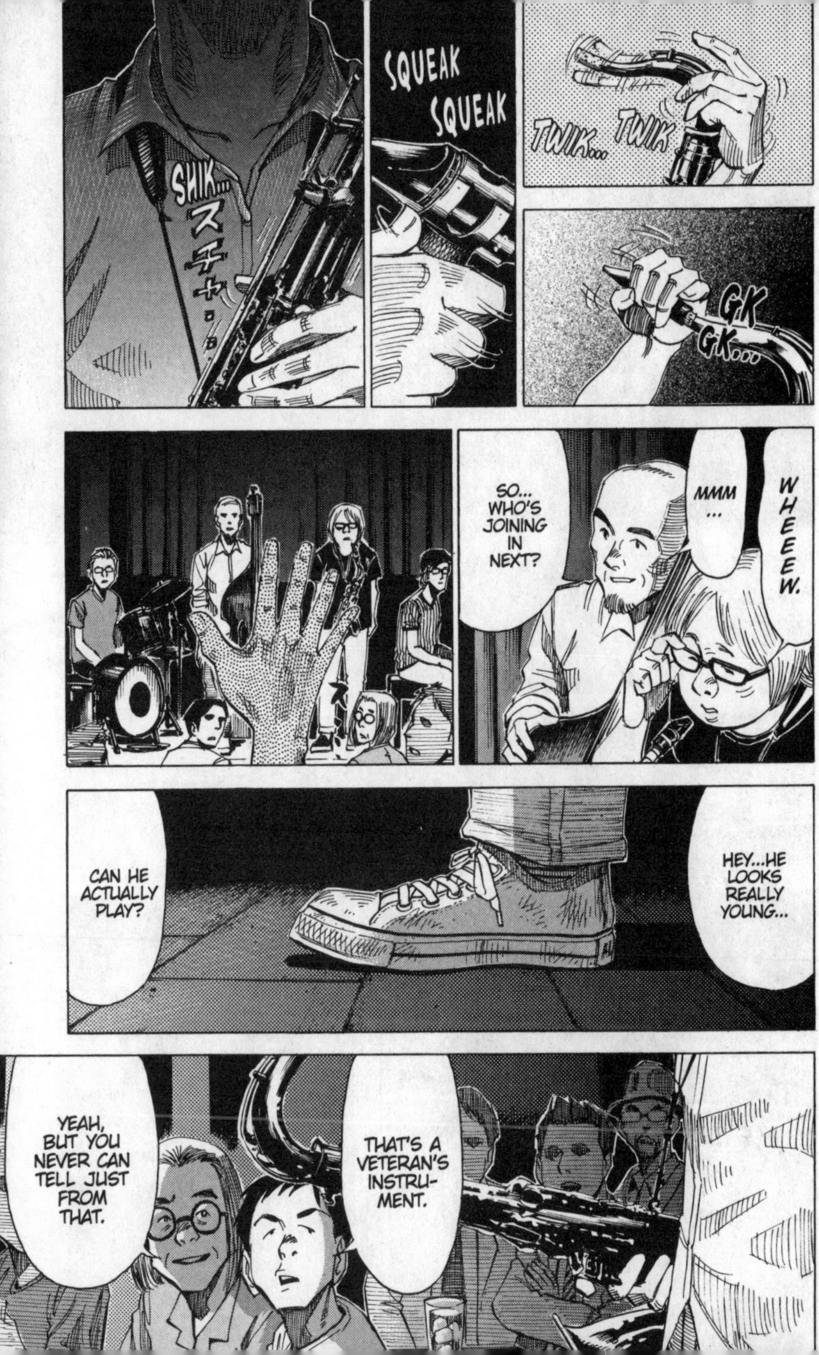
TWIK... TWIK
GK GK...
SQUEAK SQUEAK
SHIK...
スチャ
WHEEEW.
MMM...
SO... WHO'S JOINING IN NEXT?
HEY...HE LOOKS REALLY YOUNG...
CAN HE ACTUALLY PLAY?
THAT'S A VETERAN'S INSTRU-MENT.
YEAH, BUT YOU NEVER CAN TELL JUST FROM THAT.

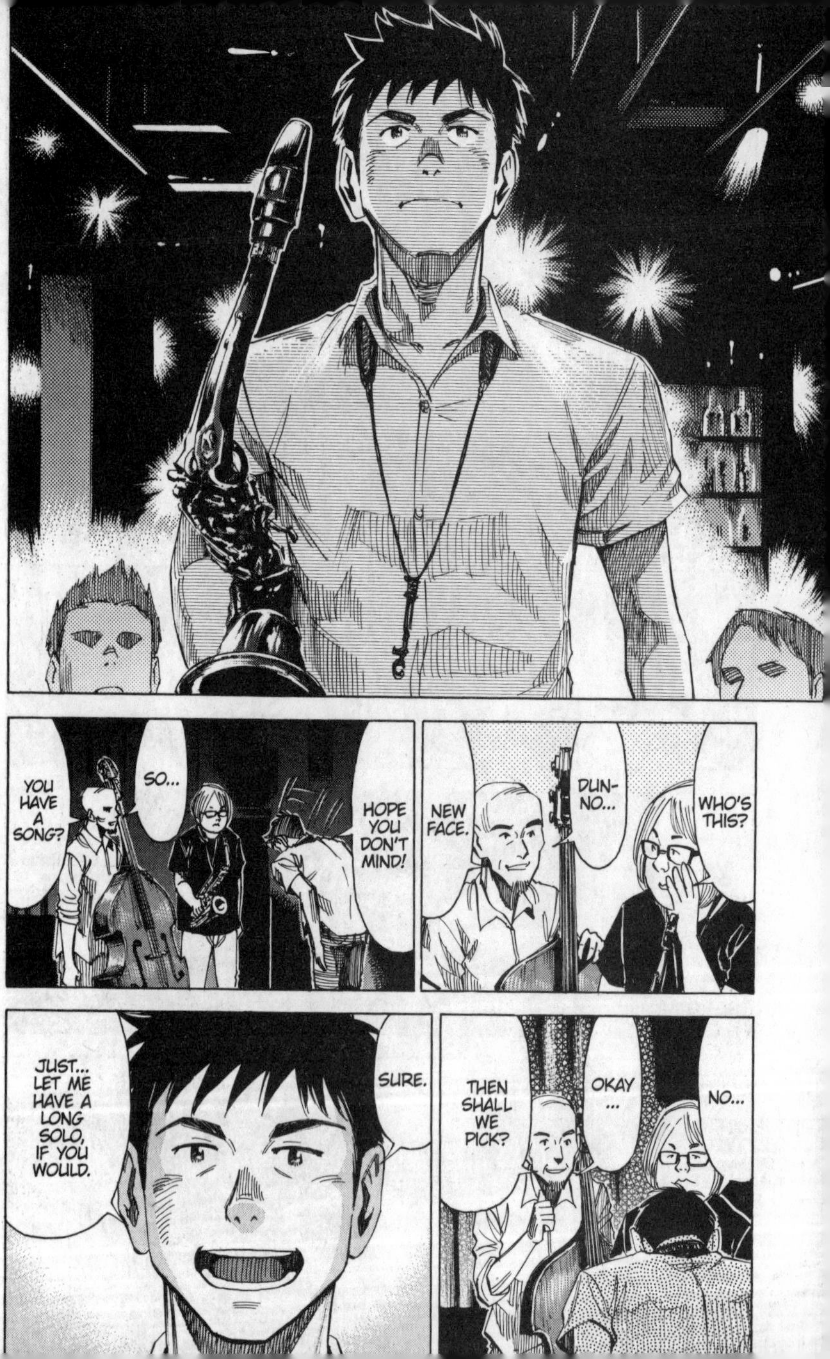
WHO'S THIS?
DUN-NO...
NEW FACE.
HOPE YOU DON'T MIND!
SO...
YOU HAVE A SONG?
NO...
OKAY ...
THEN SHALL WE PICK?
SURE.
JUST... LET ME HAVE A LONG SOLO, IF YOU WOULD.

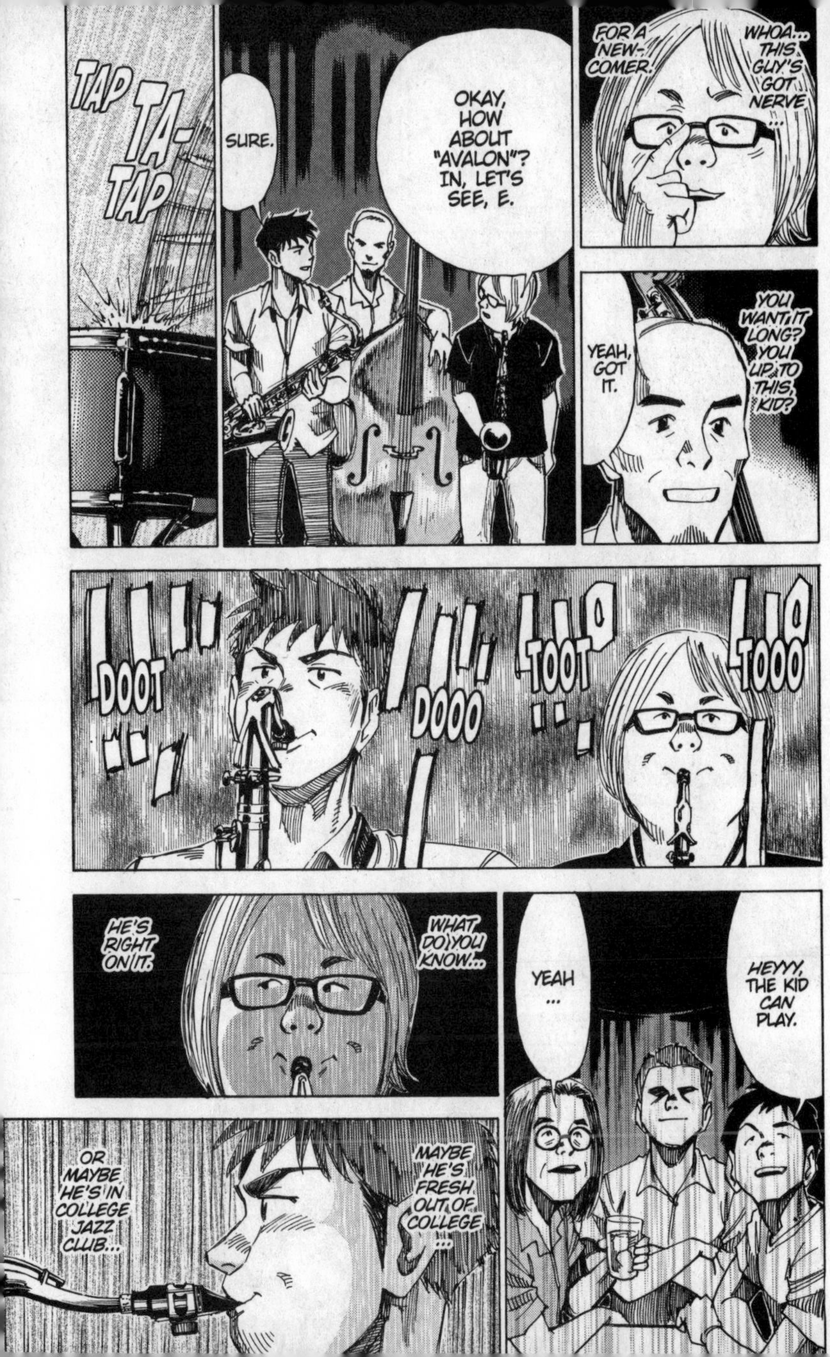
WHOA... THIS GUY'S GOT NERVE...
FOR A NEW-COMER.
YOU WANT IT LONG? YOU UP TO THIS, KID?
YEAH, GOT IT.
OKAY, HOW ABOUT "AVALON"? IN, LET'S SEE, E.
SURE.
TAP TA-TAP
TOOO
TOOT
DOOO
DOOT
HEYYY, THE KID CAN PLAY.
YEAH ...
WHAT DO YOU KNOW...
HE'S RIGHT ON IT.
MAYBE HE'S FRESH OUT OF COLLEGE ...
OR MAYBE HE'S IN COLLEGE JAZZ CLUB...

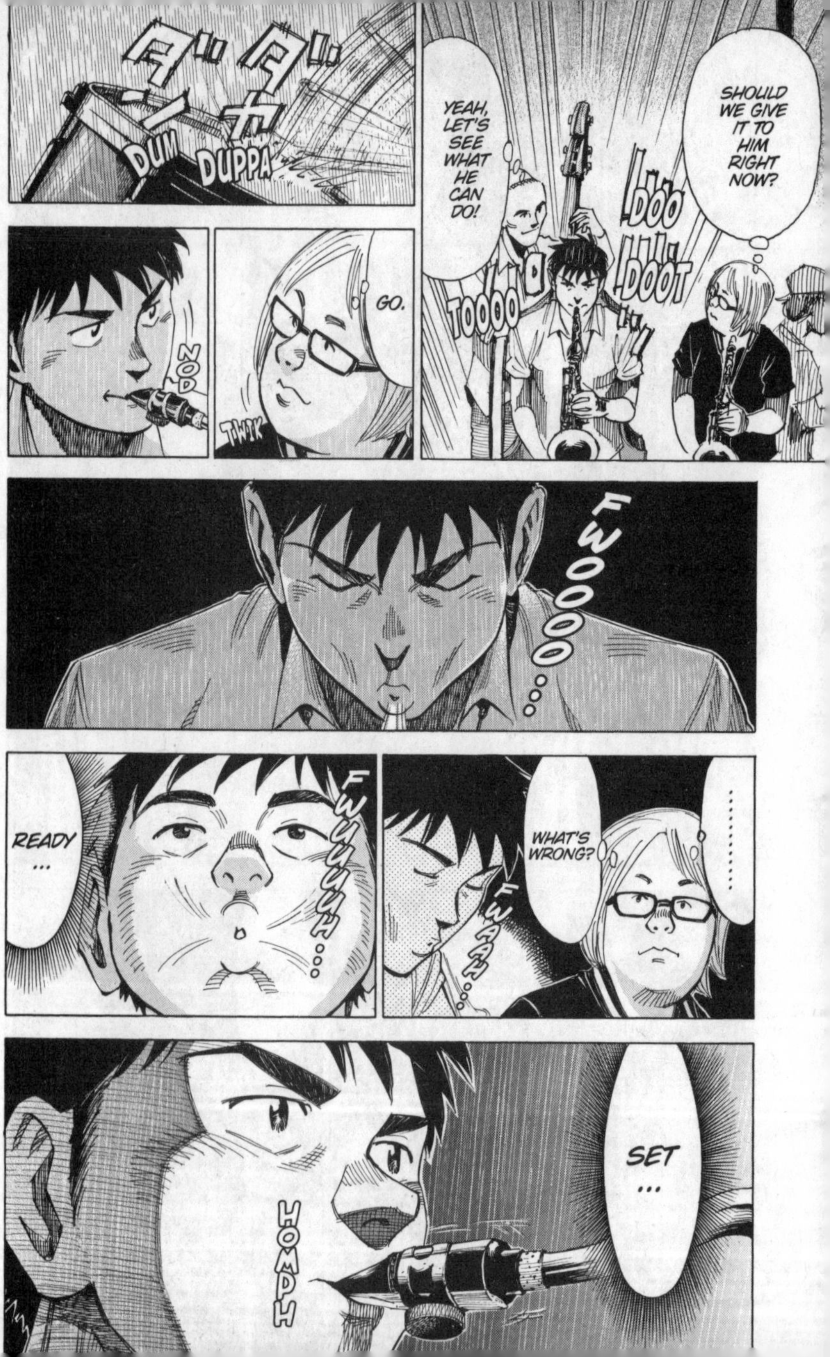
SHOULD WE GIVE IT TO HIM RIGHT NOW?
YEAH, LET'S SEE WHAT HE CAN DO!
DOO DOOT
TOOOO
DUM
DUPPA
GO.
TWIK
NOD
FWOOOOO...
......
WHAT'S WRONG?
FWAAAH...
READY ...
FWUUUUH...
SET ...
HOMPH

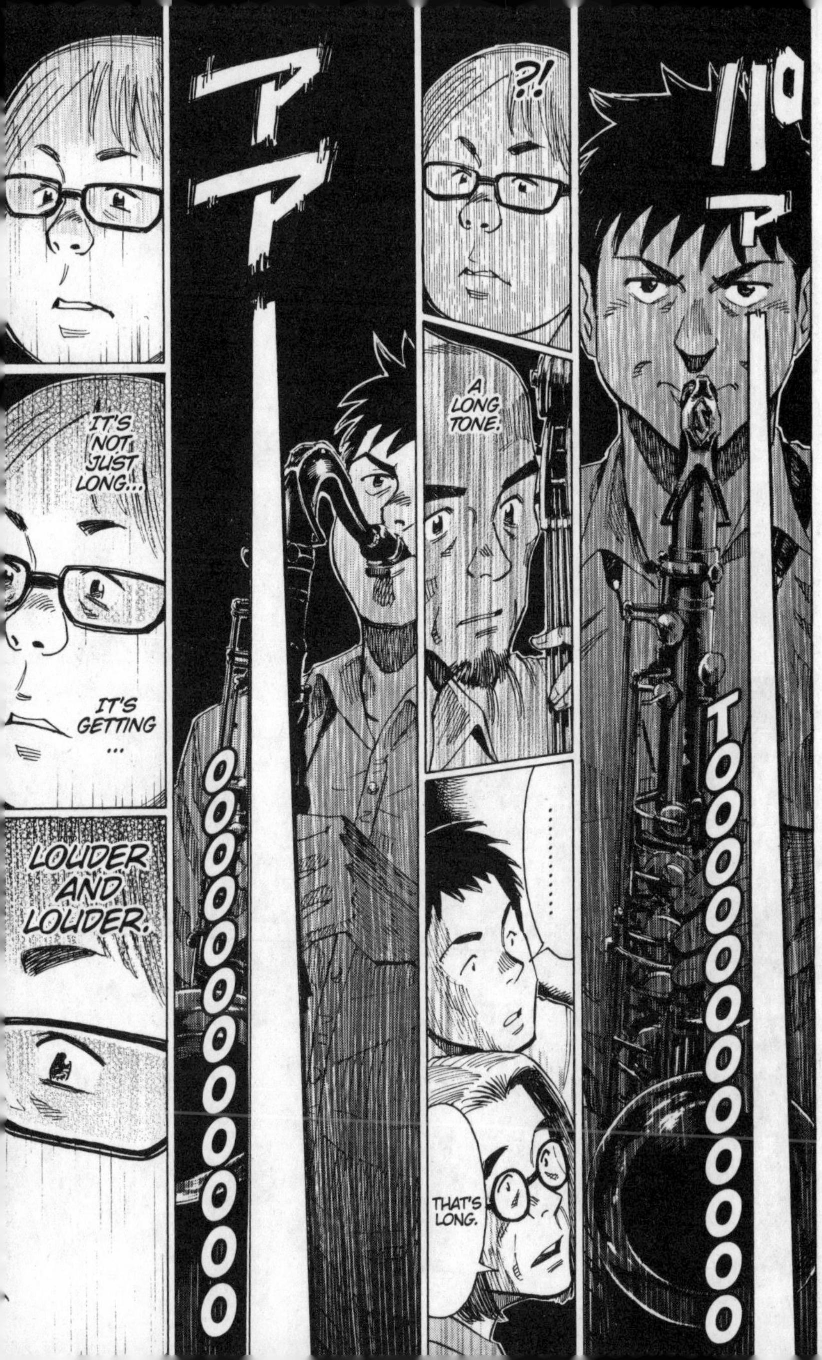

パ
TOOOOOOOOOOOOOO
?!
A LONG TONE.
......
THAT'S LONG.
ア
OOOOOOOOOOOO
IT'S NOT JUST LONG...
IT'S GETTING ...
LOUDER AND LOUDER.

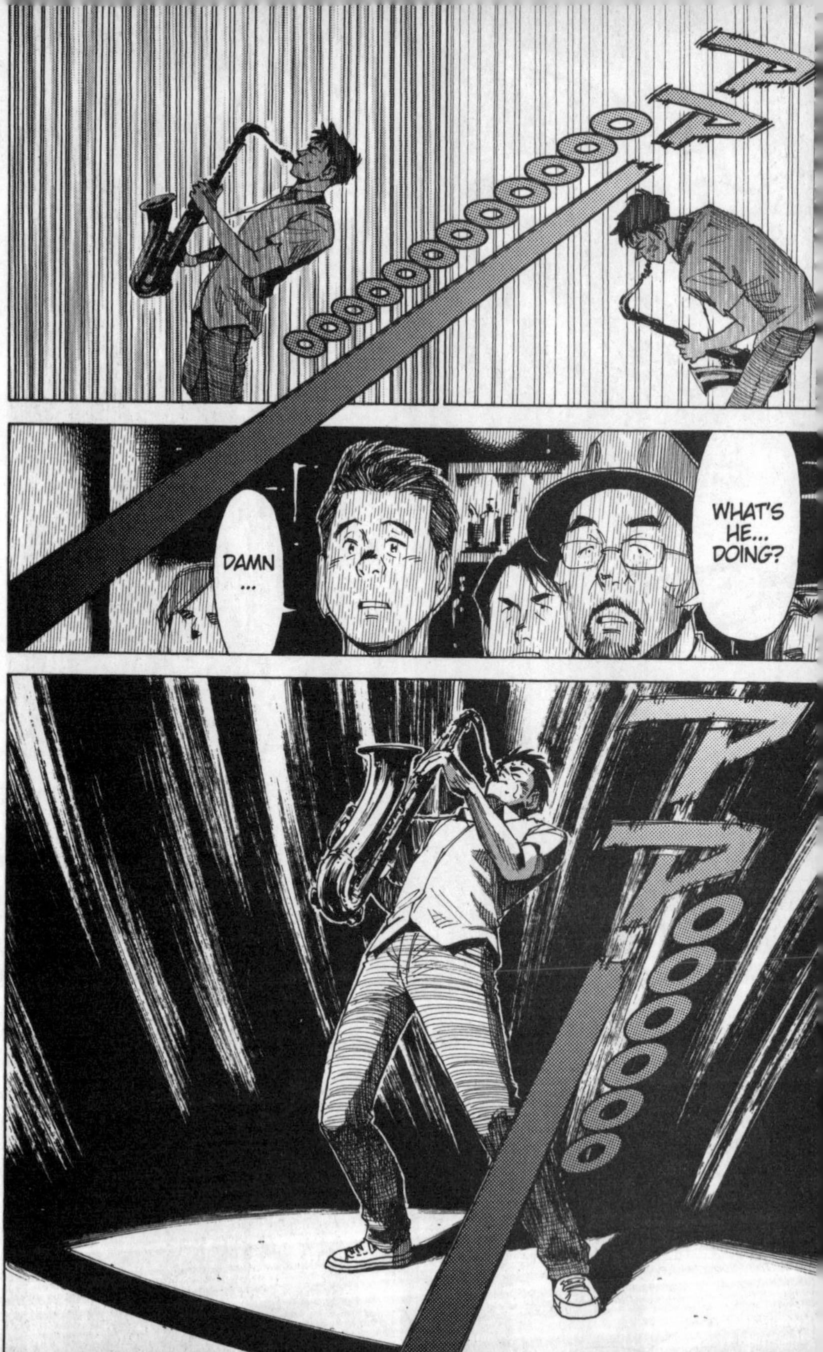
WHAT'S HE... DOING?
DAMN ...

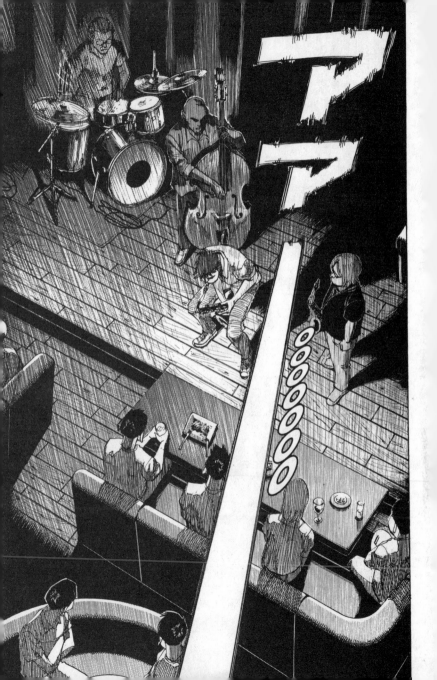

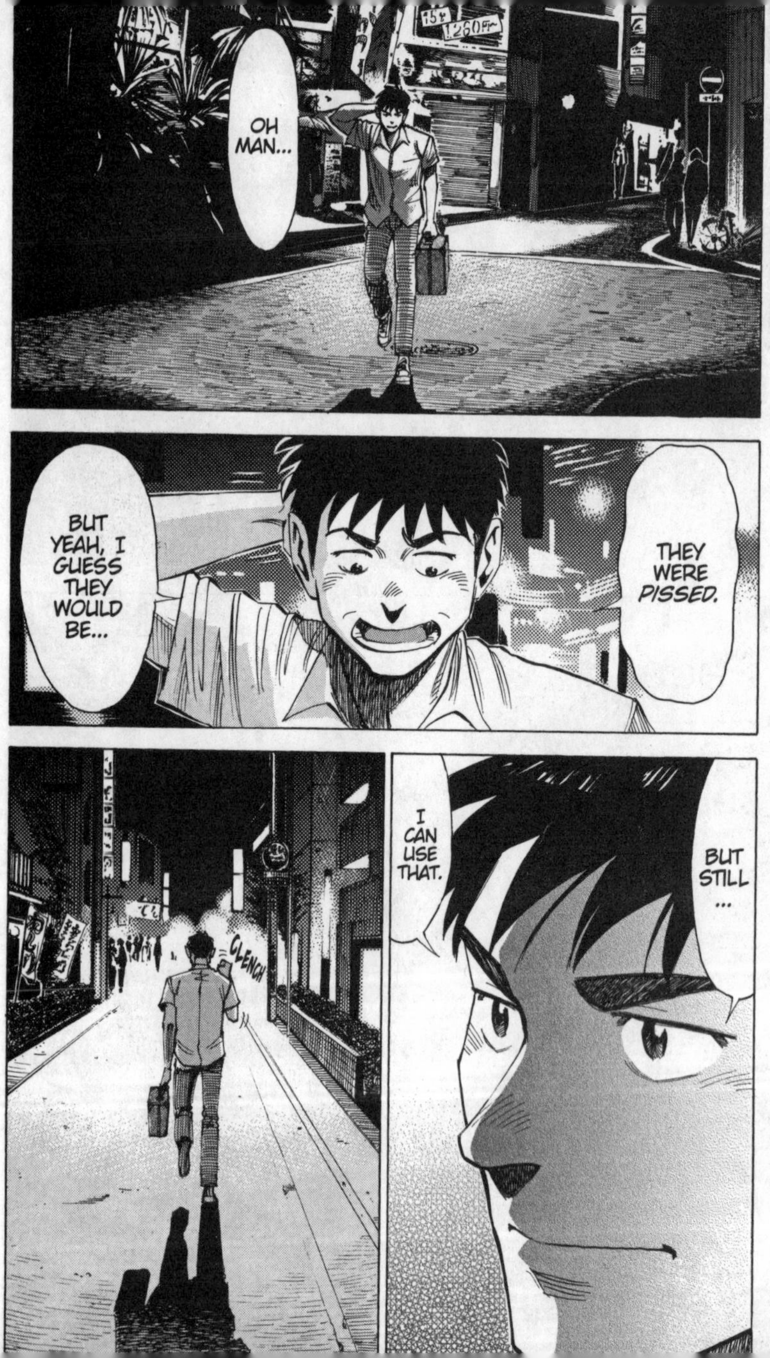
OH MAN...
THEY WERE PISSED.
BUT YEAH, I GUESS THEY WOULD BE...
BUT STILL...
I CAN USE THAT.
CLENCH

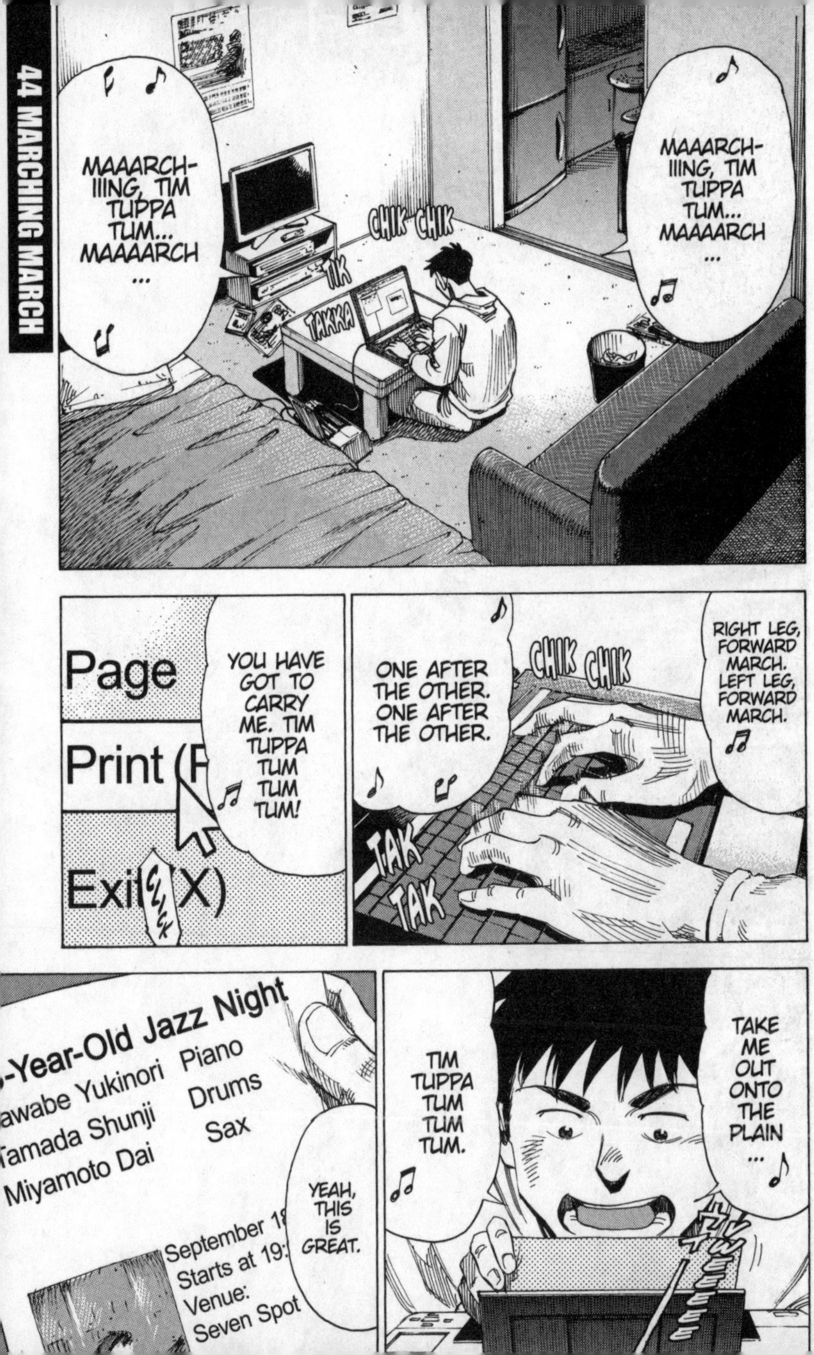
MAAARCH-IIING, TIM TUPPA TUM... MAAAARCH ...
MAAARCH-IIING, TIM TUPPA TUM... MAAAARCH ...
CHIK CHIK
TIK
TAKKA
RIGHT LEG, FORWARD MARCH. LEFT LEG, FORWARD MARCH.
ONE AFTER THE OTHER. ONE AFTER THE OTHER.
CHIK CHIK
TAK TAK
YOU HAVE GOT TO CARRY ME. TIM TUPPA TUM TUM TUM!
Page
Print (P
Exit (X)
CLICK
TAKE ME OUT ONTO THE PLAIN ...
TIM TUPPA TUM TUM TUM.
YEAH, THIS IS GREAT.
-Year-Old Jazz Night
awabe Yukinori Piano
Tamada Shunji Drums
Miyamoto Dai Sax
September 1
Starts at 19:
Venue:
Seven Spot

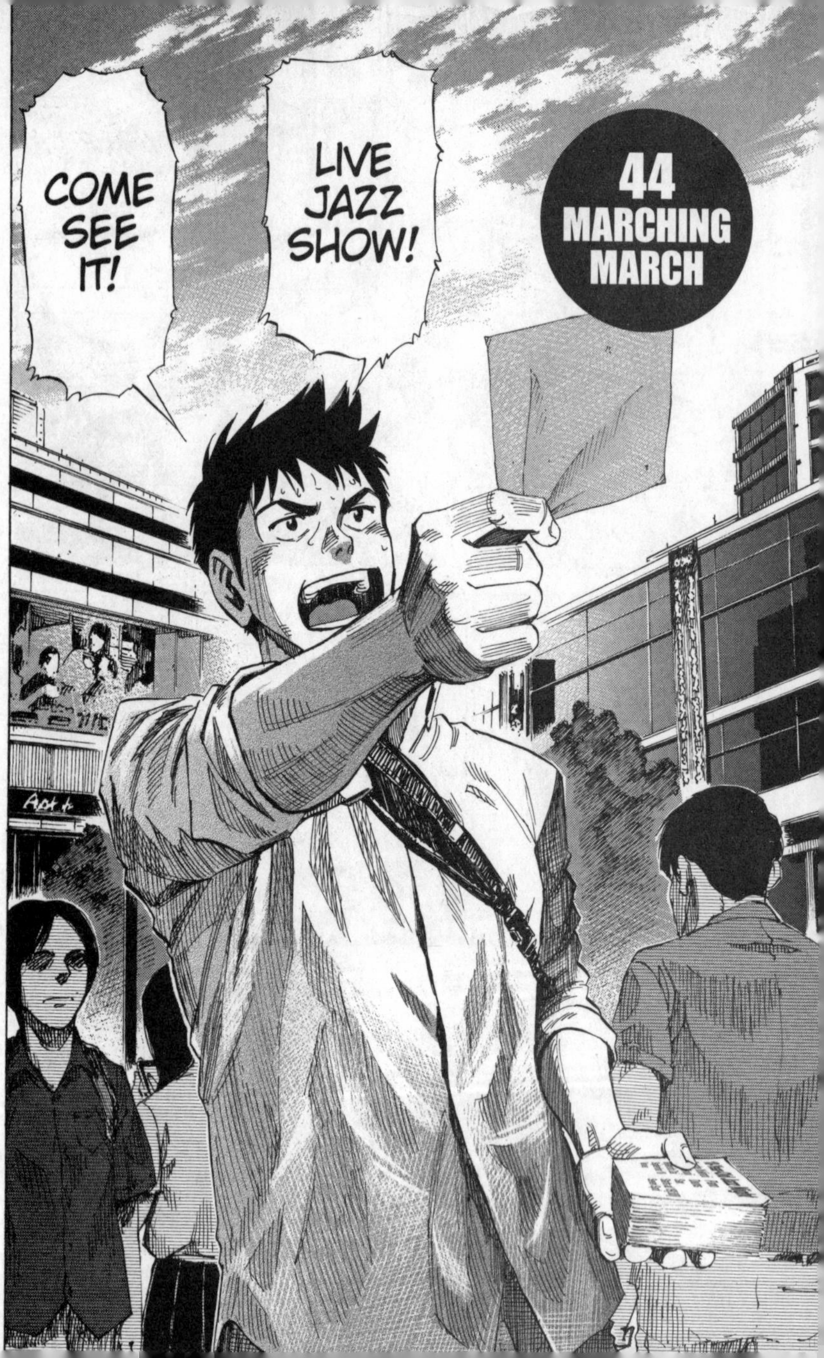
44
MARCHING MARCH
LIVE JAZZ SHOW!
COME SEE IT!

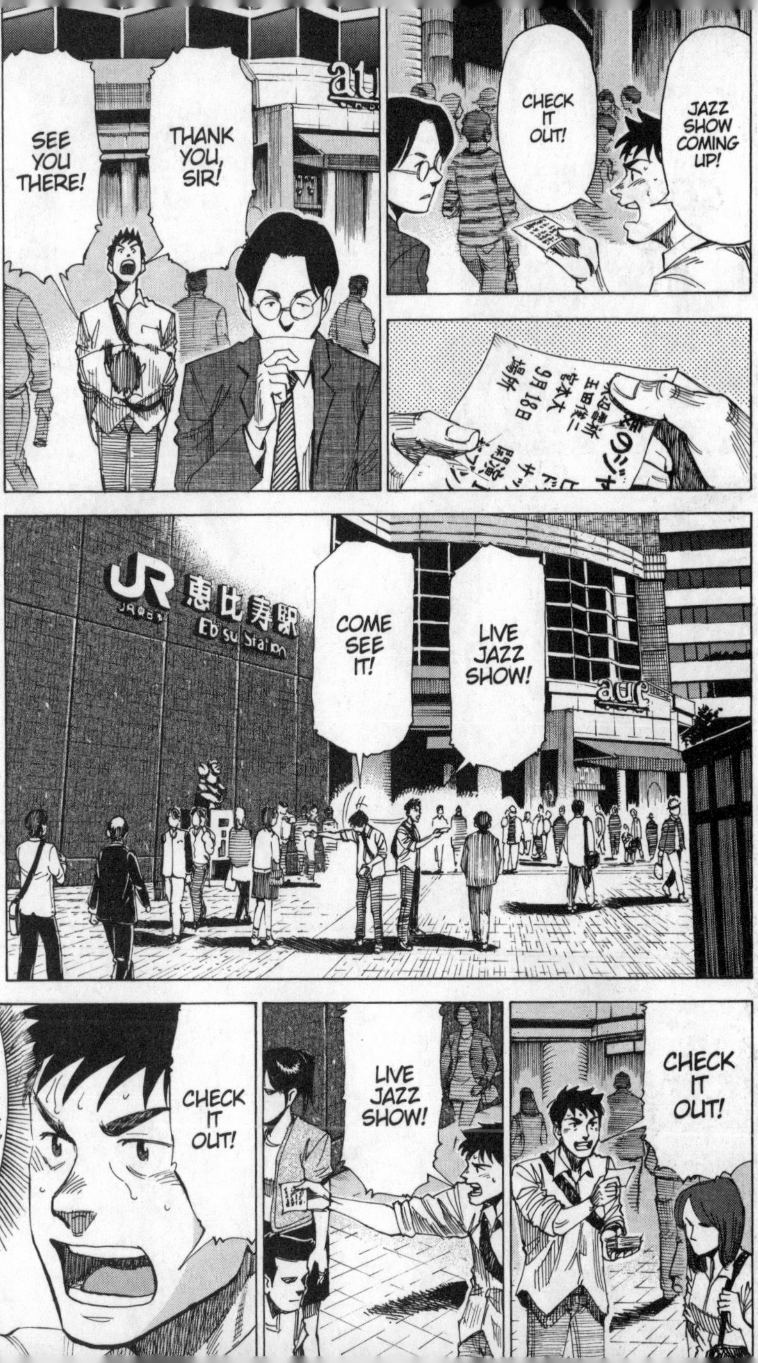
JAZZ SHOW COMING UP!
CHECK IT OUT!
宮本大
玉田俊二
9月18日
場所
THANK YOU, SIR!
SEE YOU THERE!
LIVE JAZZ SHOW!
COME SEE IT!
JR 恵比寿駅
Ebisu Station
CHECK IT OUT!
LIVE JAZZ SHOW!
CHECK IT OUT!
"LOOK, YOU'RE CRAZY."

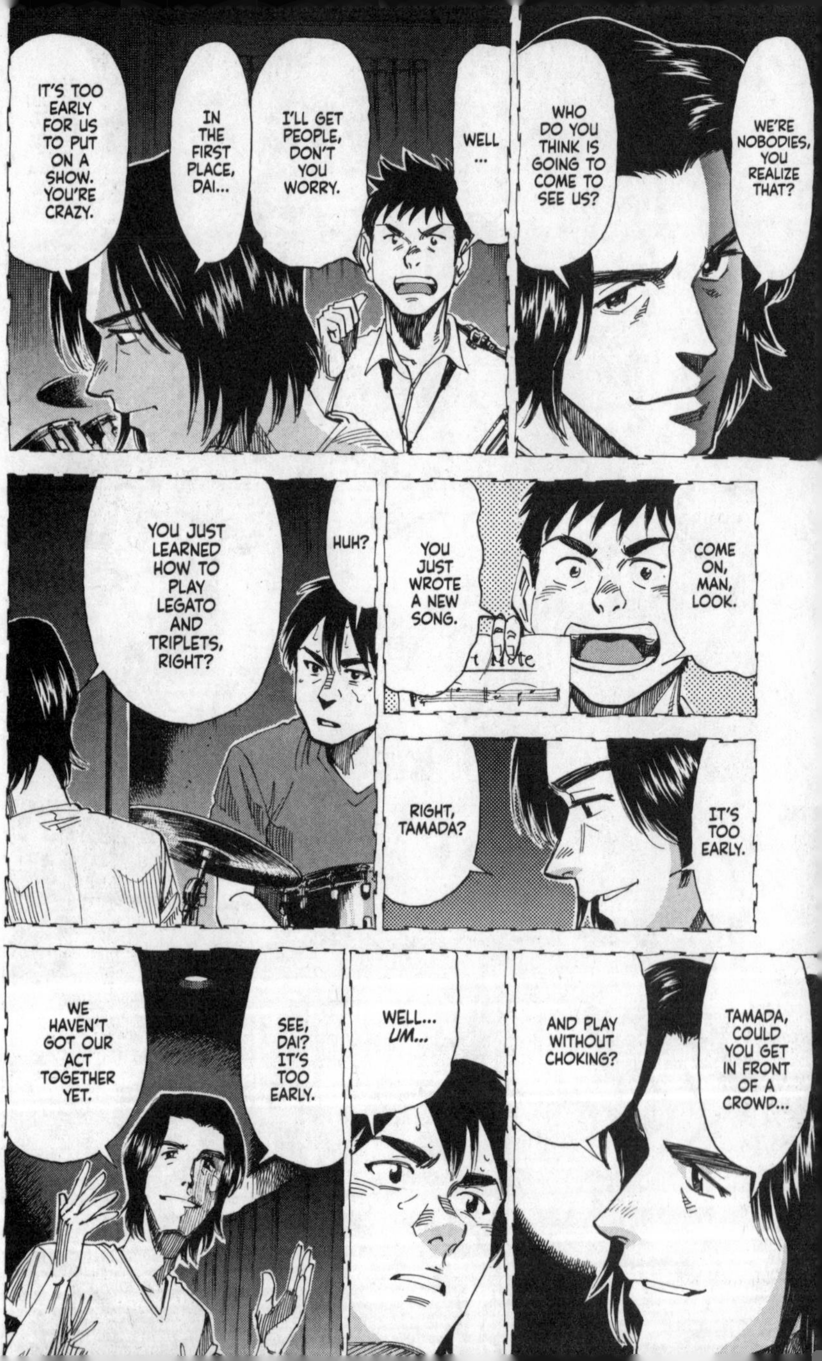
WE'RE NOBODIES, YOU REALIZE THAT?
WHO DO YOU THINK IS GOING TO COME TO SEE US?
WELL ...
I'LL GET PEOPLE, DON'T YOU WORRY.
IN THE FIRST PLACE, DAI...
IT'S TOO EARLY FOR US TO PUT ON A SHOW. YOU'RE CRAZY.
COME ON, MAN, LOOK.
YOU JUST WROTE A NEW SONG.
IT'S TOO EARLY.
RIGHT, TAMADA?
HUH?
YOU JUST LEARNED HOW TO PLAY LEGATO AND TRIPLETS, RIGHT?
TAMADA, COULD YOU GET IN FRONT OF A CROWD...
AND PLAY WITHOUT CHOKING?
WELL... *UM*...
SEE, DAI? IT'S TOO EARLY.
WE HAVEN'T GOT OUR ACT TOGETHER YET.

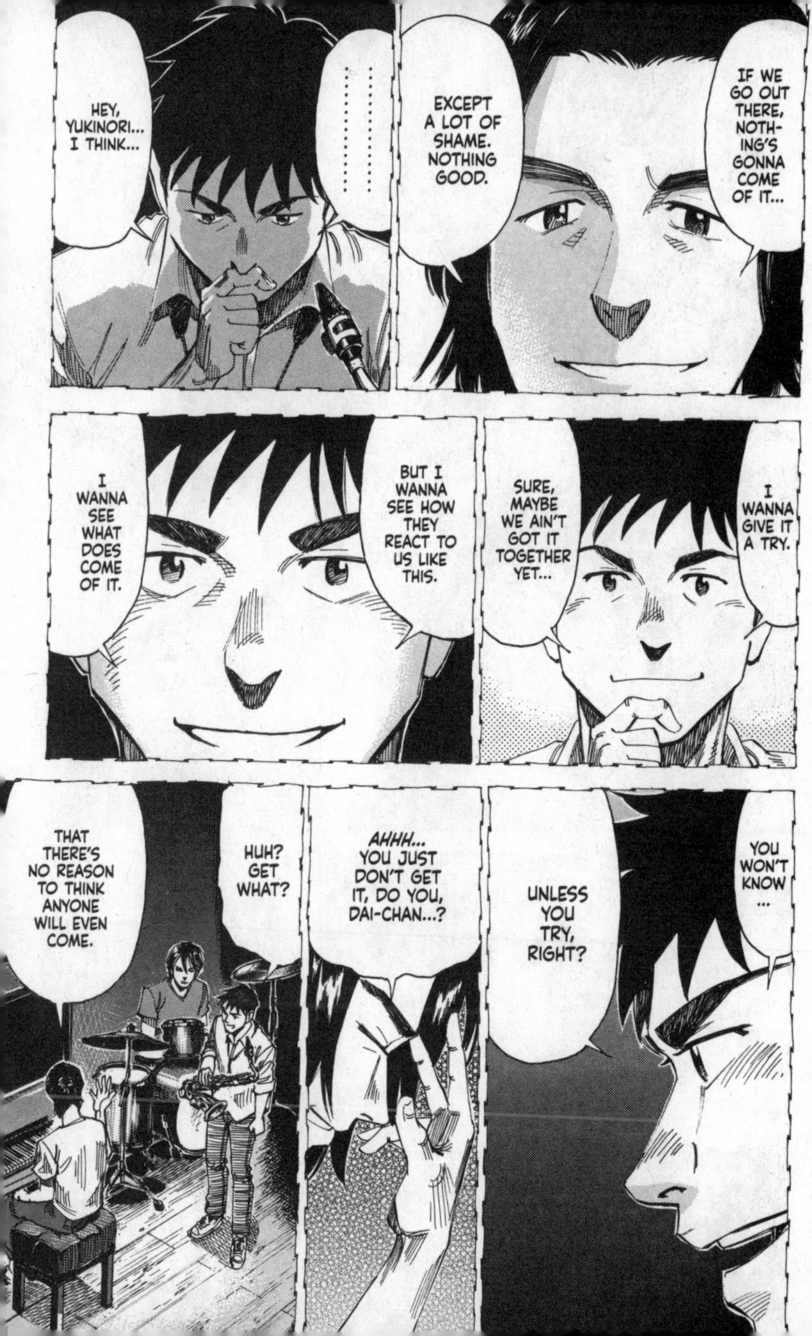
IF WE GO OUT THERE, NOTHING'S GONNA COME OF IT...
EXCEPT A LOT OF SHAME. NOTHING GOOD.
......
HEY, YUKINORI... I THINK...
I WANNA GIVE IT A TRY.
SURE, MAYBE WE AIN'T GOT IT TOGETHER YET...
BUT I WANNA SEE HOW THEY REACT TO US LIKE THIS.
I WANNA SEE WHAT DOES COME OF IT.
YOU WON'T KNOW ...
UNLESS YOU TRY, RIGHT?
AHHH... YOU JUST DON'T GET IT, DO YOU, DAI-CHAN...?
HUH? GET WHAT?
THAT THERE'S NO REASON TO THINK ANYONE WILL EVEN COME.

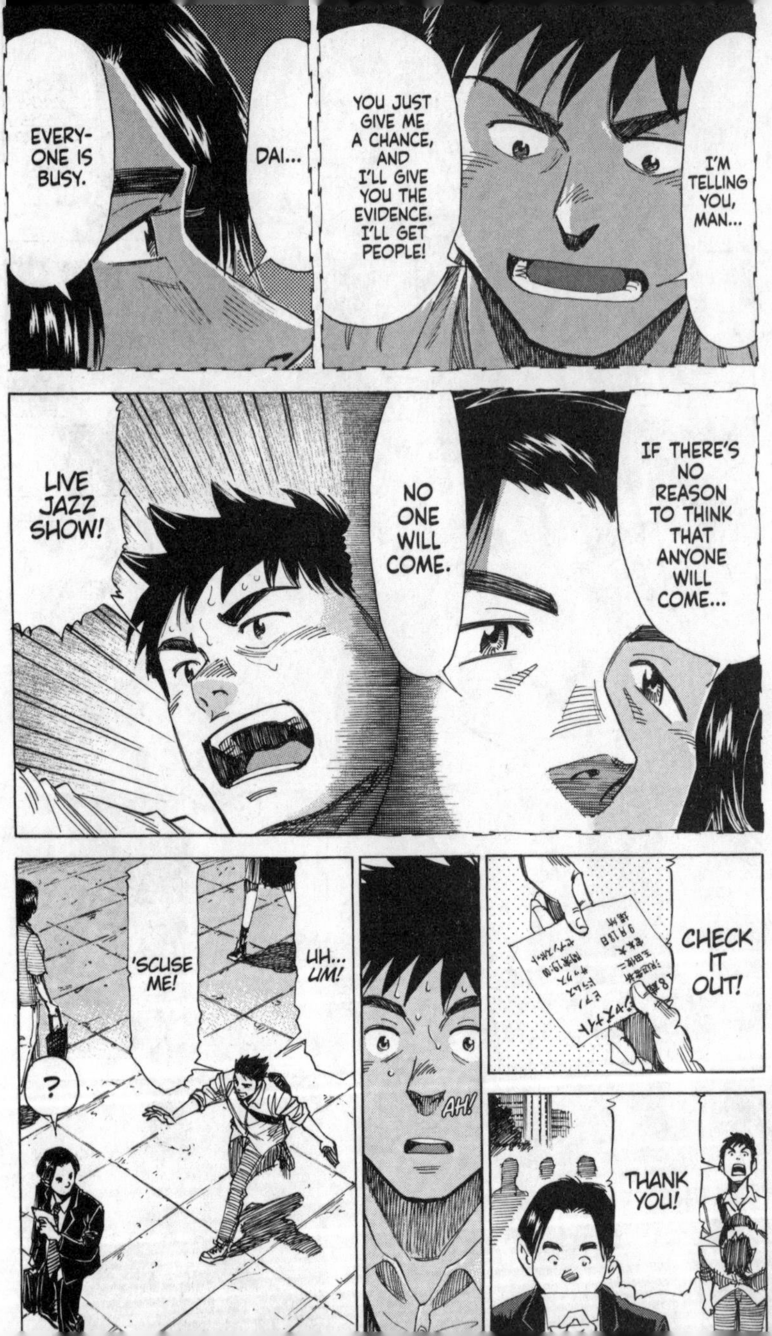
I'M TELLING YOU, MAN...
YOU JUST GIVE ME A CHANCE, AND I'LL GIVE YOU THE EVIDENCE. I'LL GET PEOPLE!
DAI...
EVERY-ONE IS BUSY.
IF THERE'S NO REASON TO THINK THAT ANYONE WILL COME...
NO ONE WILL COME.
LIVE JAZZ SHOW!
CHECK IT OUT!
THANK YOU!
AH!
UH... UM!
'SCUSE ME!
?

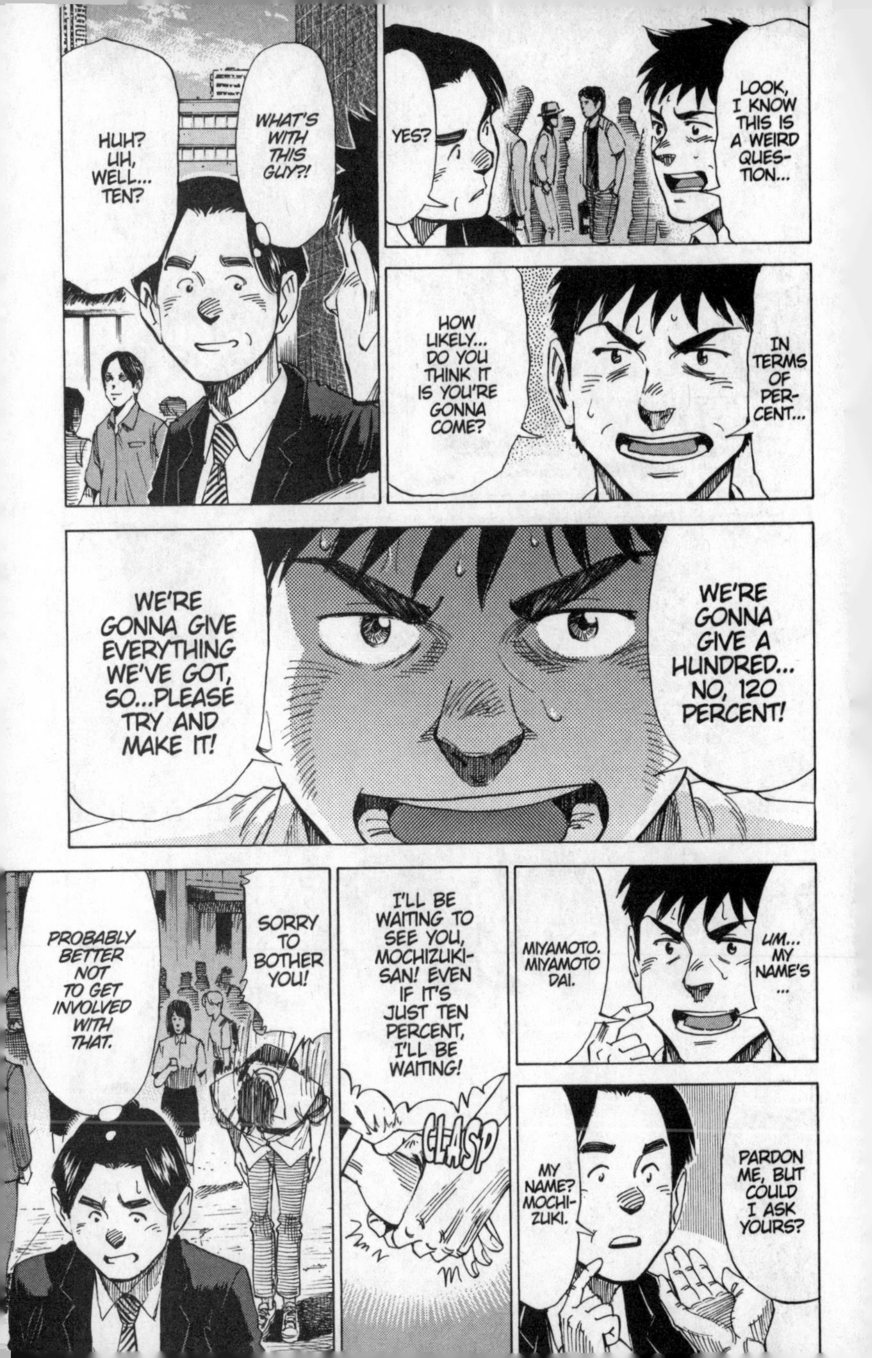
LOOK, I KNOW THIS IS A WEIRD QUES-TION...
YES?
IN TERMS OF PER-CENT...
HOW LIKELY... DO YOU THINK IT IS YOU'RE GONNA COME?
WHAT'S WITH THIS GUY?!
HUH? UH, WELL... TEN?
WE'RE GONNA GIVE A HUNDRED... NO, 120 PERCENT!
WE'RE GONNA GIVE EVERYTHING WE'VE GOT, SO...PLEASE TRY AND MAKE IT!
UM... MY NAME'S ...
MIYAMOTO. MIYAMOTO DAI.
PARDON ME, BUT COULD I ASK YOURS?
MY NAME? MOCHI-ZUKI.
I'LL BE WAITING TO SEE YOU, MOCHIZUKI-SAN! EVEN IF IT'S JUST TEN PERCENT, I'LL BE WAITING!
CLASP
SORRY TO BOTHER YOU!
PROBABLY BETTER NOT TO GET INVOLVED WITH THAT.

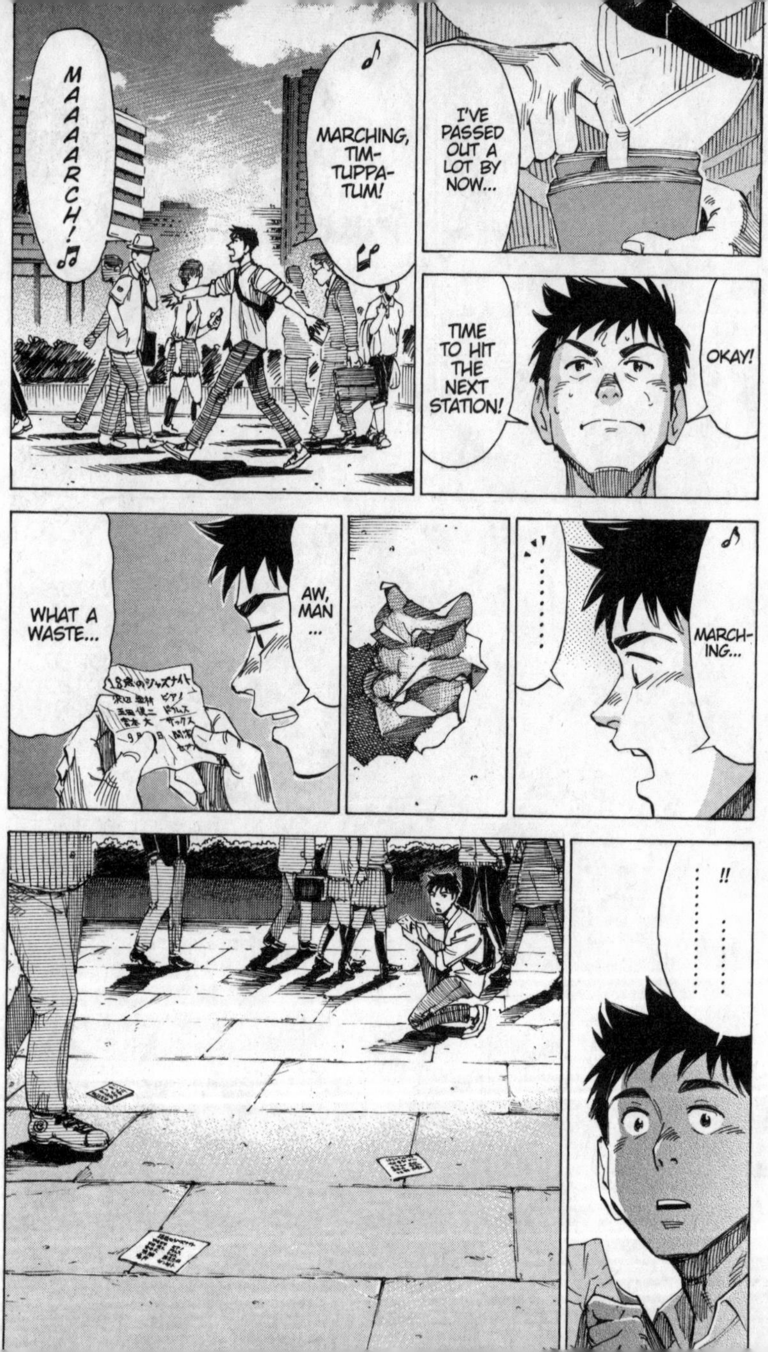
I'VE PASSED OUT A LOT BY NOW...
OKAY!
TIME TO HIT THE NEXT STATION!
♪ MARCHING, TIM-TUPPA-TUM! ♪
MAAAARCH!♫
♪ MARCH-ING...
......
AW, MAN...
WHAT A WASTE...
!!
......
......

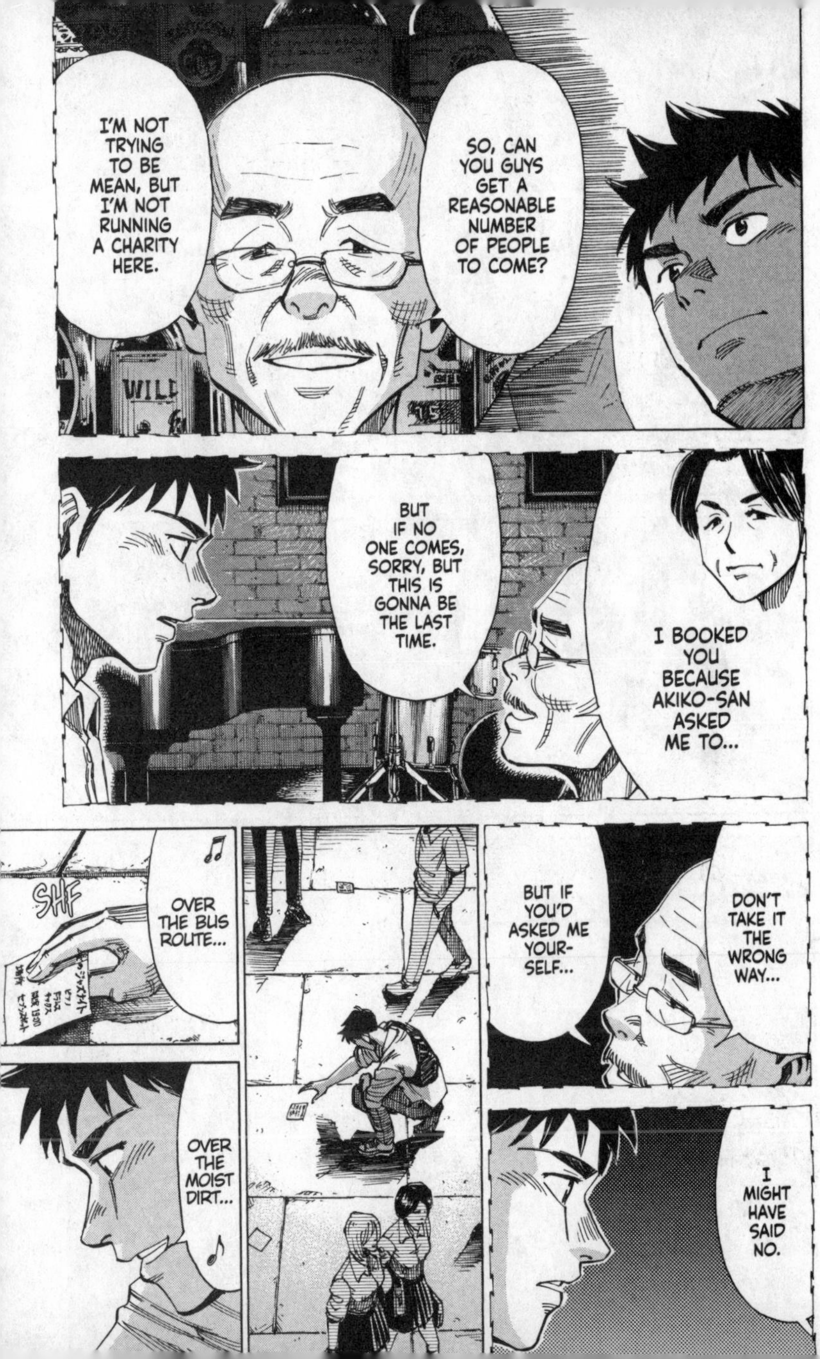
SO, CAN YOU GUYS GET A REASONABLE NUMBER OF PEOPLE TO COME?
I'M NOT TRYING TO BE MEAN, BUT I'M NOT RUNNING A CHARITY HERE.
I BOOKED YOU BECAUSE AKIKO-SAN ASKED ME TO...
BUT IF NO ONE COMES, SORRY, BUT THIS IS GONNA BE THE LAST TIME.
DON'T TAKE IT THE WRONG WAY...
BUT IF YOU'D ASKED ME YOUR-SELF...
I MIGHT HAVE SAID NO.
SHF
OVER THE BUS ROUTE...
OVER THE MOIST DIRT...

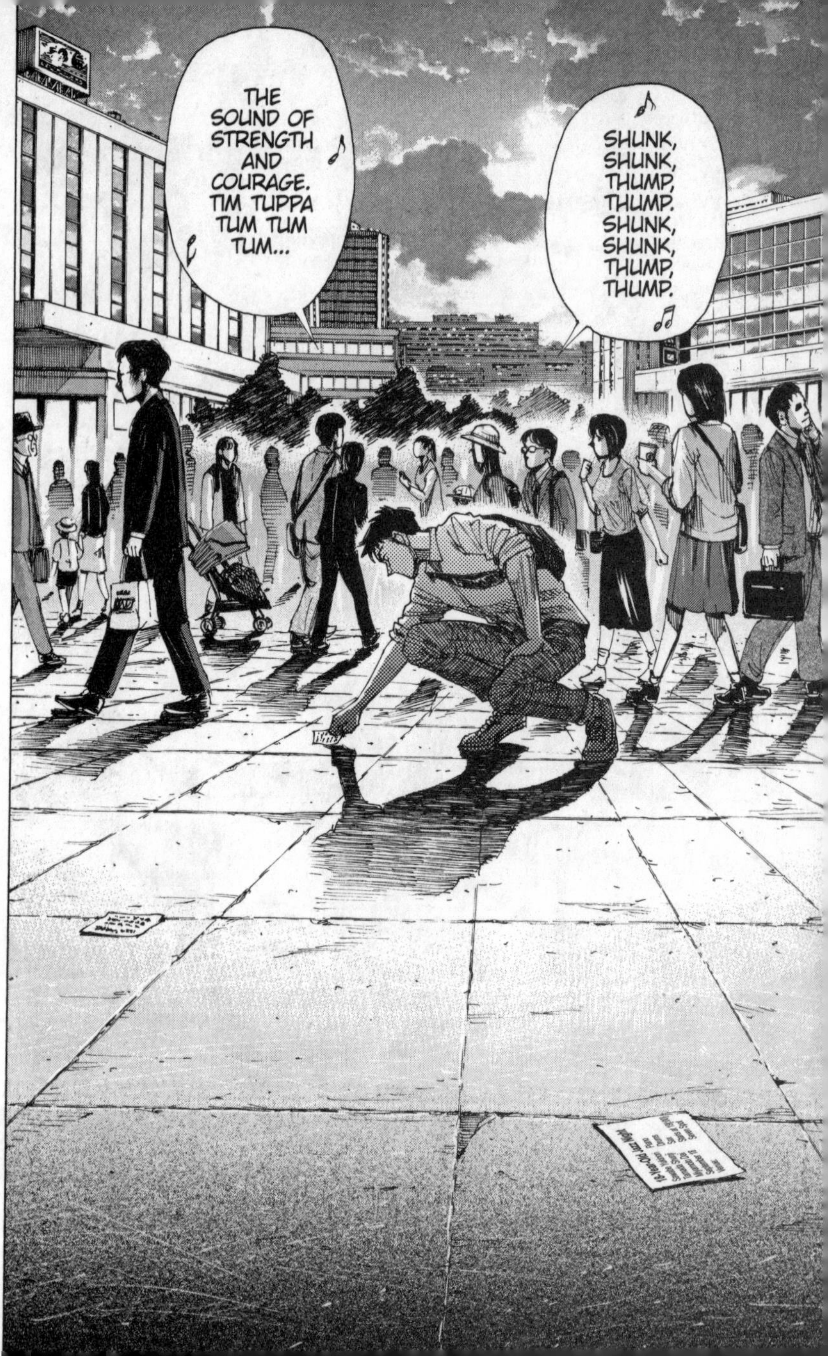
SHUNK, SHUNK, THUMP, THUMP. SHUNK, SHUNK, THUMP, THUMP.
THE SOUND OF STRENGTH AND COURAGE. TIM TUPPA TUM TUM TUM...

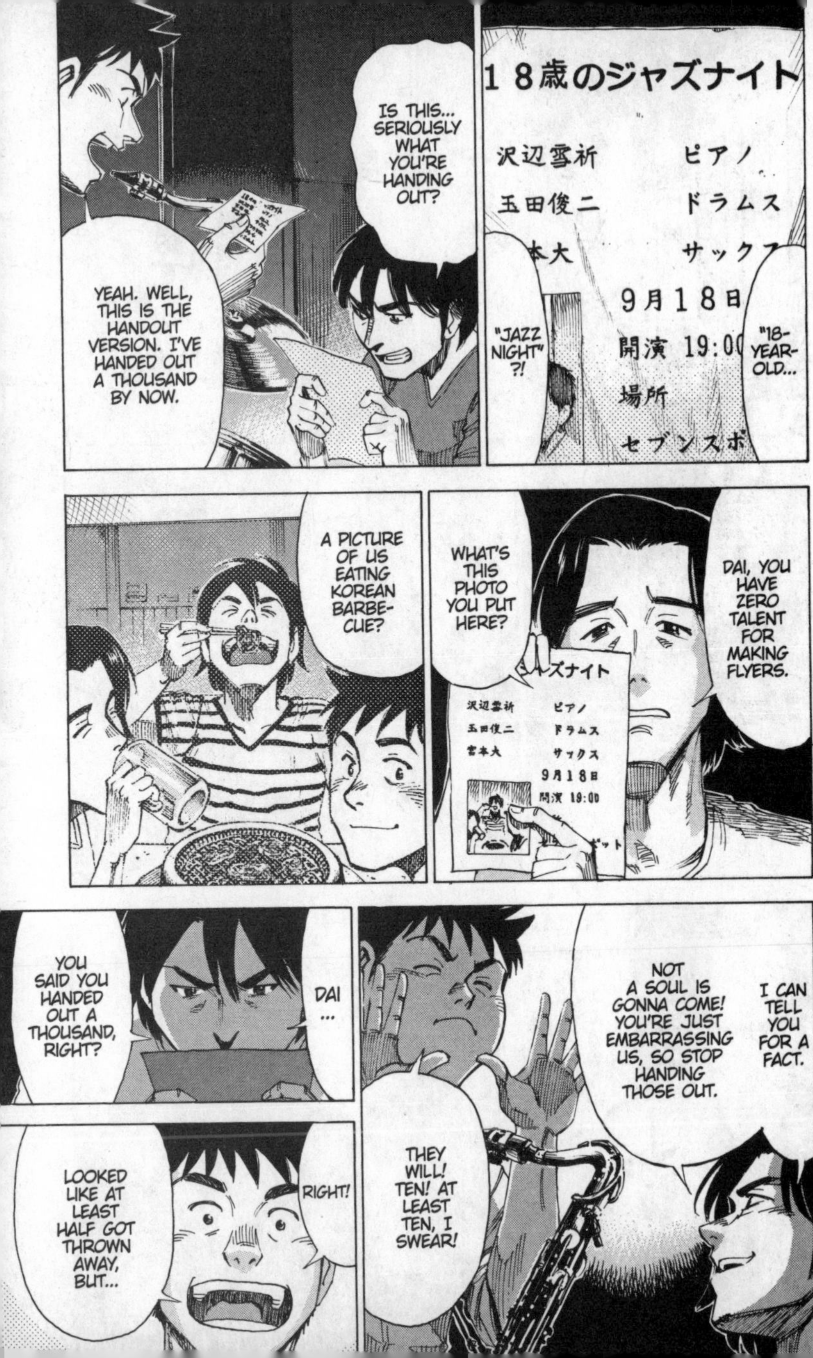

１８歳のジャズナイト
沢辺雪祈 ピアノ
玉田俊二 ドラムス
本大 サック
9月１８日
開演 19:0
場所
セブンスポ
"18-YEAR-OLD...
"JAZZ NIGHT" ?!
IS THIS... SERIOUSLY WHAT YOU'RE HANDING OUT?
YEAH. WELL, THIS IS THE HANDOUT VERSION. I'VE HANDED OUT A THOUSAND BY NOW.
DAI, YOU HAVE ZERO TALENT FOR MAKING FLYERS.
WHAT'S THIS PHOTO YOU PUT HERE?
ジャズナイト
沢辺雪祈 ピアノ
玉田俊二 ドラムス
宮本大 サックス
9月18日
開演 19:00
ポット
A PICTURE OF US EATING KOREAN BARBE-CUE?
I CAN TELL YOU FOR A FACT.
NOT A SOUL IS GONNA COME! YOU'RE JUST EMBARRASSING US, SO STOP HANDING THOSE OUT.
THEY WILL! TEN! AT LEAST TEN, I SWEAR!
DAI ...
YOU SAID YOU HANDED OUT A THOUSAND, RIGHT?
RIGHT!
LOOKED LIKE AT LEAST HALF GOT THROWN AWAY, BUT...

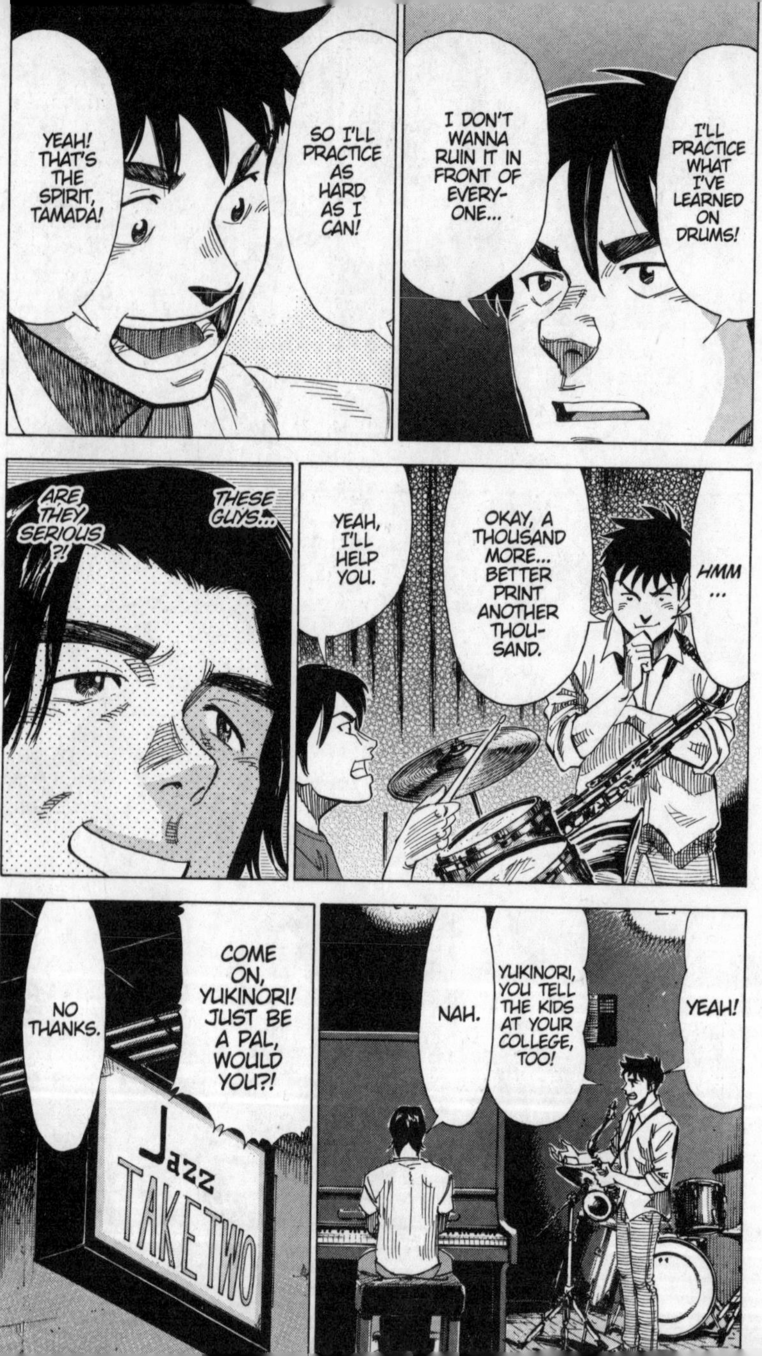
I'LL PRACTICE WHAT I'VE LEARNED ON DRUMS!
I DON'T WANNA RUIN IT IN FRONT OF EVERY-ONE...
SO I'LL PRACTICE AS HARD AS I CAN!
YEAH! THAT'S THE SPIRIT, TAMADA!
HMM...
OKAY, A THOUSAND MORE... BETTER PRINT ANOTHER THOU-SAND.
YEAH, I'LL HELP YOU.
THESE GUYS...
ARE THEY SERIOUS?!
YEAH!
YUKINORI, YOU TELL THE KIDS AT YOUR COLLEGE, TOO!
NAH.
COME ON, YUKINORI! JUST BE A PAL, WOULD YOU?!
NO THANKS.
Jazz
TAKE TWO

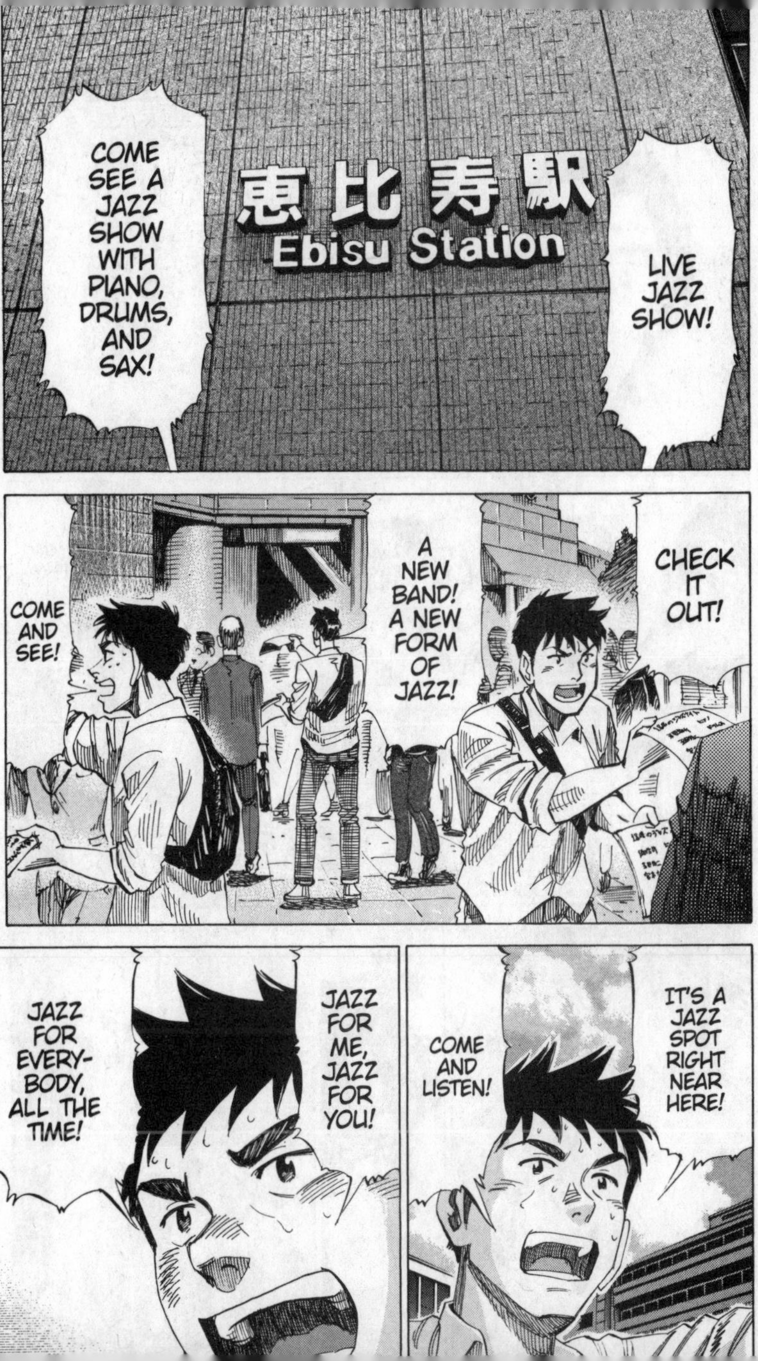
LIVE JAZZ SHOW!
恵比寿駅
Ebisu Station
COME SEE A JAZZ SHOW WITH PIANO, DRUMS, AND SAX!
CHECK IT OUT!
A NEW BAND! A NEW FORM OF JAZZ!
COME AND SEE!
IT'S A JAZZ SPOT RIGHT NEAR HERE!
COME AND LISTEN!
JAZZ FOR ME, JAZZ FOR YOU!
JAZZ FOR EVERYBODY, ALL THE TIME!

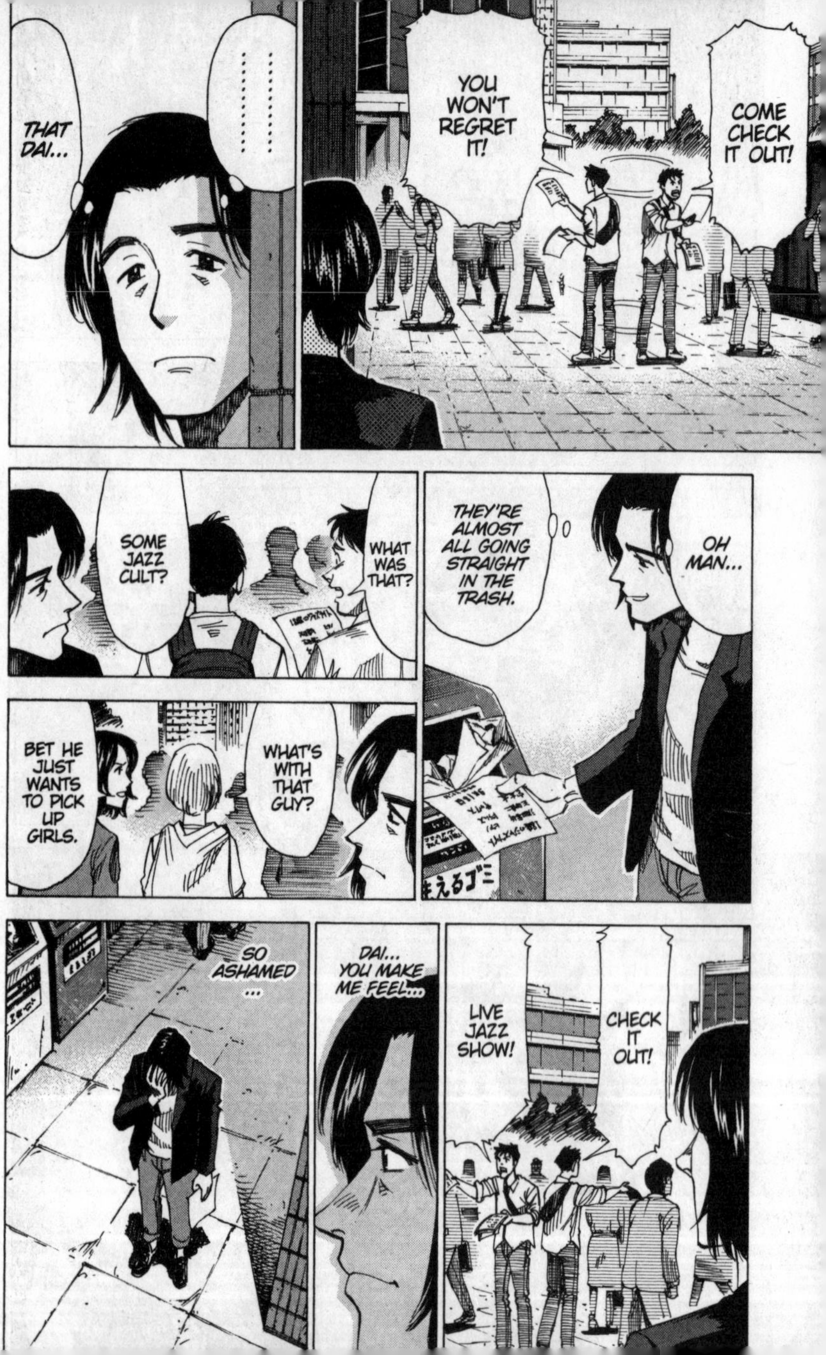
COME CHECK IT OUT!
YOU WON'T REGRET IT!
......
THAT DAI...
OH MAN...
THEY'RE ALMOST ALL GOING STRAIGHT IN THE TRASH.
WHAT WAS THAT?
SOME JAZZ CULT?
WHAT'S WITH THAT GUY?
BET HE JUST WANTS TO PICK UP GIRLS.
CHECK IT OUT!
LIVE JAZZ SHOW!
DAI... YOU MAKE ME FEEL...
SO ASHAMED ...

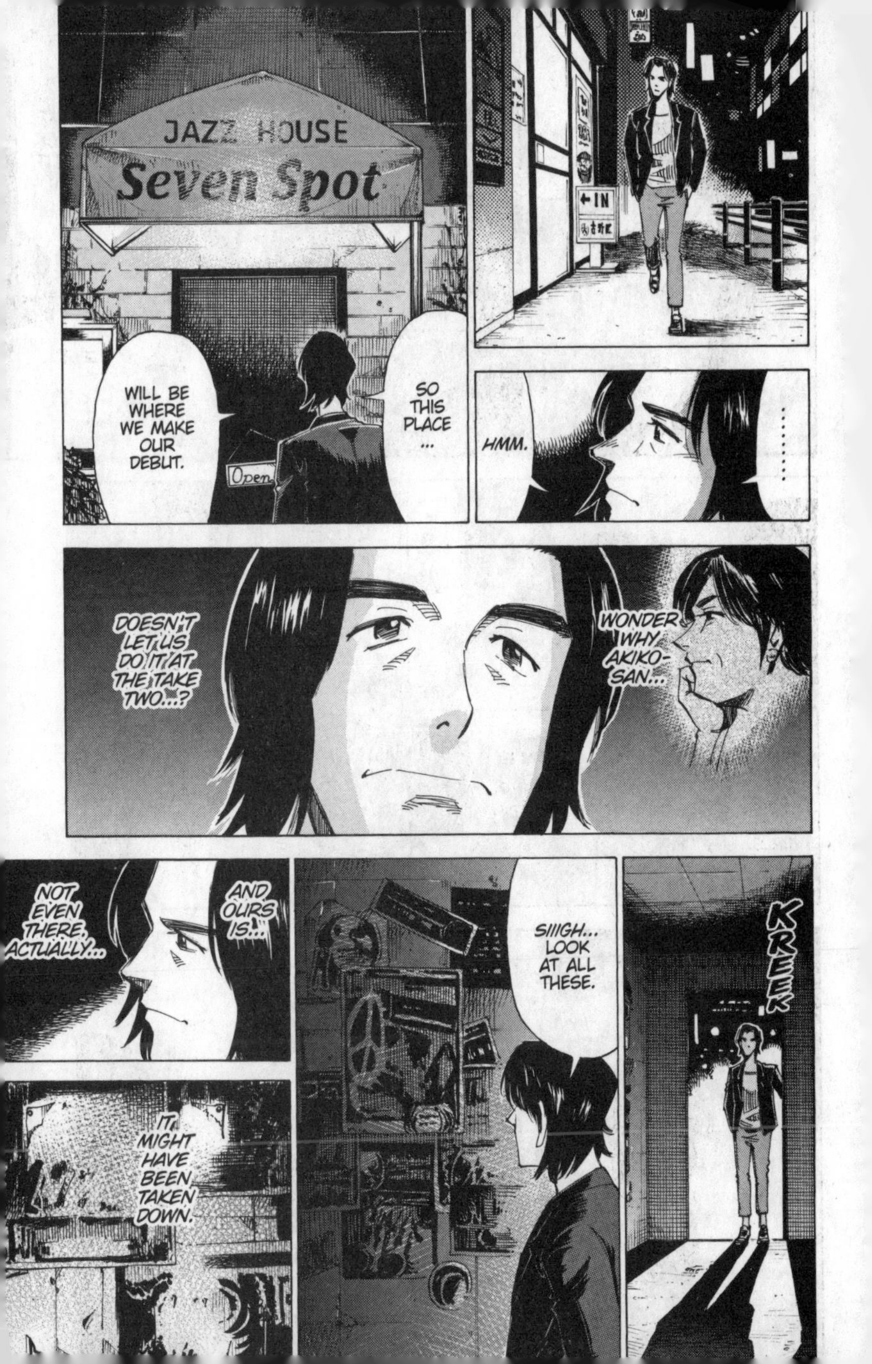

←IN
......
HMM.
JAZZ HOUSE
Seven Spot
Open
SO THIS PLACE...
WILL BE WHERE WE MAKE OUR DEBUT.
WONDER WHY AKIKO-SAN...
DOESN'T LET US DO IT AT THE TAKE TWO...?
KREEK
SIIGH... LOOK AT ALL THESE.
AND OURS IS...
NOT EVEN THERE, ACTUALLY...
IT MIGHT HAVE BEEN TAKEN DOWN.

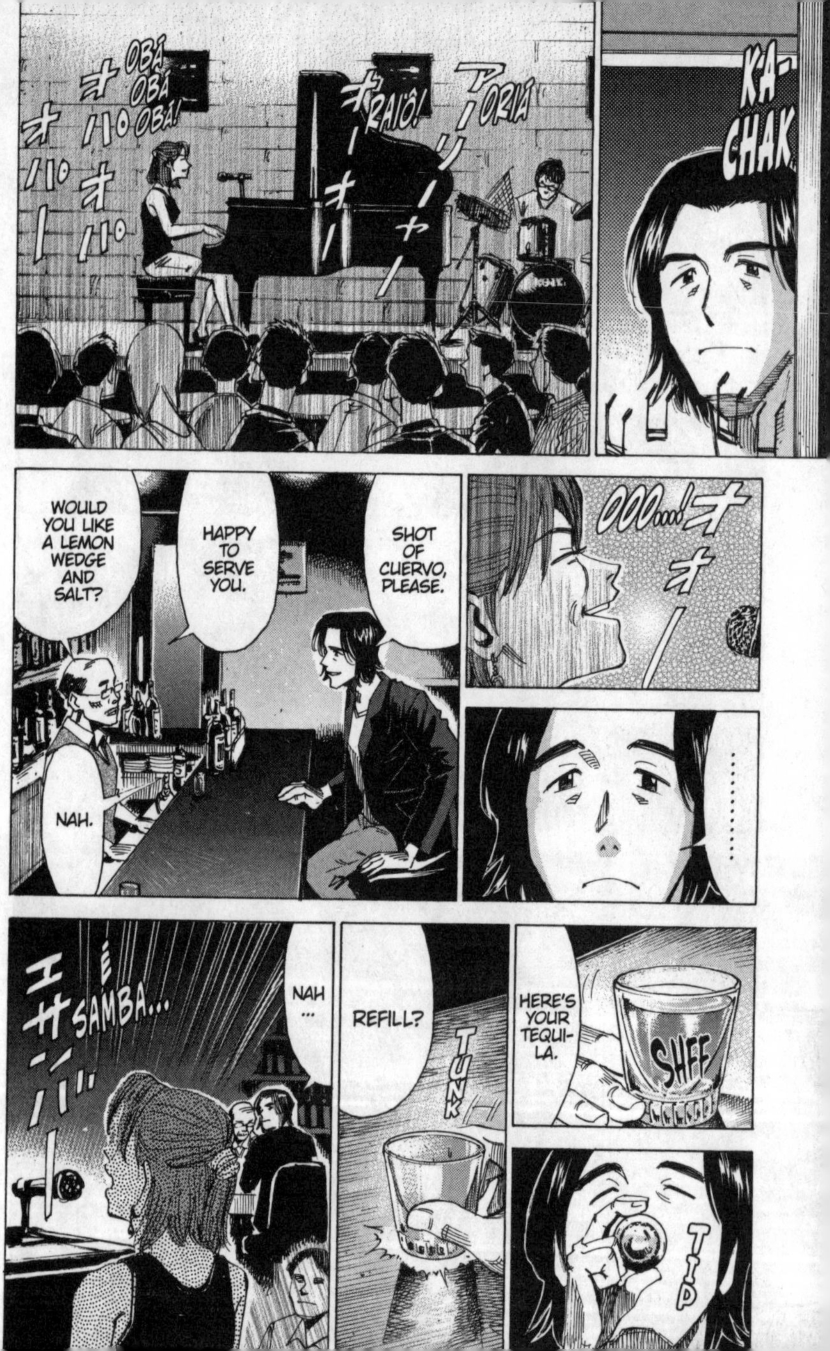
KA-CHAK.
ORIÁ
RAIÔ!
OBÁ OBÁ OBÁ!
OOO...!
......
SHOT OF CUERVO, PLEASE.
HAPPY TO SERVE YOU.
WOULD YOU LIKE A LEMON WEDGE AND SALT?
NAH.
HERE'S YOUR TEQUI-LA.
SHFF
TIP
REFILL?
NAH ...
TUNK
É SAMBA...

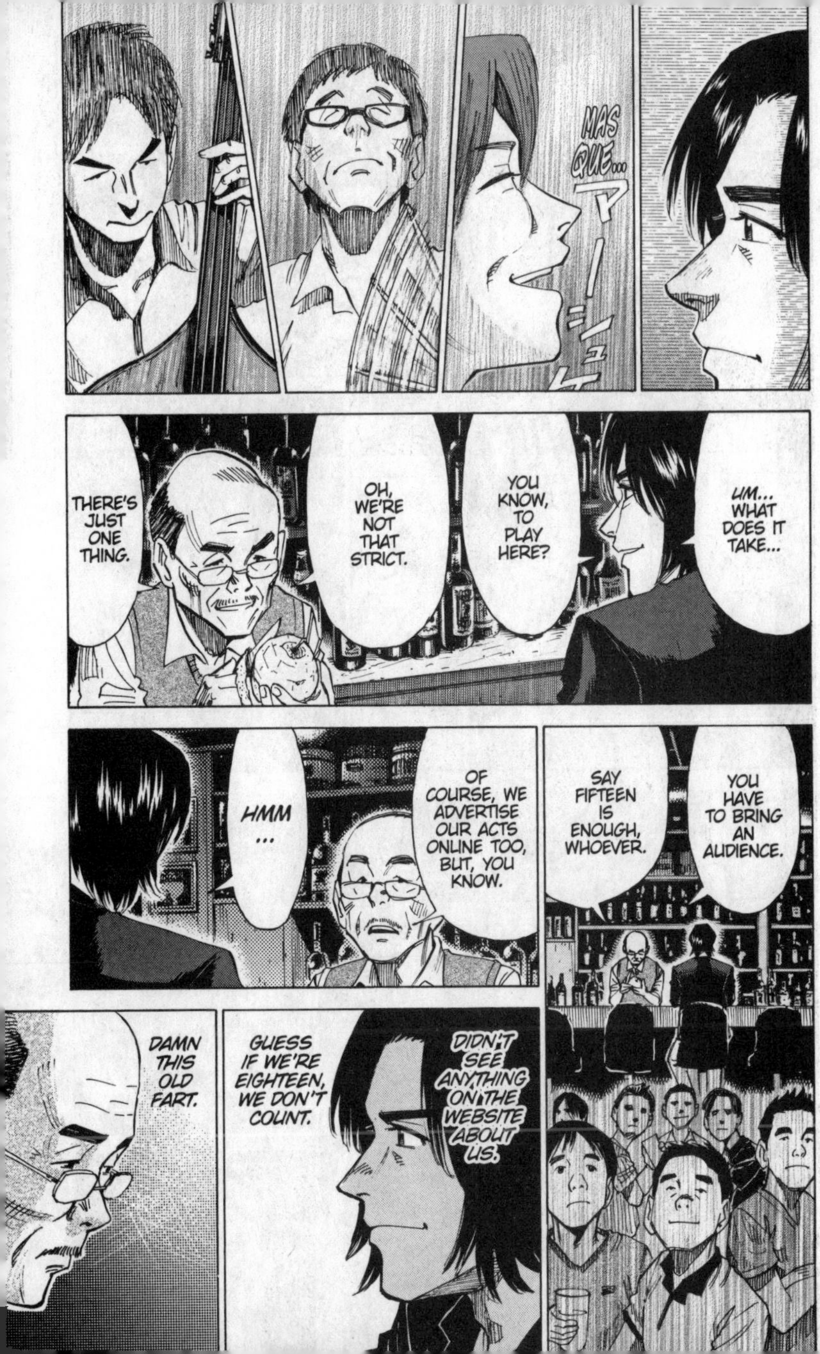
MAS QUE...
UM... WHAT DOES IT TAKE...
YOU KNOW, TO PLAY HERE?
OH, WE'RE NOT THAT STRICT.
THERE'S JUST ONE THING.
YOU HAVE TO BRING AN AUDIENCE.
SAY FIFTEEN IS ENOUGH, WHOEVER.
OF COURSE, WE ADVERTISE OUR ACTS ONLINE TOO, BUT, YOU KNOW.
HMM ...
DIDN'T SEE ANYTHING ON THE WEBSITE ABOUT US.
GUESS IF WE'RE EIGHTEEN, WE DON'T COUNT.
DAMN THIS OLD FART.

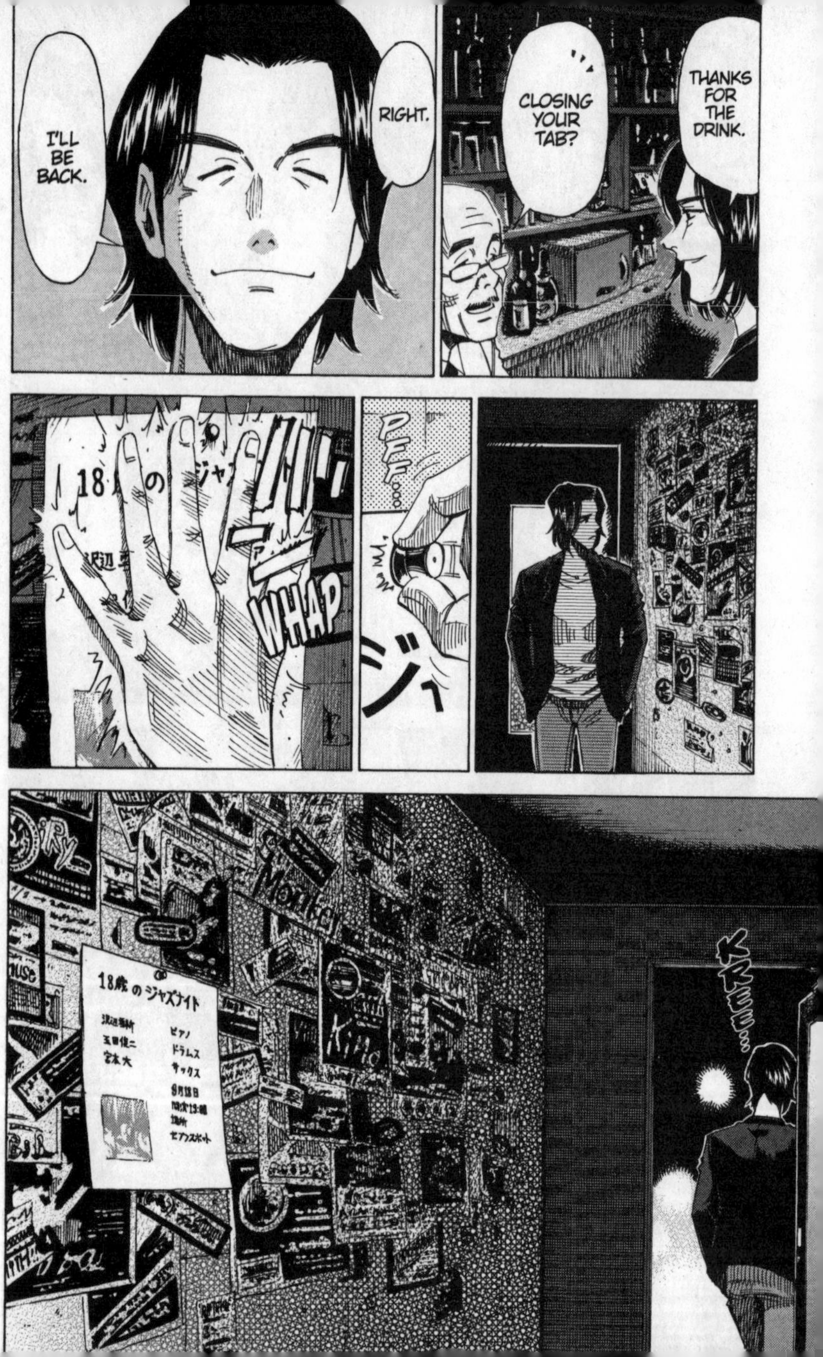
THANKS FOR THE DRINK.
CLOSING YOUR TAB?
RIGHT.
I'LL BE BACK.
PFF...
ジュ
WHAP
18歳のジャズナイト
宮本大
ピアノ
ドラムス
サックス
KREEE...

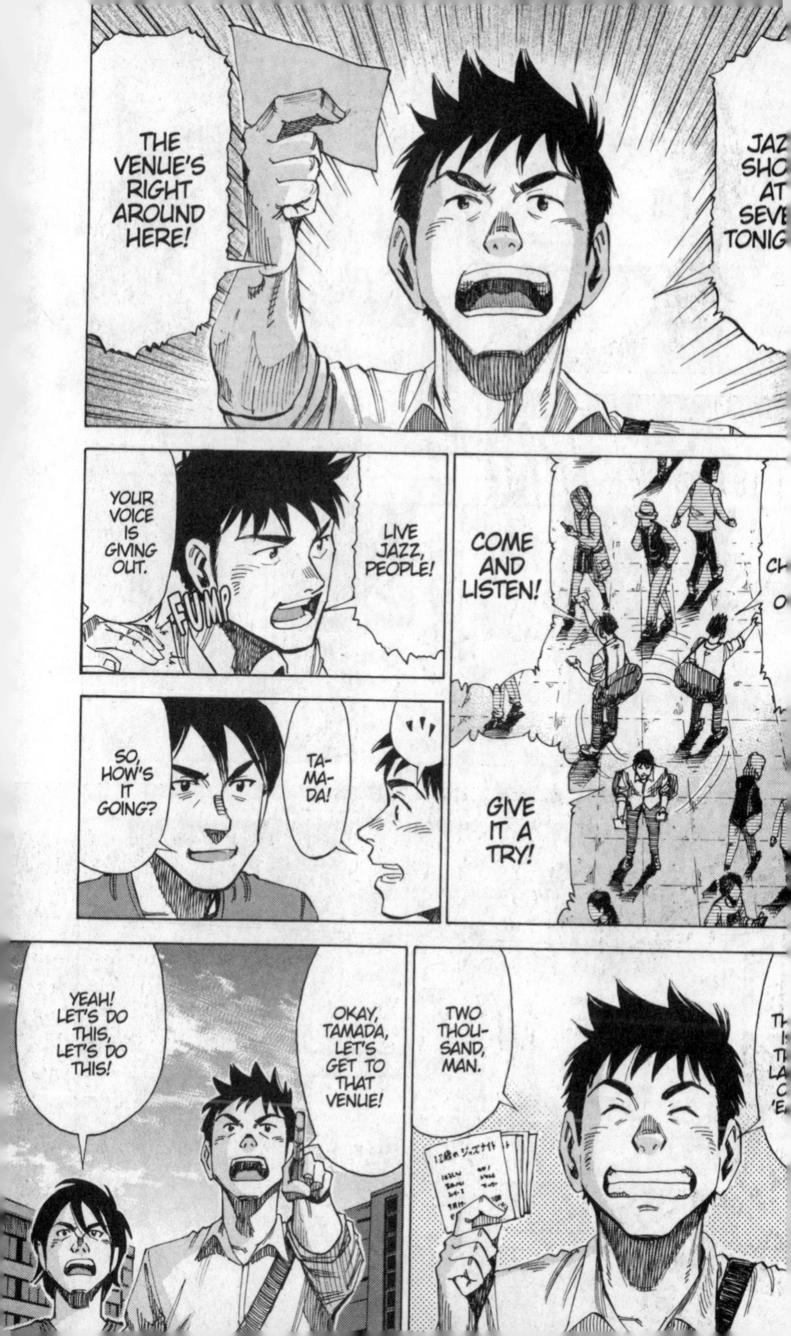
THE VENUE'S RIGHT AROUND HERE!
COME AND LISTEN!
GIVE IT A TRY!
LIVE JAZZ, PEOPLE!
YOUR VOICE IS GIVING OUT.
FUMP
TA-MA-DA!
SO, HOW'S IT GOING?
TWO THOUSAND, MAN.
OKAY, TAMADA, LET'S GET TO THAT VENUE!
YEAH! LET'S DO THIS, LET'S DO THIS!

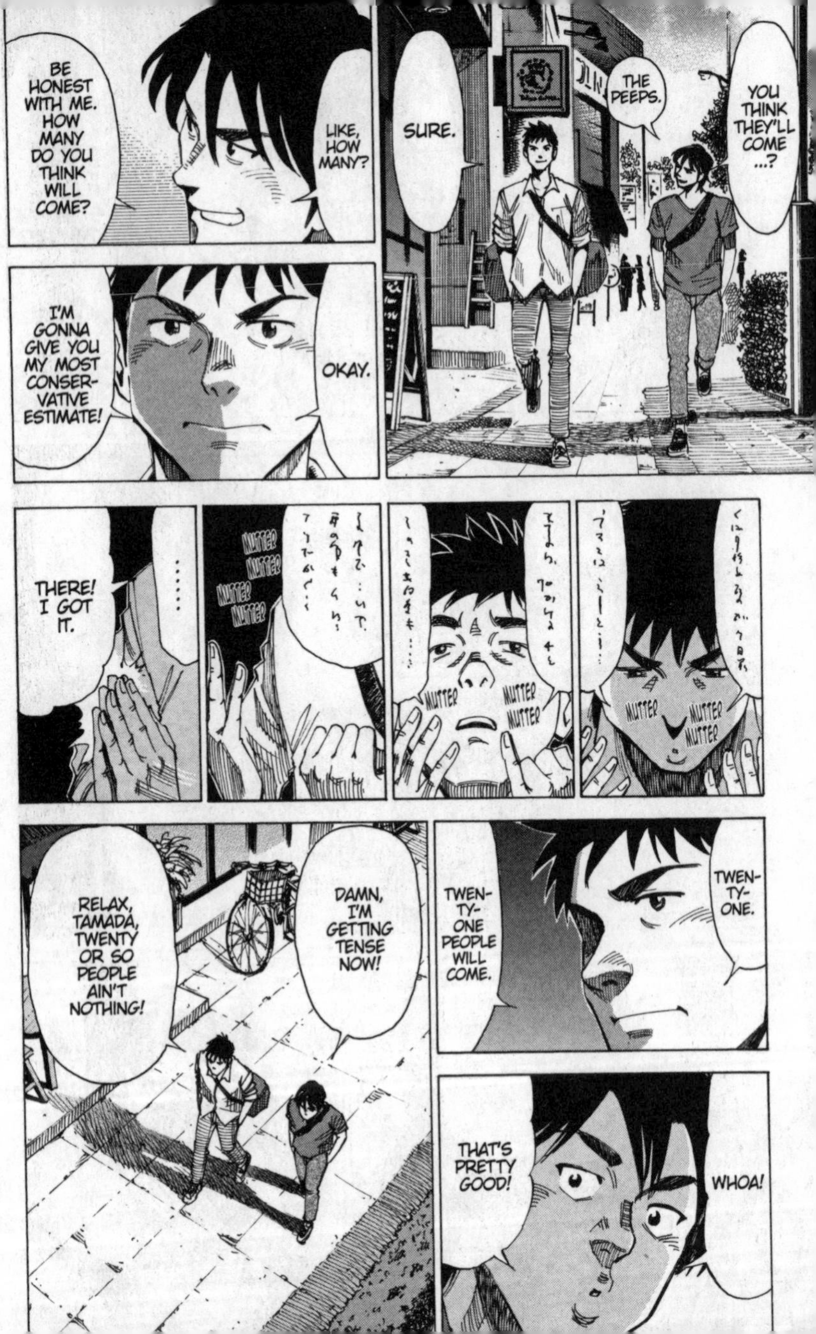
YOU THINK THEY'LL COME ...?
THE PEEPS.
SURE.
LIKE, HOW MANY?
BE HONEST WITH ME. HOW MANY DO YOU THINK WILL COME?
OKAY.
I'M GONNA GIVE YOU MY MOST CONSERVATIVE ESTIMATE!
MUTTER MUTTER MUTTER
MUTTER MUTTER MUTTER
MUTTER MUTTER MUTTER MUTTER
......
THERE! I GOT IT.
TWENTY-ONE.
TWENTY-ONE PEOPLE WILL COME.
WHOA!
THAT'S PRETTY GOOD!
DAMN, I'M GETTING TENSE NOW!
RELAX, TAMADA, TWENTY OR SO PEOPLE AIN'T NOTHING!

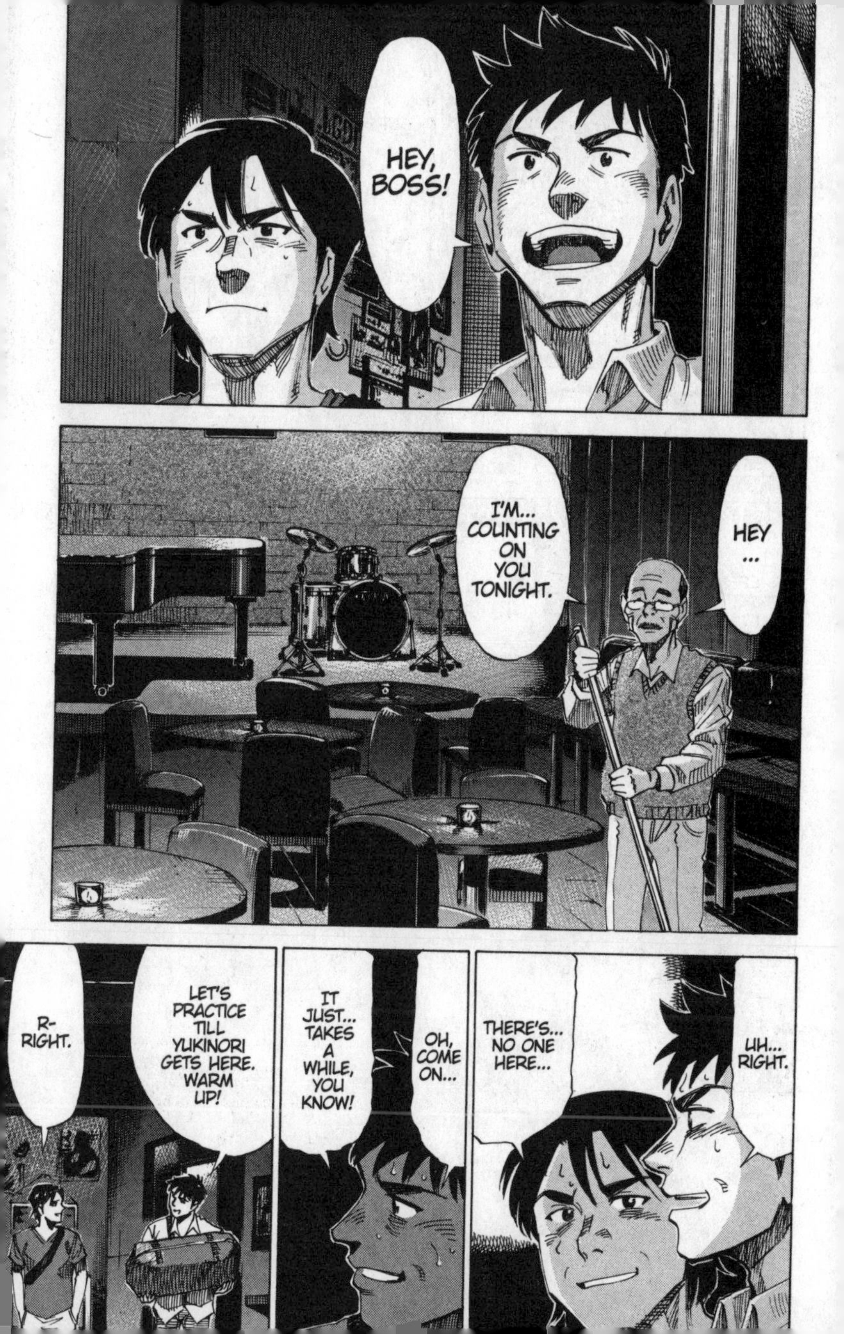
HEY, BOSS!
HEY ...
I'M... COUNTING ON YOU TONIGHT.
UH... RIGHT.
THERE'S... NO ONE HERE...
OH, COME ON...
IT JUST... TAKES A WHILE, YOU KNOW!
LET'S PRACTICE TILL YUKINORI GETS HERE. WARM UP!
R-RIGHT.

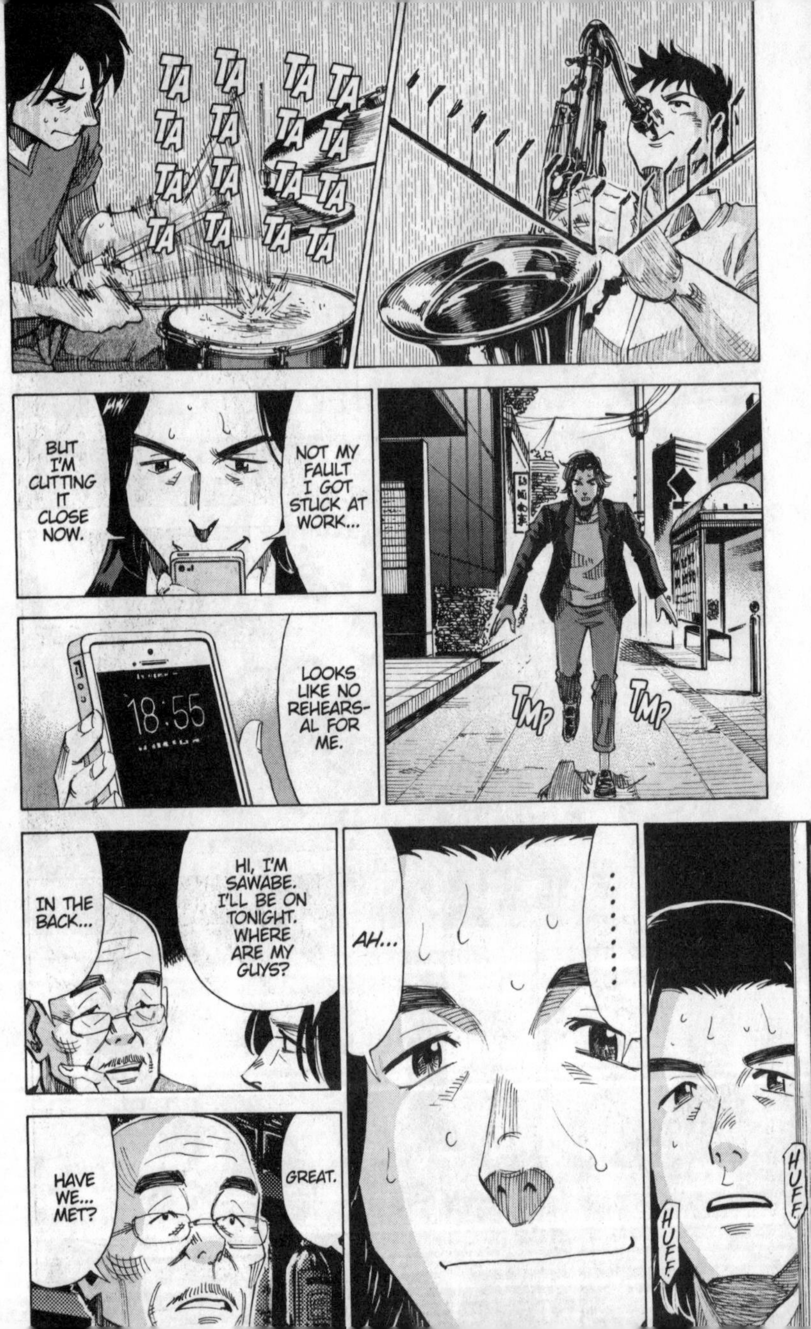
TA TA TA TA
TA TA TA TA
TA TA TA TA
TA TA TA TA
TMP
TMP
NOT MY FAULT I GOT STUCK AT WORK...
BUT I'M CUTTING IT CLOSE NOW.
LOOKS LIKE NO REHEARSAL FOR ME.
HUFF.
HUFF.
....
AH...
HI, I'M SAWABE. I'LL BE ON TONIGHT. WHERE ARE MY GUYS?
IN THE BACK...
GREAT.
HAVE WE... MET?

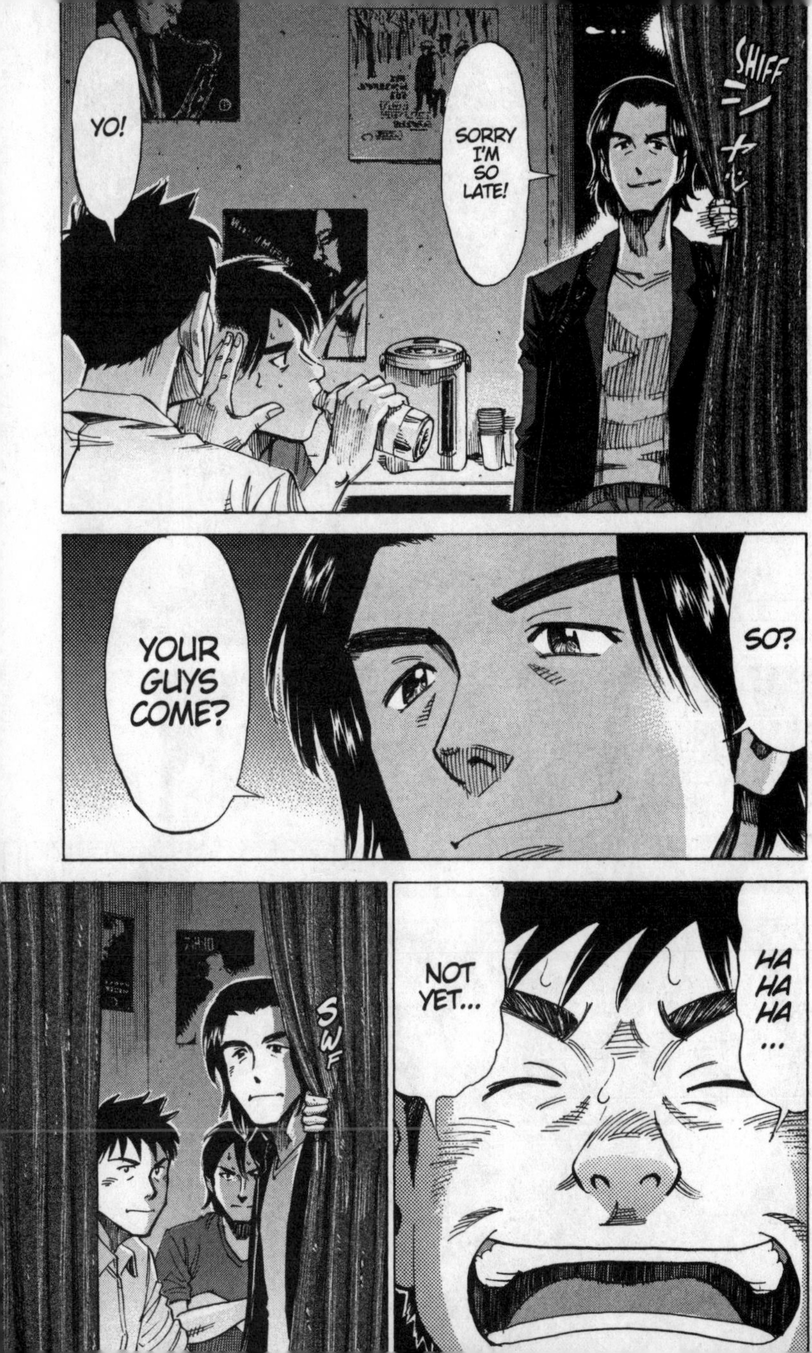
SHIFF
SORRY I'M SO LATE!
YO!
SO?
YOUR GUYS COME?
HA HA HA ...
NOT YET...
SWF

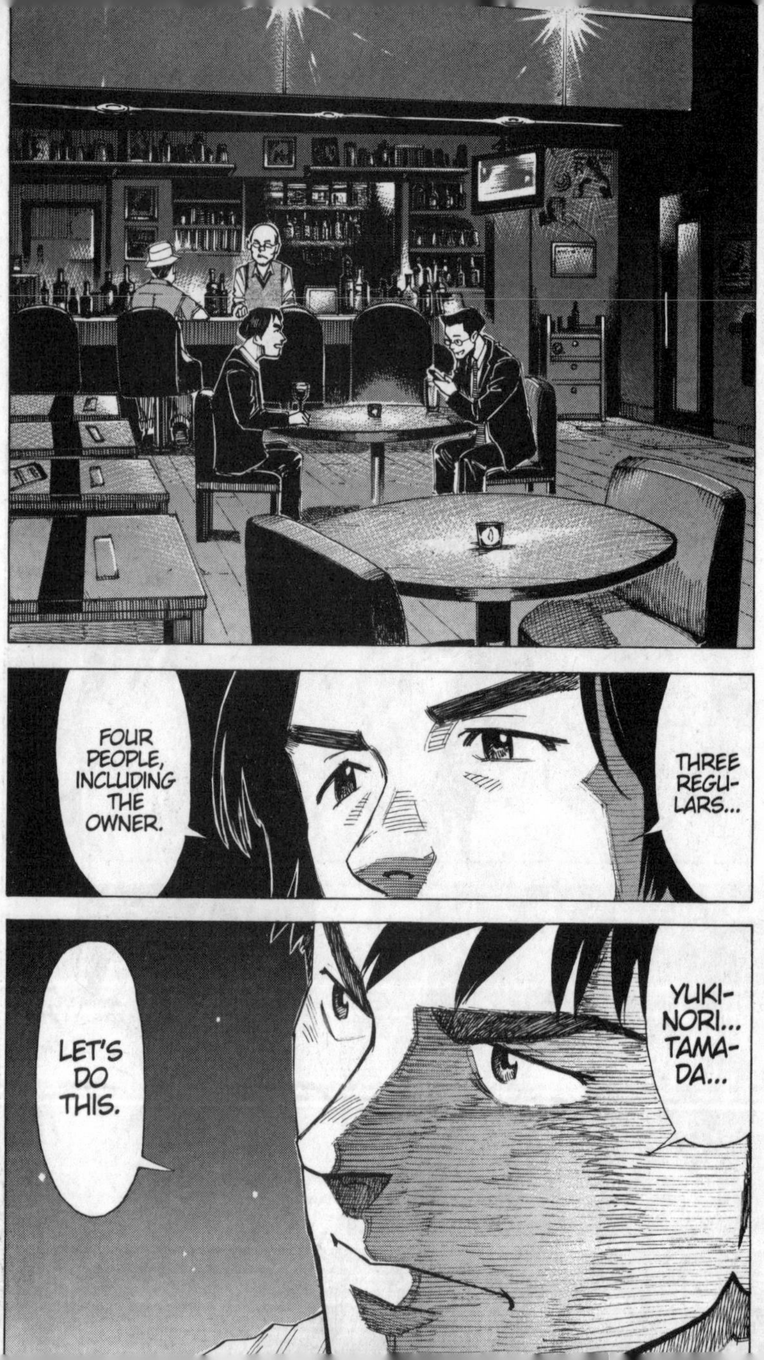
THREE REGU-LARS...
FOUR PEOPLE, INCLUDING THE OWNER.
YUKI-NORI... TAMA-DA...
LET'S DO THIS.

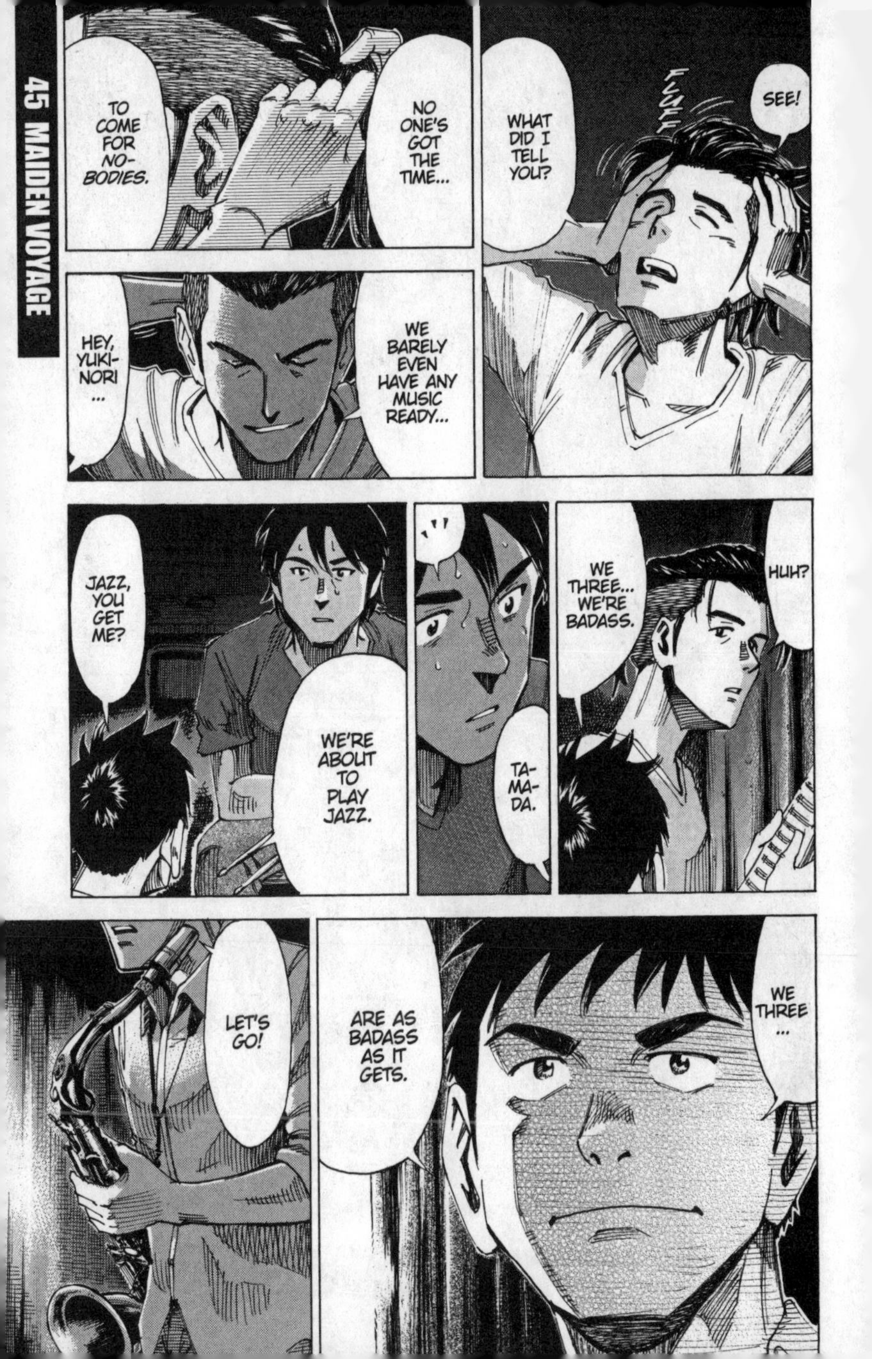
SEE!
FLUFF
WHAT DID I TELL YOU?
NO ONE'S GOT THE TIME...
TO COME FOR NO-BODIES.
WE BARELY EVEN HAVE ANY MUSIC READY...
HEY, YUKI-NORI ...
HUH?
WE THREE... WE'RE BADASS.
TA-MA-DA.
WE'RE ABOUT TO PLAY JAZZ.
JAZZ, YOU GET ME?
WE THREE ...
ARE AS BADASS AS IT GETS.
LET'S GO!

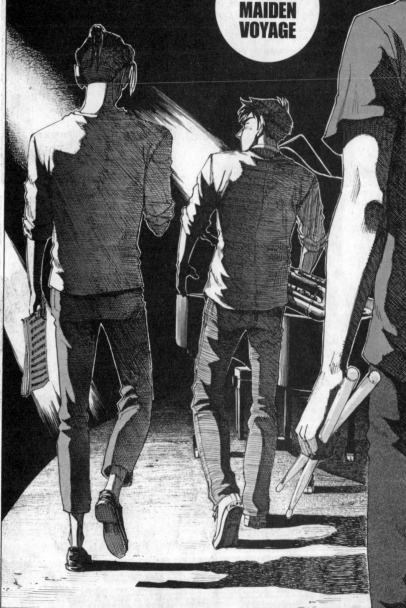

45
MAIDEN
VOYAGE

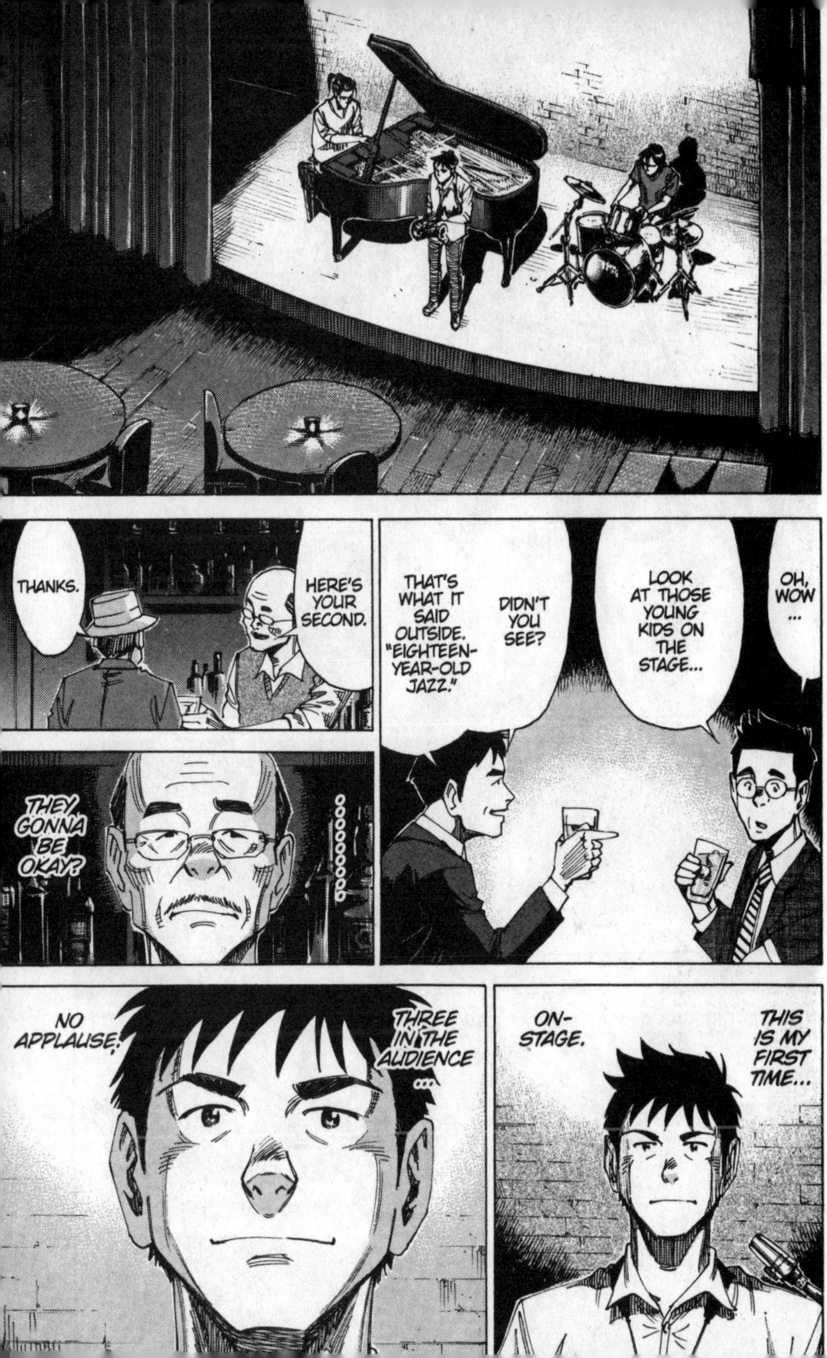

OH, WOW ...
LOOK AT THOSE YOUNG KIDS ON THE STAGE...
DIDN'T YOU SEE?
THAT'S WHAT IT SAID OUTSIDE. "EIGHTEEN-YEAR-OLD JAZZ."
HERE'S YOUR SECOND.
THANKS.
THEY GONNA BE OKAY?
THIS IS MY FIRST TIME...
ON-STAGE.
THREE IN THE AUDIENCE ...
NO APPLAUSE.

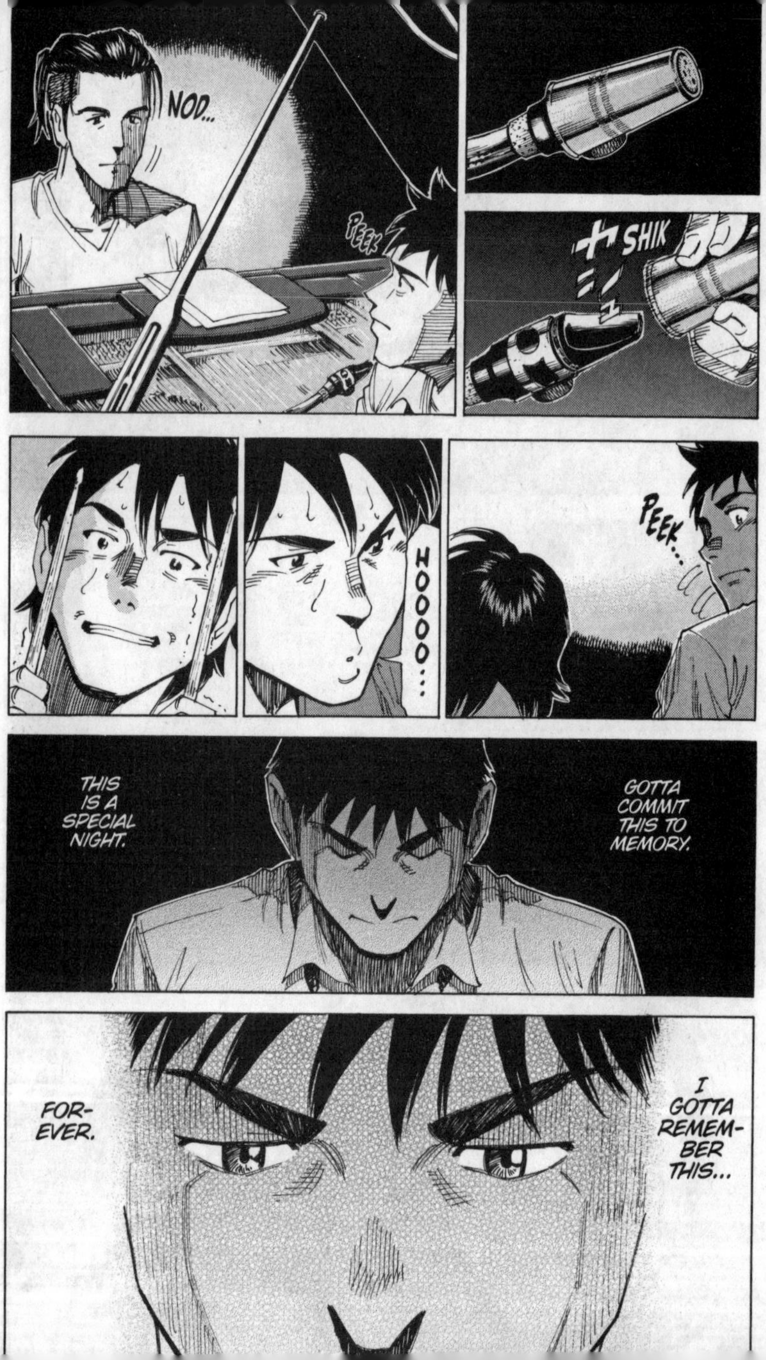
SHIK
NOD...
PEEK
PEEK...
HOOOO...
GOTTA COMMIT THIS TO MEMORY.
THIS IS A SPECIAL NIGHT.
I GOTTA REMEM-BER THIS...
FOR-EVER.

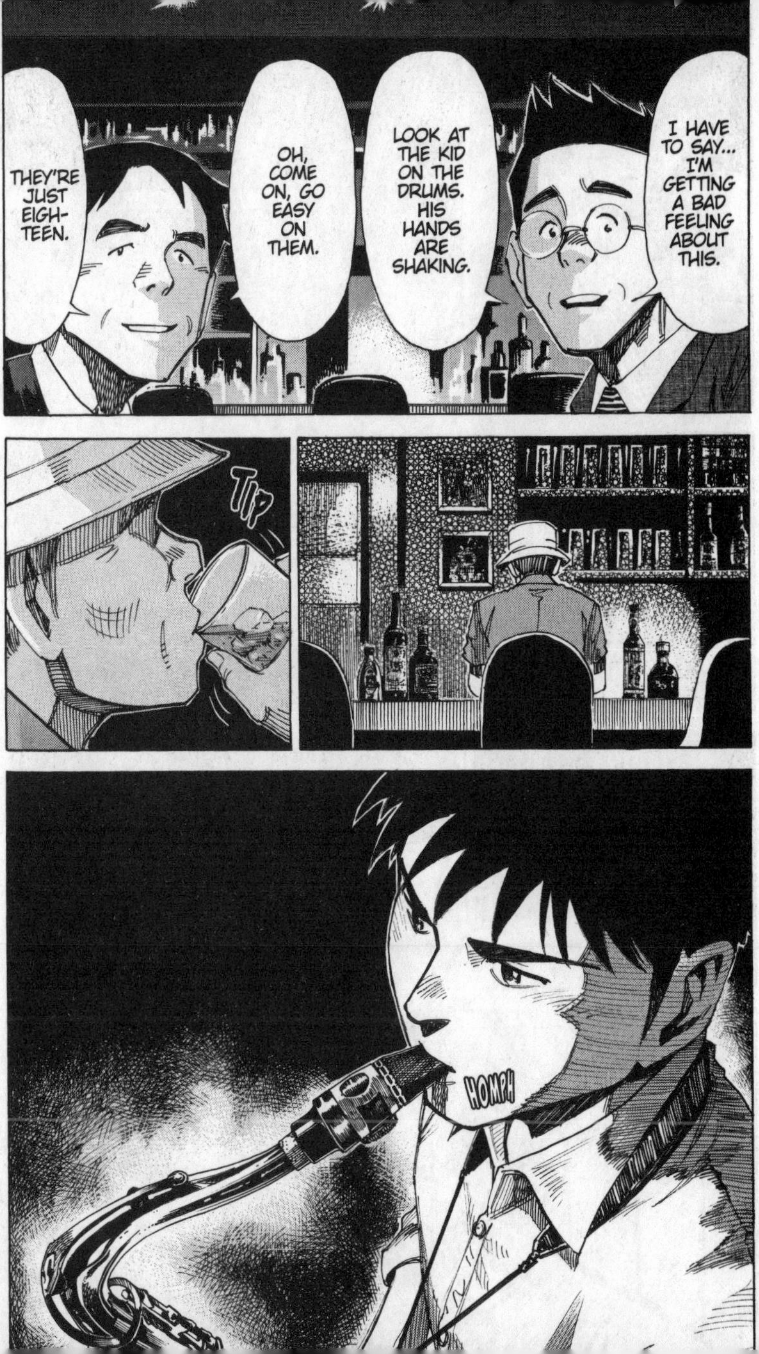
I HAVE TO SAY... I'M GETTING A BAD FEELING ABOUT THIS.
LOOK AT THE KID ON THE DRUMS. HIS HANDS ARE SHAKING.
OH, COME ON, GO EASY ON THEM.
THEY'RE JUST EIGH-TEEN.
TIP
HOMPH

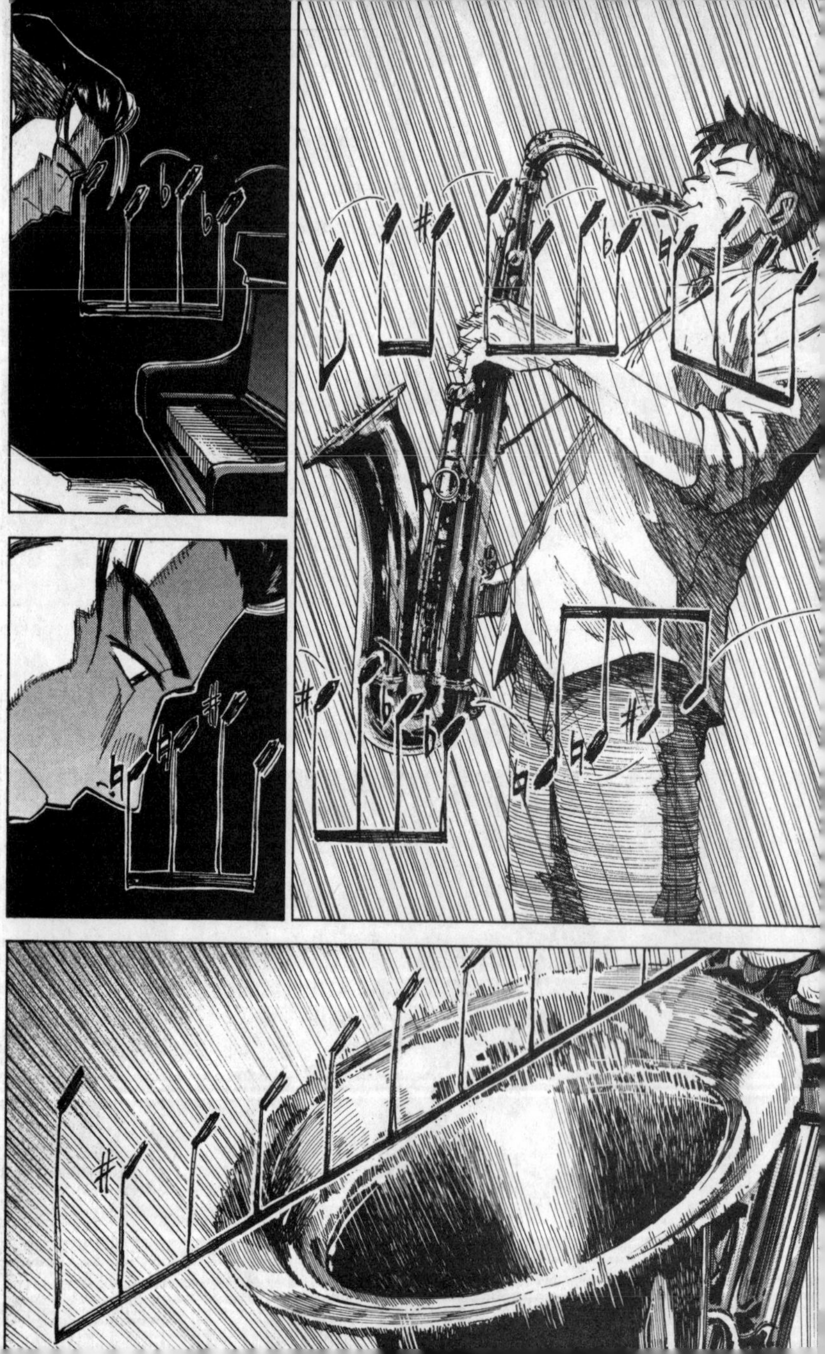

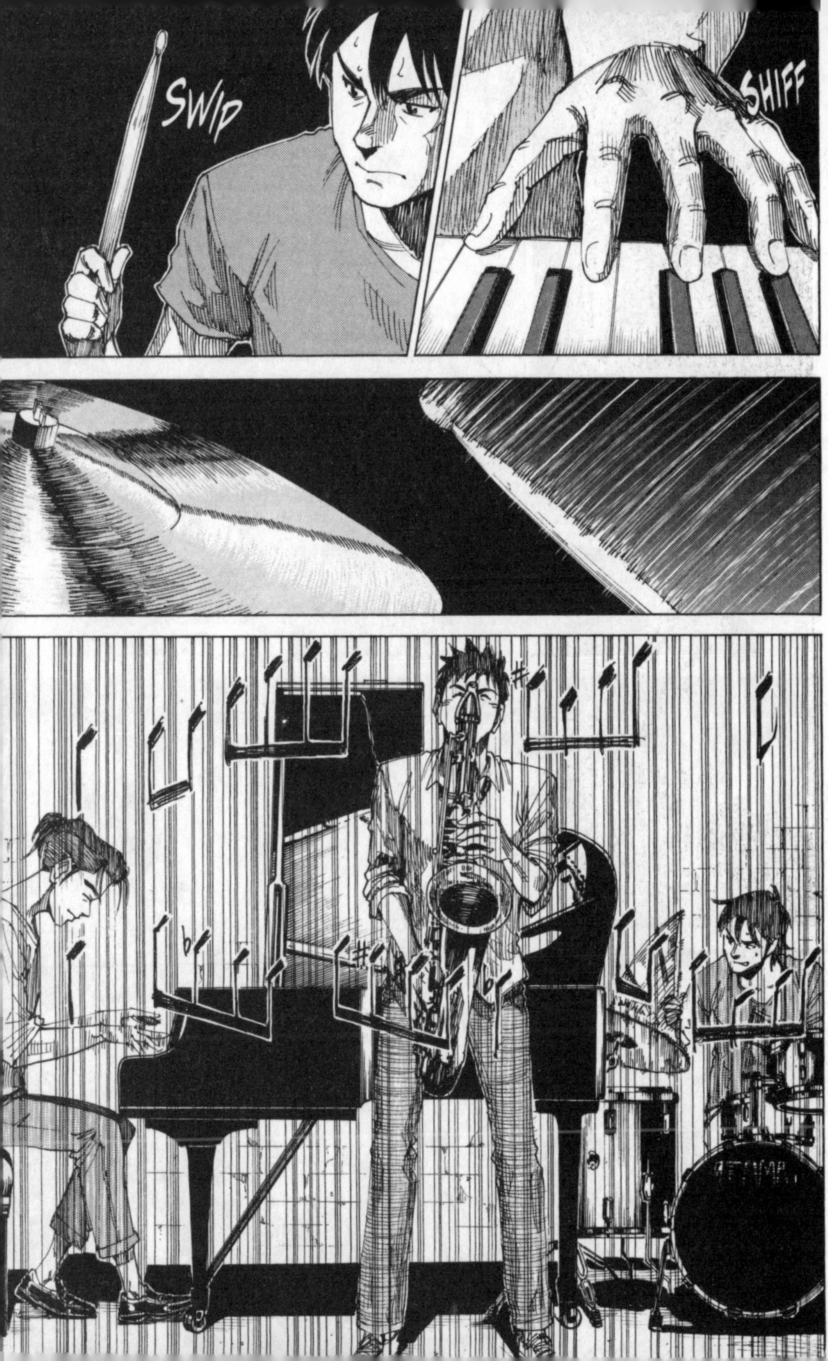
SHIFF
SWIP

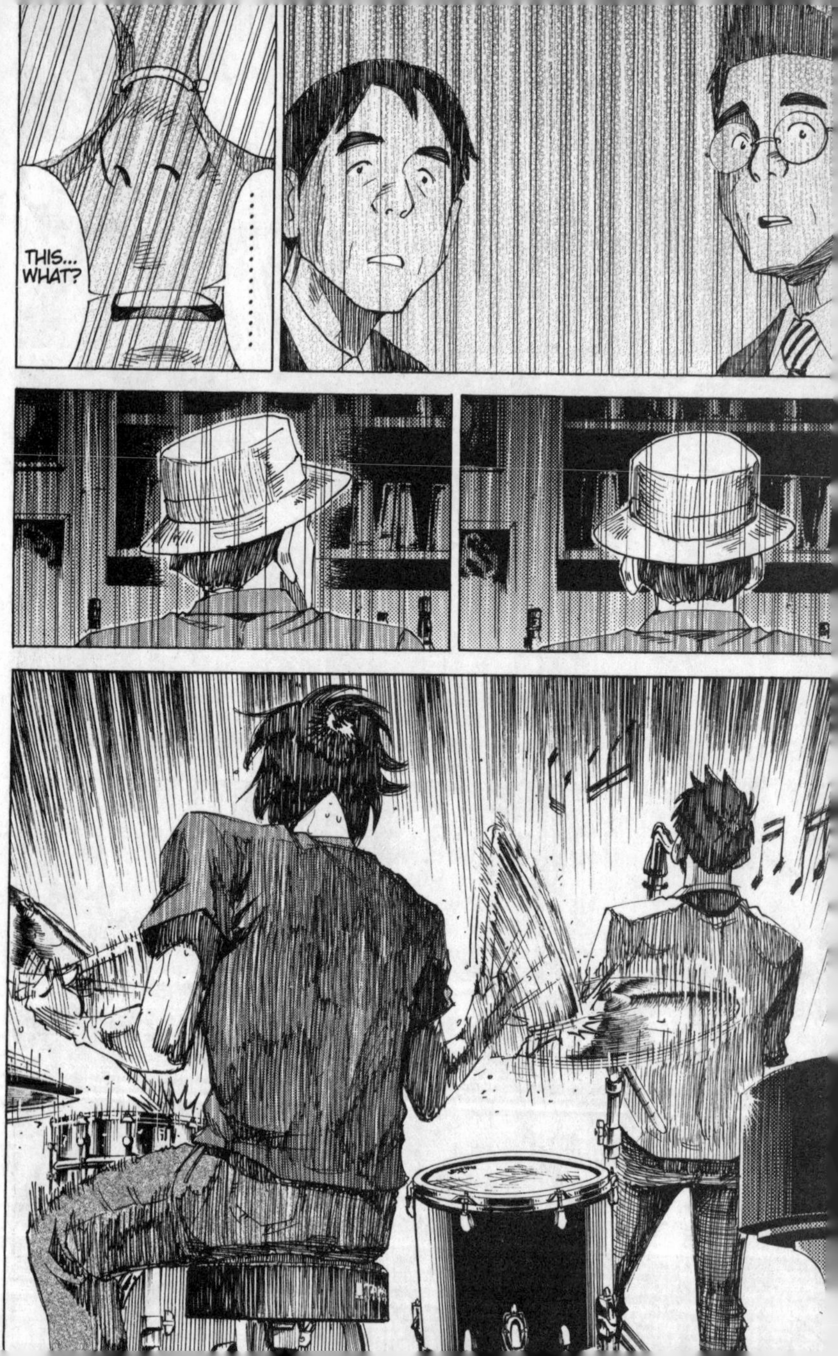
THIS... WHAT?
......

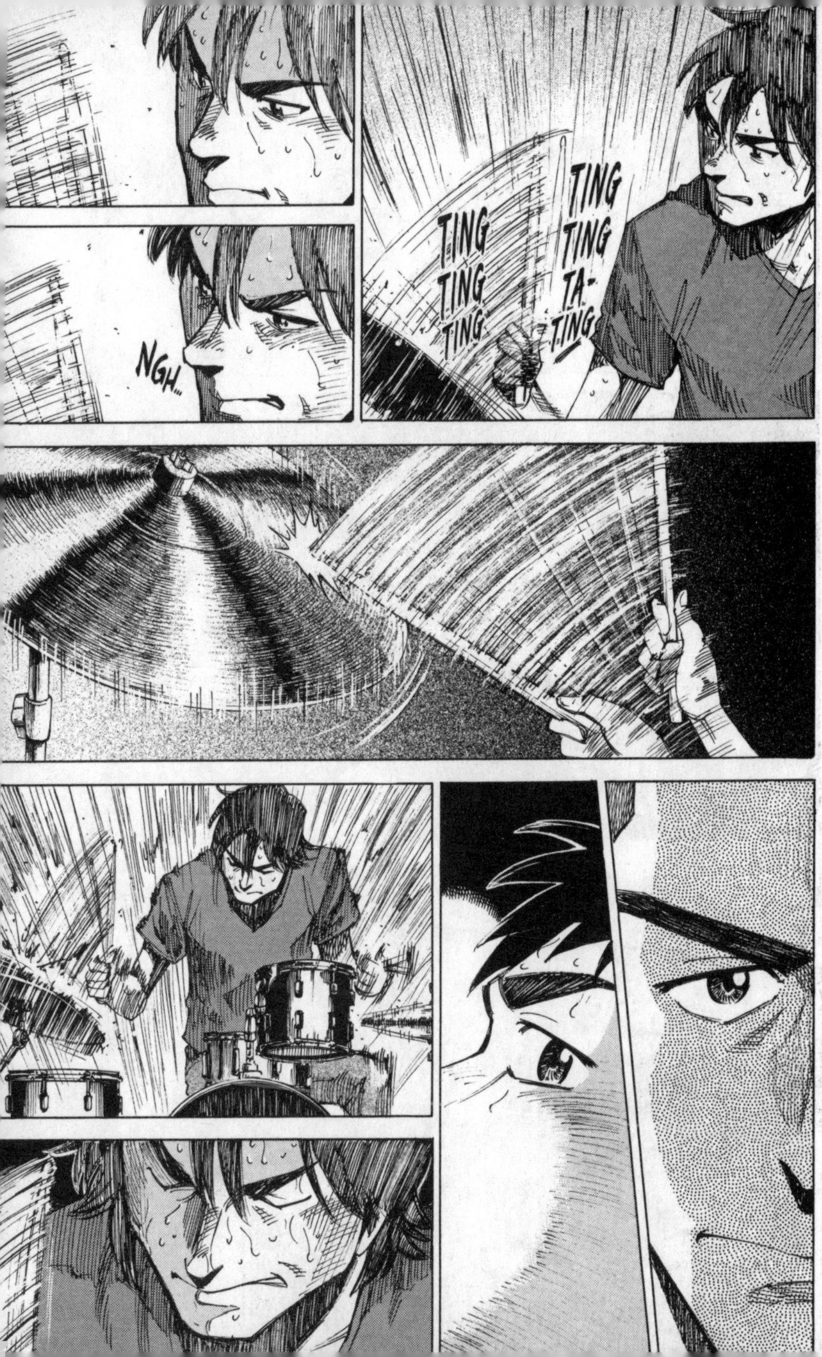
TING TING TA-TING
TING TING TING
NGH...

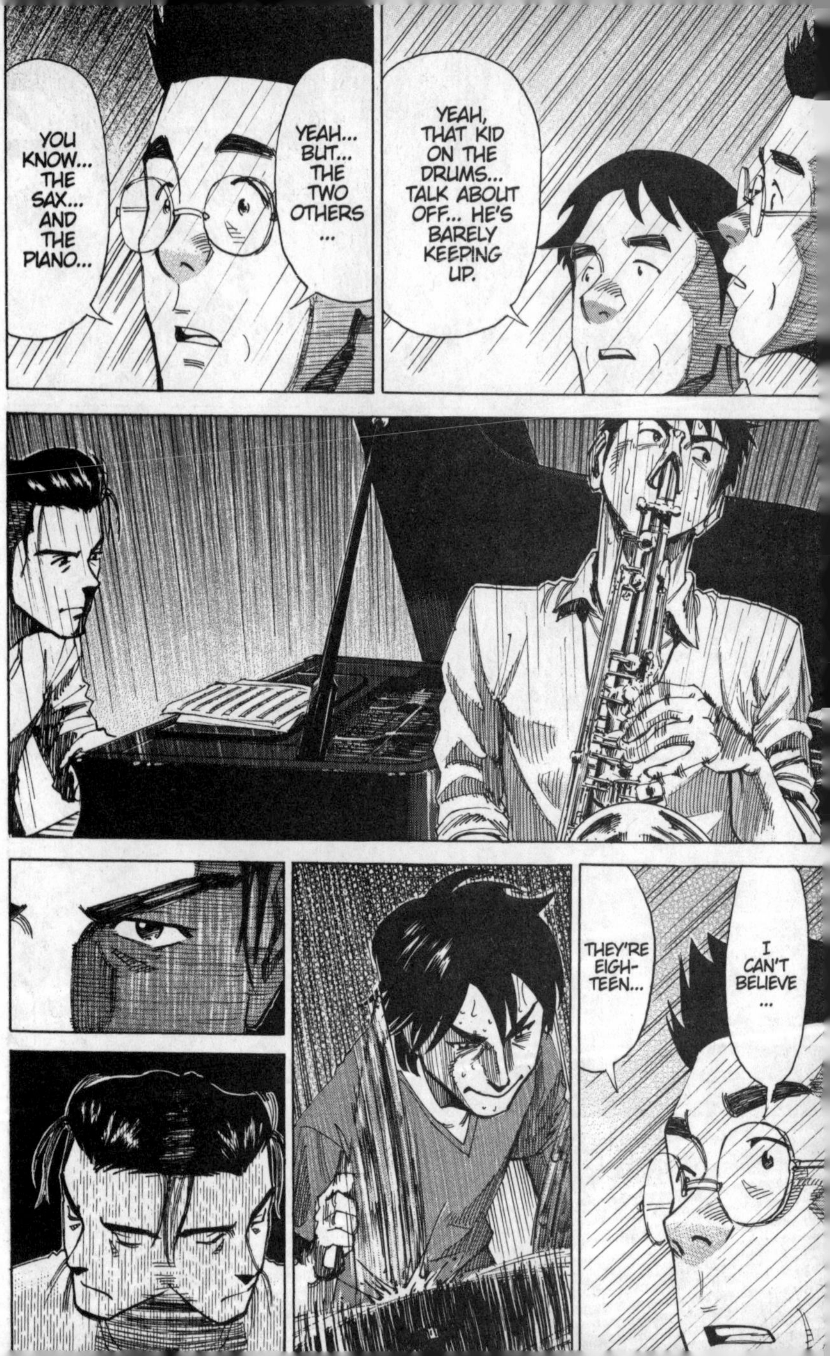
YEAH, THAT KID ON THE DRUMS... TALK ABOUT OFF... HE'S BARELY KEEPING UP.
YEAH... BUT... THE TWO OTHERS ...
YOU KNOW... THE SAX... AND THE PIANO...
I CAN'T BELIEVE ...
THEY'RE EIGH-TEEN...

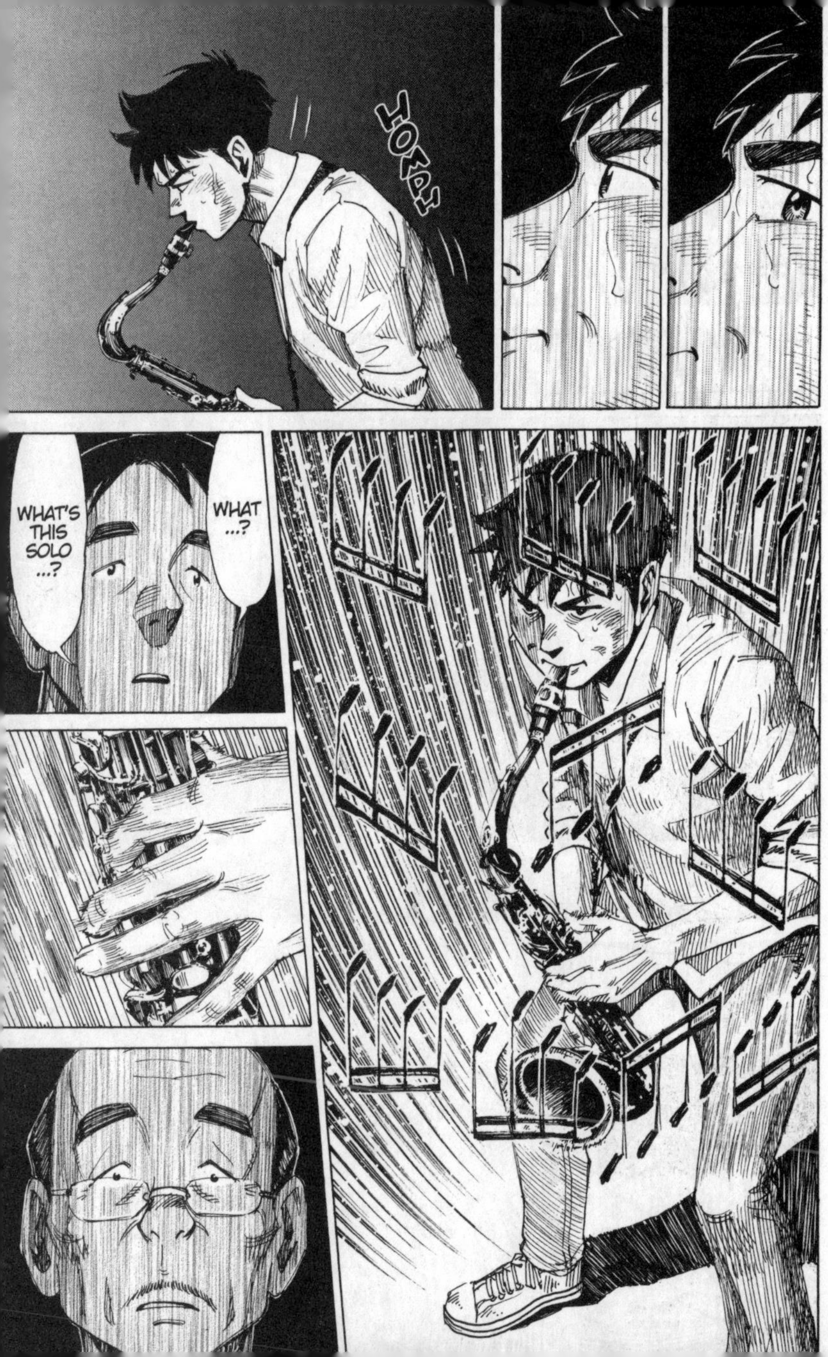
HOMP!
WHAT ...?
WHAT'S THIS SOLO ...?

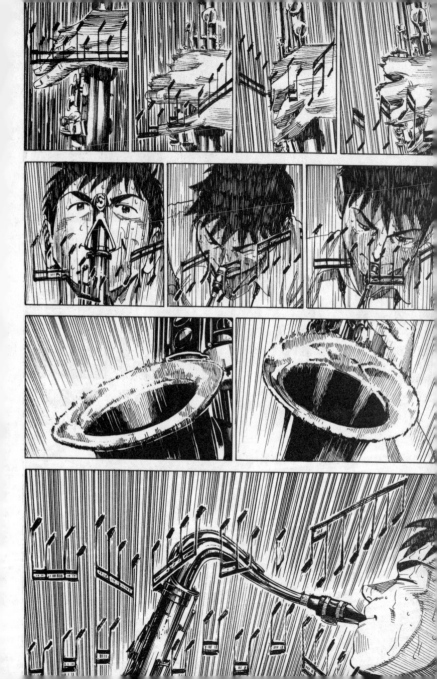

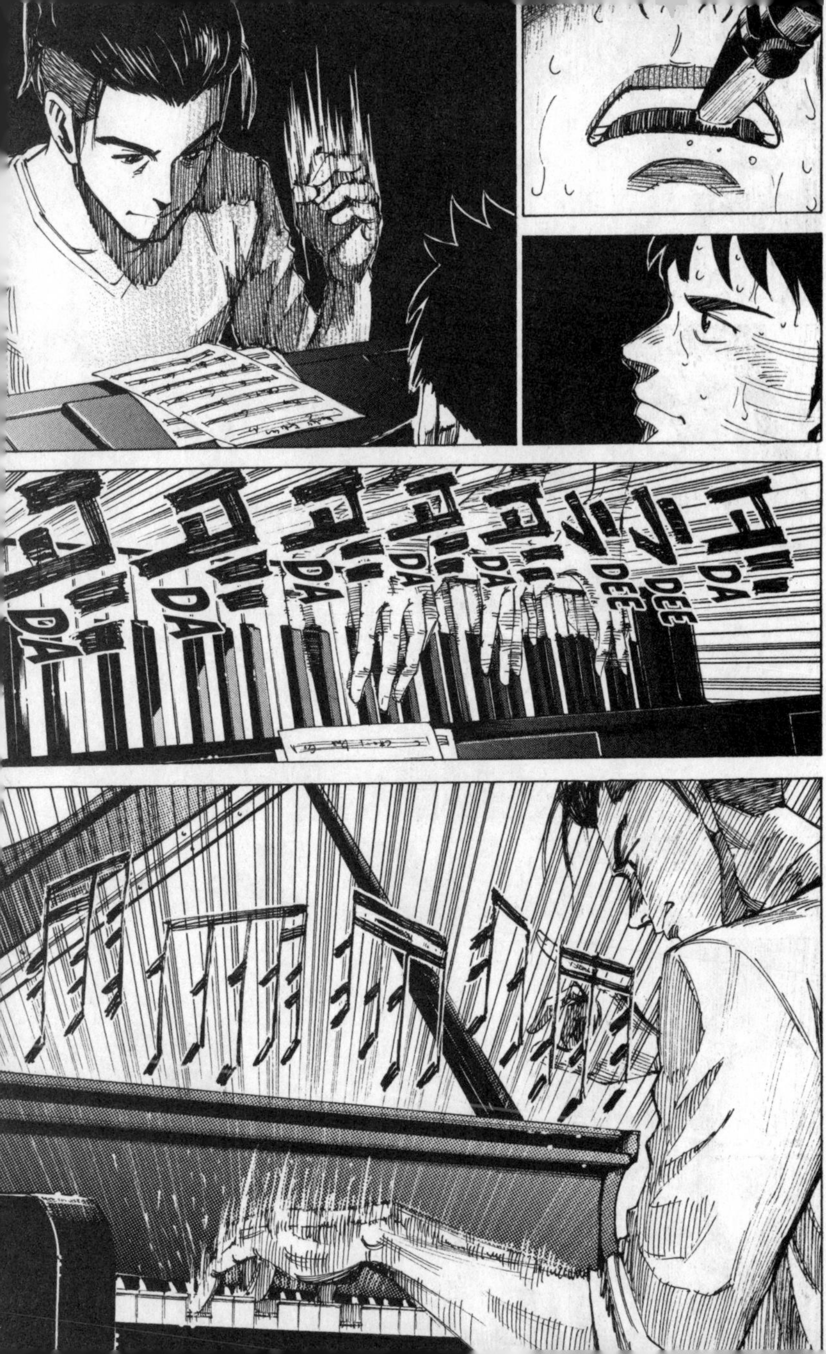
DA DEE DEE DA DA DA DA DA

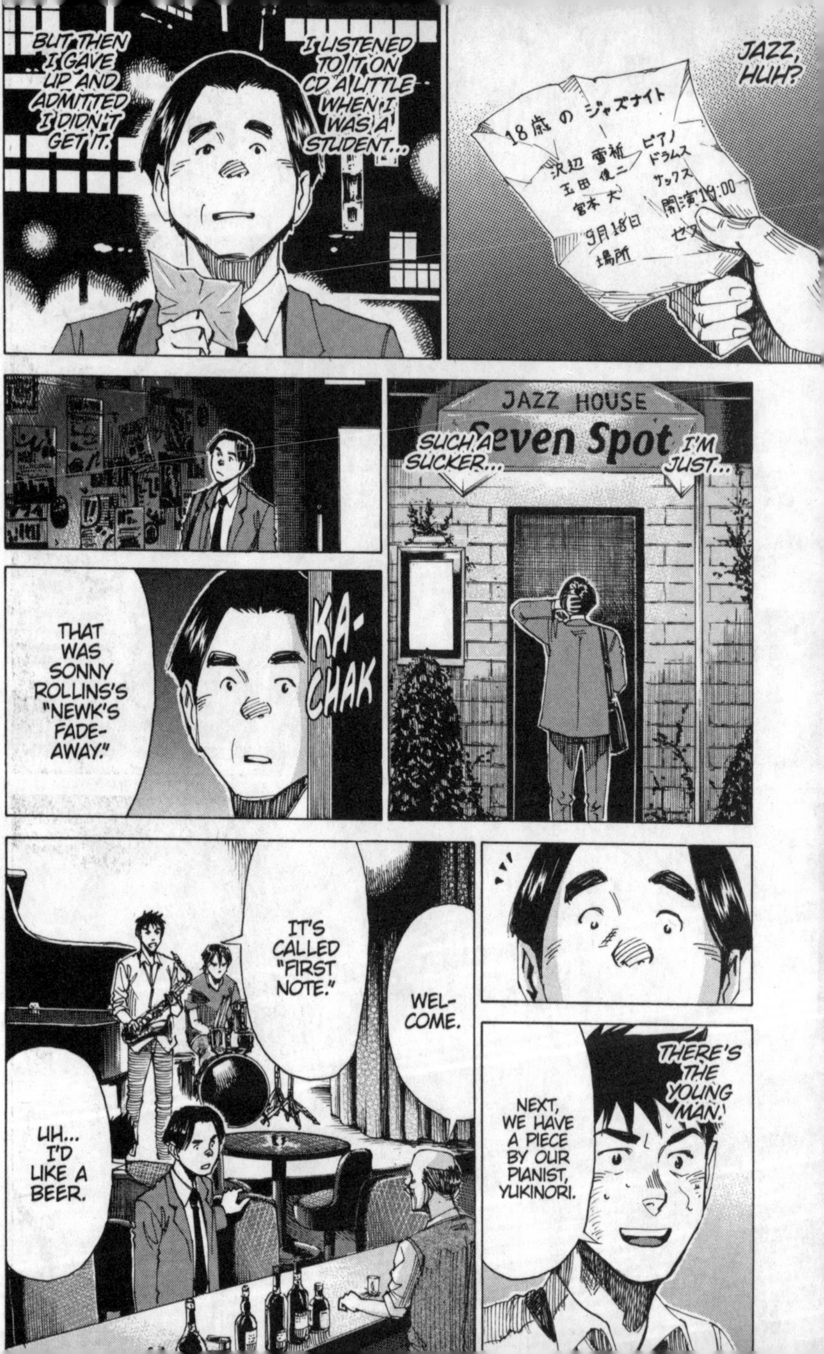
JAZZ, HUH?
18歳のジャズナイト
沢辺雪祈 ピアノ
玉田俊二 ドラムス
宮本大 サックス
開演
9月18日
場所
I LISTENED TO IT ON CD A LITTLE WHEN I WAS A STUDENT...
BUT THEN I GAVE UP AND ADMITTED I DIDN'T GET IT.
JAZZ HOUSE
Seven Spot
I'M JUST...
SUCH A SUCKER...
KA-CHAK
THAT WAS SONNY ROLLINS'S "NEWK'S FADE-AWAY."
THERE'S THE YOUNG MAN.
NEXT, WE HAVE A PIECE BY OUR PIANIST, YUKINORI.
IT'S CALLED "FIRST NOTE."
WEL-COME.
UH... I'D LIKE A BEER.

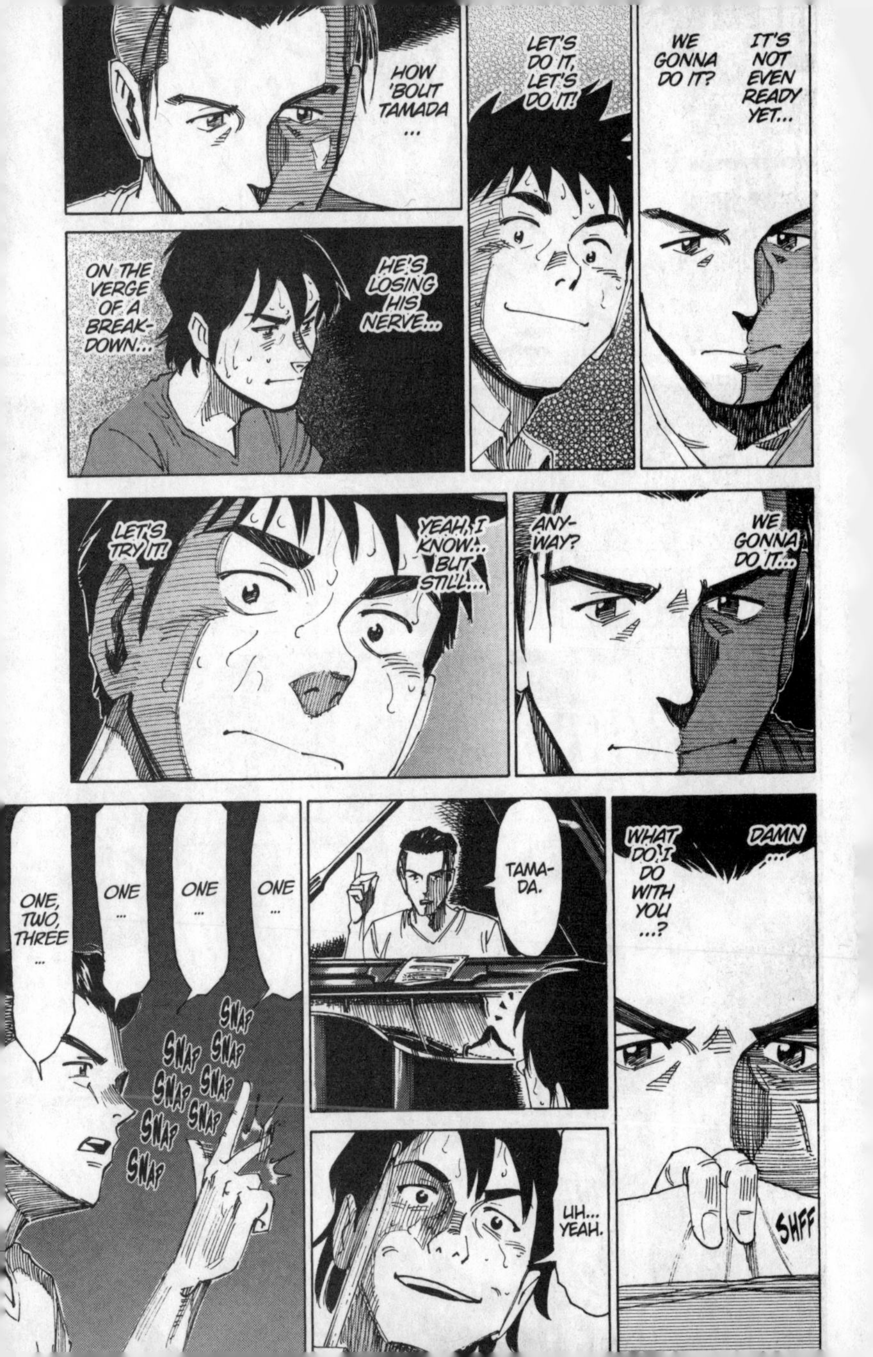
IT'S NOT EVEN READY YET...
WE GONNA DO IT?
LET'S DO IT, LET'S DO IT!
HOW 'BOUT TAMADA ...
HE'S LOSING HIS NERVE...
ON THE VERGE OF A BREAK-DOWN...
WE GONNA DO IT...
ANY-WAY?
YEAH, I KNOW... BUT STILL...
LET'S TRY IT!
DAMN ...
WHAT DO I DO WITH YOU ...?
SHFF
TAMA-DA.
UH... YEAH.
ONE ...
ONE ...
ONE ...
ONE, TWO, THREE ...
SNAP SNAP SNAP SNAP SNAP SNAP SNAP SNAP

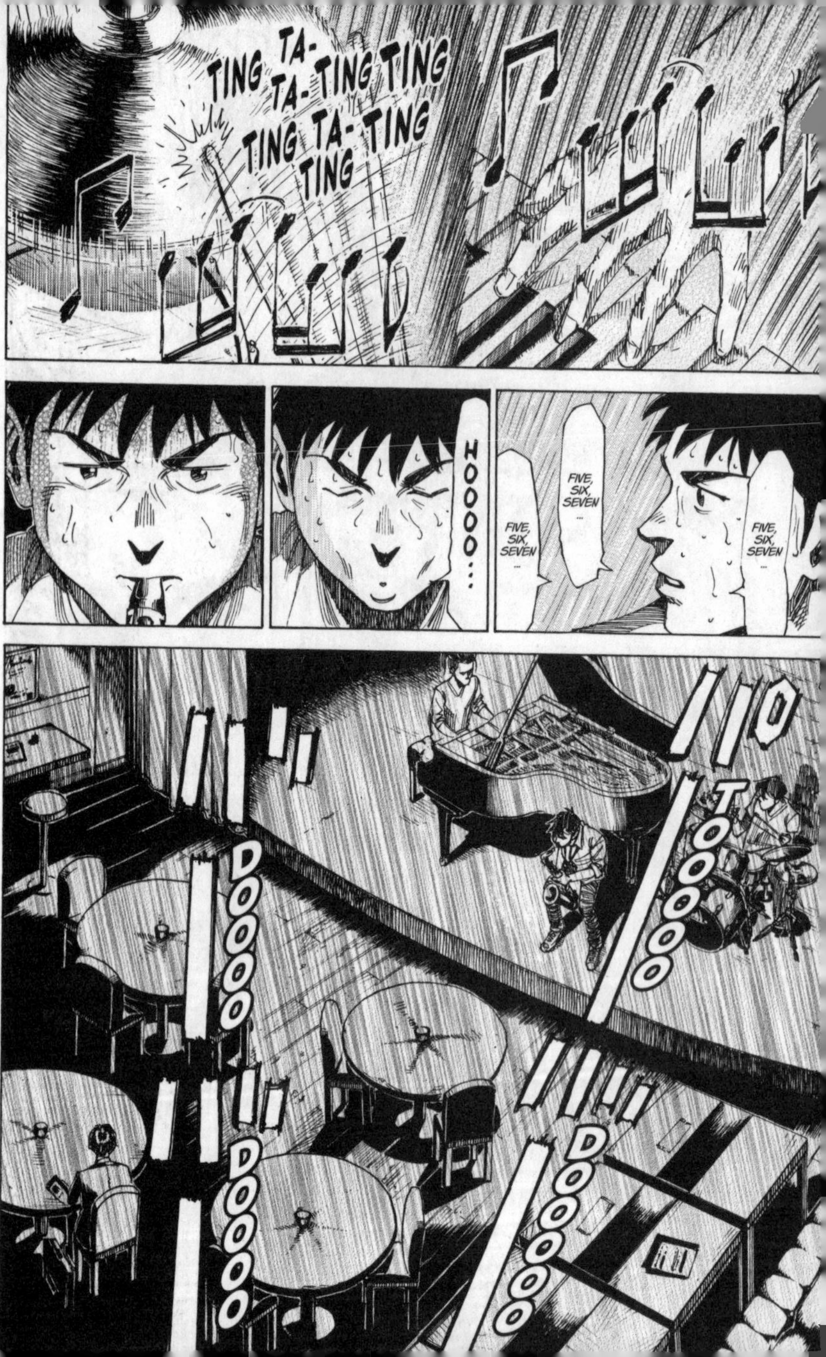
TING TA-TA-TING TING TING TA-TING TING
FIVE, SIX, SEVEN ...
FIVE, SIX, SEVEN ...
FIVE, SIX, SEVEN ...
HOOOO...
TOOOOOOO
DOOOOO
DOOOOOOO
DOOOOOO

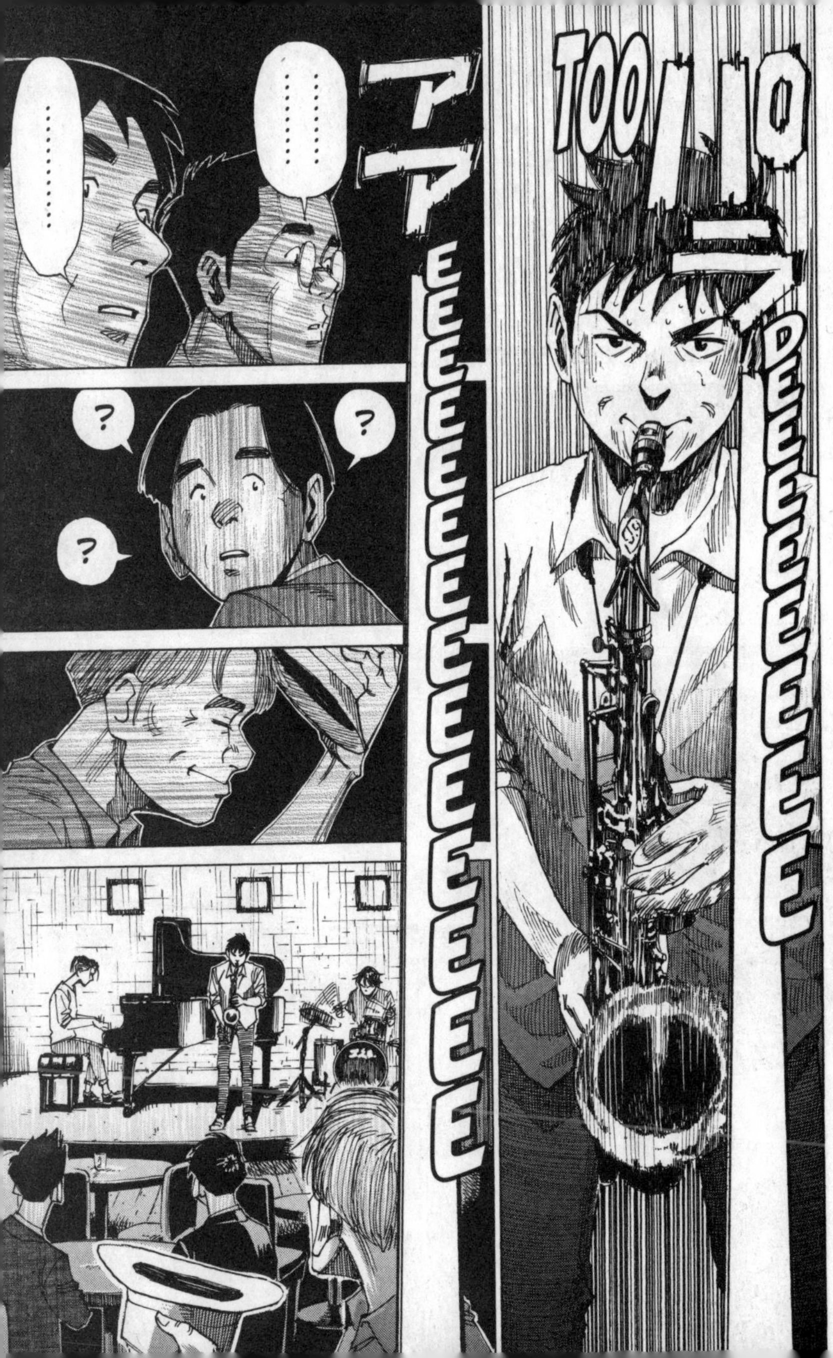
TOOO
DEEEEEEEEEE
アア
EEEEEEEEEEEE
……
……
?
?
?

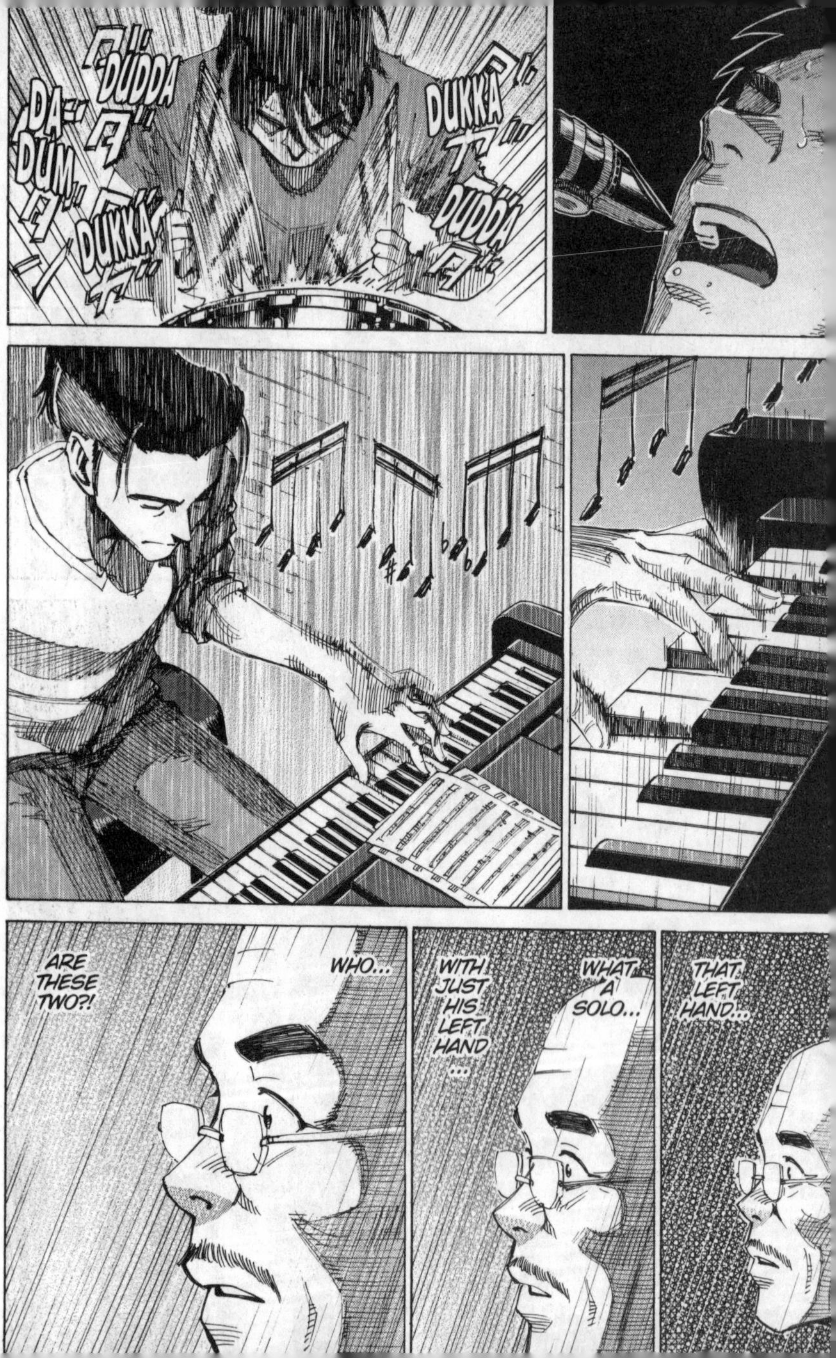
DUKKA
DUDDA
DUDDA
DA-DUM
DUKKA
THAT LEFT HAND...
WHAT A SOLO...
WITH JUST HIS LEFT HAND...
WHO...
ARE THESE TWO?!

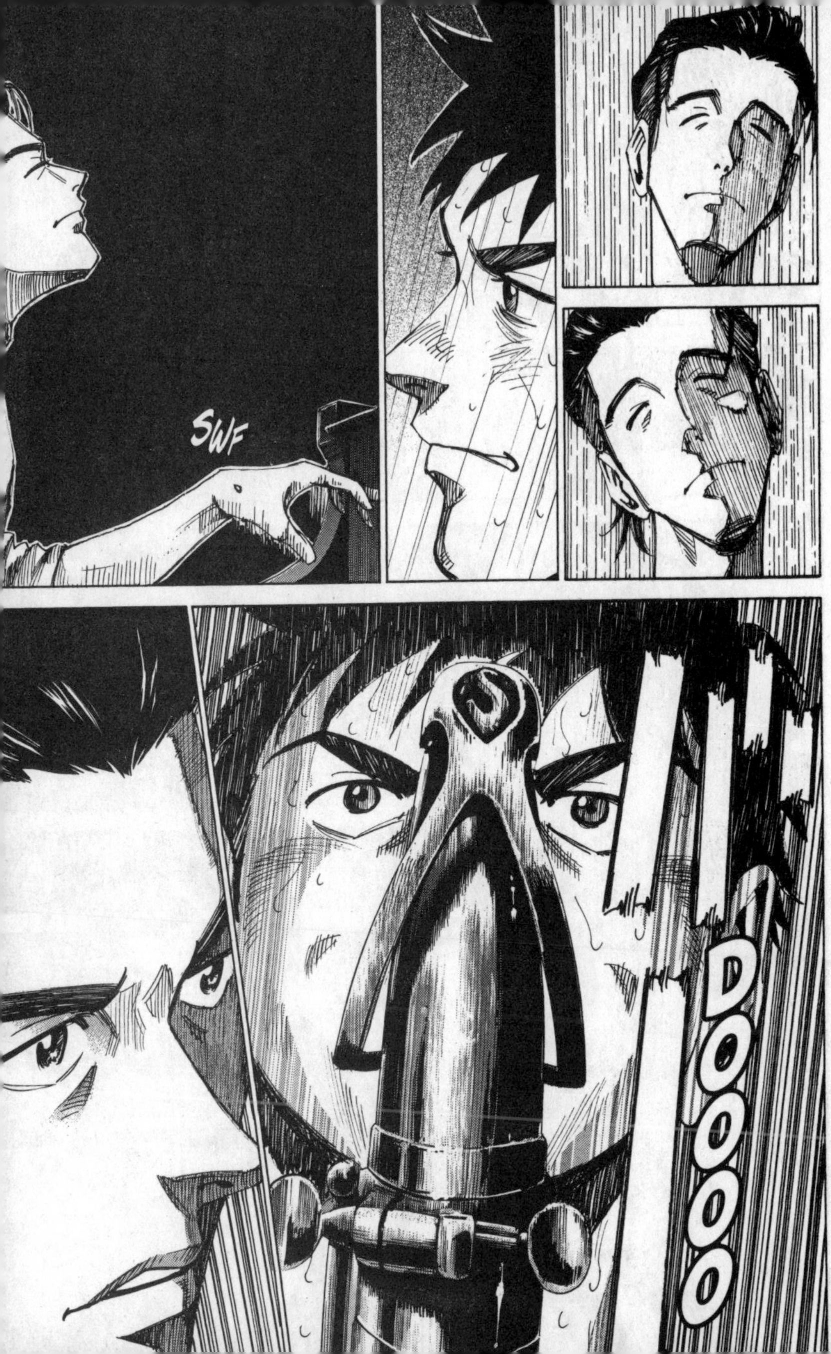
SWF
DOOOOO

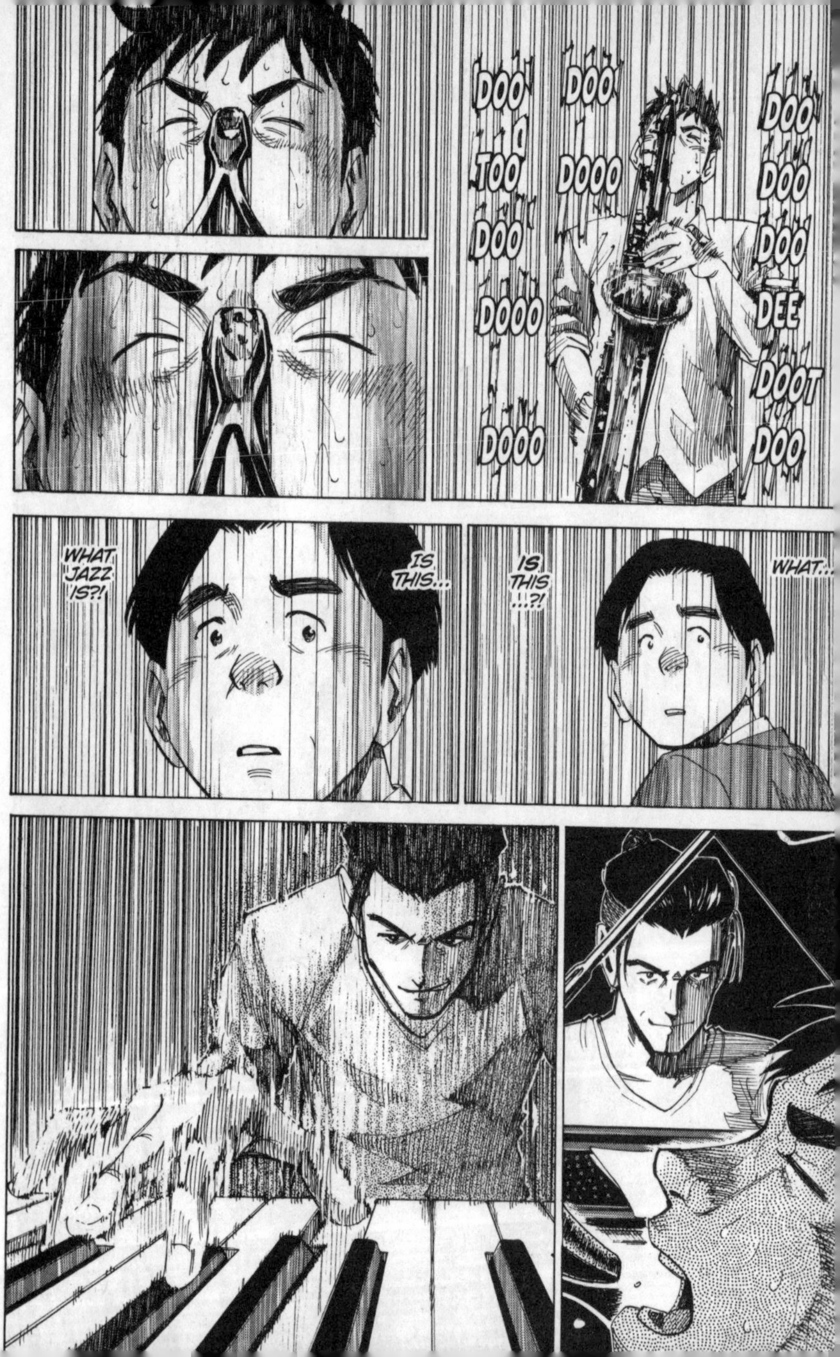
DOO DOO DOO DEE DOOT DOO
DOO DOOO
DOO a TOO DOO DOOO DOOO
WHAT...
IS THIS ..!?!
IS THIS...
WHAT JAZZ IS?!

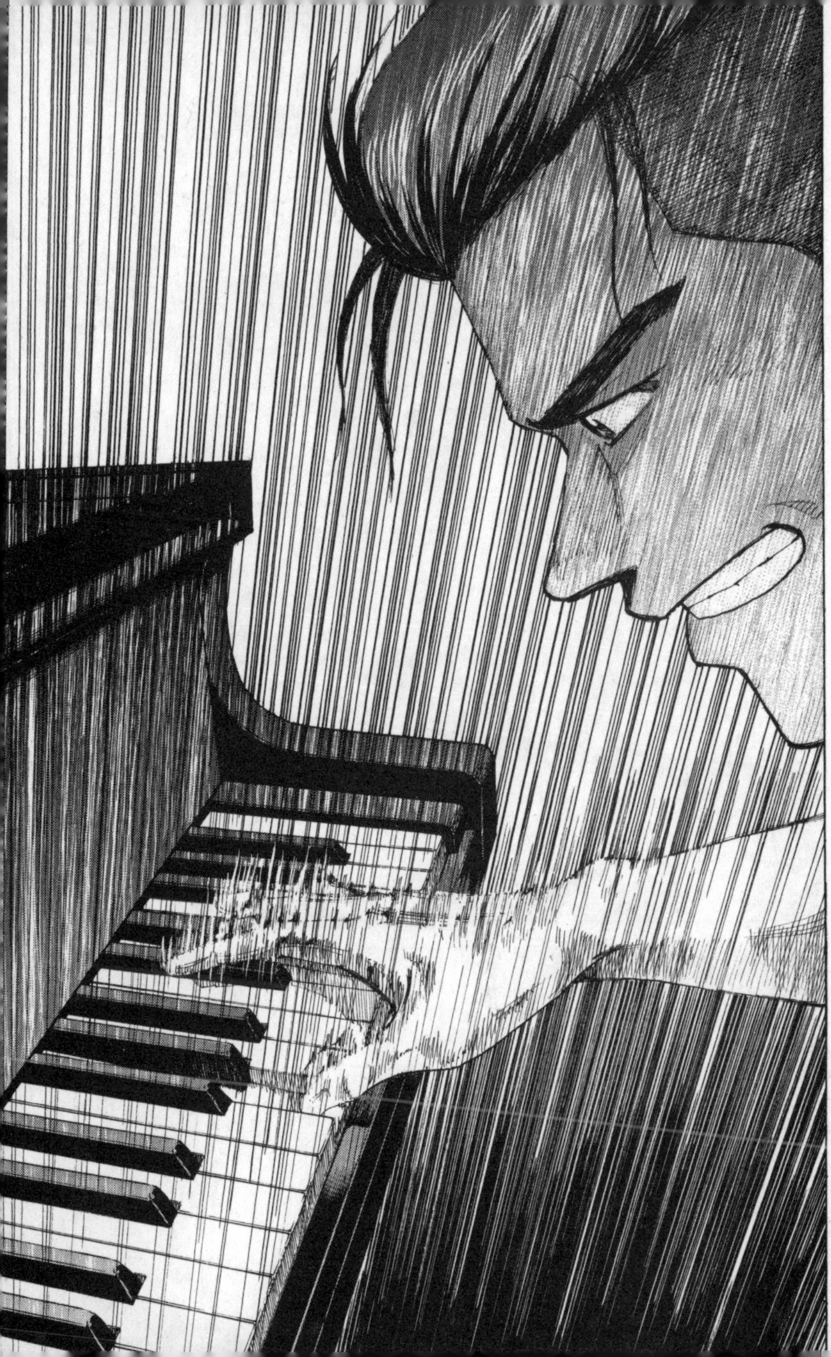

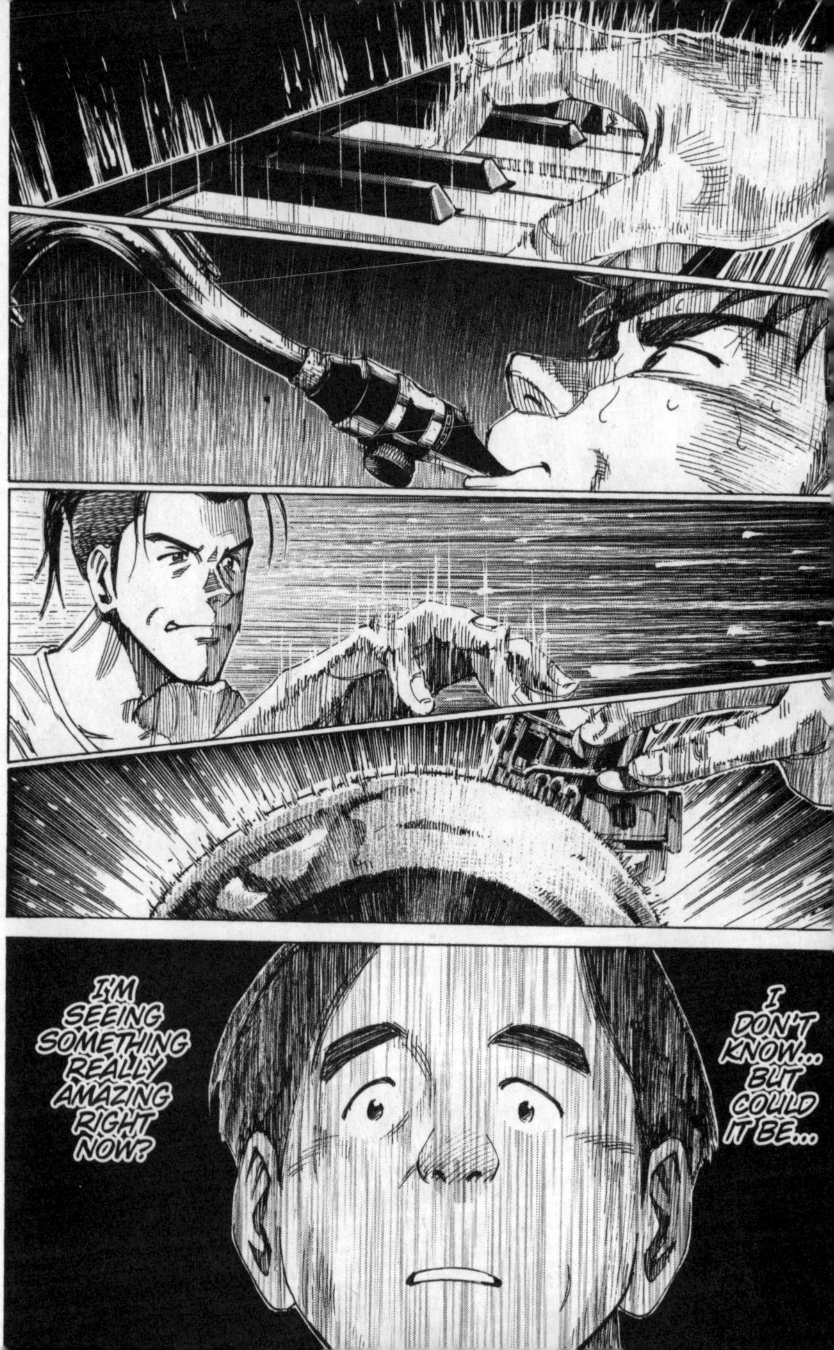
I DON'T KNOW... BUT COULD IT BE...
I'M SEEING SOMETHING REALLY AMAZING RIGHT NOW?

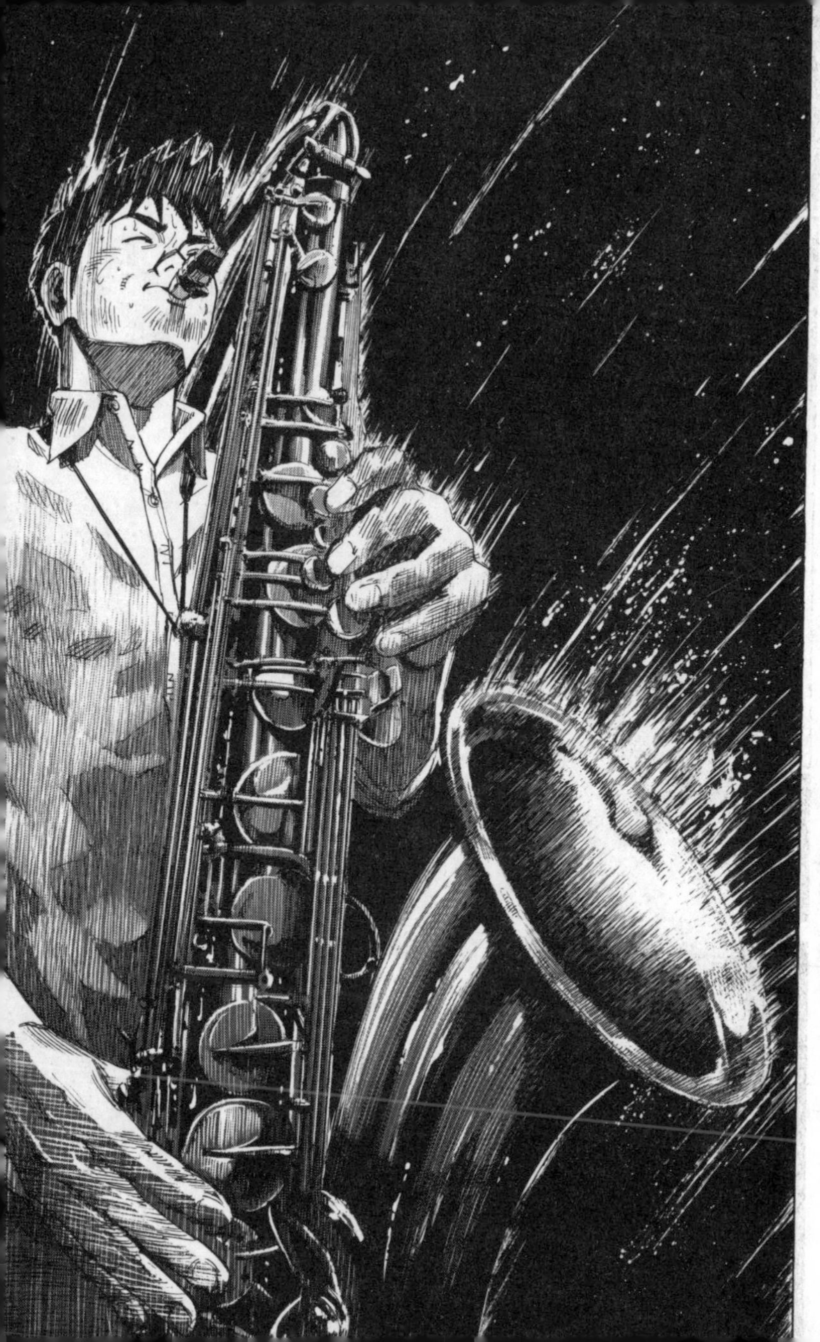

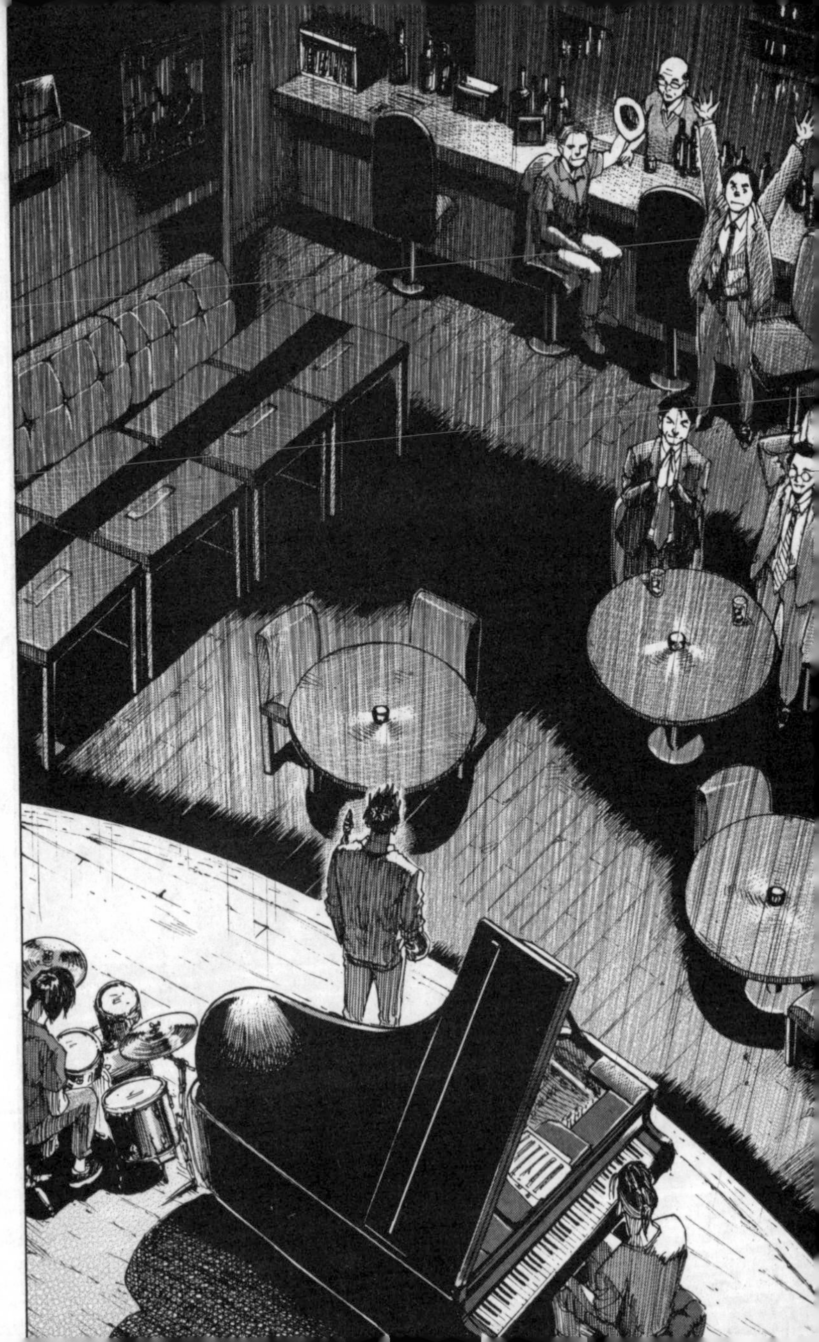

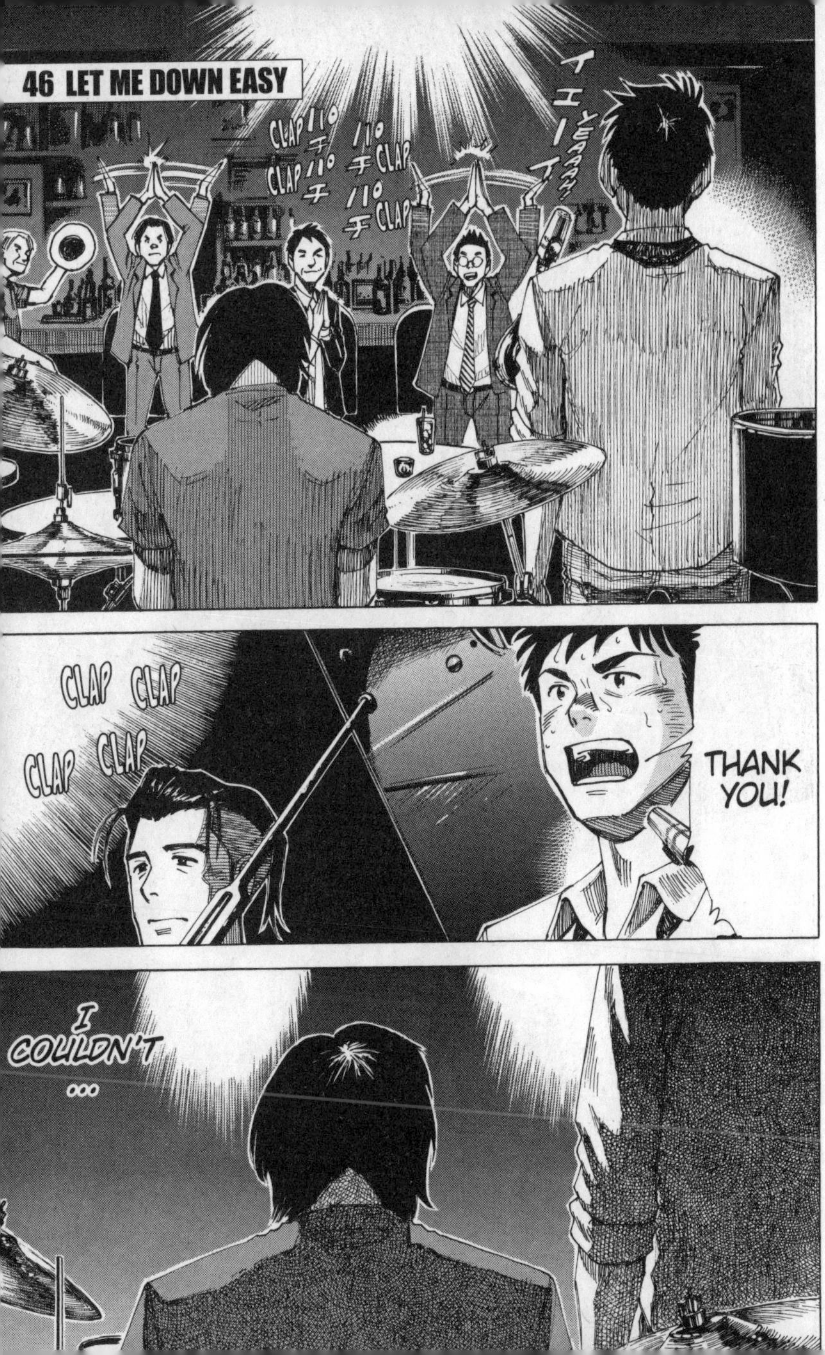
46 LET ME DOWN EASY
YEAAAH!
CLAP
CLAP
CLAP
CLAP
THANK YOU!
CLAP CLAP
CLAP CLAP
I COULDN'T
...

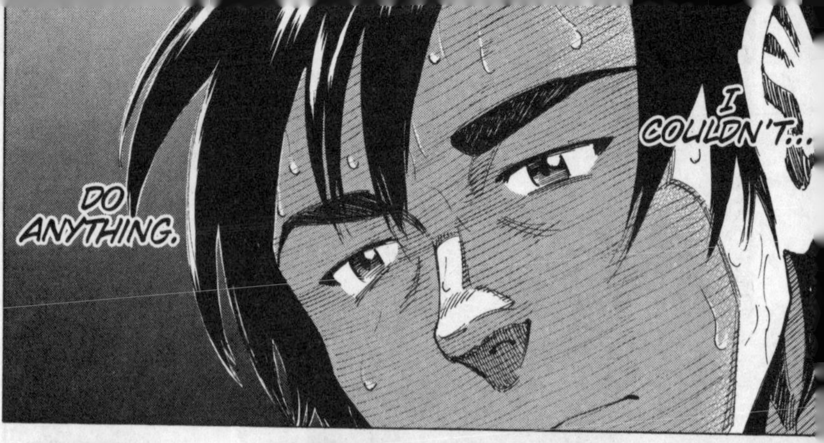
I COULDN'T...
DO ANYTHING.
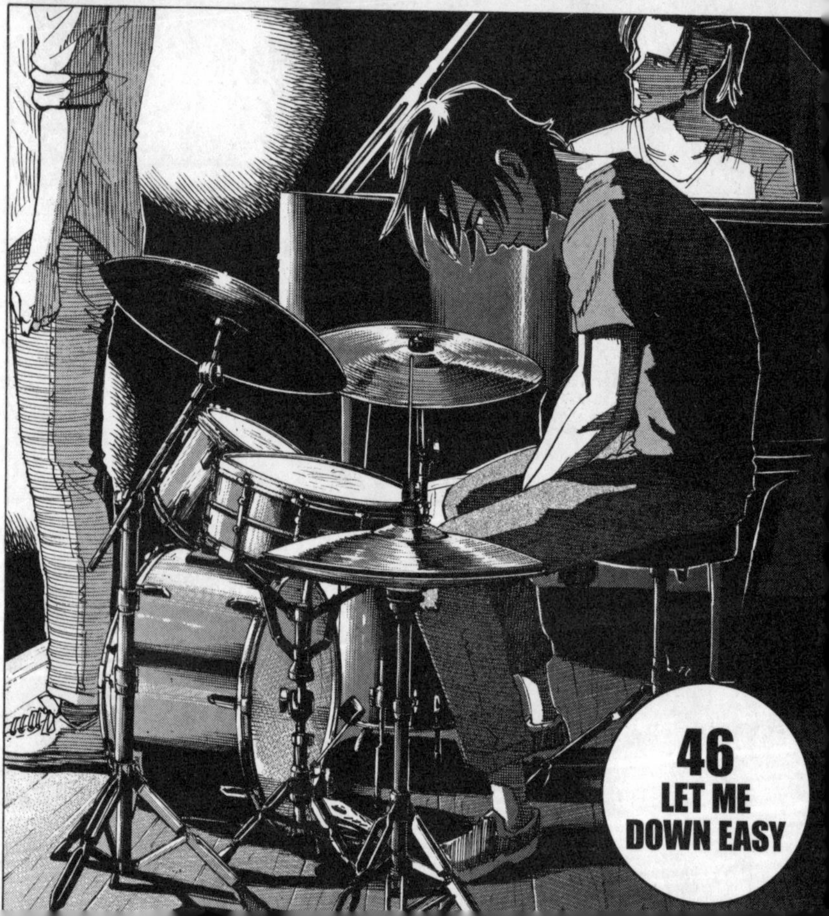
46
LET ME DOWN EASY

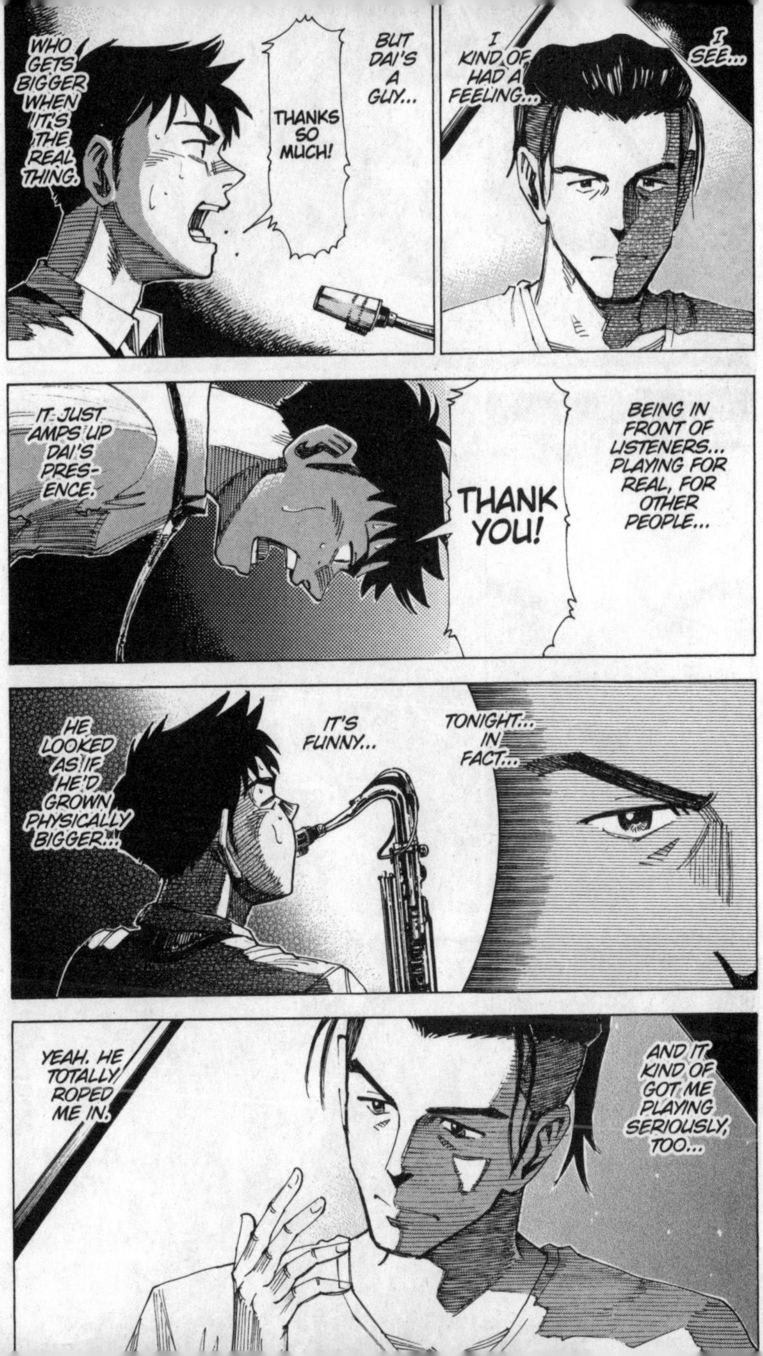
I SEE...
I KIND OF HAD A FEELING...
BUT DAI'S A GUY...
THANKS SO MUCH!
WHO GETS BIGGER WHEN IT'S THE REAL THING.
BEING IN FRONT OF LISTENERS... PLAYING FOR REAL, FOR OTHER PEOPLE...
THANK YOU!
IT JUST AMPS UP DAI'S PRESENCE.
TONIGHT... IN FACT...
IT'S FUNNY...
HE LOOKED AS IF HE'D GROWN PHYSICALLY BIGGER...
AND IT KIND OF GOT ME PLAYING SERIOUSLY, TOO...
YEAH. HE TOTALLY ROPED ME IN.

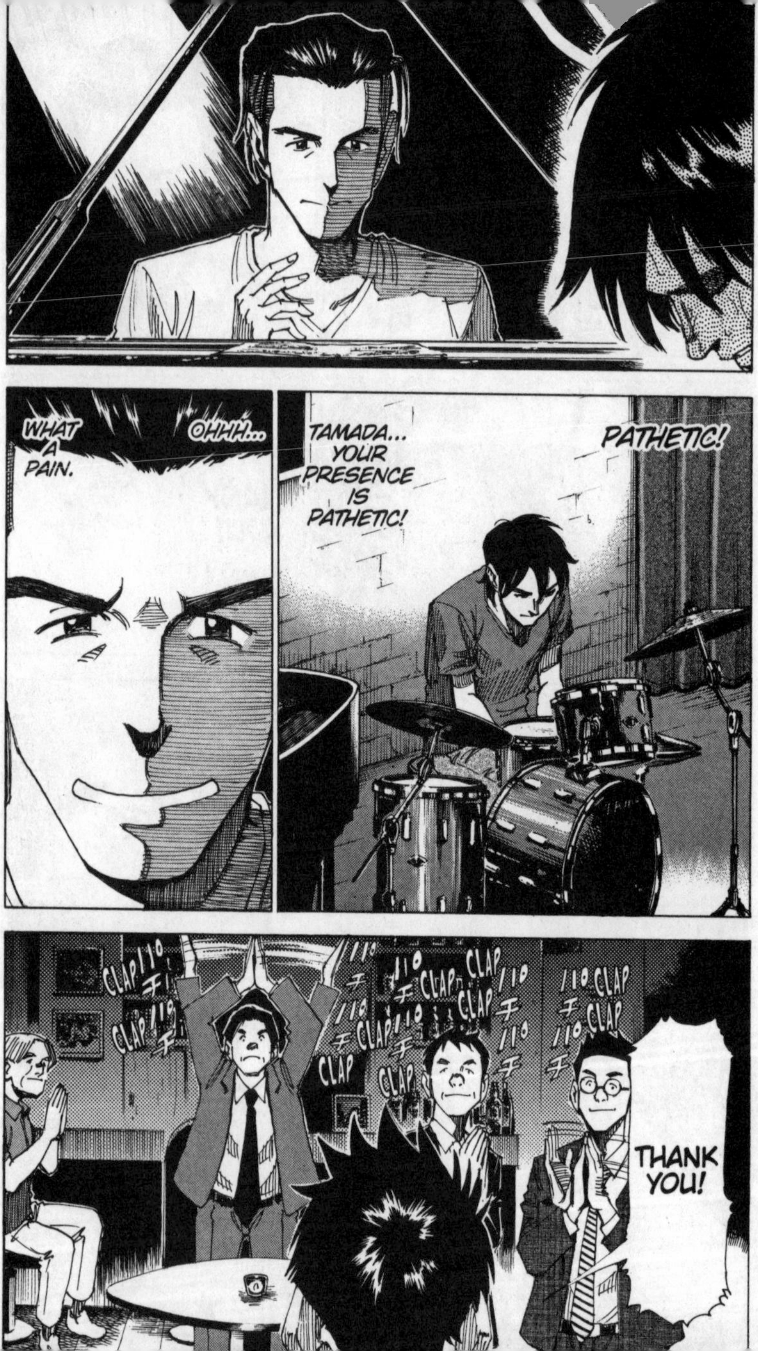
PATHETIC!
TAMADA... YOUR PRESENCE IS PATHETIC!
OHHH...
WHAT A PAIN.
THANK YOU!
CLAP CLAP
CLAP CLAP
CLAP CLAP
CLAP CLAP
CLAP CLAP
CLAP CLAP

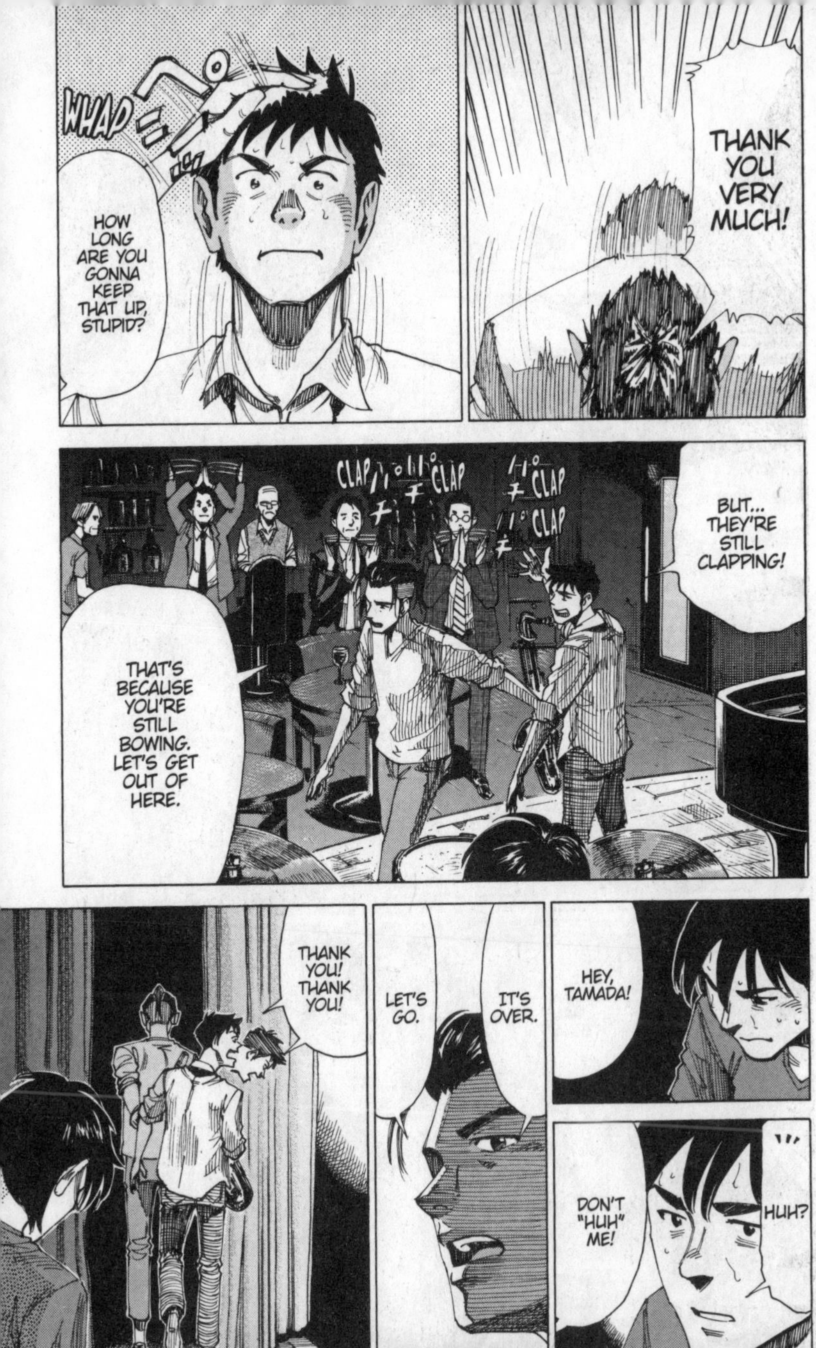
THANK YOU VERY MUCH!
WHAP
HOW LONG ARE YOU GONNA KEEP THAT UP, STUPID?
BUT... THEY'RE STILL CLAPPING!
CLAP
CLAP
CLAP
CLAP
THAT'S BECAUSE YOU'RE STILL BOWING. LET'S GET OUT OF HERE.
HEY, TAMADA!
HUH?
DON'T "HUH" ME!
IT'S OVER.
LET'S GO.
THANK YOU! THANK YOU!

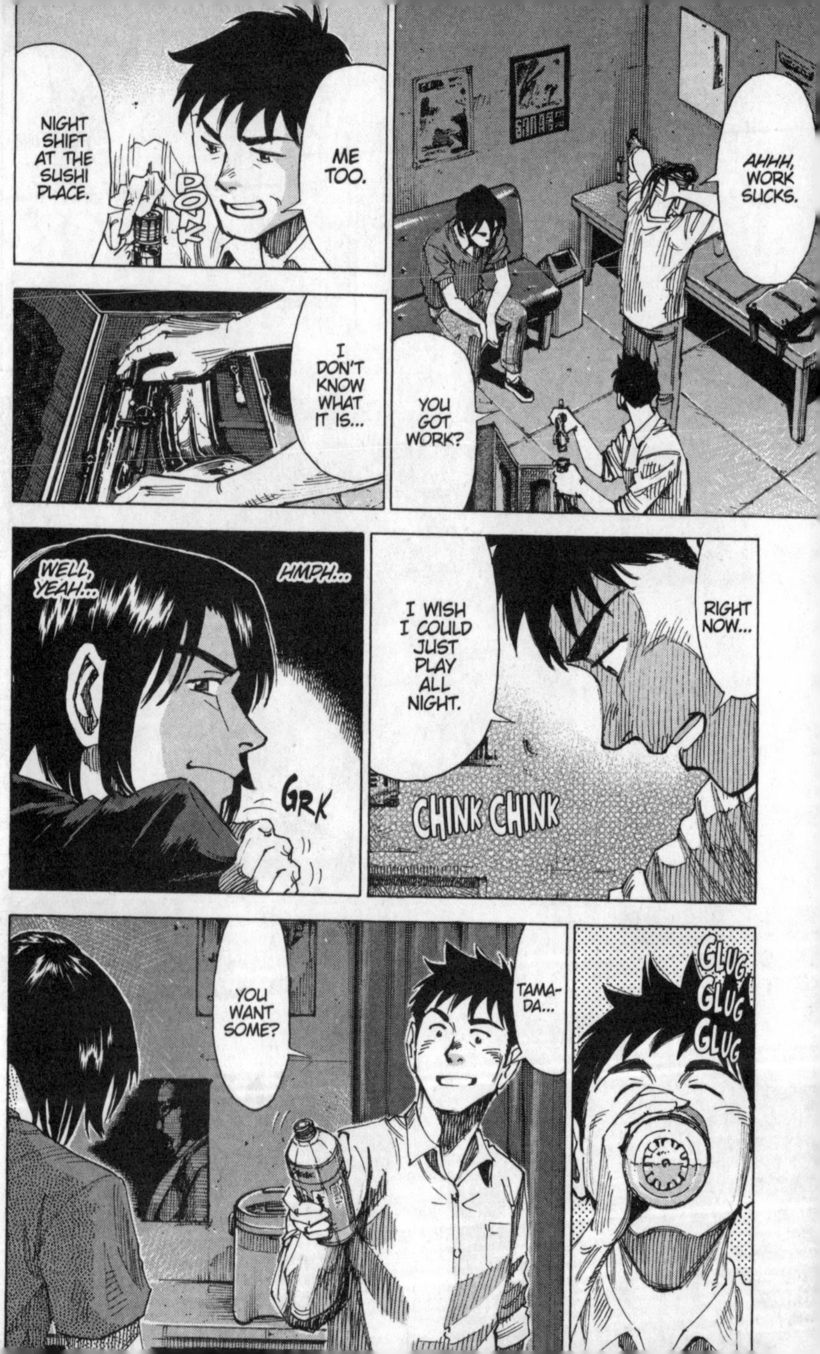
AHHH, WORK SUCKS.
YOU GOT WORK?
ME TOO.
PONK
NIGHT SHIFT AT THE SUSHI PLACE.
I DON'T KNOW WHAT IT IS...
RIGHT NOW...
I WISH I COULD JUST PLAY ALL NIGHT.
CHINK CHINK
HMPH...
WELL, YEAH...
GRK
GLUG GLUG GLUG
TAMA-DA...
YOU WANT SOME?

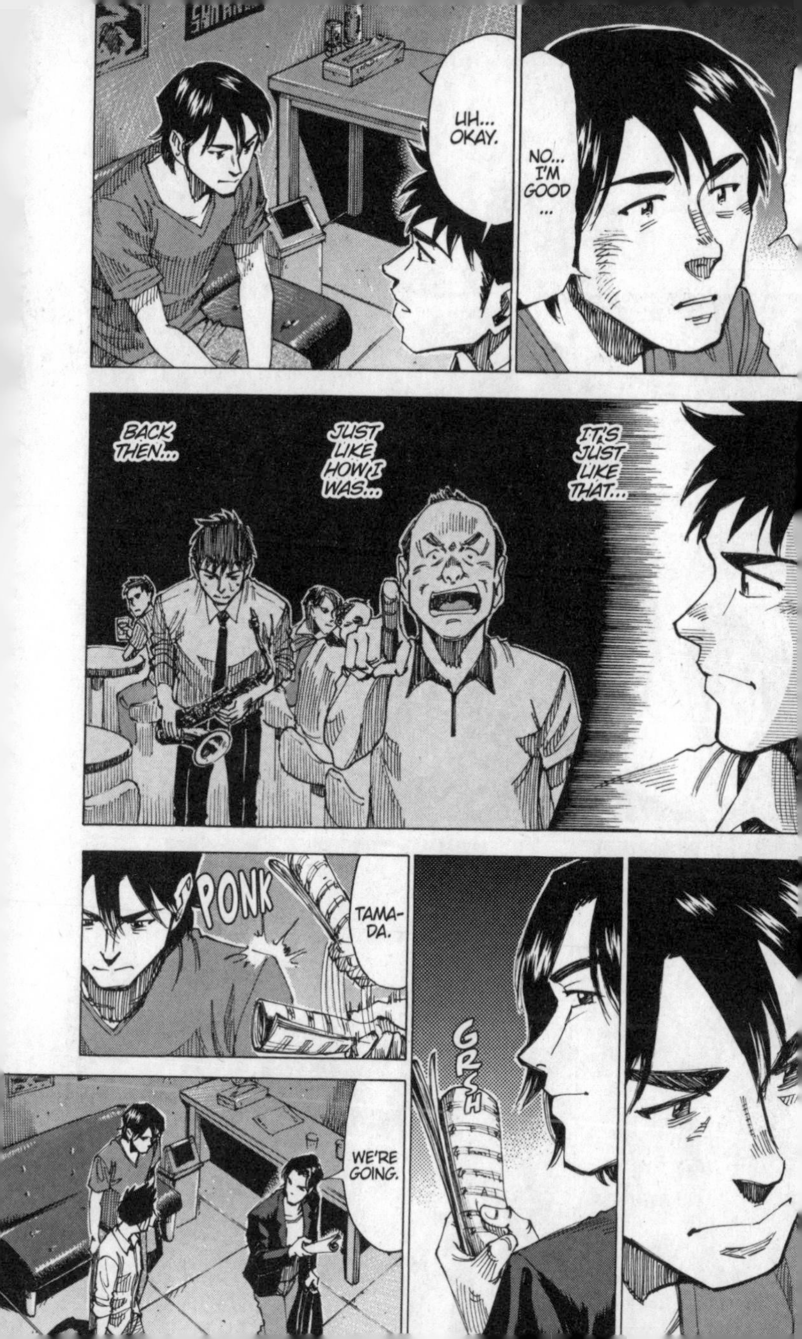
NO... I'M GOOD ...
UH... OKAY.
IT'S JUST LIKE THAT...
JUST LIKE HOW I WAS...
BACK THEN...
GRSH
TAMA-DA.
PONK
WE'RE GOING.

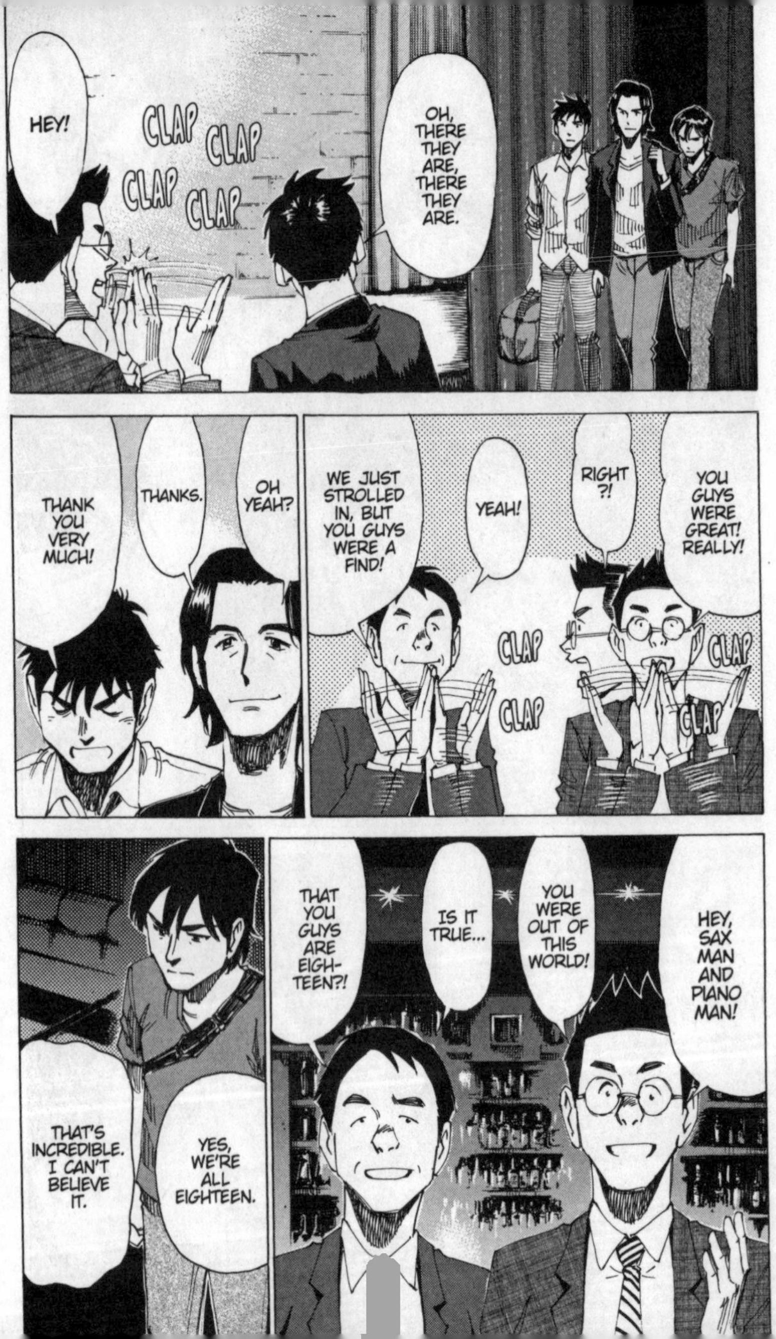
OH, THERE THEY ARE, THERE THEY ARE.
CLAP CLAP
CLAP CLAP
HEY!
YOU GUYS WERE GREAT! REALLY!
RIGHT?!
CLAP
CLAP
CLAP
CLAP
YEAH!
WE JUST STROLLED IN, BUT YOU GUYS WERE A FIND!
OH YEAH?
THANKS.
THANK YOU VERY MUCH!
HEY, SAX MAN AND PIANO MAN!
YOU WERE OUT OF THIS WORLD!
IS IT TRUE...
THAT YOU GUYS ARE EIGHTEEN?!
YES, WE'RE ALL EIGHTEEN.
THAT'S INCREDIBLE. I CAN'T BELIEVE IT.

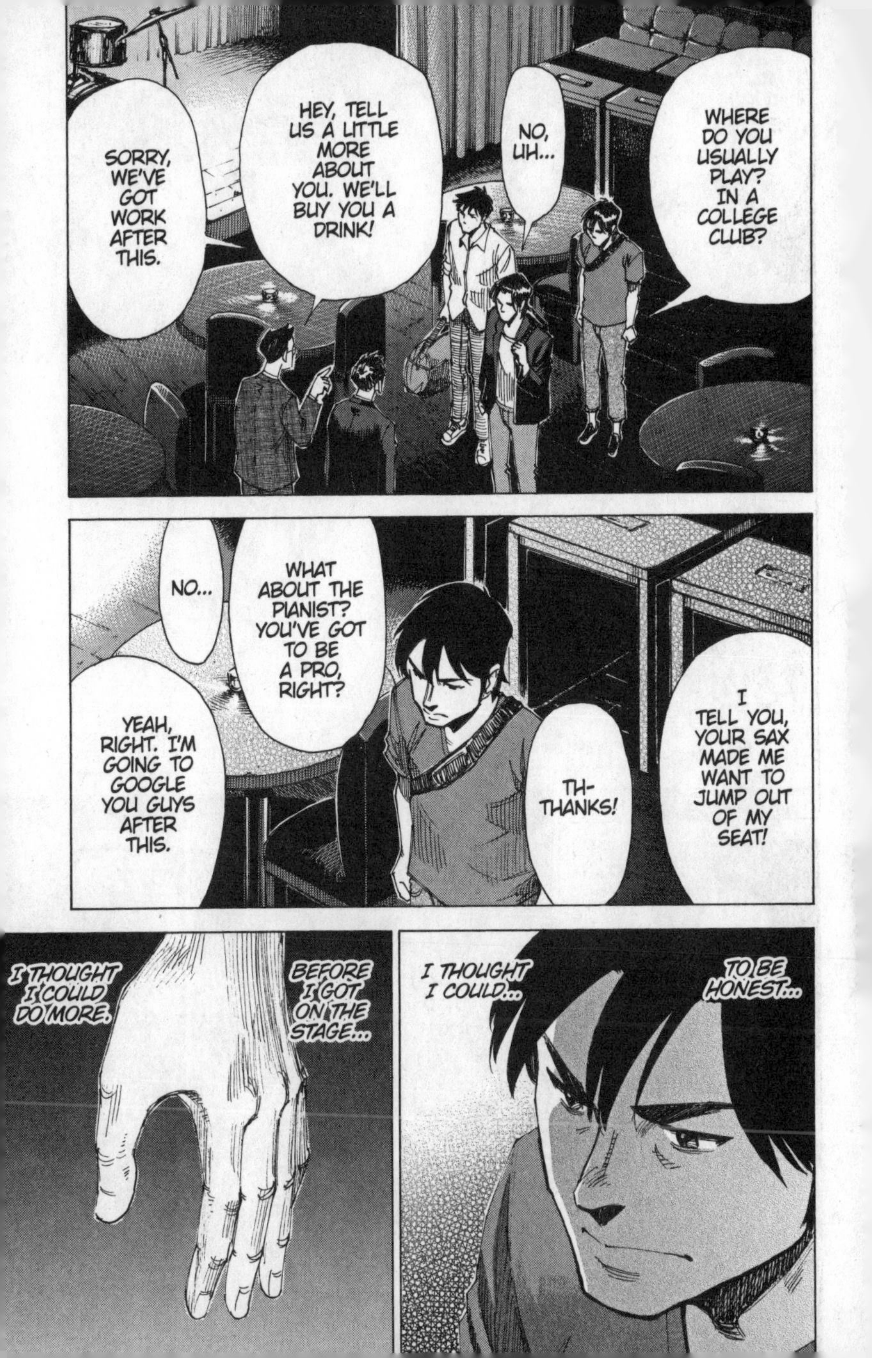
WHERE DO YOU USUALLY PLAY? IN A COLLEGE CLUB?
NO, UH...
HEY, TELL US A LITTLE MORE ABOUT YOU. WE'LL BUY YOU A DRINK!
SORRY, WE'VE GOT WORK AFTER THIS.
I TELL YOU, YOUR SAX MADE ME WANT TO JUMP OUT OF MY SEAT!
TH-THANKS!
WHAT ABOUT THE PIANIST? YOU'VE GOT TO BE A PRO, RIGHT?
NO...
YEAH, RIGHT. I'M GOING TO GOOGLE YOU GUYS AFTER THIS.
TO BE HONEST...
I THOUGHT I COULD...
BEFORE I GOT ON THE STAGE...
I THOUGHT I COULD DO MORE.

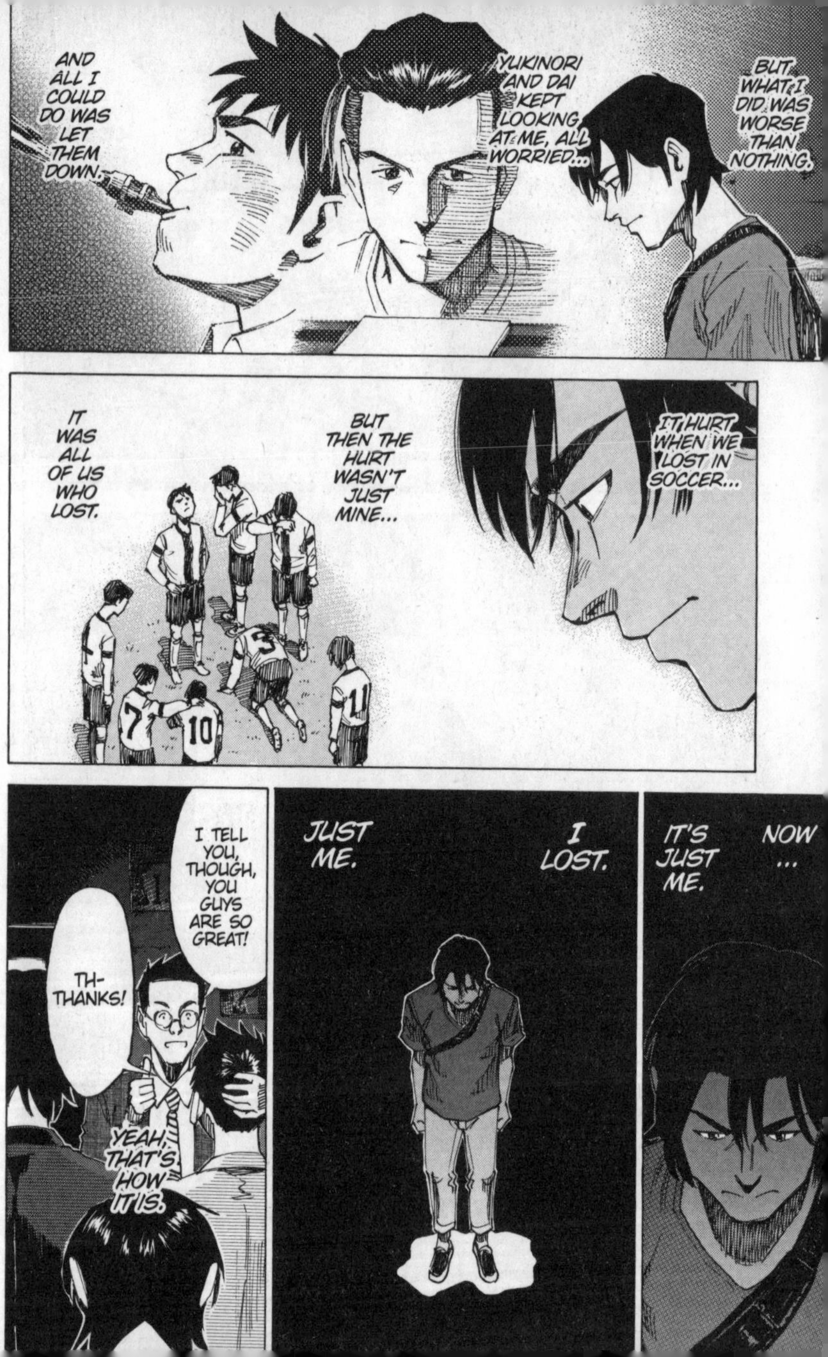
BUT WHAT I DID WAS WORSE THAN NOTHING.
YUKINORI AND DAI KEPT LOOKING AT ME, ALL WORRIED...
AND ALL I COULD DO WAS LET THEM DOWN.
IT HURT WHEN WE LOST IN SOCCER...
BUT THEN THE HURT WASN'T JUST MINE...
IT WAS ALL OF US WHO LOST.
NOW ...
IT'S JUST ME.
I LOST.
JUST ME.
I TELL YOU, THOUGH, YOU GUYS ARE SO GREAT!
TH-THANKS!
YEAH, THAT'S HOW IT IS.

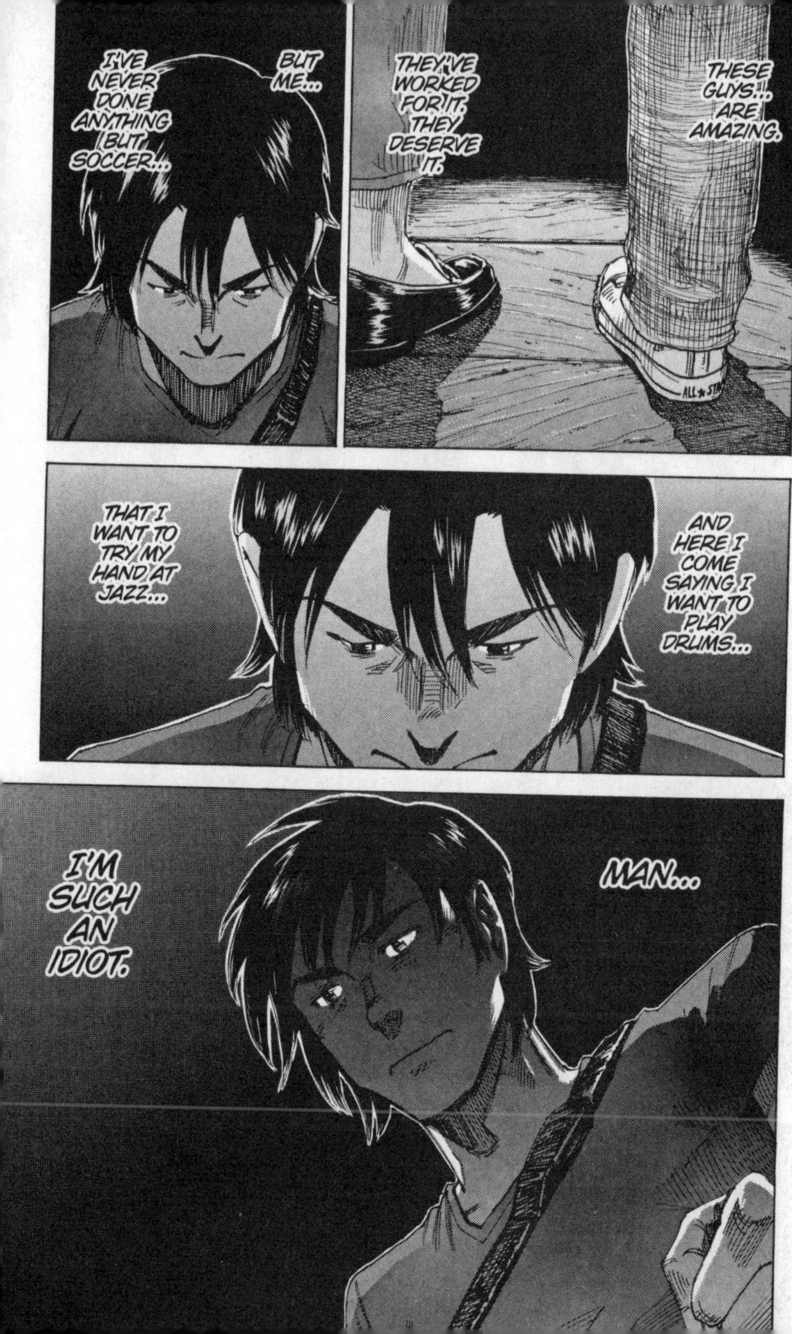
THESE GUYS... ARE AMAZING.
THEY'VE WORKED FOR IT. THEY DESERVE IT.
BUT ME...
I'VE NEVER DONE ANYTHING BUT SOCCER...
AND HERE I COME SAYING I WANT TO PLAY DRUMS...
THAT I WANT TO TRY MY HAND AT JAZZ...
MAN...
I'M SUCH AN IDIOT.

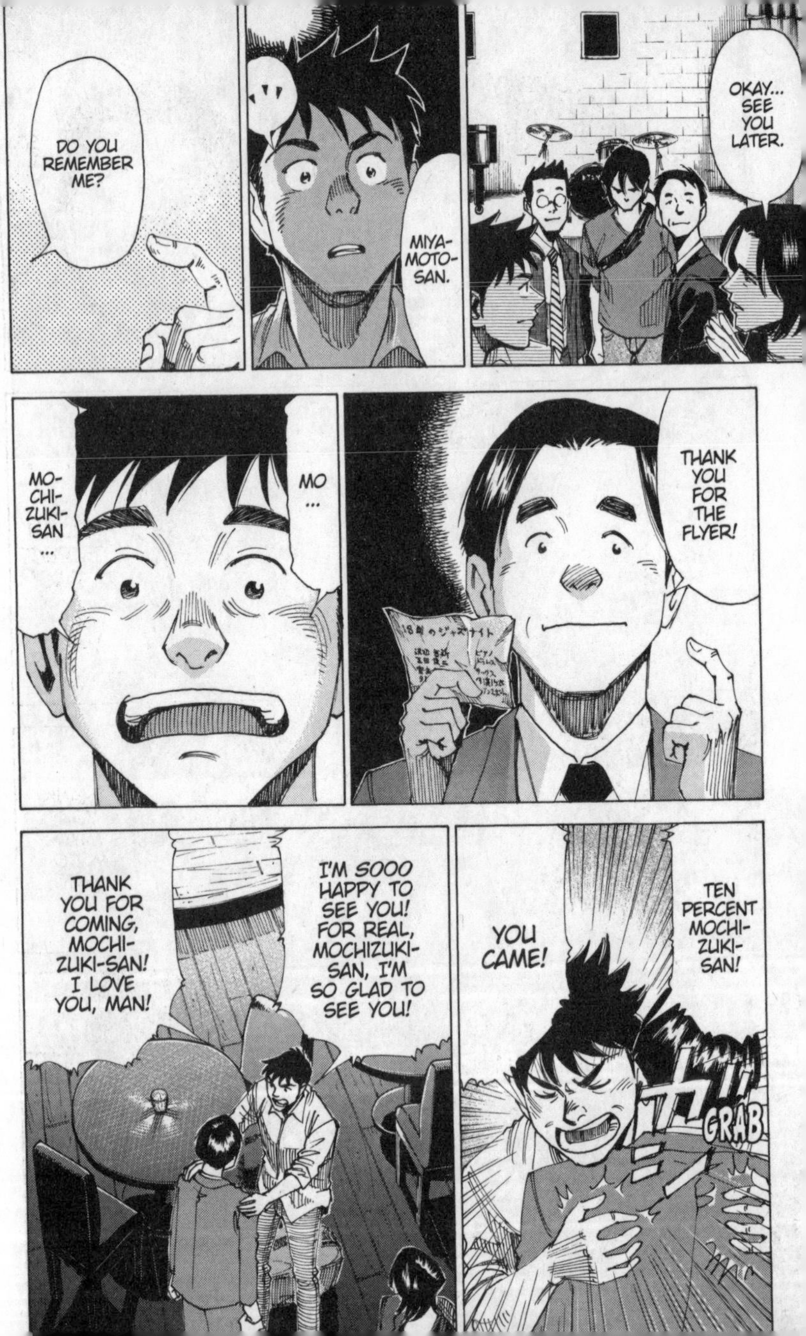
OKAY... SEE YOU LATER.
MIYA-MOTO-SAN.
DO YOU REMEMBER ME?
THANK YOU FOR THE FLYER!
MO...
MO-CHI-ZUKI-SAN...
TEN PERCENT MOCHI-ZUKI-SAN!
YOU CAME!
GRAB
I'M SOOO HAPPY TO SEE YOU! FOR REAL, MOCHIZUKI-SAN, I'M SO GLAD TO SEE YOU!
THANK YOU FOR COMING, MOCHI-ZUKI-SAN! I LOVE YOU, MAN!

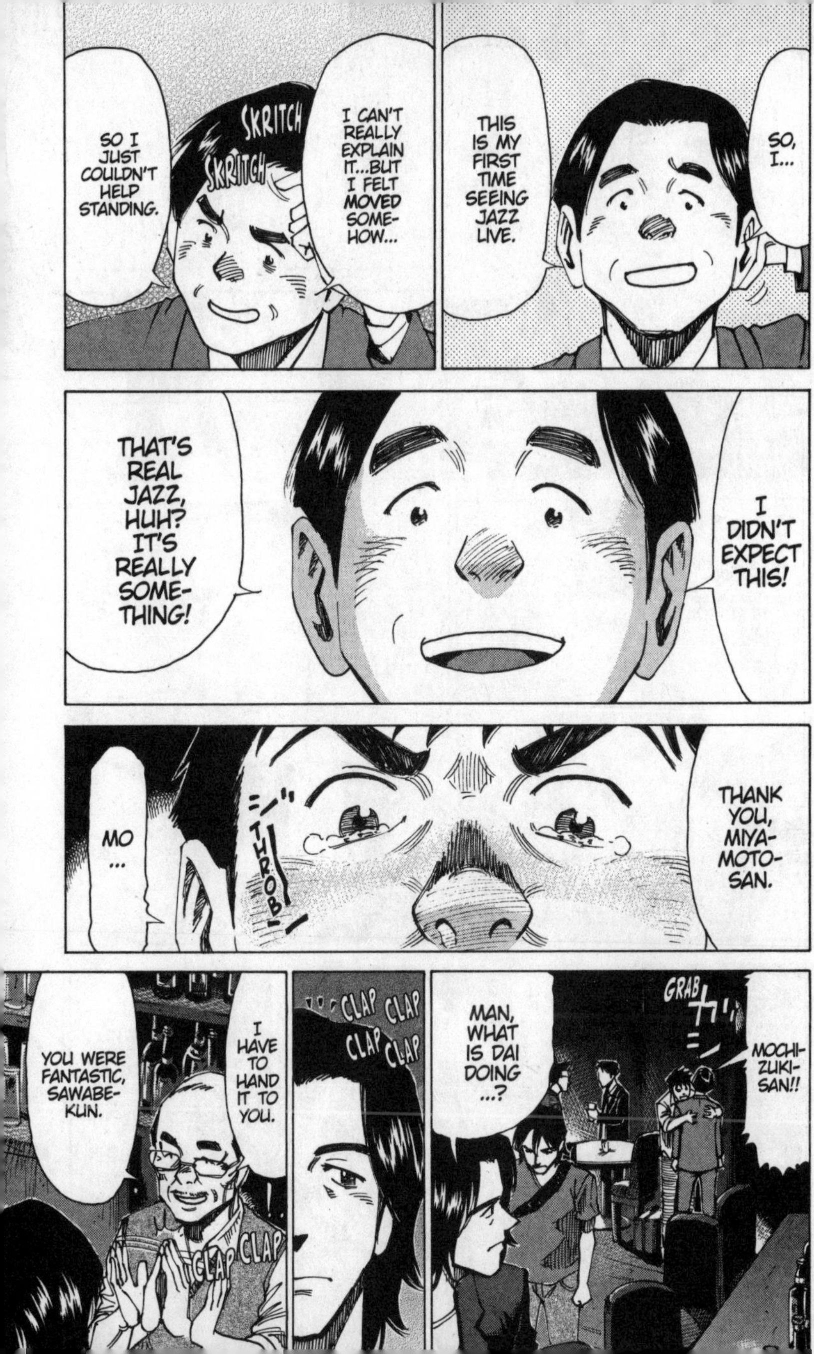
SO, I...
THIS IS MY FIRST TIME SEEING JAZZ LIVE.
I CAN'T REALLY EXPLAIN IT...BUT I FELT MOVED SOMEHOW...
SKRITCH
SKRITCH
SO I JUST COULDN'T HELP STANDING.
I DIDN'T EXPECT THIS!
THAT'S REAL JAZZ, HUH? IT'S REALLY SOMETHING!
THANK YOU, MIYAMOTO-SAN.
THROB
MO ...
GRAB
MOCHIZUKI-SAN!!
MAN, WHAT IS DAI DOING ...?
CLAP CLAP
CLAP CLAP
I HAVE TO HAND IT TO YOU.
YOU WERE FANTASTIC, SAWABE-KUN.
CLAP CLAP

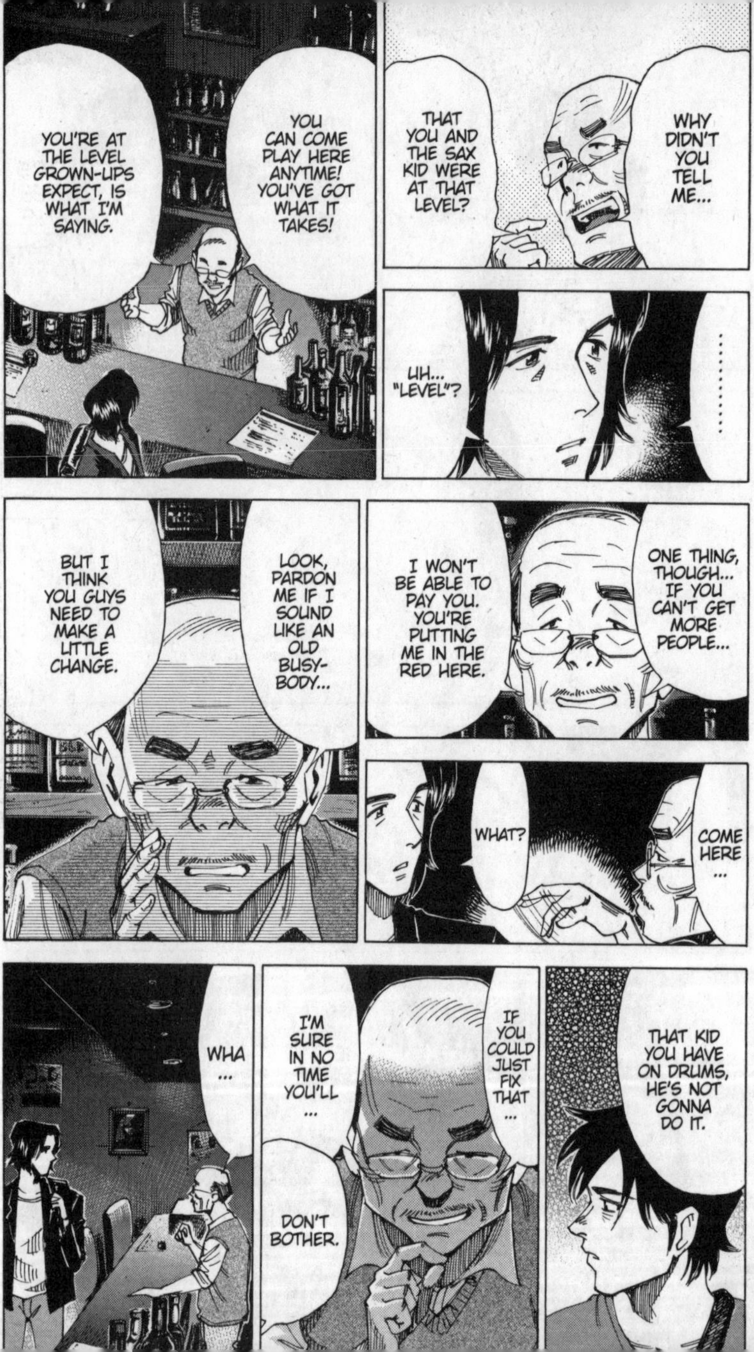
WHY DIDN'T YOU TELL ME...
THAT YOU AND THE SAX KID WERE AT THAT LEVEL?
......
UH... "LEVEL"?
YOU CAN COME PLAY HERE ANYTIME! YOU'VE GOT WHAT IT TAKES!
YOU'RE AT THE LEVEL GROWN-UPS EXPECT, IS WHAT I'M SAYING.
ONE THING, THOUGH... IF YOU CAN'T GET MORE PEOPLE...
I WON'T BE ABLE TO PAY YOU. YOU'RE PUTTING ME IN THE RED HERE.
COME HERE ...
WHAT?
LOOK, PARDON ME IF I SOUND LIKE AN OLD BUSY-BODY...
BUT I THINK YOU GUYS NEED TO MAKE A LITTLE CHANGE.
THAT KID YOU HAVE ON DRUMS, HE'S NOT GONNA DO IT.
IF YOU COULD JUST FIX THAT ...
I'M SURE IN NO TIME YOU'LL ...
DON'T BOTHER.
WHA ...

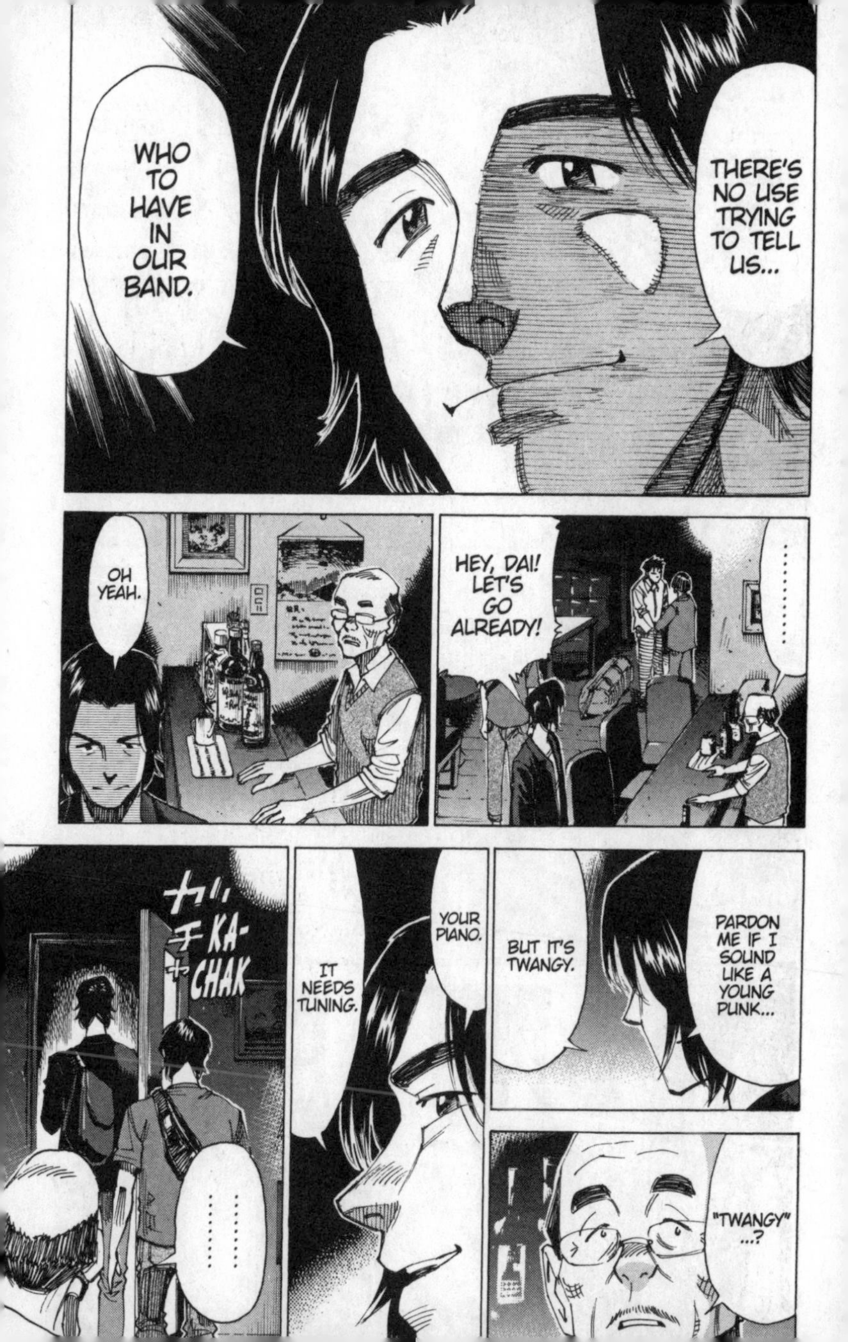
THERE'S NO USE TRYING TO TELL US...
WHO TO HAVE IN OUR BAND.
......
HEY, DAI! LET'S GO ALREADY!
OH YEAH.
PARDON ME IF I SOUND LIKE A YOUNG PUNK...
BUT IT'S TWANGY.
"TWANGY" ...?
YOUR PIANO.
IT NEEDS TUNING.
KA-CHAK
......

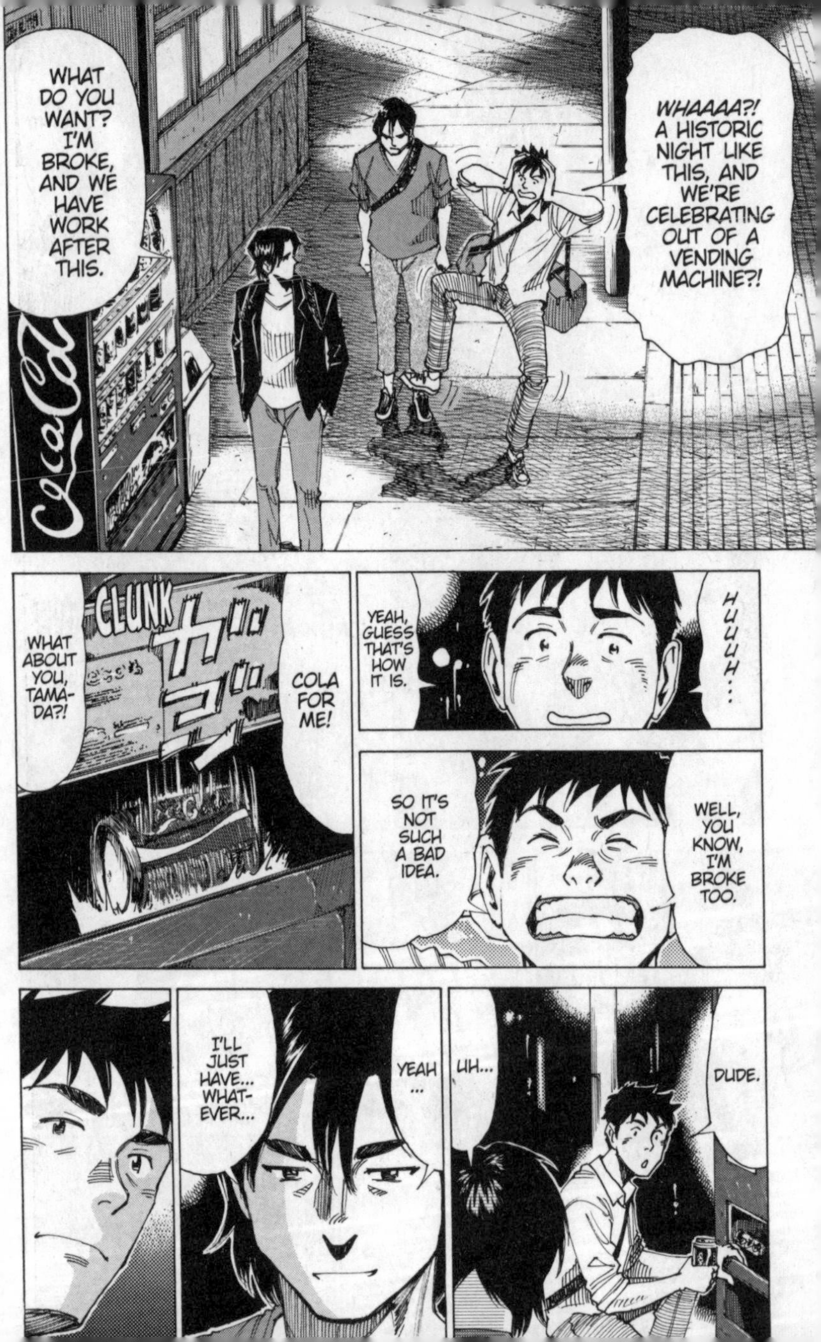
WHAAAA?! A HISTORIC NIGHT LIKE THIS, AND WE'RE CELEBRATING OUT OF A VENDING MACHINE?!
WHAT DO YOU WANT? I'M BROKE, AND WE HAVE WORK AFTER THIS.
HUUUH...
YEAH, GUESS THAT'S HOW IT IS.
WELL, YOU KNOW, I'M BROKE TOO.
SO IT'S NOT SUCH A BAD IDEA.
COLA FOR ME!
CLUNK
WHAT ABOUT YOU, TAMADA?!
DUDE.
UH...
YEAH...
I'LL JUST HAVE... WHAT-EVER...

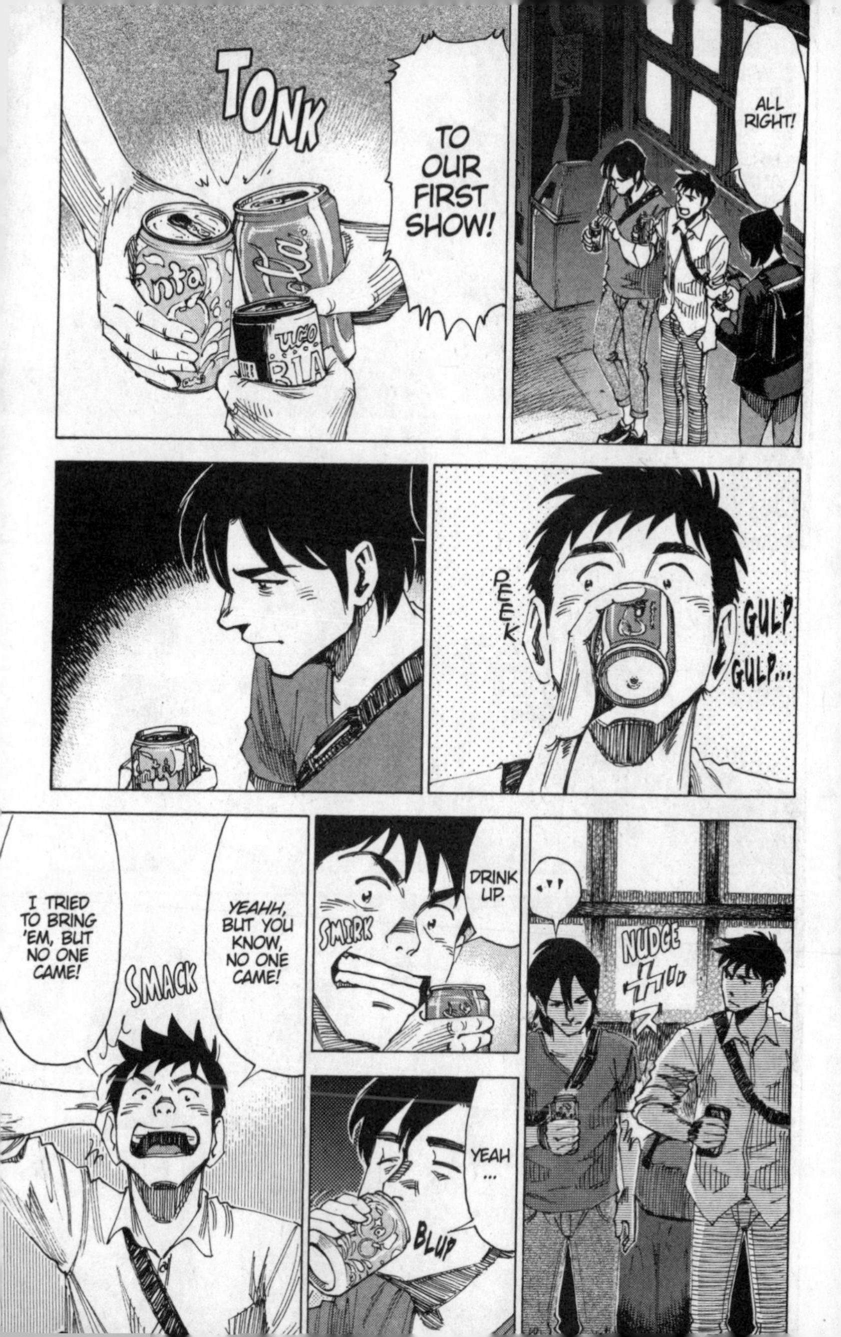
ALL RIGHT!
TONK
TO OUR FIRST SHOW!
PEEK
GULP
GULP...
NUDGE
DRINK UP.
SMIRK
YEAH ...
BLUP
YEAHH, BUT YOU KNOW, NO ONE CAME!
SMACK
I TRIED TO BRING 'EM, BUT NO ONE CAME!

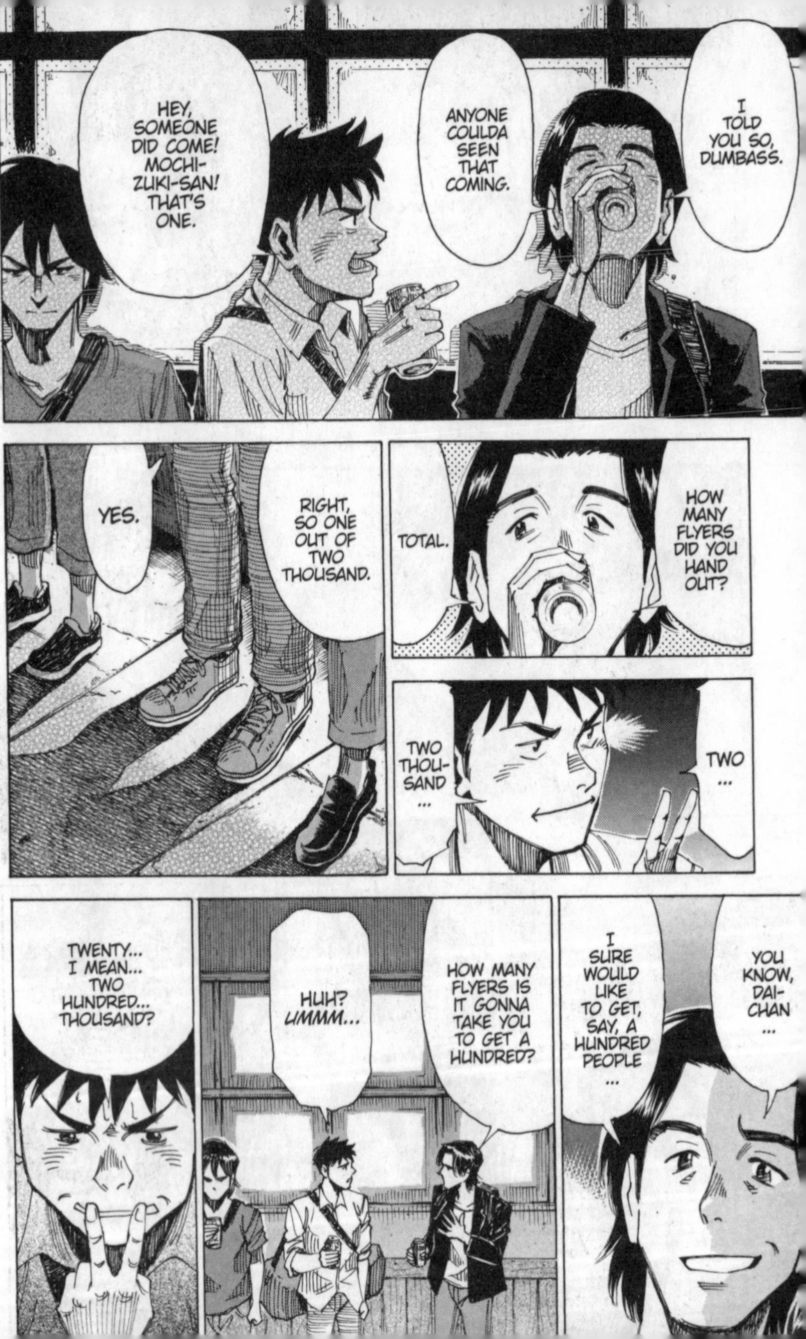
I TOLD YOU SO, DUMBASS.
ANYONE COULDA SEEN THAT COMING.
HEY, SOMEONE DID COME! MOCHI-ZUKI-SAN! THAT'S ONE.
HOW MANY FLYERS DID YOU HAND OUT?
TOTAL.
TWO ...
TWO THOU-SAND ...
RIGHT, SO ONE OUT OF TWO THOUSAND.
YES.
YOU KNOW, DAI-CHAN ...
I SURE WOULD LIKE TO GET, SAY, A HUNDRED PEOPLE ...
HOW MANY FLYERS IS IT GONNA TAKE YOU TO GET A HUNDRED?
HUH? *UMMM...*
TWENTY... I MEAN... TWO HUNDRED... THOUSAND?

NGH...

DO YOU SEE NOW HOW WRONG YOUR APPROACH IS?

B-BUT...

THE WAY YOU'RE DOING IT IS ALL BACKWARDS!

YOU GET WHAT I'M SAYING, DAI-CHAN?

I MEAN...

ALL YOU THINK ABOUT IS WHAT YOU WANT TO DO! YOU WANT TO PUT ON A SHOW, YOU WANT TO HAND OUT FLYERS!

DON'T GIVE ME "BUT," DAI! YOU KNOW WHAT YOUR PROBLEM IS?!

?

?

NGH...

SORRY.

IT'S NOT GONNA WORK LIKE THIS! I CAN'T TRUST YOU WITH THIS CRAP! YOU HEAR ME?!

IS TRASH.

I KNOW MY DRUM-MING...

I... I'M SORRY.

I KNOW I'M DRAG-GING YOU DOWN...

THAT DOESN'T EVEN COVER IT...

I MEAN...

GOTTA GET OUT.

I...

TAMA-DA...

HEY...

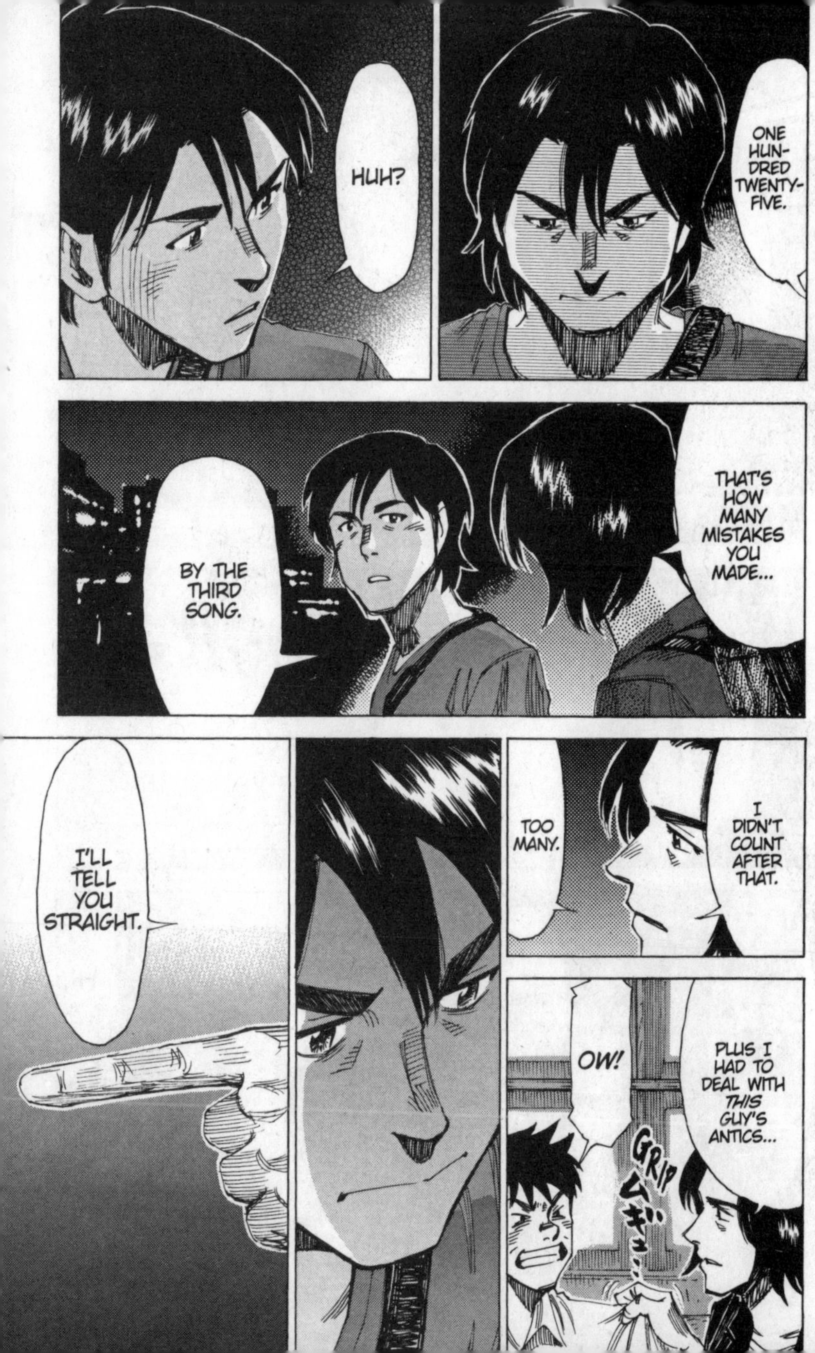
ONE HUNDRED TWENTY-FIVE.
HUH?
THAT'S HOW MANY MISTAKES YOU MADE...
BY THE THIRD SONG.
I DIDN'T COUNT AFTER THAT.
TOO MANY.
PLUS I HAD TO DEAL WITH *THIS* GUY'S ANTICS...
OW!
GRIP
I'LL TELL YOU STRAIGHT.

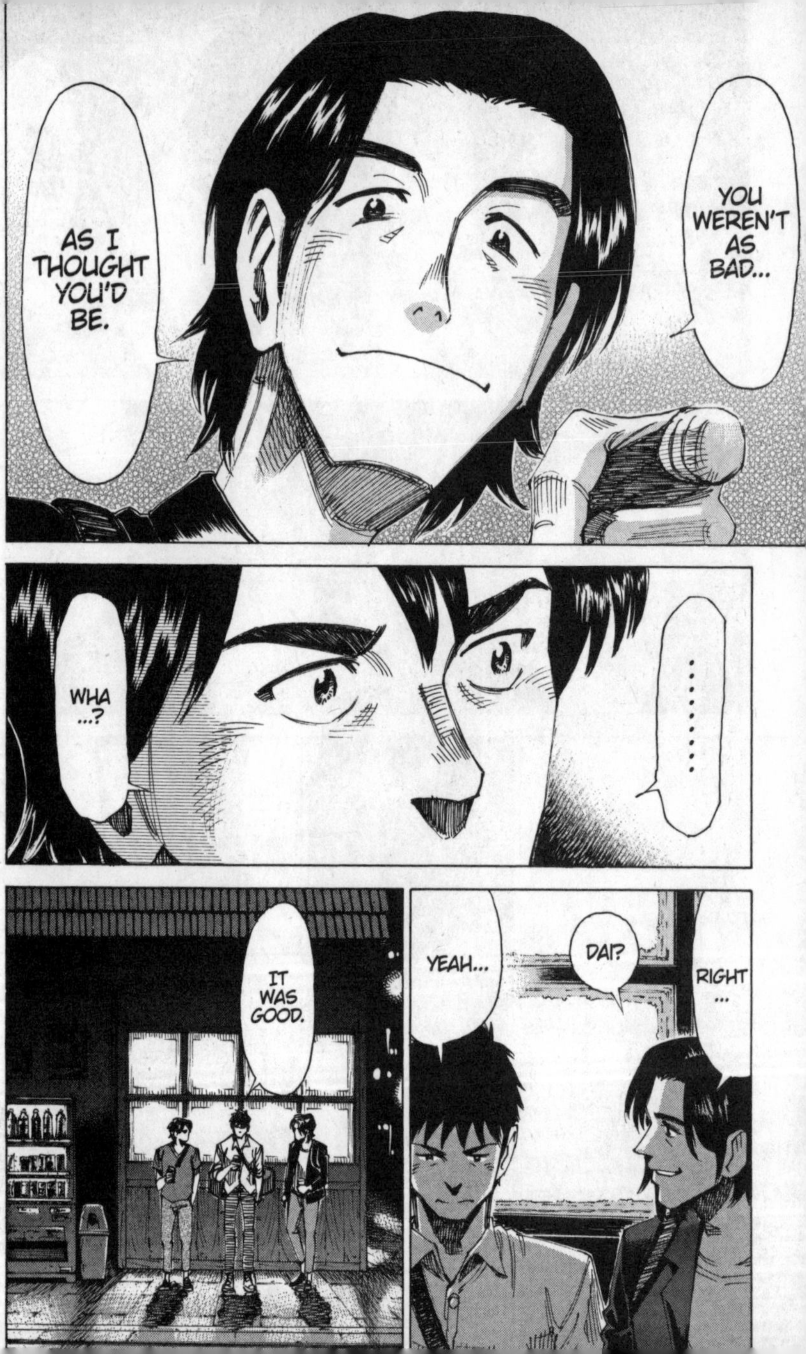
YOU WEREN'T AS BAD...
AS I THOUGHT YOU'D BE.
......
WHA...?
RIGHT...
DAI?
YEAH...
IT WAS GOOD.

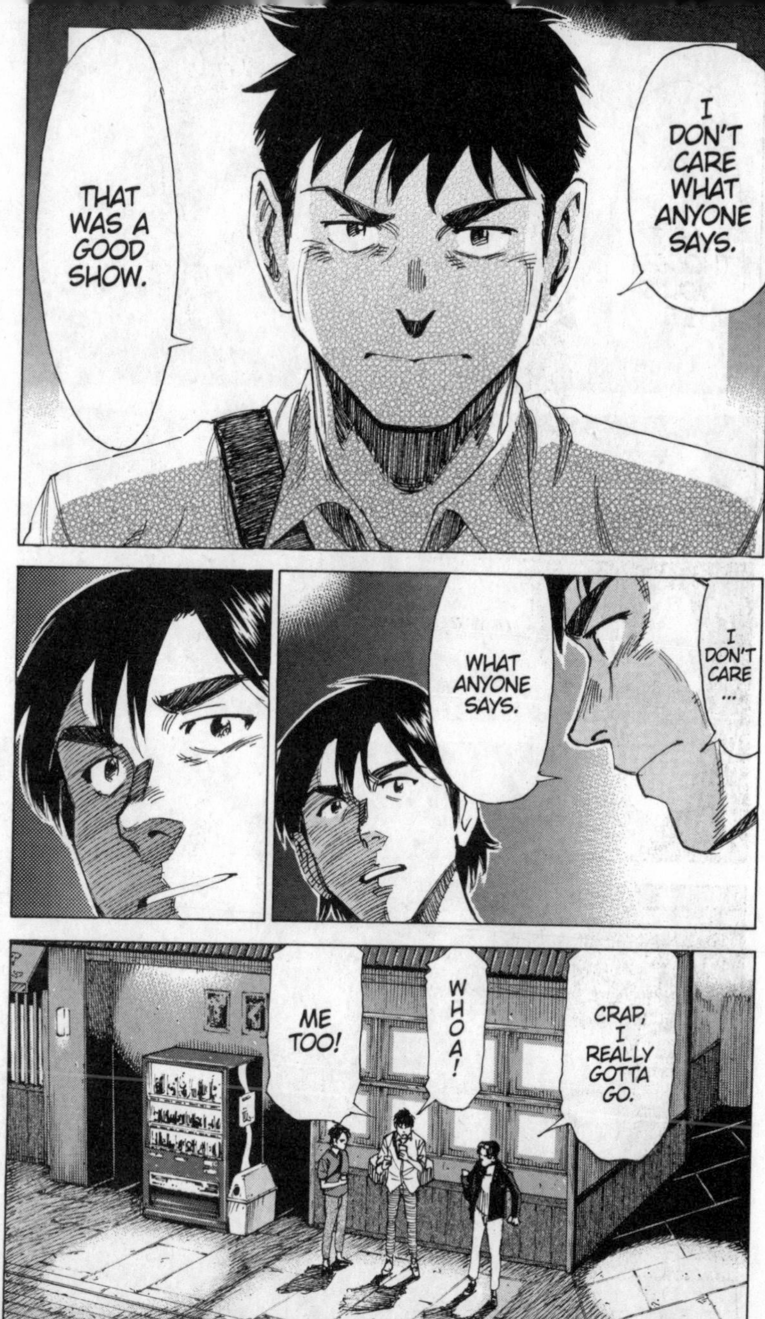
I DON'T CARE WHAT ANYONE SAYS.
THAT WAS A GOOD SHOW.
I DON'T CARE ...
WHAT ANYONE SAYS.
CRAP, I REALLY GOTTA GO.
WHOA!
ME TOO!

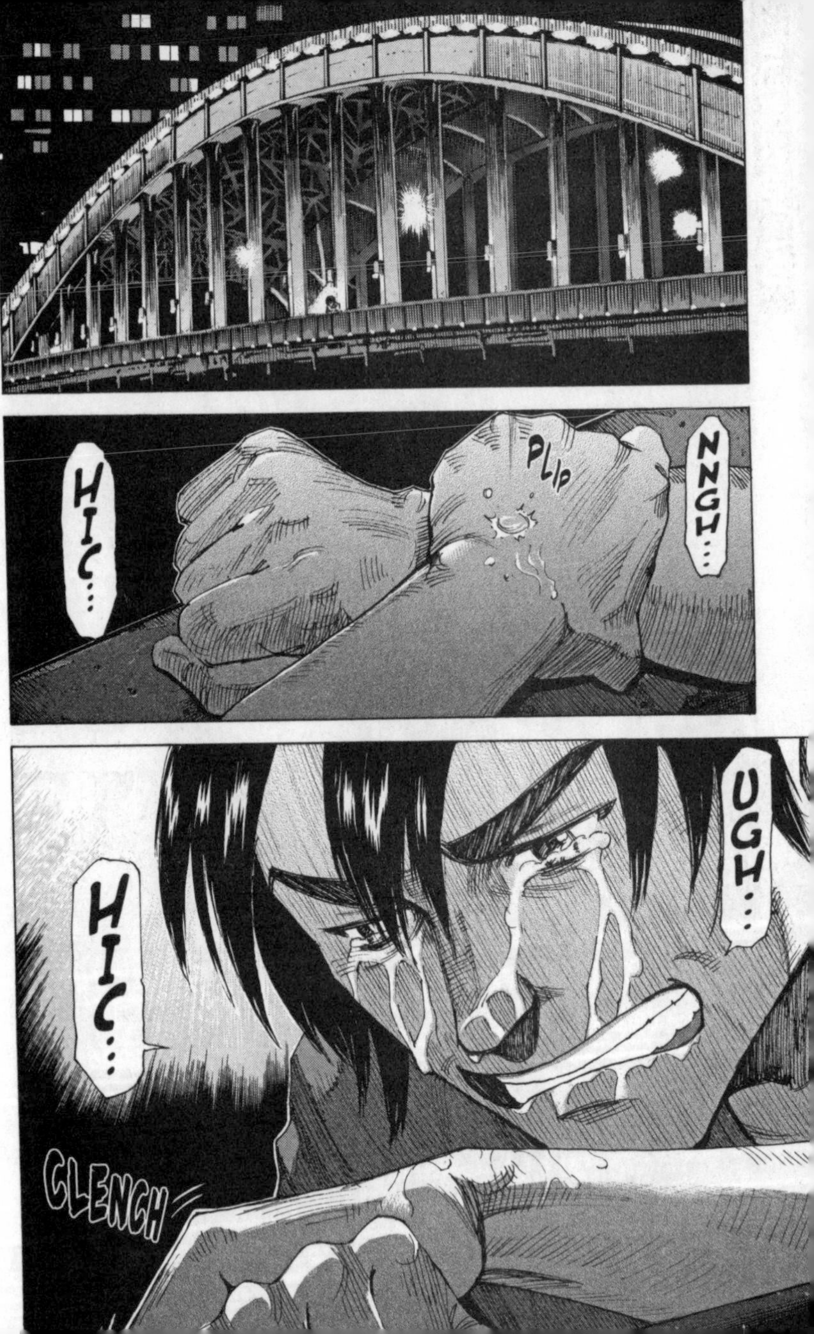
NNGH...
PLIP
HIC...
UGH...
HIC...
CLENCH

47 THE SONG IS YOU

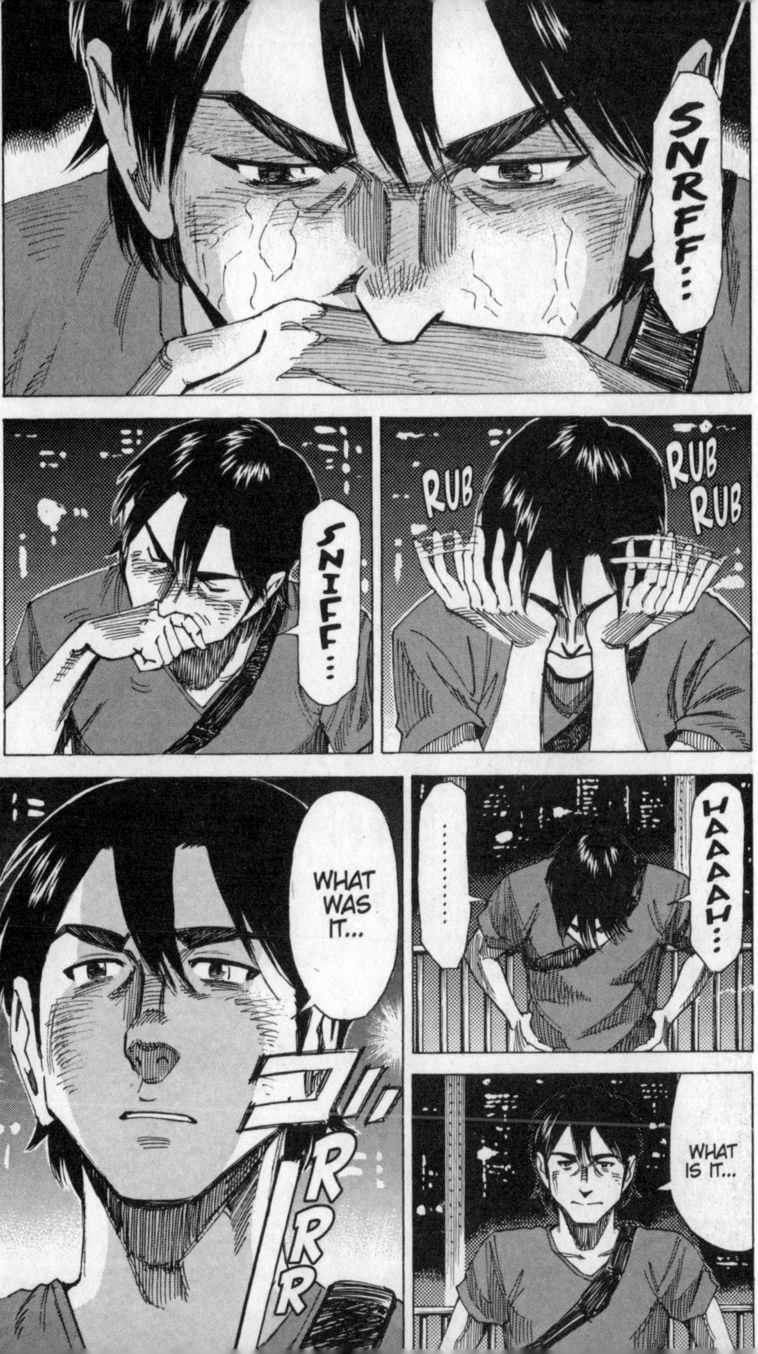
SNRFF...
RUB
RUB
RUB
SNIFF...
HAAAAH...
......
WHAT IS IT...
WHAT WAS IT...
RRR

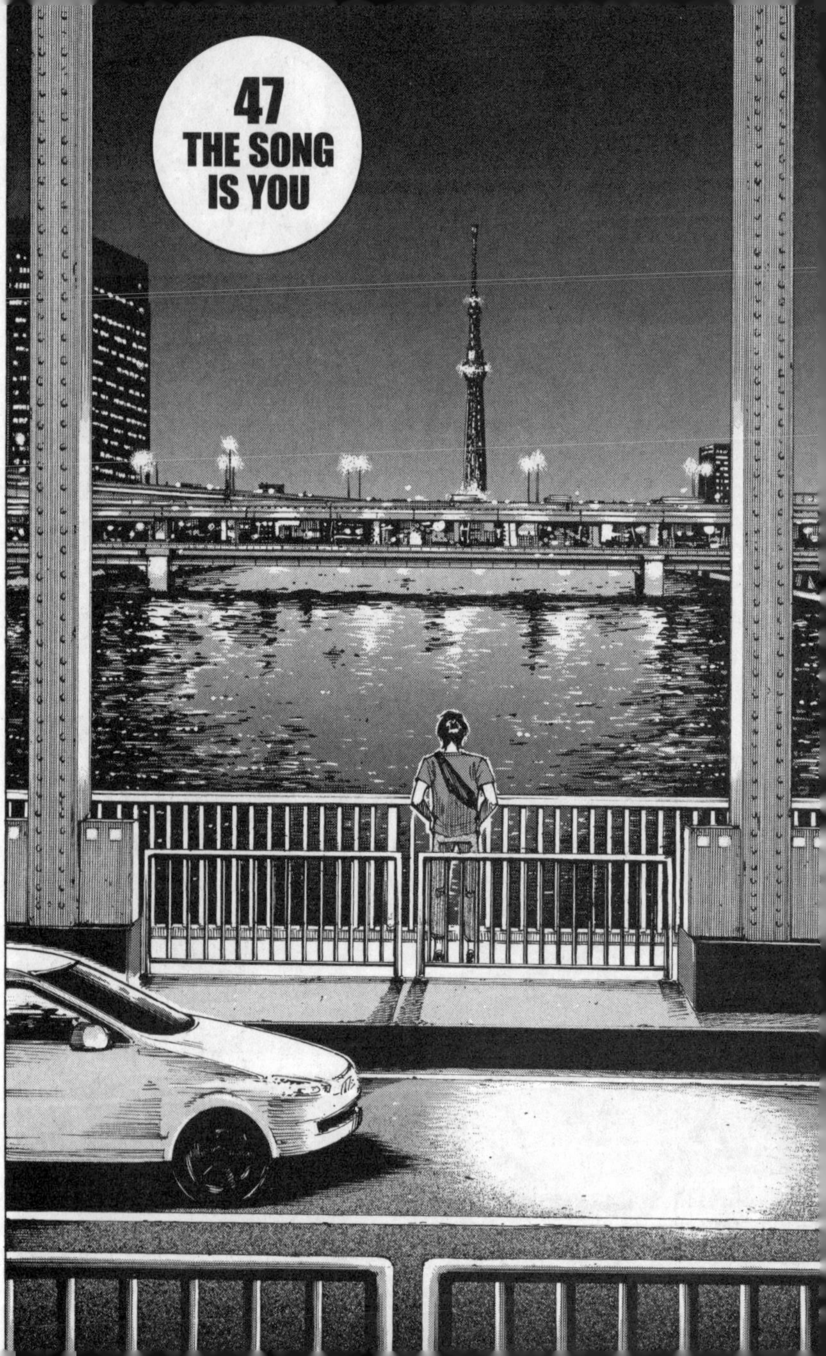
47
THE SONG IS YOU

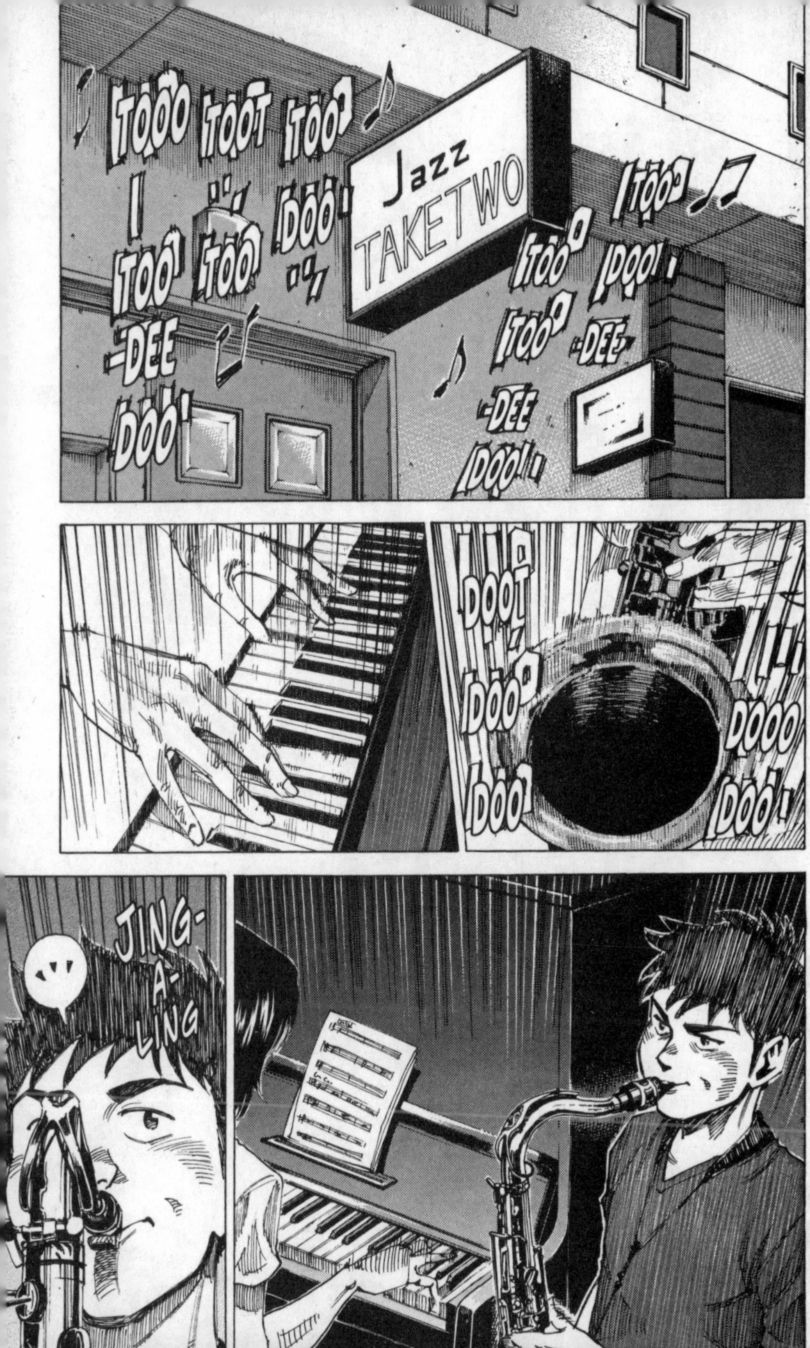
TOOO
TOOO
DOO
TOOO
-DEE
-DEE
DOO
Jazz
TAKETWO
TOOO TOOT TOOO
TOO TOO DOO
-DEE
DOO
DOOO
DOO
DOOT
DOO
DOO
JING-A-LING
...

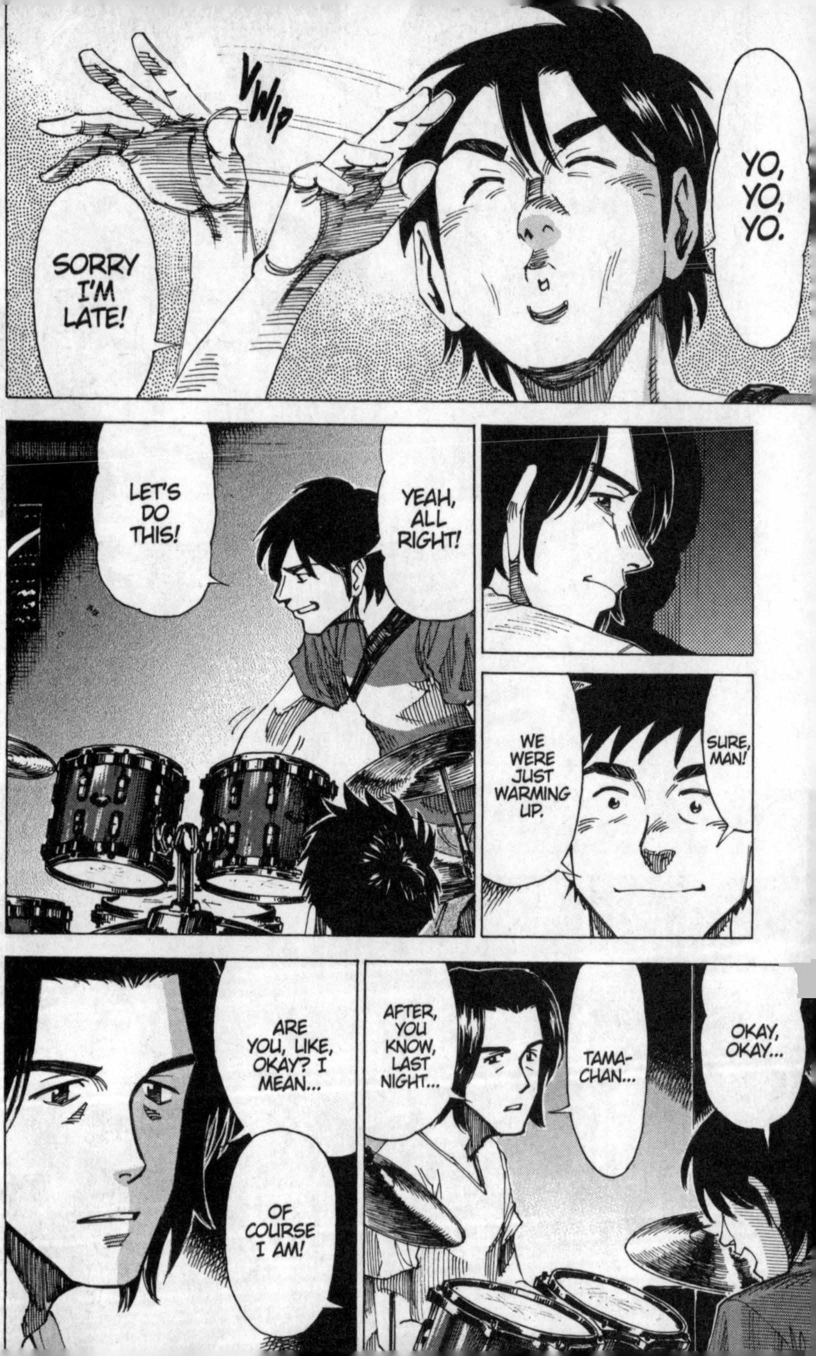
YO, YO, YO.
VWIP
SORRY I'M LATE!
SURE, MAN!
WE WERE JUST WARMING UP.
YEAH, ALL RIGHT!
LET'S DO THIS!
OKAY, OKAY...
TAMA-CHAN...
AFTER, YOU KNOW, LAST NIGHT...
ARE YOU, LIKE, OKAY? I MEAN...
OF COURSE I AM!

YEAH!

GOLD-EN!

I'M GOLD-EN!

CHIK

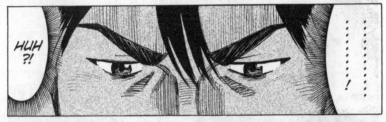

HUH ?!

！

DOOT

DOOO

TOO

TOOOO

BOOO

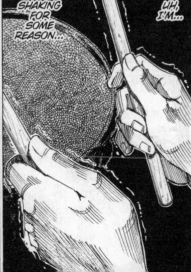

SHAKING FOR SOME REASON...

UH, I'M...

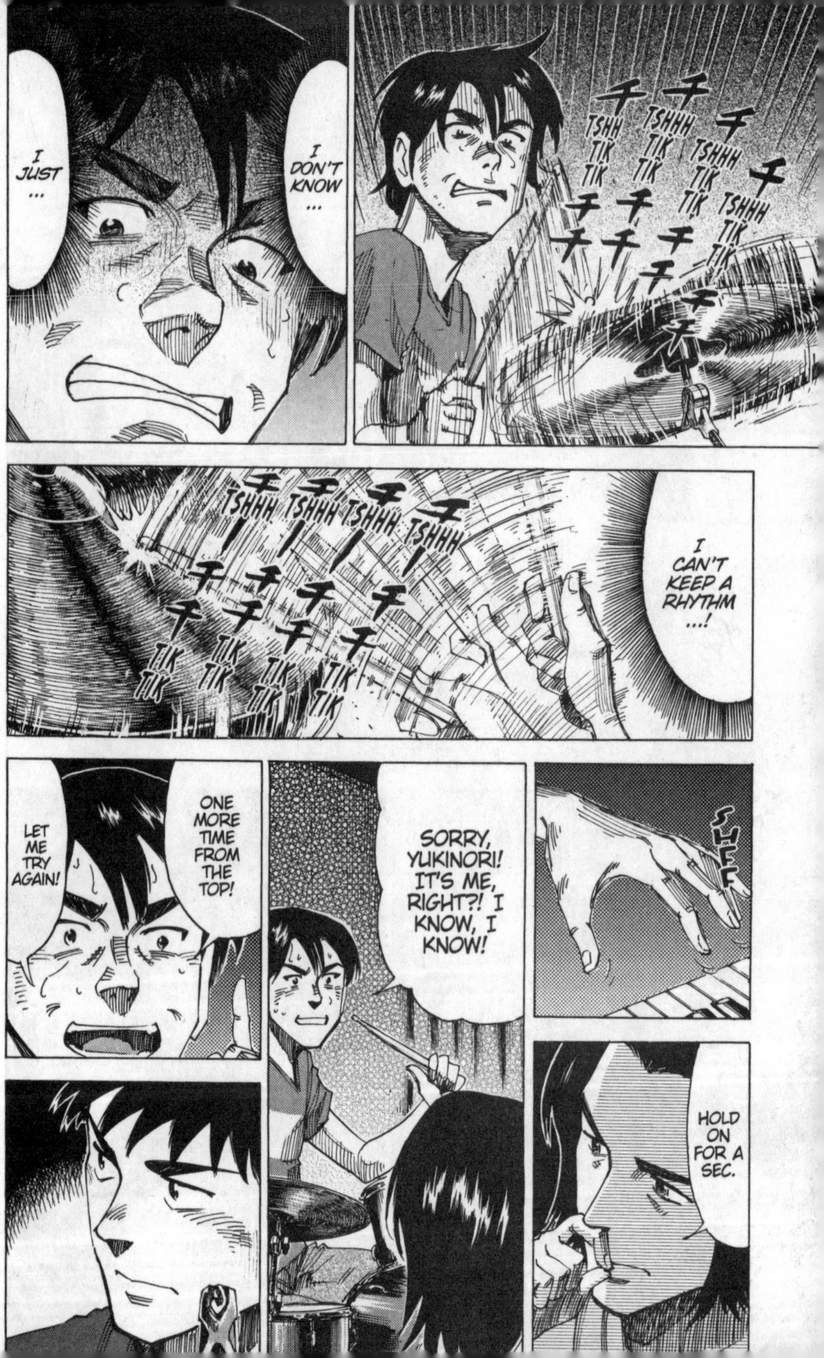
チ TSHH TIK TIK
チ TSHHH TIK TIK
チ TSHHH TIK TIK
I DON'T KNOW ...
I JUST ...
I CAN'T KEEP A RHYTHM ...!
チ TSHHH
チ TIK TIK
SHFF
HOLD ON FOR A SEC.
SORRY, YUKINORI! IT'S ME, RIGHT?! I KNOW, I KNOW!
ONE MORE TIME FROM THE TOP!
LET ME TRY AGAIN!

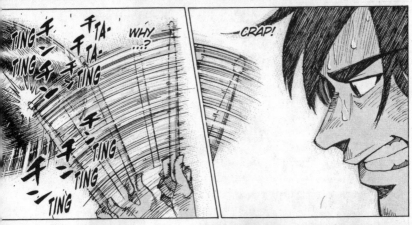

TING
TING
千
千
TA-
TA-
TING

TING
千
千
千
TING
TING

TING

WHY
...?

—CRAP!

CELL PHONE... GIMME A MINUTE... I'LL GO GET IT.

OH...I... FORGOT MY...

......

TAMA-DA.

HOLD ON...

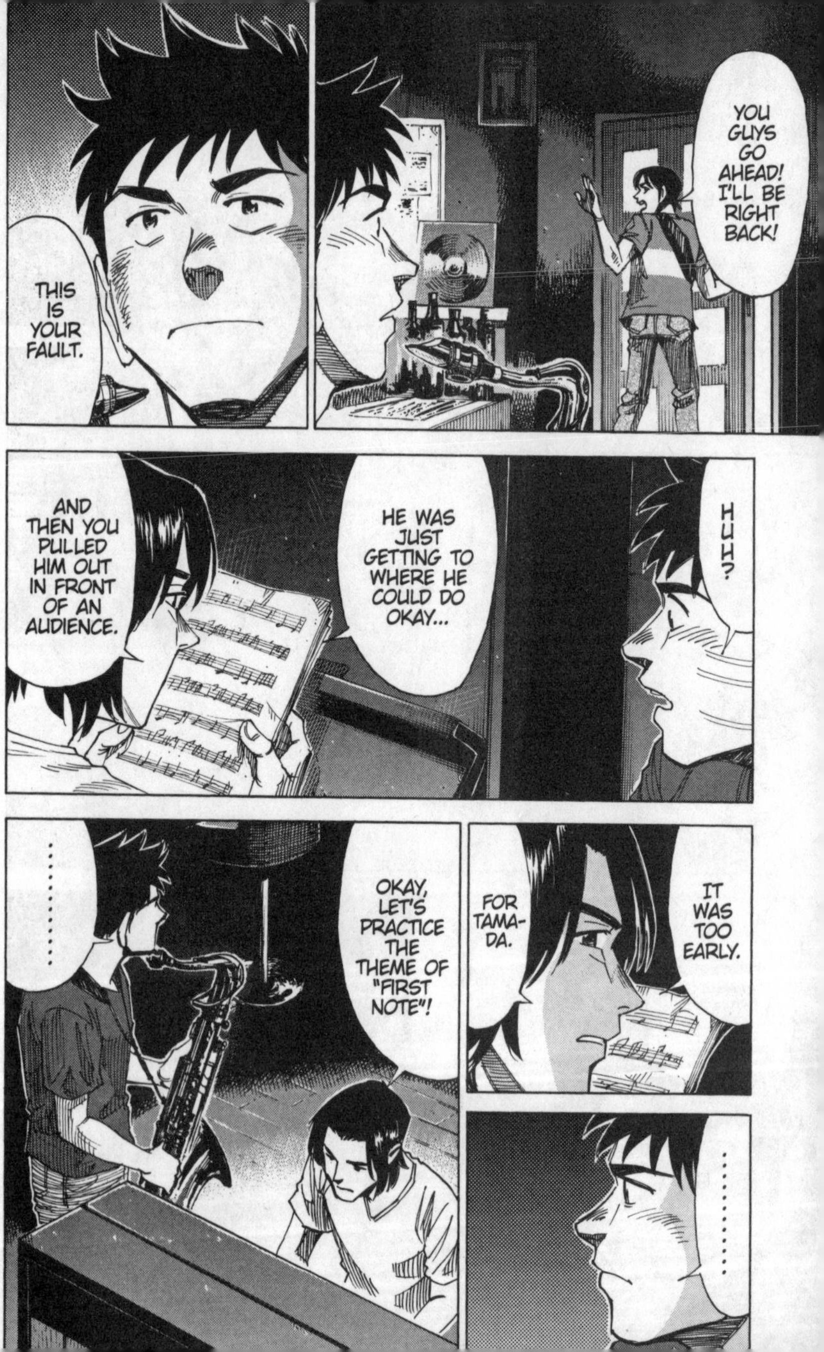
YOU GUYS GO AHEAD! I'LL BE RIGHT BACK!
THIS IS YOUR FAULT.
HUH?
HE WAS JUST GETTING TO WHERE HE COULD DO OKAY...
AND THEN YOU PULLED HIM OUT IN FRONT OF AN AUDIENCE.
IT WAS TOO EARLY.
FOR TAMADA.
......
OKAY, LET'S PRACTICE THE THEME OF "FIRST NOTE"!
......

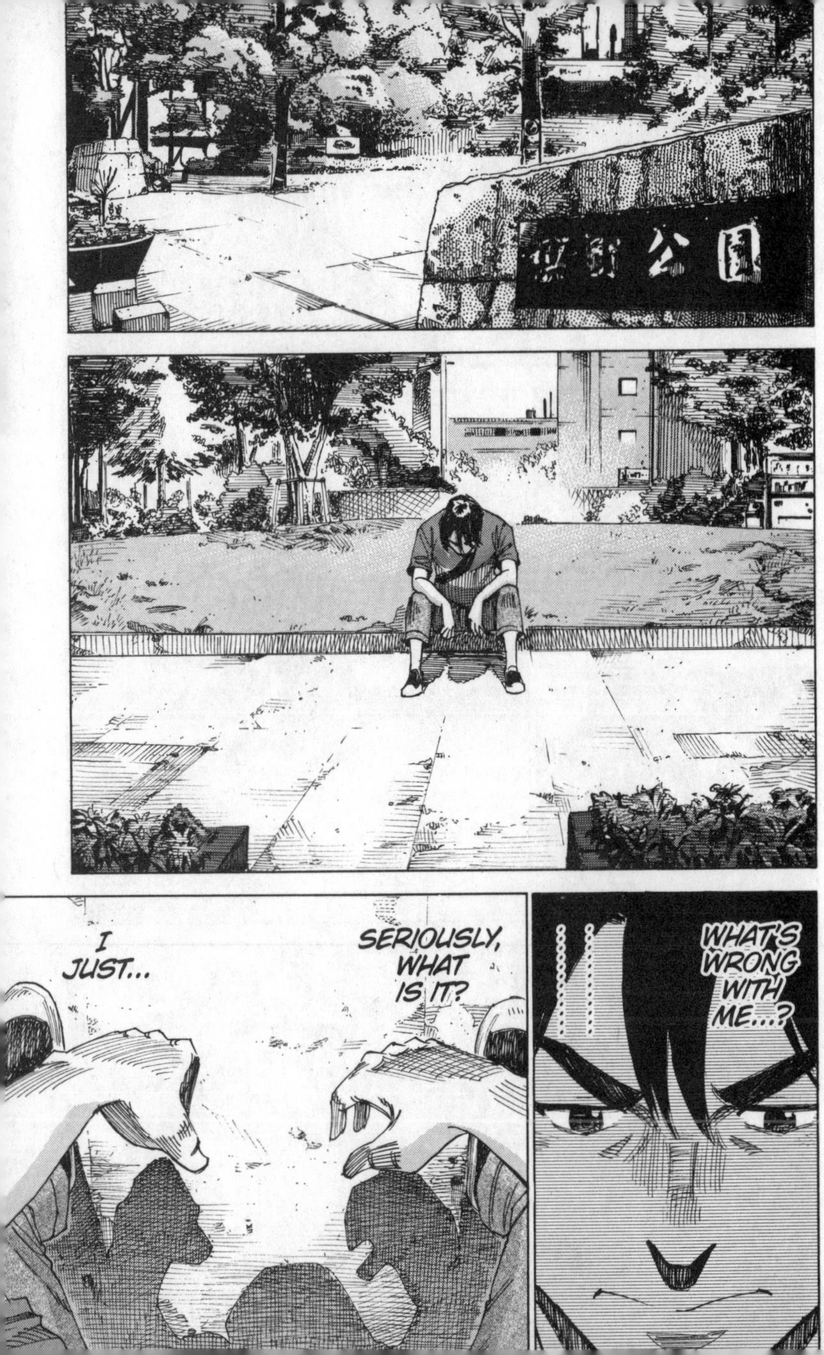
WHAT'S WRONG WITH ME...?
SERIOUSLY, WHAT IS IT?
I JUST...

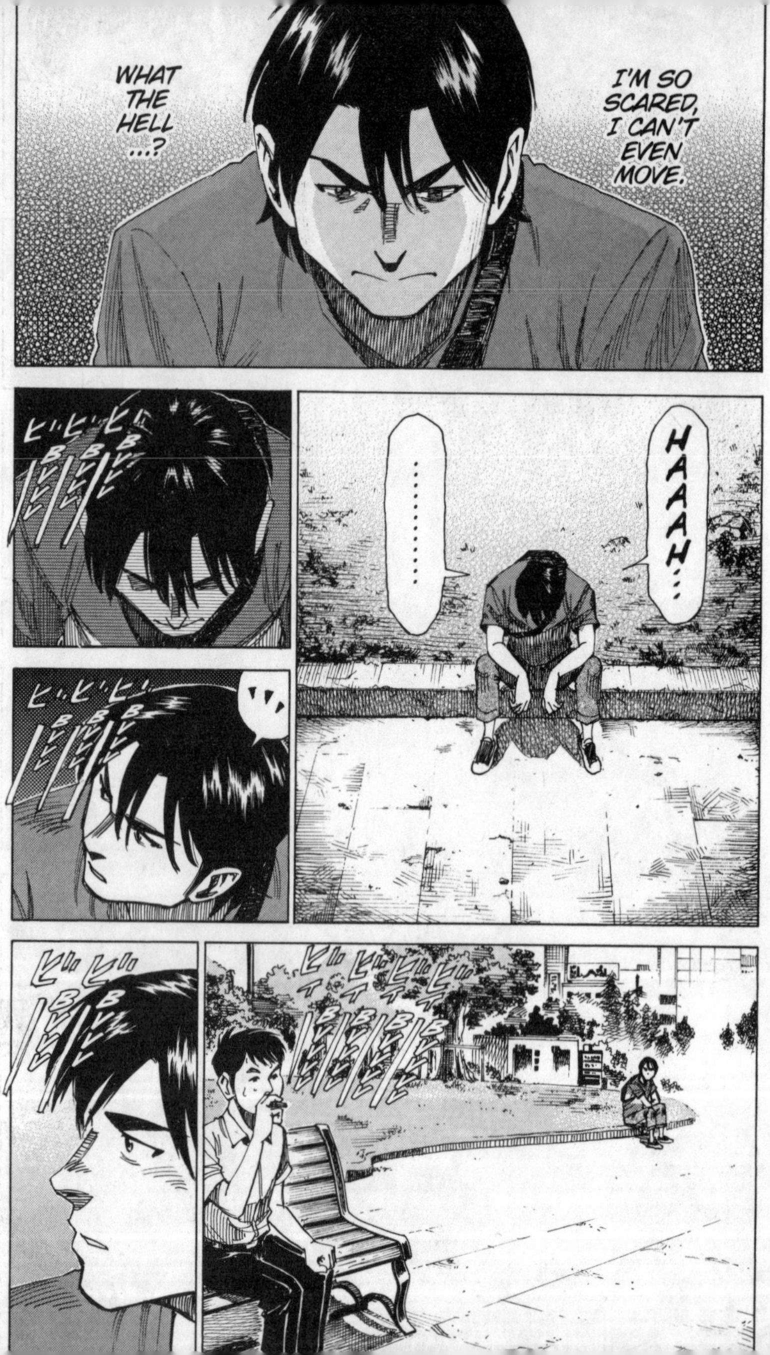
I'M SO SCARED, I CAN'T EVEN MOVE.
WHAT THE HELL ...?
HAAAAH...
......
BVVVV
BVVVV
BVVVV
BVVVV

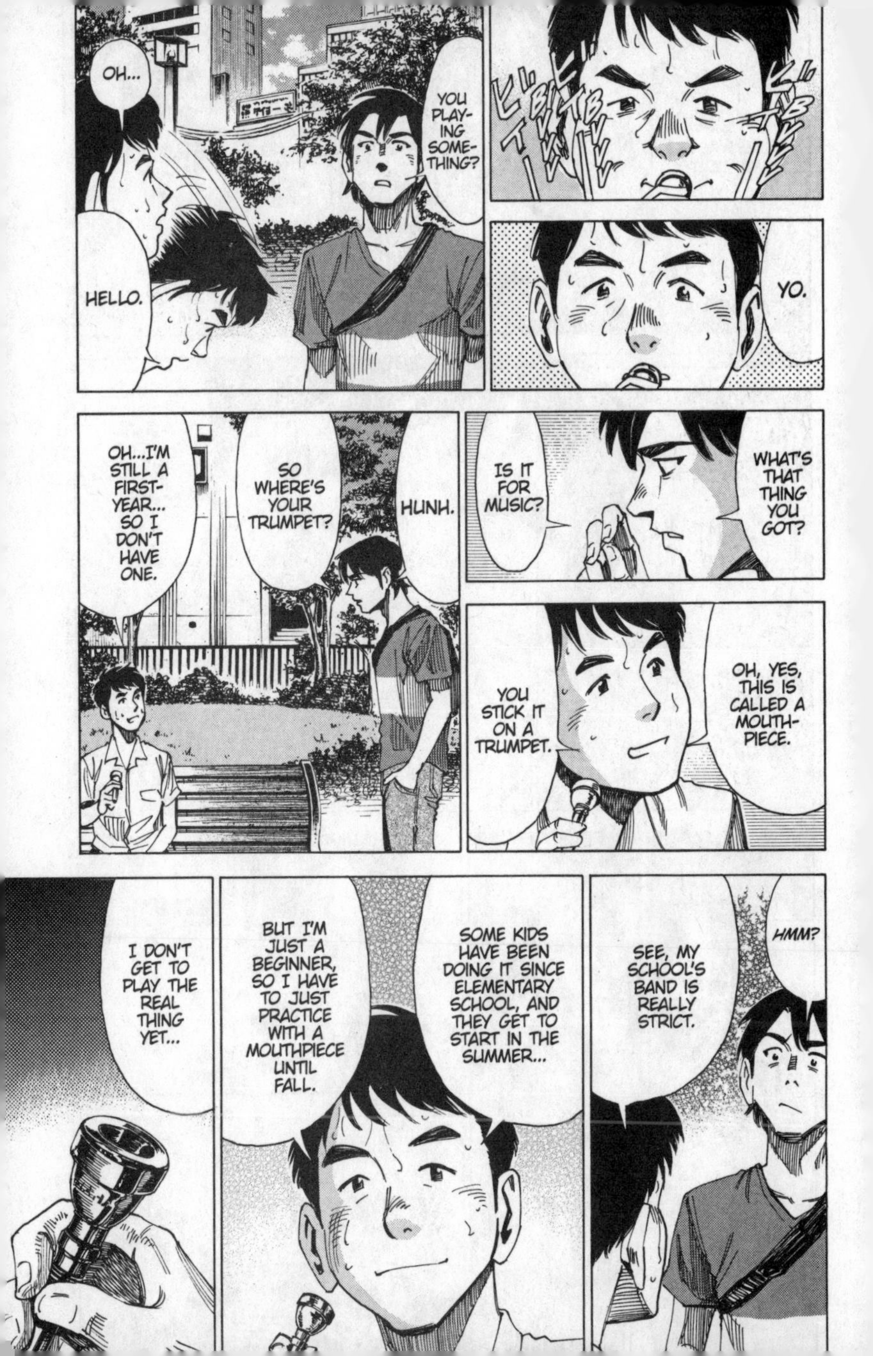
YO.
YOU PLAYING SOMETHING?
OH...
HELLO.
WHAT'S THAT THING YOU GOT?
IS IT FOR MUSIC?
OH, YES, THIS IS CALLED A MOUTHPIECE.
YOU STICK IT ON A TRUMPET.
HUNH.
SO WHERE'S YOUR TRUMPET?
OH...I'M STILL A FIRST-YEAR... SO I DON'T HAVE ONE.
HMM?
SEE, MY SCHOOL'S BAND IS REALLY STRICT.
SOME KIDS HAVE BEEN DOING IT SINCE ELEMENTARY SCHOOL, AND THEY GET TO START IN THE SUMMER...
BUT I'M JUST A BEGINNER, SO I HAVE TO JUST PRACTICE WITH A MOUTHPIECE UNTIL FALL.
I DON'T GET TO PLAY THE REAL THING YET...

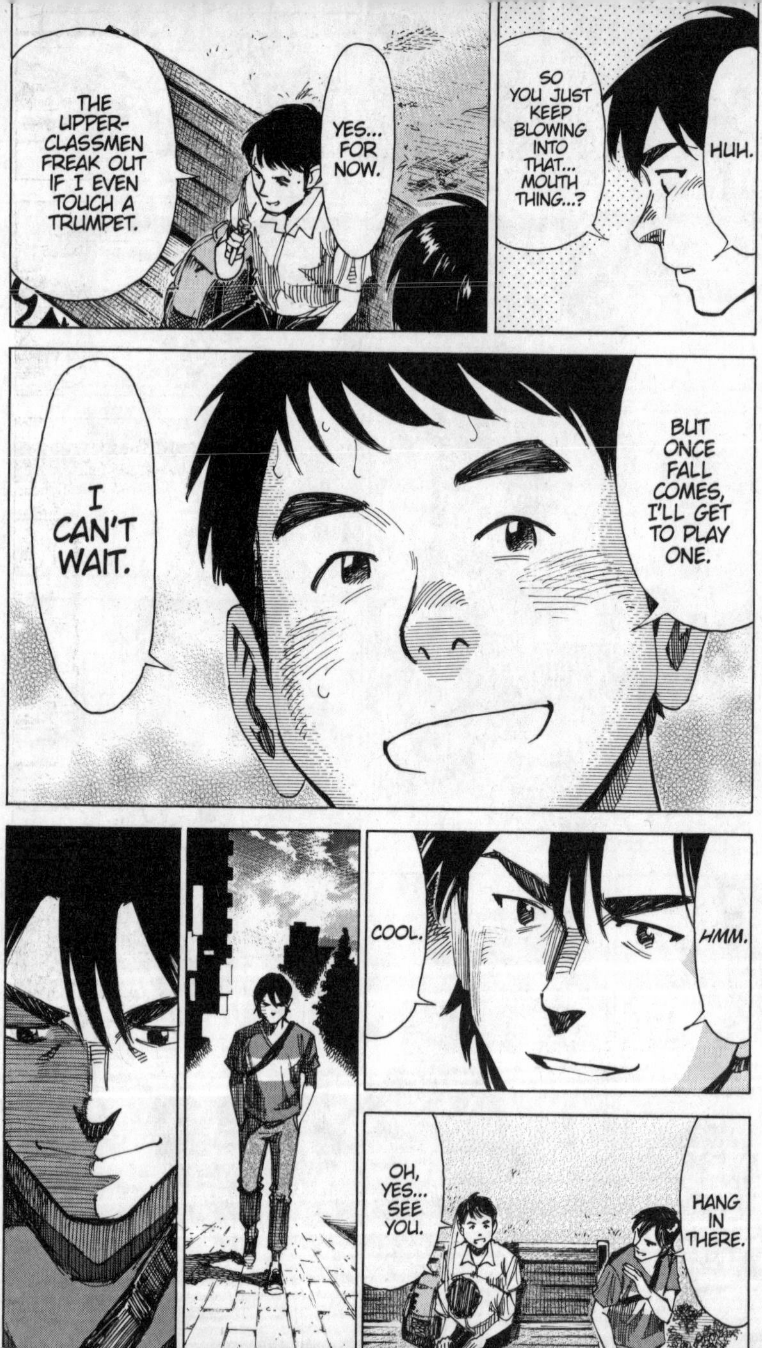
HUH.
SO YOU JUST KEEP BLOWING INTO THAT... MOUTH THING...?
YES... FOR NOW.
THE UPPER-CLASSMEN FREAK OUT IF I EVEN TOUCH A TRUMPET.
BUT ONCE FALL COMES, I'LL GET TO PLAY ONE.
I CAN'T WAIT.
HMM.
COOL.
HANG IN THERE.
OH, YES... SEE YOU.

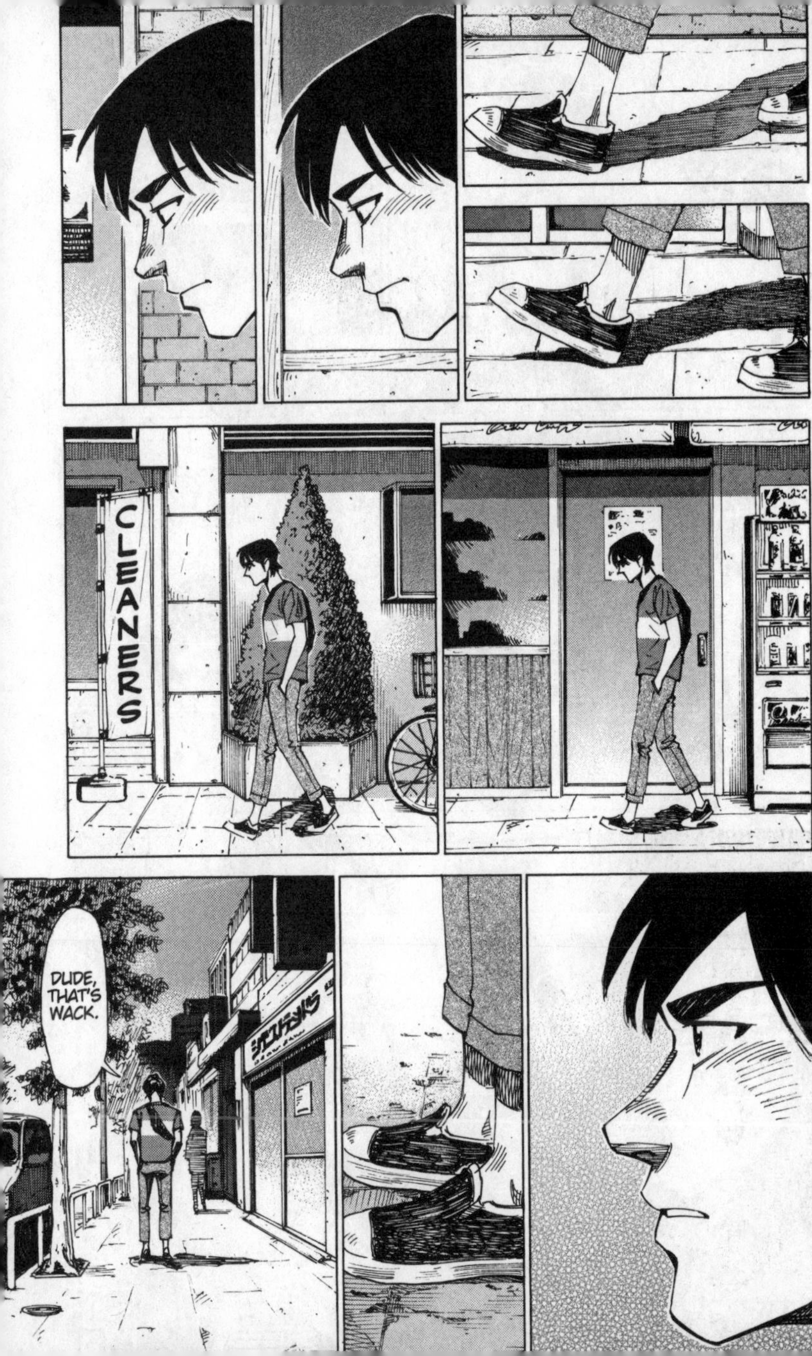
CLEANERS
DUDE, THAT'S WACK.

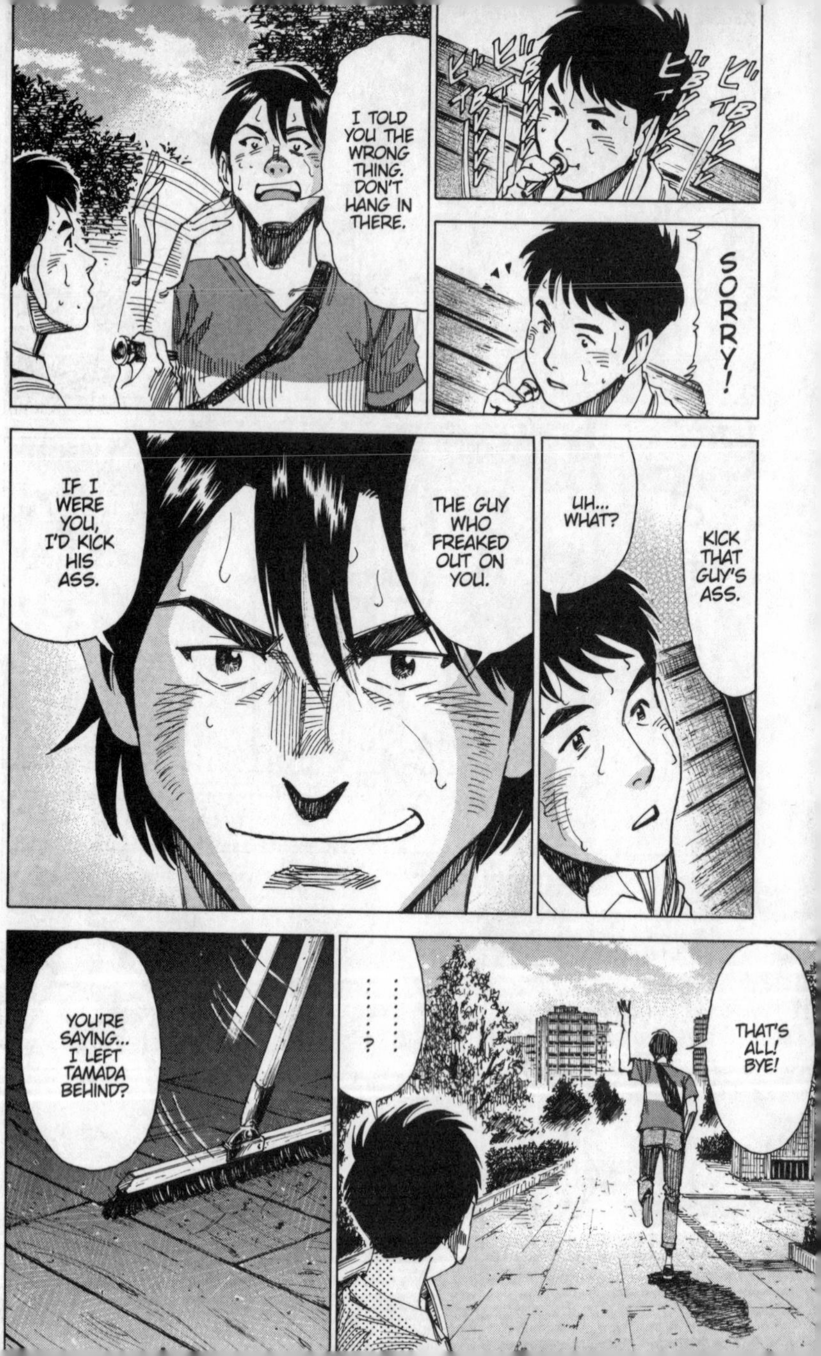
SORRY!
I TOLD YOU THE WRONG THING. DON'T HANG IN THERE.
KICK THAT GUY'S ASS.
UH... WHAT?
THE GUY WHO FREAKED OUT ON YOU.
IF I WERE YOU, I'D KICK HIS ASS.
THAT'S ALL! BYE!
......?
YOU'RE SAYING... I LEFT TAMADA BEHIND?

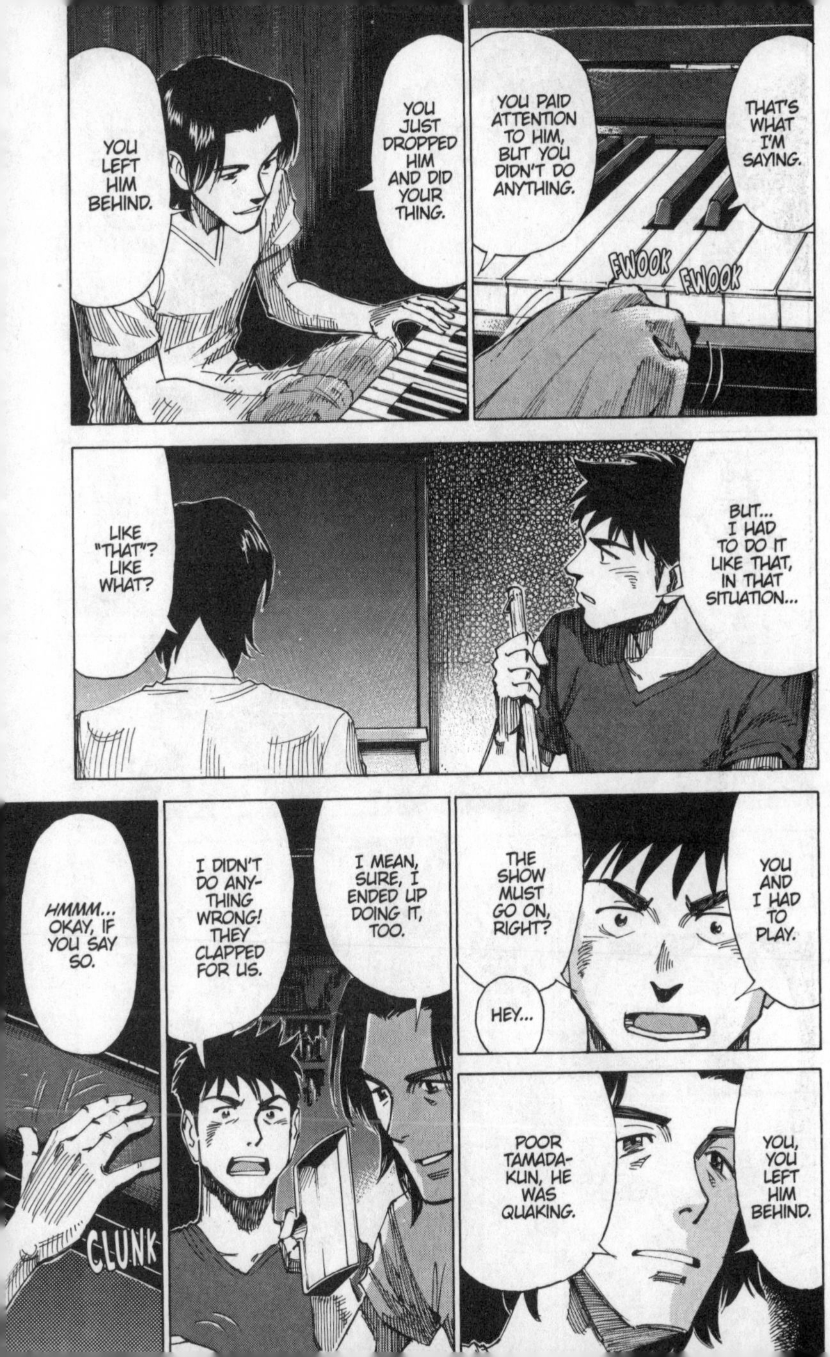
THAT'S WHAT I'M SAYING.
YOU PAID ATTENTION TO HIM, BUT YOU DIDN'T DO ANYTHING.
FWOOK
FWOOK
YOU JUST DROPPED HIM AND DID YOUR THING.
YOU LEFT HIM BEHIND.
BUT... I HAD TO DO IT LIKE THAT, IN THAT SITUATION...
LIKE "THAT"? LIKE WHAT?
YOU AND I HAD TO PLAY.
THE SHOW MUST GO ON, RIGHT?
HEY...
YOU, YOU LEFT HIM BEHIND.
POOR TAMADA-KUN, HE WAS QUAKING.
I MEAN, SURE, I ENDED UP DOING IT, TOO.
I DIDN'T DO ANYTHING WRONG! THEY CLAPPED FOR US.
HMMM... OKAY, IF YOU SAY SO.
CLUNK

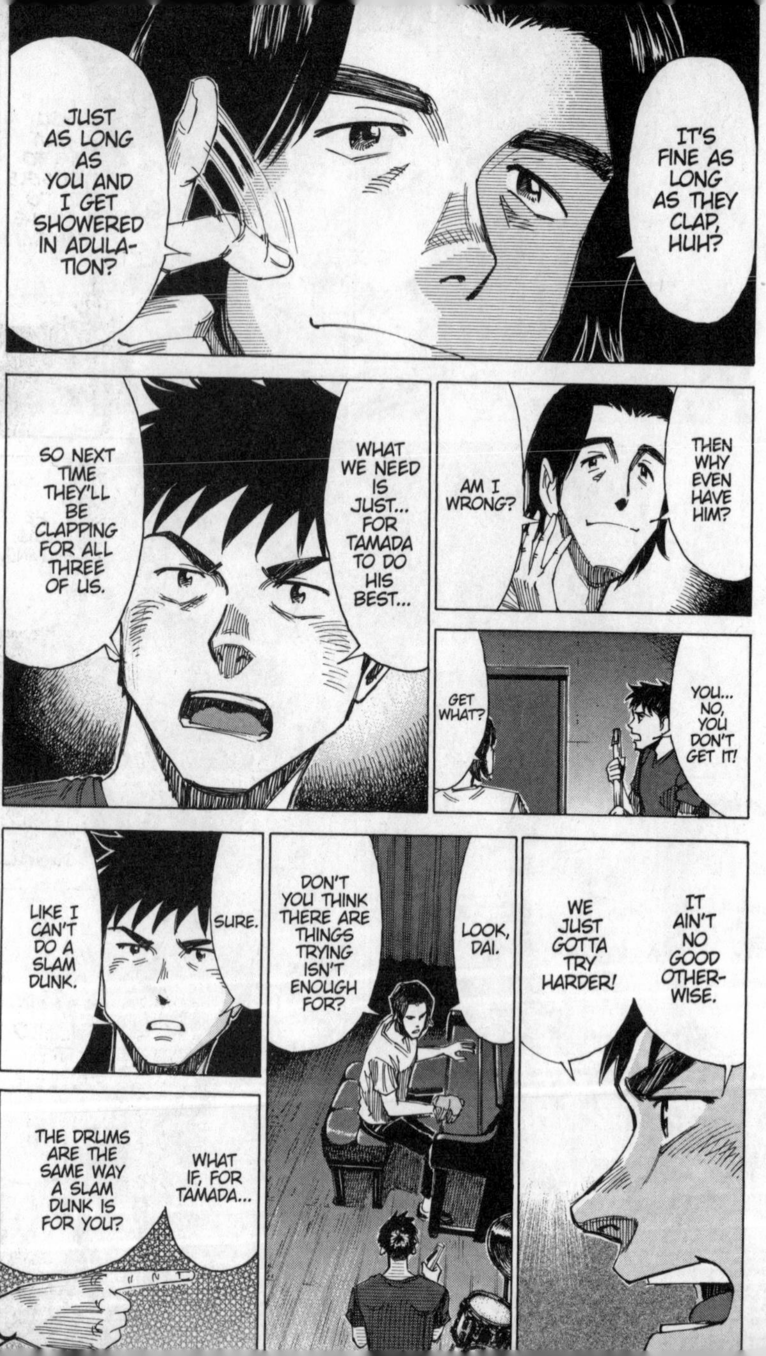
IT'S FINE AS LONG AS THEY CLAP, HUH?
JUST AS LONG AS YOU AND I GET SHOWERED IN ADULATION?
THEN WHY EVEN HAVE HIM?
AM I WRONG?
YOU... NO, YOU DON'T GET IT!
GET WHAT?
WHAT WE NEED IS JUST... FOR TAMADA TO DO HIS BEST...
SO NEXT TIME THEY'LL BE CLAPPING FOR ALL THREE OF US.
IT AIN'T NO GOOD OTHER-WISE.
WE JUST GOTTA TRY HARDER!
LOOK, DAI.
DON'T YOU THINK THERE ARE THINGS TRYING ISN'T ENOUGH FOR?
SURE.
LIKE I CAN'T DO A SLAM DUNK.
WHAT IF, FOR TAMADA...
THE DRUMS ARE THE SAME WAY A SLAM DUNK IS FOR YOU?

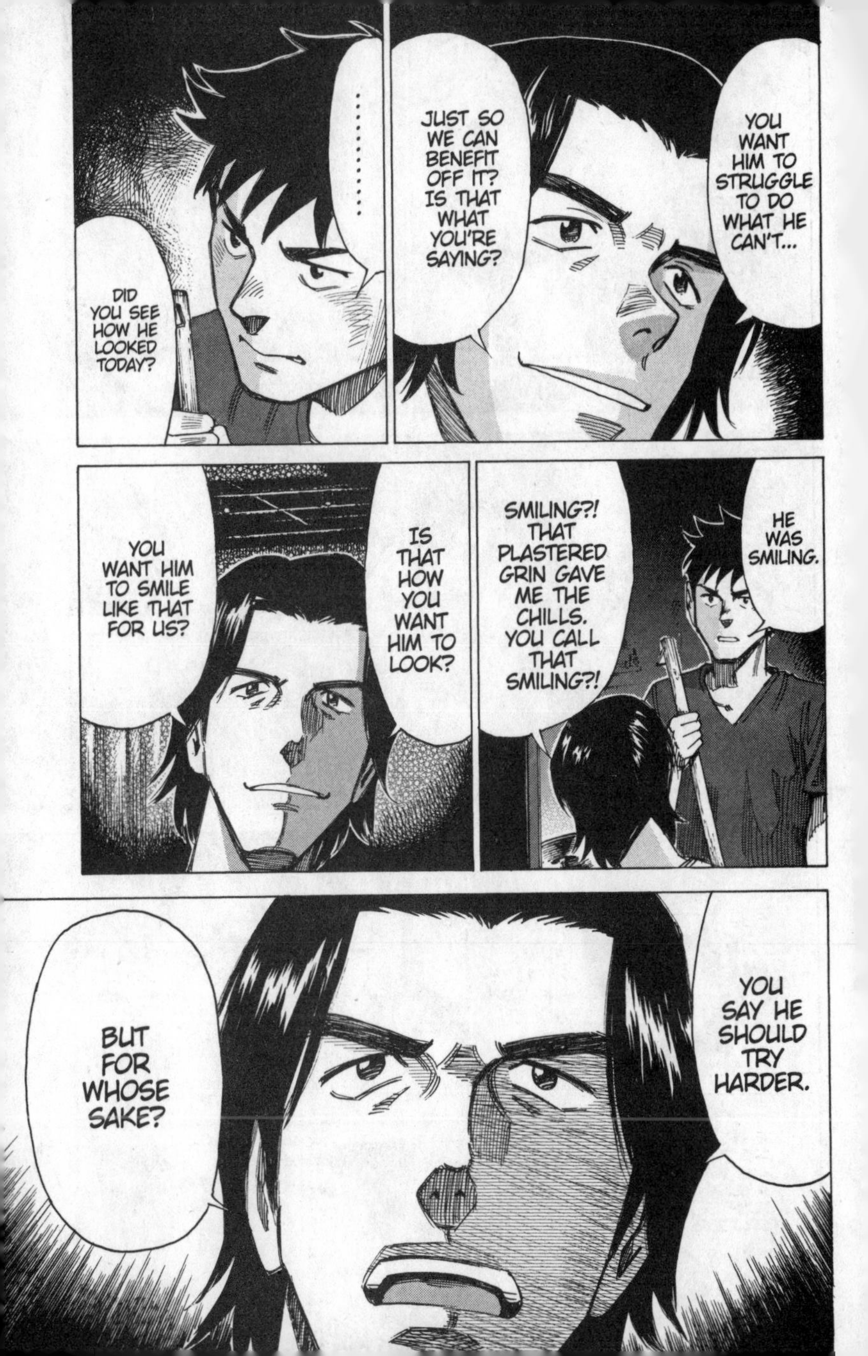
YOU WANT HIM TO STRUGGLE TO DO WHAT HE CAN'T...
JUST SO WE CAN BENEFIT OFF IT? IS THAT WHAT YOU'RE SAYING?
......
DID YOU SEE HOW HE LOOKED TODAY?
HE WAS SMILING.
SMILING?! THAT PLASTERED GRIN GAVE ME THE CHILLS. YOU CALL THAT SMILING?!
IS THAT HOW YOU WANT HIM TO LOOK?
YOU WANT HIM TO SMILE LIKE THAT FOR US?
YOU SAY HE SHOULD TRY HARDER.
BUT FOR WHOSE SAKE?

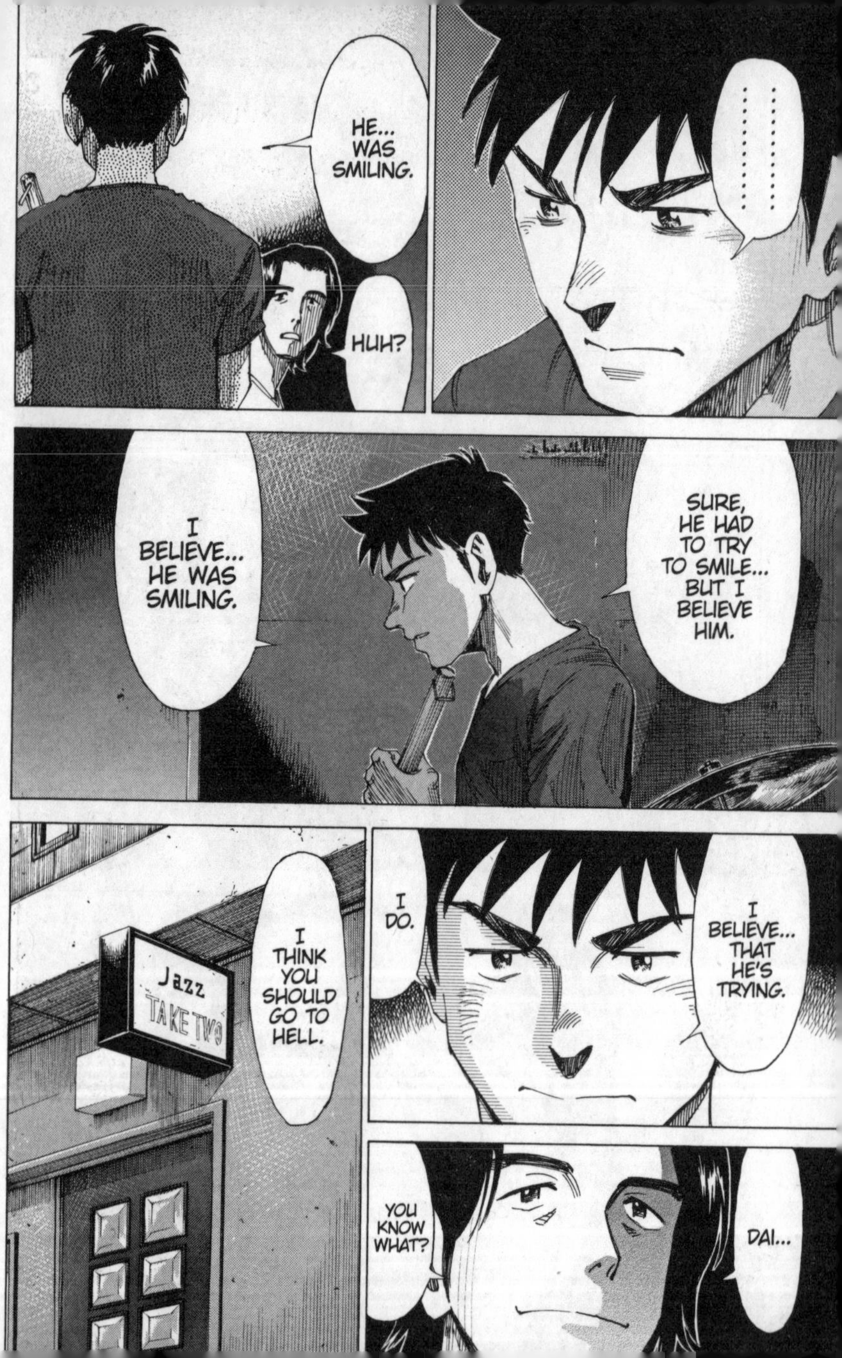

......
HE... WAS SMILING.
HUH?
SURE, HE HAD TO TRY TO SMILE... BUT I BELIEVE HIM.
I BELIEVE... HE WAS SMILING.
I BELIEVE... THAT HE'S TRYING.
I DO.
DAI...
YOU KNOW WHAT?
Jazz
TAKE TWO
I THINK YOU SHOULD GO TO HELL.

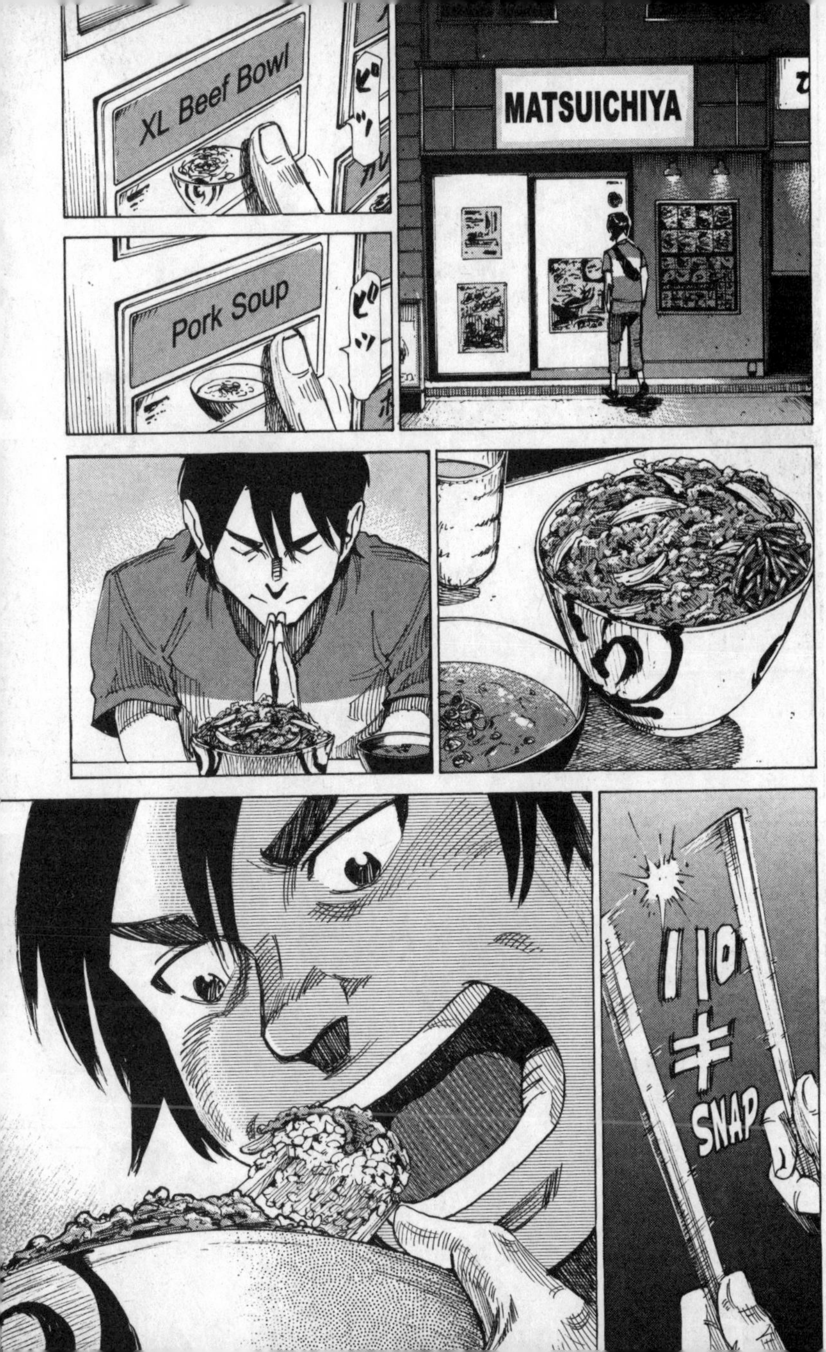
MATSUICHIYA
XL Beef Bowl
Pork Soup
SNAP

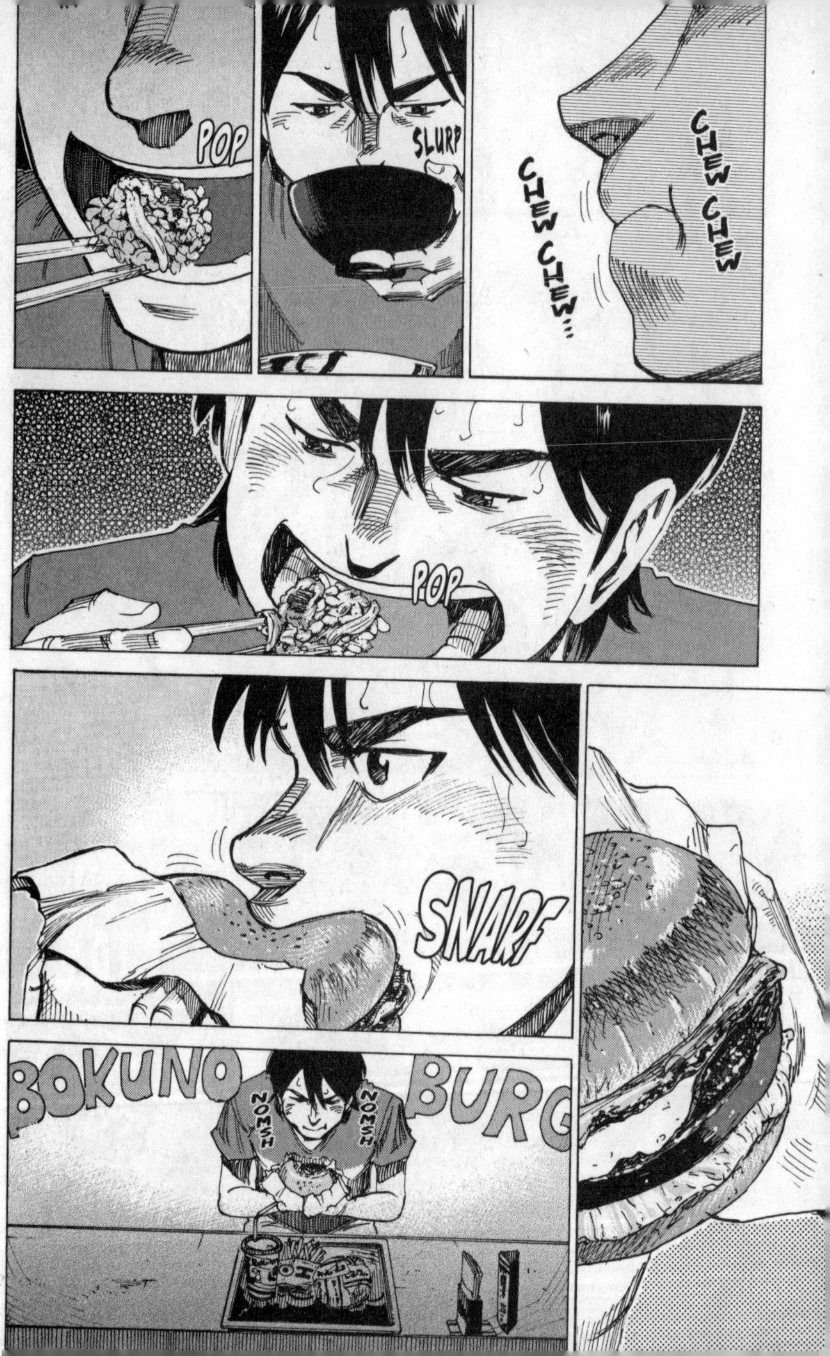
CHEW CHEW
CHEW CHEW...
SLURP
POP
POP
SNARF
BOKUNO BURG
NOMSH
NOMSH

ONE LARGE CREAMY RAMEN, ONE ORDER OF POT STICKERS!

SLURP

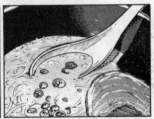

PUFF... PUFF... PUFF HUFF

Thk

POP

CHEW CHEW CHEW CHEW

SLURRRP

GULP...

GULP...

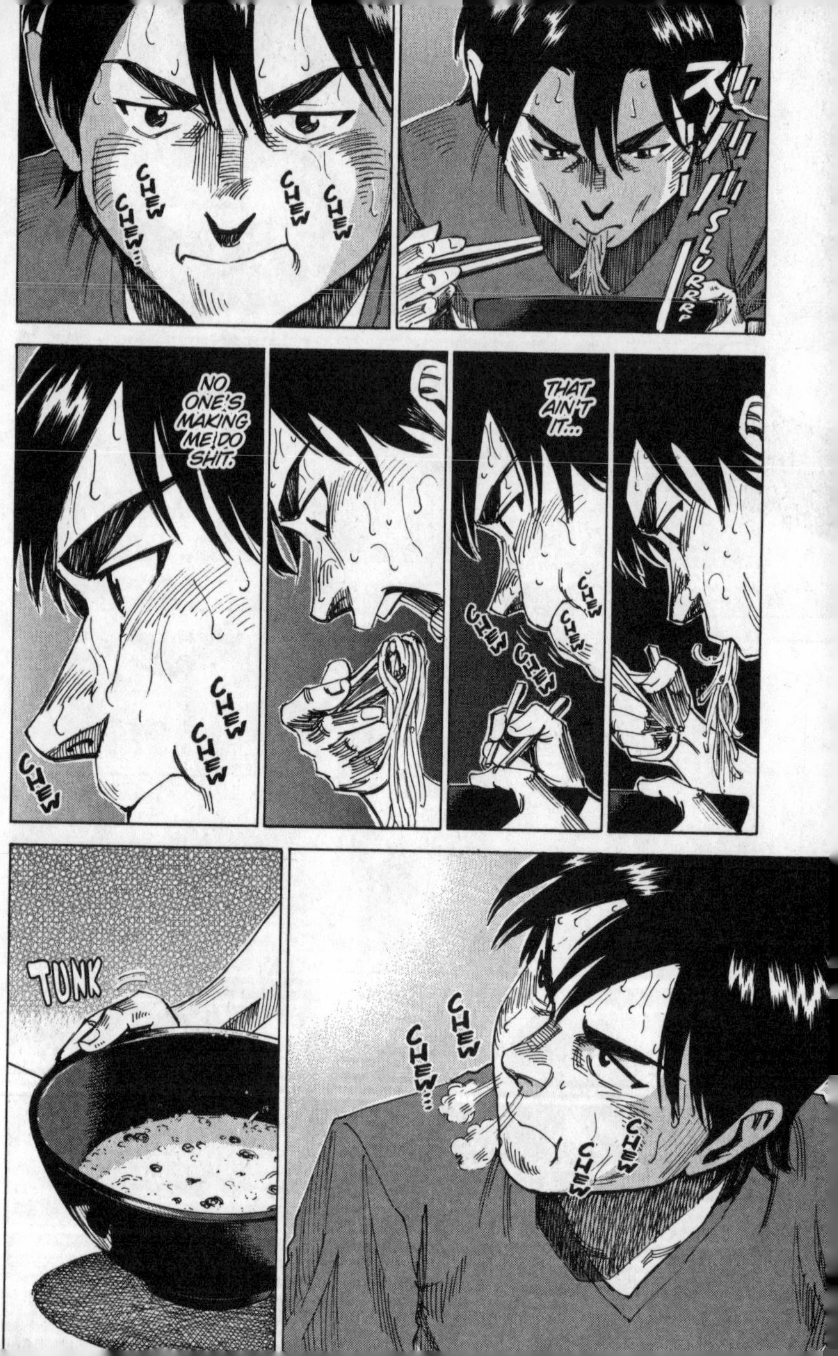
ズ
SLURRRP
CHEW CHEW
CHEW CHEW...
THAT AIN'T IT...
CHEW CHEW
CHEW CHEW
NO ONE'S MAKING ME DO SHIT.
CHEW CHEW
CHEW
CHEW CHEW
CHEW CHEW...
TUNK

'CAUSE I WANT TO.

I DO IT...

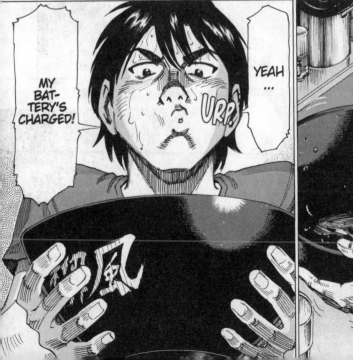

MY BAT- TERY'S CHARGED!

YEAH ...

URP!

TUP

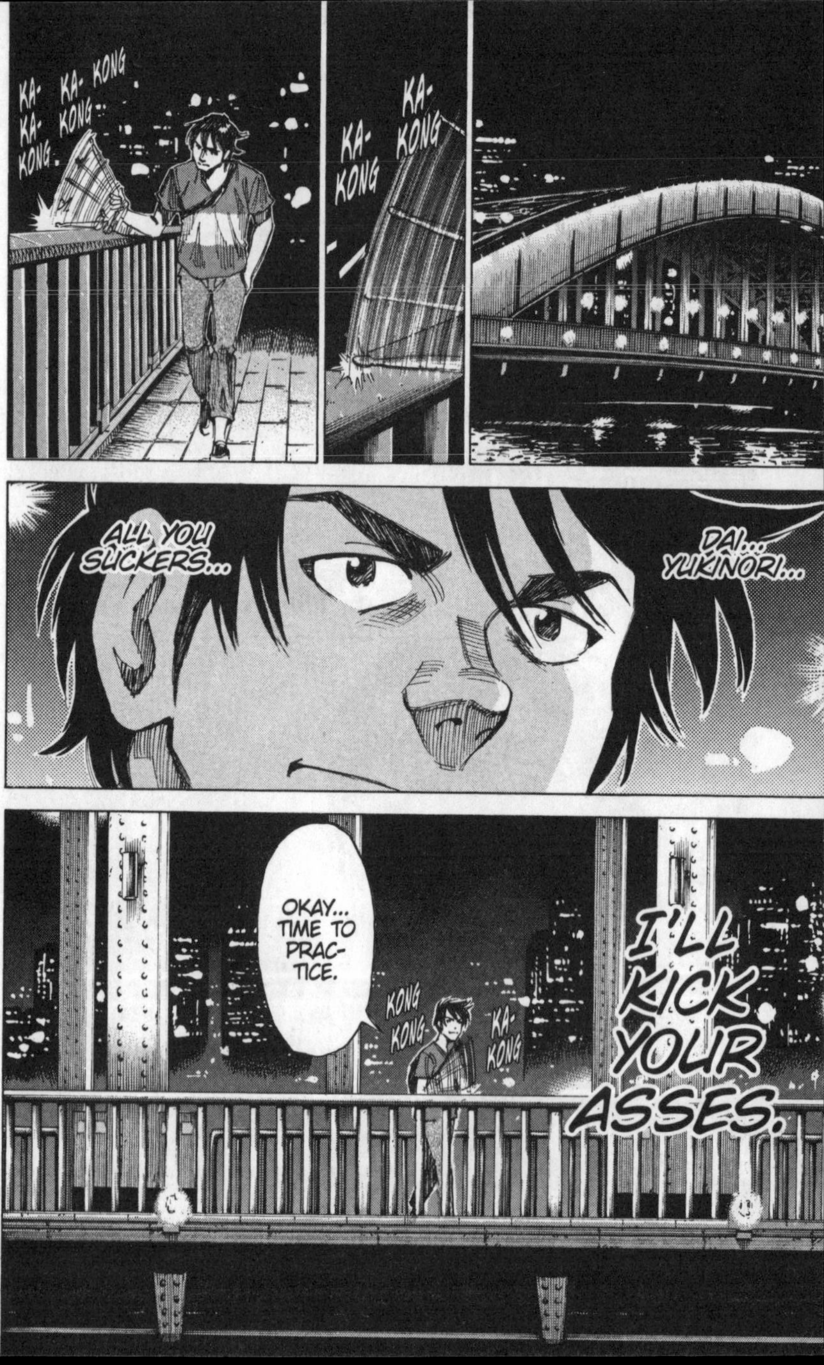
KA-KONG
KA-KONG
KA-KONG
KA-KONG
KA-KA-KONG
DAI... YUKINORI...
ALL YOU SUCKERS...
I'LL KICK YOUR ASSES.
KA-KONG
KONG KONG
OKAY... TIME TO PRAC-TICE.

48 I'LL SEE YOU AGAIN

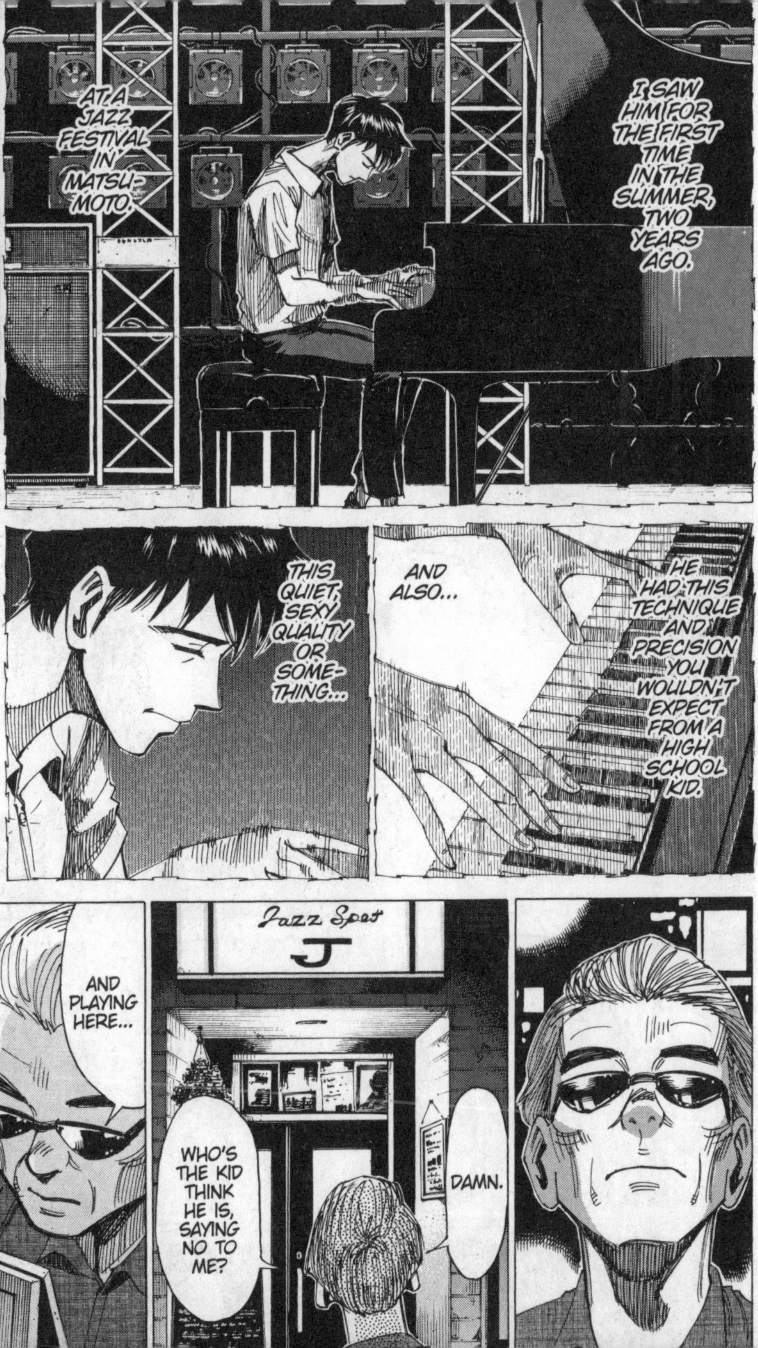
I SAW HIM FOR THE FIRST TIME IN THE SUMMER, TWO YEARS AGO.
AT A JAZZ FESTIVAL IN MATSU-MOTO.
HE HAD THIS TECHNIQUE AND PRECISION YOU WOULDN'T EXPECT FROM A HIGH SCHOOL KID.
AND ALSO...
THIS QUIET, SEXY QUALITY OR SOME-THING...
Jazz Spot
J
DAMN.
WHO'S THE KID THINK HE IS, SAYING NO TO ME?
AND PLAYING HERE...

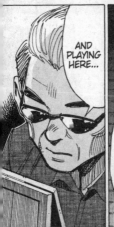

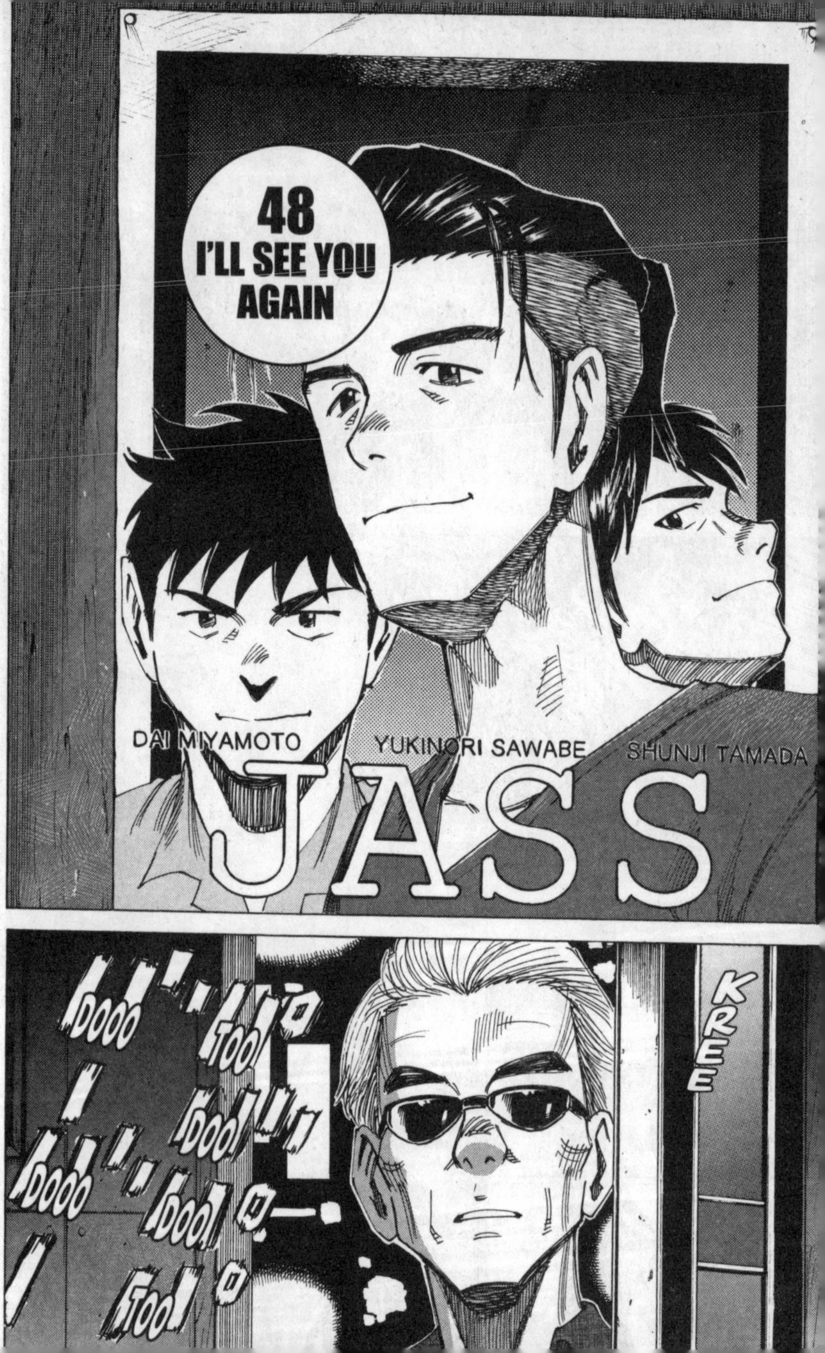
48
I'LL SEE YOU AGAIN
DAI MIYAMOTO
YUKINORI SAWABE
SHUNJI TAMADA
JASS
KREE
DOOO
TOO
DOO
DOOO
DOO
TOO

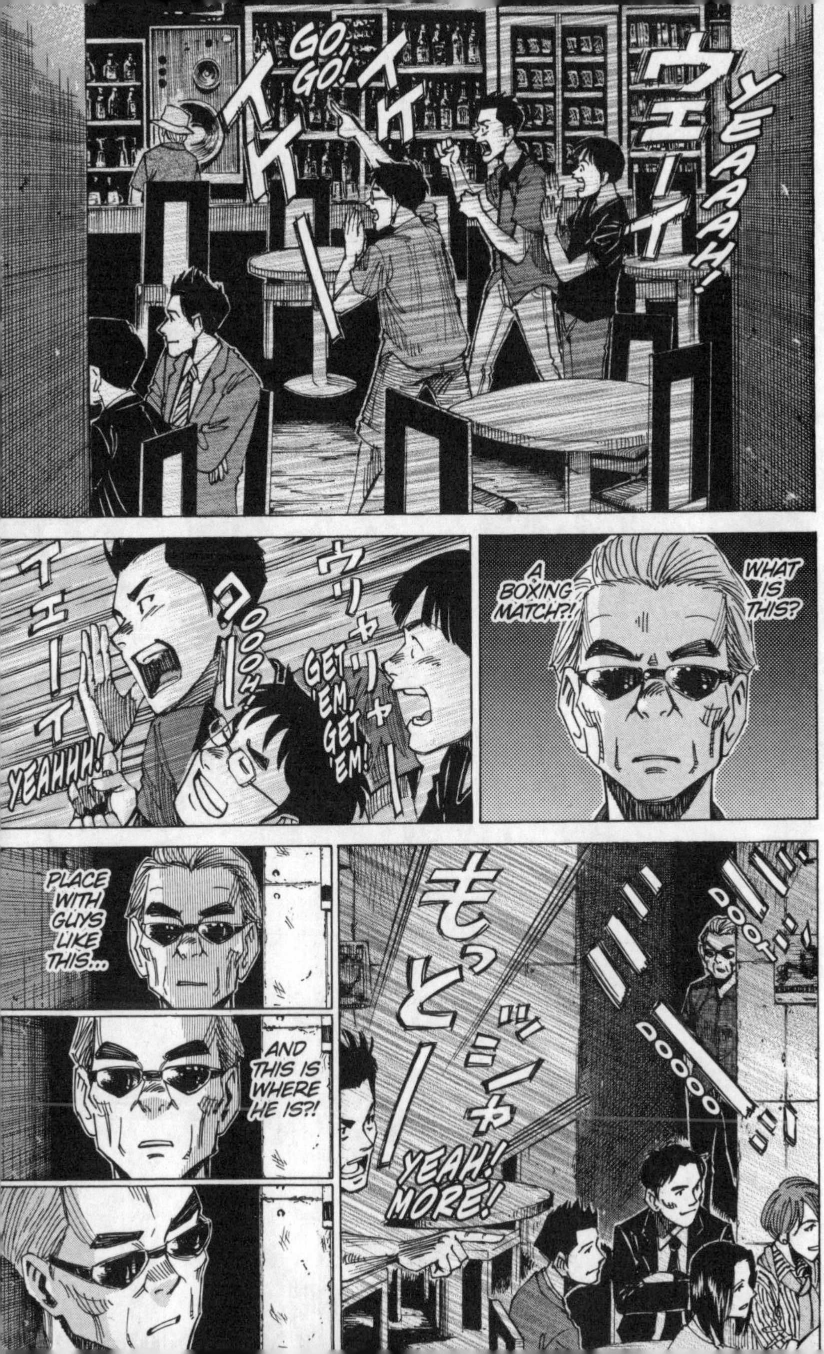
YEAAAAH!
GO, GO!
WHAT IS THIS?
A BOXING MATCH?!
GET 'EM, GET 'EM!
OOOOH!
YEAHHH!
DOOOT!!
DOOOOO
YEAH! MORE!
PLACE WITH GUYS LIKE THIS...
AND THIS IS WHERE HE IS?!

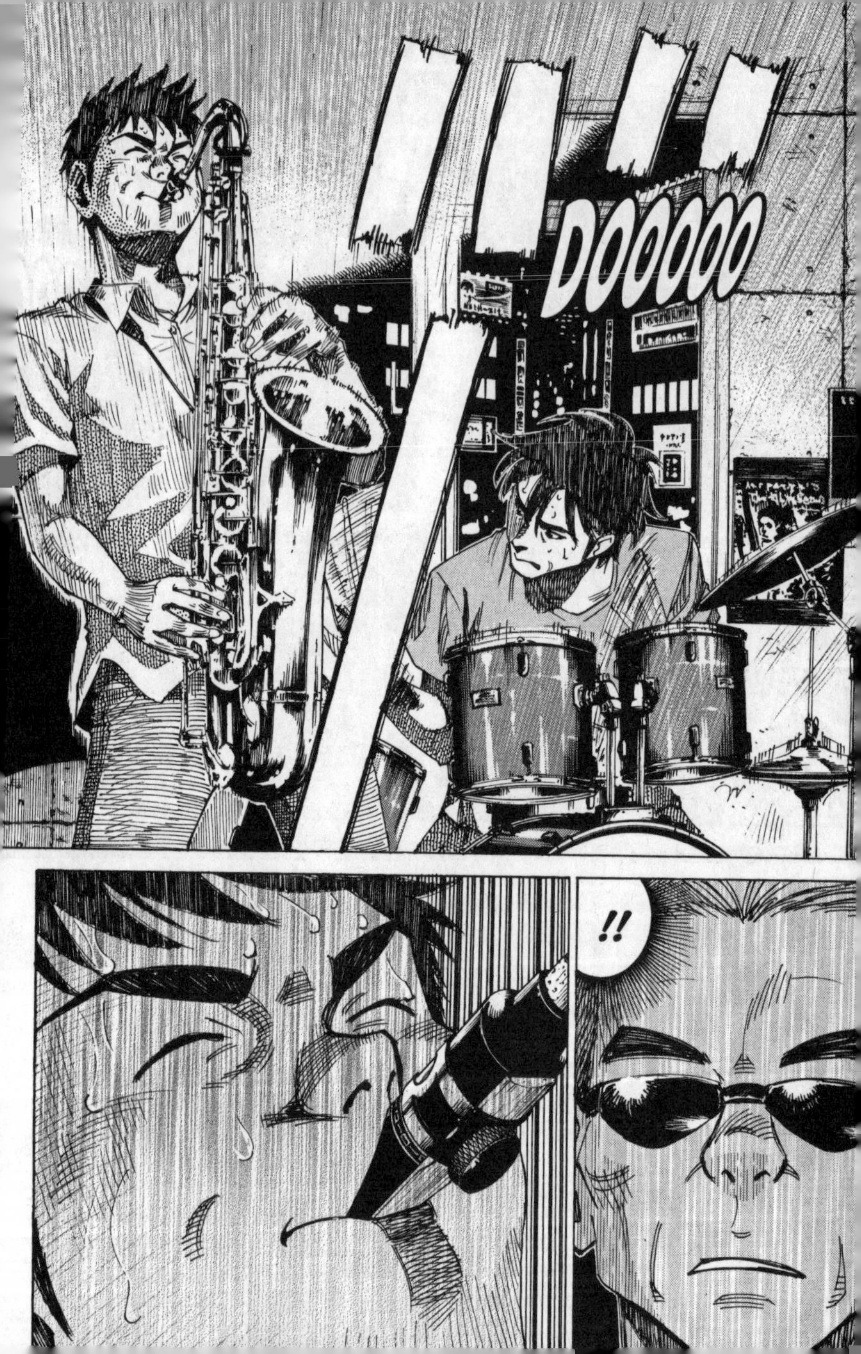
DOOOOO
!!

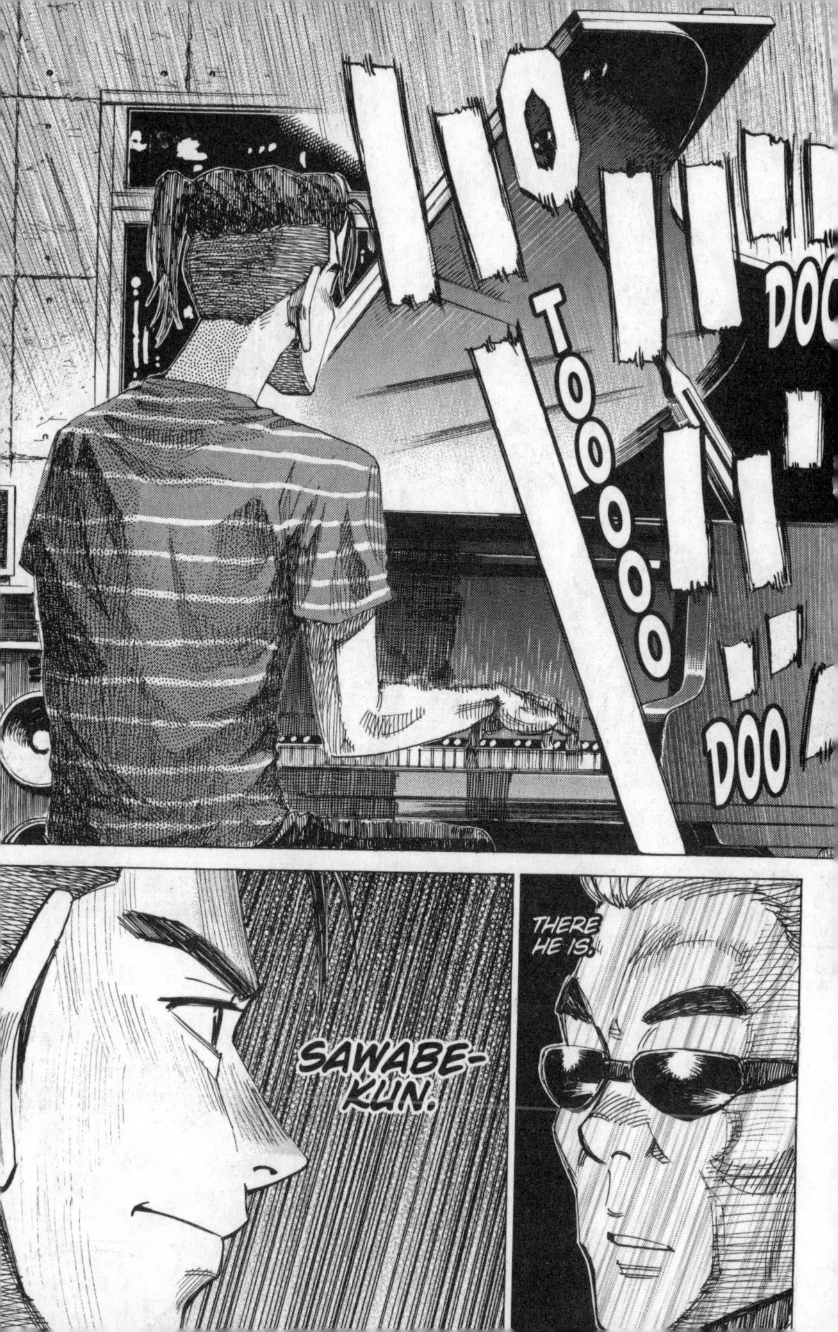
DO
TOOOOOO
DOO
THERE HE IS.
SAWABE-KUN.

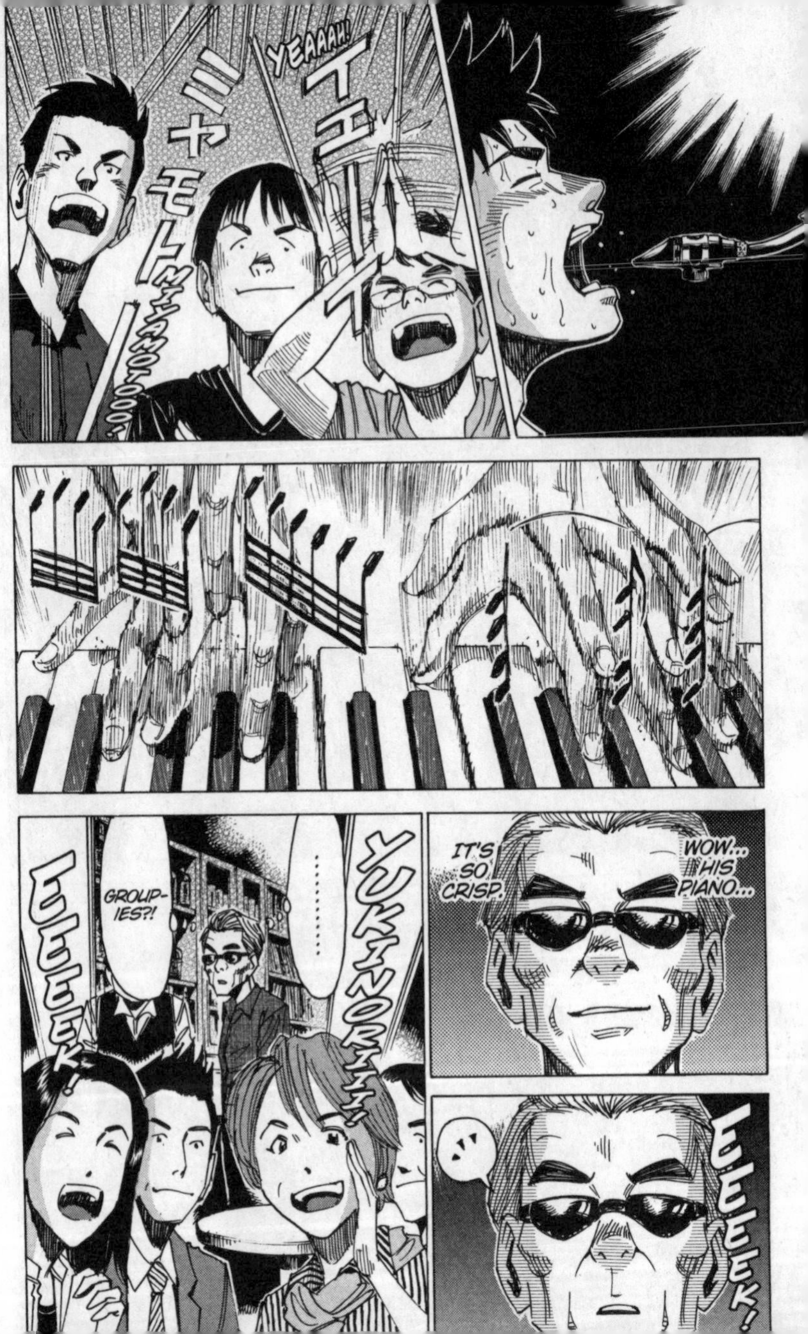

YEAAAH!
イェーイ
MIYAMOTOOOO!
ミヤモト
WOW... HIS PIANO...
IT'S SO CRISP.
!
EEEEK!
YUKINORIIII!
......
GROUP-IES?!
EEEEEK!

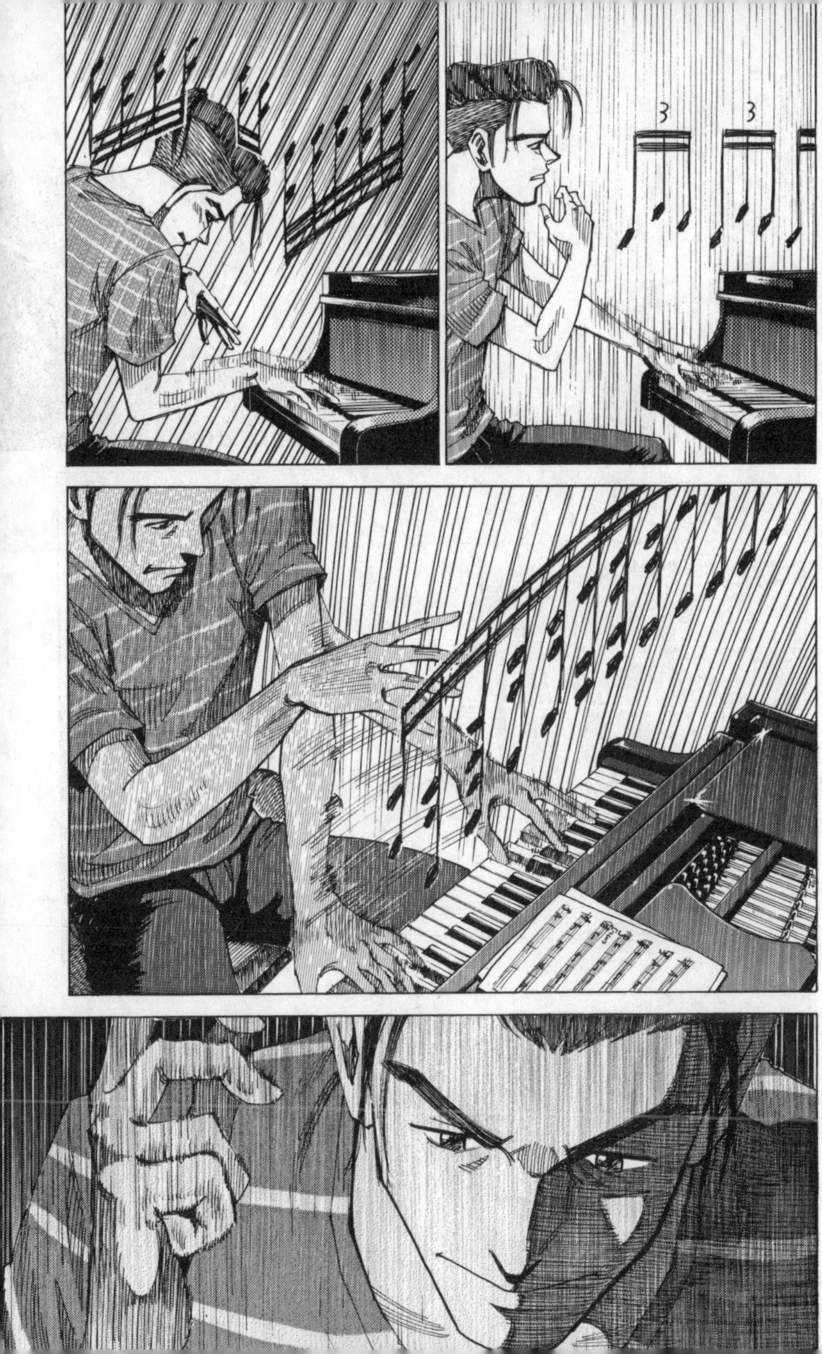

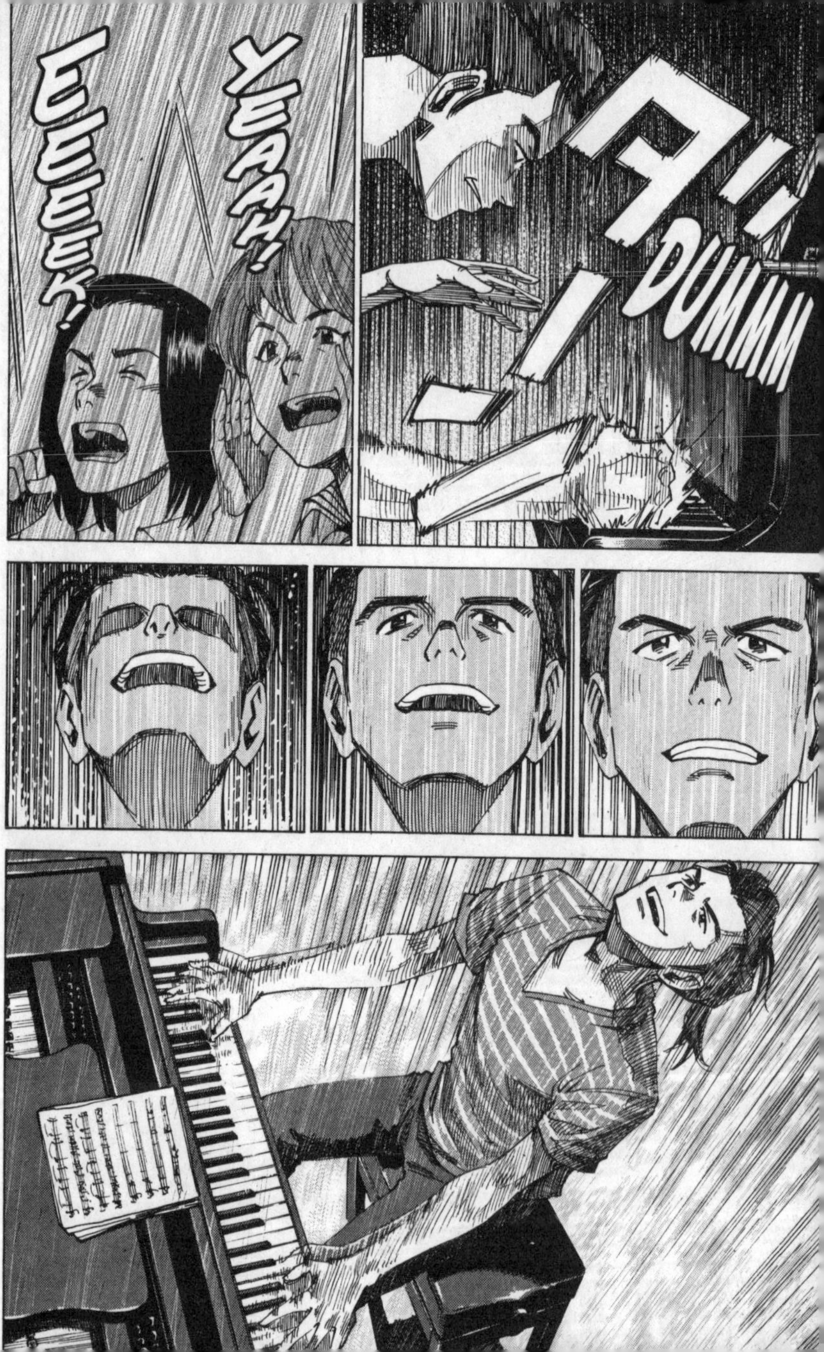
DUMMM
YEAAAH!
EEEEEEK!

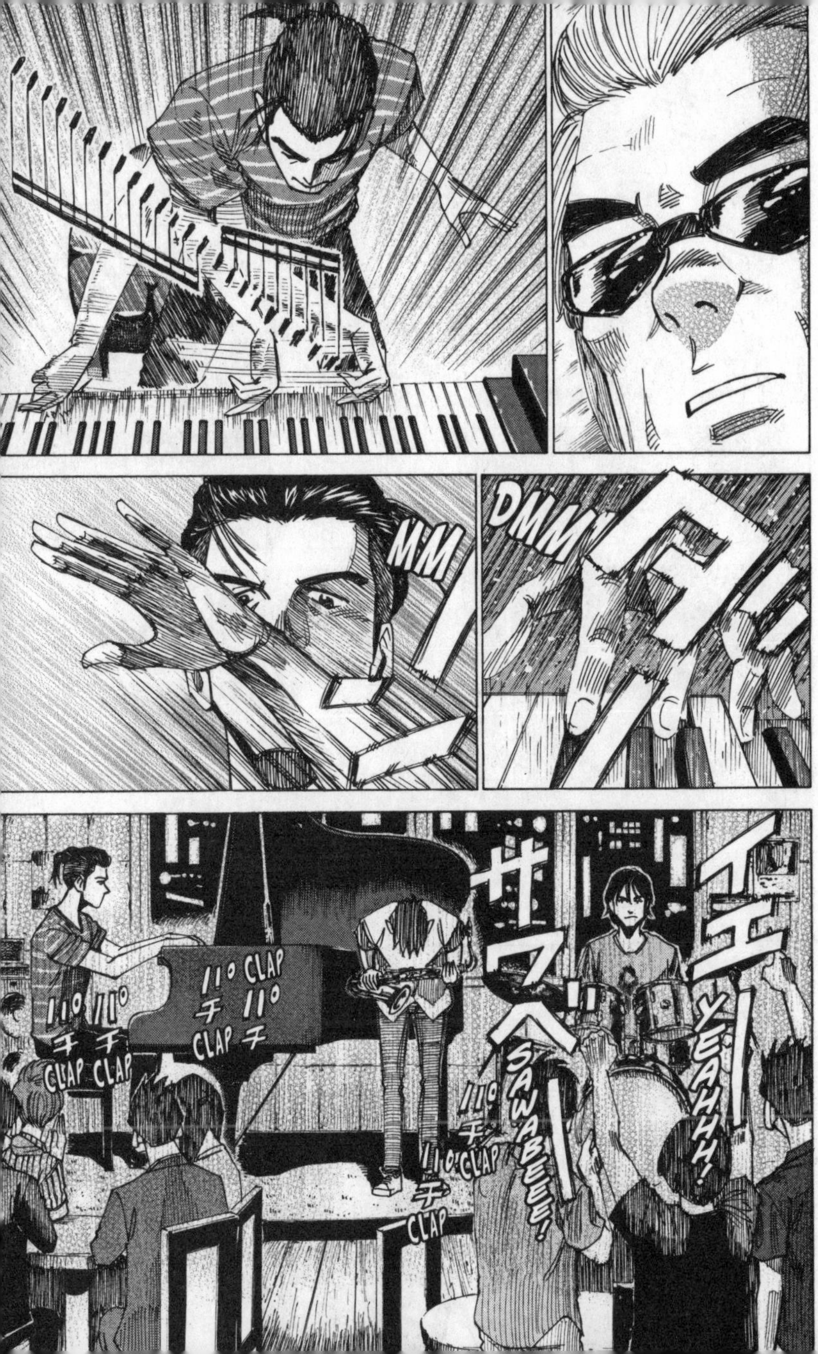

DMM
MM
イエー
YEAHHH!
サワベー
SAWABEEE!
パチ CLAP
パチ CLAP
パチ CLAP
パチ CLAP
パチ CLAP
パチ CLAP

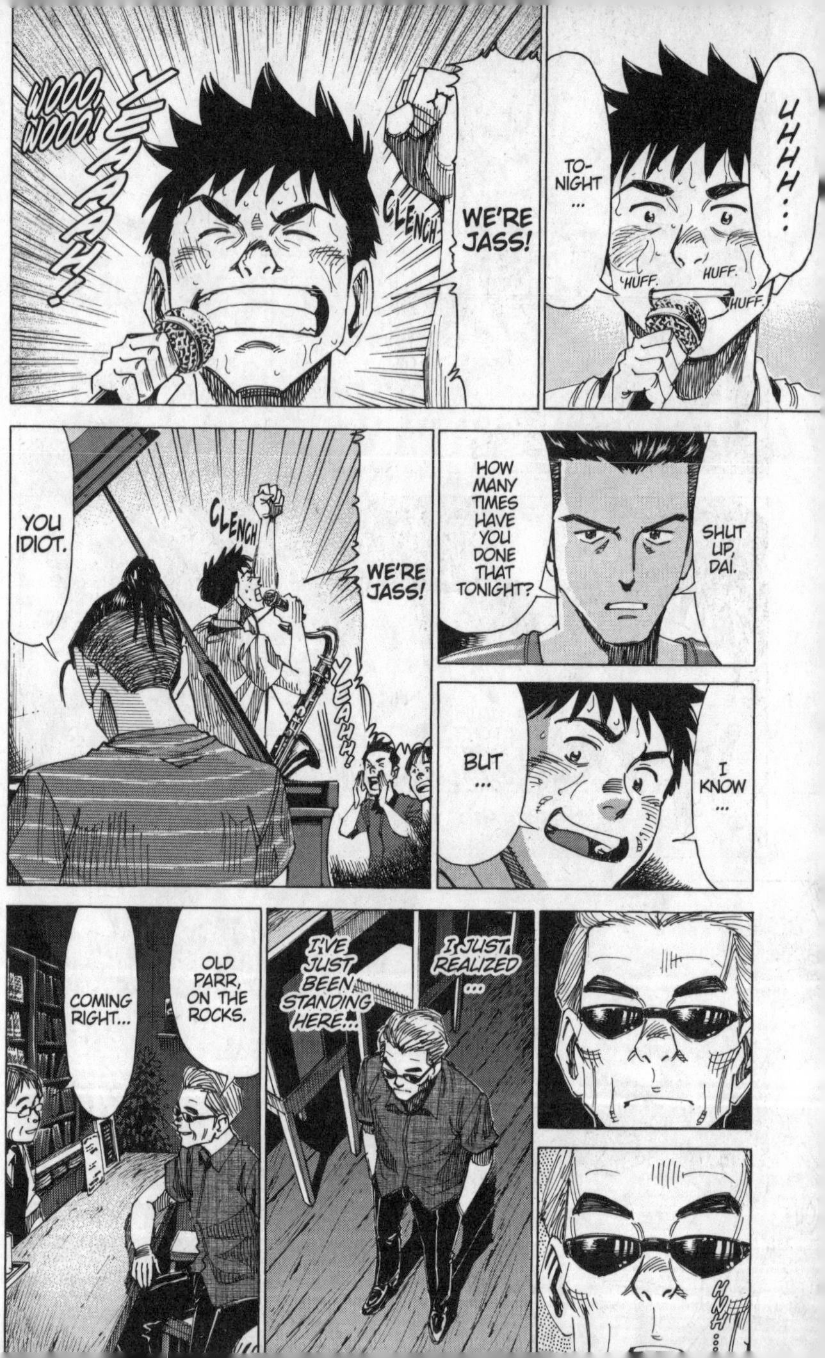
UHHH...
TO-NIGHT ...
HUFF.
HUFF.
HUFF.
WE'RE JASS!
CLENCH
YEAAAAAH!
WOOO, WOOO!
SHUT UP, DAI.
HOW MANY TIMES HAVE YOU DONE THAT TONIGHT?
I KNOW ...
BUT ...
WE'RE JASS!
CLENCH
YEAHH!
YOU IDIOT.
HNH...
I JUST REALIZED ...
I'VE JUST BEEN STANDING HERE...
OLD PARR, ON THE ROCKS.
COMING RIGHT...

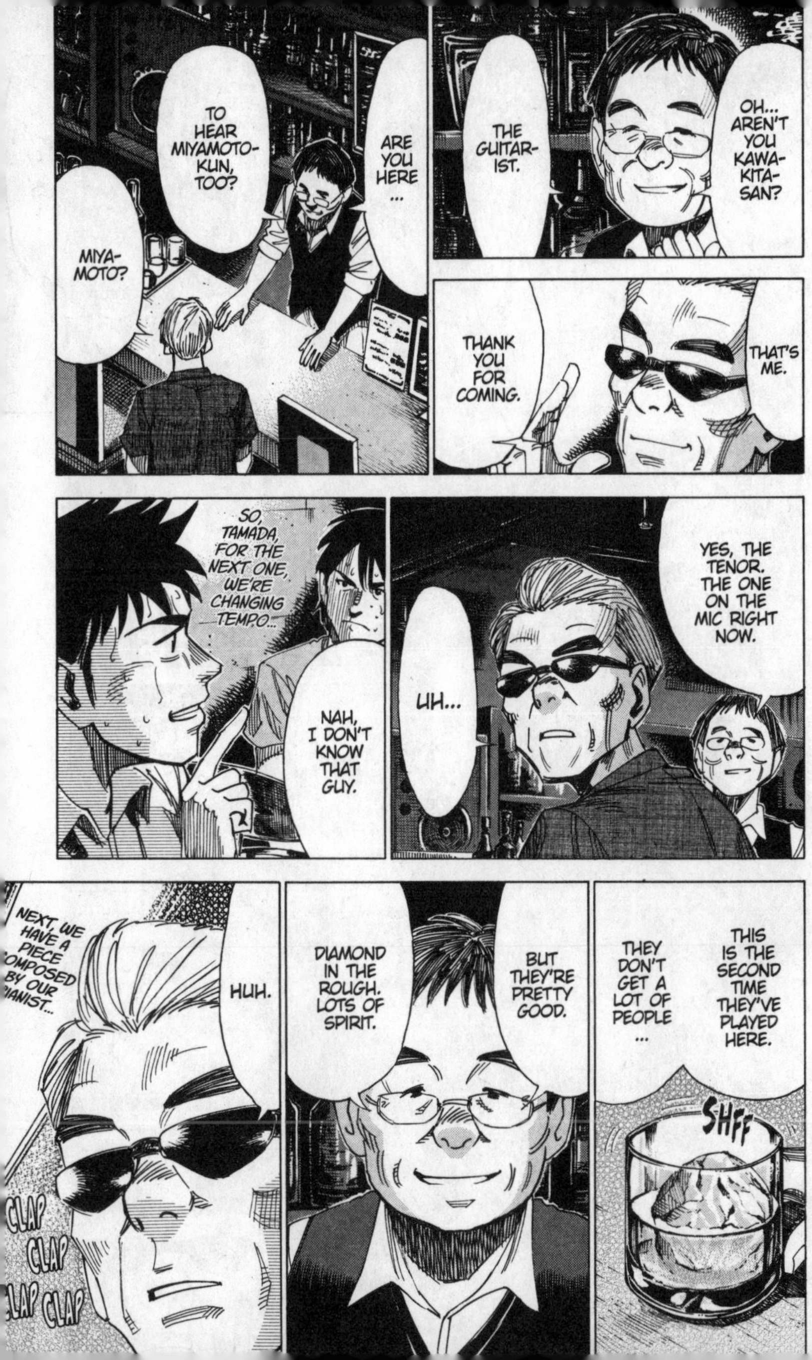
OH... AREN'T YOU KAWAKITA-SAN?
THE GUITARIST.
THAT'S ME.
THANK YOU FOR COMING.
ARE YOU HERE...
TO HEAR MIYAMOTO-KUN, TOO?
MIYAMOTO?
YES, THE TENOR. THE ONE ON THE MIC RIGHT NOW.
UH...
SO, TAMADA, FOR THE NEXT ONE, WE'RE CHANGING TEMPO...
NAH, I DON'T KNOW THAT GUY.
THIS IS THE SECOND TIME THEY'VE PLAYED HERE.
THEY DON'T GET A LOT OF PEOPLE...
SHFF
BUT THEY'RE PRETTY GOOD.
DIAMOND IN THE ROUGH. LOTS OF SPIRIT.
HUH.
NEXT, WE HAVE A PIECE OMPOSED BY OUR IANIST...
CLAP CLAP
LAP CLAP

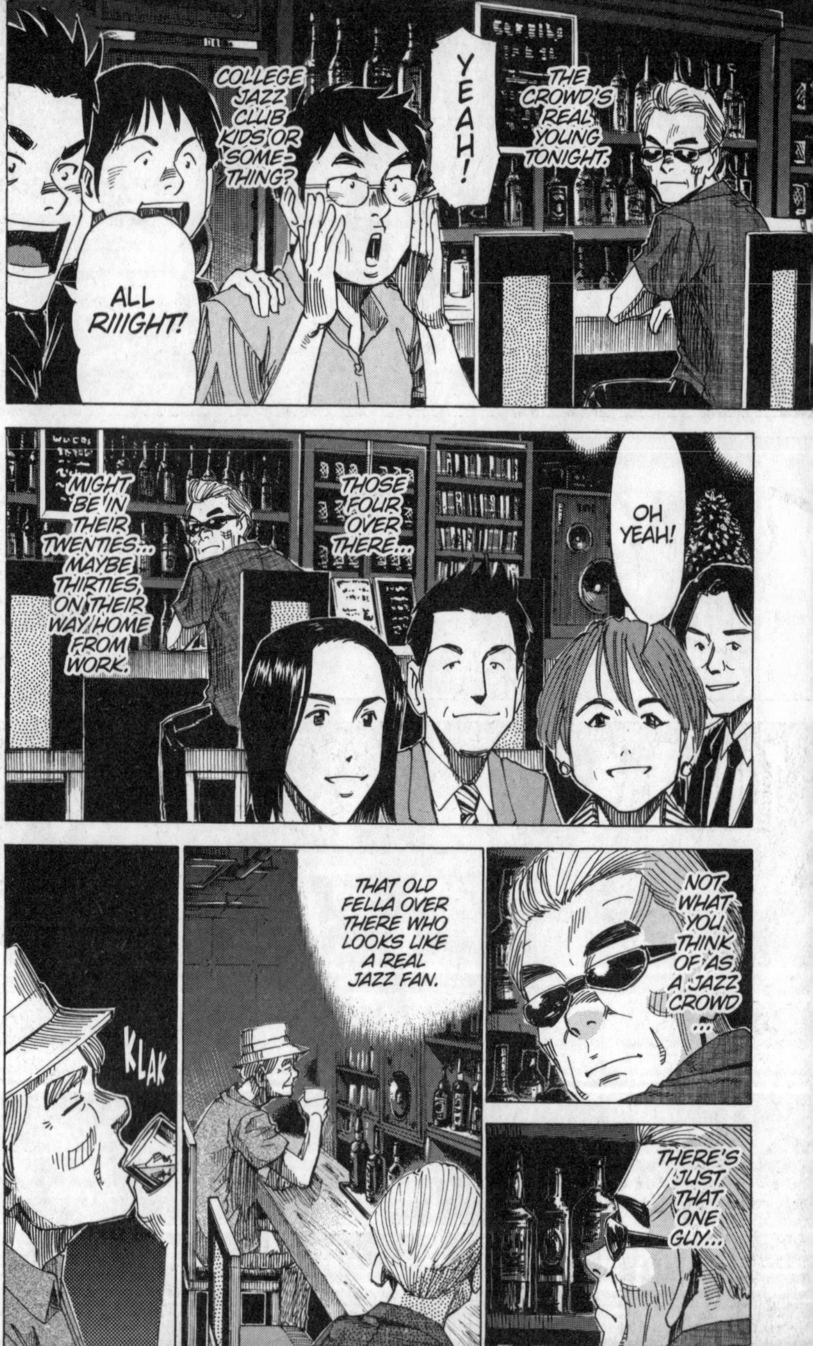
THE CROWD'S REAL YOUNG TONIGHT.
YEAH!
COLLEGE JAZZ CLUB KIDS OR SOME-THING?
ALL RIIIGHT!
OH YEAH!
THOSE FOUR OVER THERE...
MIGHT BE IN THEIR TWENTIES... MAYBE THIRTIES, ON THEIR WAY HOME FROM WORK.
NOT WHAT YOU THINK OF AS A JAZZ CROWD...
THERE'S JUST THAT ONE GUY...
THAT OLD FELLA OVER THERE WHO LOOKS LIKE A REAL JAZZ FAN.
KLAK

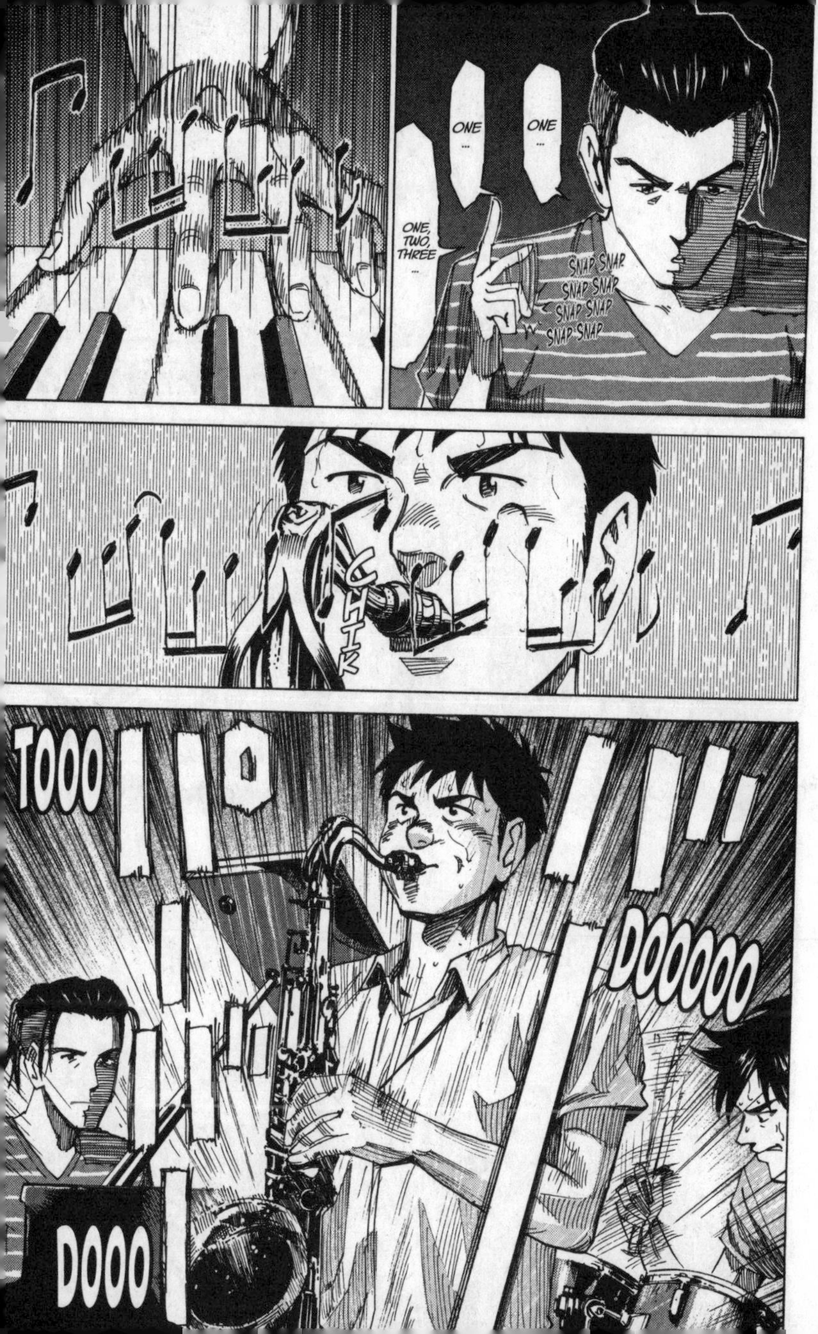
ONE ...
ONE ...
ONE, TWO, THREE ...
SNAP SNAP
SNAP SNAP
SNAP SNAP
SNAP SNAP
CHIK
TOOO
DOOOOO
DOOO

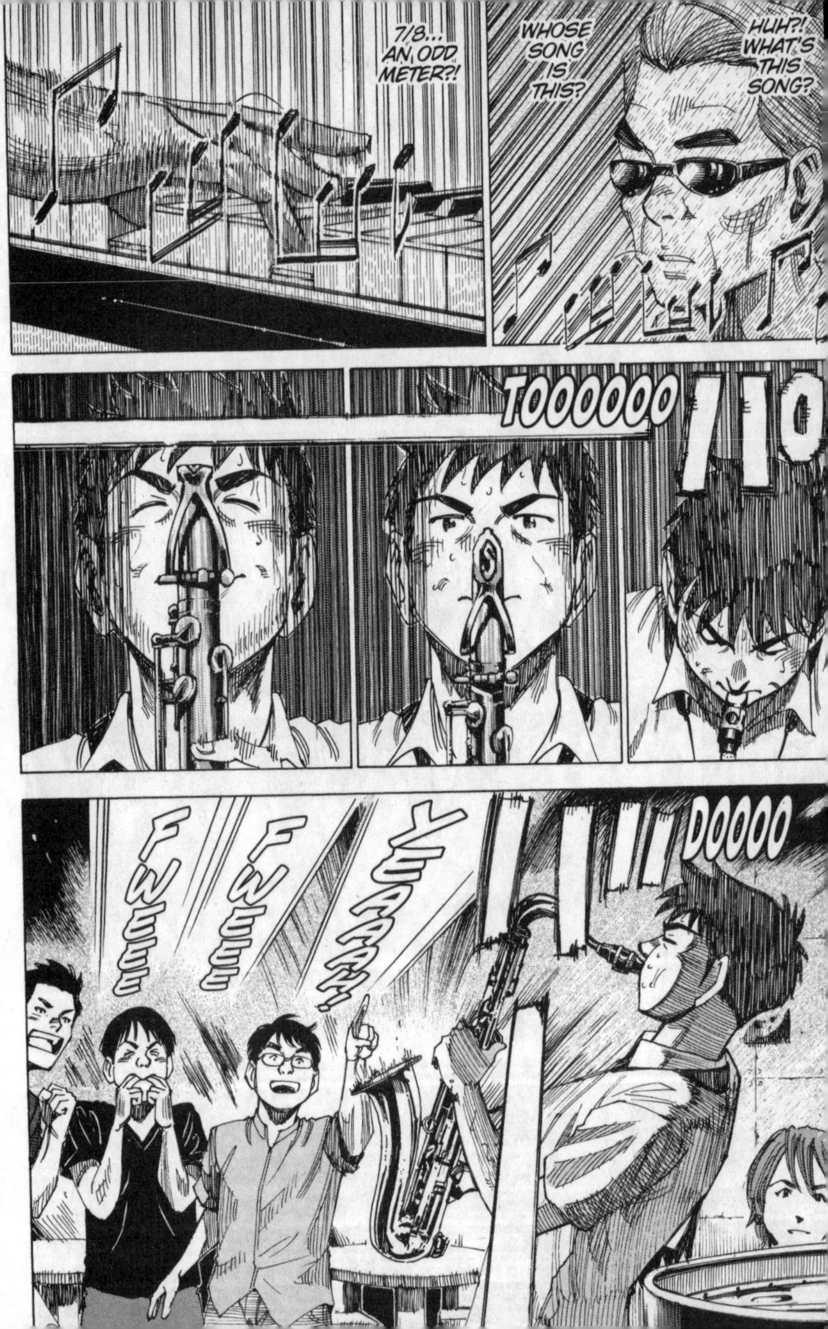
HUH?! WHAT'S THIS SONG?
WHOSE SONG IS THIS?
7/8... AN ODD METER?!
TOOOOOO
DOOOO
YEAAAAH!
FWEEEE
FWEEEE

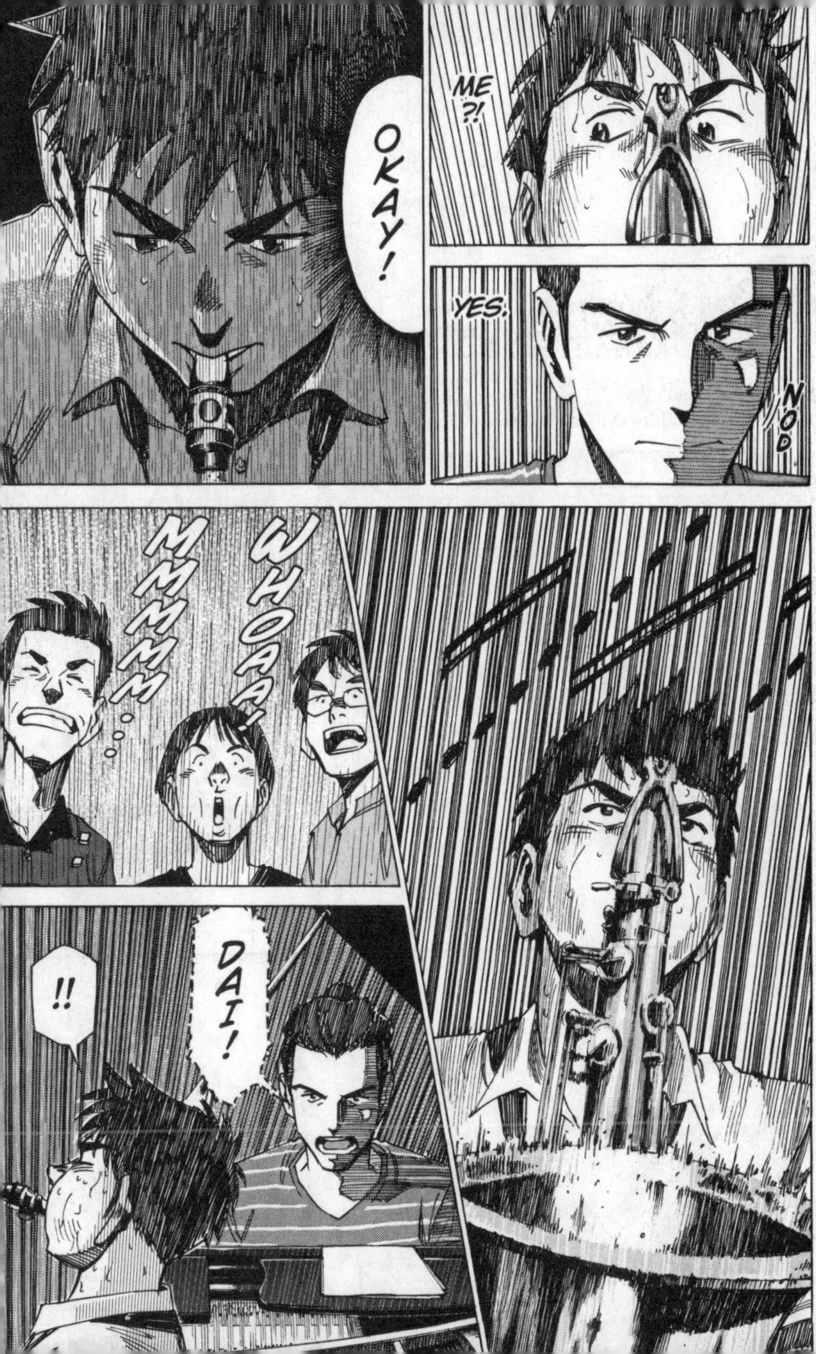
ME ?!
YES.
NOD
OKAY!
WHOAAA!
MMMMMM
DAI!
!!

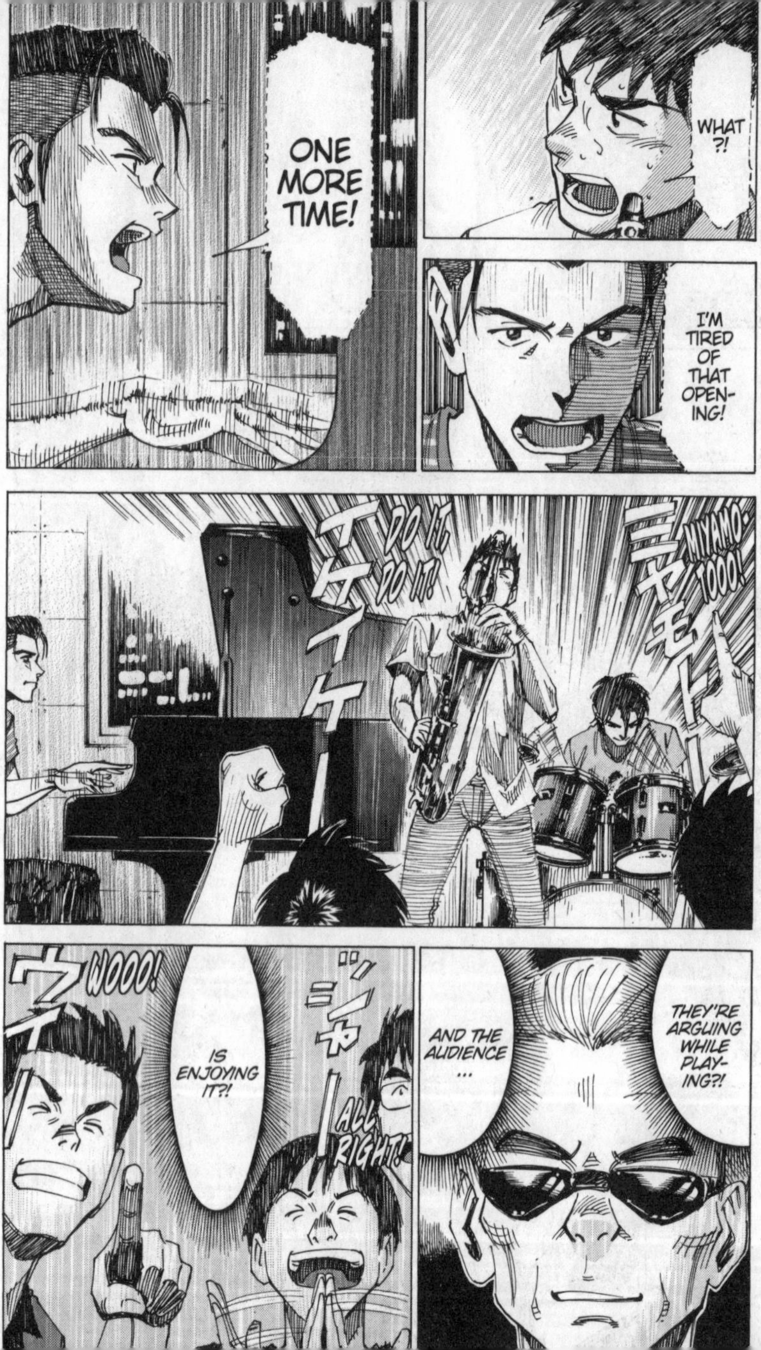
WHAT?!
I'M TIRED OF THAT OPENING!
ONE MORE TIME!
MIYAMO-TOOO!
DO IT, DO IT!
THEY'RE ARGUING WHILE PLAYING?!
AND THE AUDIENCE ...
IS ENJOYING IT?!
ALL RIGHT!
WOOO!

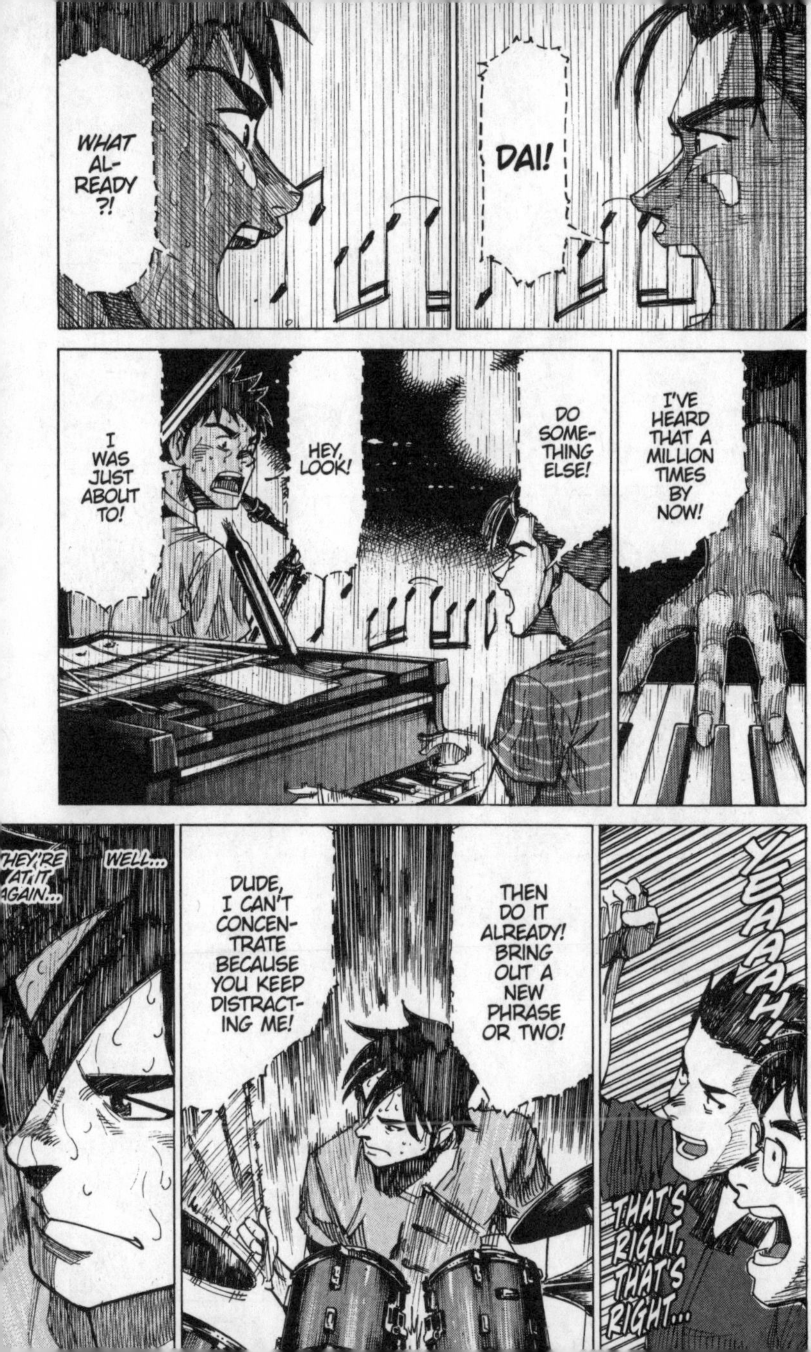
DAI!
WHAT AL-READY ?!
I'VE HEARD THAT A MILLION TIMES BY NOW!
DO SOME-THING ELSE!
HEY, LOOK!
I WAS JUST ABOUT TO!
YEAAAAH!
THAT'S RIGHT, THAT'S RIGHT...
THEN DO IT ALREADY! BRING OUT A NEW PHRASE OR TWO!
DUDE, I CAN'T CONCEN-TRATE BECAUSE YOU KEEP DISTRACT-ING ME!
WELL...
THEY'RE AT IT AGAIN...

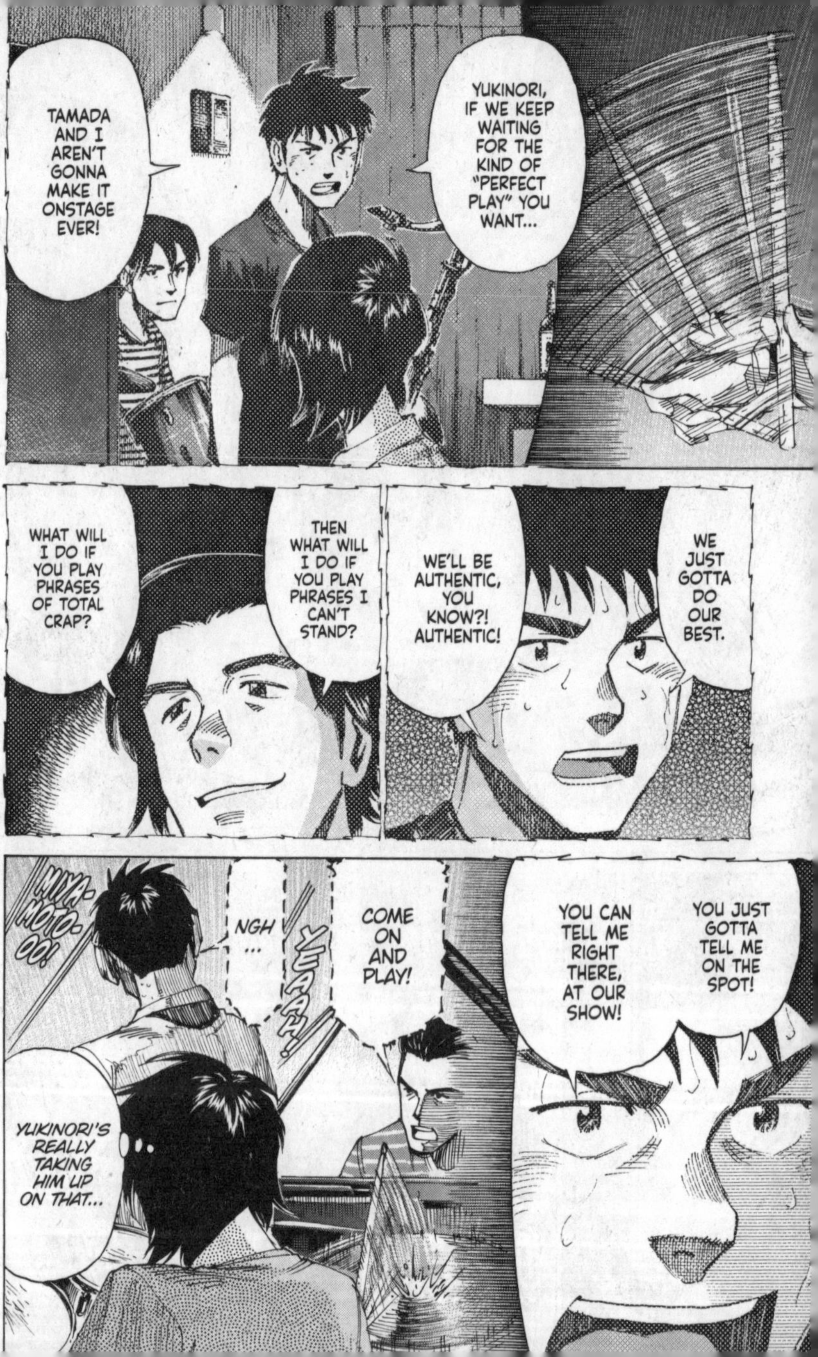
YUKINORI, IF WE KEEP WAITING FOR THE KIND OF "PERFECT PLAY" YOU WANT...
TAMADA AND I AREN'T GONNA MAKE IT ONSTAGE EVER!
WE JUST GOTTA DO OUR BEST.
WE'LL BE AUTHENTIC, YOU KNOW?! AUTHENTIC!
THEN WHAT WILL I DO IF YOU PLAY PHRASES I CAN'T STAND?
WHAT WILL I DO IF YOU PLAY PHRASES OF TOTAL CRAP?
YOU JUST GOTTA TELL ME ON THE SPOT!
YOU CAN TELL ME RIGHT THERE, AT OUR SHOW!
COME ON AND PLAY!
YEAAAH!
NGH ...
MIYA-MOTO-OO!
YUKINORI'S REALLY TAKING HIM UP ON THAT...

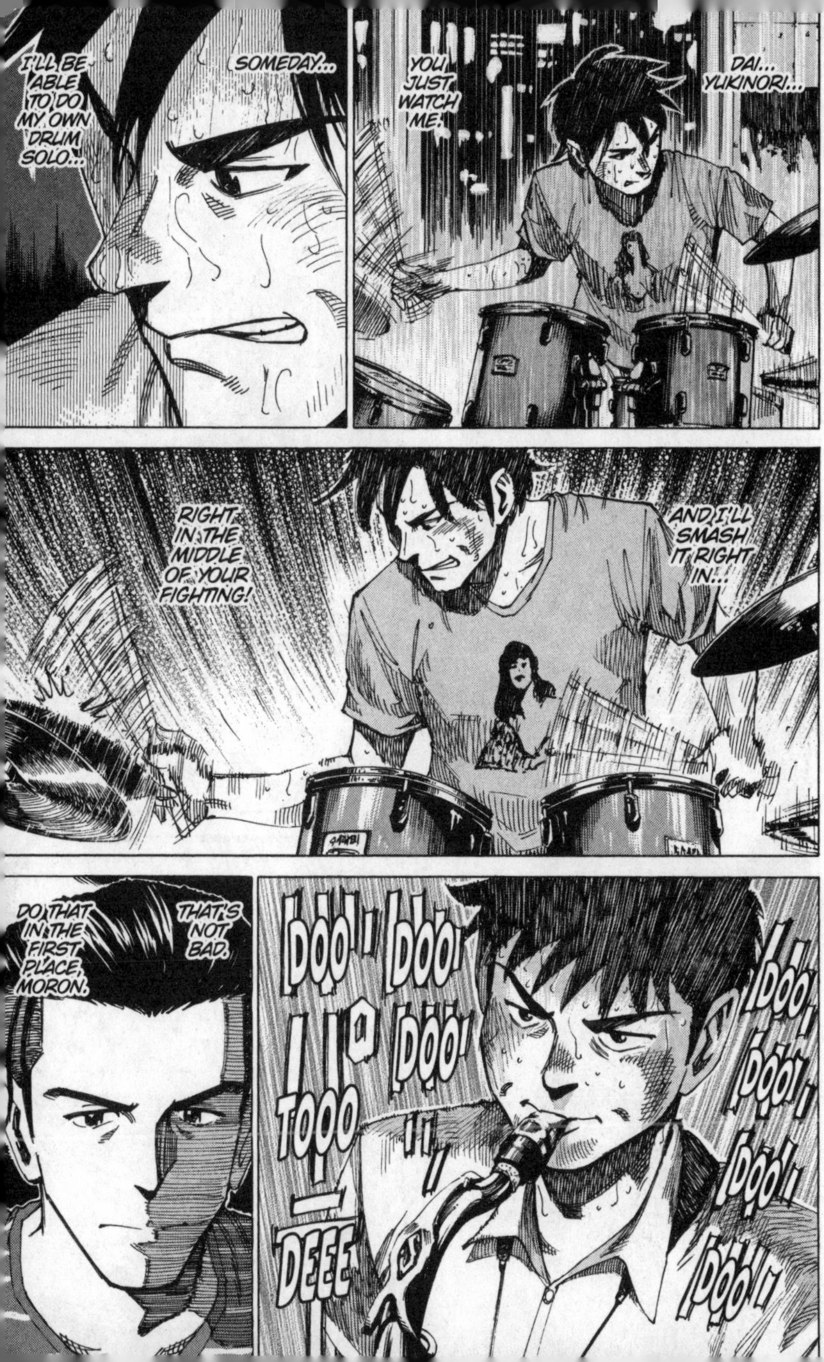

DAI... YUKINORI...
YOU JUST WATCH ME.
SOMEDAY...
I'LL BE ABLE TO DO MY OWN DRUM SOLO...
AND I'LL SMASH IT RIGHT IN...
RIGHT IN THE MIDDLE OF YOUR FIGHTING!
DOO DOO DOO DOO
DOO DOO
DOO TOOO DEEE
THAT'S NOT BAD.
DO THAT IN THE FIRST PLACE, MORON.

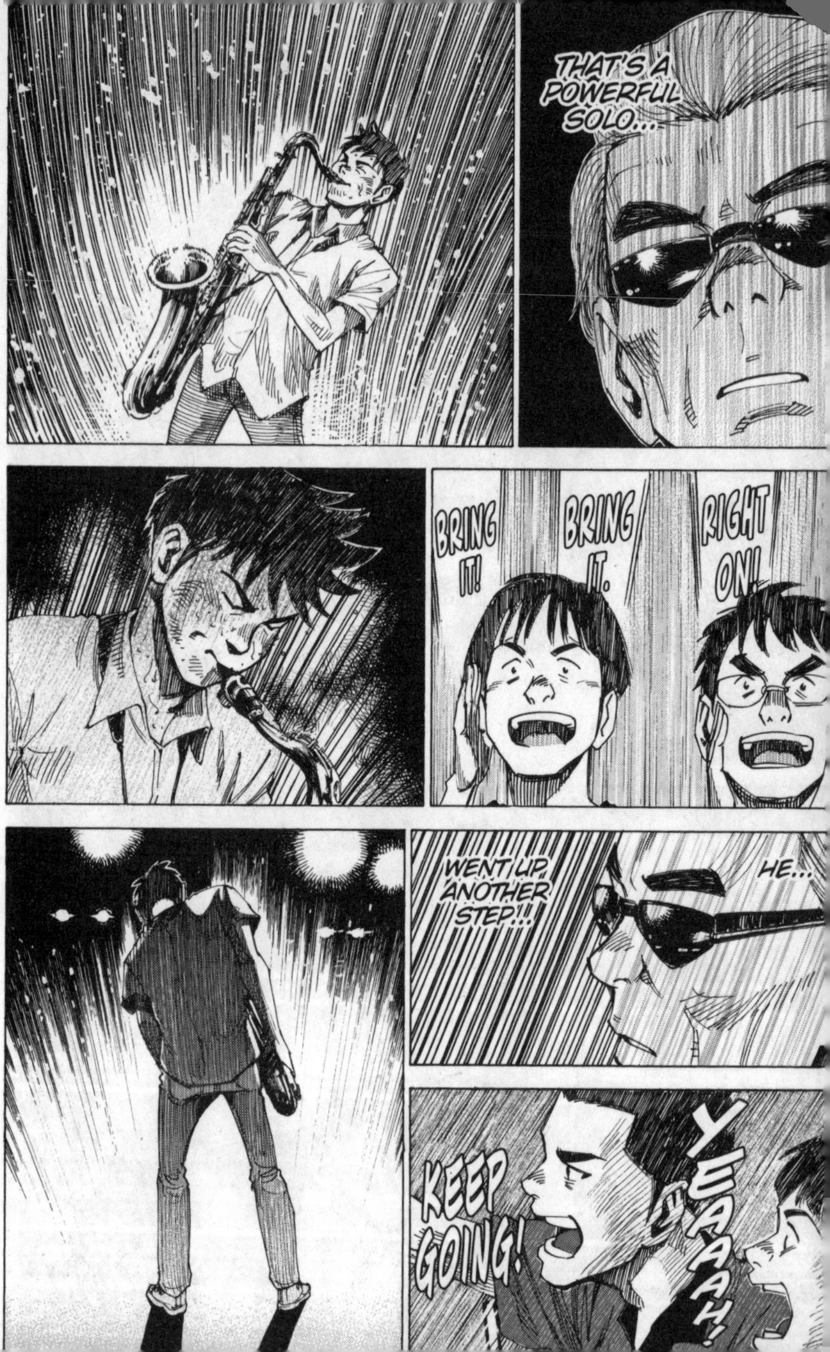
THAT'S A POWERFUL SOLO...
RIGHT ON!
BRING IT.
BRING IT!
HE...
WENT UP ANOTHER STEP!!
YEAAAH!
KEEP GOING!

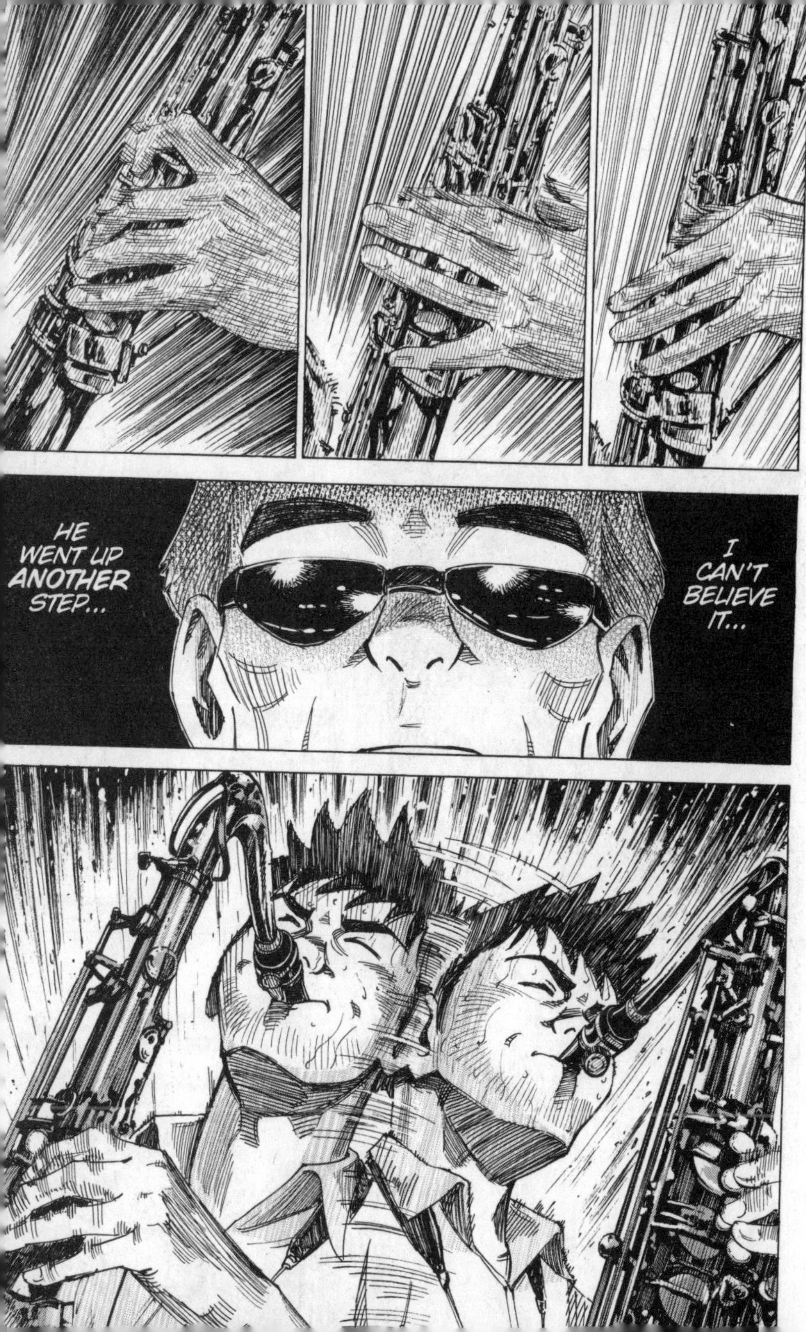
I CAN'T BELIEVE IT...
HE WENT UP ANOTHER STEP...

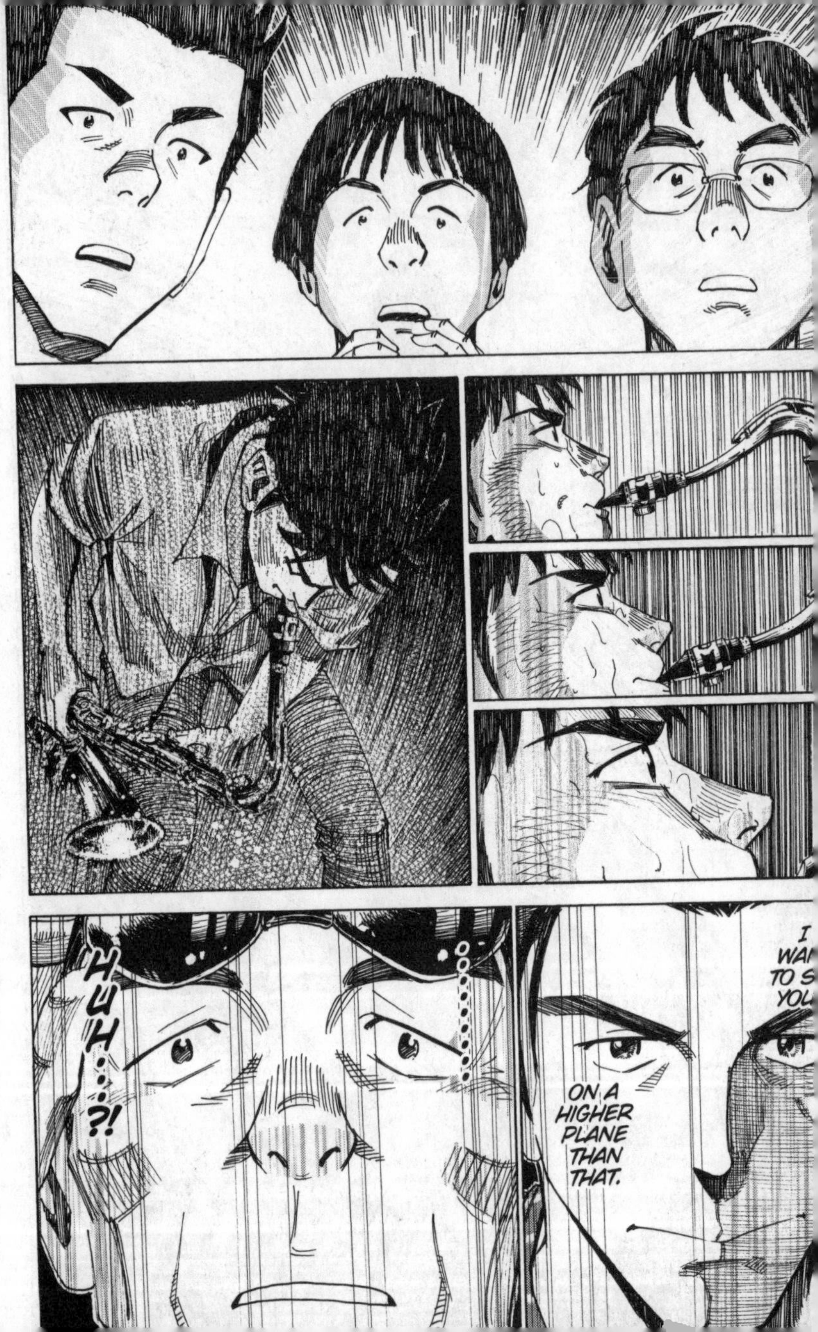
I WA
TO S
YOU
ON A HIGHER PLANE THAN THAT.
HUH...?!

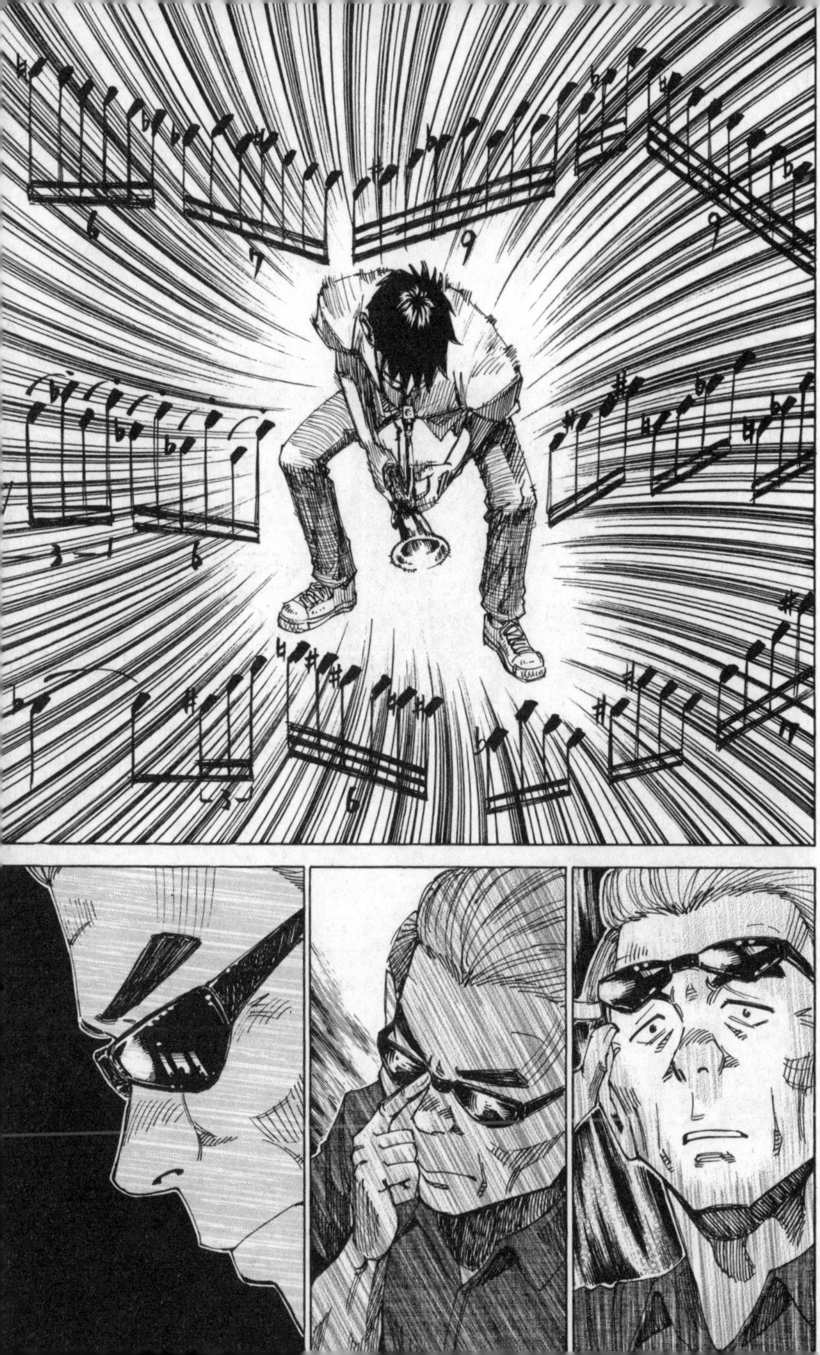

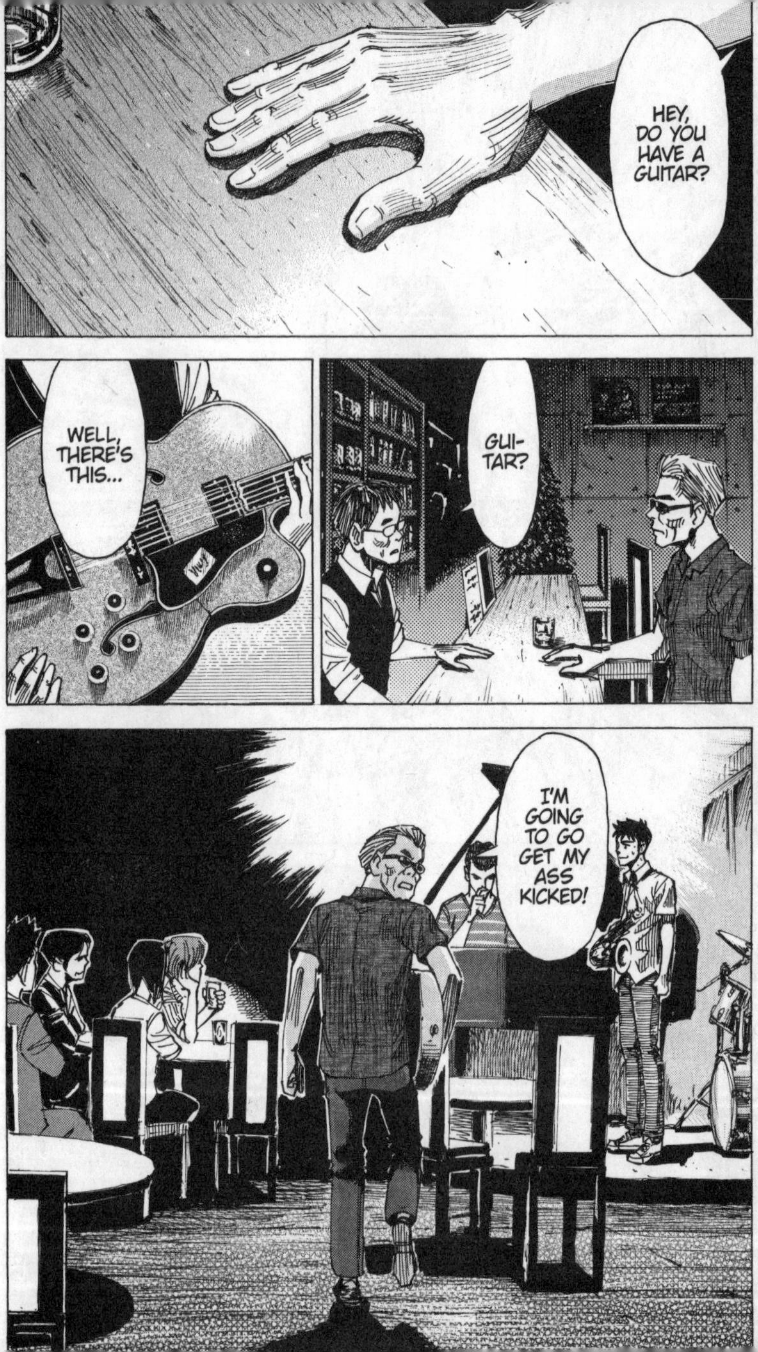
HEY, DO YOU HAVE A GUITAR?
GUI-TAR?
WELL, THERE'S THIS...
I'M GOING TO GO GET MY ASS KICKED!

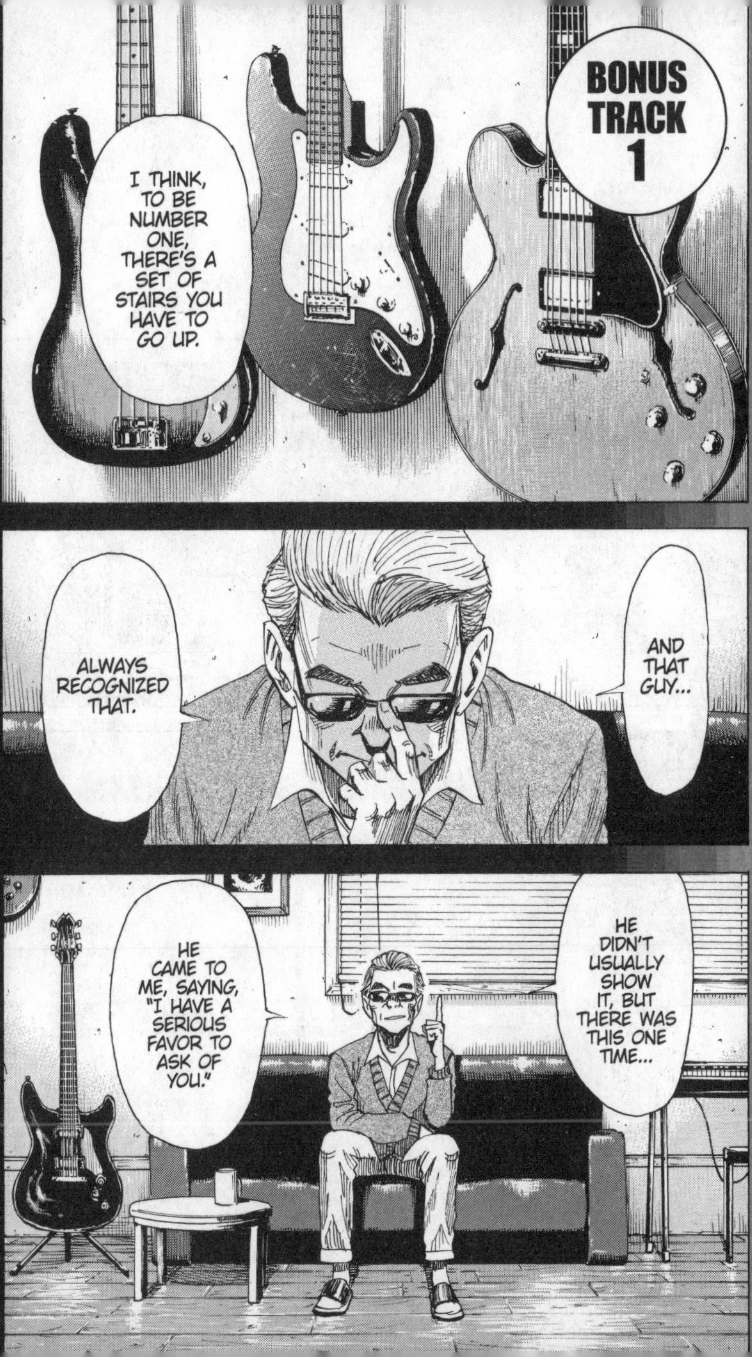
BONUS TRACK 1
I THINK, TO BE NUMBER ONE, THERE'S A SET OF STAIRS YOU HAVE TO GO UP.
AND THAT GUY...
ALWAYS RECOGNIZED THAT.
HE DIDN'T USUALLY SHOW IT, BUT THERE WAS THIS ONE TIME...
HE CAME TO ME, SAYING, "I HAVE A SERIOUS FAVOR TO ASK OF YOU."

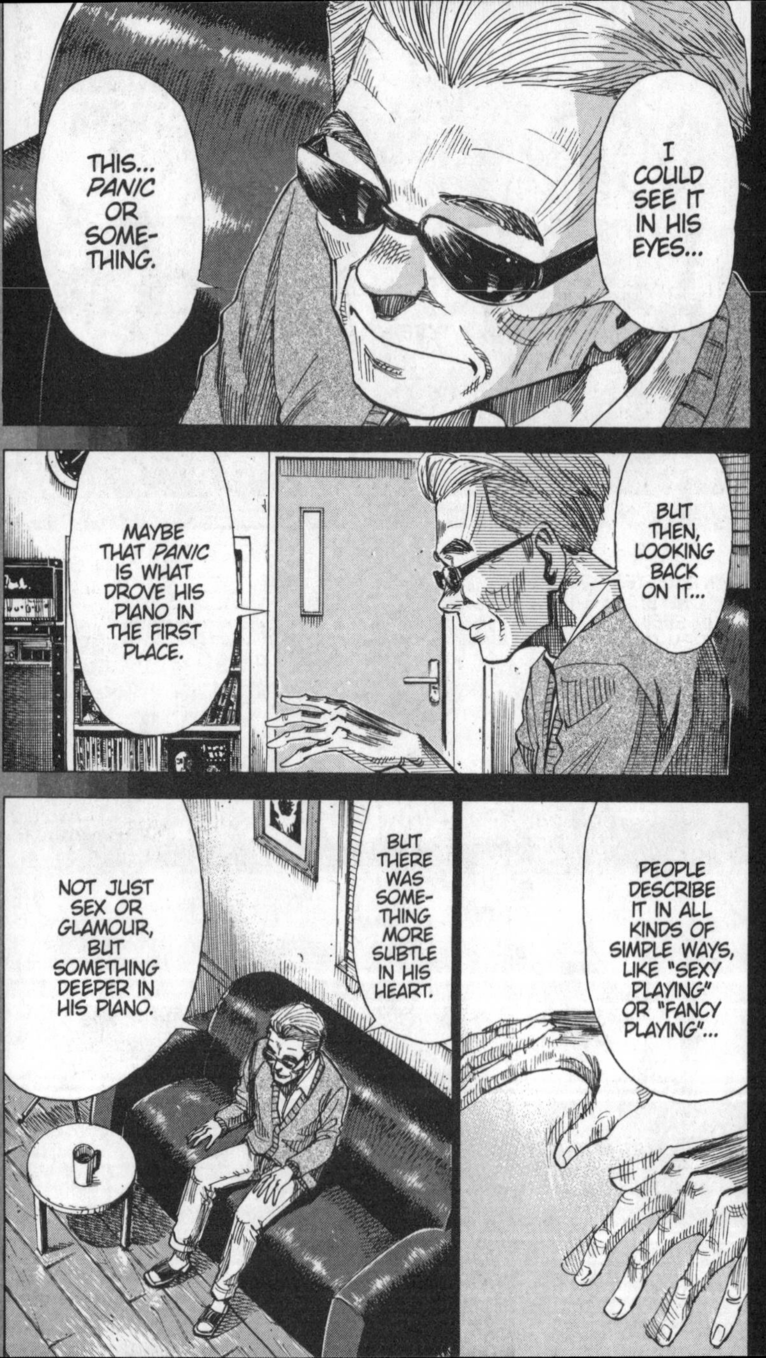
I COULD SEE IT IN HIS EYES...
THIS... *PANIC* OR SOMETHING.
BUT THEN, LOOKING BACK ON IT...
MAYBE THAT *PANIC* IS WHAT DROVE HIS PIANO IN THE FIRST PLACE.
PEOPLE DESCRIBE IT IN ALL KINDS OF SIMPLE WAYS, LIKE "SEXY PLAYING" OR "FANCY PLAYING"...
BUT THERE WAS SOMETHING MORE SUBTLE IN HIS HEART.
NOT JUST SEX OR GLAMOUR, BUT SOMETHING DEEPER IN HIS PIANO.

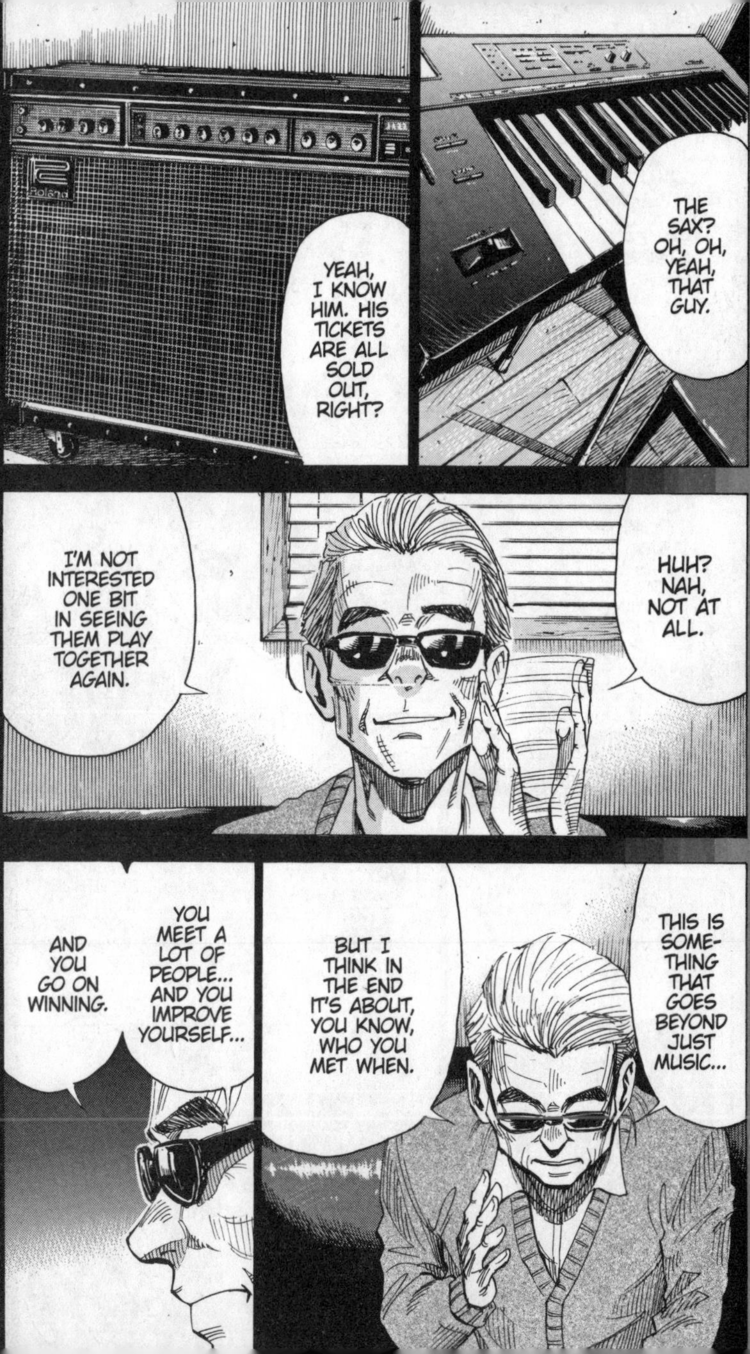
THE SAX? OH, OH, YEAH, THAT GUY.
YEAH, I KNOW HIM. HIS TICKETS ARE ALL SOLD OUT, RIGHT?
HUH? NAH, NOT AT ALL.
I'M NOT INTERESTED ONE BIT IN SEEING THEM PLAY TOGETHER AGAIN.
THIS IS SOME-THING THAT GOES BEYOND JUST MUSIC...
BUT I THINK IN THE END IT'S ABOUT, YOU KNOW, WHO YOU MET WHEN.
YOU MEET A LOT OF PEOPLE... AND YOU IMPROVE YOURSELF...
AND YOU GO ON WINNING.

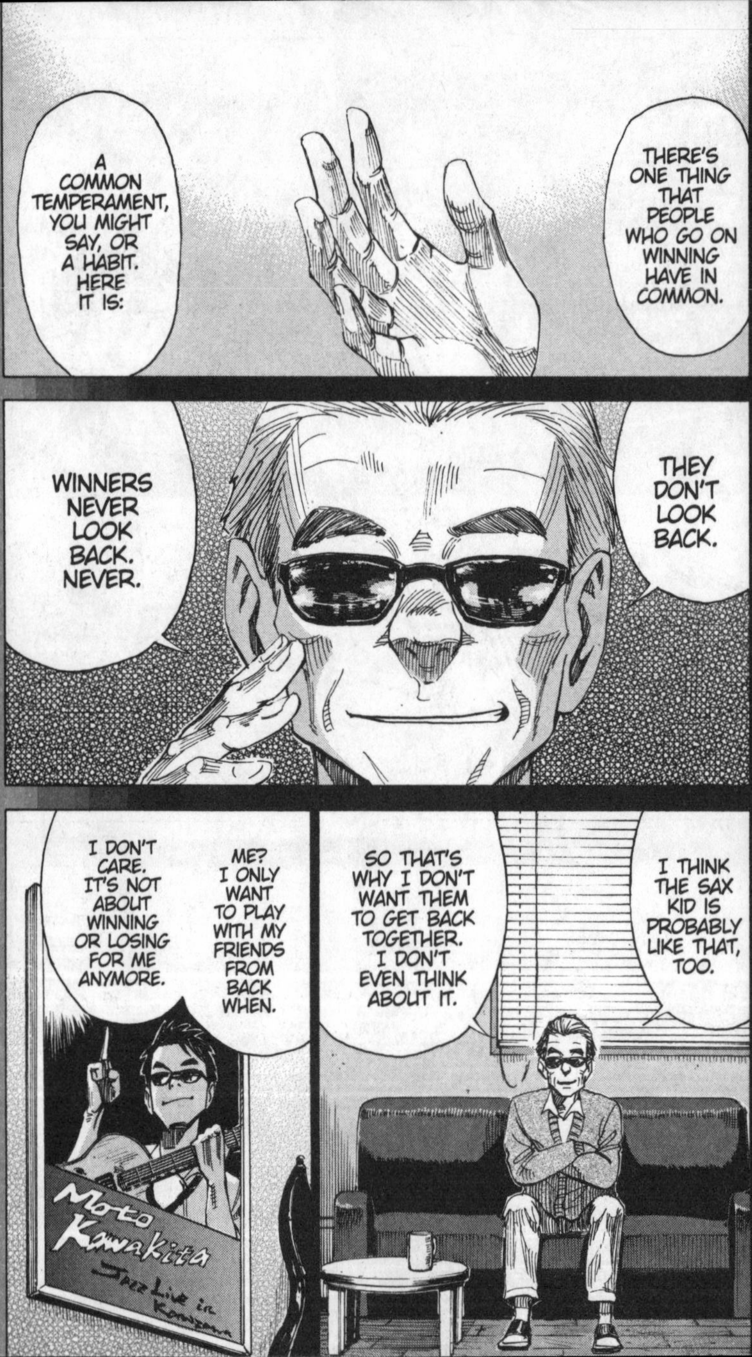
THERE'S ONE THING THAT PEOPLE WHO GO ON WINNING HAVE IN COMMON.
A COMMON TEMPERAMENT, YOU MIGHT SAY, OR A HABIT. HERE IT IS:
THEY DON'T LOOK BACK.
WINNERS NEVER LOOK BACK. NEVER.
I THINK THE SAX KID IS PROBABLY LIKE THAT, TOO.
SO THAT'S WHY I DON'T WANT THEM TO GET BACK TOGETHER. I DON'T EVEN THINK ABOUT IT.
ME? I ONLY WANT TO PLAY WITH MY FRIENDS FROM BACK WHEN.
I DON'T CARE. IT'S NOT ABOUT WINNING OR LOSING FOR ME ANYMORE.
Moto Kawakita
Jazz Live in

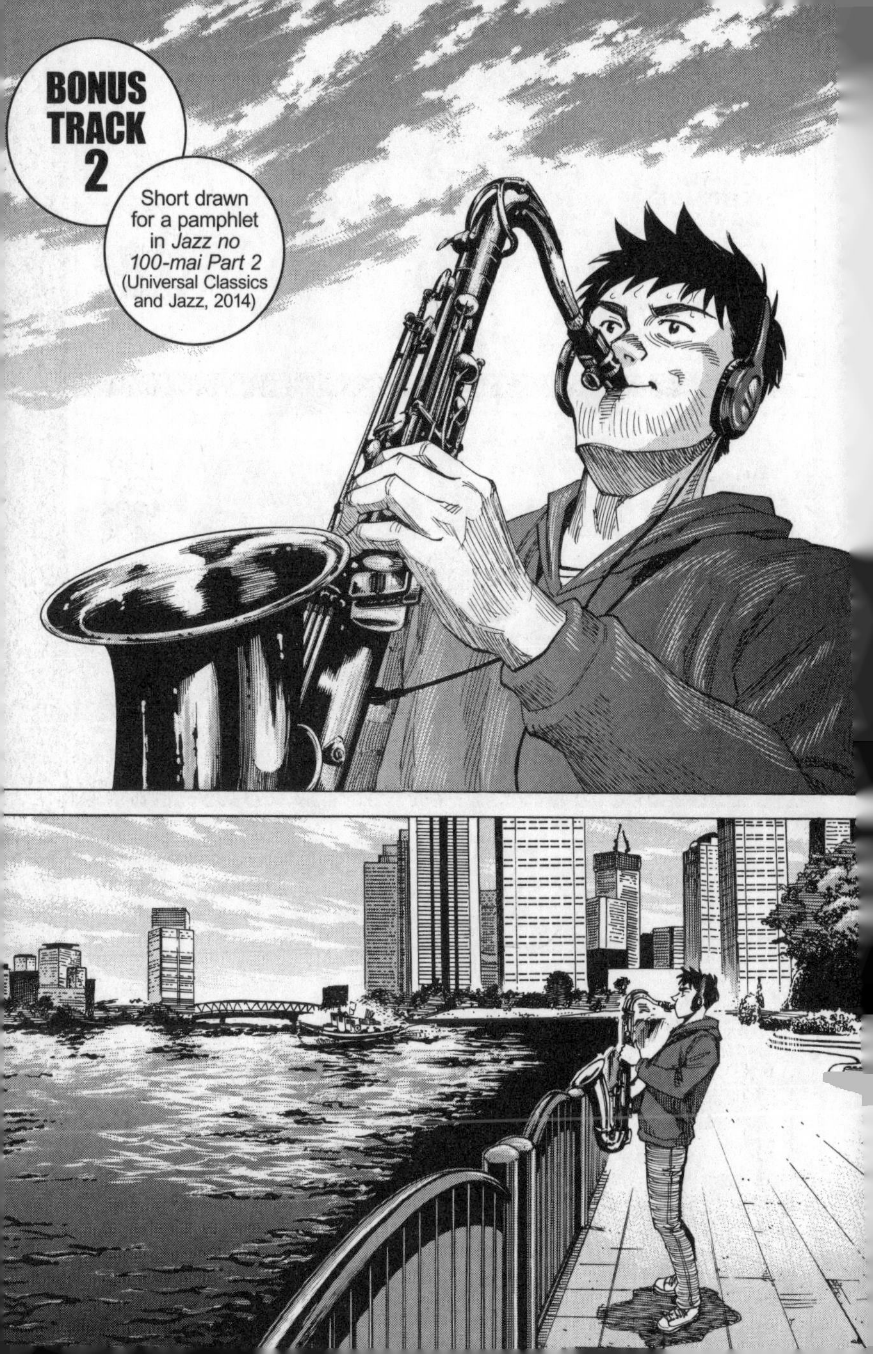
BONUS TRACK 2
Short drawn for a pamphlet in *Jazz no 100-mai Part 2* (Universal Classics and Jazz, 2014)

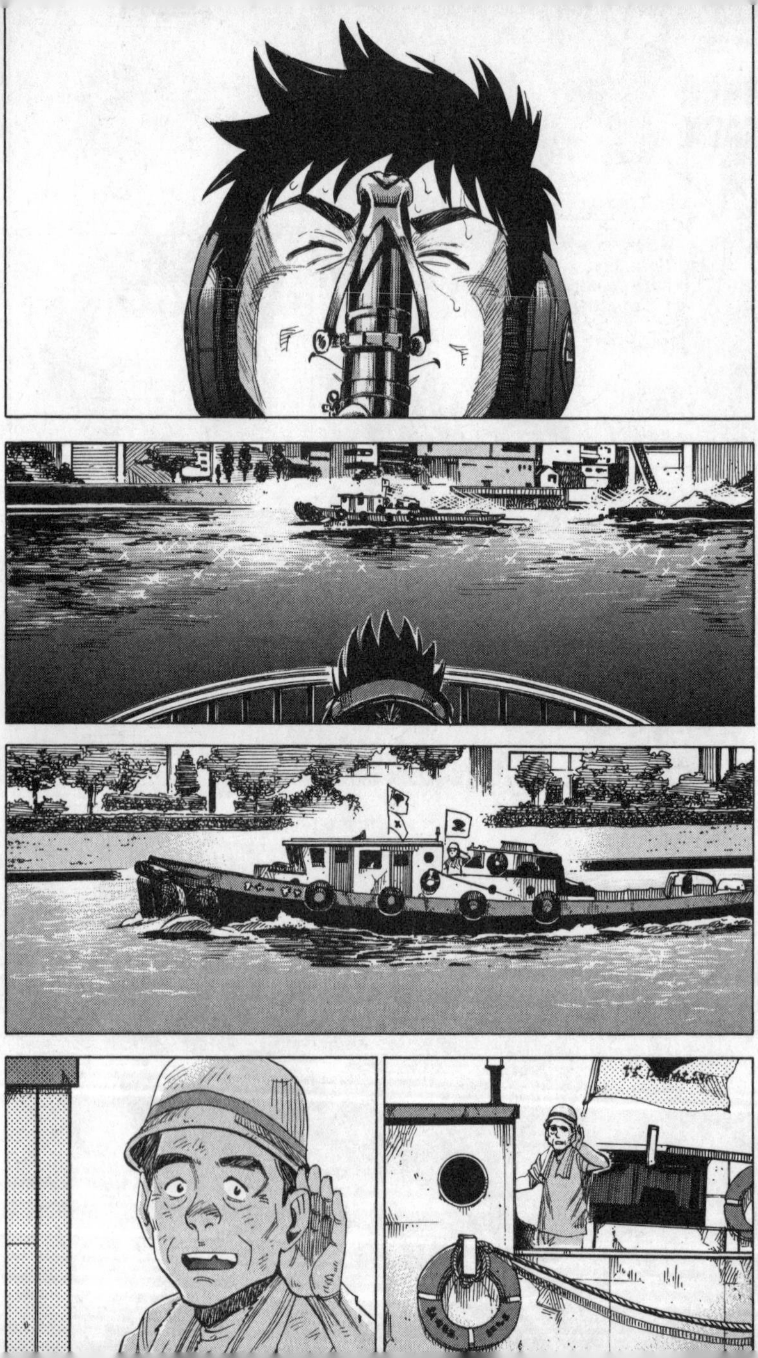

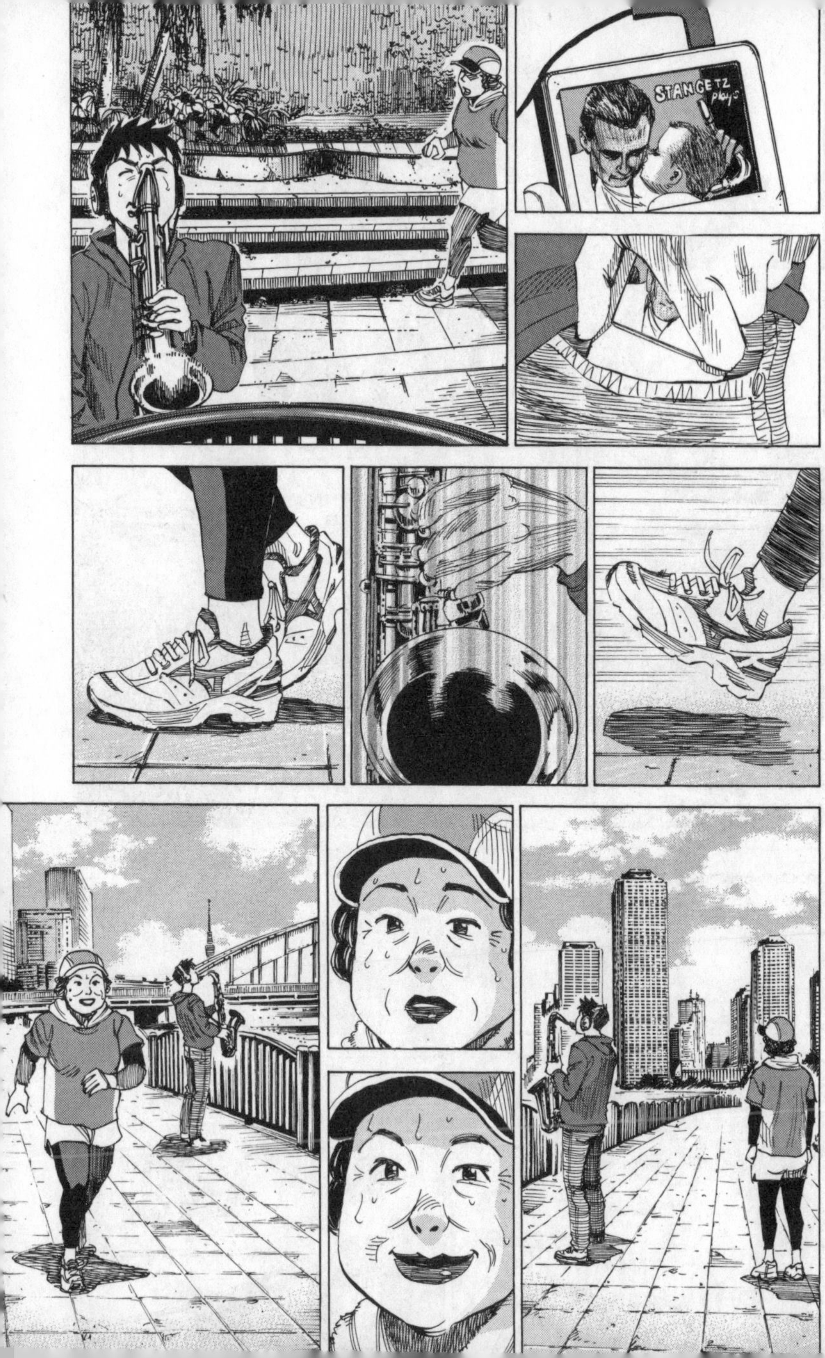
STAN GETZ
plays

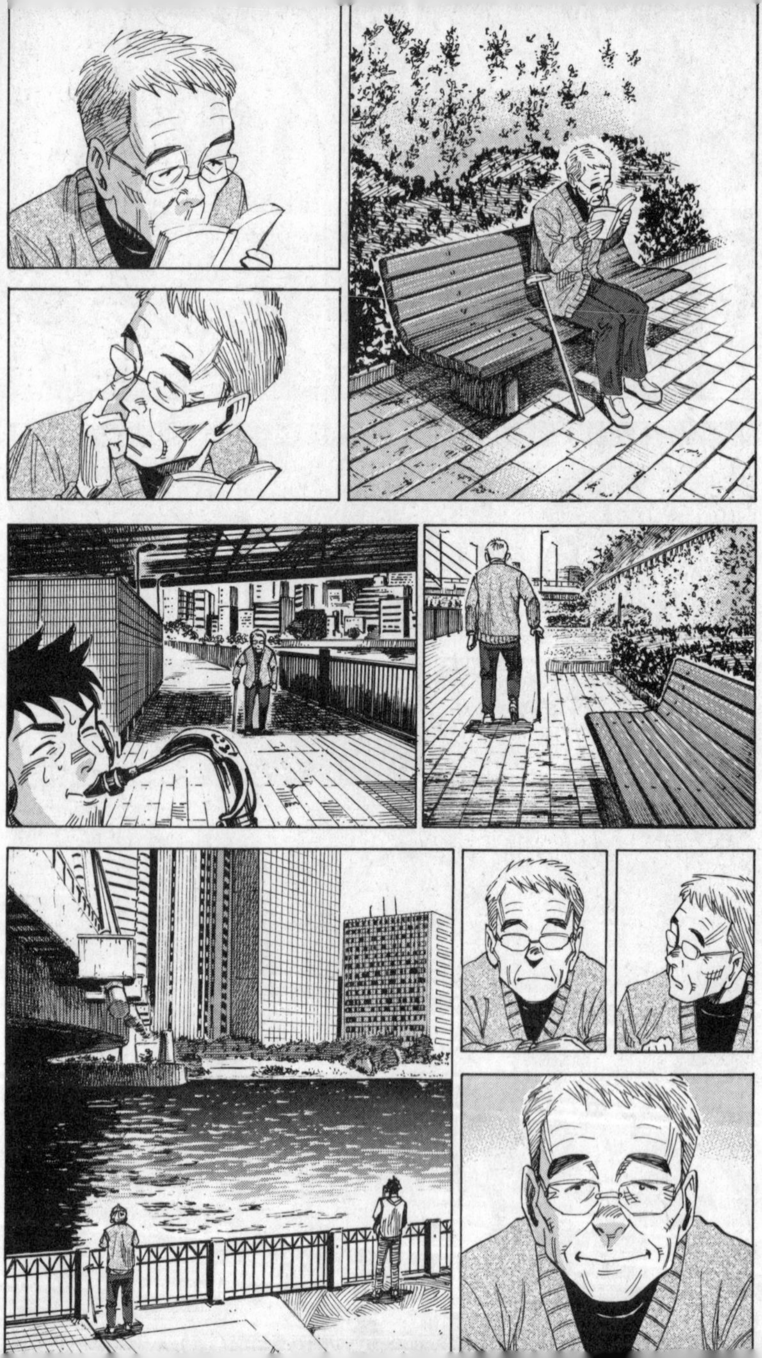

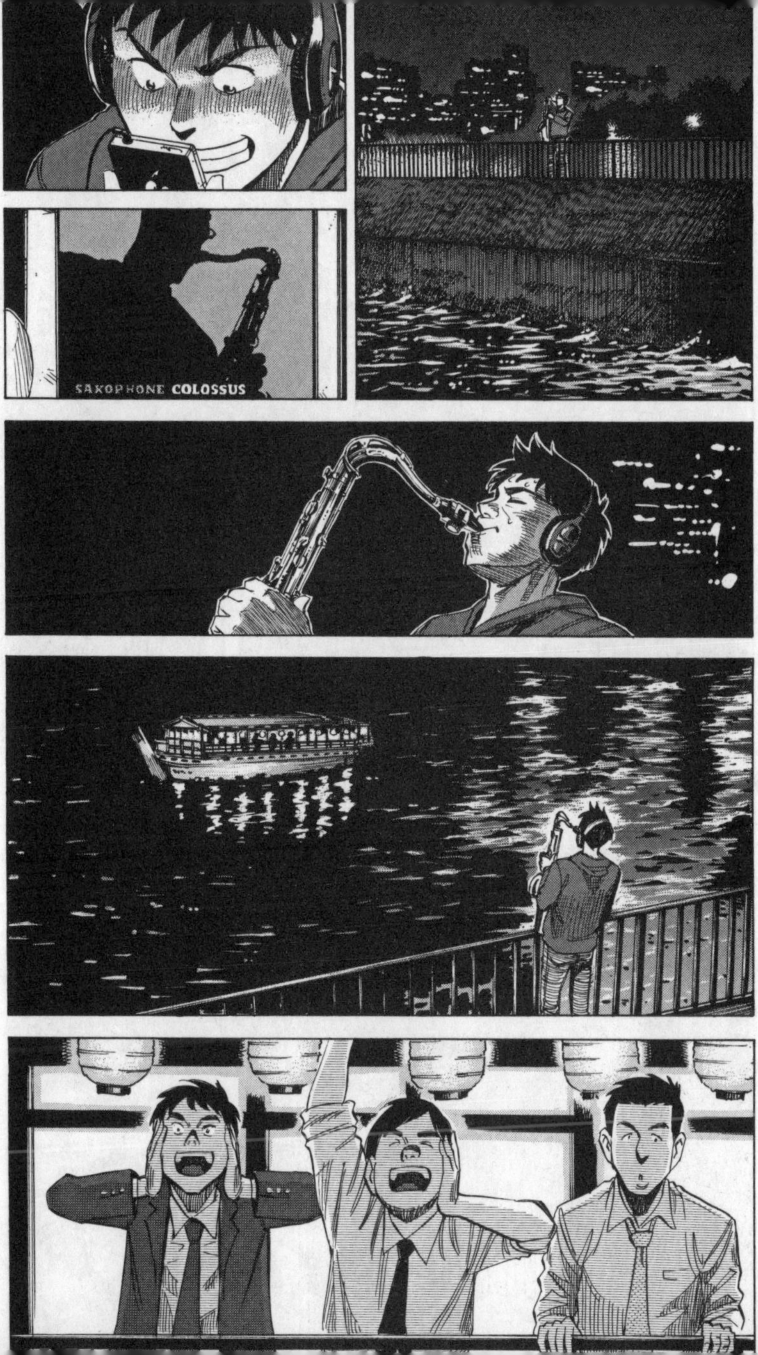
SAKOPHONE COLOSSUS

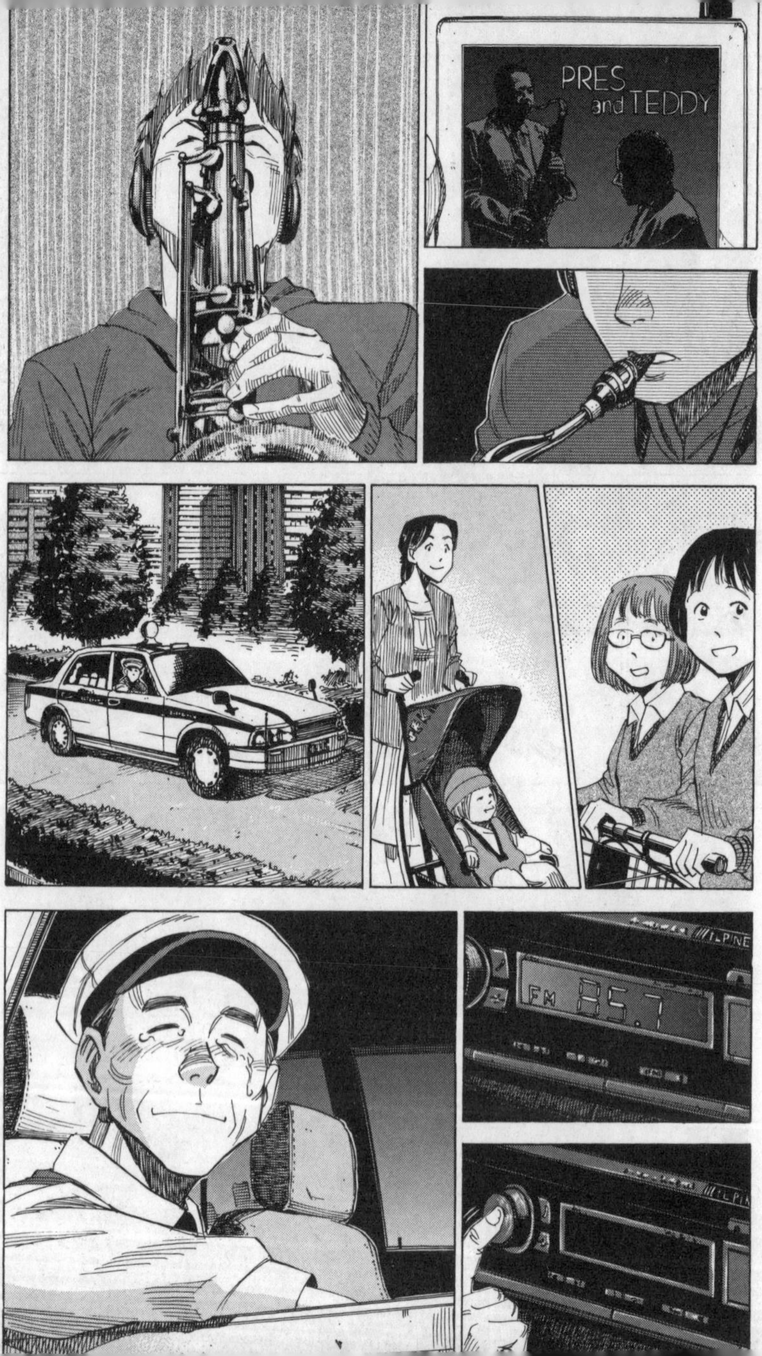
PRES
and TEDDY
FM 85.7

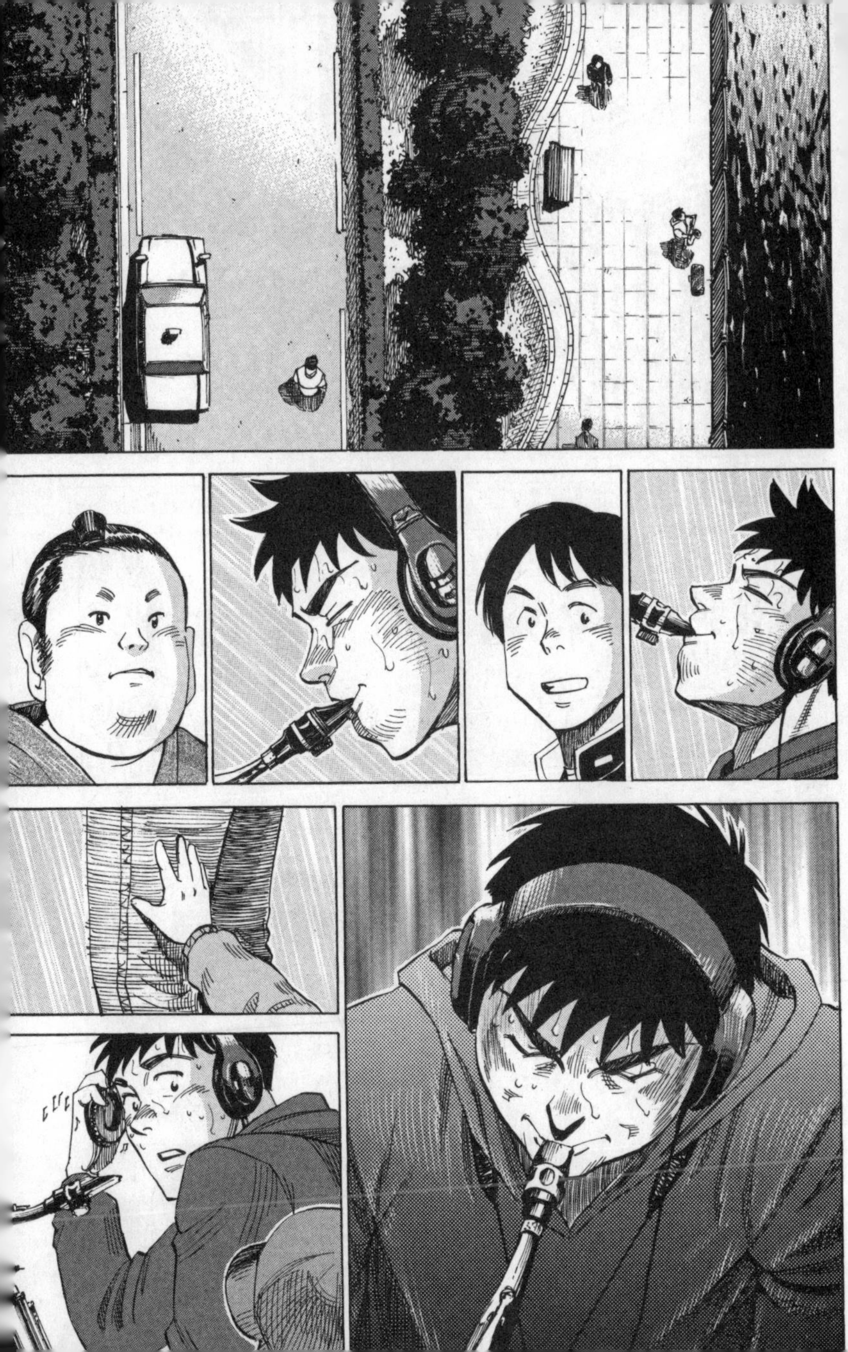

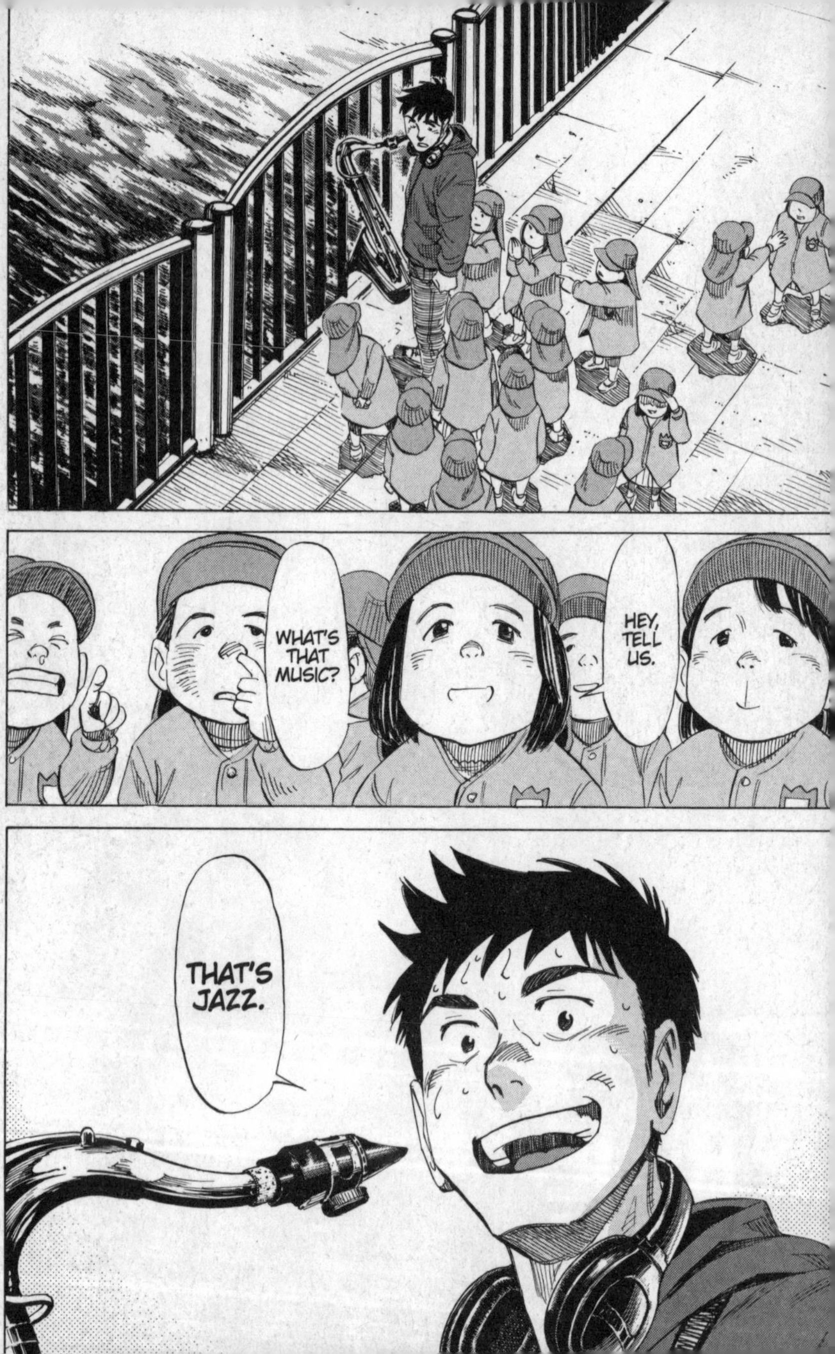
HEY, TELL US.
WHAT'S THAT MUSIC?
THAT'S JAZZ.

BLUE
GIANT

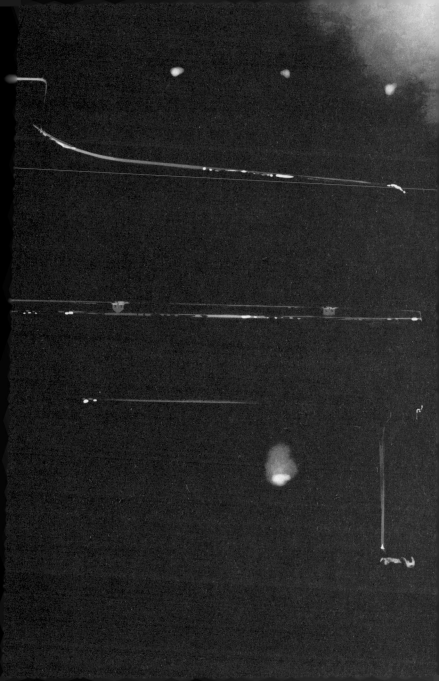

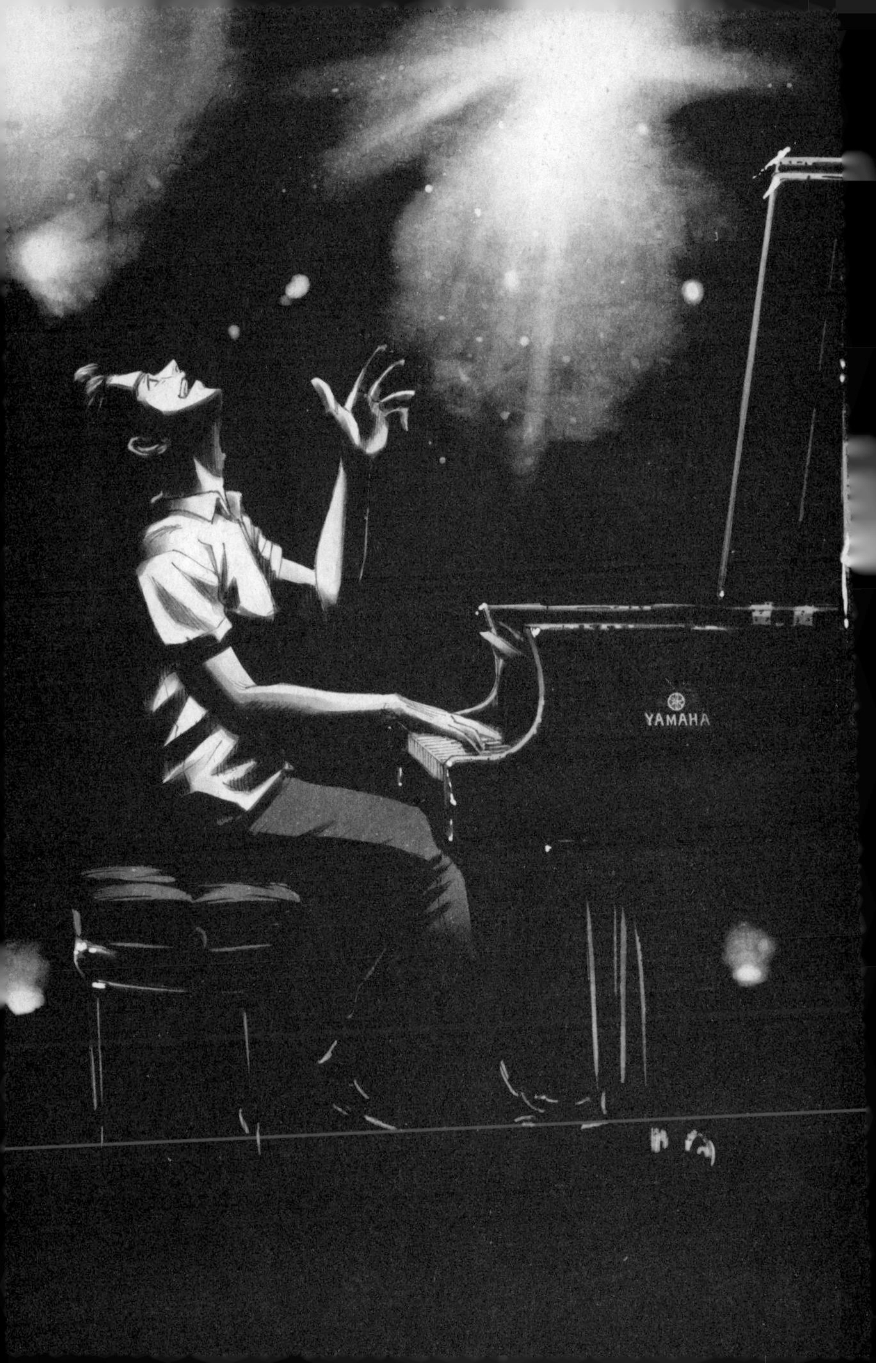
YAMAHA

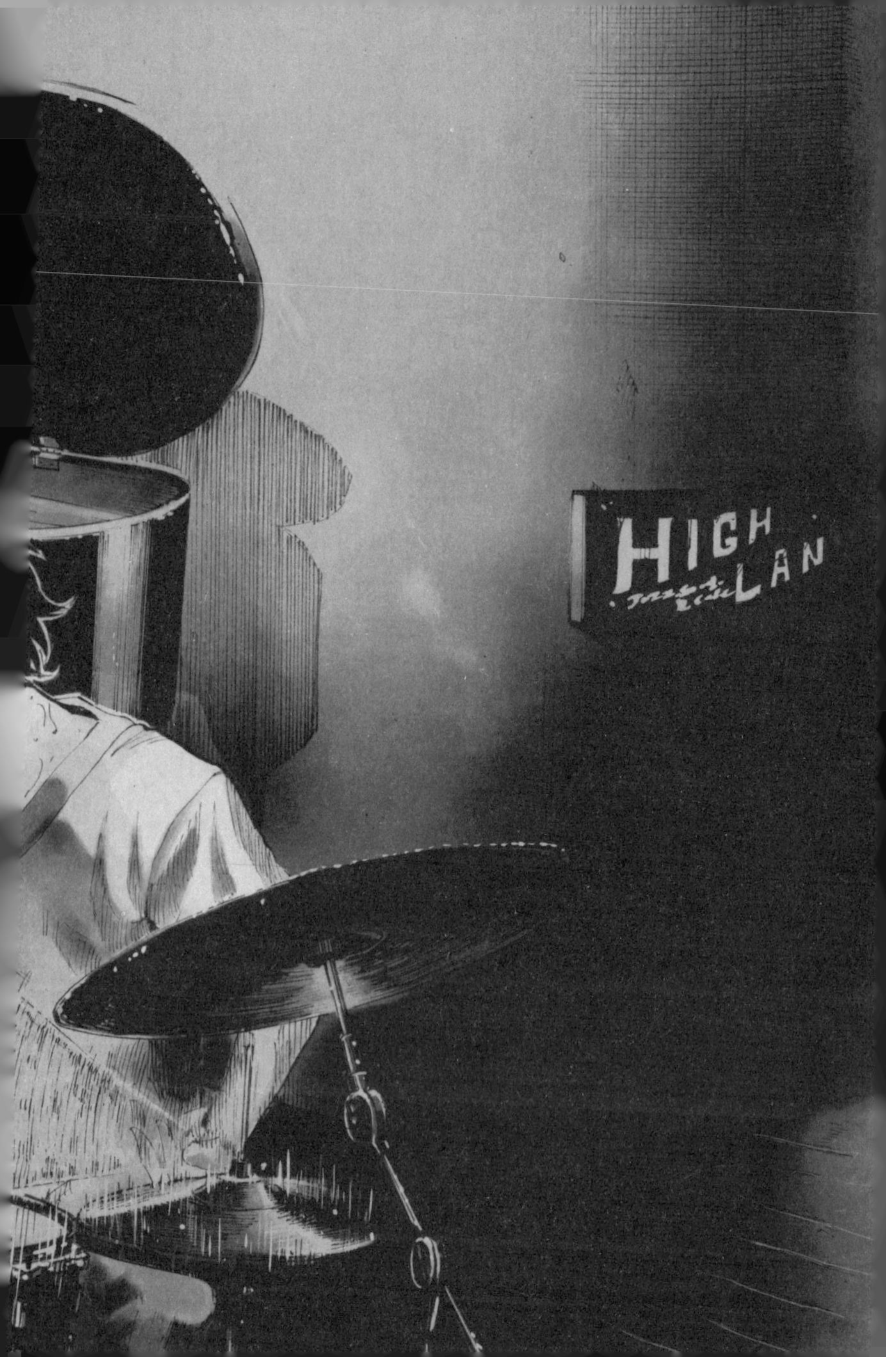
HIGH
LAN

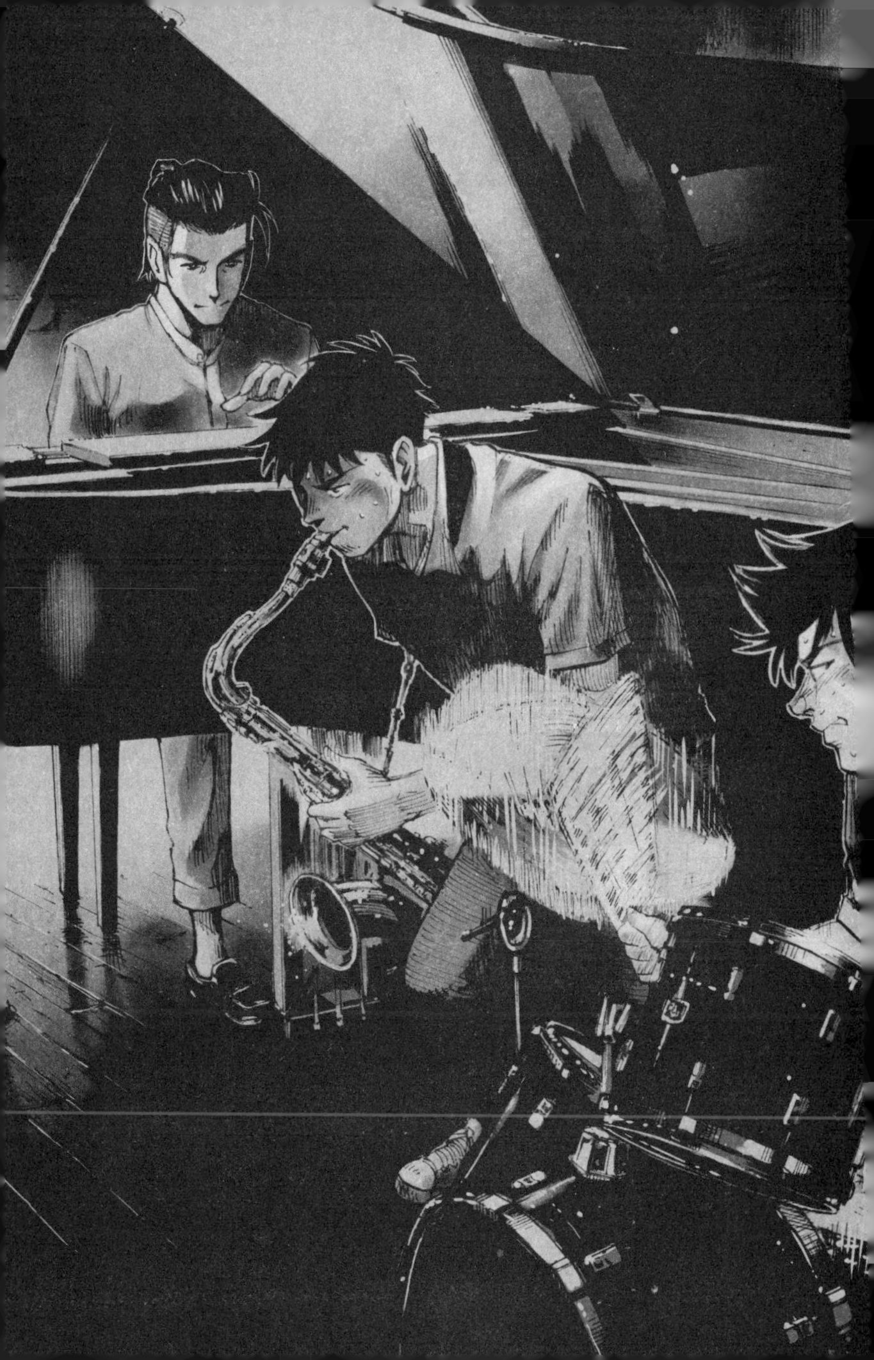

BLUE
GIANT

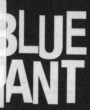